REUBEN COLE WESTERNS COLLECTION

The Complete Series

STUART G. YATES

HE WHO COMES

Reuben Cole Westerns Book 1

AUTHOR'S NOTE

By 1905, when the bulk of this story is set, the use of the telephone was well established. From 1901, Brown and Son was installing telephones in schools throughout Kansas for teachers to use when wishing to contact parents. It is no distortion of history to imagine telephone use in other areas of the United States at this time.

The camera was made popular by Eastman from 1900, with his invention of the 'Brownie.' By 1905 there would be many such cameras in everyday use. Indeed, from earlier periods, we have many historically valuable images from the Old West, most markedly from the period of the Civil War.

Similarly, the idea of 'supermarkets' has to be considered as it would appear that Kestler has created such a store in this novel. The 'Piggly Wiggly' stores in which customers could purchase all their needs under one roof were not established until 1916, but Kestler's is *not* a supermarket in the truest sense of the meaning. It is a large store, providing a range of merchandise for ranchers and farmers, so it should not be confused with those large hypermarkets in which we now do the bulk of our shopping.

I hope these brief explanations add rather than detract from your enjoyment of this tale.

For Janice, who has made my life complete.

CHAPTER ONE

Reuben heard the noise that woke him in the night and thought it must be the wind taking hold of the broken yard door, which never could shut properly, causing it to bang repeatedly. Turning over, he tried to ignore it but when the noise came again, he sat bolt upright, senses straining, the dark pressing in on him like a living thing. As he waited, body coiled like a spring, he realized one very important detail: there was no wind that night. Not so much as a breath.

He sat rock still for some considerable time, mouth slightly open, heart pounding in his ears. The large, sprawling house, built by his father some fifty or so years ago when people called this piece of dirt The Wild West, seemed suddenly an unfriendly, alien place. Someone had broken in, violated his privacy. But who could it be, he wondered. This was Nineteen-hundred and five. The outlaws were all gone now. Dead, buried or forgotten. The telegraph wires hummed, cattle wandered across the plain without fear of marauding savages and he had even heard it say people had seen a horseless carriage trundling through Main Street. A German invention somebody said. Reuben Cole was not quite sure where Germany was. The modern world was as much a mystery to him.

He swung his legs out from under the blankets and waited legs bare from the knees down, his nightgown thin, shivering. Nights were cold out here. Cold and friendless. Reuben did not have many friends. He was a loner, not lone*ly,* as he was ever quick to tell anyone interested – of which there were few – but the path he had chosen kept him apart from company and he liked it that way. Nobody with whom to answer. Get up when he liked, go to bed when he liked, farted and—

There it was again. A footfall, without any mistake.

Reuben remained alert, struggling to keep his mind from freezing over. He had killed men, but that was a long time ago, out there in the open world where the questions and answers were cleaner and simpler, unlike in here, alone in the hideaway he had made for himself.

He knew he would have to go and confront whoever it was. A thief, an opportunist. Reuben had little idea how much anything in the house was worth, other than ... He squeezed his eyes closed. The old painting his daddy had bought from that strange old coot over in Paris, France. The artist had died years before and his paintings, especially that large Water-Lillie one, had fetched a pretty sum. The one hanging on the dining room wall was probably worth more than the entire house.

He eased the drawer of his bedside cabinet open, careful not to make a sound, and reached inside. His hand curled around the familiar, maple wood butt of his Colt Cavalry. He took it out, gently checked the load and stood up.

He gathered himself, breathing through his mouth, eyes clamped on his bedroom door. Dawn's grey light was just beginning to find its way through the night but even so, Reuben's eyes were now well accustomed to the dark.

He took a step toward the door.

There followed an almighty crash from downstairs, so loud he almost jumped into the air. Damn it, what could that be?

Footsteps crushing shattered glass.

He knew what it was. That old Chinese thing Daddy had brought back with him from one of his many trips abroad. Ting or Ying or something. Old anyways. So big, you could plant a Love Oak inside it and still have room for an Elm.

Someone was hopping around down there, the sound unmistakable. Whoever it was must have bashed their knee against the side table holding the vase and Reuben imagined the intruder gripping his offended knee with both hands, swallowing down his curses.

The accident decided everything for him.

He tore open the door, all thoughts of maintaining silence gone. Taking the steps two at a time, he careered into the wide-open foyer and saw two men, one disappearing out the rear entrance, the other bent over, clutching his knee. He turned as Cole came in. His face turned white as ash, a soundless scream developing in his open mouth. Cole hit the man across the side of his head with the Colt, harder than he meant to, and he winced at the sound of breaking bone sounding off like a gunshot.

'Peebie? You all right in there?'

The owner of the voice came in from the dining room. Big bellied, small headed. In his hand was something that looked like a machete. Reuben shot him high up on the left shoulder, spinning him round in as fine a movement as any ballet dancer ever could complete. 'Oh, no, help,' he managed to squawk, 'he's killed *Peebie!*'

The big guy retreated before the shock of the gunshot struck home. Once he became aware he was hit, his body would shut down and he'd be as petrified as one of those fossilized trees up in Arizona Cole had read about. Blundering back into the dining room, crashing through the door, hitting the floor hard, the wounded man nevertheless managed to scramble to his feet. Reuben went after him but had not taken a single step before a grip as strong as a vice closed around his ankle. He looked down.

The dawn light, slowly but inexorably conquering the dark, bathed the original intruder in an eerie, unnatural light. Mouth open, his white teeth gnashed amongst the ruin of his cheekbone, and he gurgled, 'I'll see you in hell...'

Trying to shake him off proved useless, so Reuben put a bullet through that grinning skull and ran into the dining room in pursuit of the other one.

Something as hard and as heavy as a blacksmith's anvil hit him across the back of his head, catapulting him forward into a huge, gaping hole of blackness.

He was out cold before he hit the parquet-laminated floor.

CHAPTER TWO

Kicking off his boots, Sterling Roose stomped into his sparsely furnished office and, ignoring anything around him, went directly to the coffee pot and peered inside.

'Not the most observant of folk are you.'

Roose whirled, hand reaching for his revolver, and froze before he managed to clear the holster primarily due to it being a Remington New Model Police revolver with a five and a half inch barrel. This detail had never much bothered Roose up until now. The last time he had drawn his gun in anger had been almost twenty years earlier on that unforgettable evening when he and Reuben Cole laid out five Mexican bandits in the main drag. This, however, was not that warm, dry evening. This was a warm, dry morning and he was older, slower. Furthermore, the man sitting at his desk had a big calibre Smith and Wesson trained unerringly towards his midriff. He let his breath rattle out in a long, slow stream and straightened up. 'All right. You've made your point, stranger, now do you mind telling me what you're doing in my office?'

'The door was open.'

'That's no answer.'

'True.' The man smiled and Roose took the opportunity to study him. Clearly, he had been on the range for a prolonged period, his face swarthy with the sun, a three or four-day growth of beard not totally disguising his solid jaw, the thin mouth. Ice blue eyes twinkled from under heavy brows, and he was not young. Deep lines cut through his cheeks and around his eyes. He appeared a hardened individual, one well versed in using the gun in his hand, a hand encased in worn, kid gloves smeared, like the rest of his clothing, in the dust which invaded everything in that town. 'I'm here to talk to you about Maddie.'

'Oh.'

'Yes ... *oh*. Now, unbuckle that gun belt and sit down real slow. I have some things on my mind that you need to hear.'

'I don't even know who you are.'

'Well, that's one of the things we can discuss, now ain't it.' He waved the gun slightly. 'The gunbelt ... *real* slow.'

Things all seemed to tumble into a mess of confusion from that moment. The door burst open violently, the force almost tearing it from its hinges and Mathias Thurst, Roose's young deputy, bounded in. Wearing nothing but his sweat-stained long-johns, Thurst, like his boss, did not at first see the angular figure of the stranger sitting behind the sheriff's desk. With his arms flapping around like those of a broken wind-mill, he strode in, gunbelt draped over one shoulder, hat hanging by its neck cord around his throat. He wore one boot, the left one held in his left hand.

'Sheriff, oh please, you gotta come quick,' he began, his words gushing out as if from an untapped oil strike, 'It's Mrs. Samuels, she came riding in like a crazy thing on that little buggy of hers and she is telling everyone she has ...' His voice trailed away as his eyes lighted on the stranger and, in particular, the big-barrelled Smith and Wesson which was now turned on him

Roose took the opportunity, swept up the small cast-iron coal shovel with which he used to keep the pot-belly stove stoked up with fuel, and with all the power he could muster, smacked it, with a good deal of satis-faction, across the stranger's jaw.

Shrieking, the stranger clutched at his right cheek and fell over the chair. Crashing to the ground, the gun skating over towards Thurst, he writhed and moaned loudly. Thurst meanwhile stooped and picked the big Smith and Wesson up. ''T'ain't even loaded, Sheriff.'

Not listening, Roose nimbly darted behind his desk and cracked the shovel two or three more times across the stranger's skull. 'Swine,' he hissed. Satisfied the stranger would not be causing any more trouble, he stood up, breathing hard and glared at his young deputy. 'What was you hollerin' about, Thurst?'

It took a moment for Thurst to answer, eyes on stalks, studying the bloody and inert body of the stranger.

'*Thurst,* open your ears!'

'I ... Darn it, Sheriff, you think you might have killed him?'

'I don't care if I have,' said Roose, face flushed, sweat sprouting across his forehead. He threw the small shovel away and hoisted up his trousers. 'He was already here when I came in this morning. Had that gun on me. Don't know who he is.'

By now Thurst was next to the body, fingers pressed under the man's broken jaw. 'I don't get no pulse.'

'Thurst, can you leave it and tell me why you came in as if all the hounds of Hell were snapping at your heels.'

Thurst stood up again, shaking his head. 'Darndest thing I ever did see.' He turned to fix his gaze upon his boss. 'Mrs. Samuels, you know the one, she cleans a number of the big properties around here? Well, she went over to Reuben Cole's place and found him all beat up, just lying there in his own dining room she said.' He looked down at the body and shook his head again. 'Just like him, I guess.'

'Reuben Cole? Beat up? You sure that is what she said?'

'That's it. She's over in Drey Brewer's coffee house being comforted by them Spyrow sisters. I was on my porch when she came flying by in her buggy, pulled up real sharp and started squawking at me, almost *demanding* I come and get you. Hence my unkempt appearance, boss. I do apologize for that.'

'Don't you go fretting about any dress code, son.' He pointed at the crumpled body next to the desk. 'You, er, tidy up in here after we've put that idiot in a cell. Put his gun on my desk.'

'It's not loaded.'

'I heard you, but I wasn't to know that was I?'

'No, I guess not.'

'Well then,' Roose tugged off his jacket and flung it over the back of his chair, 'let's get him inside the jail, then I'll call on Doc Evans to fix him up.'

'He don't need no doctor, Sheriff. He needs a preacher.' Another shake of his head. 'Or Jesus, to raise him.'

CHAPTER THREE

E asing open the door to the coffee shop, Roose nodded towards Dray Brewer behind his counter, and saw Mrs. Samuels all huddled up, crying into a sodden handkerchief, two elderly and thin ladies dressed in black each with an arm around her, cooing soothing words. 'It'll be all right now, Jane, you just take your time. None of this is your fault, you've done what you can. Best leave it to the authorities now, they'll know what to do ... Oh, Sheriff Roose! A most timely intervention!'

Doffing his hat, Roose pulled up a chair and shuffled it towards the ladies. The two elderly ones made way for him, leaving the third, Jane Samuels, to regard him through eyes puffy and red with too much crying. 'Oh Sheriff, it was terrible. Poor man.'

'Is he dead?'

'No, no I am sure he isn't. I did what I could, made him comfortable, and then rushed over here as fast as I could, telling that young Thurst boy to fetch you.'

'You did the right thing, Jane,' said one of the Spyrow sisters soothingly.

'I hope so, but ... Oh, Sheriff, he has a bump the size of an egg on the back of his head.'

'Did you see who might have done it?'

'No. There were long gone, I shouldn't wonder. Whoever did it gave

14

him a terrible beating. And the house ...' Seized by a renewed wave of anguish, she bawled into her handkerchief, 'All those lovely things that his daddy collected. So awful it is, *awful.*'

'There, there Jane, try not to upset yourself so,' said the sister closest to Roose. 'Can't you do something, Sheriff?'

'Miss Spyrow, I will do all I can to find the perpetrators, have no fear. But Mrs. Samuels, I have to ask you again. You are absolutely certain ... *is he dead?*'

Her face came up and she seemed to gather herself, taking a few shuddering breaths. Roose prepared himself for the worst. He knew Cole well. They'd ridden the range together back in the days when the Indians roamed free and tenderfoots were struggling to start a new life. He couldn't count the times Cole had saved his life, and now he too was—

'No, he's not dead, Sheriff. I told you. I tended to him, got him into bed. It was a struggle I don't mind telling you. He's a *big* man.'

'He ain't that big, but even so ...'

'Well ... I had to strip him naked, Sheriff. Bathe his bruises, so I know what I saw.'

The two sisters squealed, clamping tiny hands against their startled mouths.

Unable to hold her gaze, Roose turned away, face burning. He called across to Brewer in a shaky voice. 'Any chance of a coffee?'

The coffeehouse owner nodded, but before preparing Roose's order, he said, 'After what Mrs. Samuels said, I called across to the stable boy, Percival, to go and fetch Doctor Evans so Mr Cole could be better cared for.'

'That was good of you, Dray. Thank you.'

'I think one or two of his ribs were broken,' said Mrs. Samuels.

'I ain't never known Cole to be bettered,' Roose mused in a low voice. He swiveled in his chair and looked at the still sobbing woman. 'There must have been more than one of 'em, taken him by surprise perhaps.'

'Yes, I shouldn't wonder. There was one of those baseball bats lying beside him, with blood and bits of hair stuck to it.'

Another shriek, one of horror this time, from the accompanying sisters.

Roose contemplated this news for a moment. Most of his dealings recently had been with settlers over in the west of the county, people who were moving from the already growing cities further to the north. Some were questionable types, mainly living on the wrong side of the law, coming down from Missouri with prices on their heads. Already ideas were ruminating in his brain, suspicions mounting. If desperate men, on the brink of starvation, were beginning to reconnoitre and burglarise outlying properties, he was going to have a huge job on his hands to protect the disparate population.

'I think I might need your husband, Nelson, Mrs. Samuels. I'm going to need a good group of men to deputize. He'll be at the head of my list.'

'Nelson is too old to be going riding around searching for lowlifes, Sheriff. His army days are done.'

'Nevertheless, he was one of the ablest scouts the army ever used, and I could sure as h—' He cut off his choice of word sharply as the withering glares of the Spyrow sisters turned upon him. Squirming in his chair, he cleared his throat before he continued uneasily. 'What I mean is, he was a good scout back then, Mrs. Samuels, and the skills he had are not ones you ever forget. And he ain't old – he's two years younger than me.'

'Well, there you are, Sheriff. *Too* old by far.'

Roose returned to the sheriff's office, chewing on a cheroot, feeling he'd been dragged backwards through the sagebrush. Sweeping the floor, Thurst, bareheaded and bare-chested, glistened with sweat. He stopped sweeping as Roose came through the door and leaned on the broom, placing his chin on the end of the pole. 'Sheriff. He's dead.'

Roose felt a tightening around his gut, heartbeat accelerating, the heat of the day not helping him at all. 'That's unfortunate.'

'I'd say the way you went about him with that shovel meant there weren't ever gonna be any other result.'

'Thurst, you get on with your sweeping, then go and get yourself kitted out for an overland manhunt.'

'I'm considering not doing any of those things, Sheriff.'

'Say what?'

'The way I see it, I reckon you murdered that gentleman and I am—'

'He wasn't no gentleman, Thurst, let's get that straight right from the off. He was here to do me harm.'

'All righty, but even if he wasn't so great a guy, he's still dead and you still killed him. I think that's murder, right there and that's the truth of it, Sheriff.'

'He had a gun on me, you pond-weed.'

'An unloaded gun.'

'Like I said before, I wasn't to know that. The guy was here to kill me, that was for sure, and I wasn't about to stand around and let him do it. If you hadn't burst in on us it would be me setting out my patch in the cemetery, not him.'

Mathias Thurst stood staring, not at Roose, but into the jail beyond and the bundled up heap that once was a man. Roose followed his deputy's eyes and considered his options. What would he have done if Thurst hadn't arrived at that most convenient of times, he wondered. What did the man have to say about Maddie or anything else for that matter? Surely sure the man was Maddie's husband. Roose had been more than friendly with the man's wife for some time. Of course, Roose knew Maddie was married, but he believed it was all over between them, so what had galvanized her husband into a confrontation he could not say. Clearly, he needed a little face-to-face with his lover of over six months, to bring some light to the situation. Right now, however, he had other, more pressing worries, Thurst being the main one.

Roose blew out his cheeks and measured his deputy with a cold look, hands on hips, well away from the New Model Police sitting in its holster, set ready for a cross-belly draw. 'Mathias, we can work all this out, we truly can, but at the moment we have got a manhunt to get started. I aim to find those responsible for breaking into Cole's home and beating him close to death. I will need you.'

'I ain't going,' said Thurst without pausing for a moment to consider Roose's words. 'I'm done with this and done with you, Sheriff.'

'Now hold on just a minute there, Thurst, this isn't all about you and me! We can deal with this when we get back.'

'How will we do that?'

'Well, I'll make a sworn statement ... Present it to the circuit judge. You can witness it or even give your own account of what happened.'

'After we get back from the manhunt?'

'Yes! That's exactly right. This unfortunate incident will keep – it's not as if he's going anywhere is it?'

'And what if I don't come back?'

'What if you don't … What are you talking about? Of course, you'll come back!'

'What I mean is, what if I was to be the victim of an accident, a stray bullet, a rattler sliding underneath my blankets? What then, Sheriff? It would just be your word and …' He chuckled, a strangely humourless and eerie sound in that small, dusty room. 'Nobody would ever question any of it, would they, you being such an upright citizen and all.'

'What do you take me for, Thurst? I'm as law-abiding as anyone.'

'Why you set to him the way you did?'

'Listen, it's complicated all right. He's Maddie's husband – *was* Maddie's husband.'

'So that's why you killed him?'

'Thurst, you've got this all wrong! I was acting in self-defence.'

Thurst turned away, setting the broom against the side of the pot-belly stove. 'Well, I've made my mind up. I ain't going. I'll stay here until you get back, hold the fort so to speak. And I'll do something with the body – it is liable to get somewhat ripe in this heat.'

'Thurst, there is no need to—'

'There is every need Sheriff. I ain't dumb and I ain't gonna risk my life because you killed a man.'

And that was that. Roose could see it in his deputy's eyes. He was not going to be persuaded, one way or the other. Roose let his shoulders relax and strode forward, pushing past Thurst. He pulled down three Winchesters from the open cabinet and stuffed his pockets with cartridges. 'I'm taking Samuels with me and probably Ryan Stone too. Both of 'em served in the army and they know what it is like to be out on the open-range.' He stacked the Winchesters into the crook of his arm and glared at his deputy. 'You've let me down, Mathias. When we get back, we'll sort this out. And it won't be to your advantage.'

'At least I'll still be alive.'

Roose went to say something, thought better of it and stomped outside into the glaring heat of yet another airless day.

CHAPTER FOUR

They rode sluggishly across the endless plain, all three men wearing broad-brimmed Mexican sombreros. Hunched over their scrawny mounts, whose own legs buckled under the weight of their riders, the relentless heat drained all strength and made even the most simple of physical actions an epic in determination and effort. The lead man was huge and rode a mule. Against each of the animal's flanks banged and clanged bulging canvas bags, the noise from which reverberated across the scorching landscape, a landscape bereft of shade.

'Soloman,' said the second in line, his voice weak and scratchy, 'we have to find a spot to rest, if not for us then the horses.'

Solomon rolled his huge shoulders, pulled off his hat, and dragged a sleeve across his brow. He was bald save for a few wisps of oily black hair, which he had once, some while ago, swept over his pate in an attempt to disguise his lack of anything on top. It hadn't worked and he had given up the struggle and surrendered to the inevitable. Compared to his bulk, the head was so small people called him 'pin-head', but never to his face. Such a thing would be suicidal, for Soloman was a man well versed in killing. It was something he enjoyed.

He reined in his mule. The animal, when it decided it wanted to, slowed to almost stopping, but not quite. 'I ain't too sure where any of that shade might be, Pete.'

Pete came up alongside him. The sweat rolled down his face, cutting tiny rivulets through the grime covering every inch of him. 'We should never have come this way. We should have taken the trail. It's known to us and we—'

'They'd have caught up with us.'

'*Who?* Sheriff Roose? It would be hours, maybe even days before he worked out what had happened.'

'Well, I wasn't taking no chances.'

'That was Reuben Cole,' said the third man, bringing his horse alongside the other side of Solomon. 'I saw the portrait of his daddy above the fireplace before I put my Bowie through it.'

'Reuben-whoever-he-was is dead,' said Solomon with feeling. He recalled the deep, almost sexual satisfaction he derived from slamming his boot into the man's ribcage.

'You don't know that for sure,' said Pete.

Turning in the saddle, Solomon gave Pete a withering glare. 'I beat him real good, Pete. No one could survive the beating I gave that piece of bar-filth.'

'Yeah, so you say, Sollo, but we don't know that for s—'

'*I* know it. I ain't never been bettered in no fight and not many have ever got up again after taking a beating from me. He's the same. He's *dead*, I tell you – D-E-D, dead!'

'Well, that makes the case for Roose coming after us even more definite, don't it?' The others looked at the third man. Pencil-thin, his face, hands and any other piece of exposed flesh were burnt almost to a crisp, every patch of his clothing, both covering his torso and his legs, soaked through with sweat. 'What?'

'You don't have to state the obvious, Notch.,' said Pete, 'we all know what Roose will do.'

'Yeah, but like I say,' put in Solomon, turning his eyes to the distant horizon and the mass of dry grey scree that divided them from it, 'he won't discover the body for days. We have plenty of time to make it to Lawrenceville and deliver this here booty to Mr Kestler. It'll be a payday like no other.'

'If we ever make it,' said Notch, shaking his water canteen for grim effect. The sound of a few dregs of liquid splashed around inside. 'I ain't barely got a mouthful left in here.'

'Me neither,' said Pete, downcast.

'Will you two stop squawking! Lawrenceville cannot be more than half a day's ride away, so we are not going to die from thirst out here.' He gingerly dipped his right hand under his filthy shirt to feel the pulsating wound where Cole had shot him. The bullet had gone clean through. 'I always was lucky when it comes to getting shot, but this hurts like sin.' He looked at his bloody fingers and licked them.

'I hope you is right about us not dying out here, Sollo,' groaned Pete, head hanging further down onto his chest, voice sounding defeated.

'I am right, damn you, Pete! You ain't been shot but all you do is moan like some old woman. Now buck up and let's continue before we really do fry out here.'

With that, Solomon kicked the mule's flanks several times. Eventually, it moved a little faster, but not by much. It plodded across the hard, arid ground where nothing grew, everything covered in a uniform grey dust which reflected the glare of the sun's rays, bouncing them back into the faces of both men and beasts. Solomon pulled off his neckerchief and covered most of his face with it and, to give further relief from the brightness, pull his sombrero down as far as he could without causing it to fall off. In this way, he could protect himself from the scorching glare as much as possible. The others followed his example, set their shoulders, and continued, resigned to what they had to do. Too far to go back the way they had come, there was no other choice but to follow Soloman's lead.

It may have been two hours later, although it probably felt like two *days* when Pete thought he heard something, reined in his horse and strained to listen.

There! Beyond the distant crest, the sound of ...

Narrowing his eyes, he saw it, stark against the white sky. A trail of grey trailing backwards from its point of origin. Not a fire. Smoke. 'Smoke by Jiminy! *Smoke!*'

The others reacted, Soloman the first to do so, jumping down from his mule when it refused to come to a total standstill. 'Darn it, wish I had me a telescope. Smoke you say?'

'No mistaking it,' cried Pete, unable and unwilling to keep the triumph out of his voice.

'Maybe it's Injuns,' said Notch forlornly. 'They send smoke signals, don't they?'

'No it ain't Indians, that's the railroad,' said Soloman, spinning around and throwing his sombrero high into the air. 'The railroad to Lawrenceville! Boys, we is saved!'

The others gawped at him but they knew it was true.

They were saved.

CHAPTER FIVE

Roose came out of Doc Evans' home, which doubled as his surgery and stood on the porch, looking down the street towards a voice he recognized.

It was Maddie. Dressed in a cornflower blue dress, with a tiny pillbox hat set upon her mass of tumbling golden locks, she drove a small buggy, calling, 'Sterling, what in blazes is going on?'

One of the things he truly adored about Maddie was the way her beautiful looks did not quite match the coarse sounding voice. She was a wildcat, both in and out of bed, and he smiled with a mixture of pride and joy as she drew closer. She was as hard as they come while always managing to look as pretty as a picture.

However, in her eyes today burned something he did not recognize.

She pulled up close and yanked back the wheel brake. Studying him for a few moments, her voice cracked as she spoke. "I went to your office to call in on you being as you left me without a word this morning.'

'Ah, yes, I'm sorry about that but—'

'And when I got there, your young deputy and another youth is manhandling a body out of the cell. So I stops, all of a flutter as you would expect,' – he did and he pulled off his hat and went to explain but was intercepted yet again – 'when I look and see who it was.'

'Who it ... Well, I have to admit he did mention you by name so I assumed he was a jealous lover.' The lie came easily to him, for he knew full well the dead man was her husband but he couldn't tell her that. Roose shot her a coy smile. 'I am well aware you have several other gentlemen friends.'

'He was *more* than a friend, Sterling! It was Gunther.'

'Gunther?'

'Yes, you dimwit – Gunther Haas, *my husband!*'

For one terrible moment, Roose believed he could be in danger of over-acting as his mouth opened and his eyes bulged. Gaping grotesquely, he forced a strained, 'Husband?' She nodded and, to give her words more emphasis, she sniffed loudly, produced a silk handkerchief from her sleeve and blew her nose into it. Roose ran a shaking hand across his mouth. 'Oh jeepers.'

'Yes, you may well say 'oh jeepers'!' She gave her nose another blast then climbed down from the buggy seat and stepped up to him, hands on her hips, head tilted, mouth set in a thin line. 'You seriously telling me you didn't know who he was?'

'I swear it.'

'All right, if that is so, you tell me what Gunther is doing in *your* jail, dead as a post.'

Hearing the raised voices and Maddie's heartfelt sobbing, Doc Evans stepped from out of his surgery, assessed the situation, and helped Maddie inside. He set her down at his kitchen table while Roose, following like a chastised dog, stood in the doorway, arms folded, wondering how he was going to survive the next few minutes.

'There, there, Mrs. Haas,' said the Doc in soothing tones as he set a glass of water down before her, 'try and drink that and don't upset yourself so.'

Mumbling her thanks, Maddie did as suggested. She sat quietly, dabbing at her eyes and nose with the handkerchief, inhaled breath shuddering in her throat.

Turning from her, Doc Evans' eyes settled on Roose, the unspoken question hanging there.

"She's had some bad news,' said Roose, unable to hold the doctor's stare. 'Very bad.'

'He's *dead,* damn your eyes, Sterling Roose!'

Turning from one to the other, a deep frown forming ever more pronounced, Evans shook his head. 'Who is dead?'

'Her husband.'

Evans gaped and looked at Maddie, whimpering. 'Your husband? Why I never even knew he was back in town. How long is it since you—'

'Over three years.'

'Well, I'll be.' Shaking his head, Doc Evans went over to a large, glass-fronted cabinet, opened it and carefully extracted a bell jar bottle, about three-quarters full of a brown liquid. He pulled out the stopper and filled a small glass from the bottle and handed it over to Maddie. 'Medicinal brandy. I'm guessing you could do with that right now.'

She nodded her thanks, paused for a moment, then tipped the contents of the glass straight down her throat.

Evans gave Roose a startled look, Roose responding with a slight shrug and a knowing raising of the brows.

'Thank you, Doctor,' she said, thrusting out the glass towards Evans. 'Another if you don't mind.'

Roose suppressed a chuckle as Evans poured out a second healthy measure. Maddie took her time with this one.

'I'm sincerely sorry for your loss. I shall ask Miss Coulson, my nurse, to accompany you home. You shouldn't be alone after such a shock.' He turned to Roose. 'I'm assuming there was foul play, so any idea who might have done such a thing?'

'Oh yes,' said Roose with a slight smile, 'I have a very good idea.'

Maddie refused the offer of being accompanied home. Instead, she got Roose to steer the little buggy out of the town limits and bring it to a halt on the top of a nearby knoll, under the shade of several trees.

'You killed him, didn't you?'

'Now why would you think such a thing?'

'Because I saw the look in your eyes when the good doctor asked you.'

Roose cleared his throat, taking out his tobacco pouch. 'I had no idea he was your husband.'

'Would that have made any difference?'

25

'Maybe, Maybe not,' he drizzled a line of tobacco onto a paper and deftly rolled it into shape. 'He had a gun on me, was most likely set on shooting me dead. I did what I had to do.' He studied her. 'How come you never mentioned him all the times we've been together?'

'We were estranged.'

'E-what?'

'Estranged. Separated. He'd started playing around with some Mexican harlot called Beatriz Gomez a few years back so I threw him out. Best thing I ever did. It was always my intention to tell you, Sterling ...' A fluttering of the eyelashes. 'I promise.'

'Bah, it don't much matter to me none.' He put the cigarette into his mouth, struck a lucifer on the dull metal tin in which he kept his papers, and touched the flame to the end. It flared and Roose took in a pull of smoke and blew it out in a long stream. 'What's done is done. I have more important things to think about. And I need your ranch hand to help me out.'

'Cougan? He's a live one, that man is just like his pa.'

'I knew his pa. Knew him well.'

'Then you'll know his son still blames us all for what happened to his family down in Louisiana. They were hanged, fleeing from the plantation there were all working on. He doesn't take too kindly to white folks, especially the law-making kind.'

'I don't make the law, Maddie, I just dish out its justice. Reuben Cole was beaten half to death by a bunch of drifters last ni—' He stopped when he saw her face, those eyes widening, lips trembling. For a moment it seemed to him she was about to faint. 'Are you all right?'

Taking a moment, she pulled out a small silk handkerchief from her sleeve and dabbed it at her mouth. 'Cole? Is he ... I mean, beaten half to death you said.'

'Yeah ...' He swept his eyes over her. If he wasn't mistaken she seemed more disturbed by the news about Cole than she had about her husband. 'But you know Cole ...' A look of alarm ran across her features.

'Well, *yes*, I know him, but not in that way, Sterling.'

'I never said you did, Maddie,' Roose said slowly, eyes locked on hers now. 'What I meant was, he is as tough as they come and they may have tried their darndest, but they didn't succeed in killing him.'

'Ah yes, yes of course.' She forced a tiny chuckle and returned the handkerchief to its resting place. 'So, what happened exactly?'

'They broke into his house and have run off with almost all of his family heirlooms, probably worth a goodly sum, and I aim to bring 'em back to pay their dues.'

'Yes. Yes, of course ... But why do you need Cougan?'

'Because he is one of the best local shootin' men and I might have need of his services. I have a couple of trackers, but I doubt they'll be much good in a firefight.' He laughed as he studied the burning end of his cigarette. 'Fortuitous of you to come into town when you did. Perhaps it's a sign.'

She sniffed loudly, emotions recovering. 'Poor Gunther. You had no need to kill him.'

'I had every need. He would have killed me.'

'Well, we'll see what the judge has to say about that.'

'Judge? What what do you mean by that?'

'I *mean* I aim to let justice take its course, Sterling. I'm only repeating your own sentiments on the matter.'

'You are a vixen, Maddie! I told you I had no choice.'

'We shall see. There are bound to be witnesses.'

'What? Who have you spoken to? Whoever it was, they have got it wrong, I swear to you.'

'No Sterling, I haven't spoken to anyone, not yet. But I think I might have a fair idea where to start.' She smiled. 'Now, if you're not going to kiss me, take yourself back into town and then you can get on with your manhunt.'

They waited until late in the afternoon before they spotted Cougan coming into town astride of a large and powerful looking colt. He was a large, heavily muscled man, who wore a grey army shirt, and army blue pants held up by broad braces. In his waistbelt was a Navy Colt and, in its sheath slapping against the horse's rump, a Spencer carbine. If it wasn't for the ridiculously small bowler set askew on top of his close-shaven pate, he looked for all the world like a man on a mission.

'Dear Lord, he is one big bruiser,' said Nelson Samuels, waiting on his own horse next to Roose.

'He is a fister,' said Roose, 'so try not to rile him too much.' He looked askew at the other man he had pressed into service, Ryan Stone, a tall, wiry-looking man with sharp features. He looked mean and Roose felt a knot tightening in his middle. 'You're not looking too pleased with our companion's arrival, Ryan. Why's that? Had dealings with Cougan before?'

'Our paths have crossed.' He leaned over the side of his horse, hawked and spat into the dirt. 'Never did like him. A loud-mouthed boaster is what he is. What possessed you to bring him along?'

'He's the finest shot this side of the Mississippi. No other reason. See that big old Sharps he's lugging? He can take a rattler's eye out at a thousand yards with it.'

'That's a Spencer carbine, Sheriff,' said Samuels slowly. 'Not that it matters if he can use it.' Samuels shifted his weight in his saddle. 'Let's just do the niceties and get this thing done. My wife is all shook-up because of Reuben Cole and she wants those men apprehended.'

'Or killed,' muttered Ryan, his eyes never leaving Cougan as the big man reined in not half a dozen paces from them. He did not speak.

Roose didn't either, giving Cougan the briefest of nods before turning his mount around and kicking it into a lazy trot. Thinking things through, he wouldn't mind at all if those men were killed. Killing had always been something of a bed-fellow for Sterling Roose.

CHAPTER SIX

They left Fort Concho in the late August of Eighteen-seventy-four. The orders were despatched some days previously and Reuben Cole, together with Sterling Roose, stood outside the main entrance to their barracks on the evening prior to their departure, smoking and gazing out towards the vast prairie surrounding them.

'Heard it's about Comanch,' said Reuben, letting the smoke stream from between his lips. He was not a great smoker, allowing himself one in the evening before he settled down to sleep. "Again," he added, unable to keep the bitterness out of his voice.

'Heard a bunch of Cheynee and Arapaho have joined 'em. Broke out the reservation to follow a band of Kiowa. There's a lot of 'em, maybe two thousand.'

'If that's true, we're in for a long ol' haul this time, Sterling.'

'It's always a long ol' haul when it comes to Comanch. They don't take prisoners. And this time, according to the Colonel, neither do we. The government want 'em back in that reservation and we are to do whatever is necessary to succeed in that demand.'

'You know a lot about this, don't you?'

A mischievous glint played around Roose's eyes. 'To tell you the truth, Rube, I was listening at Colonel Mackenzie's door after I saw that express rider come blazing across the parade ground. A few of us crept across and listened to what he had to say.'

'That was brave of you. If Sergeant Dixon had found you he'd have—'

'Shoot, Rube, Dixon was the first one over there.' He chuckled. 'I'm guessing he was hoping for an easy retirement. His wife's expecting their first.'

'Maybe he'll get compassionate leave.'

'Against Comanches? Are you kidding me? No, they need every one of us out there, to push 'em up against the Red River, causing them as much hardship as possible and so force 'em back where they came from. But Lone Wolf is leading 'em and he is as hard as the mountains which hem us in from every side. He won't go down without a fight.'

As they streamed out of the main entrance, with Reuben and Roose at the van, the sun blazed overhead, beating down with an intensity that was almost too harsh to bear. As scouts, they wore broad-brimmed straw hats and buckskin clothes which afforded some protection. Ben Cougan, the third scout, had brought himself a parasol which he now twirled daintily between his sausage-thick fingers. 'Got me this from a young whore down in El Paso. Best thing she ever gave me – she was as ugly as an old coot.'

'So says the Greek Adonis,' chuckled Roose.

'What was that you said?'

'Nothing Ben,' said Roose with a grin, 'only commenting on your supreme good looks and how you can charm the prettiest of young things into your bed.' He winked.

Cougan glared, not believing a word of it. He was a dangerous, unpredictable individual, but Reuben had knocked him on his backside on more than one occasion, and said simply, 'Leave it, Ben.' That was enough.

The undulating landscape was an arid, broken plain, the compacted earth punctuated with clusters of rocks and clumps of sage. An acrid smell caught at the back of men's throats and the three scouts pulled up their bandanas to cover nose and mouth.

They set a steady pace, threading their mounts through the rough ground, knowing the most dangerous thing to do out here would be for a horse to turn an ankle in a hidden depression. The occasional rattler hissed its warning and sometimes the rare sight of a soaring eagle caused them to look skywards. Apart from these nothing else stirred and the only sounds were the plodding of hooves and the groans of cavalrymen close to the edge of boredom.

'I don't like this,' said the young second-in-command, Lieutenant Nathan Brent, fresh-faced and immaculately turned out despite the heat. He'd ridden up to the scouts who walked some hundred paces ahead of the column.

Roose, leaning forward, hands on the pommel of his saddle, gave him an encouraging look, liking his eagerness and his innocence. 'What exactly don't you like, Lieutenant?'

'Look at it,' he swept his arm dramatically in a wide arc, 'we're too open. Commanches could be hiding in a gulley, just waiting to attack.'

'Hit and run, you mean?' interjected Cole.

'Yes! Precisely.'

'What do you suggest, Lieutenant?' asked Roose, stretching out his back. 'We could spread out, but I don't believe there are any Indians out here.'

'They're more likely to be hiding amongst those rocks,' said Cole, pointing towards a distant range of low jagged mountains, which sprouted from the grey earth like giants' teeth. 'The summits are virtually unscaleable, but there's a whole system of caves, crags and hidden pathways where any number of men could hide.'

'Then we should check them out, seeing as we are heading in that direction.'

Cole looked uncomfortable and gave Roose a look.

'That's a good two-hour ride, Lieutenant. We wouldn't be back until nightfall.' He looked around, reached inside one of his saddlebags and pulled out a pair of German, precision-built binoculars. He scanned the plain over to his left, grunting when he found what he was looking for. 'Yonder is a small knot of trees and gorse, which will provide the horses with a little relief from the sun. My advice would be to make camp there and await our return.' He continued to swing the glasses to cover every direction.

'And post pickets,' said Cole. 'Your very best men.'

. . .

The three scouts rode at a fair pace across the flat earth, setting a course least sprinkled with broken rock fragments. As they drew closer to the base of the mountains, the scree increased dramatically, forcing them to skirt to the east as they searched for a way into the mountain network.

Giving way to a large depression, the landscape changed suddenly, with grassland and small areas of woodland replacing the uniform greyness of the plain. It was here they spotted a small cluster of timber buildings. Reining in, Roose again brought his binoculars to his eyes. 'All righty, we have here a cabin. It appears well built, and recent, with a fenced in area to the rear. Probably vegetables and the like. There's a small barn and a stable but I can't see any horses ... There's a well, and to ...'

His voice trailed away as he slowly lowered the field glasses and turned to face Cole who sat, waiting in silence.

'What?'

'There's something behind the well ...' He put the glasses to his eyes, adjusting the focus ring slightly. 'It looks ... I can't quite make it out as it's obscured by the well ...'

'Let's go down there,' said Cougan, pausing for a moment to spit over his horse's neck. 'There ain't nothing moving for a hundred square miles in this dead and dying land. Look at it – nothing grows except twisted gorse bushes and the like. Why would anyone live out here?'

'They have worked hard, whoever they are,' said Roose, continuing to scan the settlement, 'they have planted a good deal of wheat. Real farmers, not eager amateurs. Look at those fields, that ain't the work of someone who doesn't know what they're doing.'

'So where are they?'

Roose lowered the glasses again and answered his friend's question with a simple shrug.

'I'm going down there,' said Cougan as he deftly collapsed the parasol and placed it just behind the saddle pommel. 'The longer we sit out here the more likely we is to get fried. Besides, they might have some grub, a good cup of coffee, wholesome bread.' Licking his lips, his patted his ample stomach, reached behind him and pulled out his Spencer carbine from its sheath. 'You comin'?'

'I don't like it,' said Roose. 'It looks well tended and all, but why is there no one about?'

'Maybe they're inside, eating.' Cougan kicked his horse's flanks and set off down the slight incline. I'll go take a look-see.' Soon he was cutting a trail through the grass.

'We follow him?'

'Nope,' said Cole. 'We go in from the flanks. You take the right. Sweep round in a wide arc and when you come through the other side of the grass, dismount and move in slow.'

'You expecting trouble?'

'I don't know what to expect,' said Cole, checking his Winchester with deliberate care, 'but something is not right. All the horses gone, that causes me a good deal of concern, Sterling, I'll tell you that much.' He took a long drink from his water canteen and eased himself from the saddle. 'I'll go in on foot. If you hear shootin', forget what I said about moving slowly and ride in hard and fast.'

Chewing on his bottom lip, Roose took one final sweep with the binoculars, shook his head, and cantered away to the far side.

CHAPTER SEVEN

G roaning with the effort, Cole sat up in bed as Maddie came into the room. Head tilted, she studied him disdainfully with pursed lips and jutting chin. 'Just look at you, Cole.'

'Good mornin' to you too, Maddie.'

He struggled to make himself more comfortable, grunting and groaning, trying to find the best position. She came up close, pulling him to her as she puffed up one of the three pillows behind his back, before easing him gently against the now well-padded headboard. 'You look like you need a helping hand.'

'Anything from you would help just fine.'

She stepped back, brushing away a strand of hair from his forehead. 'Don't let Sterling hear you talking like that.'

'When are we going to tell him?'

Maddie made a face, shot her head towards the bedroom door then back again. 'Sssh, you fool! He's just outside, talking to the others. He'll be here in a minute.'

'Answer my question.'

'Not now, you idiot! Earlier, when he told me about what had happened, I think he suspected something.'

'Why would he do that?'

'Damn it, Cole! Are you actually stupid, or what? Because of my reaction to what they did to you. I almost broke down with worry.'

'There's no need to worry about me, Maddie. I've had a lot worse, believe me. So, what did he say?'

'Nothing, thank the Lord. I think I managed to divert his attention when I told him I'd be reporting what happened to Gunther to the judge.'

'Gunther? You mean he's back?'

Taking her time, checking and rechecking the door as she did so, she told Cole about what had happened in the jailhouse. He listened without comment and when she'd finished, she smoothed out the blankets over his chest. 'Anyways, he's all set to go riding through the prairie looking for the men that did this to you. I mean, *look* at you, Reuben!' For the first time, tears appeared under her bottom eyelids, and a tiny trail spilt down over her cheek. 'Darn it, I didn't want to cry, but ... *damn you, Reuben!*'

He reached out to her as her fists bunched and seized both her arms. She gasped. 'It wasn't my fault, Maddie! They came in the night, looking to steal whatever they could. Broke two or three of Pa's finest things. I shot and killed one of them, but the other did for me as he hid behind the door. I guess I wasn't thinking so straight.'

'When do you ever?'

'I am with you, Maddie. I'm in love with you.'

She stopped, the colour as well as the tension falling from her face. For a moment it seemed to Cole she was about to cry again. He went to speak but before he could say anything more, she recovered and tore herself from his grip. 'What do you know about love, Reuben? You've spent half your life on the trail, the other half moping about in this great big empty house of yours.'

'Until you came along.'

'*Until I* ... Reuben, we've spent a few brief moments together.'

'And in those moments I've realised just how much I need you.'

Her eyes sparkled with a mix of surprise, sadness and something else ... He wished it was hope. A shared desire to be together. He'd felt it as she lay in his arms the last time they were together. The way she'd snuggled into him, her voice so soft, so sweet. He knew what they had transcended mere physicality. Now, with that wide-eyed expression, he could see it again.

She went to speak then caught her breath as the sound of approaching footsteps made all further conversation impossible.

'Well, well, there's a pretty picture.'

It was Roose, framed in the doorway, hat tilted to one side, thumbs in his gunbelt. Maddie, swivelling around and giggled, which sounded to Cole forced, false. If Roose picked up on it, he neither said so nor changed position. 'Sterling, you are a dumb ass,' Maddie said. 'I'm only here giving Reuben my comfort, which is more than you're doing. I mean *look* at him.'

Pushing himself from the doorframe, Roose strode forward, the sound of his boots ominous in that small, dark room. 'Let some light in,' he said, rolling himself a cigarette.

Maddie quickly went over to the main window and opened up the shutters. Instantly, rays of sunlight streamed in, picking out the haze of dust hanging in the air. 'My, this place needs a good clean,' she said.

Roose grinned at his old friend. 'It's true what she says, Reubs – you do look all beat up.'

Unconsciously, Cole felt the swelling around his jaw. The worst of the pain was across his ribs where they'd laid into him with their boots. He didn't feel it at the time, having had the back of his skull cracked open like an egg. The bandages he wore were caked in dried blood. 'I might have to shave my head to get this thing off,' he said, prodding at the lint dressing.

'Leave it,' snapped Maddie, slapping away his hand. 'Have you no sense? The doctor said to rest, so rest.'

'She's right,' said Roose, lighting up his cigarette. He blew out a long stream. 'I have three good men waiting outside. We aim to ride out and pick up their trail. We have a witness who said they saw three men high-tailed it north-west. The only town within a hundred miles of north-west is Lawrenceville.'

'That ain't the most welcoming of towns, you know that.'

'It's still pretty much lawless. But the railroad arrived two years ago so things are bound to have improved. A man called Kestler is the constable there.'

'You know him?'

'Know *of* him. Heard a few things. Not all of them complimentary.'

Reuben made to throw back the blanket covering him, but Maddie was there first, 'What do you think you're doing, Reuben Cole?'

He laughed. 'I'm getting up, putting my boots on and going with them.'

'No you ain't,' said Roose quickly, acknowledging Maddie's wild, pleading look. 'You'd only hold us up.'

'You know that's not true. I'm the best-darned tracker in this whole county.'

'That you are, but you're in no shape to help. I can handle it.'

'Yeah, I'm sure you can, but with me riding alongside you, we'd handle it a lot better.'

Roose let out a blast of smoke. 'No, Reuben. I can't take the risk. The doc said—'

'That's right, Reuben,' cut in Maddie, 'the doc said you have to rest, that you can't take the risk of opening that head-wound up again. You need to *mend*, Reuben.'

'Maddie,' said Cole, doing his best to keep his temper, 'why don't you go outside for a moment, make sure those other boys have their canteens well filled with water.' She glared at him. 'Please, Maddie.'

She gave up the fight. Not looking too pleased with any of it, she stormed out, her long dress sweeping across the floor, sending up more clouds of dust.

Watching her go, Roose turned to consider his friend. 'She seems mighty concerned with you, Reubs.'

'She always has had a soft-spot.'

Nodding, Roose threw down his finished smoke and ground it with his boot. 'As far as I was aware, you don't know each other that well.'

'Well, that's true, Sterling. Dang it, are you jealous or something?'

'Jealous? No. Why, should I be?'

'Not at all, old friend.'

'Well, that's all right then.' He readjusted his belt. 'I aim to bring those varments to justice, Cole. You can count on me.'

'I know I can. This isn't about your abilities. You know that.'

'Remember back in Seventy-four when we rode across the great plain with Cougan.'

'Oh Lordy, why you thinking of that?'

'I don't know. It came to me the other day, the memory. So clear. Almost as if I was re-living it.'

'Well, you sure as anything don't want to do that.'

'I know, but ...' He heaved in a deep breath and sat down on the bed next to his old friend. 'These thieves, they've taken almost the self-same route. It got me to thinking, that's all.'

'Thinking about those times, Sterling ...' He shook his head. 'They're not dreams, they is nightmares.'

'Got a report come in across the wire. A whisper, to be honest. A group of Comanch have broken out again.'

'What?' Cole sat up, ignoring the pain, but gritting his teeth nevertheless. 'How many?'

'I don't know. Half a dozen. Some youngster's been whipping up things, getting some of the old boys agitated. They robbed a bank in a little town about fifty miles out of El Paso. Killed two tellers and wounded a young woman.' He looked into Cole's eyes. 'A pregnant woman. She's lost the baby.'

Snapping his head away, Cole bit down on his bottom lip. 'This ain't *ever* gonna end.'

'There's a chance we will come across 'em as we chase down the others. If we do ...' He leaned forward. 'Cole. You remember back then when we found that deserted house?'

Cole grunted, nodded his head once.

'You remember how we went in? You remember what we found?'

'What is it you're trying to say, Sterling?'

'I'm not sure I could go through that again.'

'It's haunting you, ain't it?' Roose nodded, not able to look his friend in the face any longer. 'Then let's talk it out and banish those ghosts forever.'

CHAPTER EIGHT

The memories returned, as vivid as if they were from yesterday. Cole listened intensely, all discomfort forgotten as Roose returned to that moment thirty years ago when they came upon a deserted homestead.

Roose took a wide berth, keeping the pace of his horse steady, using the long grass as partial cover from anyone who might be watching from the cabin. From a distance of around two to three hundred yards, he kept the settlement in plain view, stopping every so often to train his German-made precision field glasses on the cluster of buildings. He saw Cougan striding through the grass, rifle in hands. From twenty paces away, the big man had dismounted and now marched defiantly on, going straight through the open door of the cabin, paying no mind to the bundle behind the well. Intrigued, Roose once more focused in on what appeared to be a pile of clothes.

Until he saw the naked arm.

He dropped the glasses from his grip and kicked his horse into a canter, cutting a wide swathe through the gentle swaying grass, stirred by a hot breeze blowing in across the fields.

A shout, more of a strangulated bark, and Cougan appeared in the cabin entrance, staggering like a drunkard, his hands empty, the rifle gone. Roose turned his horse and jumped down at the run, levering his carbine, dropping to his knees when within calling range and training the weapon on the door.

'Cougan?' He waited, either for his companion to move or say something. There was no discernable reaction, however, only the swaying from side to side. Cougan's face, ashen-grey, seemed to have turned to stone, mouth and eyes wide open, but no life there. He was, Roose mused with chilling certainty, like a ghost. Already dead.

Something moved beyond the bulk of the inert Cougan. A shape, a man perhaps. Roose fired a single round into the blackness of the cabin, the large calibre bullet streaking over Cougan's left shoulder. A muffled cry followed by silence.

'Cougan?' Roose hissed again. More urgent now, as he levered another round into the Spencer and cocked the hammer. He sucked in a breath and steadied himself. Waiting, always the hardest part when shooting, Roose listened out for any sound of movement from within.

There was nothing.

Keeping low, Cole approached the side of the cabin from the mountainside. He dropped to his belly some dozen paces or so and slithered forward. The bundle of clothing behind the well caught his eye and from this angle and distance, he could clearly see it was a body. A young woman, contorted in the unmistakable pose of death.

Cougan came out of the doorway and stood swaying like a willow. Cole rolled away, deciding to take the rear of the cabin. Reaching the corner, he got to his haunches and checked his Winchester. He was about to move when the boom of Roose's carbine brought him up short and he waited, mouth open, straining to hear anything.

A low groan from inside the timber building. Definitely a man, possibly badly hurt.

Or possibly also a trick, to lure Roose indoors.

Taking a few urgent breaths, Cole chanced a look around the corner.

There was a man, kneeling in the stable doorway on the other side of the rear yard. Cole darted away again behind the cover of the cabin wall. He waited, eyes squeezed shut, recalling the man's look. Long hair, blue shirt, buckskin pants. An Indian, possible Comanche or Kiowa. He chanced another look.

Beyond the yard fence, they were taking the horses away at a gallop. Perhaps half a dozen men, some doubled up on their own mounts, leading the roped together animals across the far fields, kicking up a lot of dust as there the grass was not in such lush condition. Perhaps the settlers, or farmers more like, had left it fallow for the following season. Cole clamped his mouth shut. They'd never be farming this land again.

He chanced another look towards the stable. There were two of them now and, as yet, they hadn't spotted him, so he dipped back, flattened himself against the wall and bided his time. As soon as they broke cover, he too would move.

He had no way of knowing how many more renegades were lurking amongst the settlement. He'd estimated at least six of them making off with the retreating horses. Reports had said around a dozen Indians had broken free from the reservation, so somewhere milling around were a further six warriors. If Roose had hit one in the cabin, there were still five or so more to contend with.

Cole pressed the Winchester against his chest and measured his breathing. Comanche and Kiowas were just about the best for moving silently. They could already have made the rear entrance to the cabin.

So, sucking in a deep breath, he moved.

With no subsequent movement or sound emanating from inside the cabin, Roose decided to lower his carbine. Cougan continued to maintain his curious swaying motion, but Roose felt that almost certainly the man was dead. His big body leaned against the door frame, the only thing to prop him up. But it was the man's missing rifle that worried Roose the most.

Head down, he broke cover and ran half-crouched to the well, throwing himself up against its curved wall. From this angle, he had perfect cover to protect himself from anyone in the cabin shooting at him. Not from the stable, however.

There were two men in the open doorway and they were running also.

As they ran, another man appeared in the stable entrance, covering them with a partially-drawn bow.

Roose threw himself to his left as the arrow hit the well wall and veered off in a skyward direction. They'd spotted him, cutting off his chance to move.

Waiting, imagining the Indian with the bow nocking another arrow, he sprang up from his position and put three rapid shots into the stable opening. The bullets slapped into the woodwork, sending up a shower of jagged splinters, but no cries, no blood. Swinging his Spencer again to the cabin he put a further three rounds inside. Spent, he threw the carbine down and drew his Colt Cavalry. Just then more firing opened up. It was close.

Cole sprang out from his cover, standing, legs apart, Winchester lined up as three shots rang out across the wide open area between the rear of the cabin and the stable door.

He saw them. Two warriors, hatchets in hand, quiet as an owl swooping for its prey.

Three more shots thundered into the cabin and Cole responded, pouring steady shots into the charging men. Each bullet struck home, hitting first one man, then the other, full in the chest, throwing them backwards and Cole put two more bullets into each of them, heads erupting in a fine spray of pink mist and white, shattered skull fragments.

A man came out of the stable, drawing a bow and Cole shot him, dropping him like a stone.

The silence descended, eerie, other-worldly and Cole stood and viewed it all, dispassionate, unmoved. He'd fought Comanche for many years. This was nothing new for him. He knew what these warriors were capable of, their ruthless aggression almost legendary. Even in death, they appeared terrifying.

Footsteps clumped around inside the cabin and Cole whirled, going to one knee, his revolver in his hand, the Winchester by his side empty.

The rear door to the cabin remained closed. A voice, one he knew, called from beyond it. 'Cole? It's me. Don't shoot.'

The door eased open and Roose stood there, white as death. 'It's bad,

Cole.' He pushed his Colt its holster, angled for a cross-belly draw. 'Very bad.'

Without a word, Cole scooped up the Winchester and pushed past his friend and into the cabin interior.

It took a moment for his eyes to adjust to the change in light.

A large room, where once the family would have sat around the table, eating supper, sharing the laughter, the rigours of the working day. Ordinary conversations. Father, hard-working, wiry, strong. His two sons, gangly, not yet fully filled out. The wife. Plain, but determined. A daughter.

Cole knew all of this. He could see them.

The daughter was outside, next to the well. She must have broken free and run for her life. An arrow in the back.

Is that how it was?

He didn't know about the girl, but he knew about the others.

The wife lay spread-eagled across the table. Naked, her body defiled, her mouth open in a soundless scream, features contorted in pain. After they'd had their fill of her, they'd opened her up like a ripe melon with a heavy-bladed Bowie, straight to the breastbone.

If they had witnessed it, the male members of the family could not have helped her. Both boys were hanging by the feet from the rafters. Naked, the blood running in thick black streams down their bodies to mingle with their matted hair.

Between them, propped against the cold fireplace, the father. They'd wrenched his arms sideways, and lashed his limbs to the mantle to make him appear like a bird of prey, hovering over the dead. They'd hacked off his hands and his feet leaving him to bleed out in a torment of horror, watching what his wife had to endure, unable to help.

'What do we do?'

Cole turned to his friend. Something passed between them. A sadness, but also an acceptance. They had come too late to help these people and that was something that would stay with them forever.

'We bury them,' said Cole dispassionately, 'then we burn this place to the ground.'

Roose cleared his throat, averting his eyes from the horrors around him. 'And Cougan?'

Grunting, Cole went over to their companion. The knife still jutted from his back. It might have been the same knife they'd used on the woman. Cole put one hand flat against Cougan's back and pulled out the broad blade, the flesh making a sucking sound in its desperate attempt to keep the cold metal inside. It came out with a sickening plop and Cole pushed Cougan forward and he toppled, like a great tree, and smacked into the ground, face down.

'After we've buried 'em, we hunt the others down.' Cole turned and stared at his friend. 'Alone. You and me. And when we catch 'em, I'll do to them what they did to these poor folk.'

Roose's eyes came up and he knew that his friend spoke the truth.

CHAPTER NINE

'Things were a lot different then,' said Cole after both men had shared their memories of a quarter of a century before. He stared into the distance, recalling those images, the burning desire for revenge springing to life once more. 'Darn it, *I* was different.'

'And now it's happening again.'

'Hardly the same Sterling. Those who have broken out of the reservation, they'll be nothing like those others.'

'We never did catch up with the leader.'

'He died, I heard it say. Lone Wolf. Someone shot him and threw his body in a sunken hole somewhere down New Mexico way.'

'You believe it?'

Blinking, Cole frowned as he studied his friend. 'What do you mean by that?'

'Just seems strange, that's all. That these others have—'

'Didn't you tell me that it was some young fella who stirred them up, persuaded them to break out?' Roose nodded. 'Well then, it ain't gonna be Lone Wolf. Even if he didn't die with a bullet in his brain-pan, he'd be as old as a coot by now. A shambling wreck. He'd be ... good Lord, he'd be nearer ninety years of age.'

"They live a long time I heard it say.'

'Not *that* old, Sterling. And even if he was still alive, I doubt he'd be able to mount a horse and ride. He'd be old and tired and *long* past it.'

'Isn't that what we are, Cole? Past it? Do you think we still have what it takes?' He pulled in a ragged breath and something rattled in his chest, like nails in a rusty bucket. 'I have to tell you, I ain't sure. Maybe we've just outgrown this business, this land. This life.'

Unconsciously, Cole touched the rear of his skull and the heavy bandaging. He gave a chuckle. 'You might be right there, Sterling my old friend. You might be right.'

For a moment the depressed atmosphere bore down on them both like a living thing. It took Cole an effort to shrug it off, but shrug it off he did, and he gathered himself, the lines around his eyes hardening. 'Sterling, let me come with you. If you go out there in this state of mind there's no telling what might—'

'*No Cole*! I told you, you're in no state for riding out on the range,'

'Oh, and you are? I took a bash on the head, Sterling, but you ... What you have cuts a darn sight deeper than anything that's happened to me.'

'You're to stay in bed,' it was Maddie, coming through into the bedroom after more than likely listening to their conversation from out on the landing. 'You have to rest. Doctor's orders.'

'Doctor can go—'

'No he can't, Cole,' she said, coming up close. She pressed a hand down on Roose's shoulders. 'I'm none too happy with you going either, Sterling. It's dangerous.'

'No one else is prepared to do it.'

'It makes no sense.' She swept up her skirts and flopped down on the bed. 'So, they broke in and took a few things. None of it is worth dying for.'

'No one is going to die,' said Roose, but nothing in the tone of his voice was convincing anyone.

Maddie sighed. 'You're stubborn, Sterling. Stubborn and stupid.'

'You could just wait for me,' suggested Cole, looking from one to the other. 'That way we could track 'em down together, and if there was any fighting then I could—'

'Trail will be cold by then' said Roose, shaking his head but not daring to hold his friend's eyes. 'It has to be now. If they get away, they'll be back. Yours ain't the only big house stacked full of treasure.'

'Hardly treasure, Sterling.'

'You know what I mean. If we let 'em go every young tearaway from here to Carson City will think they can just ride in here and do whatever they want. I have to find 'em and bring 'em to justice. You know that, Cole.'

Cole grunted, looked at Maddie and, shrugging his shoulders, raised his brows in acquiescence.

She stood arms folded, watching them trot away, leaving Cole's land, taking the well-worn trail north. She watched them until they were mere dots and, even then, she remained where she was, wishing it was all a dream, that she would wake up and find everything was as it should be. Safe. *Normal.*

'He'll be all right.'

Turning she peered down the wide hallway to where Cole himself stood, rock still, a hand pushed out to support himself on the balustrade.

'I wish I could believe you.'

'It's not like it was,' he said, trying his utmost to reassure her. 'All them years ago, when we were out there, the world was different. A savage, untamed land, with dangers around every corner. It ain't like that anymore.'

'I overheard you and what you were saying. There's been a breakout.'

'Yeah, but even that is nothing—'

Maddie held up her hand and cut him off. 'I heard you. Times are different. But I still don't feel I can relax.' One last glance outside, then she swung around and walked straight up to him, taking his face in her hands and kissing him. 'You should be in bed.'

'If you'll come with me.'

Cocking her head, she couldn't help but smile. 'You think you're up to it?'

'Help these old bones up the stairs and I'll show you.'

47

CHAPTER TEN

They made camp in the bottom of a large dip, where acacia trees gave them adequate shade, and there was grass and water for the horses. Breaking out biscuits and bacon, Notch soon had a fire burning and he mixed the food in a black pan and fried it. The smell of the cooking caused them all to salivate. Notch poured them coffee and they drank with gusto.

'How are you now, Sollo?' asked Pete, leaning back against a well-knotted tree, stretching out his legs with an expression of sheer delight on his face.

'I'm fine." He rolled his damaged shoulder as if to underline his words. "We're a few hours away from Lawrenceville, but it's best if we are rested and fed before we go in. I want us on high alert, boys.'

Notch looked up from stirring the biscuits and fat, 'Why you say that? Expecting trouble?'

Soloman shrugged. He lay flat out on his back, hat over his eyes, arms behind his head. His stomach rumbled loudly. 'Maybe. I don't trust Kestler as far as I can spit.'

'I thought you said you knew him from years back?'

'I do. But that don't make him any less than the snake he is. He's never been totally trustworthy.'

'Then why did you hook up with him?' asked Pete, incredulous.

'Yeah,' said Notch, his voice a low grumble, 'it cost old Peebie his life, didn't it. Was it worth it?'

A heavy silence fell over them, the only sound the sizzling of the fat in the pan. Notch stirred through it half-heartedly. 'That should never have happened. You said the house would be empty.'

'Kestler *told me* it would be empty.'

'And you believed him.'

'I had no reason to doubt him.' Soloman sat up, face red, the anger brewing. 'Understand this, Notch, Peebie's death was not my fault.'

'Never said it was.' Notch shifted position, his mood dark, sombre. 'This is ready. Wish we had some bread.' He scooped out piles of biscuits and bacon onto tin plates and handed them over. Pete took his without ceremony and instantly started cramming huge spoonfuls greedily into his mouth. Soloman took his plate with much more grace, nodding his thanks, and taking his time with his eating.

'I was in the Lucky Dime saloon,' said Soloman, not looking up. 'I'd been spending time there drinking and gambling. Peebie was doing better than any of us and we had enough money to find us a decent bunkhouse, with grub and a whore or two. On the third morning, Kestler came in. He's a big man, and he seemed to fill the room. Everyone went deathly quiet. He crossed to the bar, ordered whisky for him and his boys, and then he noticed me. Grinning, he came over and put down his glass in front of me. He told me he was pleased he'd bumped into me, that I should drink his drink. I was down to my last few dimes. I guess he knew that. I drank and his smile got wider. He told me he had a deal he'd like to discuss with me, seeing as we went way back.' Soloman played with a clump of congealed biscuit and grease. He studied it for a long time before popping it into his mouth. Licking his lips, he pushed the empty plate away and lay down on his back again. 'We'd first met some years before, taking one of the last great cattle herds up to Wyoming. The railroad followed pretty darned quick after that, put a lot of us out of business. But on this last drive, Kestler and I got friendly. He was making his money selling that beef, and he'd made a lot of it. Said he was going to become sheriff, marshal even, of a frontier town called Lawrenceville. Well, he'd almost done it by becoming a constable there. Now, there he was, telling me his plan.'

Notch put away his plate. 'To break into those big old houses?'

Soloman grunted. 'There was riches in abundance – they was his words. *In abundance.* Apparently, he was bedding one of them cleaners who visited the homes on a regular basis and she told him everything he needed to know. Would you believe it, she even took pictures.'

'Pictures?' Pete laughed, wiping his mouth with the back of his sleeve. 'Shoot, I have seen them. Photographs is what they is called. They is like paintings, only without the colours.'

'That's right,' said Soloman. 'He showed me some taken from the house we broke into. He said he wanted the big vases and the paintings. Said they was the most valuable, but there was also porcelain figures too. From Germany. He wanted them. We was to be extra careful and we—'

'You told us all that,' said Notch, sounding irritated. 'Didn't stop Pete here smashing that big old blue vase though, did it.'

At this, Pete looked up, grease oozing from both the corners of his mouth. 'Notch, that was Peebie.'

'My ass,' spat Soloman. 'I knew it was you.'

'It was that guy coming in the way he did, taking us all by surprise. I thought the house was empty, just like you said it was! Then, him shooting Peebie and all ... I just wanted to get out as fast as I could.'

'You said you didn't know who that guy was, didn't you, Sollo?' asked Notch. 'Did Kestler know?'

'Nope. Kestler never gave me no names, just told me to get some boys, break in and get out. Then we was to do the same to two other houses. He drew me a map. Had it all worked out.'

'Reuben Cole. If I'd have known then ... I don't think I would have signed up to any of this. Indians call hiom 'He Who Comes'. You know why?'

'No doubt you're gonna tell me.'

'Because he never stops.'

'Never stops what?'

'Stops hunting you until you are dead and buried deep.' He shuddered. 'If I'd have known...'

'You're full of it,' spat Soloman. 'He's dead. I told you.'

'You don't know that – as *I told* you!'

'Pah ...' Soloman rolled over onto his side. 'Kestler wasn't bothered either way. Said he was gonna recruit another gang to do the same further north.'

'Another gang? What is this, Soloman? You never said nothin' about no other gang!'

'Ease up, Notch,' said Soloman, turning over again and re-settling his hat over his eyes. 'We ain't likely to come into contact with them. They're in the north I said.'

'Even so, I don't like the idea of us sharing.'

'Well, whatever happens now,' said Soloman, his voice sounding tired, resigned almost, 'we have a lot of explaining to do. One, we ain't got no vases and two, we never hit the other houses. Kestler ain't gonna be too happy about any of that.'

'But Peebie's death changed everything,' said Pete quietly.

'Sure did,' said Soloman with feeling, 'but I doubt Kestler will see it that way.'

'I swear, I'm truly sorry about that big old vase. You really think he'll be mad?'

'More than mad,' said Soloman. 'He is gonna be pissed.'

CHAPTER ELEVEN

Most mornings Lance Givens would step onto his large, covered porch and gaze upon his land. He'd close his eyes and breathe it all in, giving thanks to God for the many benefits bestowed upon him. It was something of a ritual and if for any reason, he forgot or omitted to send out his prayer to the cosmos, the guilt would gnaw away at him for the rest of the day. In saying that he rarely forgot. A man of strict habits, one might conclude, by viewing him every morning, that he was obsessive. This particular day, without thinking, he pushed through the main door and smiled as the warmth hit him. His eyes were closed. When he opened them, his smile disappeared.

Five riders, in a dark smudged line, were on the distant horizon, moving slowly bit inexorably towards his home.

They were crossing land which was fenced off and had been for well over thirty years. Givens had claimed this land half a lifetime ago, had worked and sweated over it, forging it into the sprawling ranch it now was. To have gained access, these intruders must have broken through the perimeter fence which demarked where the range ended and his ranch began. They'd called him a sod-buster back then. Now they called him 'Mr Givens'. Out here, he was the law. Despite the twentieth century promising wholesale change for the country, this particular plot was locked into days gone by. Givens didn't even possess a telephone.

Perhaps he should.

Swinging around, he stepped back inside. Mooching about in the dining room, laying the table for breakfast, old Shamus looked up and caught something in his master's demeanour. He tensed. 'Trouble, Mr Givens?'

Givens, breaking open the rifle cabinet, took out a Henry repeating carbine and loaded it with the same methodical precision he always used when dealing with firearms. 'Could be.'

Without a word, Shamus went to the same cabinet and pulled out a rifle. No words passed between the two men but when his wife wandered down from the first-floor bedroom, yawning, rubbing her eyes, and spotted them the atmosphere changed. 'What is it?'

Givens worked the Henry's lever. 'Don't know. Riders. They must have broken through the fence and they're heading this way.'

'*Riders?* You mean outlaws?' A strangulated yelp came out of her throat and she clamped a hand over her mouth.

'Go to your room,' he said, voice in control. Confident and strong. How he always was. 'Lock the door and do not open it for anyone.'

'Oh no, Lance, what if they ...'

He forced a smile, but it wasn't entirely convincing. 'Deborah, lock the door. There's a Colt in my dresser. It's loaded. Use it if you have to.'

'Best do what Mr Givens says, mistress.' Shamus eased in the last round in his gun and worked the lever. 'I'll cover you from the first-floor landing.'

Grunting, Givens went to return to the outdoors but checked that his wife was doing as he'd commanded. He saw the trails of her nightdress disappearing up the last few steps of the broad, sweeping staircase and he sighed. He then went outside.

There were only three men now. He blinked a few times. He knew he hadn't imagined their original number and this development concerned him. Thinking the others must have circled to the rear of the house, he checked either side but saw nothing. They were moving fast. Experts.

He dropped to one knee and settled the barrel of the Henry over the porch balustrade. He let them come on. They rode high in the saddle, backs ramrod straight. As they drew closer, he hissed in a breath.

'Indians,' he muttered to himself.

The central figure was young, much younger than his two companions, who were gnarled, grizzled old men, faces tanned and hard like leather, the lines of age deep cracks in their stretched skin. One sported a top hat, out of which sprouted a large black-tipped feather. The other wore his hair long. Both were dressed in old army jackets, the blue dye faded to a dull grey. The younger one wore a white shirt tucked into newly pressed black jeans. A face chiselled out of granite, his features determined. All eyes were bright and alert, darting from side to side, checking for any danger.

At twenty paces they reined in, the horses snorting furiously. This had been a long ride.

'Howdy,' said the young one, putting a forefinger to his forehead. 'Sure is a beautiful morning.'

'You're trespassing,' said Givens, keeping the rifle trained on the young man whom, he suspected, was the leader.

'Oh,' said the man in white, twisting in his saddle, looking to each of his companions in surprise. 'I didn't know that. We thought—'

'This is my land. You must have broken through a fence to gain access.'

Tilting his head, the man in white shook his head, 'No, no, I can assure you, we did not break through anything, sir.'

'Then how did you get through?'

The man chuckled. 'Well, there was a gap, in your fence. We just assumed—'

'There was no gap. I checked the whole perimeter yesterday evening. It's kind of a routine, you see. My men and I.'

This last point was not lost on the others. They grew tense and the older ones grumbled and looked around, agitated. The man in white, however, did not allow his gaze to shift an inch. 'You and your men?' He nodded. 'And where might they be right now?'

'Mister, that is no business of yours. Your *only* business is getting off my property.'

'Like I say, we didn't know this land was—'

'Well, you do now, so scoot!' To give his words greater emphasis, he eased back the hammer. 'Now.'

'That's mighty unfriendly of you, sir. Mighty unfriendly.'

The scream came first, belonging to Deborah, an ear-piercing sound filled with horror, followed by a single gunshot. Shamus' voice crying out, 'Oh no, *please no!*' and a fusillade of small calibre fire.

Givens instinctively stood up and turned to the direction of the shots.

The man in white shot Givens in the back of the head and it was over.

The others whooped, jumped from their horse and tore into the house. Taking his time, the man in white eased himself to the ground, pulled out a load of hessian sacks from behind his saddle and stepped up onto the porch. Givens, at his feet, had his face pressed against the wood planking, eyes wide open, the blood blossoming around his head. The man in white stooped down and plucked the Henry from Givens' dead hands, eased down the hammer and went inside.

After helping himself to some freshly brewed coffee, the young man went to the foot of the stairs. The cries of a woman in distress filtered down to him. He shouted, 'Boys, quit with your recreationals and come down here to help take the stuff.' One of the men from upstairs grunted, another laughed. A single shot put an end to the woman's cries.

They came down, out of breath, one of them stuffing his shirt into his pants, beaming proudly. 'My, she was a beauty!'

'Here,' the man in white threw over a clump of sacks towards the men. 'We have to move fast. It's still early, but he has neighbours and they would have heard the shots. Why didn't you use a knife?'

'The old coot heard us, tried to shoot me.'

'So you put a half dozen bullets into him?'

'I don't know what half a dozen is, Brody, but I shot him to pieces if that is what you mean?'

The man in white, identified as Brody, shrugged and turned away from the big Indian. 'What you did has probably woken up everybody within a hundred square miles and they will soon be heading out this way to investigate.' Shaking his head, he wandered into what he believed could be termed a library, given the number of books lining the walls. He turned and met his companion's hard stare. 'Mr Kestler wants jewellery and silverware, so get to it. The others are already working and you are wasting time – now *move.*'

Ignoring the other's look of outrage, Brody stepped into the library and marvelled at the learning contained in so many leather-bound volumes. Reaching into his pocket he extracted the list he'd been given. Scanning it, he saw no mention of books, which, to his mind, was criminal. On the desk, however, was one item he could readily tick-off. A perfectly made figure of a couple enjoying an afternoon stroll. Two exquisite porcelain figures, the man in a tricorne hat, the lady in a white, flowing dress, the floral motif on the fabric beautifully rendered. Brody shook his head in awe. To have the skill and artistry to produce such a piece of miniature brilliance was something he could only admire.

He savoured the other delights waiting to be discovered in that large, rambling house.

CHAPTER TWELVE

Roose and his men picked up the trail with relative ease. All three were expert trackers, but Nelson Samuels was the most accomplished. It was he who spotted the signs before the others. 'They are heading towards Lawrenceville, that is for sure.'

'It's a half day's ride. We will overtake them if we carry on.'

'The horses need resting.'

'They can rest after we've run those loathsome vermin down.' Roose unconsciously checked the revolver at his waist. 'We have them in our sights and I won't allow them to slip away.'

'You said this was a manhunt, Sterling, not a *death*-hunt.'

'You can ride back if you wish,' said Roose. 'You'll be paid for your time.'

'Ain't no need to say that, Sterling. I'm here to do a job, but I ain't an assassin.'

Roose scoffed, 'Nor me.'

The big man called Cougan stretched out his back. 'You did this with my pappy, didn't you, Sheriff?'

'Sure did.'

'You was hunters of men back then, so I heard tell?'

'This ain't the same thing.'

'Well then.'

'Well then *what?*' Roose rounded on his old friend's son, eyes flashing dangerously. 'They very near killed Reuben, breaking into his home, violating him and his father's memories! And how many other homes have they raised? Answer me that?'

'We don't know about that, Sterling,' said Samuels. 'We don't know anything about these idiots.'

'I know they tried to kill Reuben. If we let 'em go, we'll be sending a signal to every vagabond between here and the Missouri Breaks to come and help themselves to whatever we got!'

'I'm not saying we don't catch 'em, or let 'em go, Sterling. We bring 'em back for trial, that is what I meant.'

'And if they resist?'

Samuels left the question hanging unanswered. He shrugged and turned from Roose's accusing glare.

'Then we kill them,' said Ryan Stone in a flat, unemotional tone.

Roose grunted, flicked the reins and moved on in the direction of Lawrenceville.

When Roose was safely out of earshot, Samuels gave Stone a jab in the arm. 'You up for this, Ryan? Killing these men in cold blood?'

'Shoot Mr Samuels, it's like Mr Roose said – they darn near killed Mr Cole. I say, lay 'em out dead, then I can claim the bounty. Hot dang it, we could be rich.'

'Or end up in hell.'

'Hell don't put food on the table, Mr Samuels.'

'He's got a point,' said Cougan. He steered his horse behind Stone and Roose, setting his gaze towards the horizon.

Samuels remained watching them in silence. It was a long time before he fell in line.

From their vantage point on a towering cliff, Stone had an uninterrupted line of fire as the three robbers idled along across the open prairie.

'You can shoot 'em from this range?'

Stone gave Roose a sideways glance. 'I can shoot 'em, not sure if I could kill 'em though.'

'What about you, Cougan?'

The big black scout pushed back his hat and whistled soundlessly. 'I'd only wing one of 'em at best. The others would spook and ride like they was on fire towards the town.'

'They'd warn everyone that we're coming,' added Stone.

Roose rolled over onto his back and gazed at the sky. 'All right, that being the case, we could wait until they come out of the town. My reckoning is they are going to meet up with someone there, sell their ill-gotten gains, then move on.'

'Who'll do the buying?' asked Samuels, using Roose's field glasses to study the three robbers.

'My guess is Kestler. Nothing goes on in Lawrenceville without his say-so. He has that place wrapped tighter than a Fourth of July firecracker.'

'Kestler is not a man to trifle with, Sterling. You know that.'

'I do, which is why I say we wait for them to come out. There are only two possible exits. East or West. Northern limits are blocked by the mountains. East is back this way, which I do not think they will take due to their fear of being pursued.' He chuckled at this. 'West is their only option, so we go there, set up an ambush, and wait.'

'What about south?' asked Stone, not taking his eyes from his quarry.

'South is a wide open plain with little water and no shade. It has to be West.'

'So we don't shoot 'em now, Mr Roose?'

Smiling, Roose studied both of his eager young sharpshooters. 'No, Ryan. We shoot 'em when they come out.'

'You're insane,' said Samuels, lowering the glasses and shaking his head as if grieving. 'You've already made your mind up to kill them, haven't you.'

'I haven't decided anything. Not yet.'

'Of course you have.' He glared at the others. 'You all have! Dear God, I never thought it would come to this.'

'Me neither, Nelson, but it has. What must be done has to be done.'

'Killing them, like dogs? And without a trial? Is that what we must do?'

'We've been through this, Nelson. You can leave the shooting to me, Cougan, and Ryan if it'll help your conscience.'

'*Help my* ... Sterling, can you hear yourself? Conscience? What you're planning to do here is murder. Nothing more, nothing less.'

'You think them boys would have thought twice about killing Cole? *They* have no conscience, why should I?'

'Because you're a *lawman,* Sterling. Or at least I thought you were! This is not the old days. This is the Twentieth-century. We have laws and men like you are meant to enforce them, not corrupt them.'

'So say-eth the preacher man.'

'You're out of your mind, Sterling.' Samuels threw down the field-glasses and stood up. 'I'll not be part of this.'

'Sit down, Nelson,' said Roose, sitting up, his revolver materialising in his hand. 'I can't have you high-tailing away. Not now. We're too close.'

'What, you gonna shoot me, is that it?' He pointed to the rapidly diminishing figures out on the range far below. 'Your gunshot will alert them, Sterling. You wouldn't want that, now, would you?'

'I said *sit down*, you old bag of wind. If they hear it or not, I ain't bothered. I'll shoot you dead right now if I have a mind to.' He pulled back the hammer determinedly. 'Sit down until they are out of sight, then you can skedaddle.'

'Sheriff,' interjected Cougan quickly, 'you fire that big old police special and those bandidos will bolt for sure.'

Samuels, ignoring this exchange, turned to see Stone staring at him, that same unconcerned look in his eyes. 'Are you just gonna lie there, Ryan and say nothing?'

'Nothing to say, Mr Samuels. I want the bounty, simple as. And if you go back home, then that leaves all the more for me and Cougan here. Mr Roose can't take any, he's the law. I'll be sitting pretty.'

'With blood on your hands!'

Stone shrugged, sighed, and straightened himself up. 'My daddy died last winter, his chest all clogged up with blood and pus. Mama never has got over it. Like an old lady, she is. Mary, my eldest sister, she tries her hardest to cope, but Belinda, our youngest, is not well either. Doc says she has the same as Pa had.' He sniffed, dragging the back of his hand across his nose. 'I gotta do what I can to help my family, Mr Samuels. You go on home if you needs to, but I have an opportunity to make a difference to my loved ones, and I will.'

Looking down, unable to answer any of these points with any conviction, Samuels allowed his shoulders to droop. He turned to Roose and nodded his head. 'Put your gun away, Sterling. I'll go as soon as they are well out of earshot.'

Roose acquiesced and returned his New Model Police to its holster. 'We'll give 'em a half hour then make it over yonder, to the western boundary, and set up amongst the rocks.'

'And what if he tells folk back in town what we is planning on doing?' demanded Cougan, standing at his full, impressive height, agitated, breathing irregular.

From this angle, Roose thought he looked remarkably like his father and, more to the point, appeared just as headstrong and unpredictable. 'He won't,' he said quietly.

'We can't take the risk.'

'What are you saying exactly, Cougan,' spat Samuels. 'I told you, all I want is to go back, take no part in this. I'll not say anything to no one.'

'You will to your wife, we all know it. You cling to her skirts like you is her child. You'll blab to her and she'll tell the whole world and its wife.'

'Hold on there, Cougan,' said Roose dangerously. 'If Nelson says he won't tell, he won't tell.'

'I ain't so sure,' growled the big man and dived for the large Bowie knife at his hip. The great blade flashed. Ryan Stone yelped and scurried backwards on his backside as the big man lunged forward, preparing to swipe Samuels across the throat.

Roose moved before anyone else could even gather their wits. Looping one arm around Cougan's knife hand, he cracked his foot behind the big man's knees. As Cougan buckled and tried to twist himself free, Roose plunged his own knife deep into the big man's back, slicing upwards, the blade cutting through vital organs, piercing the lungs and into the heart. The blood welled over his fist and he held on, pushing ever deeper until he felt the strength leaving Cougan's body. Roose released his hold.

Without a sound, Cougan dropped to the ground, dead.

The others gaped at what had happened, horrified at the swiftness of Cougan's death. Roose stepped back, breathing hard, regarding the corpse with loathing. 'He sure did inherit all of his father's bad habits.'

Ashen-faced, Stone managed a strangulated mumble, 'I ain't ever seen such a thing. What do we do now?'

'Bury him,' said Samuels. He appeared shaken, face drained of colour.

'No. Leave him for the buzzards,' said Roose. 'I'll not waste any more of time on him.'

'Sterling, for the love of decency, you have to—'

'I don't *have* to do a single thing, Nelson, except what I came out here to do. Now leave it all well alone.'

Conversation over, Roose returned to his place, pulling his hat over his eyes and stretching out his long legs.

Stone looked with incredulity towards Samuels, who merely shrugged, slumped down on top of a large boulder and put his head in his hands.

Nobody spoke as, just under an hour later, Roose and Stone eased their horses down from the mountainside and began their crossing of the range to the far western edge of the town of Lawrenceville. Samuels, having said some simple words over the dead Cougan, rode away in the opposite direction without a backward glance.

He made good going, calculating he need only camp out for one night before he returned home to his wife and a good, hearty meal. No doubt she would be full of questions and Samuels already went through a number of scenarios as he set a steady pace along the trail. Cougan's death troubled him. He knew Roose had saved his life, but the enormity of the violence shocked him, left him numb, forcing him to question the Sheriff's sanity. He'd seen a wildness in his old friend's eyes, a loss of control. At the same token, he thanked God for it. Cougan would have murdered him within a blink and would have done so with less conscience than Roose had displayed. A tremor ran through him. He'd rather forget it, as best he could. His only fear now was that his wife would somehow tease it out of him.

Deep in thought, he did not notice the five riders coming out of the heat haze towards him.

By the time he did, it was already too late.

CHAPTER THIRTEEN

Perhaps the most prominent feature of the town was the train station. Two lines, a waiting room, wrought iron canopy and, at that moment, a huge locomotive hissing steam awaiting departure, a man filling the tender with water. The engine throbbed, beating like the heart of some prehistoric beast. Soloman pulled up his horse and breathed in the vapours. 'I don't know what it is, but that smell makes me feel like I'm home.'

Notch sniggered. 'That ain't no home I'd ever like to visit.'

'Notch, I wouldn't invite you anyway.' Soloman sniffed loudly. 'When was the last time you washed?'

'Christmas morning, as always. Don't see no point in washing away my natural oils, Sollo. It's what protects me from diseases.'

'Well you is ripe, my old friend. I reckon when this is done, we book ourselves into a warm, inviting bordello, and ease ourselves into a tin bath full of fancy French perfumes.'

'Hot dang,' cried Pete, tearing off his hat and beating his thigh with it. 'I like the sound of that, by Jiminy! You think Kestler will give us enough dollar to do all that, Sollo?'

'More than enough. He'll be mad about the vase, but the rest will cheer him up.'

'Let's hope so,' said Notch, sounding unconvinced, shooting a derisory sideways glance towards Pete.

They slowly moved away from the bellowing of the locomotive beast and eased their way into Main Street.

Kestler's base of operations did not require a signpost to identify it. Next to the first saloon, they came to a large merchandise store, which bore the legend 'R KESTLER & Co'. Under the shade of an awning, three gunhands leaned against the veranda balustrade, chomping on tobacco or smoking, looking bored. They stiffened as Soloman and the others rode up.

'Howdy,' said Soloman.

The gunhands did not speak.

Soloman shifted his weight in his saddle, the leather creaking. Surveying the street, he noted how quiet it was. What few shops were still open, none appeared to have any customers. It was early evening, the air thick with heat. Maybe that was the reason. He caught Notch's feverish look and tried again. 'I'm looking for Mr Kestler. Is he about?'

'Nope.'

This from the tallest of the three men. He leaned over the balustrade and spat into the dirt next to Soloman's horse. The animal snorted and stamped its foot.

'Do you know where I might find him?'

'Nope.'

He'd tried. Friendly, polite. None of these came easily to Soloman, but he'd done his best. He exchanged another glance with Notch and drew his revolver in one, flowing movement. 'Then do your best to remember, boy, before I put a hole so big in you that fancy new train down at the station could ride right through you.'

The three gunmen stood gawping at Soloman's audacity. The tallest tried his best to laugh, but nothing came out except a strangulated squawk.

Notch and Pete drew their guns.

Soloman grinned. 'I'm waiting.'

'No need for any of that, Soloman.'

Half a dozen pairs of eyes snapped to where a baritone voice boomed.

A man dressed in black trousers and waistcoat, watch chain stretched across his ample belly, pulled off his Stetson and mopped his brow with a handkerchief.

'Well how do you do, Mr Kestler,' said Soloman, the relief noticeable in his voice. He dropped his gun back into its holster. 'I was thinking we might have come into the wrong town.'

'Hardly likely, Soloman, seeing as Lawrenceville is the only sizeable settlement in these here parts.'

'I was talking about the reception committee.' He nodded towards the gunmen, who remained nervous, eyes fluttering from Kestler to the others.

'Well, they are raw, Soloman. Unlike yourself. A seasoned campaigner.' He chuckled at his joke. 'Tell your partners to get themselves a drink in the saloon while you and I discuss business in my office.'

'Sounds good to me,' said Pete, holstering his gun.

Notch did not follow suit. He stood, glaring at the gunhands. A friendly tug on the shoulder from his partner eventually made Notch turn and stomp off towards the saloon.

'He's edgy,' noted Kestler, taking Soloman by the elbow and steering him towards the entrance to the large store.

'It's been a difficult few days, Mr Kestler.'

They went inside. Soloman gasped.

A vast space opened up before him, the ceiling so high a double storey house could be placed inside. There were aisles stuffed with every conceivable piece of equipment, from simple hammers and nails to entire ploughs with harness. Every space seemed filled. Sacks full of grain. Great rolls of cloth. Clothing. Boots. Hats. And guns, of course. Lots of guns. Above all, it smelled wholesome, the air rich with sweet, seasoned timber, a smell designed to encouraged a customer to linger, browse and buy.

Soloman whistled through his teeth. 'Dear Lordy, Mr Kestler, this is a mighty fine shop.'

'It's what is known as a supermarket, Soloman. Got the idea after I visited New York city some months back. You like it?'

Soloman shook his head in awe, pirouetting to take everything in. 'It's incredible. But, where is everyone? The town seems almost deserted so how are you gonna make this a success if no one comes in?'

'Ah, Soloman,' Kestler clamped a big hand on Soloman's shoulder. 'It's evening, people have all gone home. Tomorrow it will be bustling again. And of course, now that the railroad is here, soon this entire town will be taking on the look of a city. Already there is building work going on close to the rail station. You might have seen it?'

Soloman frowned, thinking, but he couldn't recall seeing any such building work. Then again, he wasn't particularly looking. 'No, sorry, can't say that I did.'

'Well, not to worry.' Kestler moved through the main aisle towards a broad counter behind which a bespeckled man in a waistcoat and rolled up sleeves was counting money from out of a cash register. He didn't look up as the others approached and Soloman noticed the man's lips moving as he silently counted the cash.

'This is Doc Haynes. He's my chief cashier. A man who knows every inch of this here establishment.' Kestler turned around to face Soloman and leaned back against the counter. 'So, my friend. Did you get it?'

The moment Soloman had dreaded through the entire journey to Lawrenceville was here. He swallowed with some difficulty, spread out his hands, a forced a pathetic smile. 'We had a problem.'

'Ah,' Kestler, nodding, turned askance towards Haynes. 'A problem?'

Did the cashier stop counting, if only for a second? Soloman tensed. The atmosphere was changing. Gone the friendly warmth of the interior, replaced now with a frosty chill. 'Yeah. The house we broke into, the one you told us about ... What you didn't tell us was that the owner was Reuben Cole.'

'Ah. Reuben. He has something of a reputation.'

'It was Notch who recognised him. Said he was an old-time Indian scout for the Army. Hard as they come. A killer.'

'Yes, so I understand.' He drew in a large breath. 'So you killed him?'

'I kicked him to pieces. He shot poor old Peebie right through the head.'

'Yes, but you *killed* him?'

The cashier stopped counting altogether. Soloman waited, trying to steady himself as his heart slammed up into his throat. 'I believe so.'

'Well then,' Kestler clapped his hands together. 'We have no further need to worry do we?' Again, a quick glance towards Haynes who now stood, head down, palms flat on the counter. 'And the items, Sollo? You managed to acquire the items?'

'I have 'em all, tied up with the horses. Except for the vases. The big blue ones.'

An arched eyebrow. A slight draining of colour from the lips. 'Oh?'

'Yeah. Pete, he sort of panicked ...'

'Panicked?'

'Yeah, with Cole coming in and all, shooting Peebie the way he did. Poor Pete sort of got all nervy, knocked into 'em. Smashed 'em.'

'Smashed them?'

Soloman nodded and looked across to Haynes whose own head had come up, eyes filled with a murderous glare. Soloman took an involuntary step backwards. 'Mr Kestler, it was an accident. We got everything else.'

'The painting?'

'Yes, I got that. No problem. Figures too, beautiful things. And serving dishes, as your orders. Solid silver. Soup bowl. Great big thing, with a ladle. All in solid silver. French, I think you said.'

'Yes. Lots of French things. Cole's father was something of a collector.'

'So, from what I'm guessing, you know Cole?'

'I've never met the son, but I have met the father on numerous occasions. Before his untimely death, of course.' As the corners of his mouth turned down, Kestler took on the demeanour of a deeply disappointed man. He sighed long and loud. 'I'm saddened though, Soloman by what you have told me. I thought I could trust you.'

'You *can*, Mr Kestler. You can.'

'Hmmm .... Well, I am not happy. Those vases, they were worth a lot of money. I had customers lined up, all the way from Paris, France.'

Soloman gaped at that. 'Oh, really?'

'Yes, *really*. I have a reputation to maintain, Soloman. I need men on whom I can depend.'

'On whom ...' Soloman's voice trickled away. 'Mr Kestler, this was one mistake. I'm sorry, it won't happen again.'

'Get rid of this Pete fellow.'

It was Haynes, his voice like a slab of ice piercing the heavy air. Soloman turned to him, eyes bulging, his stomach rolling over. 'Get rid of him? What does that mean exactly?'

'It means,' said Kestler, folding his arms, looking smug, 'we can't afford to have idiots working for us, Soloman. Your choice of accomplices was not a good one. You need to vet them much more circumspectly. Understand?'

Soloman didn't. The man was talking in some fancy, made-up way and he could not make head nor tail of his words. He ran a finger under the collar of his grubby, sweat encrusted shirt. 'I, er, don't think I do, Mr Kestler. What does circum, er, circumthingfully mean?'

'You need to take more care in who rides with you,' said Haynes, eyes unblinking, his stare able to freeze bones to the marrow. 'So get rid of him.'

'The other one too. The jumpy one.'

'Notch? But I can't ...' Soloman puffed out his chest. Not used to being spoken to this way, not by anyone, he wasn't about to be railroaded into something he didn't want to do. His hand dropped close to his gun. 'All right, Mr Kestler, we made a few mistakes and I'm sorry. So, if you'll be paying us what we're due, we'll be on our way.'

'On your way?' Kestler chuckled. 'Soloman, you work for me. You can't simply walk away.'

'And I can't simply 'get rid' of my boys. So pay me the money we is owed and that'll be an end to it.'

'No,' said Haynes.

'What did you say?'

'He said 'no', Soloman. I have a business to run and you are part of it. Now, do as you are told or you won't get a single penny.'

'Get rid of them,' said Haynes and added, with deliberate slowness, 'then all of the payment will be yours.'

Running a hand over a face seeping with sweat, Soloman instantly saw the attraction of such a proposition. 'I've known Notch for years,'he spluttered, pressing a trembling hand against his mouth. 'He's my friend.'

The other two men stared. Neither spoke.

A thousand conflicting thoughts roared around inside his head and, with each passing moment, the stress levels increased. Pulling off his bandana, he mopped his brow, puffing his breath through ballooning cheeks. 'I hate you, Kestler. You hear me? You should have told me about Cole and who he was.'

'Just do it,' said Haynes, looking down at the money. 'With less of the dramatics.'

'Just who are you, mister?'

Shaking his head, Haynes returned to counting out the piles of dollar coins and bills.

The conversation was over.

CHAPTER FOURTEEN

Nestling amongst a jumble of jagged rocks, Roose and Stone did their best to stay comfortable, knowing they may well be there for some time. Shade was minimal, a fact not missed by Roose. 'Always had me a wide-brimmed sombrero when I rode with the Army,' he said, readjusting his own headwear, a battered Stetson.

Stone, bareheaded, pulled off his bandana and fashioned a sort of cap which he positioned on top of his skull. 'Stupid. I should have brought something.'

'Too late now,' said Roose, pushing himself up against a large boulder in order to get a good view of the town below. He took up his field glasses and focused in on the main street. Few people were about, one of two wagons moving slowly along, but no sign of the burglars.

'How long do you reckon we should wait?'

'Beats me,' said Roose, lowering the glasses. 'A few hours at least. If my guess is correct, they are down there doing some sort of deal after delivering their stolen goods.'

'Yeah, but who to?'

Another shrug. 'Not sure it matters, but I'm guessing Kestler.'

'Yes, the one you mentioned. He runs the town, so you said.'

'He does, but I ain't ever heard of him doing anything illegal.'

'Always a first time.'

Roose looked at his young partner and chuckled. 'That there is. You learn fast, son. It is to the advantage of a lawman to get inside the head of those he pursues and that is what you is doing.'

'Is that what you did when you hunted Comanch? Get inside their heads?'

Roose turned away. 'Comanch is different. They don't think like White folks. That's what makes 'em so dangerous.' His eyes grew cloudy as he looked back to a time steeped in brutality and death. 'They is a proud and noble people, but if you cross them they will not rest until you are under their knife. They give no quarter and they expect none.'

Finally satisfied with his protective cap, Stone took the chance to sit up and peer down to the township of Lawrenceville. 'They must have been dangerous times back then.'

'Times is always dangerous, son, if you do not keep your wits about you,' he patted the New Model Police in its holster, 'and always have your best friend forever close.'

Nodding in agreement, Stone settled himself back down amongst the rocks. He closed his eyes.

'If you can sleep, do so,' said Roose. 'I'll wake you if anything happens.'

As he did not possess a timepiece of any description, Roose had to rely on his age-old abilities to calculate the hour by the passage of the sun. Satisfied they had waited for well over three hours and with the evening hurrying on, Roose roused his young companion with a sharp dig in the ribs with his boot. Stone cried out, arms flailing, and sat up, disorientated. 'What? What is it?'

'It's late and there's no sign of anyone. I've been watching and watching but there ain't nothing.'

Stretching out his limbs, Stone climbed uncertainly to his feet. 'It's almost evening. You should have woken me earlier, Mr Roose.'

'The day's moving on, yes, but you were sleeping like a baby.' He gave Lawrenceville one last look through the field-glasses then dropped them back into their leather case. 'I'm going down there.'

'What, into the town?'

Roose grunted before he checked his revolver. 'We'll go in nice and slow, but from the other side. It's an easier approach, given that we won't need to take our horses on such a treacherous downward route. Take a look.'

Stone craned his neck to take in the twisted, rutted path that snaked down towards the town. Given its steep angle of descent, it did indeed appear perilous.

They moved off, Roose in the lead. Having covered almost three-quarters of the distance between their hilltop lookout and the eastern entrance to the town, Roose brought his horse up to a jerking halt, right hand raised. 'Dismount,' he said, voice reverting to the tone of authority that served him so well in his army days. Without waiting for his younger companion, he dropped from the saddle and scurried over to a clump of sage and got down on his knees. Silently, Stone followed, something which didn't go unnoticed. 'Good,' acknowledged Roose and brought up his field glasses. He trained them towards the open prairie and sucked in air through his teeth. 'Shoot,' he said and passed the binoculars to Stone.

There were riders, moving at a leisurely pace, the man at the lead of the group distinctive in a blazing white shirt. Alongside him, the horse tied to his own, the rider manacled, stripped to the waist, was Nelson Samuels.

'Oh no, they captured Mr Samuels.'

Roose took back the glasses and looked again. 'All right, at least he's alive. They must be taking him into town, maybe to question him.'

'Question him? About what?'

'Who he is, why he's out here all alone, why he's packing a rifle that can take your eye out at a thousand yards.' He pushed the binoculars into their leather case and closed the lid. 'Whatever they ask, they will get their answers and Nelson will tell them everything they want to know.'

'You can't know that Mr Roose.'

'By the look of that band, son, I'd say it's pretty clear who they are – the bunch of Comanch that recently broke out of the reservation.'

'But why are they coming here?'

'Same reason those ones who broke into Cole's place came here – to get paid.'

'By Kestler?'

Grunting, Roose went back to his horse. 'Son, I'm going down there. Maybe I can find out what's going on, negotiate with 'em.'

'Mr Roose,' said Stone, voice verging on breaking, frantic with concern. 'If what you suspect is true, those men won't want to negotiate with you about anything.'

'Yes, they will because you is going back to telegraph for help. There is a detachment of U.S. cavalry at Carson City. You send word there to a man called Willets. Captain Willets. I served with his uncle, Sean Willets, so if you mention my name he'll respond more quickly.' He turned, eyes burning. 'You tell him to send a troop to Lawrenceville, you hear me. And you tell 'em to get here *fast*.'

'Maybe I should go straight to Mr Cole. He'll know what to do.'

'Cole is convalescing. Don't trouble him with any of this.'

'But Mr Cole is—'

Without warning, Roose's hand shot out and seized the young man by his shirt front. 'You do as you are damn well told, you hear me!'

Stone, rigid with surprise and fear, eyes bulging, sweat breaking out on his brow, rapidly nodded his head.

Roose let him go and swung up into his saddle. 'I didn't mean to scare you, son, but this is something I must do on my own. Now get out of here, keep your head down, and don't stop for anyone. You understand me?'

'Yes sir,' said Stone, bringing his heels together, right hand springing against his head in as close an imitation to a salute as he could make.

Wheeling his horse away, Roose cantered off, back ramrod straight, determination evident in every part of his body.

Stone watched and wondered if life was ever going to be the same again.

CHAPTER FIFTEEN

It was Pete who first reacted when Soloman came through the batwing doors. He nudged Notch who sat absently dealing out cards for a game of Patience. 'He's back,' he said.

Notch gave Soloman a frown as his friend approached their table. 'Well? What did he say?'

'He ain't happy,' said Soloman, dragging a chair from under an adjacent table and sitting down next to Notch. 'Not happy at all.'

'But did he pay us?'

'Not yet. He wants to check through what we managed to get.'

Laying down his undealt cards, Notch allowed his eyes to roam away from Soloman to settle on the gunhands propping up the bar. 'He sure does seem to have quite a few men, don't he? Maybe he's expecting trouble of some kind. I don't like this, don't like it at all. You think he's set on double-crossing us?'

Grunting, Soloman folded his arms. 'We need to talk. There are some complications.'

'Oh? Such as?'

'Such as we need to go out back and talk.' He glanced over at the bar. 'Nothing within earshot.'

'You got a plan?' asked Pete, leaning forward. His lean, hungry looking face was streaked with dirt and sweat. Soloman sniffed and turned away. 'Yeah, I know I stink,' Pete sulked, picking up on Soloman's reaction. 'Thought we was getting a bath?'

'Later. We talk first.' Soloman stood up and readjusted his sagging trousers.

'Let's make it quick,' said Notch, 'because I too need a bath.'

Crossing over to the bar, Soloman asked the barkeeper if there was a rear entry. Puzzled, the man somewhat reluctantly pointed to a door at the foot of the large curving staircase that led to upstairs rooms. The landing, which led to a series of closed rooms, was supported by solid wooden posts with empty tables between. 'Not the most popular of places this, is it,' commented Soloman. The barkeeper ignored him. Giving his thanks, Soloman caught the gunhands' scowls and winked. Gesturing for his companions to follow, he went through the door.

The sun was swiftly descending by now and already the air was filled with the sound of insects as Soloman pushed through the door and stepped into a high-walled courtyard, filled with oak barrels and crates. He watched as Notch and Pete joined him.

'Close the door,' he said.

It was Pete who did so, turning his back for one moment.

The only moment Soloman needed.

He drew the heavy bladed Bowie knife from its scabbard positioned in the small of his back and plunged it straight into Notch's midriff, slicing upwards to the breastbone. Notch, so startled he did not have time to yell out, stood there, looking down at the blade in disbelief. Stepping past him, Soloman smacked Pete across the jaw with his revolver, smashing him back against the door. Grunting, mouth cracked open and full of splintered teeth and frothing blood, Pete did his best to remain on his feet, clawing for his gun. Soloman's knee rammed up into his groin and Pete buckled and crumpled, squealing.

On his knees now, trying to dislodge the knife, Notch bleated like a goat. Soloman came up to his victim's front, put a hand around the knife handle and a boot against Notch's chest and hauled backwards with all his strength. The blade came out, making a sickening squelching, sucking sound as it popped free.

'Why,' hissed Notch before Soloman put the blade into his throat and finished him.

Writhing on the ground, it was clear Pete would not be going anywhere, so Soloman took his time, straddled him, and stabbed his former companion repeatedly until he moved no more.

Soloman stood up, hands and shirt front splattered with blood. He was shaking, but at least it was done. He'd honoured his part of the deal, now Kestler must honour his.

But first, he needed that bath.

'What is it now?'

Hearing the approaching clump of cowboy boots on the boardwalk, Kestler, sitting at his dinner table and about to tuck into a plate of steak and eggs, lowered his head in despair.

'Boss,' called one of his men, coming into the room at a run.

'What do you want, Bart? Can't it wait?'

'Not really,' said Bart Owens, coming up to the table. 'I'm sorry, Mr Kestler. Truly.'

'Just get on with it.'

'It's them Indians you hired.' Kestler looked up, interest piqued. 'They is outside, horses laden down with sacks and all.'

'Well, that's good news. 'bout time I had some *good* news.'

'They got someone with 'em. They said you'd be interested.'

'Who is it?'

'Beats me.' He forced a smile. 'I, er, think they'd like you to go have a look-see, boss.'

Throwing his chair back with such great force that it toppled over and crashed to the floor, Kestler stood up. 'Looks like I'd better get straight to it, then.'

'Boss, I'm sorry, if I'd have—'

'Ah, shut up, Bart!'

Kestler pushed past him, fuming.

Outside, the steely grey evening lent an eerie aspect to the riders waiting in the street. Drained of all colour, it was difficult to make out their features. Kestler, however, recognised their leader almost immediately, his white shirt acting like a form of spotlight, drawing his attention. Beside him was a stranger, unlike the other riders, head bowed, hands lashed behind his back, naked except for a piece of flimsy, filthy material hiding his nether regions. He was a bloody mess.

'Evening Mr Kestler.'

'Evening Brody.' Kestler said, acknowledging the rider in the white shirt. He stepped down into the street, went up to Brody's horse, and stroked its nose. He nodded towards the naked stranger, who appeared semi-conscious. 'Who's this?'

'Well,' Brody brought up his left leg and crossed it over his right, 'we found him out on the range as we were coming here. Something about him ...' Tutting, he shook his head. 'Had himself a big rifle. Looked tasty, When I asked him about it, he became all cagey, like. Wouldn't answer, said he had to get back home to Freedom.'

'Freedom? That's the town where I sent you to break into those houses.'

'Exactly, Mr Kestler. So, we decided to rough him up a little so he'd tell us exactly who he is and what he's doing such a long way from home.'

Kestler stepped closer to the stranger and looked him over. Not a young man, his lily-white body was nevertheless well-muscled, as if he took good care of himself. 'What's his name?'

'Calls himself Nelson Samuels. Of course, he didn't give that up straight away.' Brody cackled. 'We had to tease it out of him.' This comment brought great amusement to the other riders.

'I don't know that name.'

'He then told us he was part of a team on the trail of the men who broke into Reuben Cole's house and stole some of his best wares.'

'That would be Soloman's attempt to do my bidding.' Kestler wandered across to one of the other riders and felt through one of the many sacks dangling over the horse's rump. 'Unlike yourself, Soloman's venture was something of a disaster,' said Kestler, in a satisfied tone. Brody was the 'real deal'. A man who did as he was told, who got results. 'Did he tell you where the other pursuers are?'

'He told us they were close, coming into town, hot on the gang's trail. That the leader, a man called Roose, was determined to kill the one known as Soloman. Maybe even you, Mr Kestler.'

At this, Bart Owens cleared his throat, 'Maybe we should prepare a welcoming committee?'

Nodding, Kestler clapped his hands together. 'All right, take this one,' he jabbed his fingers towards Samuels, 'and put him in one of the stables over at the livery. When his friend Roose comes along, we'll reintroduce them.'

'After we have some fun?' asked one of the other riders, a big man, aged, grizzled, a deep scar running down the left side of his face.

'Fun?' Kestler arched an eyebrow towards Owens. 'Just get this one tied up in the livery. We'll worry about Roose when he appears.'

'I think we could ambush Roose before he gets into town,' said Brody. 'If he is determined to kill both Soloman and you, it might be best to do as your man here says and stop him before he gets too close.'

'Especially if he has one of those Sharps rifles,' added the scarface. 'With that, he could shoot you from a distance.'

'Yes, all right,' said Kestler, twisting his mouth into something akin to a smile. 'Meanwhile, I want you to take all of the goods you got into my mercantile store. Doc Haynes will sort through it, then pay you.'

From across the street, half hidden behind the side wall of a carpenter's shop, Soloman watched the Indians half dragging a naked man into the livery stables. Others unloaded their horse, together with the bags draped over Soloman's horses. He debated whether or not to stride over and shoot them down dead, but common sense proved the victor on this occasion. There were too many of them. And, unlike Pete and Notch, these men seemed tough and so would prove a much more dangerous proposition. He'd need to bide his time, but with the bags of loot and stolen goods now inside the mercantile store, hopes of recouping any money for his efforts seemed increasingly like nothing more than a distant dream.

Unfortunately, as he stood mulling over his dwindling options, Soloman's nature asserted itself. He knew he would be going up against men who were as violent as he, but the draw of the money was a powerful one, urging him forward, demanding he do his utmost to gain what was his by right.

The men reappeared from the stable, not much more than dark shadows now as night continued to conquer the light. They were laughing with one another as they made their way to the mercantile store. Checking his revolver, Soloman decided to act quickly. He would interrogate the man in the stable first, find out what was going on, then charge into the store, killing whoever got in his way. The time for niceties was over. The time for action was here.

A stream of light pierced the darkness and Soloman's attention was drawn to the mercantile store entrance. The men entered, the glow from inside friendly and inviting. He chuckled. He would be the uninvited guest, the unexpected one. But not one that any person inside would welcome. He went to emerge from his hiding place, but before he could cut across the street a movement over to his right forced him to quickly return to behind the wall.

A figure appeared out of the shadows and scurried towards the stable. As he squinted, trying to focus in on who it might be, he caught the sound of a dress swishing across the ground.

It was a woman.

CHAPTER SIXTEEN

S he'd been walking for some time, deciding against taking her colt up into the hills, which is what she normally did. This particular evening, with the stars so bright and the air so mild, she wanted to stroll through the streets of what used to be a friendly, convivial town. Since Kestler and his boys rode in all those months ago, beat up poor old Stefan Moss, the sheriff, and sent him packing, everything had changed. Lawrenceville was now a miserable place to live. People moved away whenever they could, but recently Kestler's men kept a much tighter rein on people's movements. Things took a turn for the worse on the fateful night Kestler took a shine to her, approached her in the street, and invited her for dinner.

'I'm a married woman,' she said, not that that was her only reason for rejecting his advances. Kestler disgusted her. And not only his reputation. He was overweight, a whisky drinker, an arrogant, spiteful man, well used to getting his own way.

'You're a sweet young thing,' he'd said to her, swaying as he spoke, much the worse for drink. He stroked her cheek. She flinched. 'Aw, don't be like that,' he'd said, feigning being hurt. 'You entertain me and I'll reward you handsomely. What's your name, my little sweety.'

'I'm not your anything.' He blew a raspberry and she looked away as a rush of whisky breath wafted over her. 'It's Mrs Childer if you must know.'

He chuckled, 'First name is what I meant.' He made a grab for her, which she easily dodged. He almost fell on his face as he lost balance.

'My, you're a feisty one,' he said, leaning against the wall of the saloon out of which he'd emerged to accost her. 'I like that.'

She stepped away but had only managed two steps when he was at her again, pulling her around by the arm to face her. 'Mrs Childer, I am an honourable man,' he was wagging his finger in front of her face, 'Please, do me the service of accepting my invitation to dinner.'

'No.'

Again she went to turn away and again he turned her by the arm. 'I won't ask so politely again.'

'Mr Kestler, I am sure you are well used to getting whatever it is you set your heart on, but I have no intention of accepting your invitation, or anything else for that matter.'

'How does five hundred dollars sound?'

She stopped. Everything stopped, except her mouth which hanged open as if yanked downwards by an invisible cord.

Kestler laughed. 'That's got your attention, eh?' He moved in close, snaking his arm around her waist. 'I mean it. Come to dinner and I'll give you five hundred dollars. It's a present, Mrs Childer, not a payment if you get my meaning.'

She went to strike him, but it was a half-hearted effort and, despite him being drunk, he managed to block her blow and gripped her wrist. 'I'm not a whore,' she hissed.

'I never thought you were. But I'm guessing five hundred will ease your situation.'

Ease her situation five hundred dollars undoubtedly would, but how did he know that? Back home, with his face forever in his hands, her husband Stacey would nightly hurl out abuse at God, the world, and every person in it, blaming everybody but himself for the failure of his bean crop. He'd put everything they had in purchasing the seedlings. Planted them, cared for them, watched them day and night. They'd shrivelled and died. People in town had warned him about the bad choice of land, how irrigation was virtually impossible, how the previous owners of their homestead had experienced similar calamities, first with wheat, then corn. Nothing grew out there, everyone said. Stacey ignored them, dug in the fertiliser, worked in whatever goodness he could. All for nothing. Now those beans, together with all their savings, lay dying in the dust.

So five hundred dollars could give them a new start. A chance to leave, start over in a more forgiving place. She'd always had ambitions to open a store dealing in dry goods. Such a payment could set her up, help purchase enough stock and pay for the initial rental.

Kestler, aware of her hesitation, like the predatory animal he was, swooped. 'I'll make it seven hundred and fifty. Come dine with me this evening. Seven o'clock shall we say?'

She took a deep breath. Seven hundred and fifty dollars. She couldn't earn that in a year working for doctor O'Henry as his receptionist. Not even two years. She'd be a fool to reject this offer if it was only dinner. She suspected, however, for that amount, Kestler would demand a lot more. The thought turned her stomach.

'Listen,' he said, as if reading her mind, 'it'll just be dinner. If anything develops, then that will be just fine. But, I'm not looking for you to do anything you would not want to.'

'Just dinner?'

He nodded, grinning. 'I'll even pay you up front.' He turned away slightly, teetering for a moment before he gathered his strength and pulled out a wallet from inside his coat. He extracted a roll of dollar bills. She gaped, never having seen such a pile of money before. Without a word, he peeled off several bills and pressed them into one of her hands. 'That's two hundred. Come tonight, I'll give you the balance. My house-keeper is a wonderful cook.'

Gazing at the money in her hand she had a sudden urge to pinch herself. This couldn't be happening. *Two hundred dollars? Just like that?*

'If you decide not to come,' he said, beginning to move away uncertainly on legs which barely seemed capable of keeping him upright, 'I quite understand. But keep the money.' He reached the saloon steps, held onto one of the posts adjacent to them and slumped down on his backside. 'Come to the store. We'll take a buggy out to my place.' He looked up, bleary-eyed. 'And your name, Mrs Childer. What's your name?'

'It's Amy,' she said as she moved away, light-headed, unsure of the propriety of her decision, but knowing that the lure of so much money was too powerful to refuse.

After her evening with him, however, her thoughts were to change.

Stacey was drunk when she arrived home after her so-called 'dinner date'. He did not notice her cut lip, dishevelled bodice. As she stumbled around in the dark, found the washing basin and threw water over her face, his snoring grew louder and she thanked God that he could not hear.

It had all happened so unexpectedly.

Kestler, standing outside the mercantile store, well dressed in a neatly pressed morning suit, gold watch chain stretched over his ample stomach, greeted her with a warm, open smile. The heavy smell of cologne invaded her nostrils as she stepped up close. A darn sight more acceptable than whisky fumes, she told herself. He took her hand, kissed it in the finest manner, opened the door and motioned her inside.

The inside of the store was vast, lit by numerous gas lamps which gave off a thick, oily smell and cast weird, contorted shadows across the walls and ceiling. Everywhere she looked she could pick out the various types of products for sale, from claw hammers to wash basins and everything in between. 'You run a successful business, Mr Kestler.'

'I do indeed,' he said, slipping his arm around her and guiding her to the counter. He lifted up the hatch and led the way through a door in the rear to reveal a small room, candles giving off an inviting glow. A table was laid for two, but there was no food or plates, only waiting cutlery and napkins. 'I have decided it best to dine here, rather than at my home. My housekeeper will arrive later with our dinner.'

Smiling she waited until he pulled out a chair for her. He was certainly a gentleman, as unlike Stacey as she could imagine. Stacey was roughly hewn, his hands large, calloused, his body tight with muscle from the many hours he laboured in the fields. But his brains were addled, the drink rendering him little more than a mulling fool nowadays. Kestler, although clearly a drinker, seemed far more in control of himself. Successful and sophisticated.

'You are so very attractive, Amy,' he said, producing a bottle of wine from a cabinet in the corner. He poured a generous measure into a delicately cut glass. She smiled, a little coy, sweeping away a lock of hair, and raised the glass as he clinked his own against hers. She drank, the wine tasting crisp, sweet and unlike anything she had ever sampled before. 'I'm surprised your husband let you out so late, to meet a strange man.'

'Stacey was asleep, as usual.'

'Ah yes. He spends a good deal of his time asleep, so I hear.'

About to take another sip, she paused, eyes studying him through hooded lids. Slowly, she lowered the glass. 'What else have you heard, Mr Kestler?'

'That you're lonely. Unhappy. A husband who pays you no attention does not lead to a satisfactory relationship.'

'Is that right?' She sat back in her chair, the heat rising to her jawline. 'You've been asking about me, is that it?'

'I'm *interested* in you, Amy. As soon as I first saw you something happened to me,' he punched his chest, 'in here, in my heart.'

'Well, that's all very complimentary, Mr Kestler, but I don't really think I can—'

Without warning, he reached across the table for her, seizing both her wrists in his hands. Taken completely by surprise, she gave a startled shriek. He pulled her towards him. 'Amy, I'm only asking for you to give me a chance. Please, We can have several evenings such as this, develop our friendship.'

She struggled in his grip. 'Mr Kestler, you're hurting me.'

But she saw then there was something in his eyes. A change, all of his self-control disappearing with each passing moment. 'You don't understand.'

'I understand perfectly,' she said, voice breaking as she tried to pull herself free from his hold. But he was surprisingly strong and then, unbelievably, he was leaning across the table to plant a wet kiss on her mouth. Squirming, she managed to turn her head so that his lips smacked against her cheek. 'I can look after you,' he cried, his face so very close now, the broken veins on his bulbous nose appearing large at this distance. 'Please, just give me the chance to show you. I can't resist you, Amy. I can't.'

Summoning all her strength, she at last managed to tears herself free and jumped to her feet. Crying out, she made to run, but he was there, moving faster than she could ever imagine, catching her around the waist, turning her, kissing her again, this time with success.

He was moaning and she could feel his hardening manhood pressing against her. Ripping her lips free, she slapped him hard across the face.

Gasping, he recoiled, clutching at his rapidly reddening cheek. 'You bitch,' he said.

She hit him again, rocking him back against the table. Turning she made a grab for the door handle. He caught her, strong hands gripping her arm, bringing her round to face him. This time it was his turn to strike, a forceful back-handed blow across her mouth which rattled her teeth. Her legs buckled under her, strength seeping from her muscles, and another back-handed slap from the opposite direction sent her to the floor.

Head spinning, she had only the vaguest notion of where she was or what was happening. Material ripped, hot lips pressed against an exposed nipple. Hands clawed at her dress, her undergarments. Through a swirling mist, she saw him groping for his own pants, the belt pulling away, the flies opening.

From somewhere she trawled up enough strength to swing her booted foot into his groin. He screamed, staggered backwards and hit the table again. Curled up in a ball, hands clamped over his crotch, eyes squeezed tight shut, tears sprouting, he wailed like a baby.

Rolling over onto her knees, she pressed the back of her hand against her mouth, felt the blood, cursed herself for being so stupid. Using the door handle for support, she hauled herself to her feet and looked at him writhing on the ground. 'I'll kill you if you ever come near me again,' she said and went out into the store.

Moving like a drunkard, she waltzed through the aisles, bashing into the occasional display, sending stacks of pots, pans, culinary utensils and crockery crashing to the floor. Unconcerned, she continued to the main door and stepped out into the night. The cold, night air hit her almost as hard as Kestler's blows, but it revitalised her, cleared her head. She managed to get to her buggy and, without a single pause, flicked the reins over the colt's back and soon she was riding away into the night, leaving Kestler hurt, pride broken, alone in his room, to recover.

And now, here she was. She'd watched them take the semi-naked stranger into the stable. Waiting, she now moved closer. Since that night, Kestler had attempted no further advances, but she continued to seethe about the money. He owed her and, from her standpoint, she had every right to it. Perhaps this was a way to make some form of redress. So she crept up to the stable door and eased it open.

CHAPTER SEVENTEEN

The shadows were long as Roose came into town, walking his horse slowly down the middle of the main street. Shops and stores on either side were now closed for business, the last few owners sweeping away the dust from their porch entrances. One or two looked up as he passed by, their faces framed by the flickering lights from the interior of their businesses. Roose, eyes straight ahead, made for the only building which appeared open. The saloon. A chipped and faded sign across the front bore the name 'Lucky Nights' which he thought somewhat amusing, given the virtual absence of customers.

A solitary man sat on a rocking chair adjacent to the batwing doors. He busily filled a bone pipe as Roose dismounted, tied up his horse, dusted off his jacket and took the steps to the boardwalk. The man looked up. 'Evening,' he said in a lazy drawl, settled the pipe stem between his teeth, struck a long match and set it to the filled bowl.

Roose tipped his hat. 'I'm looking for a Mr Kestler.'

The man paused in concentrating on lighting his pipe. His face clouded over. 'And why might that be, mister?'

'Is he inside?' Roose went to take a step forward.

'I asked you a question, boy.'

This remark amused Roose as he was considerably older than the pipe-smoker. 'All I wanna do is talk to him.'

'Well, you can wait here while I go and have a look-see.'

'Kinda touchy, ain't you?'

'Just doin' my job, boy,' said the man, discarding his pipe and standing up.

Roose noted the brace of Army Colts in the man's waistband. 'And what job might that be?' Without waiting for a reply, he pulled back his coat to reveal the badge pinned to the left lapel of his waistcoat. 'This here is mine.'

Pursing his lips, the pipe-smoker turned and dipped through the doors without another word.

Roose waited. There was little noise emanating from inside, perhaps because it was early, or perhaps because few people frequented this establishment. The entire town had a sadness about it, even the buildings appearing sullen, uninteresting. It stank with the air of decay and Roose doubted it would remain inhabited for much longer and would fade away, like so many other frontier towns through the West. As the big cities of San Francisco and Los Angeles grew, so the numerous towns which sprang up along the newly laid railroad lines to house the many labourers died. Ghost towns they called them. As he waited, Roose wondered how many souls had come to such places in search of dreams and new beginnings only to have those aspirations crushed, trampled into the dust.

He gave a jump as the double doors sprang open. The pipe-smoker stood in the doorway, but he was no longer alone. A large man filled most of Roose's view together with several other men, mean-looking, all of them toting tied down guns, hate-filled bearing down on the sheriff.

Maintaining his calmness, Roose inclined his head slightly. 'Mr Kestler, I assume?'

'That's right,' said the big man, 'but you have me at a disadvantage, sir. Who may you be?' He wore an embroidered shirt, sleeves rolled up, a glistening film of sweat covering his furrowed brow. Grease around his mouth declared he'd only just finished eating.

'Name's Roose. Sterling Roose. I'm sheriff of Freedom, a small town some fifty miles or so east from here, on the trail of several varmints that broke into and stole some valuable artefacts from my friend's home. Reuben Cole is my friend's name. Perhaps you've heard of him?'

Kestler gave the impression of thinking for a moment. Poking the tip of his tongue between his lips, he savoured the remnants of his dinner before shaking his head slightly. 'Can't say I have.'

'Well,' Roose looked around him, noticing two further men appearing from the side of the saloon. They must have come from the rear entrance. Both sported Winchesters, 'Thing is, Mr Kestler, I followed the trail of those men straight to this town.'

'Oh, you did?'

'Yes, I did. Perhaps you could let me have a look around, discover any signs that they might still be here.'

'They ain't.'

'Oh.' The men behind him were drawing closer. 'And how would you know that, Mr Kestler?'

'Because I know everything in my town.' As if given some unspoken command, the others eased past their boss, fanning out on either side of him. Four to the front, two to the rear. Roose knew the odds were stacked against him.

'Yes, of course, you do. So perhaps you could tell me which way they headed ... If they have left town, that is?'

The unmistakable sound of Winchester levers engaging accompanied Kestler's broad smile. Roose allowed his shoulders to droop. There was little he could do unless he made a fight of it with his certain death the inevitable outcome. He slowly put up his hands. A tall gangly gunfighter stepped up to him and pulled out Roose's handgun.

'You on your own?' asked Kestler as the others moved up to Roose and took him by the arms.

'I am.'

'A manhunt with only one in the party? I don't think so. We already have one of your boys over in the barn.' Roose's eyes widened despite his best efforts to conceal his surprise. 'So, I reckon there's more of you.'

'Well, there ain't.'

The first fist erupted into Roose's guts with the force of a mule's kick, doubling him up. He gasped and retched as he hung in the firm grip of the men holding him. 'You'd be wise to tell us everything you know,' said Kestler before giving the gangly one a nod. Grinning, the tall gunfighter hit Roose in the midriff again with his left, then followed it up with a right cross to the jaw that almost lifted Roose off his feet.

Hanging in the men's arms, Roose managed to bring his head up as

Kestler stepped closer. 'How many more of you are there?' All he received was a slight shake of the head. Kestler nodded again to the tall, gangly one, 'Rough him up a little more, Bart.' Requiring no further encouragement, Bart Owens pulled back his fist in preparedness for another punch. Before he could deliver the blow, a voice came out of the darkness.

'Leave him to me, Mr Kestler.'

Brody emerged from the darkness, his white shirt casting him in its own particular aura. Beside him were his men, gnarled, aged native Indians, eyes feverish, bodies tense with expectation.

'We're more than capable,' said Owens, unable to keep the anger out of his voice.

'You'll kill him before he speaks,' said Brody.

'I have known men like this one,' said the scarface, studying Roose intensely. 'They never speak unless the right pressure is applied.'

'And you can give that pressure?' asked Kestler.

'I can.'

'Then do it. I don't like the idea of more of these scum wandering around my town.'

Reluctantly Owens stepped away as the Indians took hold of Roose and dragged him into the night.

'We will take him just outside of town,' said Brody, then added with a grin, 'so nobody can hear his screams.'

CHAPTER EIGHTEEN

From out of the far distance, Samuels heard something. It might have been the rustling of rats but something told him differently. He eased himself up to a sitting position, grunting with the pain lancing through his ribs. They'd beaten him expertly, pummeling his ribs and guts before stripping him, pressing the broad-bladed knife over his manhood. 'It will only take a second,' said the one in white, that sadistic grin set like a permanent feature on his face. Using the blunt edge, he lifted up Samuels' member. 'A quick flick of this blade ...' He chuckled. 'It'll hurt, my friend. It will hurt a lot. So tell me all that you know.'

Within a few minutes, Samuels revealed everything. That there were two more men in his party, that he wanted no more of it, that Roose's plan was to kill them all, especially the ones known as Soloman and Kestler.

He left nothing out, even telling the man in white it was Reuben Cole's house that had been burgled and that Cole, as soon as he had recovered from his attack, would be out on the range himself, hunting them all down. If anything happened to Roose, Cole's revenge would be terrible.

'Sounds like quite a man,' said the man in white, returning his knife to its scabbard at his waist.

'He is. He's an Indian fighter from the old days.'

The man in white looked at his companions. 'You heard of him?'

Two of them nodded, a tall, heavy set man with a deep scar running down the side of his face, spoke in low, concerned tones, 'He is well known to us. From the old days. He tracked our fathers, put many of them in the ground. My people call him 'He Who Comes'. Nothing can stop him, Brody.'

'Is that right.' Brody stood up. 'Kestler needs to hear this. We'll take this one into town.'

And so they did and now, sitting in the darkness of the stable, the smell of wet hay thick in his nostrils, Samuels held his breath, straining to hear the scurry of the rats again. The scurry when it came, however, was not that of a rat.

A figure squatted down in front of him.

'I watched them bring you in.'

A woman, sounding scared. He couldn't make out her features in the dark, but something told him she was kind. Young. A blade flashed and she was cutting through the cords binding his wrists. 'We're getting out of here,' she said in a whisper. 'I don't know who you are or what you're doing here, but any enemy of Kestler's is a friend of mine.'

Rubbing his wrists, Samuels climbed to his feet. She helped him. Acutely aware of his nakedness, he leaned away. 'I can't walk around like this.'

'I have blankets in my buggy. My home is out of town and once we're there, we can work out what to do.'

'What to do? There's nothing we can do.'

'Oh yes there is,' she said through gritted teeth. 'We can kill him.'

Amy Childer helped Samuels hobble through the slurry of stinking, rotting straw and hay, the array of strong odours assailing them from all directions. Amy, swallowing down the bile, brushed sweat from her brow and reached out a hand to push open the stable door.

A man stood there, his impressive bulk nothing but a large, looming black shape in the doorway, blocking their exit. Amy almost squealed and reeled backwards, Samuels groaning in her embrace. How had Kestler managed to find her, to follow her at this exact point in time? Was he like that magician she had seen in the theatre one time. What was he called? A mind-reader? Hypnotist? She couldn't quite recall, remembering only how Stacey had laughed so loudly. The last time he had done so, she recalled. Maybe this was to be her last time also. Her last time for anything.

'You'd do best to keep quiet,' said the man. It wasn't Kestler's voice, she knew that. He stepped in close and shot out his left fist straight into Samuel's face, felling him like a tree. He lifted the injured man with ease, draping him over his broad shoulders. 'Stay close.'

'But who are you?'

'Don't you worry about that,' he said. 'I'll get us out of this mess.'

'My buggy's over yonder,' she said, pointing vaguely to her left.

'We won't be needing your buggy,' he said.

She froze at his words, taking a moment to find the courage to say, 'Why not?'

'Because,' he said, drawing his gun and easing back the hammer ominously, 'we're going to visit Mr Kestler and he's gonna reward me handsomely for putting paid to your little scheme.'

'You can't. For the love of God, you can't!'

He pressed the muzzle against her forehead, 'Oh yes I can, little missy. I need to get back into his good books, and this is the perfect way to do it. Now, walk ahead and make straight for his store. One false move and I'll put a bullet in your spine.'

'You miserable cur.'

The big man chuckled. 'I've been called a lot worse, little missy, but that'll suit me just fine. Now walk on, I'm tired and I want this done.'

Someone was talking as they came through the doors of Kestler's mercantile store. The voice sounded raucous, words delivered with deliberate slowness. 'I need those guarantees, Mr Lomax. I need them by tomorrow so I can ...' The voice drifted away as the speaker, standing behind the counter, with the earpiece clamped hard against the side of his head, saw the intruders and reached for something hidden underneath. 'I'll call you back Mr Lomax ... No, I will call *you back*!' He replaced the earpiece on its cradle and levelled the revolver he'd taken from its hiding place towards the three strange looking characters advancing upon him through the murkiness of the store. 'Y'all just hold on right there,' he said.

'Name's Soloman,' came the voice of the large man holding another over his shoulder. 'I'm here to speak with Mr Kestler.'

'I know who you are,' said the man as he moved from behind the counter and stepped through the open hatch, gun in hand, eyes narrowed. 'What is it you want, Soloman.'

'I want to talk to Mr Kestler. I have some things to tell him, and these two here might give me some leverage. I upset Mr Kestler, let him down with my boys. They were green, made mistakes. I don't make mistakes and these here are my proof.' Grunting, he lay his burden on the ground.

'Who is she?'

Soloman lifted his head, sensing Amy trembling beside him. 'She was gonna help this one get away. Said she wanted to make Kestler pay for what he did.'

The man with the gun was close now. Tall, well dressed, he studied Amy, running his eyes over her, pursing his lips. 'I believe you had a dinner date with our mutual friend. Mrs Childer isn't it?'

'Hardly a friend, whoever you are.'

'Name is Haynes. They call me Doc Haynes, on account I used to look after people's feet back in San Francisco.'

'*Feet?*' Soloman blurted, unable to keep his amusement to himself. 'I reckon I've heard everything now.'

'Mr Kestler is in the saloon next door,' said Haynes, his voice turning icy cold. 'My advice is to go and tell him what you told me while I wait here and entertain this little lady.'

Soloman hesitated, rubbing his face with agitation, 'I reckon I'll wait.'

'You'll be waiting a long time, friend. Mr Kestler likes his drink. Best go and talk to him before words of any kind make very little sense to him.'

'I'll take the lady.'

The gun came up, 'No you won't. She'll be just fine here with me.'

An age seemed to pass between them before Soloman gave in, blowing out a long sigh. He swung around and stomped off towards the door. As he opened it, Hayne squeezed off a single shot, the heavy slug hitting Soloman high up in the shoulder, the impact projecting him into the street.

The body made a heavy clump as it landed in the dirt. Amy screamed and Hayne struck her hard across the face, sending her crashing to her knees. 'Why is it always me who has to tidy up the ends of this pathetic little business.'

With the sound of Amy's whimpering filling the store, Haynes prodded Samuels with the toe of his boot. He ejected the spent cartridge from his Remington and slipped another into the cylinder.

Approaching voices caused him to look up and all at once a gaggle of loud, well-armed men erupted through the doors, headed by a reeling Kestler. 'What is all the shootin', Doc?'

'We've had a visitor.' Haynes nodded towards Amy still on her knees, head down. 'Seems like Mrs Childer here wanted to rescue your prisoner. Soloman found 'em and brought them to us, hoping he could ingratiate himself back into your good books.'

'Well, he did for his two idiot partners,' mumbled Kestler, approaching none too steadily. 'But even so, I can't trust him, not after this. Where is he?'

'Outside. I sent him on his way with a bullet in his back. Get one of the boys to finish him off.'

'Outside?'

'Yeah. In the street. It's a surprise you didn't see him.'

Troubled, Kestler snapped his fingers, 'Rogers, go and take a look.'

Rogers, chomping on a bone pipe, mumbled something inaudible and went through the main door. It wasn't long before he came back in. 'Ain't no one there, Mr Kestler.'

Kestler snapped his head around to Doc Haynes, who pushed through them all.

Outside, in the dark, he could just about make out the imprint of where Soloman's heavy body had hit the ground.

But of Soloman himself, there was no sign.

CHAPTER NINETEEN

Kestler sat in his saloon, turning a half-filled glass of whisky between his palms, staring at the dishevelled Amy Childer sitting opposite him. Standing at his shoulder was Doc Haynes, tapping his foot impatiently. 'She was going to skedaddle before Soloman waylaid her. She'd have ridden over to El Paso, warned the authorities. We don't need U.S. Marshalls snooping around. We can ill-afford any—'

'*All right, I hear you!*' Kestler rocked forward and threw the whisky down his throat. As the fiery liquid percolated through his guts, he grew calmer. 'I hear you. What do you suggest?'

'Kill her, bury the body out in the prairie. Coyotes will get rid of any evidence.'

Amy squirmed in her chair, the only sound emanating from her mouth a muffled squeak. Her jaw and mouth were swollen to twice their normal size, a vicious looking bruise of deepest purple covering the lower half of her face.

'What about the husband?'

They both looked up to Bart Owens, standing there, toying with Roose's gun.

'What about him?' asked Haynes. 'From what I hear, he's a drunk. He won't even notice she's gone.'

'But what if he does?'

Haynes and Kestler exchanged a look. 'Mitch,' said Kestler, 'take a ride over there, make sure Mr Childer won't say anything to anyone.'

Tipping his hat, Mitch Rogers put his bone pipe into his waistcoat pocket, turned, and left without a word.

'Mr Kestler,' said Owens, appearing awkward, unable to look Kestler in the eye, 'I have to say … Some of the boys, they is mighty edgy with them Comanch around the place.'

'*Them Comanch,*' put in Haynes quickly, 'have served us well. I been through what they took and it amounts to a fair amount. My contacts in San Francisco will ensure us of a good return.'

'Bart,' said Kestler, rising unsteadily to his feet, 'I know you have read all them dime novels about how Comanches roamed the plains, butchering men, women and children, but those days have gone.'

'With all due respect, Mr Kestler, they is old, and from the *old days*. They is as much a bunch of murdering savages as any who ever rode all them years ago.'

'Ah, Bart, are you listening to yourself? We are living in the modern world right now. Those days have gone. There ain't no more savages torching houses and raping females. They are civilised.' He weaved his way between tables and and reached the bar, out of breath, squeezing finger and thumb into his eyes. 'Hot diggity, I don't feel so good.'

'You should ease off the juice,' said Haynes.

'It's late,' said Kestler, ignoring his partner's jibe. 'I'm going to bed. Bart,' he swung around to level his bleary, bloodshot eyes on the tall, lean gunman. 'Take her out into the prairie and finish her, just as Doc suggests. Watch out for coyotes.'

'But Brody and those Comanch are out there.'

'*Don't answer me back, Owens!*' Kestler took in a shuddering breath. 'Just do as you're told.'

Pulling a face, Owens reluctantly took hold of Amy by the shoulder and hauled her to her feet, ramming the gun into her back. He pushed her through the batwing doors and they both disappeared into the early morning darkness.

. . .

They camped amongst the rocks, Scarface lighting a fire around which they huddled. Roose, trussed up so well he could barely move, watched them keenly. Brody, some way off, stood staring out across the plain. If Roose could somehow manage to loosen the leather thongs which bound his wrists and ankles, he could perhaps overcome one of them, take their gun, kill Brody. The rest would run. He was sure of that.

As sure as he was that any idea of escape was futile.

He put his head back against the cold rocks. These men were experts. There was little chance of him loosening his bindings. He'd been trying unsuccessfully to do so since the moment one of the Indians secured his limbs together. Nothing gave then, nothing gave now. It was useless and he cursed himself for not making a fight of it back in the town. True, he'd be dead, but he'd take some of those curs with him. His predicament now could only result in one outcome. His head dropped to his chest, despair engulfing him. If he could see Maddie one more time, then none of this would seem so bad. A fool he was for leaving her. A fool for coming out here on this mad errand. A fool for not waiting for Cole to recover. Together, they could have put them all into the ground. Fate had worked against him, as always. Damn this hopeless situation and this accursed life.

Something caused Stone to turn over and sit up from his bedroll, senses alert. A movement in the darkness, the glint of eyes shining bright as candles in the night. With extreme care, he reached out for his revolver and eased back the hammer. A coyote, perhaps more than one, circling him. He should have made a fire, but fear of being seen prevented him from doing so. Perhaps that was a mistake.

He swept his hand across the ground, found a small rock and climbed to his feet, ready to open fire if one of the coyotes attacked. He launched the rock towards the eyes. A yelp, followed by the desperate retreat of the animal and once again, Stone was alone.

Releasing a long sigh, he relaxed and went to return to his makeshift bed when he saw something out the corner of his eye. A light, way over to the west. This time it burned from no animal. Moving across to an outcrop of boulders, he heaved himself to the top and peered through the night. A campfire. Unmistakeable. Whoever it was had revealed their position, just as he had avoided doing so. He gave up a small prayer of thanks. Could it be Roose, returning from his meeting with Kestler? With no way of knowing, all he could do was wait. Something unwanted stirred inside, however. A feeling, a suspicion that perhaps it wasn't Roose. Perhaps men, sent by Kestler to track Stone down. Uneasily, he slinked back to his camp and hurriedly rolled up his blankets. He'd ride back to Reuben Cole's without delay. If it was Roose, then that would be all to the good, but if not ... Gritting his teeth, he worked feverishly and soon, with his horse well packed, he set off at a steady pace across the wide-open prairie, the approaching dawn nothing but a light grey smudge on the distant horizon.

Bacon rind and grits sizzled in a blackened pan, whilst Brody, stretching out his limbs, instructed two of his companions to bring Roose forward.

'We have no time to play with you, my friend,' said Brody as the others cut through Roose's bindings and pulled off his jacket and shirt. His lily white body shivered in the cold, morning light. Soon, as the sun rose, the temperature too would increase. His skin would blister and burn. He stood, limp, defeated, as they cut through his trousers and left him quivering there, like a plucked turkey, ready for the pot.

Slowly, Brody drew out his broad-bladed Bowie. He tested the edge with his thumb and hissed. 'How many of you were there, my friend, hunting us?'

Roose's eyes came up, dark, defiant. He may well have accepted his fate but he was damned if he was going to tell this monster anything at all. Grinning, Brody nodded to his men, who held onto Roose by the arms and legs. Four men, all of them cackling like febrile, malicious children, impatient for the sport to begin.

Brody moved up close, the blade before his face. 'You will tell me, just like your friend did.'

Roose wanted to scream. So, they'd overtaken Stone. The game was up.

'So why not save yourself some pain, eh? Or do you like pain?' Roose muttered something, shaking his head once. 'No, of course not. But *this* pain, it is going to be like nothing you have ever experienced before.'

Taking his time, Brody placed the blade flat against Roose's withered stomach and gently lowered it towards his manhood. He continued, all the while his eyes locked on Roose's, whose teeth chattered as the true horror of what was about to happen struck home.

Turning the blade, Brody rested the tip against Roose's rectum.

'I'll ask you one more time, my friend. How many men came with you, and where are they now?'

Roose merely glared.

Brody pushed and the accompanying scream rang out across the plain louder than any thunderclap.

Flat on his ample belly, Soloman looked down from his vantage point to where Brody and his men were just putting the finishing touches to their torture of Sterling Roose. Rolling over, he looked to the sky for a moment, ran a calloused hand over his face and sat up. Across from where he was, Amy Childer sat with her back against a blackened tree, the tears cutting through the grime of her pretty face.

'This ain't gonna end well for anyone,' Soloman said and stood up. He waddled over to her and flopped down on the ground. 'Listen, what I did by knocking out that S.O.B down back there, rescuing you, that means they'll be coming for me, to kill me.' He rolled his shoulder and winced. 'Lucky for me that bullet only winged me. Two times I been shot here, and two times the bullet has not stuck. That ain't nothing unusual. I've mostly been lucky my whole life. And now I've met you.'

Her eyes came up. There was malevolence in her look, determination too. 'If you believe you are any better than those ghastly men of Kestler's, you've got another think coming, mister. I thank you for knocking that scoundrel down the way you did, but I also know that other one went to kill my Stacey. My life has no future now, so you may as well kill me and get it over with.'

He gaped at her. 'Kill you? Why would I wanna do that? Nah, I ain't gonna kill you. Listen, I think if you take me to your place, we can hole up there for a while, then I'll make my plans.'

'You're not holin' up anywhere that has anything to do with me, mister.'

'So I just cut you adrift, is that it? You sure is unappreciative of my kindness.'

'Your kindness? You were gonna turn me over to Kestler and let him do whatever he wanted until you realised he would cut you no deal. You're all the same – murderers, cheats and scoundrels the lot of you!'

'You sure are some kinda wildcat. I like that in a woman.'

She snapped her head away, fresh tears tumbling down her face. 'Shoot me. That's the only thing I want from you.'

'Well, it ain't gonna be the only thing you get.'

She looked at him, horrified. 'No. Please, I'm begging you ...'

'I can't figure you, woman. One minute you're begging me to shoot you dead, next thing you is resisting my advances. What is it you want exactly?'

'To go back home. Bury my husband, then leave this godforsaken place once and for all.'

'On your own? Ma'am, this may be the twentieth century an' all, but from what I've just witnessed, there is still plenty of mean individuals roaming this land. Best if you go home and wait for me.'

'Wait for you?'

'Why not? It's a good proposition. I will look after you, treat you well ...' He winked. 'And satisfy you, I can guarantee you that.'

'You think a lot of yourself, don't you.'

'Ma'am, from where I'm sitting, you don't have much choice. I would love to share my life with you, settle down, maybe build up a business. Kestler has given me some ideas to work on so this all might just work out well in the end.'

She considered him for a long time. 'All right. I can see you are a man of talent, unlike Stacey who drinks himself into a stupor every night. The likelihood he is dead, shot by that stringy one with the pipe. Crazy thing is, I couldn't care less. My life has been going nowhere fast these past years, perhaps I do need a new direction.'

'I'll give you any number of directions, I promise you.'

After she'd provided him with basic directions to her homestead, she scurried away whilst he, checking his guns, swung in behind Brody and his men, careful to keep his distance, sure they would be winding their way back to Reuben Cole's now they had finalised their business with their prisoner. Both they and Soloman needed Cole dead, for he was a heap of trouble and once he knew his partner was dead, vengeance would drive him relentlessly on, like one of the steam engines dissecting the prairie and opening it up to the modern world. He'd have to die, decided Soloman. Brody and his men too.

CHAPTER TWENTY

S tone spotted the dust cloud as he gained the ridge. They were a considerable distance from him, but there could be no mistake. Whoever had lit the campfire was coming his way. Pursuing him. From the amount of dust, he knew there were more than one, so that ruled our Roose. And they were riding fast. He wished he had Roose's field glasses to pick out just who they were. Cursing his bad luck, he spurred his horse and broke her into a gallop, heading for the only place to go he felt safest – Reuben Cole's.

Sitting out on his sprawling veranda, Cole stared across the vast landscape bordering his ranch. Since the previous day, he felt restless, stomping around the big house aimlessly, ignoring the pleadings of Maddie to rest. 'I've done enough resting,' he told her and spent a lot of time cleaning his guns, checking his saddle and bridle, ensuring his canteens and grain sacks were prepared and ready.

'You're not going out there,' she said, stepping onto the veranda. Her sleeves were rolled up, a scarlet scarf tied around her head, face flush with exertion.

'What you been doin' in there?'

'Cleaning. Not sure who that woman was who you had coming in, but there is a lot of work to do to get this place straight.'

He smiled, despite the heaviness he felt in his heart. 'You don't need to do any of that, Maddie.'

'Sure I do,' she said, coming over and sitting down on his lap. She snaked her arms around his neck and kissed him passionately. 'You need a woman to look after you, Cole.'

'Well, I'm hoping I've found one.'

They kissed again, but suddenly she tensed and pulled back, troubled. 'When will we tell Sterling?'

Shifting position, Cole looked away, awkward, uncomfortable. 'I don't know. It's gonna be just about the most difficult thing I've ever done.'

'Worse than hunting Indians?'

'Much worse,' he said without hesitation. 'He's my only true friend. I know how much you mean to him.'

'It's not something either of us planned, Cole.'

'I know that. Don't make it any easier though.'

She put her head on his shoulder, caressing the back of his scalp, and they both drifted off into their own, private thoughts.

At first, looking up a few moments later, Cole believed the swirl of dust was a mere devil, kicked up by the wind which often came out of nowhere to assault the ground. As he focused in, he realised it was an approaching rider. He patted Maddie's arm. 'Go into the study, Maddie, get yourself a Winchester from the rack.'

Stiffening, she sat up and followed his gaze. 'It could be Sterling.'

'It could, but he's galloping as if the hounds of hell were on his tail.' He reached down to his side and picked up his own repeating rifle and levered a cartridge into the breach. 'Fetch that gun and stay indoors.'

Sensing his tension, Maddie immediately disappeared inside and Cole stood up.

He waited, all of his attention on the rider.

It was not Roose. Absent were the tell-tale black frock coat and the battered old Stetson that Sterling always wore. This rider was bare-headed, dressed in a pale blue shirt and denim trousers.

Dropping to one knee, Cole flipped up the fold-down rear sight and squinted along the length of the barrel until he had the rider in his view. He gave a start as the man drew closer. '*Stone,*' he gasped and stood up.

Stone pulled his mount up sharply, the horse kicking and neighing, eyes wide with alarm, nostrils flared. The young man jumped down before the dust had settled and raced up to Cole.

'They're coming, Mr Cole. Five of 'em.'

'Coming? Who's coming?'

'The men who ... Ahh, I have to say it, Mr Cole.' Without warning, the tears sprang from his eyes and he slumped down on the bottom step which led to the veranda. Holding nothing back, his pent-up emotions burst forth like the waters from a broken dam. Pressing his face in his hands, he wept uncontrollably.

'Son,' said Cole quietly, sitting down next to him. He gently slipped his arm around Stone's shoulders. 'Try and tell me what in tarnation is going on.'

Battling to suppress his body-jerking sobs, Stone eventually brought his head up, gulping in air, calming himself down. 'Mr Roose and me made to go into the town. Lawrenceville. Mr Samuels, he said he couldn't be involved in any killing, so he left. But then, as we moved down towards the town, we saw the Indians. Comanch, I think. They had Mr Samuels with 'em. Mr Roose, he became ... I don't know how to explain it, but he changed. Already he'd ...' Stone squeezed his eyes shut. 'Cougan, you remember him?'

'I do. His pa rode with us years before.'

'He ... Mr Cole, I ain't ever seen anything like what happened. Cougan got real agitated when Mr Samuels said he was coming back here. Cougan drew a knife and was gonna kill poor Mr Samuels—'

'He was gonna *what?*'

'It's true, I swear to you. But Mr Roose, he just came up behind him and put his own knife deep into Cougan's back, killed him right there and then. Then, he just lay right down there on the ground and went to sleep, as if nothing had happened.'

Cole shifted his eyes towards the open range. 'Sterling has been acting kinda strange these past months. Like he's losing control of his senses.'

'I heard it said that sort of thing often happens to old folk. But Mr Roose ain't so very old, is he?'

Cole didn't answer, merely blew out a breath. 'Carry on with the story, son.'

'Well, when we saw them riding down with Mr Samuels, Mr Roose told me to come back here, tell you to send for soldiers and go into Lawrenceville and arrest that Kestler. Then he went there.'

'Sterling went into the town?' Stone nodded, sniffing loudly. 'To take on Kestler on his own?'

'That was his idea, I think. He said he was gonna just talk, persuade Kestler to let Mr Samuels go. But ... Mr Cole, he was different. He was cold. Like he was someplace else.'

'Shoot,' said Cole, rubbing his face, thinking hard. 'He was setting to kill him. I know that from the old days, how Sterling would become like a man possessed.'

'There's something else.'

Cole nodded. 'I thought there might be.'

'They're following me. Those Comanch. They've been on my trail all night and day. I've led 'em straight to you, Mr Cole.'

Then something curious happened.

A grin spread out across Cole's face. 'That's just about the best thing you could have done, son.' He turned to the young rider. 'You take that big Sharps gun of yours and get up on the balcony with Maddie. When I give the signal, you pour down lead into those renegades until there ain't no more of 'em left standing.'

'What will you do?'

Cole stood up, put the Winchester over his shoulder, and smiled again. 'I'm gonna give them the biggest shock of their lives.'

From where they reined in their horses, the large house appeared deserted. Scarface crossed his hands on the pommel of his saddle and leaned forward. 'He must be inside.'

'Tracks tell us he came this way,' said another, reading the signs in the dirt.

'Then we'll just have to go inside and fetch him out,' said Brody. He smiled at the others. 'Once we have him, we can search through the house and take anything Soloman left behind. Mr Kestler will be more than pleased.'

'He has yet to pay us,' said Scarface with meaning.

'He will have no worries about that.' He studied the upper storey and something about it made him wary. 'I'm not sure, but I think maybe he is in there, watching.'

'Watching?' Scarface drew his revolver. 'Let's just go inside and kill the old coot.'

Brody grunted his assent and edged his horse forward.

From the balcony, Maddie and Stone rose to their knees from their prone positions and opened up on the Indians, the fusillade deafening and almost continuous.

Screaming out orders above the tumult, Brody reeled his horse away, returning fire into the balcony from his Colt with wild, unaimed shots. A heavy slug tore into the Indian beside him, flinging him to the ground. Another screamed, bullets peppering his chest. 'Spread out,' shouted Brody, frantically kicking his horse's flanks, whilst his other two companions dispersed in the opposite direction.

As he struggled to control his incensed mount, Brody stared into his fastly approaching death.

A horse came thundering from the far flank, pounding across the ground, on a collision course with Brody and his men. He gawped in disbelief, not knowing what to do, uncertain why the horse would be charging with such determination. Such control.

Soon, within a few blinks, he saw the reason.

A man, hidden from view by pressing himself flat against the far side of his horse's flank, rose up into the saddle, the Winchester aiming, firing. Measured shots, some going wide due to the horse's jolting forward momentum, but enough striking home to throw the remaining Comanches from their saddles as they desperately tried to get away.

Cole threw the spent Winchester to the ground, drew his Cavalry Colt from his cross-belly holster and put a bullet into Brody's right shoulder, pitching him over the back of his horse, which reared up, screaming, and bolted across the dried, hard-packed ground.

'Cole!'

Steadying his horse, Cole circled around the writhing body of his would-be assailant, and looked up to see Maddie standing on the balcony, bare forearm pressed against her brow. 'Cole, for pity's sake ...'

'It's all right,' he spat and dropped from his saddle.

Brody squirmed, blood pumping from the ghastly wound high up in his chest. His own revolver lay tantalisingly close but, as his feverish eyes locked upon it, Cole kicked it further out of reach. He eased back the hammer of his gun. 'What did you do to my friend?'

From somewhere, amidst the sea of pain washing over him, Brody grew aware of Cole's voice. The words. Their meaning. He forced a grin. 'Go stuff yourself,' he said.

Running his tongue across his lips, Cole shook his head and returned the Colt to its holster. 'Problem is, boy, I rode down scum like you across this land a quarter of a century ago, so I know all about your ways. I know you would have taken great delight in torturing my friend.' He nodded at Brody's bowie knife sheathed at his hip. 'You would have used that, splitting my friend from stem to stern. I seen it. I know it. And now,' he paused for effect before reaching behind him to pull out his own heavy-bladed knife, some twelve inches of cold steel long, 'now, the same is gonna happen to you.'

'I will not tell you anything, gringo.'

'Oh yes you will,' said Cole, 'you'll tell me everything.'

Within five minutes of setting to work, Cole learned everything he needed to know. He didn't hear Maddie's screams or see Stone throwing up. He didn't hear or see anything. Only what Brody said. And then Cole split the man open and let him bleed out in the burning sun of a that long, awful day.

'Burn the bodies,' Cole told Stone afterwards, rechecking his weapons and rolling up his bed blanket. 'Then, go into town and send a telegram to the Army over in Carson City, tell 'em what is going on down in Lawrenceville. That Kestler is bankrolling his shares in the railroad by stealing valuables from the big houses surrounding Freedom. You think you can do that?'

'Sure I can, Mr Cole. I'll use the telephone. It'll be quicker.'

'Good,' said Cole. The quicker the better, he thought to himself. He had no idea how many men Kestler had working for him. He'd need all of his wits about him, as well as all of his skills. Despite the bruising and aching joints from the initial burglary causing him a lot less discomfort, a tiny doubt lingered. The attack on Brody and his Comanche associates had taken a lot out of him. No matter how difficult it was to admit it to himself, he knew age was against him. Riding on his horse in the old Apache way had seriously taken it out of him. His back had all tightened up and his thighs burned like they were sat in a pail of steaming hot water.

'You can't go,' said Maddie, appearing as if from nowhere, her eyes wet with tears. 'I'm begging you, Cole. You can't.'

'I have to,' he said without looking up from his preparations. 'You know that.'

'I don't know any such thing! You go down there alone, you'll end up dead, Just like Sterling.'

Cole stopped tying up his bedroll and bit his lip. 'That precisely why I have to go, Maddie. He was my friend. To die like that ...' He shook his head a swallowed down the rising grief. 'I'm gonna make them pay for what they did. It's what I have to do.'

'If you get back, you stubborn old mule, I won't be here.'

He turned his face up and stared into her wet beautiful eyes. 'Yes you will.'

'No I won't, damn you!' She flew into him, her fists beating at his chest, the tears cascading down her cheeks. 'I can't lose both of you.'

He went to hold her, to press her to him, to bring her some comfort and reassurance. Violently, she tore herself free, features twisted into a mask of pure, raging fury. 'I swear it, if you go, I will leave.'

They held one another's stares for a long time before Cole gathered up his belongings and strode outside to his waiting horse. Aware she was standing there, glaring at his back, he nevertheless steeled himself not to turn around. Instead, he hauled himself into the saddle and gently eased his horse out across the range towards the town of Lawrenceville and the reckoning which awaited them all.

CHAPTER TWENTY-ONE

The town proved not as busy as he had expected. True, there were people around, shops open, the livery stable and merchandise stores doing a brisk trade, but there was something missing. Friendliness, warmth, call it what you will, these things did not feature in the downcast and unhappy faces of the populace. At its heart, there was a tangible indifference, an acceptance of their lot. This was not a happy place.

There were two men sitting outside the first saloon Cole came to, hats pulled down over their faces, legs, encased in knee-high riding boots, stretched out, their tied down guns declaring to the world exactly who they were. Swallowing down his rising anger, Cole got down from his horse and tied the reins to the hitching post. This was a little like stepping back in time. The lawlessness that once clung to the West seemed to have found its last stronghold in this dreary, uninviting town.

As he clumped up the steps towards the double batwing doors, both men roused themselves and regarded him with icy stares. He tipped his hat and went inside.

Being late afternoon there were few customers inside. A couple of other gunslingers were at a round table playing cards, bored expressions on their faces, cigarette smoke hanging over them in ominous clouds. A half bottle of whisky sat in the centre of the table, a sprinkling of dollar coins splayed around it. A woman wearing a tight bodice of the brightest scarlet looked up from her position astride one of the gunslinger's laps and gave Cole a smile. The man followed her gaze. He did not smile.

As Cole went directly to the bar. He heard the exchange of comments from the card playing table. At the same time through the doors stepped the two from outside. Cole closed his eyes, doing his damndest to stay calm. He did not yet seek a confrontation, but being intimidated might just put the flame to the fuse. Blowing out a long sigh, he caught the barkeeper's eye. 'Do you serve coffee?'

'We serve anything you want, stranger.'

'Black coffee.'

Nodding, the barkeeper moved to the far end of the bar to prepare the order and Cole heard them coming closer.

Two from the table, two from the doors.

He kept his eyes fixed firmly ahead and could see them clearly in the long mirror on the wall behind the counter.

'That's a mighty fine rig you're wearing, mister,' said one of them.

Cole turned and studied the man sidling up to him. Tall and gangly, at his waist, a well worn Remington New Model Police revolver in a tooled holster, arranged for a cross-belly draw. It was Roose's gun. Cole kept his growing fury to himself, the almost debilitating urge to reach over and snuff out the man's life difficult to control. But he managed it. Instead of killing the man, he shrugged. He too sported a cross-belly rig. 'Could be we're twins.'

The others laughed, but the tall guy frowned. 'What's your business here, mister?'

Ignoring the threatening tone, Cole felt some relief as the barkeeper returned with his coffee. He took a sip and nodded in appreciation. 'That's good.'

'I asked you a question.'

'Well ...' Cole replaced the cup on its saucer and turned it around, aware of the man's impatience and liking it. 'I'm passing through.'

'Passing through to where?'

'Home.' The others were not joining in, allowing the gangly one to do all the talking. Perhaps the baiting might increase shortly, so Cole took his time, trying to ease the tension. He said, as calmly as he could, 'Friend, you seem awful agitated. Have I done something to offend you? If I have, then I apologise.'

The one on his left cleared his throat, 'Yeah, come on Bart, let's leave it now, huh.'

'On your way home,' said Bart, brushing aside his comrade's words. 'And where's home?'

'Tucson. Left the army about a month ago, and I'm taking my time riding the range for one last time.'

'Left the army?'

'Yes, sir. I've been a scout for them for the past thirty years or so, but my time has ended. Fort Concho will be closing soon, now that the frontier is tamed.'

'Is that what you did, mister?' asked the one on his left. A younger man, his youthful face glowed with impish curiosity. 'You were out fighting Indians and all?'

'I did, yes. But that was some time ago.'

Another man leaned forward, 'What do you make of that Buffalo Bill and his Wild West Show?'

Cole chuckled and finished his coffee. 'Is that what it's called? I wouldn't know.'

Leaning across the counter on his right elbow, Bart appeared more serious than ever. 'So what do you make of him, that Buffalo Bill? You had dealings with him?'

'Not as such, no. Saw him from a distance once, many years ago. I never did consider him as anything more than an opportunist.'

'An oppor-what?' asked the young one.

Cole looked at him. 'Maybe not him directly, but people like him ripped the very heart out of the Indian by what they done.'

'How they do that?'

'They took away their means to live. Their relationship with the buffalo goes back way beyond when the White Man first came into this land, but we saw fit to destroy them. Or, at least, try to. The Indian lived with the buffalo, used its meat, its fur. Even its sinews. All the White Man did was cut off its hide and leave its flesh to rot out in the prairie.'

'Sounds like you're an Indian-lover, mister.'

Cole gave Bart a dismissive glance. 'If we hadn't taken away their soul, their way of life, we would not have had all the troubles we've had, and none of the killing.'

'All because of killing the buffalo?'

'Mainly, in my view.'

'But you fought Indians?' said the young one. 'You knew them for what they were. Murdering scum.' The others grunted in agreement. 'I have heard some more broke out of the reservation. Comanche.'

'They should all be strung up,' said Bart through his teeth. 'They ain't nothing more than animals.'

'I take it you've never met one? Face to face, I mean. Talked. Tried to understand 'em?'

'And you have?'

Cole nodded. 'On many occasions.'

Bart turned away and spat into the spittoon at his feet. 'Like I said, an Indian-lover.'

'I don't excuse what they have done, to settlers and the like,' Cole continued unabated, 'but I do understand it. You take away wood from a carpenter, what's he gonna do? Become a farmer? After a lifetime of making things with his hands ... It's the same with the Indians. The *Lords of the Southern Plains* is what they called the Comanche. But that was back then when this was their land. Now it's ours, but at least the buffalo is coming back.' He pushed himself away from the counter and stretched his back. 'Do you know of anywhere that has rooms?'

The barkeeper, to whom Cole spoke, wiped his hands on his apron. 'Penny Albright has rooms. You'll find her two streets down on the right of the Crosskeys Mercantile Bank.'

Cole tipped his hat and placed a dollar on the counter. 'Keep the change.'

'I thought you was passing through?'

Turning his smile to Bart, Cole regarded the man's rig, deciding there and then he would be the first to die. 'I'll need a good night's rest first. Then, after a hearty breakfast, I'll be on my way.' He nodded to each in turn. 'I'll be seeing you.'

He left, pushing through the batwings and stood to scan the town. The gunslingers moved close up behind him, their spurs pinging loudly in the quiet saloon interior. Without a backward glance, Colt went to his horse and eased himself into the saddle.

He found the boarding house without much trouble.

Penny Albright was not what Cole was expecting. He didn't exactly know *what* he was expecting, but the trim, middle-aged woman with a strikingly beautiful face and green eyes that twinkled mischievously who greeted him when he called was certainly not it!

She showed him to his room, which was small, bright, and furnished with a good deal of comfort and cleanliness. A sudden urge to jump on the bed and bounce up and down on the mattress gripped him, but he managed to remain standing, drinking her in. He checked her hand and saw she wore a ring. What's more, she noticed him checking and he blushed.

'My husband is a surveyor, Mister ...?'

'Cole. Reuben Cole.'

'Are you feeling all right, Mr Cole? You seem somewhat pinky.'

'Pinky?' He felt along his jawline, the heat still there from his blushing. 'No, no, I'm fine.'

'No, I meant the bruising.'

'Ah!' He forced a laugh, his discomfort growing by the second. He slumped down on the bed, suddenly tired, the pain in his ribs returning with a vengeance. He pressed his hand against his right side without thinking. Her expression grew more concerned. 'I, er, had an accident out on the range. Nothing serious.'

'You look tuckered out if you don't mind me saying, Mr Cole. I shall bring you a hot meal to your room so as you do not need to go downstairs. I have only one other guest, a travelling salesman out of Kansas City. He too will be leaving in the morning.'

'It's a busy little town then?'

She went to speak, then pressing her lips together, stopped herself. He frowned. 'It used to be a *good* little town, Mr Cole. Until certain unsavoury elements came here and made their presence felt. A lot of people have since left.'

'Ah, yes. I think I met a few in the saloon when I first arrived.'

'Gunmen?' He nodded and again became aware of her eyes settling on his own handgun. 'That perhaps is something you know a lot about, Mr Cole?'

'I'm an army scout, ma'am. Ex-army. I've ridden across every square inch of this territory and men like those in the saloon have been my companions for way too long.'

'Not friendly companions I hope.'

'Indeed not, ma'am. I have little truck with men such as those. What exactly are they doing here, do you know?'

'They are the employees of a man called Kestler. Randolph Kestler. I shall not go into the details, for he is a man of un-Christian habits and has brought no end of spite and malice to Lawrenceville. He has shares in the railroad and is looking to expand the tracks further into New Mexico and beyond, gaining profit from the transportation of steers. He has made huge investments and courted the avarice of cattle barons from right down to the Mexican border. For them to trust him with moving their herds, he would need an orderly town and many have sprung up all along the railroad, but not many are made *orderly* in the way this one is.'

'I see.'

'I'm not sure you do, Mr Cole.'

'He's a businessman, looking to develop his company.'

'A businessman who develops his company by raising money using any means he can to get it.'

'Dishonestly, you mean?'

She pursed her lips, clearly in some discomfort with discussing all of this with a perfect stranger. Cole understood and did not press the point. How was she to know who he was? In all reality, he could even be another employee of Kestler's, sent to sound out public opinion. He sighed and stood up, throwing down his hat and pulling off his coat. He winced as a stab of pain shot through him and she hurried to his side and helped him.

'You need rest, Mr Cole.'

'Thank you, Mrs Albright.'

She watched him as he stretched himself out on the bed.

Within a blink, he was fast asleep.

CHAPTER TWENTY-TWO

The wind whipped tiny dust devils in the main street and the horses tied to the hitching rails scraped at the ground, whinnying in discomfort as tiny shards of gravel slapped into their faces or heavier pieces stung their rumps.

Kestler, sitting on his rocking chair smoking a large cigar, stood up and stretched himself out. 'Storm coming,' he said to nobody in particular.

He went to turn away and go back inside. The promise of a hot meal and a glass of bourbon in front of the fire was extremely seductive, but something made him stop. He slowly turned, half expecting to see nothing but the horses all jittery, longing to be inside a stable. Instead, he saw a man. Tall, dressed in buckskin coat and long boots, a bandana covering most of his face, the broad-brimmed straw hat fluttering so strongly it looked as if it might take off at any moment.

'Can I help you, stranger?'

'Could be.' He pulled down the bandana to reveal his craggy features, hard as flint.

Something about the voice, the steel in it, caused Kestler to tense up. He did not flinch as somebody moved behind him.

Bart Owens stepped up next to his boss. 'Who's this?'

'I don't know.'

Owens cleared his throat and took a step forward. 'Hey, I know you. I met you last night. You was looking for a room. If you're looking for something else, we ain't got—'

'Roose Sterling.'

'Who—'

Kestler put a warning arm on Bart's arm. 'Go get the boys, Bart.'

Something passed between them and Bart, picking up on the fear in his boss's voice, whirled and half-ran back inside.

'I don't know where he is,' said Kestler, rolling his shoulders, placing his thumbs in his waistband, inches from his revolver, 'if that's what you're asking.'

'Sure you do.'

Without warning the wind dropped, as suddenly as it had started, and the relief from the horses was palpable. The tension inside Kestler, however, went up several notches. 'I said I don't.'

The man remained silent, even as four others appeared on the porch, stamping their boots, glowing in anger. Perhaps their card game had been interrupted, or their drinking. Perhaps both. Clearly, whatever the reason, their temper was up and they were red-faced and itching for a fight.

'I'll have to ask you to leave, mister. People like you ain't welcome in this town. And,' a quick glance to the others, 'as it's *my* town, I have the authority.' He leaned forward, jutting out his chin, 'So get the hell out.'

'Is that what you said to Sterling before you ran him out, and fed him to those savages?'

Blinking, Kestler straightened himself up. 'What savages?'

'Around five of 'em. They took Sterling, split him in two before they pegged him out and cooked him in the noonday sun. Next, you'll be telling me you didn't have anything to do with it.'

'I didn't. Who are you, mister?'

'Thing is,' the stranger rubbed his chin, 'I went to the reservation before I came here. Spoke to a few people there. It's kinda unusual for Comanch, or any of 'em, to break out nowadays. No reason. Except ...' His hand dropped, 'except when they'd been offered the chance to make some money.'

Someone whistled faintly. Another coughed nervously. A third made his excuses and went back inside. Kestler never allowed his eyes to leave the stranger. 'I don't know what you're getting at.'

'Is that right? Well, let me enlighten you. You've been employing gangs to purloin various estates around these parts, paying them a pittance against the value of the items they steal. I know.' He pointed inside the big saloon. 'I was in here just last evening. Saw one of my daddy's paintings on your wall in there.'

'*One of your daddy 's...?* Mister, my advice, turn around and get out. Now.' He grinned, before giving some added emphasis to his threats, 'Before you get hurt.'

The stranger, however, ignored Kestler's words and continued unabated, with a galling nonchalance. 'My daddy's things, they ain't what brought me back. It's what you did to Sterling. You see, he was a friend and just before I cut out the eyes of the young varmint that led those Comanch, he told me who'd put him up to it.' He rolled his tongue around the inside of his mouth and spat into the dirt. 'It was you, Kestler.'

'Young varmint? Mister, you seem to be cooking up a wild story.'

'Went by the name of Brody.'

The gunhands either side of Kestler stiffened. Bart jutted out his jaw. 'Brody? What did you say you did to him? Cut out his eyes?'

'A lot else besides, after I'd killed those who rode with him.'

'That's hogswill,' said one of the others.

'That's what you'll be soon enough, boy.'

A bone-chilling coldness settled over everything.

Kestler, a big man, ponderous belly sagging over his belt, was confident in his skills. He had killed many men, some, like now, face to face. Something about this man, however, irked him. He had never known anything like this, never gone up against a man such as this. There was something so different about him. A calmness. A latent propensity for violence. The air of danger, of someone of whom he should be wary.

Pushing these doubts and anxieties aside, Kestler gave a laugh and took his chance. He moved, as fast as he could, to draw his gun, but before his fingers had even curled around the butt of his Remington, a bullet struck him between the eyes. He crumpled, not registering anything, and he fell with a colossal crash to the porch floor, sending up a cloud of ancient dust to hover like a shroud over his corpse.

For a moment nobody moved. Everything had happened so quickly. And now Kestler was dead. One minute that well-known sneer, that dismissive arrogance, now nothing remained except an empty husk.

Bart Owens recovered first. He clawed for his gun, the same gun he had taken from Roose, the gun the stranger knew so well. Two bullets slapped into Bart's chest, sending him spinning wildly backwards through the double swing doors to collapse in the saloon. A woman screamed.

The others hesitated.

'He was your boss,' said the stranger, 'he ain't no more. So give it up. You're all out of work.'

He stood with the Colt in his hand, a tiny worm of smoke trailing from the barrel.

For a moment, it seemed nobody would respond, or do the sensible thing. The world stopped. No one spoke or breathed. Then, gradually, the thaw set in. Men's eyes flickered and shoulders relaxed. They exchanged glances and, one by one, they turned away leaving the stranger to consider the body of the dead Kestler. A tiny upturning of one corner of his mouth was his only reaction.

The unmistakable clunk of a revolver's hammer cocking caused Cole to freeze.

'Drop your gun and turn around, nice and slow Mr Cole.'

He did so, the Cavalry hitting the wooden floor with a heavy thump.

'You're darned good, I'll say that for you' said the man. He wore a black waistcoat, white shirt sleeves rolled up past his elbows, spectacles pushed back on top of his head. The gun in his hand barely moved. 'But perhaps your days are over Indian fighter. I doubt I could have crept up on you this easy back when you were out on the plains, hunting down Comanche.'

'Just do what you need to.'

A grin before the man's head erupted in a huge crimson and white ball of blood and brains.

Before the broken corpse toppled to the ground, Cole was diving, hitting the floorboards and rolling over. Sweeping up the Colt Cavalry, he managed to put three rounds towards the man standing some twenty or so paces away in the middle of the street, his Winchester already levering in another cartridge. Head down, Cole drove through what remained of the batwing doors as bullets smacked into the wall either side of him.

He took a moment, eyes fanning over the terrified customers hiding behind upturned tables or cowering in the corners. A gunman with the stem of a white bone pipe sticking out of his shirt pocket scurried over. 'It's Soloman,' he said. 'He put me down just outside Stacey Childer's place. I owe him for that,' he gave emphasis to his words by rubbing the back of his skull.

'This is my fight,' said Cole, taking the chance to reload his gun.

'Don't matter who kills him,' said the pipe-smoker, 'but one of us has to – he ain't gonna stop.' He grinned. 'You've put me out of work, Mr Cole, seeing as you killed both my employers. That one who had the drop on you? He was Kestler's partner, man name of Doc Haynes. Soloman, he's the one who broke into your home. If we help one another, maybe you can let me take my share of the loot they stole.'

'Some of that loot is mine.'

The man raised his hands, 'Hey, I don't mean yours. All I need is enough to set me up in a little tavern down Mexico way. This life ain't for me. I need a change of scenery.' He rubbed the back of his head. 'He hit me so hard, just as I was about to put that poor Childer out of his misery. Least I think it was Soloman. When I came to, everyone had gone. But whatever, I never did like the look of him.'

Another smile and he sprinted towards the doors, bent double, gun in hand. He took a quick glance outside, before rolling out into the open.

Cole followed across the saloon and flattened himself up against the wall adjacent to the shattered doors. Through the splintered woodwork, he managed to watch the man with the pipe scampering around the corner and out of sight.

Two evenly placed Winchester rounds swiftly followed and told him all he needed to know.

He looked back into the saloon. Any remaining people were making a quick and determined exit through the rear door. Beside this was a flight of stairs, leading to several closed rooms, rooms where undoubtedly the whores entertained their customers. Cole ran towards the stairs and took them two at a time.

He tried each door in turn and each one proved to be locked. Cursing, he swung around and shouted down to the barman who was sitting down behind the counter, knees pressed up to his chest, rocking. 'Keys,' he shouted.

The barman looked with vaguely indifferent eyes.

'I want the keys to these doors!'

His only chance of escape, he convinced himself, was to break out through one of the room windows, drop to the street below, and try to outflank the mysterious Soloman. A wild chance, but the only one remaining to him he realized as further measured shots rang out from outside, accompanied by shrieks and cries. He was killing the fleeing customers. The man was incensed. A homicidal maniac. Deranged. Cole sucked in a breath, went up to the first door and kicked at the lock with all his strength.

It splintered but remained firmly closed.

Another kick, then another. Cole, breathing hard, knew he had little time. Another kick. The door gave slightly. A couple more should do it.

A bullet hit the doorframe, sending up a tiny shower of wooden shards. He threw himself face down on the floor as another bullet struck the wall where he had only moments ago stood.

From where he lay, the angle would be impossible for Soloman to get off a good shot. If he moved, however ...

He heard a cackling laugh from below, a sound, which brought a chill to his very soul. The man was actually enjoying the killing.

The first bullet came through the wooden floor of the balcony inches from Cole's leg. Soloman was underneath, firing off shots in measured intervals, punctuating each shot with a burst of laughter.

'I'm gonna kill you, Cole. I should have killed you back in your house. Thought I had, but you is one tough old bird.' The lever worked. 'But now, your day of reckoning is nigh.' The hammer cocked. 'Goodbye old timer. Enjoy your time in hell.'

The rapport boomed through the saloon.

Cole winced, squeezing his eyes shut, waiting for the searing pain.

It never came.

The acrid smell of cordite hit his nostrils and he slowly released his breath. He waited, straining to hear Soloman moving below. But there was nothing. Taking his chance, he sat up and peered down into the saloon.

There, by the double swing doors stood Stone, the big Sharps in his hands.

———

Amy Childer steered her little buggy down Lawrenceville's main street, Stacey sitting beside her. There was a gaggle of bystanders outside the livery stable, women and men looking aghast, faces white as chalk.

'What's been going on?' Amy asked.

'Gunfight,' said one old woman. 'A stranger came and now they are all dead.'

'All?'

'Kestler,' said another, 'and that horrible Haynes. All of 'em dead.'

'Big fat one went in there and a young fella shot him dead.'

Amy turned her face towards the saloon and saw two men emerging, both tall, one dressed in buckskins. The 'big fat one' had to be Soloman. She thanked God for that. And for Kestler too. Now perhaps, if she could keep Stacey sober, she could make something of her life. Nodding to the tiny huddle of onlookers, she eased her little buggy into the street and away from the town deciding, there and then, never to return.

They tied up what remained of the stolen antiques to the back of a purloined mule. A buggy driven by a striking woman drew up. Cole doffed his hat.

'I've been told there was shooting.'

'Some,' said Cole. 'It's all over now.'

'I was wondering ... There was a man named Soloman. He's been terrorizing my husband and I. Was he ...?'

'Yes, ma'am. He won't be troubling you no more.' Cole frowned, gestured towards the man slumped next to her. 'Is that your husband?' She grunted. 'I was told Kestler sent someone out to kill him.'

'Yes. I knocked him down with the flat of a shovel.'

Cole laughed. 'I'm guessing that is the least he deserved. What you planning on doing now, ma'am?'

She shrugged. 'Getting as far away from here as possible. Start anew. It's gonna be hard, my husband being as he is.'

'Ma'am...' Cole went over to the mule and dipped inside one of the sacks. He brought something wrapped in thick canvas out and went over to the woman. He carefully opened up the wrapping and pressed a beautifully carved figure into her hand. 'This here is a Meissen figurine, all the way from Germany. It was my daddy's and is probably worth more than this whole town put together. I reckon in San Francisco you could raise enough money for any kind of life you wanted.'

Mouth hanging open, a single tear rolling down her face, she looked deep into Cole's eyes. 'I couldn't ... This is more than generous, but I couldn't...'

''Course you can,' he said with a smile and patted her hand. 'I've seen enough killing this day to make me sick to my stomach. This'll go some way in making it all seem worthwhile.'

He stepped away and watched her closely as, sniffing loudly, she carefully put the figurine in the back of the buggy and moved away.

'My oh my, that was a fine thing you did there, Mr Cole.'

'You think so?' asked Cole, raising a single eyebrow towards Stone. 'So was what you did for me.'

Stone smiled awkwardly.

They returned to their grisly work. The bodies they piled up in an open wagon and together they took it to the undertaker's, whose boarded-up store appeared deserted, but they left it there anyway.

Without a word, both men began their journey back home.

Cole rode, leaving his past behind him, the decision now made. The killing had to end. With Roose dead, everything he had known was gone.

Except for Maddie.

Maddie who had begged him not to go, who warned him she would not be there when he returned.

If he returned.

Before either of them did, however, they went to search for Roose.

For the last time, Cole used his old tracking skills and when they reached the place, Stone cried. Cole, in silence, dug the grave.

The town, as they trotted into Main Street later that day, looked much the same as it ever did. Passing the sheriff's office, they saw young Thurst pinning up a couple of wanted posters on the board outside. He looked at Cole over his shoulder and stopped. He turned. 'You found him?'

Cole nodded and turned his gaze towards the end of the street. 'I buried what was left of him.' Something caught in his throat and he reached for his canteen and took a large drink, wishing it was something stronger. 'I'm sure gonna miss him.' People were going about their daily business, shopping, conversing, passing the time of day. If he had a photograph of this place from a quarter of a century ago, it would look exactly the same. Except that back then Sterling Roose would be part of it. Cole thought about that for a moment before pushing it to the back of his mind. They had had a good run, better than most, and Cole always knew something like this would happen in the end. For men like Roose and he, that was how life ran its course.

'What happens now?'

Snapped out of his reverie, Cole looked at Thurst. 'Elect a new sheriff, I guess.'

'Oh.' Thurst turned his face to the ground. 'Mr Cole, I admired Mr Roose a good deal. I'm gonna miss him.'

'Me too, son. Me too.' He gestured towards the sign for Sheriff above the door. 'You would make a fine sheriff, Stone.'

Stone gaped. 'Mr Cole ... I don't think ...'

'Nonsense, son. I'll put your name forward. But for now,' he inched his horse away, 'I have something a little more pressing to see to.'

He flicked the reins and moved gently forward, wondering what he would find waiting for him back home.

Breaking into a canter, he left the town limits and headed in the direction of his large home. The one his father had put so much energy into building. Cole never truly appreciated how cold the house was, nor how it could be warmed by the love of a good woman. Now, even that was lost to him. He should have tried harder, begged her to stay. However, he did not. His foolish pride once more got in the way and now, he truly was alone.

He came over the rise and reined in his horse, heart banging so hard against his chest he thought it might burst out.

There, just inside the gate was her buggy. In the stable yard, the horse munching on something. Something tasty no doubt. Something the little mare would always have.

Because she was there.

Maddie had not left.

As if sensing his approach, she appeared on the porch, framed in the doorway, the sleeves of her dress rolled up, a bandana around her forehead to keep her flowing blonde hair out of her eyes. She stood with a bucket in one hand and a mop in the other. She set them both down, put her hands on her hips and, even from this distance, he saw the flash of her smile.

Flicking the reins, his heart swelling, Cole kicked his horse into a gallop and the grin on his face was broader than it had ever been before in his entire life.

The End

THE HUNTER

Reuben Cole Westerns Book 2

*For Janice, as always, with all my love
and also for Ray, again, who always loves a good Western.
Enjoy!*

CHAPTER ONE

The Mid-West, 1875.

O n that final morning, Charlie, as he did most days, dug through one of the several vegetable patches which punctuated the fields around the sides of the family home. Soon, if these latest crops proved as successful as the last, he would begin to expand cultivation into entire fields. He'd brought with him the plough he'd always planned on using in his smallholding back in Kansas. The prospect of hitching it to a team of strong horses and cutting furrows in this good earth was at long last a very real one. Closing his eyes, he paused in his toil and allowed himself a moment to dream a little, relishing the thought of establishing a fine working farm. Already the wheat was doing well and soon there would be potatoes and any number of Brassicaceae. His was not a labour of love, but one born out of necessity – without these crops there would be no food for his family to eat. Failure meant they would all die. This land, sprawling untouched and uncultivated, had to be tamed if it was to give up its undoubted treasures. Life in Kansas proved restrictive, with increasing bureaucracy hampering opportunities to truly thrive. The opportunities out west were continuing to attract those willing and able to put in the effort to succeed. So, determined to fulfil his aspirations, Charlie packed up his wagon and headed west, with his wife Julia, their two sons and fourteen-year-old daughter. It was a journey they should have made years before but, now that they were here, the future looked bright. All he would need to do was continue his labours until completed and the fields made ready. So, with muscles already screaming, he sank the spade deep into the soil and turned it before dropping to his knees to attack the weeds with a short-handled fork.

From inside one of the log cabin's two newly built rooms, still smelling sweetly of freshly hewn timber, the sound of his wife singing drifted across to him. He smiled. Back in Kansas, she had sung in the church choir, and he knew how much she missed her time there. But she had always been supportive of his ambitions, her quiet strength bolstering him whenever he floundered in self-doubt.

On the far side of the wheat field, his two sons were busy erecting the fencing which separated their land from the endless plains beyond. Half a dozen years previously the constant fear of attacks by marauding Comanches meant that such endeavours would not be possible. Now, safely interned in their reservations, the Lords of the Southern Plains no longer posed a threat. Recently news filtered through that Apaches continued to fight against government forces down in southern Texas, but everyone felt assured that within a short time even they would be safely penned in. Murmurings of continuing problems in the far north made little impression on those settling on the land bordering New Mexico. Perhaps it should.

The fork hit something hard and unyielding so Charlie returned to using the spade, easing the blade underneath a stubborn rock and levering it from the soil's embrace. He took a moment to drag his arm across his brow but did not allow his exhaustion to dampen his spirits. Soon the whole family would be working on the harvest, bringing to an end their first successful year of farming. As if to underline the good fortune with which they were all blessed, daughter Amber came drifting by, beaming broadly. "Morning, Papa," she said, her voice as pretty as she herself. Charlie grinned his response and returned to using the fork on his assault of the weeds.

Amber went over to the well and carefully lowered the pail into the dark depths. From inside the log cabin the sound of Mary, his wife, singing at the top of her voice made this day something beyond special.

A distant noise, more of a squawk than a human voice, caused Charlie to raise his head. Frowning, he thought he saw movement on the horizon. Dust, the first indication of riders. He hauled himself to his feet, blowing out his breath loudly. Constant bending and straightening were taking its toll on his joints, the only blemish on an otherwise perfect family life. He focused in again on the smudge of brown billowing in the distance. Definitely horses. Who could they be? He'd heard rumours of disquiet amongst some of the Indians on the reservations, a yearning to return to the great days of the past, when the Comanches roamed this land before being forcibly ejected. Surely the days of senseless violence were now gone, buried along with the many hundreds, if not thousands who had lost their lives on both sides? Disquiet was leading to outbreaks of fighting in the north as the discovery of gold meant many more white folks would be encroaching upon Indian territory. He gave up a little prayer of thanks that he'd brought his family to the relative calm of New Mexico. Establishing a small-holding back east had given him enough skills and knowledge to turn his hand to full-blown farming and it looked, finally, as if things were turning his way.

"Pa, Pa, for God's sake, get inside!"

The two riders were now fully in view. They weren't Indians but his two sons, riding as if the very hounds of hell were snapping at their heels, beating their horse's flanks with their hats, both boys red-faced, grimacing. "Pa, get the Winchesters!"

Charlie couldn't quite understand what all the fuss was about. He stood and watched, slightly bemused, as the boys brought their stampeding mounts to a grinding halt, hurling themselves from their mounts before they fully stopped, and racing into the cabin. He heard his wife shout, "Boys, take off those filthy boots, I don't want—"

"Pa?"

Charlie turned towards the sound of his daughter's voice. She sounded afraid and he looked at her standing beside the well, the pitcher full, water slopping over the brim. She was staring open-mouthed at something beyond his shoulder. As he went to follow her gaze, an arrow struck her in the throat and she fell in silence, a look of abject horror on her pretty face. He knew she was dead before she hit the ground, but this knowledge didn't help galvanise him into action. Instead, he stood rooted, unable to react. He heard the thundering of approaching hooves, could taste the acrid tang of horse sweat at the back of his throat, but his limbs failed to respond. Realising outsiders were invading his land, hell-bent on destroying everything he held dear, he somehow managed to tear his gaze from the nightmare before his eyes and noticed the semi-naked warrior leaping from his still running horse, to smash into him. Flaying about beneath the frighteningly powerful Indian, Charlie did his best to ward off a strike from a flashing hatchet. But even as he squirmed and gripped his attacker's wrist, a burst of fire erupted in his side. The Indian whooped in triumph, spittle drooling from his mad, grimacing mouth, brandishing the knife which dripped blood. Charlie's blood.

From somewhere, rough, strong hands were gripping him by the shoulders, dragging him across the ground. He heard a gunshot, screams. His wife's screams. Cries and groans of pain.

Those who held him pulled him into the interior and he saw, through a mist of pain, his handsome, strong sons being disembowelled, his wife pawed and slapped, bleating warriors filling his once beautiful home, their nakedness an abomination to his eyes.

They hauled him to his feet and forced him to watch. At some point within the horrors enacted around him, he lost consciousness, only to be punched awake again, grinning faces looming close, hot blades slicing through his flesh. Dear God would it never end as those monsters danced and yelped amongst the blood.

Long afterwards, the white hunters despatched those few warriors who dawdled behind their comrades. Cougan paid for the intervention with his life and they buried him along with the others. Sterling Roose said some words but Reuben Cole, who stood in the yard and peered in the direction of the fleeing Comanches who raced away with Charlie's stolen horses, barely heard a word of it. "I'll do to them what they did to these poor folks," he said through gritted teeth and rolling tears. His partner Roose sucked in a breath. "We'll need to report back to the troop," he said, voice distant, all of the strength wrested from it.

"You go," said Cole, reloading his rifle. "Tell the Lieutenant what happened here and get a squad to scout in a wide arc, warning other homesteaders what could happen. In the meantime, I'll head 'em off. Catch me up as best you can."

Cole went to move away but Roose held him back by the arm. "You can't take them alone, Reuben. For pity's sake..."

Cole levelled his gaze upon his companion. "You bet your sweet life I can, Sterling."

With that, he strode back the way he had come, untethered his horse, and mounted up.

Roose watched his friend leave and knew that for those fleeing warriors all the furies of Hell would soon be visited upon them. He'd seen it before and knew all too well what Reuben Cole was capable of.

As he stood, his eyes never leaving Cole's slowly diminishing form, he remembered the first time it had happened and a shudder ran through him as the memories stirred around in his mind. Having seen it before, he thanked God he would not be a witness to what Cole would do when he caught up with those Comanche raiders.

CHAPTER TWO

Some years earlier

Hyram Clay was a big man, slow to anger, but also slow in reactions. The first punch cracked into his jaw despite it being well telegraphed, and he staggered backwards, impressed by the weight of the blow and the size of the black man moving in closer towards him.

"I'll not stand your insulting anymore," said Cougan, flexing his shoulders, slamming a right fist into Clay's ribs. The big man's breath rushed out from his mouth and the left cross put him down on the floor where he sat on his backside, staring in dazed disbelief at the blood dripping in between the cracks in the wooden boards.

"Darn it, he sure is something," said Sterling Roose from where he sat, long legs stretched out under the card table. The two men opposite, cards held close to their faces, barely muttered a reply. Around ten or so dollars was spread out across the tabletop before them and neither man was willing to take the chance of any of it going walkabout.

"That Clay had it coming," continued Roose, almost to himself now. "A more arrogant, self-serving individual I have yet to meet."

"Cougan's an ignorant bastard," said one of the card-players unexpectedly, thumbing through his hand. "I would prefer it if he were the one spitting teeth."

"Me too," said his companion, frowning at his own hand. "I'll see your fifty-cents and raise it another fifty."

"Shoot," hissed Roose, glancing down to the empty space next to his elbow. All of his money was gone and a quick glance at his card-hand confirmed he would have been looking at a tasty win if he had the means to cover his opponent's bet. He threw down his cards. "I'm out."

"Shame," said the man opposite, grinning as his partner covered the stake and laid down his cards. "A pair of sixes."

Giggling, the other spread out his own hand and beamed. "*Two* pairs." Roose groaned inwardly. He could have beaten either hand. He looked up to see Cougan taking Clay by the throat, lifting him to his feet. A thrust of his bull-neck and his forehead connected with Clay's nose, the audible snap of bone sending a tremour through Roose's scrotum. Clay screamed and Cougan slammed in a swinging left hook and it was all over, Clay crumpling in an unconscious, bloodied heap on the barroom floor.

A hand pressed down on Roose's shoulder, causing him to jump in alarm. His hand was already reaching for the Colt Cavalry at his waist when he saw who it was and immediately relaxed.

Reuben Cole settled down in the chair next to his friend. "You're tense."

"Just been watching Cougan take that ape Clay apart, so I was a bit preoccupied."

Nodding, Cole stared at the large black man who, having felled Clay, was now busily rummaging through the man's pockets. "Seems like it was something of a grudge."

"Both of 'em are mean."

"And dangerous." Cole cast a caustic eye over the two card players opposite. "Sterling, Captain Phelps wants to talk to us about some rustling going on close to the border. Army horses. He's not impressed and wants the perpetrators brought in and hanged publicly in the fort parade ground."

"Should make a great spread for Harper's Weekly."

"Interestingly, I think he's planning on just that very thing."

"Full of laughs is our Captain Phelps."

"He's full of stomach acid and a vicious razor-rash across his neck. He therefore ain't in the best of spirits."

The two of them left the bar, noting Cougan moving across to the counter to order a large whisky with the money extracted from Clay's breast pocket. No doubt more trouble would soon follow.

Kicking the dust off their boots, the two scouts mounted the steps to the captain's office, nodding to the guard outside. The young private stiffened, twisted his body and gave a light rap on the door. A gruff voice from within invited his visitors inside.

It was a large, well-ordered office, smelling of oak and cigar smoke. The oak came from a broad desk and several cabinets arranged against the walls. The tobacco aroma wafted from the fat cigar Captain Phelps chomped on as he bent over a large map spread out in front of him. He wore a well-creased grey shirt, uniform trousers held up by wide braces. On his chair, hanging from one arm, was his army jacket. As the two scouts moved closer and brought their heels together, he scrutinised them under his heavy brows. A big man, rumour had it he had once fought the heavyweight prizefighter Tom Allen. His broken nose and heavily scarred face gave the story some considerable weight.

"Gentleman," said the captain, waving them closer, "we have a situation and we need to get it sorted as soon as is physically possible."

The two scouts moved up to flank the broad-shouldered officer. The map covered the northern part of New Mexico and its border with Colorado.

"Beyond Willow Springs," continued Phelps, "is a half-abandoned trading post, one of many along the old Santa Fe trail. It was recently converted to a water station for the railroad. Just over a week ago, a locomotive pulled in to top up its boiler. Coupled to it were three U.S. army carriages, with around thirty or so horses being brought down from Denver. There was a small detail of soldiers guarding the cargo as nobody thought anyone would dare hijack it."

"But someone did," said Cole.

"There were six guards. Four were shot and killed, a fifth wounded. The sixth, a weassly private by the name of Parrott managed to get away and raised the alarm. He made his way here and got himself patched up. It's a miracle he did what he did or we may not have known about the theft for weeks."

"Was he badly hurt?"

Phelps shrugged. "Don't know and I don't care. It's the horse-thieves the government want, Cole."

"What about the train driver?"

Phelps blew out a thick bloom of smoke and straightened out his back, his gaze settling on Roose. "They shot him too, together with the stoker, and the brakeman."

Frowning, Roose looked down at the map. "Indians?"

"I doubt it. The reservations have not reported any breakouts." Phelps clamped his teeth down on the cigar and looped both thumbs through his braces. "These are a bunch of ruthless individuals who have run off with Army horses, with a view to selling 'em. We believe they're running them down to the Mexican border."

"To sell them to the Mexicans?" Roose shot a glance towards Cole. "Seems a bit extreme, don't you think? What could thirty horses bring? Two hundreds dollars a head, *if* they is thoroughbreds."

"Oh, they're more than that Roose," said Phelps. "They is breeding stock. Stallions. What you have here is the basis for a regiment of the best-damned cavalry mounts this part of the world has ever seen."

Roose whistled. "No wonder the Army want 'em back."

"They want 'em back, but they want the men who did this even more. You're to bring 'em in, alive, for a hanging here at the fort."

"Hold on," said Cole slowly. "They is clearly no bunch of amateurs and they must have had some inside information to have known the train was full of prime breeding stock."

"Indeed," said Phelps.

"So how many men are we talking about."

"Our witness said there was at least ten of 'em."

"Ten. Killers."

"Seems that way."

"And you want us to go up against ten, armed and very capable desperadoes?"

"Can't think of anyone else who'd succeed in such an endeavour, Cole."

"Well that's mighty gracious of you Captain, but how in Hell do you expect us to bring ten such individuals in *alive*?"

"I'm giving you six good men, Cole. All you need do is pick up their trail and hunt 'em down."

"I see..." Cole thought for a moment. "So, this survivor, the one named Parrott, he knew which way they went?"

"Roughly."

"You don't suspect him of being the insider, Captain? I mean, it sounds incredibly fortuitous that he should survive, knows how many there were *and* which way they went."

"God's good mercy, Cole. That's what it is."

The interview over, Cole and Roose stumbled outside into the blinding sunlight. Squinting towards one another, both of them blew out long sighs. Cole was the first to speak.

"Did you believe a single word of that hogwash?"

"I'm not sure what to believe, Cole. The captain, He's..." He shook his head, eyes downcast as if he were reluctant to meet Cole's frosty gaze. "You've known him longer than most."

"At a distance, Sterling. I've never broken bread with him, nor never felt the urge to do so."

"Why not?"

"Rumour has it he was with one of them renegade squadrons that ran wild with Anderson over in Kansas during the War. I heard him talking about Jesse James once, how he'd met him, became something of a friend. Makes me wonder if a man like that could ever turn his hand to legal matters."

"So, you knew him, back in the War?"

"Let's just say, I learnt some things, most of 'em unsavoury. After the War, I know he joined the army somehow managing to keep his past something of a secret. But he has a big mouth and has been known, during periods of drunkeness, to spout off about Anderson and James. When I was with Terrell hunting down those bushwackers, I never did come across him. That was later."

"Jeez, Cole, you think he's involed in something illegal ... like stealing horses, for example?" Rubbing his chin, Roose lost himself in thought for a moment. "Maybe it was him who put Parrot up to it?"

"Who knows. All I know is, orders is orders and as long as we are in the employ of the United States Army, that is what we do."

"Yeah, but can we trust him?"

"Trust ain't got much to do with it, Sterling." He blew out a long breath. "If we can pick up the horse-thieves' trail, and the men we have riding with us are good, then we might just—"

"Cole, regardless of who comes with us, It's a suicide mission."

True. Putting aside what you just said, if Parrot, this so-called insider, gave the thieves information, He'sbound to know who the thieves are. We catch up with him, we"ll know who we're going up against."

"They was probably provided with all kinds of securities, like a small army of Federales waiting to give them a helping hand."

"Federales won't cross the border."

"True enough, but how are we to stop them horse-thieves before they cross the Rio Grande?"

"By talking to the man who gave them the information in the first place." He sniggered. "We don't have to be geniuses to work out who it was."

"I think You're right – It's Parrott, the surviving soldier. I thought that when Phelps first mentioned him, but how could a lowly soldier have that sort of information? And even if he did, how could he be sophisticated enough to brew up such a plan in the first place?"

"I believe you're right, Sterling, but, as I said, I also believe he will be able to point us in the right direction, so let's pay the doc a visit and see how bad Parrot's wounds were."

CHAPTER THREE

"Oh yeah, he was here," said the Army surgeon, a man known to be more connected to a bottle than to his profession. He stood in long-john underwear and soiled vest, barefooted, pouring out a large tin cup of coffee for himself from a battered metal pot. Cole noted how the man's hand shook as he brought the cup carefully to his cracked lips and sipped steaming coffee into his mouth.

"Was?" Sterling exchanged a quick look with his friend. "How long ago did he leave?"

"Can't say precisely." The surgeon smacked his lips and moved across to his cluttered desk. The two scouts were standing in an unkempt, disorganised surgery, which stank of something unsavoury. Cole guessed it might be a mix of urine and vomit. He certainly hoped it wasn't what the surgeon used to clean up the mess after his operations. A sagging bed along the far wall was bleached pink, a pile of blood-stained instruments sitting in filthy liquid resting on a three-legged stool beside it. The surgeon caught Cole's disturbed look and cackled. "Had to see to a young corporal this morning, got himself kicked in the guts by a horse he was supposed to be looking after."

Roose Sterling cleared his throat. "Did he live?"

The surgeon grinned at Sterling's incredulous tone. "Used one of them new fancy sewing techniques from England. They been talking about making the gut *antiseptic*. Some personage called Lister is supposed to have developed techniques which stop people getting infected during and after surgery. Anyways, I tried it, soaking the cat-gut in carbolic. He had internal bleeding, you see. Terrible state he was in."

Sterling Roose let out a tremulous breath. "Yeah, but like I said, did he live?"

"Up to now. You wanna see him?"

Sterling paled at the thought. "Er, not right now, thank-ee."

Chuckling, the surgeon slumped down in his chair. "As for Parrot, I doubt you'll find him on post. He was talking to me about making his way back home, but by the way he half-sprinted across to the livery, I doubt if he were telling the truth."

"How did he seem?" asked Cole.

"Afeared. Wild, crazy eyes, dancing all over the place as if he were expecting some horror to visit him."

"Horror?" Sterling rolled his shoulder, looking ill at ease, shooting his eyes towards the open door of the surgery. "What kind of horror?"

"Nothing of the ghostly kind," the surgeon answered, chuckling to himself again. He seemed to take great amusement in almost everything that went on around him, a fact Cole found galling.

"Where do you think he might have headed for?" asked Cole. "You said he mentioned home."

"Beats me. I'm not sure he'd have anywhere in particular to go. He wasn't from around here, as no doubt you already know. He skedaddled away from that attack on the horse-train as fast as he could go, was picked up by a patrol a couple of miles to the north and brought here to give his testimony."

"Which Captain Phelps took," said Roose, more a statement than a question.

"Indeed."

"Best bet is to ask around the bunkhouses," suggested the surgeon. "Someone might have heard something. The only place he mentioned to me was Willow Springs."

"I doubt he'll head back that way, but thanks anyway." Cole nodded towards the various surgical instruments laid out across the waiting bed, dried blood covering most of the bare metal. "You have a good day."

Stepping out into the daylight, Cole paused un the act of rolling himself a cigarette, setting his eyes straight ahead as a cavalry sergeant strode purposefully across the parade ground towards them.

"That's Burroughs," said Roose in a low voice. "Second Troop Sergeant."

Bringing himself smartly to attention, the big, powerful looking sergeant, gave a quick salute, giving most of his attention to Cole as he spoke. "I'll be accompanying you on the hunt for the horse-thieves, Mister Cole. Men are mustered, horses saddled, provisions packed. Captain Phelps said they would be moving towards the Mexican border so we will need to leave right away."

"I been thinking I might talk to this Parrott first, find out a little more about who these thieves are."

Burroughs frowned, looking confused. "Parrott has left the fort, Mister Cole. He'sheaded for a little town called Rickman City."

"That's interesting," said Cole. "How you know that?"

Burroughs shrugged. "He told virtually the whole fort before he left. His wounds were nothing more than a few scratches, and he probably got those from the brambles he hid amongst whilst those murdering scum made their escape with the horses."

"You talked to him at length?"

"Nope. Why would I do that?" Burroughs turned his pained looking expression back the way he had come. "We should be getting going. They already have three days lead on us."

"All right, Sergeant," said Cole. "We"ll meet you at the entrance. Ten minutes."

Another salute and Burroughs turned on his heels and marched off.

"What are you thinking now, Cole?"

Smiling towards his friend, Cole finished making his cigarette, lit it, and inhaled deeply. "He didn't talk with Parrott at length and yet he knows where he went and that he wasn't badly hurt."

"So what?"

"Strikes me that our good sergeant there had something of a conversation with Parrot. Interesting, Don't you think?"

"Can't see that any of that matters, Cole, but it does make me feel uneasy."

"Me too."

"All I know is I have an uncomfortable feeling all the way down my back about all of this. When we ask a question, It'sbrushed aside. Makes me feel we're being pushed to get this job done quick."

"I agree, Sterling. Whatever happens, we need to be on our guard that's for sure."

CHAPTER FOUR

Roose let his eyes roam over the men who would be part of the group joining himself and Cole. The gaunt looking Indian leaning against a hitching rail was the only one who filled him with confidence. He'd introduced himself as Brown Bear and when he heard Cole's name his eyes lit up. "Reuben Cole?" he asked excitedly.

"You know him?"

"From years ago when we were both young men."

"All righty then." Smiling, Roose went off to find the sergeant.

Burroughs could barely conceal his irritation when Sterling Roose informed him of Cole's departure to the north. "He tends to do things his own way," explained Roose, holding the sergeant's glare.

"But we have *orders,* or don't you believe in such things?"

Roose looked away, not wishing to enter into a debate about the morality of following orders which made no sense. "Oh, I'm sure he'll catch up with us – when he's ready."

"North you said? North where?"

"Who knows. As I said, he tends to do things his own way. As for us, Sergeant, I suggest we head towards where those thieves might have gone."

Swallowing down any further comments, Sergeant Burroughs ordered his men forward and the small clutch of uniformed men trailed slowly out of the fort's entrance.

Roose turned to the Shoshone scout who knew Cole. "I sure hope Cole knows what He's doing."

"He usually does," said Brown Bear, his face a mask, inscrutable.

They moved on.

Cutting across the arid plain, they made good progress, the men purposeful, alert and professional, which was just how Roose liked it. He wanted men who were well used to travelling across the plains, men who could handle camping out under the stars and were alert to danger. This continued to be a wild, untamed land, with or without the Comanches.

Movement cut into his thoughts and Roose tensed as the sergeant came up alongside, breathing hard. "I know you said Mr Cole does things his own way but you must have some idea about how long he will be away?"

Roose swivelled in his saddle, the fort already nothing more than a speck on the horizon. "Only he knows," he said and returned his gaze to straight ahead.

"I thought he was your friend?"

"He is, but Cole is his own man. When he has the bit between his teeth, there ain't much anyone can do to turn him away from his path."

Burroughs grunted but remained quiet for the remainder of that day.

On the next morning of their journey, as Roose rubbed down his horse, both man and animal shivering in the ice-cold air, he double-checked the soldiers rising from underneath their blankets. He counted them and frowned. Adjusting his trouser braces, Burroughs caught Roose's look as he came over, "I sent two of them back to the fort."

"Oh? Why would you do that?"

"We forgot hard-tack and flour. We only have some grits for this morning's breakfast."

Roose watched the sergeant's broad back as he wandered down to the nearby stream next to which they had camped the night before. Something didn't feel right. He found it hard to believe that one as experienced as Burroughs would forget such essentials. That uncomfortable feeling running down his spine grew worse.

CHAPTER FIVE

The single, well-rutted narrow street of Rickman City, silent, dreary, and sleeping, snaked ahead of him. Cole stretched out his back and leaned forward to run his hand over his horse's neck. He estimated the time as a little after six, taking his calculations from the slowly rising sun peeping over the top of distant mountains to the east. He expected the town to begin waking up shortly, for the citizens to emerge and set about their daily routines. He also doubted the numbers would be all that large. The entire town had an emptiness about it that spoke to him of abandonment mingling with a good deal of sadness.

He went to kick his horse forward when a figure caught his attention. A man, of indiscernible age, standing on the porch of what might have been his home. Dressed in longjohns, he had a holstered six-gun belted around his scrawny waist and, atop his head, a huge crowned hat, battered and sweat-stained. Some fifty or so paces from where Cole sat, his eyes contemplated him, unblinking and wary. Cole tipped his own hat and moved his horse along the street.

Within a few strides, Cole decided that this solitary citizen might be the best place to start, so he gently eased his horse towards him. As he drew closer he saw how old the man was, face deep-lined and ruddy, exposed skin on his arms and chest baked hard as leather by the unforgiving sun.

"Mornin'," said Cole, pulling back on his reins some half a dozen paces from where the old man stood, unmoving. His response was the tiniest of tilts forward of that craggy head. "I'm wondering if you might point me in the direction of the sheriff."

The man stood ramrod still until, at last, he sucked in a long breath, turned his face to his left, hawked, and spat into the ground in front of the porch. "Ain't got one."

"Ah. Constable then?"

"Nope."

"Any sort of law official?" A vacant look was the only reply. Shifting his weight in his saddle, Cole sighed. It was clear he wasn't going to gain anything meaningful from this curious, unfriendly individual so, shrugging his shoulders, he moved to turn his horse away.

"Rickman's the only law we've ever had," the man's voice crackled. "Only law we've ever needed."

Cole, buoyed up by this sudden change, pulled up. "Rickman? Would he be the one who gave his name to this town?"

"He would."

"So where might I find him?"

"Yonder." A thin, almost skeletal arm rose up, bony finger pointing past Cole's shoulder to the hillside behind him. Cole followed the direction.

"He has a house up there?"

"Nope. He's in the cemetery. Dead."

Not sure if this was meant as an attempt at humour or not, Cole pulled a face. He was close to losing his patience with this annoying little man, who was clearly the local idiot, brains addled, no doubt wandering around in a daze during the early hours. "Well, thanks for your help."

"You could try his son."

Ignoring him, Cole touched the brim of his hat, kicked the horse's flank and eased once more down the street.

"Before they all move on," came the old man's voice, raised by a fraction above the crackling whimper he'd used for his previous utterances.

Intrigued, despite his simmering annoyance, Cole stopped and looked. "All gone where?"

"They're leaving. Like everyone else."

"All right. It is clear you take great delight in dragging out a tale, so I'll oblige you. Why are they leaving?"

The man's mouth cracked into a wide, toothless grin. "Silver's run out. Why else."

"Ah-ha, of course."

The first spark of interest brightened the old man's features. "You know about the silver?"

"Doesn't everyone?"

"Well, I thought ..." His eyes narrowed. "Are you teasing with me stranger?"

"Me teasing you? I think you got that all twisted, old-timer."

"If you is teasing me," he slapped the holstered gun, "you'd best know I served in the Mexican War. I have seen men die. Many times."

"That I believe, and in my defence let me assure you, I ain't teasing you. Most ghost towns in these parts are the results of lodes petering out, be they silver or gold. This one ain't quite deserted yet, or else you wouldn't be here, now would you?" He nodded to the gun. "And I am a-certain you can handle that as well as any Jesse James or somesuch."

"Jesse James is not a man I would care to join hands with."

"Well, in that my good sir, you have much to commend yourself."

"You know him?"

The question caused Cole to lean back, surprised. "Some."

"He is an associate of yorn?"

"I would not go that far. I have come across many a desperado in my time, including him. I am an army scout, employed to guide troops through the Territory and am at present searching for an individual who has absconded from post."

"I see."

"I take it, as the town be slowly dying, that there won't be anywhere for me to find some refreshment."

"You could try the hotel down the main street. Not everyone has run off as yet."

"Well, that's kind of you." He tipped his hat again. "Thank you."

He turned away, aware of the old man's eyes boring into him, but decided not to look back.

. . .

Cole went down the street, a strange empty feeling percolating around inside him. The meeting with the old man had left him disturbed as well as confused. None of it felt right. In this deathly quiet place, where nothing stirred, not even the breeze, why would that old man be standing there, half-dressed, almost as if he were waiting. His clipped way of talking, that half-mocking tone, testing Cole's patience, edging him towards ... towards what? A violent reaction? What would be the reason?

Chewing at his bottom lip, Cole directed his horse towards a three-story building, exterior freshly painted, the sign proudly declaring this was the "Beacon Hotel". Tying up his horse, he took his Henry repeating rifle from its scabbard and stomped up the steps to the main door.

He rattled the handle. The door remained firmly closed.

Pressing his face up against the glass, he peered into the murky interior. Unable to make out anything save for the ghosts of armchairs and a small reception desk, he pounded his gloved hand on the window, stepped back and peered upstairs.

Something, a figure perhaps watching him from one of the rooms, darted back out of view. Cole raised his voice, "Hello there. I need a room for the night ..." He waited but when he received no reply, he banged on the door once more before turning.

The old man stood there, causing Cole to give a little start. Now wearing store bought pants and blue-checked shirt, the man appeared more presentable. His eyes too were changed, brighter and more alert. The gun, at his hip, was now tied down, his right hand hanging loosely beside it, giving the appearance of an almost nonchalant preparedness.

"What is it you want, mister?"

Cole studied the old man through narrowed eyes. "Just a place to stay. I told you. I'm passing through, is all, but I need a moment to rest, take a bath, maybe catch up on some sleep."

"Passing through?"

"That's what I said."

"Nothing more?"

"Could be. What's it to you?"

"I'm the sheriff."

Cole almost guffawed, disguising his amusement with a bark of a cough. Clearing his throat a little more, he said through the fist pressed to his mouth, "You never said."

"You didn't ask."

"Well ... I do recall asking if there was a sheriff."

"Maybe I omitted to tell you our sheriff is retired. Until now, that is."

"All-righty, so now I know who the sheriff is, perhaps you can help me."

"With your passing through?"

"Yeah... Could be you might be able to give me the information I require." He smiled, but it froze on his face as two others appeared, emerging from either side of the hotel. Each man held a Winchester aimed unerringly towards him. "I was going to say such information would send me on my way, but I see you have other plans."

"That's right," the old man said, stepping close. "I'll take your guns if you don't mind."

The sentence was punctuated by the Winchester levers working a new round into the breaches. With little choice but to comply, Cole slowly raised his arms and the old man took the Henry first, followed by the Colt Cavalry. He pulled the revolver smoothly from the holster angled inwards at Cole's left hip.

At a signal from the old sheriff, one of the gunmen moved up and took Cole's weapons. "Now," said the old sheriff, "perhaps you could tell me what that information is exactly."

"I think I have a mind to leave that to myself ..." Cole smiled again. "If *you* don't mind."

Nodding, the sheriff looked at the much younger, taller man cradling Cole's guns. He grunted, "That's such a shame," then swung his right fist hard into Cole's face, sending the army scout reeling backwards. Off-balance, he stumbled against the hotel steps and fell on his backside, gasping.

It took nothing more than a blink to recover, the blow not being all that powerful. It was the surprise which stunned him. Now, with the red mist falling over his eyes, he started to scramble to his feet, fists bunched. One of the gunmen stepped forward to block his advance. Slipping under his outstretched arm, Cole landed his fist solidly into the man's guts, folding him like a penknife. The second gunman, however, gave Cole a good deal more respect and used his Winchester to jab the scout in the midriff. A rush of breath erupted from deep within him as Cole pitched forward. A vicious upward smash of the stock ended any hope of resistance and he fell again but this time, head swirling, made no effort to get up. He couldn't.

Vaguely aware of rough hands lifting him under the armpits, Cole hung helplessly in their grip. From somewhere a door opened and the musty, thick smell of wet straw hit the back of his throat. A brutal, dismissive shove and he collapsed amongst a mound of the stuff, too dazed to move. The door banged closed and he lay there, in the semi-gloom and allowed the darkness to envelop him.

He did not know how long he remained unconscious. As senses returned, he summoned enough strength to prop himself up by the palms, shook his head to clear it of the mush masquerading as his brain, and looked around him.

The barn was large, airless, boarded up windows and huge double doors allowing mere slits of light to give some relief from the gloom. It had clearly not been used for some time and the remnants of stale horse sweat and rotting straw hung heavy in the atmosphere.

He was in a stall, the high walls blocking out much of his surroundings. Climbing to his feet, he instinctively checked his holster and groaned when he discovered it empty. It came back to him with a jolt as he remembered what had happened, how his stupidity had lulled him into believing the old sheriff was not the unscrupulous individual he eventually turned out to be. He gingerly rubbed his swollen chin and swore he'd never underestimate any old person again.

Leaning on the top of the closest wall, which separated him from the adjacent stall, he caught sight of a figure, huddled against the opposite side. A man, awake, his eyes flashing white in the dark, giving him a hunted look. Perhaps he too had faced death, survived, but knew it would soon return.

Settling himself with several deep breaths, Cole stepped out from the stall and surveyed his surroundings more closely, paying particular attention to the double doors. He thought he heard noises from without but before he could move over and try to figure out who might be talking, the man with the wild eyes spoke.

"You're not army."

Frowning, Cole moved closer and considered him keenly. Despite the murkiness, Cole managed to pick out details. Although the man's shirt was grubby, drenched in sweat and blood, Cole recognised it as standard cavalry issue. The yellow stripes running down the side of his trousers confirmed it. "But you are."

"'S'right." He shifted position and sat up with his back flat against the wall. "Came here for help and received several broken ribs for my trouble. What is it you done?"

"As far as I know, I just asked the wrong questions." Cole got down on his haunches and scanned the man from head to toe. He was certainly in bad shape and it was clear more than just a few ribs were broken. Teeth, nose, and eye socket more than likely. "Name is Cole. I am an Army scout, on the trail of a bunch of escaped renegades. Came this way looking for an absconded cavalry trooper by the name of Parrot."

The man's expression remained impassive as his mouth cracked into something resembling a smile. "Looks like you found him."

Cole nodded, expecting as much. "So why they do this to you?"

"Burroughs wants me dead."

"Burroughs?" He shook his head. "You mean Sergeant Burroughs?"

"The very same. He came to see me once or twice, once when I was with the doc checking, so he said, that I wasn't too badly hurt. Later, he came to the bunkhouse, ordered everyone out before he interrogated me."

"Interrogated? That sounds peculiar."

"Not really, given who I am and who he is."

Nodding, Cole considered the man's story so far. "I should have guessed he is in this sorry mess right up to his neck. Sergeant Burroughs is the slimy piece of driftwood who put me onto this place."

"That sounds like him. He has a lot to hide, Mister. Too much to let anyone live who might have gotten wind of what he's been doing."

"Stealing Army horses."

"Arranging them to be stole, yes. I was his man on the inside, the one who made sure the engine brakes were well and truly on when those murdering scum came charging up to us. Burroughs never made no mention of any of that."

"So that's why they let you live, because it's clear you was in on it with Burroughs from the start?" Parrot nodded and immediately winced. "So why they did this to you?"

"I got wind of him about to double-cross me, so I took his money and high-tailed it out."

"His money?"

"This ain't the first string of horses he's traded to the Mexicans, although these is the first Army mounts. He's been doing it for years and has accumulated quite a tidy sum. Well," Parrot chuckled, "most of it I now have. I was gonna make a deal with him, but when I showed up here that measly sheriff had his boys beat me near to death. Seems like Burroughs had planned for every eventuality."

"This was supposed to be a safe place for you?"

"For all of us. I wasn't the only one in on this caper. Rickman City is Burroughs' town, mister. But it's dying. Times are changing, and Burroughs is cutting his losses. Including me. But he ain't gonna order me dead until he knows where I put the money. Don't think I can guarantee a stay of execution for you though." Again, the chuckle.

"That's real swell of you, Parrot."

"Ahh, don't take it personal. I don't even know who or what you are, nor do I want to. You say you came looking for me, to take me back? Well, to hell with that. I ain't going no place except well away from here. I'll make my deal and Burroughs can have his money. You, on the other hand, are a dead man, after they've beaten whatever information they want out of you."

"There's something you should know about me, and that's what I mean to do, I do. No matter what."

"You is full of it, mister. What you gonna do locked away in here, with no means of getting out? Disappear like one of them magician folk?"

"Stranger things have happened."

"Strangest is what they will do to you when they come back. That sheriff, he is as mean as a rattler. Burroughs ain't gonna let you live, and he'll make darn sure you suffer before you breathe your last. Guess finding me has not been your luckiest of days now has it."

Cole swivelled on his heels and peered towards the double doors. "How long you think they'll be?"

"The Lord knows. That sheriff is probably waiting on instructions or is enjoying his dinner before he comes back to finish you. You being a scout an' all, they will want to cut you up into tiny pieces and feed you to the hogs so there ain't no evidence. Maybe they'll give me a portion for my supper."

Cole levelled narrowed eyes on the miserable little man as he cackled maniacally at his own wit. Without a word, Cole slammed his fist square into Parrot's mouth, shattering what few teeth he had left, jack-knifing him backwards into the straw where he writhed and wailed like a babe.

Standing up, Cole wandered back to his original stall and flopped down, eyes set on the double doors. He didn't know how long he'd have to wait but, from what Parrot had said, they would return before long. So, he sat back against the stall wall, found the driest piece of straw he could, and sucked on it.

CHAPTER SIX

They made straight for the old sheriff's office. Riding hard, they were drenched in sweat and covered with the harsh dust of the open plain, dust which had almost turned their blue army uniforms grey. They didn't care. They had no time for anything other than what Burroughs had told them to do.

"Cole's headed for Rickman City," Burroughs had told them that first early morning before any of them had taken so much as a mouthful of breakfast.

"Why would he do that?" asked Buller, one of the two troopers Burroughs had pulled away from the rest of the Troop.

"He's sharp," said Burroughs through his teeth, forever checking back into the sleeping camp in case anyone was stirring. "He put two-and-two together and came up with the right answer."

"What?"

Burroughs had turned his venomous glare towards the second trooper. "Just do as I tell you, Ashton. Ride over to Rickman City and make sure Cole has not spoken to Parrot."

"If he has?"

"You kill him and get rid of the body."

"And if he hasn't?"

Burroughs' face had split into a wide grin. "You kill him anyway."

And so, here they were. Rickman City. Outside the sheriff's office, they reined in their mounts and slipped down from the saddles.

"This is a fine old place," spat Ashton, considering the broken down dilapidated buildings which ran down both sides of the main street.

"Looks like even the rats have run away," added Buller, tying up his reins to the hitching post. As he went to negotiate the steps leading up to the office, the door creaked open and a withered old man stepped out, cigar clamped in his blue-lipped mouth, dressed in threadbare clothes, a gunbelt strapped around his scrawny waist. He titled his head and frowned.

""Morning, Sheriff," said Buller, shaking his head as his eyes roamed over the little old man standing before him. "Looks like you've had a rough night."

"Rough life more like," added Ashton and sniggered.

"What is it you be wanting, boys?"

"Now there's a warm welcome," said Buller. He moved to place a boot on the first step.

"Just hold on," said the old sheriff, drawing his gun and drawing back the hammer in one, surprisingly fluid movement.

"Hey," snapped Ashton, "you pull a gun on us, old-timer, you better be prepared to use it."

"Oh, I am more than prepared, boy. Now, ease off your own gun belts and tell me who you are and what it is you want in my town."

"*Your* town?" Buller laughed and shot a glance towards his companion. "Hear that? This is his town."

"And here's me thinking it was called Rickman City because of a certain Mister Rickman."

"Rickman is dead," spat the sheriff. "His son is leaving. That means this town is mine."

"I think our sergeant would have a lot to say about that," said Buller, turning his face towards the old man. "Sergeant Burroughs that be."

Instantly, the sheriff's face paled and for a moment, it seemed he might faint. The hand holding the gun shook alarmingly but when Buller again attempted to mount the steps, the old man recovered, eyes narrowing, mouth clamping down tighter on the cigar and the gun, now in his rock-steady grip, inched upwards. "I think me, and your sergeant might have a few disagreements about that."

"Is that so," mumbled Ashton. His hand dropped to his side, close to his own Colt.

"Since he sent that imbecile Parrot here, things have changed some. What that young soldier told me got me to thinking. Thinking I might help myself to what Burroughs has accumulated for himself."

"Accumulated?" Buller shook his head, frowning. "Old-timer, I don't think you know just who you is dealing with."

"Oh, I know well enough, boy. Now, unbuckle them belts, like I told you, before I plug you."

"Plug us?" Ashton threw back his head and guffawed.

"You talk mighty big for such a dried-up prune of a man, sheriff," said Buller. "Best you put your own gun down before I shove it where the sun don't shine."

"And you show us where Cole is," put in Ashton, all the laughter gone from his voice.

"Cole? You mean that scout that came in here asking questions?"

"That would be the very same person, I reckon."

"I got him over in the barn, with Parrot. You'll be joining him soon if you do the wise thing, boys." He grinned. "Drop those belts."

It was Buller, surprisingly, who moved first, his hand clawing for the holstered Colt at his hip. He'd managed to clear the holster about halfway when the sheriff's first shot hit him full in the chest, the heavy calibre bullet throwing the soldier backwards, clean off his feet. Squealing, Ashton went for his gun, but he didn't even get as far as his friend before two bullets smacked into him, the first in the throat, the second in the chest and he span grotesquely on his heels and fell into the dirt, dead.

Taking his time, the old sheriff came down the rickety steps, the Colt smoking in his hand. He toed Ashton's body before moving across to where Buller lay on his back, eyes staring to the sky, blood splattered across his uniform front. The sheriff stood over him, feet planted either side of Buller's stricken body. "You're not cut out for this kind of work, boy," he said.

Head rolling from side to side, blood seeping from lips already white, Buller's voice strained as he spoke. "I was only doin' what I was told. Please, please don't kill me."

"Boy, you is already dying." The sheriff shook his head. "That

Burroughs, he sends children to do what he should have done hisself." He cracked open his guns cylinder and ejected the spent shells. He replaced them, hands steady, his initial shock at hearing Burroughs' name replaced with an unnerving determination. He twirled the cylinder and dropped the Colt back into its holster. Groaning with the effort of stooping down, he relieved the dying trooper of his own handgun. Standing up again, he closed his eyes and made a face as he clamped a hand into the small of his back. "These old bones are getting more and more useless with each passing day."

"Please ..."

The sheriff looked again at the young trooper's pain-racked features. "I feel sorry for you boy, coming all this way to die like this, so I'll tell you what I'll do. I'll make you a nice plot up on Cemetery Hill, with a lovely view of them distant mountains. How's about that?"

"How's about you go and rot, old man. Rot in hell."

"Boy, the only one who is going down there, is you." He smiled. "My name is Clifton Spelling, for your information. I rode with the Youngers after the War and I did a lot of bad things, but killing you has been one of my better decisions." Buller broke into a bout of painful-sounding coughing. Sheriff Spelling clicked his tongue, shook his head and turned away.

"Please," said Buller, voice growing weaker, "please help me ... I'm begging you ..."

But Spelling was no longer listening. He had other things to occupy his mind now and made his way towards the barn for his next meeting with Reuben Cole.

CHAPTER SEVEN

Touching his jaw where the Winchester had cracked into him, Cole leaned forward, pulled up the bottom of his thick, sweat-stiffened trousers, and tugged free the Wells Fargo Colt holstered at his ankle. He checked the load and sat back against the stall wall. Over to his right he heard Parrot shuffling in the straw, groaning as he did so. "You've got a darn good right cross on you there," said the young soldier, "likes you might be a prize fighter."

"Only job I have is I work for the Army," came Cole's neutral reply. "I'm here to do that job and find who made off with them horses. Who was responsible? Seems like I've cracked that part, now all I need do is figure out where them horses have got to."

"Well, that's something only Burroughs knows."

Cole turned his head and watched Parrot climbing painfully to his feet, stretching out his back, feeling his face with trembling fingers. "Maybe you could point me in their direction?"

Chuckling, Parrot moved forward, his breath hissing. He stepped fully out of the stall. "I reckon them Mexicans who attacked the train would have killed me if I'd hung around. I wasn't about to take that chance."

"Mexicans?"

"Most of 'em, from what I could see. But, like I said, I wasn't going to wait and swap introductions." He shook his head, dabbing at the corner of his mouth then studying his fingertips. "You sure you ain't no prize-fighter?"

"Angry is what I am. What do you know about Rickman?"

"Nothing. 'Cepting he's dead."

"And the sheriff?"

"Well, between bouts of kicking me half to death, he told me his name is Clifton Spelling. That mean anything to you? He seemed to take a good of pride in telling me."

Shaking his head, Cole thought hard, casting his mind back as he looked again at the barn doors. "The only person I recall with that name was one of the Younger gang. Had an argument with Jesse James, almost lost his life. He disappeared into the Territory not long after. Word has it he had some connection with a band of train-robbers who were hunted down by the Pinkertons. Maybe ..." His words disappeared into the airless barn-air.

"Maybe that's why Burroughs chose him." Parrot shuffled closer. "Maybe it was him who was in charge of stealing them horses."

"Could be."

"He ain't no Mexican though."

"Yeah, and he's old. I can't see him charging into a fight on horseback the way he used to do with Anderson and his bunch."

"Bloody Bill Anderson? I heard that before. You think that old boy rode with him?"

"Could be. But he's long past all of that now. I'm thinking he must have been old even back in the War ... Unless of course, he's ill. Dyin' of something."

"Something catchin'? Oh no," squeaked Parrot, taking a step back-wards, frantically brushing away at his clothes. "Hey, you don't think him kicking me the way he did could mean I'll get it too?"

Cole released a long sigh. "Just get back into your stall." He gave Parrot a long look. "We'll talk some more later."

Breathing hard, Parrot stopped flapping his arms and gaped. "Later? Mister, we ain't getting out of this ..." He jabbed a finger towards the cut-down gun in Cole's grip. "You think you can stop 'em with that little thing?"

"This little thing will put a hole in you so deep you won't be getting up again, friend. Now get back into your stall before—"

The barn door opened with a loud squeal from its ancient hinges, light streaming in to pick out the straw dust hanging in the air.

Sheriff Spelling stood there, the Colt looking big in his withered hand. He cackled, a sound that sent a chill through Cole's bones. "Found your feet, eh boy?"

With his attention focused on Parrot who stood trembling in the centre of the barn, Spelling did not see Cole, nor the Wells Fargo now unerringly trained on him. It was only when the hammer came back with a snap did he shoot an incredulous look in the Army scout's direction.

"I'll be asking you to lower that gun, Spelling."

"How did you ..." He stopped, stunned by this turn of events. But only for a moment. Recovering, he cackled again. "Well, well, looks like you have the drop on me, boy. I should have asked my men to search you before they threw you in here."

"Lucky for me they didn't."

"Luck ain't got much to do with it, boy. Only the desire."

"You should know, riding with the Youngers."

A nod of the wrinkled head and then Spelling turned, crouching low, the gun coming up.

A single shot rang out and Parrot, flinging himself to the ground, hands clamped over his ears, screamed.

CHAPTER EIGHT

A winding pathway reached the house, an imposing white-boarded affair of two floors with ornamental pillars supporting the veranda roof. Broad steps, edged with white balustrades, led up to the main door set to the right, with wide, panoramic windows alongside. In the black slate roof were three dormer windows. Two large barns were adjacent to the main building, a fenced-in area nearby in which three horses stood lazily staring at the approaching visitors.

Apart from the animals, the place appeared deserted.

Cole reined in his horse and looked askance at Parrot. Slung behind the young soldier, hands tightly bound, was Spelling, the wound in his right shoulder oozing blood. "This is the place, right?"

Parrot shrugged. "I guess so, but I ain't ever been here before, Mr Cole."

Noting the use of this new salutation, Cole grunted with a degree of satisfaction before turning to study the windows of the imposing building before him. "I'll go take a look round back. Meantime, you wander up to the front porch, dismount, and knock on the door."

"What if they don't come out?"

"Then you holler as loud as you can, to get their attention."

"And if they *do* come out?"

"Then you smile and say "howdy". It ain't difficult."

Leaving Parrot to chew on those words, Cole wheeled his horse away and made for the barns, keeping his eyes keenly focused on the house. At the first enclosure he dropped down from the saddle and tied the reins around the gatepost. Placing his elbows on the top of the fence, he studied the three horses inside. They gave him a dismissive glance.

Not a breath of wind stirred, the silence falling without warning, cutting everything off, leaving the area soulless, desolate. Alert, Cole straightened up and felt the coldness creeping up his back. It was an eerie, unnatural feeling because above him the sun pulsed its heat, a heat so intense that it baked the earth iron hard and made the air as thick as steaming soup. Frowning, he allowed his eyes to scan the silent house. A single pearl of sweat dropped from his brow, stinging his right eye, forcing him to blink and flinch. As he turned, something moved behind him. A scurrying sound. He reacted instinctively, whirling around in a half-crouch, hand streaking for his gun, drawing it cross-bellied from its holster, his movement a blur.

A small, black and white dog darted across the enclosure and slipped through the open door of the nearest barn, tail between its legs, whimpering pathetically as if half-expecting Cole to shoot.

The scout remained as he was, senses straining, picking out anything else that might move or make a sound. Narrowing his eyes, he tried his best to discern any shapes lurking within the gloom of the barn, but it was impossible and of the dog, there was no more sign.

Gradually he allowed himself to relax but kept the gun in his hand. He turned and considered the house once more. The side facing him was clad in what looked like lead, making it appear even more uninviting than the surrounding atmosphere. High up, close to the roof, a single window punctuated the uniform greyness. It drew all his attention and the more he looked the more he realised someone was there, studying him.

A woman, dark-haired, dressed in a white shift.

Cole took a step forward and she responded by retreating into the blackness.

Parrot's voice cut through the stillness, splintering the tension, "Hey inside, is everything all right with y'all?"

Whatever was happening, Cole knew that everything was far from all right. Quickly giving the barn another once-over, he holstered his gun and doubled across to the steps leading to the house front door. Parrot shrugged as the scout came up beside him. "No one is home, Mr Cole."

"Oh, yes there is," said Cole and rattled the door handle. The door remained firmly closed. Stepping back, he pulled in a breath and snapped out his foot against the lock. Three times he kicked it in before it tore open, crashing backwards, the sound reverberating around the interior as if it were a cave. Nothing stirred.

Drawing his gun, Cole pressed his finger to his lips and beckoned Parrot to go inside.

Parrot puckered up his mouth, considering his options, and gave a dejected shrug before he crossed the threshold.

Cole came up beside him and waited until his eyes grew accustomed to the darkness.

But of the smell, there would be no getting used to.

The pungent aroma of death invaded his nostrils. Already Parrot was gagging, bent over, hand clamped to his nose and mouth. "What in the name of Job is that stench!"

Tearing off his neckerchief, Cole pressed it over his face. "Decay, that's what that is."

"Decay? What is that when it comes a-callin'?"

"Death. Stay close."

Cole inched forward, eyes forever scouring every corner, every feature. By now, he could pick out details, such as furniture, bookcase cabinets, an empty fireplace. Once this must have been an elegant and comfortable home, festooned with costly ornaments and, on the walls, landscape paintings and portraits. Family history. But where that family now was, he could hardly guess.

Finding a large oil lamp on a table, he struck a match and set it alight. The globe flared into life as he twisted the wheel to control the intensity of the light. It hissed reassuringly; the first sign that life continued in this otherwise empty place. He handed the lamp across to Parrot. "Take it and hold it high so we don't bash into something."

Parrot did as he was bid and slowly moved the lamp sideways, exposing more furniture and a door adjacent to the foot of the broad stairs. "We go up?"

"Check that room first."

Parrot groaned. "I think it's in there," he said, his voice crackling underneath his hand, which he still pressed over his nose.

"Could be." Cole closed his eyes, took a step closer to the door and sniffed. The bile instantly rose up into his throat and he swung away, gagging. "You're right. It's in there," he gasped.

"I can hear something too," whispered Parrot, voice trembling now. His entire body took to shaking, forcing the lamp in his hand to send dancing figures cavorting across the walls.

"Open it."

"*What?* Are you out of your mind?" Parrot stepped away. "I ain't – I *can't* Mr Cole. I just can't."

Blowing out a breath, Cole, exasperated, moved past Parrot, and pushed open the door.

The stench hit them like a sledgehammer, driving both men backwards, reeling, balking, and retching. A black swarm of fat flies buzzed around their heads, forcing them to swat and beat away at them with hands barely able to move, so rigid were they both with disgust.

In the centre of the small, airless room, slouched in a large armchair, was the body of a man, eyes gazing sightlessly from out of a blue-grey face, mouth open, congealed blood like black slug trails running from the corners, and a gaping hole in his chest filled with writhing maggots. Great clumps of flies flew around the corpse and the stench of decomposing flesh proved overwhelming.

Parrot reeled away and vomited. Cole, reacting quickly, holstered his gun and caught the oil lamp before it slipped from the young soldier's grasp.

"Ah, dear Lord," managed Parrot, groping for the stairs where he collapsed on the bottom tread and sat there, wheezing, shaking his head as if in denial of his senses. "Who *is* that?"

Cole went to speak but before he could utter a word, the creak of floorboards from the top of the staircase cut him off. Swinging the oil-lamp towards the direction of the noise, he gave a tiny cry of surprise as a figure came into sharp focus.

The figure of the woman who he had seen watching him from the window.

"It's my husband," she said, her voice low, edged with barely contained rage, "Lionel Rickman." And as she slowly descended the stairs, the rifle in her arms grew more noticeable.

CHAPTER NINE

They stood on the porch, Parrot against the balustrade sucking in air, Cole beside him with the woman's rifle firmly jammed in his back.

"Who is that?"

Cole craned his neck to look at her. Out here, in the daylight, he could see her face so much more clearly, and she was a woman of staggering beauty. Amongst her perfectly formed features, however, lay a heavy, all-consuming look of grief. Full lips so pale, startlingly blue eyes red rimmed and cheeks sunken. He turned his gaze to settle on Parrot's horse, and the old sheriff slung across the animal's back. "It's Spelling."

Her breath hissed. Cole snapped his head to face her and for a moment, he thought she might collapse. Although already ghostly white, her face seemed to drain of whatever blood remained, and she teetered backwards, strength leaking from her limbs. Moving rapidly, Cole dashed away the rifle and caught her around the waist before she collapsed. She moaned, struggling in his grip, but it was useless, and she surrendered, allowing him to take her to an ornamental wrought-iron bench standing against the wall. He lowered her onto it and stepped back, hefting the rifle in his hands. "Civil War Lee-Enfield. You know how to use this, ma'am?"

It took her a few moments to find the words, her breathing laboured.

She looked into the far distance, the tears rolling unchecked down her cheeks. "It's not loaded."

Blinking in surprise, Cole checked the weapon and found she spoke the truth. Carefully, he propped the rifle against the balustrade. As he did so, Spelling showed the first signs of life since Cole had shot him back in town and bundled him like a prize kill over the back of Parrot's horse. "She's a mad woman," he croaked, "and she'll kill us all if you let her."

"Shut up before I finish you for good," snapped Cole and turned to the woman again. "Mrs Rickman, who killed your husband?"

Her face came up, the eyes so big, the mouth now trembling. "He did."

"Tell me why I ain't surprised to hear that," said Cole and looked at the old sheriff.

"It was Burroughs who gave the orders, as well you know."

Mrs Rickman got to her feet, fists bunched. "You're a liar! It was you and only you, desperate to grease your own palms with whatever money you thought we had."

Spelling, straining his neck to lift his head, groaned, "It's you who is lyin'."

"I'll get to the truth of this," said Cole, "one way or the other."

Spelling squawked and struggled against the restraining ropes lashing him to Parrot's horse. Cole went down the steps and, from his own horse, reached into a saddlebag to produce a big, heavy bladed Bowie knife.

Writhing against the ropes, Spelling stared with eyes so large they threatened to burst out of his face. "Ah, what you gonna do with that?"

Cole heard the fear in the old man's voice, and it gave him no end of pleasure. However, before he could do anything something in the distance caught his attention and he looked out over the prairie from the direction in which he'd come and saw the dust. Cursing, he used the knife to slice through the old man's ropes. Spelling squealed and dropped like a dead weight to the ground. Writhing there, he kicked and spat. Ignoring him, Cole tugged out the Henry from its sheath hanging from his saddle. "You got bullets for that rifle, ma'am."

Crestfallen, she shook her head.

"All righty," said Cole. "Parrot get this piece of filth into the house. We've got company."

"Company?" Parrot jerked his head up. "Who is it?"

"They're my boys," said Spelling, the laughter convulsing him sounding brittle and dangerous, "and they're coming here to kill yeh – *all of yeh!*"

Cole shored-up the broken door with one of the Rickman's heavy wooden cabinets then handed Parrot the gun he'd previously relieved Spelling of.

"Kind of trusting, ain't you, Mr Cole?"

"Needs must, son. Those men coming here are gonna do their best to kill us, make no mistake. You wanna use that gun against me, I'd advise you try your luck after our new guests been dealt with."

Parrot grinned. "Guests? Did you invite them, Mr Cole?"

"No, but he did." He pointed at Spelling huddled in the corner, head down, whimpering. Next to him, sat on a high-backed dining chair, Mrs Rickman cradled the rifle, watching him like a hawk. Cole went to her and gently took the rifle from her hands, replacing it with the Wells Fargo. "This'll serve you better, ma'am."

Her head came up and she held his eyes. There was no malice there, only a quiet acceptance of the situation. "How do you know I won't shoot him?"

"I don't, but I'd ask you not to, not until I can work out what's truly happened here."

"If those men break in here, my first bullet goes through his head."

Grunting, Cole nodded but left any further comments unspoken. Instead, he turned to the immediacy of their situation. "You have a rear entrance?"

She gestured towards the other door on Cole's right.

"What's in there?"

"Dining room, with adjoining kitchen." Her breath shuddered as she drew it in. "I haven't been able to go into the parlour, not since ..."

"It's all right," said Cole. Something compelled him to lay a hand on her arm. Her eyes flashed for a moment but then, almost immediately, softened. She did not move her arm away. "When this is over, we'll give him a decent burial." She said nothing. He checked the Henry's load and crossed to the dining room door. He eased it open. "They'll try and come through this way. I'll be waiting."

"Mr Cole," interjected Parrot, forcibly, his voice harsh. "Let me go in there. I need to atone, Mr Cole."

"Atone? For what?"

"For all I've done. If it wasn't for me, none of this would have happened."

"You don't know that. Burroughs would have used someone else."

"Burroughs?" It was Mrs Rickman's turn to grip Cole's forearm. "You mentioned him before, but do you mean Captain Burroughs of the U.S. Cavalry?"

Eyes widening, Cole gave a tiny laugh. "He ain't no captain, ma'am. He's a sergeant and a pretty mean one at that."

"He ... He was a friend of my husband. He dined here many times and together they discussed the breeding and transportation of horses. My husband has many contacts with the railroads and ..." Her eyes grew moist and she turned away, the back of her hand pressed against her mouth. She sobbed.

Again, Cole's hand, this time settling on her shoulder, calmed her. "When this is over, we'll—"

The sound of horse's pounding along the side of the house cut him off. Without a word, Parrot pushed past and went through the door, revolver at the ready. Cole whirled away and moved to the small window adjacent to the front door. He sucked in a breath and worked the lever of his carbine. "They've gone round back. Let's pray Parrot can hold them."

Soundlessly, Mrs Rickman stepped over to Spelling and pressed the muzzle hard against his head. He squealed, cowering away, blubbering, "Cole, Cole she's gonna murder me!"

"Quit squawking," snapped Cole, shooting Mrs Rickman a look. "We wait, you understand? We take him to Paradise, and we put him on trial. We do it right."

The sound of furious shouting broke out from the dining room. Parrot's voice, raised in alarm, cracking with fear, "Hold on boys, hold on. I'm one of Burroughs' men! Don't shoot."

Mrs Rickman screamed and reeled backwards. "He's with them!"

Cursing, Cole rushed to the door, booted it open and immediately dropped to one knee, the Henry rammed into his shoulder.

The dining room was long and narrow, dominated by a neatly laid out table with cutlery and serving bowls waiting for the next meal. Large panoramic windows faced front and back, allowing uninterrupted views of the surrounding countryside at one side, and the other coral and barns at the rear. At the far end of the room, the door to the kitchen stood ajar and Cole could clearly see the rear entrance open.

Shooting broke out, wild and furious. Had Parrot tried to dupe them then opened up, or had they dismissed his appeals and shot him anyway? Cole couldn't be sure, and he wasn't about to debate the alternatives for a second longer. He sprinted forwards, keeping low, and slammed himself against the wall adjacent to the kitchen door. Mouth open, he waited and listened.

The shooting continued, confirming Parrot's survival. At least for now. The fusillades grew less, single shots now the norm, no doubt initial surprise giving way to a determination to kill.

Cole slipped into the kitchen and almost cried out when he spotted the body. Under the roughly hewn preparation table lay a black woman, sprawled on her back. The sickly grey pallor of her skin attested to the fact she'd been dead for some time. Something terrible had occurred in this house and Cole suspected it had little to do with Spelling or Burroughs.

A scurrying of feet. A gunshot. A muffled scream. Cole snapped his head to the open rear door, held his breath and inched forward on his knees.

The brightness of the scorching sun temporarily blinded him, but only briefly. Within two seconds, he saw Parrot doubled up on the ground clutching at his leg as it pumped blood. His handgun lay beside him, no doubt empty. Two men emerged from behind piled up hay bales, spilling out empty shells from their own weapons. Cole recognised them as the ones who had laid into him and dragged him to the barn. Their faces set, streaked with sweat, they did not notice Cole stepping out into the yard until it was too late.

He moved forward, Henry at his hip, working through the lever, shooting both men several times, blowing them backwards, perforating their bodies with bloody patterns of death.

A strange eerie silence descended. Cole slowly reloaded the carbine before moving across to Parrot. He looked down at the young trooper, giving his wound a swift once-over. "I'll tourniquet that and you'll be fine."

Moaning, Parrot tried his utmost to raise his head. The tears tumbled down his face. "Oh Mr Cole, I thought I had them, but they were too fast for me. I'm sorry. So sorry."

"Calm down, son. You did fine. Your bravery gave me the time to get the drop on "em."

"What I said, Mr Cole, it was a ruse. You understand? You believe me, don't you?"

"I do, son. Yes. Now let me go and get something to patch you up." He stood, swung around and gasped, seeing Mrs Rickman standing in the kitchen doorway, the Wells Fargo in her hand. Her face, deathly pale, seemed carved from granite.

"Mrs Rickman," Cole said, hand coming up in the universal gesture of peace. He took a step towards her.

She brought the Wells Fargo up, steadying her aim with two hands.

"Don't," Cole whispered, not daring to believe what she was planning to do. "Mrs Rickman, there's no need to—"

"It's over, Cole."

Cole blinked, not believing what he heard and turned his head to see Parrot, gun in hand, easing back the hammer. He was grinning.

Then Mrs Rickman fired the Wells Fargo and Parrot grinned no more.

CHAPTER TEN

S he took him inside the barn, the same barn the moth-eaten dog had disappeared into all that time ago. To Cole it seemed a lifetime since he reined in his horse at this lonely, cold place. So much had happened since. Death mainly. Mrs Rickman's husband, the maid, two gunmen and Parrot. Parrot whose treachery and trickery had almost cost Cole his life. If it hadn't been for Mrs Rickman. "My name is Julia," she'd told him before she took his hand and led him to the barn. And another death.

The body swung grotesquely from a frayed, ancient rope, the eyes bulging, and the tongue blue with the neck stretched impossibly long. Flies buzzed around the corpse.

"My son," she said simply, betraying little emotion.

Shaking his head, Cole looked around. "I'll cut him down."

"No," she said. Her voice put paid to any objections.

Cole studied her. Not even the ashen hue of her skin could mask her loveliness. "What happened here, ma'am?"

"Julia," she said. He nodded, and she drew in a deep breath. "Belinda, my maid, she overheard my husband talking with Burroughs. I didn't want to believe her when she told me. Poor girl, she was so frightened, but she made me listen. I struck her. Can you imagine? I could not accept what she was telling me. That my husband was in cahoots with

Burroughs, stealing horses from the Army, taking them down to Mexico. I never thought to question why horses were always corralled here. I simply believed it was all part of his business." She gave a short, scoffing laugh. "Well, I was right in that, wasn't I? It *was* his business, but not one which I would have ever considered him capable of indulging in. Putting it bluntly, Mr Cole, he was up to his neck in illegal dealings."

"So, to keep it all from you, he decided to murder the maid?"

She nodded, turning away to return to the open door. From out of the gloom emerged the dog, tail between its legs, eyes to the ground. It virtually slid up to her on its belly, snaking around her ankles, whimpering pathetically. She reached down and tickled the animal behind an ear. "He tried to conceal it, but it all went wrong. Our son caught him in the act of strangling her. They fought, a gun went off and Belinda ..." She sniffed loudly. "Overcome, James followed him into the parlour and, well, you have seen the outcome."

Cole stepped up alongside her, pausing for a moment to watch her tickling the dog. "That's James, in the barn?" She nodded. "I'm sorry. No one should experience such loss."

"I'm fine," she said, and he frowned at the distance in her voice, her apparent coldness. She caught his expression and forced a smile. "He was not my biological son, you understand? His mother died from fever three years ago."

"So, you and Rickman, you have only recently married. Still, it's a lot to take in."

"No, Mr Cole. We never married." She laughed again as he raised his eyebrows. "I didn't take you for a prude, Mr Cole. I wouldn't have thought such a thing would have shocked you."

"Well, I ..." He shuffled his feet and preferred watching the dog than keeping his eyes fixed on her face.

"I moved in around nine months ago and at first everything was fine. We even talked of marriage and James, he seemed to accept it. He was still grieving, and I guess you could say I helped him with that. I'd lost my own parents back in sixty-eight from cholera. This is a brutal world, Mr Cole as well you know."

"Indeed, I do, ma'am."

"Julia."

He nodded. "I'll set to burying 'em. Spelling can help."

"I don't want that piece of rat-filth moving through this place. No, you and I will do it, then we'll go down into Paradise and I'll turn myself in."

"Turn yourself in? For what?"

"For what I did, Mr Cole." She stood up, the dog immediately nuzzling her for more affection. Instead, she pointed across to where Parrot's body lay baking in the sun. "I murdered him."

"No, Julia. He got caught in the cross fire, don't you remember?"

"What cross fire?"

"Between myself and them two varmints I put in the ground. Didn't you see?"

"Mr Cole, you can't—"

"The name's Reuben and, when it comes to anything to do with killing, I can do whatever I please."

CHAPTER ELEVEN

After they'd ridden the half day's journey to Paradise and deposited Spelling at the town jail, they continued across the prairie to where they hoped to find Burroughs and his troop. Julia had insisted she accompany Cole and there was little the scout could do to dissuade her. "I want to look at him straight in the eye and tell him what he's done."

On that first night, camping out under the stars, they sat beside the fire Cole had made, she gazing into the flames, he gazing at her profile. "He won't care," he said at long last.

"I know that. But I want him to know that *I* do."

"Is that why you forced Spelling to make his confession to the sheriff?"

She picked up a tiny piece of wood and tossed it into the fire. "I didn't need to force him – he was terrified."

"He didn't seem so terrified when I first met him. The opposite in fact."

"Perhaps the thought of that noose tightening around his throat."

"Is that what you said to him?"

She shrugged, weighing another twig in her hand. "Maybe."

"I heard you talking with him, and saw his face grow white. Pretty soon after that, you said some other things and he was more relaxed. You made a deal with him?"

"It's Burroughs who must face the hangman's noose, Mr Cole. Spelling was nothing more than his lackey. I told him I'd do my best to make things go easy for him if he told me where Burroughs was heading."

"His trail is clear. You didn't have to—"

"I'm tired," she said, stifling a yawn. "We'll talk again tomorrow." With that, she threw her last twig into the flames, gathered her blanket around her neck and rolled over. Cole sat, considering her words, knowing none of them sounded in any way convincing.

Troubled, it took him a long time to find sleep.

Rising early and, after taking a meagre breakfast of grits and coffee, they moved slowly over the endless plain, neither speaking very much. Julia did not develop her explanations from the night before and Cole did not press her. On their second night a storm broke, lighting up the sky as if it were a carnival night. Julia, a lot more relaxed, jokingly told him how the gods were fighting in the distant mountains, Thorns hammer pounding the sky with rage. "Nordic gods," she added.

He shrugged, expression blank. "Nordic? I have no idea what that is."

"Vikings," she said but he merely shook his head. "All right, how about Greeks? You've heard of them surely?"

"I knew a Greek once. Can't remember much about him now. Fought with him in the War. Got a bullet through his throat and took him three days to die."

She pulled a face. "Ancient Greeks, Mr Cole, they were a tad different."

"They were?" Thankful for anything to relieve the monotony of the ride, Cole grunted, "Never was one for schooling. Learned some letters and numbers when I was little more than a corn nubbin, but never much reading to be honest."

Smiling, she explained some of it to him, how the gods and the Titans fought for mastery of the world and the gods, victorious, went to live on Mount Olympus, with Zeus the most powerful. "There are many stories about their gods. Some are exciting, some sad. There's something for everyone."

"I'm sure, but for me I just can't quite get my thinking around the idea of 'em eating their own children." He chuckled to himself. "Closest I ever got to gods and stuff was the few times my old ma sent me to Sunday school. But that was mainly to teach me my letters, like I said. I didn't learn much else, sorry to tell."

"So, you wouldn't class yourself as a religious man, Mr Cole?"

"I know the difference 'tween right and wrong. I guess that's about the only religion anyone needs out here."

"You must have seen a good deal of suffering. Evil deeds. Wrongs."

"I have, but I've also seen good, Miss Julia. I've seen folk suffering against all sorts of setbacks and coming back, stronger than ever."

"You think that is what will happen to me? After what has happened these past few days?"

"You strike me as being a resolute woman, Miss Julia. Defiant, strong. I believe you will come out of this with a new determination."

She stared at him through the flames of their second campfire. Somewhere in the distance a coyote howled, an eerie, lonely sound. The distant storm retreated still farther away, leaving a dampness in the air but no other hint that the weather had changed, albeit fleetingly.

"I won't come out the other end until I see Burroughs dead, Mr Cole."

"You'll see that soon enough."

"I pray you are right, Mr Cole. If you are not, you will see me making another killing." She rolled over, pulling her blanket over her shoulders. He watched her back until the gentle rise and fall of her breathing grew regular, deep, and complete. Only then did he settle down himself, with his arms behind his head, staring into the vastness of the night sky. Again, no sleep came to him, not for many hours.

CHAPTER TWELVE

R oose, on his knees studying the ground, raised his head to scour the horizon. From his left came Brown Bear, one of the few Shoshone scouts remaining in this part of the territory, riding his pinto pony without a saddle, a Winchester cradled in his arms. He dropped from the pony and came across to join Roose. He considered the scuffed-up earth and knelt next to the Army scout, fingers testing the earth. "Two days," he said.

"Maybe. Could be longer. Either way, we're slowly catching them up."

"And when we overtake them?"

Standing up, Roose stretched out his back. "Fortunately, that ain't my call," he said breathlessly. "Can you see anything else?"

Brown Bear ran the flat of his hand across the ground. "There are ponies here, as well as horses."

"Indians you think?"

"Some. Comancheros too, maybe. Dangerous men. We will need to be extra careful." He stood up and turned his gaze to the distant mountains. "We should tell the sergeant."

"Agreed."

They mounted up and made their way back to the tiny troop of horse soldiers plodding along through the parched earth. They looked tired and dejected, the relentless heat sucking the strength from their very bones.

On seeing their approach, Burroughs raised a hand and the men came to an untidy halt, all of them groaning, one of them muttering, "Can't we camp now, Sarge?"

Ignoring this plea, Burroughs narrowed his eyes as the two scouts reined in beside him, horses snorting. "What you find?"

"They be about two days ahead," Roose said, "moving slow, which in this heat you can understand."

"They push them horses too hard, they'll die."

"Exactly," said Roose, twisting in his saddle and gesturing to the mountains. "If we're lucky, we could catch them before they get into cover." He looked again at Burroughs. "Brown Bear says there are ponies amongst 'em. Might mean Indians."

"Or Comancheros," put in Brown Bear.

"You think Comancheros would come this far north?"

"If the price was right," continued Roose, "those murdering heathens would do almost anything. They ain't just traders, we all know that."

"I heard they is mounting raids right across New Mexico and into Texas. The Army will launch an expedition against 'em soon enough, but this ..." He shook his head. "This ain't connected."

"How you know that, Sergeant?"

Burroughs snapped his head in the direction of the scout. "Call it instinct, Mr Sterling. Sixth-sense." He grinned, "Or maybe I'm just taking on board what the good captain told me. These are horse thieves, running Army horses to the Mexican border. They ain't Comancheros trading with Comanch. If they was, they'd be doing it here," he jabbed a finger towards the ground next to his horse. "No, this miserable bunch is trading with the Mexican army and my job is to stop 'em whilst they are still within United States territory." He took in a deep breath. "Two days you said?"

"About that," said Brown Bear.

"All right, so we push on, through the night if needs be."

"Your men need rest, Sergeant," said the Shoshone scout.

"They're my men and I'll decide what's best for 'em, not some mangy redskin."

"Now hold on there, Burroughs," said Roose quickly. "Brown Bear is a sworn-in Army scout. You got no right to speak to him like that."

"I got every right."

Roose tensed and Brown Bear laid a hand gently onto his comrade's arm, easing the rising tension almost at once.

Ignoring this exchange, Burroughs rolled his tongue around his mouth, hawked, and spat into the ground. "Now, you've done your job, so you can go back to the fort and tell Cap'n Phelps this thing is all but wrapped up."

"*What?*" Roose turned his incredulous face towards Brown Bear, then back to the sergeant. "Are you out of your mind? How you gonna track 'em on your own?"

"You've shown me which way it is," said Burroughs, "the rest we can do on our own."

"Sergeant," said Brown Bear quietly, "if they have Comanches with them, you have not enough men to—"

"You let me worry about all that, why don't you? Now both of you scoot before I lose my temper."

For a few, long moment they all sat there, the two scouts speechless, struggling to come to terms with what Burroughs, rigid as a stone pinnacle, had ordered.

"Come on, Mr Roose," said Brown Bear with a deep sigh, "let us go. We are of no use here anymore."

Roose went to argue but reluctantly accepted the wisdom of his companions' words. He could see by the sergeant's demeanour he was not going to change his decision. Shaking his head, Roose kicked his horse forward and the two scouts moved past the young troopers, all of whom stared at them in disbelief.

"You is coming back, ain't yeh?" asked one.

Roose could not look at him in the eye when he said, "'Fraid not, son. Good luck to you."

"But how do we know which way to go?" called another.

"Or what's waiting for us when we get there?"

"Shut up your mealy mouths," barked Burroughs. "We'll get by just fine."

Ignoring him, Roose kicked his horse even harder and broke into a gallop, Brown Bear moving in smoothly behind him. Soon, the troop was nothing but a dark smudge in that vast landscape.

. . .

It was on the third day of Cole's journey and halfway through Roose's first that they came upon each other. Cole and Brown Bear fell into each other's arms. "Darn, it's good to see you old friend," said Cole, unable to keep a tear sprouting in the corner of his right eye. "I wasn't sure if I would ever see you again."

After a lot more hugging and backslapping, they each told their stories, making camp in a small depression, Brown Bear seeing to the food whilst Roose sat with his blanket around his shoulders, munching at his bottom lip. "Seems like the one constant thread running through this entire unholy tale is Burroughs."

"That's right," said Cole, "and if I've learnt anything about him, it is that he is cold-hearted and blood-thirsty. He'll stop at nothing to get what he wants."

"Selling those horses."

"He's taking those poor young men to their deaths," said Julia Rickman quietly, her voice trembling, betraying the depth of emotion coursing through her. "Together with my husband, they distributed horses – stolen and otherwise – right across the Mid-West. They used Rickman City and our ranch as the base for their operations. That despicable Spelling co-ordinated the movement of the horses—"

"But then Spelling began to have ideas of his own," said Cole, unconsciously feeling the ghost of the swelling along his jawline.

"Perhaps, if you hadn't arrived, Mr Cole, Spelling and Burroughs would have killed each other in a gunfight."

"Possibly."

A wry smile fluttered across her mouth. "Or maybe not. And I suspect Burroughs would have emerged victorious. He has that knack."

"So, you knew him well?"

Her head snapped up at Roose's question and, for a moment, her eyes blazed. However, not only with anger. There was something else lingering there, something which made Cole edgy. "We'll stop him," he said quickly. He looked meaningfully towards Sterling Roose, his friend and fellow scout. "Won't we."

"He won't rest his men. They'll die, as Mrs Rickman says, and he'll catch up with the thieves well before they reach the border. That's three days' ride away, Cole. Even if we rode throughout each and every day, we're hardly likely to overtake him."

"I could do it," said Cole. "On my own, riding hard."

Julia's hand reached out and squeezed his. "No. You promised me we'd bring him in and that I would be there to see it."

"You will be," said Cole, smiling tightly. "But I can make up the ground much quicker on my own. With a spare horse," here he nodded at Roose, "I could ride without a break."

"And what if you do?" asked Brown Bear, returning to the campfire with tin plates stacked up with biscuits and fried bacon. "What will you do when you meet up with them? Kill them all? You think you can."

"If it comes to it, yes."

"No Reuben!" The others started at Julia's use of Cole's Christian name. "No, you promised me. Burroughs must stand trial. Remember what you said, about right and wrong?"

"The circumstances have changed," said Cole, mouth set in a hard line. "I'll take him alive, if I can."

"*You promised.*"

"I know what I said, and I'm a man of my word, Julia. You have to trust me on this."

Silence settled over them all, until Julia, struggling to keep her voice under control, said at last, "Let us all sleep on it. In the morning we can talk about it again."

With little more to say on the matter, they retired to their makeshift beds, stretching out under the stars, huddled under their blankets next to the well-stocked fire.

At some point in the night, Cole roused himself and, as quietly as he could, readied his horse. He deliberated some time before deciding on taking Julia's horse, thinking that the best option lest he strain his friendship with Roose by using his friend's mount to change over to during the long, forced ride.

As he led the horses away from the camp a figure stepped out of the darkness, causing Cole to stop and draw the Colt cavalry, the sound of cocking the hammer amplified a myriad amount of times in that cold, still night.

"Hold on Reuben, it's only me," came Brown Bear's low voice. "I am frightened. When we rode together all those years ago, you were young, strong. You learnt all about killing and loss as well as much else." He smiled. "You have grown into a skilled tracker, my friend. But going up against so many, I am not so sure it is wise."

"I have to do this," said Cole in a whisper, slipping the Colt back into its holster. "I wouldn't want to think you might try and stop me."

"No. I aim to come with you."

Frowning, Cole tilted his head. "I'll do this better alone."

"Until you meet up with them. There are Indians with them. They will circle around you before you even know what is happening. I can help."

"I left Sterling a note, explaining things."

"He'll understand."

Letting his breath out in a long, low stream, Cole shrugged his shoulders. "I see the sense of it," he said.

"Then it'll be like old times, my friend."

"Yeah, I guess it will."

Slowly, without further conversation, the two men left, moving out into the night as if they were part of it. No one left behind stirred at their departure and by the time Roose and Julia woke up, the two scouts were far away, eating up the miles in their relentless and determined journey.

CHAPTER THIRTEEN

Towards early evening, they took their horses down the arroyo, to gain some respite from the heat, which drained every ounce of their strength, leaving them lethargic, bad-tempered, and desperate for sleep.

"I thought it was meant to get cold at night," said a lean, hungry looking trooper called Nolan as he warily guided his big roan to the bottom of the gully.

The others, moving with equal caution, joined him. "It's the rocks," said Corporal Dewy, pulling up his own horse before sliding from the saddle. He arched his back and let out a loud groan.

"Rocks?" Nolan dismounted, immediately going through a series of twists and stretches to ease out the cramps from his joints. It seemed to him that he had lived almost his entire life in the saddle.

"They suck in the heat throughout the day, then give it out when the sun goes down. Get too close to 'em and you'll cook like one of your mommy's pumpkin pies."

The others laughed, but it was a dull, depressed sound. There was little good humour to be had within this group.

Hobbling their mounts, they set about preparing a makeshift camp, gathering what wood they could. Taylor, the oldest of the bunch, was their elected cook, a position he resented for he had little faith in his abilities. However, no one else ever attempted to put pan to fire, so he went about filling up a pot with water in glum silence. He pulled out hunks of dried, salted beef from his saddlebags and stirred them into the grimy water together with a curled-up piece of onion he had managed to keep back.

Some ten minutes or so later, trooper Lomax put flint to steel and managed to light the kindling stuffed beneath the stacked-up twigs and branches. Almost flat on his belly, he gently blew at the tiny embers until they flared, flames lapping over the dried-up pieces of wood. Rolling over, Lomax gazed with a look of reverence at his achievements and began to pile on bigger, heftier pieces of timber until the fire roared.

"Think you've a tad overdone that," commented Nolan, shielding his face from the heat.

"You think you can do better, then you do it," said Lomax. Always testy, his patience was near to collapsing after the relentless heat of the day and the boredom of their prolonged ride.

"I ain't saying that," continued Nolan.

"Then what are you saying?"

"Just that you needn't have put on so much wood, is all. You is might touchy this evening, Lomax. What's stirred you up, you fart-in-a-cup?"

"Quit it you two," snapped Dewy, sat on a large boulder whilst he took off his boots. He studied his threadbare socks before pulling them off. He shook his head, saying almost to himself, "I am gonna have to darn these."

"Oh shoot," said Taylor, inching across to the roaring fire with his pot full of beef and onions. "I can't get that on there, Lomax. I'll have to wait until it dies down a tad."

"Then do so, you old coot."

"You watch your mouth, Lomax, or I'll feed you your dinner through the wrong hole!"

"That's *enough*," shouted Dewy, getting to his feet. He cursed as a multitude of tiny, sharp stones cut into the soles of his feet. As he collapsed back down on the boulder, Lomax took his first swing. He was a large man, carrying a lot of weight around his gut, but he was no fighter. The punch was wild and wide, and Taylor slipped under it with no trouble. Holding the pot in one hand, his other slammed into Lomax's right floating rib with the force of a pile driver. It was not as hard as he would have wished – he was conscious of his unmade stew – nevertheless the blow was good enough to drop Lomax to his knees. He squawked and remained there, bent double, breathing hard.

"You is one fat idiot," said Taylor and settled the pot as close to the fire as he could. Moving back to the horses, he shot Dewy a sharp glance. "I've got me a pot stand somewhere. In the meantime, to save more bickering, send them two boys out to shoot some Jackrabbits."

"Jackrabbits? There ain't gonna be any around here."

"Well there just might be. It'll give 'em something to do other than taking chunks out of one another."

"Yeah, I guess. All right," he raised his head, "Nolan, you take your carbine up on the other side and see if you can shoot something for dinner. Take Lomax with you when he's able to breathe again."

As Taylor rooted around inside his saddle bags searching for the triangular pot stand he believed he had hidden away somewhere, the other two troopers stomped off, both cursing under their breath, but neither giving Taylor so much as a glance.

The camp, or what was left of it, settled into silence at last.

Sergeant Burroughs settled himself down amongst a collection of smooth boulders, some as big as a town house. He watched the horizon, the colours of the sky slowly changing, from deep purples and mauves, to oranges and reds. He had heard it say if the sky was burning like this, then the following day would be a good one. Good in what way, he wondered to himself as he fished out a slim cheroot from his shirt pocket. He lit it, drew in the smoke, and let it percolate inside for a moment before releasing it in a long grey stream.

Many years ago, his daddy, as he lay on his deathbed, made Burroughs a gift of a smooth, well-worn fob watch. The chain had long since disappeared, but the watch remained in good order. He recalled how his daddy told him the story of it being French, how an old king of that land made a collection of clocks and other timepieces and that this little silver-cased fob was part of that collection. True or not, Burroughs concerned himself rarely with such trivialities. So long as it worked, that was all that mattered to him. Daddy was long dead, but the watched ticked on. Burroughs remembered the huge feeling of relief when his daddy gave his last breath. They had never got on. Burroughs remembered the beatings when he was younger, the yelling and cursing, how his poor dear mamma would cry long into the night whilst Daddy drank himself into unconsciousness. Such things he kept pressed far back into the corners of his mind, but it all conspired to make him angry and resentful, at everyone, but mainly those who never seemed to struggle or understand the pain. Being unloved. The greatest pain of them all.

He flipped open the fob lid and gazed at the barely moving minute hand. Why was it, he wondered, did time pass so slowly when you wanted it to go fast? And wasn't it also true that when you needed more time it simply melted away? He could never understand it. He sighed, snapped the watch shut, and dropped it back into a pocket. Another long draw on the cheroot. By nightfall it would all be over, he convinced himself. Only then might he get some sleep.

Not for the first time he wondered at the justification for what was to happen. Yes, he was angry. Yes, the hate gnawed away at him relentlessly. But those men, his troopers, none of this was their fault. How had they contributed to his sorrowful existence? There was no answer because there was no justification. It was simply something that had to be done. To round off the edges. To keep everything neat and tidy. Men became lost in this vast expanse of scrub all the time, many dying, insane with thirst. Those who managed to blunder on more than likely were picked off by Utes, Kiowa, Apaches or, God help them, Comanches. Bands continued to roam. Much less than in the past, but even so, renegades still managed to make their presence felt. No one in authority would think to question any of it. And no one would ever come looking. Cole would be long dead by now if Spelling had done what had been agreed. Roose and the Indian, whose name he could never remember, would not be coming back. There was no reason for them to do so. Burroughs and his men had been swallowed up in their desperate bid to track down the horse thieves. Sacrifices needed making for the plan to be believed. Once this last piece of necessary business was complete, he would be free from fear of pursuit and could get the horses sold. Then, finally, settle down somewhere warm, somewhere quiet, and put it all behind him.

Necessary business. That was all it was.

. . .

For the umpteenth time, Lomax lost his footing amongst the scree and fell heavily, this time twisting an ankle, causing him to cry out and clutch his foot. His carbine clattered next to him.

"What in tarnation have you done *now?*" asked Nolan, taking the opportunity to stop and wipe his forehead with his bandana. "Seems like every step you take you is in danger of breaking your neck."

Rocking backwards and forwards as he held his ankle, Lomax grimaced, teeth clenched in his white face. "You sure is full of concern, ain't yeh, Nolan?"

"Concern? For you? I tell you something, I wish that old man Taylor had whipped you good, maybe knock some good manners into yeh!"

"Yer well, he caught me off guard, that's what he did. Just like him, all sneaky and cowardly."

"Cowardly? Lomax, you seem to require a hefty dose of reality." He cocked his head and smiled. "Looks like you won't be going much farther anyways. I'll continue on a way, see if I can get me a rabbit. You just sit and relax, why don't you." He chuckled at his own sarcasm and Lomax wailed in reply, eyes squeezed shut, sucking in the pain.

Continuing to enjoy his witticisms, Nolan moved away, following a well-worn path that snaked around an overhanging rocky outcrop, leaving Lomax to mumble and moan.

Each step took him farther away from Lomax's grating mewing until, at last, he could hear it no longer. He took the opportunity to stop, pull in a deep breath, and try to force himself to relax. They all needed to get away from this land, the sun, the heat. He wished he'd been one of the men chosen by Burroughs to go back and find Cole. Because that is what Burroughs meant when he ordered Ashton and Buller to find Cole. Kill him maybe. The reasons for this were a mystery to Nolan, and he preferred not to dwell on any of it. Burroughs was planning something, that much was certain, but whatever it was Nolan did not wish to know. He had enough troubles of his own, chief amongst them being Lomax. They were going to come to blows sooner or later and the thought was an unsettling one. He'd watched Taylor land that blow like a pro, but he doubted he could ever be as good. Lomax, a big man, would prove a handful and may well be the one standing over Nolan, victorious. The thought made his stomach turn over.

Something scurried from behind a rock and Nolan turned, working the lever of the carbine. He stood rooted to the spot, waiting, eyes flicking left to right, but whatever had moved was no longer in sight. The silence was total.

He relaxed and straightened himself up. The whole enterprise was nothing more than a waste of time so, putting the carbine over his shoulder, he decided to return to Lomax and convince him they should go back to camp. They wouldn't be shooting any rabbits, not this day or any other.

Before he turned the corner to follow the track back to where his companion sat, Nolan knew something was amiss.

Lomax was no longer on the boulder. No longer nursing his ankle.

He lay sprawled out in the dirt, an arrow protruding from his throat, and his carbine missing.

Breaking into a run, unable to think straight, only conscious of the dread feeling enveloping him, Nolan skidded to a halt next to his erstwhile companion and gazed into the big man's lifeless eyes. The arrow, imbedded deep, which had to mean the perpetrator of the deed must have been close. So close Lomax could probably smell his breath. But Nolan knew Indians moved deathly quiet. He'd read the stories, the Dime Novels. He listened to the old sweats back in the Fort recounting their tales of horror and gore. Indians were deadly. Moreover, they were still around, raiding settlements for horses and food. Killing.

As here. Now.

Not daring to stop, he continued running, head down, pounding up the sharp incline to the crest where, less than an hour previously, Lomax and he had come over in their search for rabbits to shoot. Less than an hour. It seemed like a lifetime ago for Nolan as, heaving in his breath, he made the top and peered down into the basin of the arroyo.

He expected to see his comrades still there. Taylor preparing their stew, Dewy no doubt filling a pipe to smoke whilst contemplating life.

They were still there, but not how Nolan had hoped.

Mesmerised through sheer terror, he watched as Indians continued with their grizzly work. One, straddling Dewy, made great drama of sawing through the top of the Corporal's head, whilst two more grappled with Taylor. A third Indian lay sprawled on the ground and Nolan felt a tiny surge of pride coursing through him at the sight. The old cook had done his utmost. He wasn't going down without a fight. But even now, as he held one of his attackers by the wrist and slammed a knee into the man's groin, the other slipped in behind and plunged a cruel looking blade deep into Taylor's back. Taylor screeched at the top of his voice, buckled, and crumpled to his knees and the knifeman drew back the blade to make the killing blow.

Seeing enough and jolted into action, Nolan slithered down the incline, wielding his carbine like a club. His race forward continued without interruption as he struck the warrior holding Dewey's scalp aloft with the stock of his gun. Falling upon the others, he snapped the stock across the knifeman's jaw, not once, but twice, smashing him to the ground, and kicked the other squarely in the throat. Dropping down beside Taylor, he put the carbine on the ground and held the old cook by the shoulders.

The old man lifted his head. There were tears in his eyes. "Run, son. Get your horse and run."

"I have to save the sarge. There'll be others."

"No." Taylor suddenly creased up, face turning purple as his body became consumed with racking coughs. "No," he said again when he'd recovered somewhat. "He's one of them. These are renegades. There's Mexicans and Texicans with 'em. Burroughs, he ..." More coughs, so rasping and painful sounding followed before the old man keeled over to his right and went into spasm, legs kicking out, body trembling.

Nolan, knowing the old cook's time had come, swept up the carbine and prepared to shoot the groaning Indian on the ground. But then he realised that up until that time, no shots had been fired by anyone. A bullet in this devil's head would alert any others and his own death would swiftly follow. So, giving Taylor one last, lingering look, he finished both stricken Indians off by smashing in their skulls with his carbine.

Wheeling away, his sickening work completed, he scrambled up the opposite incline, to try and make some sense of what Burroughs might be doing. Burroughs, his sergeant, his troop commander, had orchestrated all of it? He had led them all here to their deaths. That's what Taylor meant. The painful truth, the depth of the sergeant's betrayal, combined to almost overwhelm Nolan and for many frightful seconds he found it impossible to come to terms with. He collapsed onto the ground, rocking himself gently backwards and forwards, cradling his carbine as if it were a baby, the only thing to give him comfort.

A moan from his right forced him to return to reality. Glancing across to one of the stricken Indians, Nolan climbed to his feet and left behind the charnel house the camp had become.

CHAPTER FOURTEEN

They saw him, as the sun was nothing more than a dull orb in the sky. The speck on the horizon grew more distinct as the rider came into sharp focus and Cole, reining in his horse, brought the eyeglasses out of their leather case.

"He is a soldier," said Brown Bear, "I can see his blue trousers, the yellow stripe."

"I'm trying to make out who exactly he is," said Cole, not wanting to engage the Indian scout with largely useless explanations that he too could see the rider was a soldier. All he wanted to know was if it were Burroughs. It wasn't. It was a cavalryman he did not recognise, but by the look of him, he was fleeing from something, something massive.

Brown Bear was already drawing his Winchester from its scabbard.

"I reckon you'll need that, but not just yet," said Cole, returning the binoculars to their case. "Let's make out for that nearby cover," he pointed to a towering pile of craggy rocks.

"You're running from him?"

Cole gave the scout a withering look. "Just do as I say," he growled and eased his horse towards the outcrop. Within a blink, Brown Bear fell in behind him.

Settling their horses out of sight, Cole edged forward to a large boulder, Henry in hand.

"So, you kill him by ambush." Brown Bear looked away, his mouth turned down in disgust. "Like a snake."

"Hell, you know we have only one chance at this. Don't judge me too harshly. What we're doing here is no worse than what we did back at Saint Boniface. You remember that, don't you Brown Bear?"

"I do. I remember everything about it, how those men tried to kill me and you ... you saved my life, Reuben. I told you then, I will never be able to repay you for what you did."

"Don't start going all maudlin' over me!" He chuckled and checked the load of his rifle.

"And you plan on going up against them with that old Henry? You think you can cause much damage with that?"

"This "old Henry" as you call it," said Cole patting the brass block, "is one of the finest firearms available. It's over fifteen years old and has never let me down."

Grunting, Brown Bear forced himself to turn his attention once more on the wide-open space stretching out before them, and the rider using his reins to whip his horse's neck, urging it to gallop faster and faster.

Cole meanwhile sighted along the Henry's barrel, drew in a breath, and waited until the soldier was virtually opposite. He squeezed the trigger to loosen off single round.

The bullet hit the ground inches in front of the pounding horse's front hooves, causing the animal to scream out in terror and veer sharply away from the offending gunshot. Another bullet saw the horse rearing and bucking wildly. The rider, caught hopelessly off balance, had little time to react and fell heavily to the ground, the impact causing the breath to gush out of him. He lay still, eyes wide-open, shock and fear mixing to put him into a sort of catatonic state.

"Get his horse," said Cole, already vaulting the big boulder and moving purposefully towards the quivering soldier. He looked over his shoulder to see Brown Bear standing there, shaking his head.

"That is exactly what you did when you saved my life. It's like it was yesterday."

Cole blew out a long sigh. "Get the horse, before it gets too far away." Already, the soldier's horse was doing its best to do just that.

As Brown Bear at last reacted, Cole went up to the soldier and stood over him, working another round into the chamber of his Henry. "You with Burroughs?" he asked simply.

From somewhere within his mangled senses, a glimmer of comprehension crossed the soldier's eyes. He frowned and took in a huge gulp of air. "Who ..."

"Don't fret too much, son. I ain't gonna kill you." He smiled, bringing the Henry up to his shoulder. "Not yet anyways."

Beneath him, the soldier squirmed and made small, animal-like noises. "Please," he managed to say.

"I need to know where Burroughs is. He's all that interests me, nothing more."

"I'll take you to him."

Slowly, Cole lowered his gun. "Now *that's* a good decision."

They sat sipping coffee whilst Brown Bear relieved the horses of their saddles and took to brushing them down with a coarse cloth.

"So, you never made it to the rendezvous point?" asked Cole, eyes never leaving the young soldier who sat nursing his coffee between both hands, head down, his body seeming as if it had imploded within itself. A man close to the edge. A man crippled by fear, or the memory of it.

The soldier shook his head. "Not that I knew that was where we was headin'. Burroughs never made it clear exactly what we were riding into. I just assumed we were out to apprehend horse thieves."

Grunting, Cole finished off his drink and threw the grounds into the small fire crackling beside him. "I ran across two of your troop. Burroughs sent them for me, I reckon. He won't be seeing them again."

"That would be Ashton and Buller. Burroughs sent them after you." Cole nodded. "You did for 'em?"

"Not me. Another of Burroughs' cronies, an old coot known as Spelling. Heard of him?"

"No, sir."

Studying the young soldier, Cole sensed his words were truthful. "That man Burroughs is a back-stabber, as no doubt you now understand,"

"I do. After I seen what those savages had done to my friends, I came over the rise to see him in conversation with more of "em. Laughing he was. Head thrown back. Amongst friends."

"He was the one in charge of the horse rustling."

"Their boss?"

Cole nodded and saw the soldiers face screw up in a grimace of barely contained rage. "You put me in his direction, and I'll serve him the justice he deserves."

"I'll do it, don't you worry. Even though I must go back to that hell, I left. The way they butchered my friends ..." He shuddered and shook his head.

"Burroughs used you, like he used a lot of people. And now, perhaps he has no doubt sent some of 'em in pursuit, to kill you. He cannot afford to allow you to return to the fort and tell Captain Phelps what happened."

"Yes, I think so. I took off as fast as I could after seeing Burroughs with them devils and spotted the one I'd clubbed with my carbine wandering around like someone blind. I reckon when he'd recovered, he told Burroughs what had happened."

"Well, whatever he did or did not say, Burroughs hasn't yet sent anyone after you. They'd be here by now, but they ain't. So ..." He reached out and squeezed the young soldier's forearm. "But he will, so we have no choice."

"I know it and I've accepted it. And, you know what, I'm looking forward to seeing him again, to stare into his face and watch him die."

"I said I'd serve him justice, son. Not retribution."

"They're the same thing."

"Not always."

"In this case, they are."

Cole wanted to agree but something held him back. He didn't want to give the soldier his blessing to shoot Burroughs down dead as soon as they caught up with him. Instead, he grunted again and stood up. He stretched and gave Brown Bear a glance. "How long?"

The scout shrugged. "Once they're watered, got down some oats ... An hour."

"By then it'll be night." Cole looked down at the soldier. "You sure you're up for this?"

"Absolutely."

"And what's your name – if we're to ride together, we need to be introduced. I'm Cole."

"Good to know you, Mister Cole. My name's Nolan. Tobias Nolan, U.S. Cavalry trooper."

"That over there is Brown Bear."

Nolan frowned. "He's an Indian. How come you ride with a savage?"

"Son, he's a scout. A man. Best you remember that when the shootin' starts."

"Those that killed my friends were like him. How do you expect me to feel? They're all the same."

"Like white folk are, I suppose?"

"Eh?"

Rolling his tongue around inside his mouth, Cole leaned away and spat into the ground. "Take it from me, son, I have met much worse white people than any so-called savage. Your Sergeant Burroughs is only one example. There are many more."

"Even if that is so, all I can say is, you just keep him well away from me. And not behind me."

"Son, you keep talking that way you're gonna lose some teeth. Now pipe down, drink your coffee and think on who it was that got you into this mess in the first place."

"I know who that was."

"Good. So, remind yourself it was no Indian."

Nolan, still huddled up, seemed to sink his neck even further into his chest and offered no further comments, which for Cole was a relief. He was feeling tired and the thought of breaking the pathetic little trooper's jaw didn't fill him with too much joyful anticipation.

CHAPTER FIFTEEN

Burroughs stood amongst the dead in the arroyo, hands on hips, deep in thought. Early morning, the camp emerging from a long night's sleep. Munching down their breakfasts with gusto, Burroughs had not partaken, preferring to sit away from the others and enjoy a scalding hot cup of coffee. Now, with the day moving on, he looked at the bodies of his former comrades without a glimmer of conscience. It was not their deaths that troubled him. He was vaguely aware of people moving around him, but it was only when a hand came down on his shoulder that he started and snapped his head around. Before him was a swarthy looking individual, dressed in black jacket, pinstriped trousers, and knee-high riding boots. He wore two guns. Anyone who looked at him, however, could not help but be drawn to the most prominent feature of this man. Across his right eye, he wore a patch. From the lowest edge, a virulent red scar ran down the side of his face to the corner of his mouth, now twisted into a parody of a smile. "He has gone. No point in worrying about it now."

"He'll inform the fort, tell them what has happened."

"So what? By the time he gets there and convinces your commander to send another troop, we will be across the border, drinking tequila, and counting our money."

The man's voice was heavily accented. A Mexican and not the only one. Amongst the band of disparate individuals roaming around, together with a gaggle of violent looking Mexicans, were Indians, Americans, and one Scotsman. Burroughs, considering them from afar, received no comfort from their presence. True they, especially the Indians, had proved their mettle, but he knew full well that none of them could be trusted. He very much doubted he would be alive to drink that tequila. As soon as he sealed the deal with the Mexican authorities, any one of this bunch would slit his throat. If he were to survive, he would need to make his move almost as soon as they crossed the Rio Grande and kill the lot of them.

"Yes," he said, turning away from the swarthy man's peering one eye, "you're right. But I wish we'd put him down before he managed to get away." He blew out a sigh, keeping his feelings well concealed. Or so he hoped. This man, Javi el Torre, as he was known, was probably the most dangerous of them all.

"We will leave," said El Torre, rolling his shoulders, and pulling out a black cheroot from his coat. "We will make the border in two more days. We cannot run the horses too hard."

"They're well-guarded?"

El Torre arched a single eyebrow and lit his cheroot. "You take me for an idiot, *amigo?*"

"Of course not, I was only—"

"Have no worries about my competence, *amigo*. The horses are safe, and my vaqueros do their jobs well. You must trust me, *amigo*."

"I do, Javi. Of course I do. You took those horses in the first place, and not for the first time. You've been a good partner to me, but this must be the *last* time. I'm compromised now. I hope you understand."

"Yes, *amigo*, of course I understand." Another squeeze and this time his smile developed into a broad grin, the cheroot clamped between his white, even teeth. "We have done well, made good money. Better than robbing banks." He chuckled to himself and moved away, calling to the others to mount up and leave. Burroughs watched and wondered what the future might hold. Perhaps he wouldn't even make it to the border, El Torre believing he alone could broker a better deal with the *Federales*. If this were so, then Burroughs might have to make his move sooner than he had first envisaged. El Torre would always act in his own best interest. If he believed he had no further use for Burroughs, then he would strike.

Unconsciously, Burroughs hand moved across to the Colt cavalry at his hip.

There were over twelve of them. He, on the other hand, was alone. Choices were now suddenly very limited, and he inwardly groaned at the prospect of the violence to come, no matter how necessary it might be.

"Hey, *amigo*," shouted El Torre's voice and Burroughs turned to see the Mexican already mounted, struggling to keep his horse steady. "We must go. *Vamos!*"

Grunting, Burroughs nodded, moved across to his own horse and saw the two men standing close by, each with Winchesters in their hands. His heart almost stopped. Was this it, the moment? He slowed down, measuring each of the silent, unmoving men, and allowed his hand to dangle next to his Colt. Long ago he had cut away the holster's regulation flap, leaving the gun always ready for use.

Six paces from the men, he stopped.

"What's this?" he said.

Neither man moved. They seemed to be waiting for some sort of a signal. Perhaps from El Torre. Burroughs drew in a breath and steadied himself.

Approaching on foot, Cole and Nolan scampered over the numerous rocky outcrops, keeping low, carbines at the ready. On reaching the rise they had an uninterrupted view of the camp. A bunch of Indians, together with a ragbag collection of rough looking individuals, were preparing to move. One lean, black-clad man stood apart, staring intensely towards another group. Two riders, guns held loosely in their leather-gloved hands, were some half dozen paces from another with his back towards Cole and his associate.

"That's Burroughs," hissed Nolan and immediately brought his carbine up to his shoulder. Instantly, Cole gripped the young trooper's arm. Nolan snapped his head around. "What? I told you, I'm gonna kill him!"

"And I told you we take him in."

"No. He dies." Nolan wrenched his arm free. "After what he did, he deserves it." Closing one eye, he squinted down the length of the barrel, right index finger curling around the trigger.

Cole smacked the palm of his hand into Nolan's arm, jerking the young trooper to the left. The carbine went off, the sharp retort echoing across the plain. Cursing, Nolan struggled to turn but Cole was too quick and cracked his fist hard into his jaw. Nolan grunted and collapsed, the fight leaving his body almost straight away but, as Cole looked down again at the camp, he saw all too clearly that already things were changing.

A single shot rang out. Burroughs instinctively ducked, turned, and looked to where he believed the shot had originated. On the periphery of his vision, he caught the two gunmen moving, bent low and, taking his chance, he swung in their direction, the Colt in his hand. He fanned the hammer, dropping both the gunmen with a flurry of bullets. Then, not waiting for any reaction from El Torre or anyone else, dashed towards some nearby cover.

Diving over a clump of gorse, a bullet whizzed red-hot above his head, leaving him as to know doubt what El Torre had in store for him. Rolling across the ground, he lodged himself behind a boulder and fumbled for fresh bullets from the little hard-leather case at his belt. Replacing the spent cartridges, he twirled the cylinder and did his best to compose himself, concentrating on steadying his breathing whilst he listened and tried to assess the direction from which his attackers approached.

———

El Torre signalled for his men to spread out on either flank, which they did without argument. Confident in their numbers, they moved with a frightening fluidity, leaping across boulders, skirting around broken scrub, darting from one piece of cover to the next. As they pressed in towards their quarry, El Torre strode relentlessly forward with seeming disdain, almost as if he dared Burroughs to come out and face him. Gun in hand and teeth clamped into a maniacal grin, so intent was he on his advance he did not consider any other outcome but what he desired – Burroughs' death. Even when the first shot dropped one of his men, he did not stop. A second bullet sent a young Indian whirling around in a grotesque sort of dance and a third shot felled another, hitting him in the guts, pitching him forward, the blood pumping from between the fingers where he gripped the horrific wound. Only then did El Torre pull up short, mouth agog, not understanding any of it. The bullets were not coming from Burroughs!

Those remaining stopped also. Bewildered and confused, they scoured the surroundings, guns at the ready, by now their former confidence eroding fast, their self-assuredness nothing but a memory. Fear replaced their arrogance and as they crouched, trembling, not knowing which way to turn, Burroughs rose up from behind his cover and his handgun belched fire.

Within seconds, other gunshots erupted from somewhere beyond that immediate area. Men fell, blood spurting, and soon those unscathed broke and ran, leaving El Torre alone.

Feeding more bullets into his gun, Burroughs moved forward towards his black-clad protagonist. No longer concerned with the rest, Burroughs knew the only danger confronting him now, the only danger there had ever been, was El Torre. And El Torre waited. Grinning.

"*Amigo*," he said, "you have a friend somewhere, I think. You are clever, but you know what, you're gonna die anyway." He giggled.

Burroughs took his chance and brought up his Colt. He knew he was good, better than those gunmen had realised. They'd underestimated him, thinking him a dullard, a worn-out cavalryman with little shooting skills. Proven wrong, they died and so too would El Torre. His arrogance knew no bounds.

But if anyone was underestimating his adversary, it was Burroughs at that moment. He moved as fast as he could, but it was not fast enough against El Torre, who shot the gun out of Burroughs' hand, shattering the sergeant's right wrist for good measure. Yelping in pain, Burroughs crumpled, clutching at the offending limb, blood spurting between his fingers.

"You are a fool, *gringo*," snarled El Torre, moving closer, that annoying grin plastered on his face like a permanent fixture.

Burroughs brought up his head, the tears stinging his eyes and, consumed with a mix of anger and despair, snarled, "Damn your hide, El Torre. I trusted you."

"Like I said, you're a fool." He shrugged and brought up his gun hand. "Hold on, boy."

The words, delivered in a low, dangerous drawl caused El Torre to falter. He stopped, turned, and saw a man standing, feet slightly apart, a Henry repeating carbine in his hands. This stranger looked more than competent and something about his demeanour, the intensity of his stare, sent a flicker of uncertainty across El Torre's face. The grin subsided and when he spoke, the self-confident tones were gone, replaced with an emotion he had not experienced since a small child. Fear. His voice, thick with it, struggled to form the words. "So ... This is your friend, *gringo*? The one who kills people unseen, like a shadow?"

Nothing came from Burroughs except pain-racked moans. From the stranger with the Henry, a long drawn out sigh.

"Give it up, boy and drop the gun."

El Torre cocked his head. Afraid he may be, but his pride was the stronger. "I cannot do that."

A long moment of silence stretched out between them before the stranger said, with an emotion akin to disappointment, "I know."

Something passed between them. That unseen, intuitive knowledge that one gunfighter has for the other. The shared experience for the profession of killing.

El Torre's gun hand came up in a blur and the Henry barked, the first bullet hitting the Mexican in the chest, hurling him backwards, the second smashing through his skull, extinguishing his life before he hit the ground.

A stillness came over everything and even Burroughs stopped groaning.

Through pain-filled eyes, he watched Cole moving closer. "You're supposed to be dead," he hissed.

"Sorry to disappoint," said Cole. "Now, find your horse and let's get moving."

"I'm not going anywhere with you." Grimacing, he raised his bleeding hand. "Or with this."

"Oh yes you are," said Cole with a smile. "Otherwise I just might leave you here to bleed to death, as food for the buzzards, or," he gestured towards the shattered remains of El Torre, "for his friends to do with you as they please. Either way, it'll hurt."

It did not take long for Burroughs to decide which choice was the better one.

CHAPTER SIXTEEN

S itting in the virtually deserted saloon, Cole stretched his legs under the table and gazed into his whisky glass. He barely flinched as the batwing doors screeched open, allowing the distant sound of a brass band to float in from outside. After a slight pause, the steady thump of heeled boots on the wooden floor heralded someone's approach. They halted just before where Cole sat and at last, he looked up. Julia stood there as if she had just stepped out of a picture, dressed in a powder blue dress and matching bonnet. She gently twirled a pink parasol with floral motifs between her palms, looking for all the world as if she were preparing to go for a Sunday afternoon stroll in the sunshine. But although this was a Sunday, and the sun did shine, the idea of a stroll anywhere was not something anyone would be considering that day.

She tilted her head and sighed. "You're not going to the hanging?"

Pulling a grim look, Cole considered his drink again before throwing its contents down his throat. He gasped, slammed the now empty glass onto the tabletop, and shook his head. "Seen it all before."

"Not Burroughs you haven't." She eased herself down in the chair opposite the scout, taking care to avoid creasing her pretty dress.

"He'll be no different to all the rest," said Cole. "He'll say a few scathing words, then his neck will snap, the crowd will cheer and that'll be that."

"They have that scoundrel Spelling up there on the gallows with him. As soon as the crowd have ceased singing their hymns and the padre has spoken, they'll die. I want to see that."

"I never took you for being so hard, Julia."

"It's not hardness, Reuben. They took everything away from me. It's justice."

"You don't have to watch it to know it's being done."

"Well, I just feel that I should, that is all. I was hoping you might accompany me. Roose will be there, together with the captain."

Cole closed his eyes for a moment before lifting himself from his chair. "Very well, I'll accompany you, seeing as you asked so nicely."

"It's you who is hard, Reuben." Sighing, she stood but, for whatever reason, could not look him in the eye. "You're blind too."

With that, she span around and marched off, with Cole several paces behind, frowning, wondering what she meant.

The assembled crowd, full of expectation, beaming smiles, rubbing hands, buoyant, lifted their voices high and sang out the lines of that great favourite "Abide with Me". Pushing her way towards the front, Julia was resolute, as if on a mission, and Cole found himself having to trot to keep up with her. At last, having made the front of the assembled throng, she opened her parasol and looked up at the gallows.

"He's not here," she said as Cole moved up to her shoulder. Her words were true. Spelling stood, cutting a pathetic, withered figure, head hanging low, pale, wizened and trembling. He seemed a shadow of the callous murderer Cole encountered back in Rickman City. He looked at her. "Burroughs," she added to his silent question.

"He will be."

"I hope so. It's him I came to watch dangle."

"Julia, these feelings … I can understand them, but revenge, it's often an empty vessel."

"An empty what?" Her face snapped around to meet his. "A vessel?"

"Yeah. A vessel. Like a—"

"I know what it is, Reuben Cole. Mine is certainly not empty. I'm full of hatred for that man and what he did."

"Yeah, I know, but afterwards... Julia, what he did, what he ordered, it was wrong, of course it was, but it's eating you up."

"It won't be for much longer." She looked again at the raised platform and studied Spelling. "He's soiled himself," she said in disgust.

"Most do."

"You've witnessed a lot of these then?"

"I've had my fill, Julia, yes. There's nothing fulfilling about any of it."

"But they must be punished. Of that you cannot argue against."

"No, I ain't. It's necessary. Doesn't mean I have to like it, though." He craned his neck to survey the crowd. "Wonder where Sterling is."

She joined him in searching for Cole's close friend. A tall man, Sterling Roose would have been easy to spot, if he was there. "And the captain."

A feeling of unease grew inside Cole, spreading slowly but relentlessly up his spine. "They should be here. I would have thought they'd be standing beside both of those varmints, readying them for the drop."

They exchanged a glance before Cole pushed through the press of people and made his way towards the guard standing at the foot of the steps leading to the gallows. All he received from his question was a shrug. Enraged, his unease unbearable now, he whirled away and gestured to Julia to follow him.

Their progress was achingly slow, no one willing to give way despite Cole's obvious desperation. When one particularly obstinate individual jutted out his jaw, refusing to budge, Cole grabbed him by the arms and bodily threw him aside. Someone screamed, other voices blurted out their indignation. Ignoring them all, Cole elbowed his way through, the crowd more forgiving now. A cry from behind made him turn in time to see Julia jabbing the heel of her boot down on the obstinate man's instep. As he hopped around, Julia shoved him aside and he went down amongst a mess of outraged arms and legs. Smiling despite the situation, Cole put his head down and surged forward until, finally, he made it to the end of the assembled mob and broke into a run.

The door to the jail was hanging open and Cole, slowing down, instinctively drew his gun.

Julia almost slammed into the back of him. Out of breath, she gasped, "What is it? What has happened?"

Stepping inside, Cole surveyed the chaos of what was left of the upturned desk, the two chairs, keys, posters, everything spilled out across the floor.

He heard Julia scream, but his attention was drawn to the bodies on the ground.

Only one of them was breathing.

CHAPTER SEVENTEEN

1875

His stomach rumbled loudly. He had only coffee to sustain him and even that supply was almost done. Sighing, he finished the remnants out of the tin cup and gazed into the depths of the tiny campfire.

Memories of Julia and what happened with Burroughs percolated far more effectively than the coffee he brewed. The taste, however, proved just as bitter.

Burroughs had made good his escape, killing the captain and leaving Sterling Roose with a black eye and swollen jaw. How the sergeant had managed it without help was a mystery. However he'd done it, he had killed Phelps, but not Roose. Yet another mystery. Things he still didn't have any answers to. Incensed, Julia begged Cole to go in pursuit of him, bring him back to justice, and, after making sure Roose would be taken care of by the fort doctor, Cole had agreed. He would have done so anyway, but the look on her face was the only encouragement he needed. She'd captured his heart and he knew that whatever she wanted he would do his very best to make it so.

Even if that included killing.

He stretched out his legs and yawned. All of that was a few years ago now. Strange, he pondered, how the images came so readily to his mind, the sound of her voice running like sweet spring water through him.

Could it be that these two manhunts were so similar? He wondered if the end could be the same. Somehow, he doubted it.

With this present hunt well under way, he pushed what happened during that momentous time to the back of his mind. Those moments out on the plains, hunting down Burroughs, changed him, made him into the man he became. And it was that change which brought him here.

After packing his meagre camp, he rode across the open range, senses alert. He knew he was gaining on them, their self-assuredness their undoing. They did not consider a single man would be foolhardy enough to confront them. But then, none of them had ever encountered a man like Reuben Cole before. A man on a mission. A man capable of so much.

He came across the stripped prairie wagon late that same day. Missing its canvas cover, a front wheel broken away from the axle, the wagon's contents inside bleached by the raging sun. Horses, long gone. Taken by the same band who had butchered those unfortunate homesteaders.

And now this.

Four corpses, strewn across the ground, stomachs split open, intestines drawn out, already food for the buzzards that scattered on Cole's approach, screaming out their protests, beaks dripping with blood and torn meat. They perched close by, on a brittle branch of a withered tree, watching him. He brought his mount to a halt, reaching behind him to pull out the Winchester from its sheath. He'd reluctantly replaced his redoubtable old Henry some months ago, but this new model proved its mettle.

Scouring the surroundings, he estimated a half dozen hours had elapsed since the attack. A wry smile. He was gaining on them.

Dropping from the saddle, he examined the closest body. A young boy, perhaps thirteen. It was not unusual for such an individual to be taken for a slave, to be reared as a brave, taught how to fight so in the years to come he would be a benefit to the entire tribe. But this one had fought already. Cole saw the remnants of powder on his right fist. A good gun in his hand, an old Colt Navy. It lay beside him and something about it, and the dead boy's attitude, brought a choking sob to Cole's throat. They'd cleaved his skull, hacked off his scalp, and the buzzards had done the rest.

The others fared no better. A mother, a baby of no more than three months clasped to her bosom, teeth bared, an arrow in her head, another buried deep in her body. And, more horrifying, one in the infant too.

Cole kicked away at the earth, wishing the marauders were there now, as the tears streamed down his face.

The father had made a stand of it. They'd relieved him of his rifle after he'd died, a repeating carbine by the evidence of the cluster of spent shells lying in the dirt next to him. Their strong, reliable father. The man who would protect them, give them the strength to carry on as they moved across this hard, unforgiving land. He'd done his best, but he had failed, as most did. Made rigid by fear, he probably worked through those rounds mechanically, without thinking, desperate to push back his attackers. And missed. Every time.

They'd fallen upon him like wild beasts, their knives and hatchets cutting him like meat for the pot. There was nothing left of his face, everything gone, consumed by the birds.

Cole crumpled onto his backside and openly wept, holding nothing back.

Why did pilgrims still travel this land? Was it the lies the government had sold them, that the tribal areas were tamed, that the bad days were well and truly gone? Did those sod-busters know nothing of the break-outs, of the groups of Comanches who continued to dominate the southern plains, filled with hatred for the Whites, for the ones who had brought nothing but disease and deprivation to their lives and sought to end their ancient way of life?

No one could blame the Comanche, or any of the great tribes, for their reaction.

But no one could excuse it either, for the extent of the violence was beyond imagination. Witness to so much, Cole once again found himself overcome with the hopelessness of it all. This land surely was big enough for everyone to live in harmony, if indeed any outsider ever chose to live here. For where the Indian struggled to survive and made some success of it, white folk simply could not cope. The extremes of temperature, the lack of resources, food, water. The Indians had lived here for a thousand years and more. They knew every grain of sand, every contour, every hidden pool. A dozen generations of struggle and toil. But fresh out of Kansas, or even farther east? Nothing but dreams of a brighter future to drive them. Where was the sense in it?

There was none. And this family had paid the ultimate price. Just as those others had, in their farm. Murdered. Left to rot. Senseless.

It took him the best part of three hours to bury them. All the time, the birds watched him, jaundiced eyes taking in every detail, possibly storing it all away for future reference. Cole laboured regardless, stripped down to his waist, pausing only to take the occasional drink from his canteen. He used a spade from the broken wagon and wrapped the bodies in blankets before he put them into the holes he dug. The sun beat down with its relentless fury and he felt his shoulders burn. A strong man, nevertheless, his muscles screamed with his exertions, the father proving the most awkward, and the most gruesome. But nothing could compare with laying the tiny babe next to its mother.

With the grizzly work finally finished, Cole leaned on the spade, closed his eyes, and spoke some words from barely remembered Sunday school lessons. In the end, he gave up and uttered a phrase more akin to how he felt. "God rest them," he said, wiped his brow, pulled on his shirt, and left them in their unmarked graves.

He did not look back.

CHAPTER EIGHTEEN

He rode hard and did not camp until late. He deliberately sought out high ground and lit his campfire. Stacking it up with piles of tinder dry wood, he hobbled his horse and made himself comfortable amongst the rocks. He was tired of pursuing them. The time for action was well overdue. His hope was that they'd come for him, in the dead of night. But they did not, and he spent most of his time squashed up, cold, miserable so that when the sun lit up the new day, his body ached as if it had been pressed through a grain mill.

Rations low, he set out again with his stomach empty, its rumbling louder than the distant thunder which sounded amongst the faraway mountains. He turned his face towards them and wished, with all he had, that he was there amongst them, battling against the elements because what he faced now was far, far worse.

Hunger, which gnawed away at his belly, and water, which tasted like gravel. He forced himself to take a small sip every hour or so, slowed his horse to a canter and tried to clear his mind. This proved an impossibility. He'd put his common sense aside in his desire to dish out retribution. He should have heeded Sterling's council, but he hadn't, so he set his sights straight ahead, resolved to do what he knew he must, no matter the obstacles in his way.

. . .

A single stream of grey smoke wafted from the wooden spire of a lonely church, which stood amongst a cluster of small, derelict buildings. Yet another abandoned township, left to rot when the gold or the silver ran out. Cole, lying on the lip of a rocky outcrop, studied it through his army field glasses. Three horses were tethered outside, along with two pack mules. These were not the Comanche raiders he hunted. He knew he should avoid anything which might detract him from his mission and push on, complete the bloody work he'd set himself to do. But the trail he found seemed to suggest that the marauders had come this way, however the signs had become mixed up with another set. Whereas the marauders seemed to skirt well around the old town, another appeared to head straight for the centre. Besides, his belly ached and, convincing himself he could barter for some food, even a few handfuls of biscuits, he decided to make the detour worthwhile.

So, he rode into that tiny place, slowing to a walk as he neared the church.

Reining in, he tied his horse to a hanging piece of hitching rail and stood, listening out for the slightest sound. Hearing nothing, he pulled out the Winchester and eased himself up the rickety steps to the entrance. The boards groaned underneath his feet, putting paid to any hope of a silent entrance. Sucking in a breath, he eased down on the door handle and pushed the door open.

He was prepared to move, and he was already dodging to his left as the first bullet whizzed through the air, inches from where he had stood. Flattened against the adjacent wall, he worked a round into the Winchester's chamber. A second bullet slapped against the woodwork, forcing Cole to drop to one knee as he cried out, "Hold your fire, I'm not here to harm you!"

If he hoped his words might allay further gunfire, he was wrong. Three more bullets tore through the wall, sending out showers of splinters above his head. He broke cover and ran, bent double, across the open doorway to the other side and didn't stop until he reached the front corner of the church. Here, several of the other buildings pressed in close, but he could see no movement within any of them. Blackened gaps punctuated their walls, doors hanging off on broken hinges, windows rotten and close to collapse. No one had inhabited this place for many years. Nevertheless, someone waited inside the church and they were intent on doing him harm.

Cole chanced a glance down the narrow alley separating the church from the rest of the structures. There was no one. Across, on the other side, were the horses and mules he'd spied from his field glasses. They stared at him, uninterested despite his sudden appearance.

On closer inspection he noted that only one of the horses was saddled. The other two were bare-backed, scrawny looking things whilst the mules were loaded down with several large sacks, several blanket rolls and an assortment of pots and pans. Frowning, Cole wondered what it all meant. Shrugging off the dark thoughts developing inside his head, he made his way along the side of the church, senses on edge, expecting at any moment to be assailed by a fusillade of gunshots.

The passageway proved long, the church a large building, and little of the sun's rays managed to penetrate the deep shadows cast by the towering wall along which he shuffled. Towards the corridor's end, Cole was drawn to the uninterrupted view opening before him. He gasped. The vastness and beauty of this land never ceased to leave him breathless. He could believe his feelings for this land bordered on the spiritual, but at that moment he had something else to occupy his thoughts as a developing cloud of dust moved relentlessly towards him.

He dipped back into the shadows, wondering what he could do. Opposite him the skeleton of what appeared to be a former shop of some description beckoned to him. He crossed to it and slipped through the flimsy doorway. Looking up, the sun streamed in through the gap where once the roof had been. Surrounding him was a tangled mass of broken furniture, overturned tables, chairs, smashed cupboards, and a multitude of shattered glass, broken pots and, in the corners, piles of what looked like oats, greedily consumed by fat, fearless rats. Swallowing down his revulsion, Cole navigated a path through the detritus until he reached a rear entrance. He eased it open and found himself in another side street. Fewer buildings confronted him this time, but one appeared more substantial than the rest. A saloon, by the looks of it. Head down, he raced over to it and went through the double bat-wing doors, going into a forward roll to give himself some advantage if anyone lurked inside.

He came to rest behind a solid table and gulped in several breaths.

Around, a grey murkiness, the dust swirling like a fog cloud coupled with the all-pervading stench of decay.

And something else.

The whimpering of a child.

CHAPTER NINETEEN

H e wasn't much more than a bundle of rags, his tiny frame lost amongst his filthy clothes. A white face, skin so thin the skull protruded alarmingly, peered out at Cole as the scout crept forward, one arm outstretched, cooing, "Don't be afraid ..."

But the child was a great deal more than afraid. Terrified, he cowered away, shuffling on his backside deeper into the shadows. There, in the darkness with his huge, bulging eyes acting like beacons, he took up his whimpering again, a pathetic sound like a small, confused puppy calling for its mother.

Squatting down on his haunches, Cole stopped. He wished he had something to offer the poor child. A piece of candy would be perfect, but he had nothing, not even the tiniest morsel of food to give in an attempt to allay the child's fears. Instead, he forced a thin smile. "It's all right," he said quietly, "I'm not going to hurt you." Sight now well-adjusted to the gloom, Cole noted the boy's wrists were tightly bound together. Frowning, he threw a glance behind him before returning to the child's glowing, frightened eyes. "Did the one in the church tie you up like this?" No answer, only the briefest of sobs. "Who is in there?" Nothing again. "When I went up to the door, they tried to shoot me. What is he afraid of? Indians?"

"It's not a "he"."

The voice, so tiny, brittle, laced with fear, but a voice, nevertheless. Cole took his time, not wishing to cause further panic or distress. "A woman?" A nod and a grunt. "But I don't understand, why would anyone do this to a—"

"And she's not afraid of Indians."

"Oh? Why? Who is she?"

"She's an Indian herself."

Frown deepening, Cole slowly reached behind him. "I'm going to cut you loose," he said as his fingers curled around the handle of his heavy-bladed hunting knife. "Don't yell out or move. I promise you I ain't gonna hurt you."

Eyes fixed unerringly on the blade, the boy held out his arms and Cole sliced through the leather binding with ease. Released, the boy wrung his hands and rubbed feverishly at his wrists, clearly relieved to be free at last.

From beyond the walls, the sound of horses came to them, hooves pounding across the hard-packed earth. Instantly, the boy flung himself against Cole, wrapping his arms around the scout, burying his face deep into his shirt. Cole held him, tried his best to offer what comfort he could and calm the awful trembling that now took hold of the boy's little body.

Turning anxiously towards the door, Cole listened. Outside, riders were reining in their mounts, gabbling with each other in a language Cole instantly recognised and which almost froze his heart.

They were Comanches.

Easing out his Colt Cavalry, whilst still holding the boy close, Cole whispered, "You need to tell me what's going on here and you need to tell me now."

Looking up at him through the gloom, the boy quietly and as steadily as he could, related what had happened to bring him to that cold and dismal place.

CHAPTER TWENTY

Some weeks previously

They left Kansas sometime in late spring. The mingle of well-wishers, a mere half dozen sullen looking townsfolk, waved their goodbyes. Amongst them, old Art Dalton who had lectured Janus that he would be taking his family into "the very cauldron of Hell", given the dread stories which made their way back and chilled the hearts of even the most stalwart. He doffed his hat. Chewing on his usual wad of tobacco, he leaned to his left and spat a long stream of juice into the ground. "Some of those who went out West were eaten by their own kin," he'd said on their last night, both huddled together in a dismal saloon, cupping hot coffee laced with whisky.

"We have enough supplies to last us three months," said Janus, not sure if he was convincing his friend or himself. "We'll be fine. Joel is as good with the rifle as I am, even young Seb can shoot when he puts his mind to it. Millie can cook anything and make it as tasty as a king's feast."

"Even kings get themselves killed." Janus pulled a face. Art leaned forward and gripped his friend's hand. "Your wife hasn't long given birth. Please, Janus, reconsider. What if something were to take hold of the child, a sickness or some such thing?"

"Art, you worry too much."

"No, I'm simply being sensible. Why can't you wait until the rest of us is ready?"

Pulling his hand free, Janus blew out his cheeks, "Art, you been saying that since before last Christmas. If I was to wait for you, I'd never leave."

"Maybe that would be for the best."

"No. It wouldn't. I can no longer sit here, twiddling my thumbs. Winter has left us now and the time is ripe. By the time we get to California, it will be the perfect time to lay out a plot, build a home. The weather is kinder over there."

"And the way is filled with perils, Janus, the like of which neither you nor I have ever known. Savages. Desperadoes. Villainous individuals lay in wait for folk such as you, Janus."

"We have nothing such people want."

"You have horses. Savages want horses."

"Those *savages* as you call "em, they've all been tamed now. Taken off to reservations and the like. "

"Not all. I hear things, Janus. There's trouble coming with them big tribes."

"Well, like I say, our route is far from any of that."

"You don't know that for sure."

Shouting out a curse, Janus brought the flat of his hand down hard on the tabletop. Some of the other customers snapped their heads around and stared. "Can't you at least send us off with your best wishes, instead of all this doom talk?"

Eventually, old Art did just that and as Janus past him by the following day, the two friends locked eyes, and both smiled, albeit somewhat sad, thin ones.

Four days into the journey, Seb, who had been sat in the wagon, peering out from the rear across the prairie, turned his head. "Pa, there's someone following us."

Sitting next to his wife on the buckboard, Janus frowned and pulled the twin team to a gentle halt. Joel, riding ahead, noting the cessation of the grinding noises the wagon wheels made, eased his horse around. "What is it, Pa?"

"Could be nothing," said Janus, patting his wife's knee before jumping down. "Bring me the Winchester."

"Janus?"

The fear in his wife's voice brought him up sharp. He forced a smile. "It'll be nothing. Don't worry." He reached across and stroked the infant's head nuzzled into his wife's breast.

Joel brought up his horse and slid the repeating carbine from its sheath. Handing it down to Janus, the boy checked his own Colt Navy. "Is there gonna be trouble, Pa?"

Janus shrugged, looked towards the lone rider ambling its way inexorably towards therm. "There's only one and ..." He squinted through the heat haze. "Holy Saint Francis, I think it's a woman!"

Within ten minutes, Janus' words were confirmed as the slim, slightly built young woman, a mass of raven-coloured hair stuffed under her broad-brimmed hat, reined in her tired looking horse, and offered him a beautiful smile. "Howdy, fellow-travellers. I don't suppose you could spare me a little water?"

Over the next few days, Adeline, as she told them her name was, rode alongside, chatting ceaselessly with Janus, who had taken Joel's horse for his own. Their shared laughter rolled across the prairie and, during their nighttime camp, they sat and ate supper, made by Millie's expert hands, and seemed lost to everything and everyone else.

None of this went unnoticed by Joel who pulled Seb aside, well out of earshot. "I don't like this."

"Don't like what?" Seb, or Sebastian as was his real name, was a thin, waspish youth some four years younger than his brother.

"The way she talks to Pa. Look how close they are sitting."

Seb peered through the night and saw the pair's silhouettes, picked out by the orange glow of the fire. "How else do you want 'em to sit?"

"You know nothin'," rasped Joel and pushed his brother away. "She's getting her pretty claws into Pa, that's for sure. And Pa ..." He shook his head. "I seen it before. Last summer, when Pa went missing for a few nights, how Ma scolded him something awful when she was big and fat with little Jenny."

"I don't get it. What few nights?"

"Pfff, you have as much understanding of such things as a plank of wood, Sebastian."

"Well, if you don't explain, how am I ever to know?"

Joel rounded on his brother, seizing him by the shirtfront, and jerking him close. "Pa was seeing some girl from one of the saloons. You understand? *A girl of the night.*" Seb merely blinked. Joel growled and shook him. "It was a bordello, you get it? And she ..." He pushed his younger brother away in despair. "You're too young to understand any of it. Just know that Pa has ... *weaknesses.* And this pretty Adeline is well aware of "em."

"So, what do we do?" Seb rubbed his throat gingerly. "Tell Ma?"

"Ma already knows. No, what we do is make sure *Pa knows* that we know."

Shaking his head, Seb pursed his lips. "That's a lot of knowing, Joel."

A burst of laughter broke through the quiet of the night and Joel sighed loudly. "It sure is, but it's all we can do to avert disaster,"

A handful of nights later, disaster did indeed strike. Raised voices stirred the two boys from their sleep, Joel the first to react, shaking his brother wide-awake. Rubbing his eyes, Sebastian went to speak but Joel's hand clamped itself over his mouth. Twisting his head, he saw his brother's finger pressed against his own lips. The dawn's light was just peeking through the remnants of the night, giving everything a ghostly hue. Seb listened.

His parents were arguing, Pa using profanities in his outrage, as Ma accused him of any manner of lewd acts with the young Adeline.

"It's not what you think, Mollie."

"Isn't it? Then you tell me what it is when you don't share my bedroll at night, and even when Jenny takes up her crying, you are nowhere to be found."

His silence convinced her of what had been happening.

The boys sat up and both looked across to where their parents stood.

As they looked, with the sun's relentless climb above the horizon picking out everything in terrifying clarity, an arrow slammed into Ma's throat. She blundered backwards, clawing at the shaft, mouth working soundlessly, eyes livid with shock.

Pa wheeled around, "Indians!" he screamed. "Get my Winchester!"

Joel was already scrambling out of his bed, throwing away his blanket and grabbing his Navy Colt. He fired into the shadows, not really taking aim, hopeful the shots would scare away their attackers.

In reply, another arrow slammed into Ma's chest, pitching her backwards. She hit the ground with a horrible, hollow thump and lay still.

Joel screamed and raced towards his mother, dropped to his knees, and cradled her head. "Ma," he whispered. She was dead, and the tears rolled down Joel's cheeks and dripped into her lifeless face.

Jenny, who had taken up a dreadful wailing, seized his attention. He stood up, legs shaky, body trembling, and made his way to his tiny sister. A movement caught his eye, a single figure dashing between the rocks that surrounded their camp, and he let off two shots towards it. There came no responding retort, so he continued on his way and bundled Jenny up his arms. Returning to his mother, he paused and looked into Jenny's tiny face, all crumpled up in tears. He kissed her tenderly on the forehead. As he drew his lips away, an arrow plunged into tiny Jenny's head. The crying ceased.

Time froze. Joel, unable to move, his mind locked in a turmoil of grief and disbelief. The infant slipped from his unfeeling grasp and fell, almost as if it had never meant to leave, into the cold embrace of its dead mother. Joel felt rather than heard something looming up close, but no longer cared. Everything was ended.

From his dishevelled bedclothes, Sebastian stared at the grotesque scene playing out before him. He saw her slipping down from the rocks, the hatchet flashing in the cold morning light, the heavy blade smacking into the back of Joel's skull. She whooped with joy as the young man fell to his knees. Lifting his head by the hair, she hacked out a hunk of his scalp and raised it above her, yelping like some incensed coyote.

Pa, lost in whirl of indecision and fear, staggered to where the Winchester lay and loosed off seven quick shots, none of which hit their mark. She crossed the short distance between them, leaping onto him and bowling him over, slicing through his body with hatchet and knife, cutting, dissembling. A wild, chaotic frenzy of killing.

At last, it was over. Seb sat and watched as she came towards him. No longer the happy, laughing girl he believed her to be, Adeline drew back her lips and growled at him, a shrieking, terrifying sound, tongue lolling out, spittle frothing. She was mad, and he knew he was about to die.

Gripping him by the throat, she lifted him to his feet and pressed her face close to his. He could smell her sweet breath as she spoke, so softly, almost soothingly. "Sebastian, unfetter the horses and mules. We're leaving."

Having stripped it of all useable supplies, she broke the axle of the wagon, secured sacks to the mules, and helped Sebastian into the saddle of his dead brother's horse. "You're quite a catch," she said, checking Pa's Winchester and loading it with shells. "They'll reward me well for all of this."

Her face, smeared with blood, broke into a wide grin and Seb, no longer able to hold it all in, turned away and vomited violently, causing his horse to buck and snicker. She caught the reins, soothing the animal with her gentle voice and he looked at her and wondered how anyone so beautiful could be so devilish, so murderous. "I'm going to kill you," he managed to gasp, dragging the back of his hand across his mouth. She laughed and thrust a water canteen into his hand. "I don't know how, or when, but I will."

"In a few months' time, you'll be thanking me for giving you a new life."

"No, never."

She smiled and watched him drink. Taking back the canteen, she brushed his cheek with her hand before leading them all slowly across the prairie and away from that butcher's yard that once was the camp where his family had rested. A family he would never see again.

CHAPTER TWENTY-ONE

1875, the present.

Cole fell back and gazed at the youngster cowering in front of him. During his frontier life he had witnessed many deprivations, experienced the very worst that human beings are capable of doing to one another, but this ... The senseless murder of an infant was beyond anything he could accept. Curling his hand into a bunched fist, he glared towards the boy who sat, lips quivering, staring into the ground. "The girl. Adeline?" The boy looked up. "I think she's in the church, yes?"

He nodded. "She told me she would meet up with her companions here, that it was all planned. She's an Indian and so are they."

"A raiding party. And a damned clever one at that. They duped me, that's for sure."

"Duped you? I don't understand."

Before he could expand further, a great eruption of shouting from outside forced Cole to snap his head around towards the rickety batwing doors. His hands instinctively brought up the Winchester in readiness. "She put you in here?"

"Said I was to keep quiet, that she was gonna sell me when they came. I guess that's them outside."

"I guess so. Wait."

Without another word, Cole crept across to the entrance and peered out through a crack in the woodwork. A clutch of tethered horses was waiting in the narrow street, with one man keeping watch. He caught the rest moving through the broken remains of a building opposite towards the church, no doubt to meet up with the girl. He held his breath and waited until they were out of sight.

The man had his back to him, and Cole eased open the swing doors and slipped outside, drawing his knife. He had to move swiftly and decisively if he had any chance of taking the marauders by surprise.

Cole moved quiet as the mist, but within an arm's reach of the man the wind or something caught the door and slapped it back into its frame. Turning, the man made to shout out and Cole leaped forward, ramming the blade upwards, deep into the other's throat. They both crashed to the ground, Cole holding on, pushing the blade until it burst out through the man's gaping mouth. He writhed and struggled in his death throes as the horses, spooked by the explosion of violence, kicked, and struggled to get themselves free.

"Come on," hissed Cole towards the boy, transfixed, stricken with horror at the sight of the scout, drenched red, standing over the corpse, the blood dripping from the knife.

Without waiting, Cole took hold of the boy's hand and wrenched him from the doorway. He dragged him down the narrow passage to where the girl's horses were waiting. Not pausing for a second, Cole cut through the reins and released the mules. "We have no need of those," he said. "Which is yours?" The boy nodded towards the smaller of the two animals and Cole lifted him into the saddle.

"My Ma's things are in those sacks," the boy wailed.

"We have no time."

"But I can't just leave them. Mister, *please!*"

"What you say your name was?"

"Sebastian. Seb for short."

"Seb," Cole squeezed his thigh, "we'll come back for them, okay? I promise. Now, you ride yourself back across the plains to the far-off rock escarpment. You can't miss it. I'll get my horse and follow you."

"But what if they—"

"Just ride!" Cole drew back his hand ready to slap the horse's rump.

The shot rang out like a crack from the bowels of hell, spewing forth a single bullet of death, which struck young Seb clear between the eyes, pitching him over the horse's back. He lay there dead on the ground, eyes wide open in abject surprise.

Stunned, Cole stood rigid, unable to process what had just happened. A second bullet whizzed past his ear to hit the far wall and galvanised him into action. He whirled around in a half crouch, working the Winchester, firing blind as he launched himself to his left, rolling across the dirt. Coming up on one knee, he saw them in the open, arrogant, assured. Two men, one of them a Comanche, the other swarthy, short in stature, loading his carbine. Cole put his last bullets into them and saw them fall.

Acting swiftly, he slapped all four jittery, wild-eyed beasts on their rumps and sent them charging off in the opposite direction. He watched them go for a moment before he glanced down at the inert form of the boy. A shudder ran through him.

With no further need to check on Seb's condition, Cole swung around the far wall, pressed himself up against the hard granite and fed more cartridges into the Winchester. He had no more. Sucking in his breath, he did his best to clear his mind of what had occurred. Resolute, determined, the red mist descending, he sprinted across to where his horse stood patiently waiting, vaulted into the saddle, and spurred his mount into a gallop.

Pressed low against the horse's neck, aware that the gunshots would have brought the rest of the gang out to investigate, he did his best to keep his eyes front, moving in behind the other stampeding animals. Further security against any venomous shots from behind.

They soon came.

Gunfire, barking out across the plains. Fortunately, the distance was already too great, and the bullets fell hopelessly short of their mark. But Cole was under no illusion. Soon, they would be on his tail, desperate for revenge and, perhaps more telling, needful for seizing hold of the mules again. Hadn't Sebastian told him what was in the sacks, hanging so heavily from the animal's flanks? His mother's things. What could they be, he wondered as his horse drew alongside the others, nostrils flared, bodies heaving? The mules especially were making hard work of it and, seizing the moment, he straightened up and urged his own mount forward to overtake them. He had time, he hoped, to round them up and steer them to higher ground. From there he could root through the sacks and set up a defensive position against his pursuers. *If* he had time.

Working fast, he headed off the fleeing animals and guided them away from their intended direction towards that higher ground which might provide him with sanctuary. They responded, slowing as his voice barked out with confident authority and he managed to herd them into a small gulley. Grasping the bridle of the lead horse, he gently brought it to a halt. The others followed and soon all of them stood, snorting with indignation but nevertheless allowing themselves to succumb to Cole's reassuring cooing sounds. Sufficiently becalmed, they waited as Cole dropped from his saddle and further soothed them with gentle caresses and reassuring mewing. It took up more time than he could spare, but better this than to pursue them endlessly across the open plain.

He first relieved the nearest mule of its burden and laid the sacks over the ground. Opening them, he peered inside and whistled. No wonder the girl called Adeline had taken the time to bring all of this with her after her murderous attack. Along with the boy, she would be able to amass quite a stash.

Candelabra, silver by the looks of it, and wine goblets. Old, possibly gold. A set of dinner bells, made from brass, suspended, when set in situ, upon a branch fashioned from pure gold. A padded hammer, its stem made from black jet, completed the array. The complete collection appeared genuine to his untrained eye, but he knew enough about antiquities to estimate he was gazing upon quite a few thousand dollars' worth of artefacts.

Once he'd tethered the animals again, he gathered the sacks together and placed them in the far reaches of the gulley. Hefting the Winchester, he ascended the nearest craggy wall-face. He could already hear the distant pounding of horses. They were coming, as he knew they would be, and he quickened his climb, determined to reach a point of advantage before they were upon him.

Scrambling towards an overhang, he settled himself and looked out across the open range. He counted several horses, but their exact number was difficult to calculate due to the clouds of obscuring dust enveloping them. So, he waited, positioning himself in such a way to give him a clear line of sight for when the shooting would start.

CHAPTER TWENTY-TWO

Adeline stood over the boy's corpse and swallowed down the sobs threatening to overcome her. This was not how she had wanted it to end. Her quelled tears, however, were not for the loss of life, but for her loss of earnings. The damn scoundrel who had put paid to three lives of Dull Blade's band was now disappearing fast with her hard-fought booty.

"We will bring him back," said Dull Blade, coming up alongside her as three of his men galloped off into the distance, whooping wildly. "And when we do, we will split open his belly and feed his entrails to the buzzards."

"While he still lives."

"While he still lives." He took her by the shoulders and turned her to face him.

She peered into his strong features, the cruel mouth, and those eyes, so clear and bright, which had first enthralled her. "I should have been more careful," she said.

"Yes," he said. "You should."

"I had no idea that anyone else would ever come."

Dull Blade turned askance, focusing on the diminishing group of riders beating their mounts into ever greater speeds. "I knew it. I knew he would come. He is unlike other white men. He does not stop."

"How do you know him?"

He looked at her again. "At the first homestead we came across. He was there, and he killed many of us. Too many. I thought we could outpace him, but he is like a man possessed. He seeks our deaths." His eyes narrowed. "All of us."

"I did not know."

"It is you who brought him here. It is you who did not cover your tracks well enough. It is you who has caused the death of good men."

"But how could I—"

Without warning he struck her hard across the face, a back-handed blow of such strength it sent her reeling backwards. In a sort of drunken daze, she lost her balance and fell to the ground, blood spewing from her nose and mouth. She lay there, propped up on one elbow, glaring at him as he stood, legs apart, his face contorted with rage. In a blur, he whipped out the heavy bladed Bowie knife from which he derived his moniker and took one, menacing step towards her.

Adeline, just as quickly, drew the Colt Peacemaker hidden underneath her coat and eased back the hammer. Despite her hand trembling, at this range she could not miss.

Dull Blade stopped and gaped. Then, astonishingly, he threw back his head and bellowed with laughter. "You pathetic, weak child! You dare to think you have the strength to pull that trigger. You cannot kill me."

"It's clear that's what you're planning for me."

"No, a stripe across your lovely face so that all who gaze upon you will know how weak and stupid you are. Now," he held out his other hand, "give that gun to me, and submit to what must be."

Her gaze shifted to the front of his pants and she realised what he meant. Slowly, she lowered the gun.

"There," he said beaming, puffing out his chest, assured and aroused by his victory, "I knew you could not do it. You adore me."

He took another step and Adeline swung up the Peacemaker and put three quick bullets into him.

CHAPTER TWENTY-THREE

Unable to get a clear shot of the riders, Cole put two well-placed bullets a couple of paces in front of the lead horse. Its knees buckled as the animal attempted to wheel away, sending the warrior on its back through the air. Cole shot him in mid-flight. All around, panic ensued, with horses screaming and riders struggling to pull themselves out of range. It was a mad, suicidal scene, the men incensed with the loss of their compatriots, unable to react quickly or sensibly enough. Cole dropped a second with two shots into the chest, then scrambled down from his perch, eyes locked on the third assailant stumbling in his desperation to escape.

Throwing out his arms in a flapping motion, the horses, already well spooked, broke and ran, leaving nothing but the dust in their wake, and the last rider, scrambling away on his backside, pleading for mercy.

Moving closer, Cole brought the Winchester to bear. Desperately, the terrified warrior fumbled for the six-gun at his belt. Laughing, Cole kicked the revolver from the man's hand, and it sailed harmlessly out of reach. Without a word, he pressed the Winchester's muzzle hard against the blubbering man's forehead.

"Tell them I'm coming," Cole said through gritted teeth. "Tell them all, I'm coming, and I will not stop."

Hardly daring to believe his life might not end at that moment, the man climbed unsteadily to his feet, his wild eyes staring pleadingly towards Cole.

"Do as I say. Tell them all, I'm coming. For the boy, for those families you butchered. Tell them."

Gibbering incoherently, the man, bobbing his head as if it had become detached from his spinal column, swung around, and ran. As he did, he bleated, "*Si, si*, I will tell them *señor*. You are he who comes. I will tell them."

Cole watched him until he was little more than a flurry of dust in that great, unending vastness.

Leaving the other animals tethered together in the shade of the gulley, Cole ambled back to the old, broken town, slowing down to a walk as he came to the outskirts. He dismounted and left his horse some way off, moving silently through the narrow streets towards the church, his Winchester at the ready. On his way, he stepped gingerly over the dead and already bloated bodies of the marauders he'd killed, together with another whom he had not. He studied the ground, saw the dried spots of blood, the signs of a hurried departure and guessed it was the girl.

Approaching the door, he propped the Winchester against the wall and drew his Colt. Using the barrel, he pushed the door open and darted away, remembering all too well what had happened on his last attempt to enter.

This time there were no resounding shots.

He waited, counting his breaths, then plunged inside.

Like a shroud, the dismal darkness draped itself around him. Disorientated, he stumbled forward, bent double, and bashed his knees into the closest pew. He yelped and fell, bundling himself up close to the cold wood of the long, narrow church seat. He cursed and rubbed his knee, then listened.

Nothing.

No sound of movement, or even breathing. The church was empty.

He took his chance and stood up. Shadowy shapes lurked everywhere he looked. More pews, altar, lectern, but no sign of any person. Creeping forward, he stepped up onto the chancel. A crack of light peeked out from under a door at the far end and he went over, opened it, and went inside. A window hung open in the opposite wall of the sacristy and as Cole went to step closer, a single gunshot rang out, causing him to flinch and duck down. The gunshot, however, came from beyond the wall and when he took a quick look outside, he saw the cause.

CHAPTER TWENTY-FOUR

Adeline knew she had to move fast. Three of them had raced off after the stranger, but two more lingered behind the church, believing they expected her to make her escape in the same direction as the stranger. She doubled-back her way around the far side of the church, moving with an easy, fluid gait.

She came up behind them as they were steadily and carefully making their way into the first narrow street adjacent to where she'd left the boy. The boy Dull Blade had so mercilessly killed. Such a waste. She liked the boy, had grown used to his company as they rode across the plains. None of this was his fault and he didn't deserve to end his life in such a manner.

Unaware of her approach, the two remaining marauders went to move further into the street. Without any feelings of guilt, old-fashioned chivalry, or grand notions of morality, she emptied her Colt into them both, flinging them forward to land face down and dead in the ground.

Adeline stood, mind a blank, and stared. Eventually, she stirred herself and went to the bodies, relieving both of their firearms and spare bullets. Squatting beside them, she emptied the cylinder of the Colt and reloaded it quickly. Only then did she look up and, staring down the narrow street to where Seb lay, think about her lack of a horse. All she could hope for now was that the others had killed the stranger and would soon bring everything back to the town.

Her hopes, however, were soon dashed when she heard a singular voice crying out across the open range.

"He is coming!" The voice wailed. *"He is coming!"*

Frowning, Adeline stood up, cocked her head, and listened, trying to calculate the direction of the voice. And who its owner was. Certainly, it was not the stranger. The voice had the unmistakeable twang of the Comanche, despite him shouting in English. So, what was going on?

He came into view, bedraggled, exhausted, stumbling every few steps, like a blind man lost and confused. Quickly, she checked the direction from which he had come and, seeing nothing, strode across, caught him by the shirt front and shook him, scolding him as if he were a child. "Who? Who are you talking about? And where are my things? My horse?" With no answer forthcoming, she shook him even more violently until, close to despair, she pushed him away with such venom that he fell to the ground, cursing her in words she understood all too well. She looked into his terrified eyes and brought out her Peacemaker. Easing back the hammer, she spoke in even, determined tones. "Where is my horse?"

"He told me to come back here and tell you. Tell you all. He is coming." A sudden thought appeared to touch him, and he looked about him, alarmed, mouth quivering. "Where is Dull Blade? He needs to know."

"Seems I'll get no sense out of you ..." She closed one eye, taking an unerring bead on her squirming quarry.

The sound of splintered wood forced her to swing around and she saw him, kicking his way through the rear vestry door. The same one, no doubt, who had forced his way into the church. It was a shame her bullets missed then. She was determined they would not miss this time.

Taking his chance, the desperate warrior made a dash for it, scrambling away from her as fast as he could, swerving left and right as he did so.

Adeline cursed, span around, and shot a bullet into the man's fleeing back. He flew forward, arms spread out, making an audible grunt as he hit the ground.

"Stop right there."

She grinned, recognising his voice. He was the one, the very same interloper from before. Well, he was an idiot then, and he was still an idiot.

Adeline knew she was good with a gun. She'd grown up in camp, after being ripped from her family in a raid over twenty years ago and spent almost every day of her adolescence practising. Her old mentor, Weeping Wounds, taught her so much, but mostly instilled in her a determination to survive. When of age and the bucks came to seek her out, her pride and self-assertiveness gave her the strength to reject them all.

Until Dull Blade.

But Dull Blade had treated her badly, forever pushing her to be as obedient as Weeping Wounds told her to be independent. Succumbing to the Whites, moving into the reservation, nothing had changed. Her life proved just as stifling as it ever was. Even when the chance came for freedom, and Dull Blade led them out, convincing them all in their band that they would need to be callous, move fast, exploit every opportunity they had. Killing was as natural to him as breathing was to everyone else. Adeline, however, had her own ideas. She struck out on her own, came across that family, and took everything they had. Including the boy. Such a sweet boy, but Dull Blade killed him, showing no remorse. Now another was here, another who had taken from her. Her means for a new life. She could not let that stand.

She whirled in a half crouch, the Peacemaker coming up in her fist, ready to fire once more.

CHAPTER TWENTY-FIVE

Smashing through the door, Cole winced again as the shot rang out, and the one he'd sent scurrying away to tell of his coming dropped like a lead wait to the ground. The girl, the gun still smoking in her hand, swung around and he shot her through the arm, sending the handgun tumbling through the air as she screamed and folded to her knees. Bleating and clutching the wound, she looked up at him as he drew closer. He recognised hatred when he saw it, but he doubted he'd ever seen it to such a degree as what he saw right now in her eyes.

"Kill me, you gringo son of a—"

"Don't be so impatient to die," he growled, bringing the Colt Cavalry level with her head. "Why did you do it? A young girl like you. Make me understand."

She gave a smirk. "Make you understand? How could you ever understand? You are a White Man, a coward, and a liar. You understand *nothing.*"

"I want to understand why you killed those people. What did they ever do to you?"

"It was what they *would* do. Coming here, like so many vermin, bringing disease. Like they always have."

"So that's why you killed them? As a form of revenge?"

"Nothing so simple. I killed them to make use of them, for my people."

"Your people? You're White, you half-wit."

"Ah, yes, the insults. What will you call me next? Whore? Renegade? *Murderer?*"

"Well, that last one suits the bill. You murdered them and took that boy. Sebastian. You were going to take him back to your tribe, for payment?"

"My *tribe* is emasculated and sits and dies in the reservation. You know nothing of what you speak."

"I know you're twisted by blind hate. It is you who do not understand. Yes, you've been lied to, betrayed, had everything taken from you, but not all of us wanted that. Those people, they wanted to share this land, not take it."

"And you want me to believe that you might be such a man – an honest White Man, who wishes us to live on our land, the land you have ripped from our fingers?"

"Like I say, there are those amongst us who want peace. Not this. And not what you did to that family. For that you're gonna pay."

"Oh, you will shoot me now, in cold blood? Is that how honourable you are?"

"No. I'm taking you in for trial. That's what I do. I'm not a murderer."

"You would be better killing me right now, because that is what I will do to you, first chance I get."

Cole nodded, believing the truth of her words. Despite his insides chewed up into rage over what she had done, he knew he could never kill her like this. True, he could get away with it. There was no one who would ever dispute his story of killing her as she tried to escape, but he also knew that only a public display of justice would serve the family she had butchered. If there was to be a killing, then it had to be right.

He caught a glimpse of movement on the periphery of his vision, and he turned to see the Indian he'd let free, standing some dozen paces away, a blood trail coursing from his shoulder, and Cole's own Winchester in his hand.

"No," roared Cole, hand coming up, desperate to thwart what he knew would happen. But the Indian was beyond dissuasion. He squeezed the trigger and the bullet smacked straight into Adeline's neck.

Cole dropped to his knees, ripping away his bandana, and pressed it against the pulsing wound as the blood spewed out. She went limp as he held her in his arms, a mere flicker of life dancing in her features.

He heard the Winchester's lever engaging.

"I should kill you," said the Indian through gritted teeth. "But you let me live, and so I shall let *you* live." He lowered the carbine, turning his gaze to the girl. "But her, she is a crazy she-wolf, a killer. Let her bleed out."

"Take her horse and go," said Cole, not believing his own words. He turned once more to Adeline, cradling her in his arms, applying pressure but knowing it was useless.

As he heard the Indian moving away, Adeline's huge, wide eyes bored into his own and for a moment his mind went back, to that day only a year or so ago, when he learned so much about himself.

CHAPTER TWENTY-SIX

He'd met up with Brown Bear not far from the town limits. The Shoshone scout sat on a large boulder, whittling away at an old twig. As Cole drew his horse close, the Indian looked up. "His trail is easy to follow, like he is wanting us to find him."

"You think it's a trap," Cole said, searching the horizon for any sign of Burroughs. A dust cloud, an image, anything.

"Could be. Or maybe he doesn't care."

"Then why escape?"

Brown Bear shrugged. "Mr Roose, he is not too hurt?"

"He'll live, although I couldn't get much sense out of him. Someone bashed him over the head real good, but he'll recover. Afraid I can't say the same for the captain."

"The captain I do not care about so much. He treated us bad. You know that."

"I thought at one point he was in cahoots with Burroughs. I'm still concerned about how the sergeant managed to get away, and Spelling didn't."

"You think Burroughs had help?"

"I'm certain of it."

"But who from?"

Cole cast his eyes back towards the town. "I think we'll find out soon enough."

They both rode across the plain, making good time, the trail as obvious as the sun in the sky. Burroughs, cantering, seemed to be writing directions for them in the earth, but neither scout lessened their horses' gallop. Only when they reached the outskirts of Rickman City did they come to a halt and sat, quiet for a few moments, whilst they took in the lay of the deserted streets.

"The trail is not so clear now," said Brown Bear having dropped down to investigate the land. "Many have travelled here."

"We'll scout around. You take the near end of the main street and I'll move in from the far side. Be careful."

Brown Bear's face split into a wide grin. "I am always that, Mr Cole."

The dilapidated remains of the city were much as Cole remembered from his previous visit and, returning to the barn where he was kept prisoner, reminded him of Parrot. For a moment, he allowed himself a few, fleeting memories to stir around inside his head until, forcing himself back to the task in hand, he continued searching.

There were no signs of Burroughs amongst the fallen roofs and crumbling walls, only the ghosts of what once had been a thriving community haunting every dark, dismal corner. Beds, with covers thrown back, tables set for dinner, others with rotting food clinging to cracked and dusty plates. Clothes neatly packed away, children's toys abandoned and broken.

Meeting up again with Brown Bear, Cole received an exact same description of what the Arapaho scout had also discovered. Blowing out a breath, Cole said, "I think I know where he must be." He pointed towards a distant ridge. The top of a large building could just be made out. They set off.

Moving with a good deal more caution now, they approached the mansion, carbines at the ready. A single horse was tethered outside. Both men stopped, instinctively dropping to one knee. "He's in there," said Brown Bear.

"And his horse is an open invitation to go inside."

"If you do, he will kill you."

"That's his hope, I reckon."

"So, what will you do?"

"Surprise him."

Brown Bear frowned. "Surprise him? How will you do that?"

"By going straight through the front door."

Brown Bear gaped at him. "Are you mad?"

"You got a better plan?"

"As it happens, I have."

As with most substantial buildings in that part of the country, the old Rickman house was made almost entirely from wood. Having not been well maintained over the years, the planking was chipped and warped in places, and tinder dry due to the extreme heat. Putting flint to steel, Brown Bear ignited a clump of dried up rags and set them down along the base of the main door. Pausing only to free the horse and lead it away to safety, the flames soon took hold and within minutes, the door was ablaze.

Ten paces from where Cole waited, a shot rang out from high up on the second story and Brown Bear fell, the heavy calibre slug smashing through his right shoulder blade. The horse bolted and ran off, bucking ferociously in its terror. Brown Bear, moaning loudly, writhed in agony on the ground as the blood pumped out across the back of his shirt.

Moving fast, Cole took hold of him and dragged him away. Another bullet hit the ground, inches from where both men were. Drawing his Colt, Cole loosed off several useless shots in the general direction of the balcony from where he believed the shots originated. His actions did little good as another shot struck Brown Bear in the left calf.

"Leave me," groaned the scout, waving his hand wildly, urging Cole to move out of range.

"I'll not do that, old friend. Never."

"Please. Find some cover and from there you can..." He squeezed his eyes shut as a shudder of pain ran through him.

Looking towards the house, and the flames now leaping up the front, Cole knew Burroughs would have to make a breakout fairly soon. Until he did, however, the chances of being hit by another bullet were high. There was no cover at all in that wide-open area that led to the front entrance and Cole's only chance now was to get on his horse and retreat.

"Don't move, Cole."

His face snapped up. Walking purposefully towards him, handgun in her hand, Julia Rickman emerged from the side of the building. His jaw dropped.

"I followed you all the way up here, but you were so intent on finding him you didn't think to look behind you. It was when you were searching through the town that I came up here. I knew I'd find him."

A sudden roar of falling timber tore his eyes from her. Crashing down onto the ground, red-hot embers exploding across the compacted ground, and Burroughs came through the billowing smoke, shirtsleeves rolled up, trousers filthy with soot and dirt, his eyes shining bright in the mask of his blackened face. The fire, having consumed the door, had petered out, allowing Burroughs to emerge unscathed. He was grinning as he advanced.

"I knew we'd meet up, sooner or later," Burroughs said, swinging the big Sharps towards the scout. "Looks like your friend could do with some caring."

Brown Bear, squirming on the ground, made a pathetic grab for his holstered handgun. Burroughs, cackling with glee, kicked it from the scout's grasp. "I think I'll leave him out here to die. You too, Cole. You've been nothing but a knife in my side since the day you first decided to come after me. Well, that's all ended now. Me and Julia here, we'll be heading down Mexico way, sell them horses, make a tidy bundle. Oh yes, I have them. It's all taken care of. Only knot in that whole, neat little plan was you, taking me in to face trial. But Julia here helped me, held up the captain in the jail, set me free. Surprised?" He laughed again, enjoying his moment. "We had it all figured out from the start."

"It's true, Cole," said Julia, smiling. "My only regret was cracking poor old Roose across the head. I always liked him."

"Then you killed Phelps?"

"No, I did that," said Burroughs. "Enjoyed it, too. Always was a mealy-mouthed good-for-nothing. He wanted a bigger share than I was willing to give. Sure, he helped out with giving me Parrot, but he got greedy. He had to die."

"But you didn't kill Parrot, did you. That was you." He looked at Julia. Her face remained impassive. "What about Nolan? Was he at the jail?"

"No, no, you've got that wrong, Cole. I don't know where Nolan is. No doubt he'll show up. I can kill him then."

"You're a real charmer, ain't you, Burroughs?"

A smile, broad and ugly, was the only reply.

"So, it's true," said Cole, shaking his head. "You, Parrot, Rickman, Phelps, and Spelling were in it together, right from the start ..." He turned his face towards Julia. "Even you?"

"Not at first. After I killed my husband, I made a deal with the good sergeant here." She laughed at Cole's raised eyebrows. "What do you expect? He was never going to share any of the money with me. So ... I made my move."

"And I readily agreed," put in Burroughs.

"Our biggest concern was you, Reuben. We both knew you'd never stop, that you'd keep on coming, so we lured you out here and you came, just as we knew you would, like a little puppy running to his master's call."

Cole calculated the chances of him pulling his Colt, gunning them both down before they managed to shoot him. He knew it was an impossibility, but he also knew he could at least put Burroughs down. That would be worth it. All he'd need was a tiny distraction to give him the edge. He nodded towards Burroughs. "But you told me you hated him for what he'd done. That it was all his fault you'd lost everything."

"Yes, yes I did."

"She never blamed me, Cole," said Burroughs, the Sharps in his hands growing heavy. Cole could see it as Burroughs lowered the big rifle. "When I came to her with the plans, she readily agreed. After the way she'd been treated, how could she not."

"I'd killed them all," she said, shaking her head, growing pale. "I never believed I could make a new start."

"Not until I came to you, my lovely."

"Not until you came to me, that's right." She smiled at the sergeant. "It was like a sign from heaven that everything I'd done was worth it."

"It will be. As soon as we've sold those horses, we can buy ourselves a little ranch, make a comfortable life for ourselves. You and me. Together. Sounds good, eh, Cole?"

"Sounds lovely," Julia said before she turned her head to face him. "Except there isn't going to be a "you and me"."

Burroughs' frown burned so deep Cole thought the sergeant might split open his skull.

She shot him through the head, and he fell without a sound. Swiftly, she turned the gun on Cole before he had a chance to recover from the shock and draw his own Colt.

"Don't look so surprised, Mr Cole. I told you I wanted to see him dead."

"But ..." Cole looked from Burroughs' dead body to her, confusion reigning. "What?"

"See to your friend," she said. "There are plenty of medicines and the like in the outhouse round back." She pointed towards an area behind the Rickman mansion. "As for me, I don't want ever to see this place again." She released a long, lingering sigh. "You gonna take me in? Let me stand trial?"

He climbed to his feet and squeezed thumb and finger into his eyes. "I don't profess to understand what motivated you to do all this, but Burroughs had it coming. You helped him escape so you could kill him with your bare hands." He shook his head, the sadness welling up inside him. "You feel better?"

"I don't think that's the word I'd use, Mr Cole. I can never feel better, but at least I'll have those horses. I'll take 'em and sell 'em, start over. Unless you are thinking of stopping me."

"Not so sure I will, L...."

"Well then."

He nodded once. "Well then."

"I guess I'll be on my way."

CHAPTER TWENTY-SEVEN

1875, the present

Adeline groaned, stirring in his arms. "You're miles away," she said. Blinking, hauling himself back to the present, he looked down into Adeline's face. "You ain't gonna make it."

"No. I know it. Pleased?"

"Some."

"I thought as much," she said and smiled.

He felt her grow heavy in his arms and he knew the end was drawing near. "You shouldn't have done what you did. That family, they deserve justice."

"You're so high and mighty. The way you let that renegade go. He'll tell the whole world about you."

"Maybe so."

"And that family. What sort of justice? Seeing me hang from up there in heaven?"

"Something like that."

"Better than letting me bleed out here in the sun, I'll bet."

He looked up and breathed a sigh, no longer certain what justice was or how it could be delivered. "One thing's for sure, I ain't doing this no more."

"Oh, really? Why not."

Her voice sounded weak, her breathing laboured, something like iron nails rattling in her chest. "I've had a bellyful of it."

"Sad way to end, you holding me whilst I die."

Before he could react, she lunged for his holstered Cavalry. He tried to spring away, catch her hand, divert the bullet, but he was too late. In a blur, she put the muzzle under her chin and blew what remained of her life out the back of her skull.

He buried her in a secluded spot, with the boy alongside. He gave them no marker. The other bodies he left to bleach and bloat in the sun. He cared nothing for them. Perhaps he cared little for Adeline, but perhaps Sebastian had held some feelings for her. At least, that is what Cole wanted to believe as he quietly and slowly rode away with the horses and mules tethered up behind him.

It was a long, lonely ride and during it, he did his very best not to think of anything.

The End

HARD DAYS

Reuben Cole Westerns Book 3

For Janice
and my long-lost friend Norm, who was such a fan
of Westerns. Wherever you are, this one is for you.

CHAPTER ONE

Apaches

They brought them in, four men, bound, heads bowed as they traipsed through the fort gates. Apaches. None turned and reacted to the many derisory comments and sneers from the civilians lining up to watch them. Some of the cavalrymen who formed the prisoner detail laughed. Cole threw a sharp glance at the officer in charge. "Shut your men up, Lieutenant!"

The young man turned away, shame-faced, and barked orders at his men. Disgruntled, the soldiers gradually fell into silence, but their scathing looks continued.

Riding alongside Cole, the young trooper who had gone out into the plains to track down the motley looking Indians, leaned closer. "Mr Cole, I'm not sure we should antagonise any of my fellow-soldiers. If we hint at any sympathy for these here savages, then I'm likely to come up against some bad feelings in the bunkhouse later on."

"Sympathy?" Cole's eyes grew dark. "These boys were ripped from their homes and forced marched across a hundred miles of scrub to a reservation that bears no resemblance to anything they have known. I don't blame 'em for breaking out. But shooting the guards, that was wrong."

"And that's why they'll hang."

"I believe so if it can be proved."

"Which it will be, surely."

"Unless hatred and suspicion get in the way. We have to be certain because if we ain't then there could be trouble. There are still roaming bands of Kiowa and Comanche out there and I hate to think what they might do if we act too hastily. Besides," Cole turned in his saddle and peered at the three Apaches shuffling bare-footed across the ground, "we didn't catch 'em all. There's at least two more out there."

"Including their leader perhaps?"

Grunting, Cole studied the young soldier. "You did well out there, son. I'm impressed. What did you say your name was?"

"Vance," and he gave an involuntary salute. "I haven't long been in uniform, Mr Cole. Still learning on the job, as it were."

"Well, you sure learned a lot these last few days, that's for sure. Next time we're called out to track down anyone, I'll be asking for you."

Red-faced, Vance quickly looked away, but couldn't suppress a grin. "My, that is praise indeed. Thank you, Mr Cole."

"You sound educated, son. I wonder why an educated young man would want to seek out a life in the U.S. Cavalry, especially out here in this godforsaken land."

"Lots of reasons."

"Well, I won't press you none, but I'm grateful that you did, whatever the reasons." He smiled before pulling his horse away, gesturing to the other troopers flanking the captured Apaches. "Move 'em over to the jail boys and make sure they is bound up tight."

"They're not going anywheres," said a rough-looking corporal, laughing.

"Even so, you don't take any chances with boys like this."

As the Indians shuffled by, the lead warrior stopped and looked up towards Cole. "You are the one they call He Who Comes. To be captured by you is an honour." He turned his attention to the other soldiers. "But I tell you this. We shall not submit, and we will bring suffering down upon you." He looked again at Cole. "Even you, He Who Comes."

Remaining tight-lipped, Cole watched as the scrawny looking Apache were pushed and shoved towards the tiny blockhouse prison.

"What did he mean by that?" asked Vance, rubbing his chin, a deathly pallor falling over his face.

"I don't know but go tell that Lieutenant to double the guards tonight, Vance. Just to be on the safe side."

Saluting, Vance eased himself from his saddle, stretched out his back, and crossed the parade ground towards the slowly dispersing crowd of onlookers. After listening to what Vance had to say, the Lieutenant shot a vicious glance towards Cole, who nodded once before turning away, his unease growing.

CHAPTER TWO

Julia

That evening, she made stew and dumplings, piling up Sterling Roose's plate until it was almost overflowing. Cole, sitting opposite his good friend, laughed. "You reckon you can get all that down you, Sterling?"

"I reckon so," said the wiry looking Roose as he attacked the stew with gusto.

"My," said Julia, "seems to me you haven't eaten for some time, Sterling. You need feeding up."

Chuckling between mouthfuls, Roose reached for the nearby plate of bread rolls and tore one in half. "I guess you could say so," he said then dunked the bread into the gravy and slurped it down.

"Sterling's been helping out old Sheriff Perdew down in Paradise," said Cole, his eyes twinkling with mischief.

"Really?" Julia asked and sat back, dabbing at the corner of her mouth with a serviette. "Don't he feed you too well?"

"Usual potatoes and gravy."

"For every meal?"

Roose nodded without looking up. "Every meal."

"Sterling has his heart set on being a law-officer," put in Cole, most of his attention on the piece of meat he was sawing through.

"You're not happy in the Army, Sterling?"

"Some," said Roose. "But it ain't what it used to be."

"Is that right," drawled Cole.

"You know it ain't."

His face came up and for a moment the two friends stared at one another.

"What are you talking about?" Julia, noticing the charged atmosphere looked from one to the other. "Cole? What does he mean?"

Roose got in first. "The southern plains are all but tamed now. Within a year, maybe two at the most, even the Comanche will be in a reservation, but there are rumours of unrest in the north."

"What sort of unrest?"

"Sioux and Cheyenne," said Cole, victorious at last over the meat. He popped a large chunk into his mouth and chewed it down with some effort. "The great tribes of the Plains. They've just about had enough."

"But what has that to do with us down here?"

"Not a lot." Cole's face came up and caught Roose's cold stare. "Maybe."

Shifting uneasily in her chair, Julia's voice broke a little as she said, "You're scaring me."

"No, no," said Roose quickly, reaching out to pat her forearm. "No need to be scared. It might just ... spread, that's all, so we have to be ready."

"Not that it's gonna happen," said Cole, his eyes settling on the way Roose's fingers gripped Julia's arm.

For the rest of the meal they ate in silence, the only sounds ones of cutlery against crockery, satisfied moans and smacking of lips. When finished, Julia gathered up the empty plates and took them into the tiny kitchen before returning with a stone jug. She poured out frothy beer into chipped cups before sitting down and gazing at the two men as they drank.

"So, tell me," she said. "Those Apaches you brought in? They will hang?"

"Almost certainly," said Roose, wiping his mouth and sitting back in his hard-backed chair. Behind him the open fire crackled and spat, the stacked logs giving off an intense, yet comforting heat. "I reckon it's what they call 'an open-and-shut case' due to the survivors who will give testimony."

"I'm surprised such savages will be given a fair hearing."

"That's the law," put in Cole. He took a deep breath. "At least around here."

"That's down to you," said Roose, his voice flat. He gazed into his beer.

"Not only me," said Cole, shifting uncomfortably in his own chair.

Frowning, Julia looked from one to the other. "What does he mean, Reuben? Down to you? Down to you in what way?"

"He won't say so himself," put in Roose quickly, "but dear old Reuben here wrote to President Grant begging him to give his reassurance that Indians would be allowed due process."

"You wrote to the President?" Julia sat back, amazed.

Cole shrugged, "It was nothing," he said in a quiet, embarrassed voice.

"And what did the President say? Did he answer?"

"Not to me directly, but the fort received a communication, suggesting they proceed with caution. Trouble is brewing up north and the Government is anxious it doesn't spread."

"It will," said Roose, draining his cup, "no matter how we deal with incursions and the like down here."

"Incursions? Sterling, this is their land. They've lived here for thousands of years. We just charged right in and took what we wanted."

"Not me," said Roose, his jawline reddening. "I never posted no claim for gold or anything else for that matter."

"I didn't mean you personally, Sterling! You know that wasn't my meaning."

"Even so, gold is a mighty temptation, and them Indians have no use for it so what's the problem?" He produced a small canvas bag and set about rolling himself a cigarette.

"Ooh, just wait a moment," said Julia and jumped up to cross to the small dresser set against the wall next to the door. She came back with a small wooden chest, opened it, and produced two slim, black cheroots. "I got these from the store. Thought you might like one?" She handed it over to Roose who looked at it with wide-eyed relish.

"She ain't nothing but hospitable," said Cole, taking the cheroot Julia offered him and twirling it under his nose. "That smells mighty good, Julia."

"I thought I'd splash out, seeing as you are back safe and sound."

Having lit his cheroot, Roose leaned across and, cupping his hands to protect the match flame from a non-existent breeze, lit up Cole's also. "He does seem to do that with some regularity."

"Well," she reached out and squeezed Cole's arm, "it's good to have you here. There's a world of work to do and those horses could do with a run-out."

"I'll see to that in the morning." He caught her look and chuckled, "All right, *we* will see to it in the morning!"

They all laughed, and Julia seemed a little relieved. "I'll make coffee."

Watching her leave the room, Roose smiled as he puffed on his smoke. "She's beautiful."

"She is."

"And yet ..." He leaned in closer, lowering his voice. "If I may say so, old friend, you don't seem ... too set."

"That's because I'm not."

Roose frowned. "But I thought—"

"It was never my intention to have a relationship, Sterling. Nor hers, I reckon."

"I think you're wrong there, Cole. She's loyal, caring. Even devoted, you could say."

"My only thought was to protect her until such time as she feels able to move on."

"Are you kidding me? You'll never find another like her."

"You could be right, but I could never ask anyone to share my life right now, not the way things are. You know how dangerous it is out there."

"Yeah, but ... If she is willing to take the risk, to be with you, to make sure you don't do anything too stupid, why not allow yourself to—"

He stopped abruptly as the sound of approaching horses from beyond the front door made themselves heard.

Cole quickly pulled out the handgun from its holster hanging on the back of his chair just as Julia came rushing in, face ashen. "What is it?"

"I don't know," said Cole as Roose took down the Henry repeating rifle from the hooks above the door. "Cut the lights."

She did so, moving across to the large oil lamp on top of the dresser first. The one in the centre of their table followed, the only glow remaining was that coming from the kitchen.

The darkness seeped over them and Cole went to the shuttered window adjacent to the door and eased up the wooden bar. He peered into the night.

A voice called out, "Mr Cole? It's me, Hyrum Vance. We've got a problem back at the fort, sir."

Cole let his breath out long and slow. "All right, thanks." He turned away and if it wasn't for the dark, he felt sure he would see Julia wringing her hands, glaring at him.

CHAPTER THREE

Apache Breakout

On the ride back to the fort, Vance outlined what had happened. "Seems like the ones we didn't find came back, climbed the walls and broke into the jail." The wind lashed against them, forcing them to bend low over the necks of their horses. Vance was shouting to make himself heard, but Cole managed to get the gist of the story. Two guards had been knocked down, but not killed, a point not lost on the army scout. Even so, when they came into the parade ground, Captain Fleming was standing waiting, with a face like thunder. He hadn't had time to dress correctly and appeared somewhat comical in long-johns, riding boots and hat. Behind him, sprawled out in front of the jail, two troopers were being tended by a subaltern who cleaned their bleeding heads.

"You took your time," growled Fleming, holding onto Cole's horse as the scout dismounted.

"That's my fault, sir," said Vance quickly, stepping up beside them. "I rode out as fast as I could but got lost."

Fleming silenced him with a glowering look. "I'll settle you later, private. Right now, Cole, we have a situation. Come into my office."

Inside the cramped office, one of Fleming's men had stoked up the pig-stove in the corner and both captain and Cole pressed up close to it, warming their hands. "This is mighty welcome, Captain."

"This is only the onset of winter," said Fleming, "soon it'll feel like death."

"Maybe for those Apache too."

"I want them caught, Cole. All of 'em this time."

"I underestimated 'em," admitted Cole grudgingly. "I never expected the others to come here, least of all to attempt a breakout. They must be desperate."

"So they should be. They know the noose is waiting." Fleming shook his head. "Beats me why they didn't kill the guards. They are already as guilty as sin."

"Maybe they don't see it that way."

Fleming turned, his eyes colder than the night. "I've heard you muttering about savages before, Cole. Seems to me you're a little too soft on 'em."

"No, sir. I do not condone anything they have done; I just feel justice should be served in its proper manner."

"Same as us, you mean? Bull!" He turned away, his shoulders tense as the anger seized him. "I have fought them many times and the only justice they recognise is that delivered by a bullet. So, you get out there and bring 'em back. Dead or alive, I don't care which."

Cole turned to go without a word.

"You should take that other scout with you, to ensure success this time. What's his name, the scrawny one?"

"Sterling Roose, Cap'n. But no, I asked him to stay at my ranch, just in case."

"Just in case of what?"

"They know me. Who knows what they might do once the killin' starts ... which it will, I guess."

"Your heart ain't in this, is it Cole."

"From where I'm standing, I think those boys will try and make it down into Mexico and we'll never see 'em again. But if we start bringing down some wrath of God upon their heads, they may just repay us in kind."

"They killed a guard at the reservation. They must be brought in to face that."

"I wonder if we'd be so desperate to see justice served if the guard had been Kiowa."

Fleming blew out a breath. "Get out of here, Cole, I'm sick of your sanctimonious drivel. And, furthermore, I've decided I'm coming with you."

Cole's eyes widened. "To babysit me, Cap'n?"

"To make sure you do what is required, Cole. You're getting soft."

Stepping out into the night, Cole crossed to where Vance stood next to the horses. The young soldier brought himself stiffly to attention. "Are we setting out straight away, Mr Cole?"

"As soon as the good Captain is ready, yes."

"Oh." Vance looked over to the light burning in Fleming's office window. "I guess that means we'll be taking an entire troop with us. That'll take some time to prepare."

"Seems so, and the longer we delay the farther away those Apache get." He shook his head. "Julia ain't gonna be happy, I know that."

"Mr Cole," said Vance in a grim sounding voice, "ain't none of us gonna be happy."

CHAPTER FOUR

Arrival

I t was in the late autumn of seventy-five, some three months before the Apache breakout, that a young man, tall and lean in the saddle, rode into the town of Paradise with murder on his mind. He tied his horse to the hitching rail outside the Parody Hotel and Saloon, kicked his dusty boots against the entrance steps and pushed his way through the batwing doors just as Sarah Lamprey was coming out. Looking flushed, all full-bosomed black dress and dark purple bonnet with matching parasol, she glared at the man, stopping him in his tracks.

"Afternoon, ma'am," he said, tipping his hat.

Ignoring him, Sarah Lamprey huffed and went into the street, the young man's eyes following her hour-glass figure.

"No point you thinking dark thoughts," said a voice. The young man turned to see a large, lurching man leaning against the swing doors, huge forearms looped over their top. He grinned. "She ain't the courting kind."

"I ain't even—"

"Ah shoot, of course you weren't." Grinning, he stepped back and pulled the doors open, gesturing for the young stranger to enter.

The stranger surveyed the interior, filled with men wrapped up in thick coats, hats and scarves, a brown fug rising from their collective bodies to mingle with the acrid smoke of numerous cigarettes, cigars, and pipes. Their many voices rumbled low, like the steady progress of a distant locomotive.

It wasn't long before he gained the information he required. A gregarious and good looking individual, his blond hair flopped over one of his crystal blue eyes, giving him a boyish look. Smooth chin, full lips and an aquiline nose contributed to his comely features. He knew well enough the effect he had on those to whom he spoke. Captivated, his audience warmed to him and put him in the direction of one or two possibilities.

Riding out to the 'Celestial Ranch' owned by Francis Rancine, a wealthy cattle rancher whose business was flourishing, the young man presented himself to the portly gentleman sat behind a vast table, eyes peering out from under thick, bushy eyes, studying and dissecting the stranger before he spoke. "I am looking for hands," he said, "but you don't look much like a cow-poke, son"

"No sir, I'm more of an odd-job person, mending and fixing and the like."

"Well, we have plenty of that work to do." He shot a glance towards his charge-hand whose scowling face told the young man that this was someone who would take some convincing.

"Please, all I'm asking is a chance. I'll work for free if that's what it will take."

"Seems you is desperate, son," said the big chargehand, his stare never faltering. "Maybe you is runnin' from something ... or someone."

"No, sir, it is not that at all. I just need a new start is all. I lost my ma and pa some six months ago and ... Well, to be honest, there are too many memories back in my hometown. I need to start again, build a new life for myself."

"So, there ain't no lawmen on your trail?"

"No, sir. I swear it, on my dearly departed momma's grave." To give credence to his words, he raised his right hand, "As God is my witness, I do not—"

"All right, son," cut in Rancine, "you don't have to give us any more explanations." He looked at the chargehand again, "Seems like a week's trial wouldn't go amiss here, Hank."

"I guess not," said Hank, sticking his thumbs into his belt, a belt which sported a tied-down Colt Peacemaker. "What did you say your name was, son?"

"Emmanuel Torrance," said the young man, "but most people just call me Manny."

"All righty, *Manny*. You follow me and we'll ride over to the bunkhouse. You can meet up with some of the boys later on."

Deep in thought, he lay on his bunk, arms behind his head, waiting for the sun to set, knowing that soon the cowboys would be returning from a long day out in the fields. With his eyes wide open he stared at the ceiling, the way the knotted tree trunks held up the roof, knowing this was a well-constructed building but that it would burn easily. If the time ever came when he would need to make his escape, burning this place down would be one way to disguise his departure. The cowhands would be so intent on putting out the blaze that he could disappear without fear of anyone pursuing him, at least not for a long time. Not that they'd know where he was going, or why. Hadn't Shapiro told him all would be fine? Didn't he trust Shapiro with his life? Of course, he did and as he lay on his bunk and stared upwards, his mind drifted back to when he met the man who offered him a way out of all his worries.

He stood and watched as they brought Sergeant Burroughs in. As silent as the dead, his eyes never flickered as they pulled him from the saddle, and he caught sight of Torrance standing only two or three paces away. Of course, he was Torrance only to the people of the Rancine ranch. His real name was Nolan, cavalry trooper, one of the soldiers Burroughs used to cover his own treasonable tracks. Stealing and selling Army horses, something he'd been doing for longer than anyone knew. To help, he'd enlisted an eclectic mix of partners – including Julia's husband. They were all dead. Most of them anyway. Except for Sergeant Burroughs who would face the hangman's noose for his efforts.

Except he didn't.

He'd escaped and Nolan, fearing for his life if he were implicated, had disappeared into the vast expanses of the Colorado/Utah territories. There he'd wander into small, half-deserted towns, as anonymous as himself. He changed his name and the veil fell over him, while every night he'd dream of her, Julia Rickman. He did not believe he had ever seen a woman as beautiful as she. Such thoughts made him feel some-what better.

The days seemed endless and pitiless, however, until he met Shapiro and listened to his story before sharing his own of the man who had changed both their lives.

CHAPTER FIVE

Shapiro

It started almost immediately on the day he left home. An easy decision, given that he'd just shot his father in the guts with the old man's Colt Paterson, a gun which he had inherited from his father who had served in the Texas navy in the old days. Now, as Vernon Shapiro lay dying on the cabin floor, his son stepped away, the smoking gun in a hand that shook uncontrollably. He felt a red-hot tear rolling down his face. It was to be the last time he cried.

Ever since he could remember, Paul Shapiro held nothing but fear and hatred for his father. It seemed to him that if he merely breathed at the wrong moment, the big old man would cuff him heavily across the ear. Beatings became something of a ritual whilst his mother watched and wailed but did nothing to halt the violence. Even now, as Vernon moaned, gripping the wound in his stomach, she stood in the door, wringing her hands, saying, "Oh my, Paulie ... Oh my ..."

After the killing, Paul Shapiro rode away without a glance and soon found himself in bad company, robbing stagecoaches together with a bunch of gormless young layabouts whose propensity for violence knew no bounds. The Rangers hunted them down mercilessly and only Paul and his friend Shamus O'Donnell managed to escape into the wild untamed New Mexico territory. That was before the War but, of course, that conflict was to change everything, certainly for everyone who served in it and survived.

For Shapiro, the War proved profitable beyond imaginings. Living on the outskirts of major towns, news filtered through to him slowly and shipments of weapons would always grab his attention and soon the Confederacy were making good use of his talents. He attacked Union Army supply wagons whenever he could, using a growing gang of vicious but resourceful men to help him in his endeavours.

It was during a lull in operations that everything changed for Shapiro. He and his band were resting up in a bordello on the Mexican border, drinking whisky and tequila, the real world far away from their minds or their cares. On the third morning, Wilf Penn stepped out onto the veranda and stretched his limbs, groaning with joy at the feel of the warm sun on his face. A bullet hit him in the head, and he fell like a stone, dead before he even knew what had happened.

As the others flung themselves out of their beds and their lethargy, a fusillade of bullets erupted through the thin, adobe walls, sending up clouds of white powder and shards of broken plaster to spatter against bare arms and bemused faces.

Screaming at his men to keep down, Shapiro, sweat-stained vest the only piece of clothing he wore, rushed out into the daylight, bent double, Colt Navy in his hand, loosing off wild, blind shots as he raced towards his horse. "Get out, boys," he screeched, chancing a look towards the nearby hillside and the black smudged outlines of men kneeling there. At least a dozen, possibly more. Army, some in green vests, and his stomach rolled over at the knowledge of who and what they were.

Sharpshooters. Men well drilled and talented in the use of their chosen weapon, the Sharps breech-loader. They must have been hunting him and his men for weeks. Now, they were here, and it didn't seem to Shapiro that they were about to take any prisoners.

To underline his thoughts, as he struggled to mount his horse, three of his men burst out from the bordello door, guns barking, and the sharp-shooters on the hill took their aim and dropped each of them, several bullets slamming into each torso.

Cursing, Shapiro kicked at his horse and tried to move away. A figure stepped out, barring his way, dressed in frayed hunting shirt and knee-length boots. From under the wide brim of his hat, furious eyes gazed out, locking in on Shapiro as his shouted, "Hold up, boy. It's over."

Gawping, Shapiro threw back his head and laughed before bringing up his Colt in a blur, only to have it shot out of his hand.

"Don't be stupid," said the brown-shirted stranger, stepping up close to grip the reins, his own Navy smoking, "or I'll kill you in your saddle."

With no choice left, Shapiro, clutching at a hand ringing with pain, slid down to the ground and knelt groaning and trying his best to stem the flow of blood from his shattered fingers. "You smashed up my gun hand real good, you miserable bastard."

From nowhere, the stranger's fist cracked into his jaw and sent him reeling backwards. "Don't tempt me to shoot apart the other one, boy."

Shapiro blinked back tears. "I'll learn to shoot with my other hand and I'll kill you dead."

The stranger smiled. "If you live that long."

Closing his yes, Shapiro sucked in his pain and surrendered.

CHAPTER SIX

Nolan's Journal

It is true that without the help of Shapiro I would have ended up at the end of a noose or maybe even a bullet in the back. I'd lost my way, desperate for food and shelter, moving from one rotting gold-mining town to the next. My clothes were tattered, threadbare, and my horse, the only thing apart from my Henry rifle I owned, was suffering as much as I. In the last town I drifted into, the ostler at the saloon stables shook his head, a sad look in his eyes. "She ain't got long, young fella." He stroked her nose, peering into her eyes, and tutted. "Nah, not long at all. She's all broken down." His eyes narrowed as he studied me. "A little like you."

I put a knife in his throat, hid his body in one of the stable stalls and, taking whatever he had, saddled up a new mount and walked it outside. It was then I heard the gunfire.

It seemed the whole main street was alive with desperate men, six-guns barking, horses screaming. Townsfolk were there in numbers, some of them with ancient muzzle loaders, sending hot lead in the direction of a group of swarthy looking individuals bursting out of the tiny bank. The town of Grievance, I was to learn later, was well known for being the home of one of the most secure vaults in the whole territory. Those robbers were there to plunder its contents that much was clear, but for whatever reasons they were making a hard time of it. Two of them were already lying bleeding, maybe even dead, on the boardwalk. A couple more were running, bent double, towards their tethered horses whilst a third stood in the bank doorway, firing at anyone who came into his sights.

It was then I made the decision which was to change my life forever.

Throwing myself into the saddle, I spurred my new horse into the midst of the gunfight, my six gun in my hand, blazing away at the towns-folk and sending them scattering in every direction. They were not gunmen and they gave up their struggle without much trouble. Urging my horse on, I made it to the bank to see the man in the doorway staring at me, his eyes the blackest I have ever seen.

"Come on," cried one of his companions, struggling to keep control of not only the horse he straddled, but a second fiery stead, bucking and plunging as if seized by a fearful fit.

The man in the doorway gave me a look, holstered his gun, and raced into the street. A bank teller appeared behind him, sawn-off shotgun in both hands. He raised to discharge both barrels and I shot him through the chest, hurling him back into the bank. Keeping my own horse under control I watched the black-eyed robber hauling himself into the saddle. Again, the look, accompanied this time by the faintest of smiles. Then, whooping at the top of his voice, he broke into a gallop, his surviving gang close behind.

I followed, without hesitation.

We camped some hours later when we were certain any pursuers had long since given up the chase. The leader, as I learned who black-eyes was, introduced himself as Shapiro, the others as Mel, a young chancer from back east, and Olaf, a huge Norwegian bruiser who took an instant dislike to me. As we sat around the drinking coffee, he glared at me across the makeshift campfire until at last he could hold his patience no longer and burst out, "How come you sprang out of nowhere, puppy-dog, and shot all those people up? Who are you?"

"Steady Ol," said the younger Mel over the rim of his steaming coffee mug, "if it weren't for him, we'd be—"

"We'd be *what*? Dead?"

"More than likely."

"Well maybe that is what we will still be when he slits our throats in the night."

I stared at him. He was a massive hulk of a man, his hands like barn doors, the muscles in his neck fit to burst through his shirt collar. The thick coat he wore only served to accentuate his imposing size. "Why would I do that?" I demanded, not caring for his tone, nor his size. I was not afraid to mix it with anyone, despite having my head broken once or twice in the past.

"To claim the bounty, that's why."

"Are you crazy," cackled Mel, setting his coffee mug down. "He's as much wanted as we are after what he did."

"Perhaps more so."

It was the first time Shapiro had spoken since we found that place. Every head turned towards him. "For killing that bank teller, I am grateful, but I think you did yourself no favours."

"I wasn't looking for any."

"Then why'd you do it," snarled Olaf.

I shrugged, finishing my own coffee. "I'm in something of a fix, as you can see." I ran my hand over my tattered garments. "I ain't had a square meal for over a week and I'm just about run out of options."

"So, that's it?" The Norwegian said sceptically. He grinned, without humour. "You saw throwing in with us as a chance to better your situation? Nah, I don't believe it. You did what you did for what you could get out of it, and I don't like—"

"Olaf," said Shapiro, his voice low and thick with menace, "he saved our skin. Now you either accept that for what it is, or ..."

"Or what? You don't own me, Shapiro. If you ask me, I think you're blind to what this stranger is." He turned to me again, his eyes mere slits, his mouth a thin line. "A bounty hunter."

He went for his gun. It was an ill thought out move, sitting all hunched up, his bulk a hindrance to pulling his gun smoothly from its holster. Even as I made a grab for my gun in response, Shapiro was faster than either of us, and he shot Olaf between the eyes and ended the dispute there and then.

Squealing, Mel stood, hands raised, palms outstretched as he retreated away from the fire. "What in the hell? Shapiro, no. For pity's sake."

Shapiro put two bullets into him and as Mel fell dead to the ground, I sat there, rooted, not knowing if I was to be next. I held my breath as Shapiro turned his wild, black eyes towards me, his gun held rock still. "Drop it," he said.

I let my Colt fall from my trembling fingers and waited for my own end to come.

Instead of a heavy slug throwing me backwards, I saw him put his hand gently over the hammer and disengage it. I felt such a rush of relief I almost swooned. "Honesty," he said, his eyes never leaving mine, "is rare. By the look of you, I would say your story is a truthful one."

"It is, I swear it."

He held up his hand as he slipped his gun back into its holster. "I believe you. Unlike those two dogs," he nodded to the corpses of the others, "who would have slit my throat for a nickel. One of them sneaked out of camp two nights ago, thinking I had not noticed. I know now he went to warn the town about our attempt to rob the bank, get me killed then claim the bounty. If you hadn't stepped in when you did ..." He shook his head sadly. For a long time, he sat staring at the ground, lost in thought. I thought at one point he may have fallen asleep but then, just as I was about to say something, he sprang back into life and raised his head, eyes bright and alive once more. "Now, as we is to ride together, I want you to tell me all about yourself and why you are in such a state."

So, I told him everything, from joining the army to being drafted into Sergeant Burrough's troop. I told him how the order came to find the thieves who had stolen Army horses from farther north and were leading them down to the Mexican border in the hope of selling them. How Reuben Cole, the Army scout, had uncovered the fact that Burroughs was in on it and—

"*Wait,*" hissed Shapiro, sitting bolt upright, a darkness descending his eyes, "Cole, you said?"

"Yes. He is an Army scout, assigned to our troop to aid us in tracking down the horse-thieves." I frowned. "You know him?"

"Oh yes," he snarled before turning his head to spit into the ground. "We have had dealings ..." Once more, he fell into a dark silence. Clearly something had passed between Cole and him, something bad.

Soon we rode away from that killing ground, taking the horses and whatever we needed from the bodies. We crossed the endless open range, never pausing for rest, drinking from our water canteens on the hoof. Shapiro, intent to put as much distance as he could between us and the town of Grievance, seemed like one possessed, and when we finally camped, he told me of his plan.

CHAPTER SEVEN

The Plan

There was nothing but hard, corn biscuits to eat, but they made a feast of it, relishing every mouthful, washing it all down with the last of their coffee.

"There is a bank in the town of Paradise," said Shapiro as he gulped down his final morsel. "It holds money from the railroad company. Every Thursday, armed men come to collect cash to pay the railroad workers' wages. One of my gang, a man called Arkan Lomas, worked as one of the guards. He told me of this. My hope was we could raid the bank on that day, take the money and head for Mexico. Cole put paid to all of that." He held up his hand, rotating it to reveal the livid scar running across the back of the wrist. "He shot my gun out of my hand. I've never known shooting like it."

Pursing his lips, Nolan nodded. "I saw him go up against Burroughs and his men. Ice cold and deadly."

"Yes." Shapiro studied the scar. "I thought I was good with a gun, until I came up against him."

"What happened to Arkan?"

"Dead, along with the rest but I can easily gather together another gang. There are plenty of desperate men to be found throughout the Territories, former gold and silver miners, railroad workers, ex-army. You are not the only one to have fallen on hard times."

"So, your plan is to raid the bank in Paradise?"

"Yes. But it is not the money which drives me, although that will be bait enough for the men I recruit. No, it is Cole I want. And that is where you come in, my friend."

Nolan took a breath. "I don't see what I can do, other than telling you more about his capabilities."

"From what you have told me, you knew the woman, the one who double-crossed Burroughs, the one who escaped?"

"You're well informed, I'll say that."

"I always keep myself one-step ahead. So, you knew her?"

"Miss Julia? Well yes, I knew her, but only slightly."

"She will remember you."

"Maybe, but I don't see how I can—"

"It is simple, my friend. I want you to reacquaint yourself with her, make her your friend, your confidant."

"My what?"

Shapiro sighed. "Make her trust you. Perhaps even love you."

Nolan guffawed, "No way would she do that!"

"Maybe not your lover, but something close. I want her to betray Cole for you."

"Betray him? I don't understand."

"Do you think I have done nothing since I escaped from his clutches? I have sought him out many times, watching, listening, learning. I have even visited his ranch. An easy thing to do as he is hardly ever there. He and the woman, they share that ranch together now."

"So, she *is* his lover?" Shapiro nodded and Nolan appeared downcast, taking on a mournful expression, and shaking his head. "Then there is even less chance for me to wangle my way into her affections."

"No. I think there is every chance. He pays her no mind, leaves her to tend to his horses and land whilst he goes away on his scouting duties. She is alone and lonely." Smiling, he leaned forward, "Trust me on this, my friend. I know women, what they yearn for. You will have no problem in seducing her. You are young, handsome, and kind."

"That's hardly what I'd call myself," scoffed Nolan. "She is a sophisticated yet hard woman. She shot Burroughs without a thought."

"Because he had wronged her."

"Yes."

"As you will convince her Cole has also wronged her. Perhaps in a different way, but the outcome will be the same. Or almost."

"Do you ..." Nolan tipped back his hat and ran a hand through his hair. "Let me get this straight. You want me to convince Miss Julia that Cole is in some way cheating on her, causing her to find some comfort in my advances, then ... Then *what?*"

"Lure him in. I want her to confront him, tell him what has happened between you and her because of the way he has neglected her. He will be devastated, and his guard lowered. Then, at that precise moment, you and the others will hit the bank, and when news reaches him at his ranch, he will respond and prepare to return to town. I will be waiting, and I will kill him. He will be in no condition to defend himself due to his state of mind."

"That's a complicated plan, Shapiro."

"Maybe, but I think it will work. It all hinges on you, my friend. You will get a job at one of the bigger ranches and bide your time until you are able to make yourself known to her."

"How am I supposed to do that?"

"Find a way to make herself beholden to you so she will invite you to work on Cole's ranch. As the time passes, she will grow fond of you, I know it."

"You seem awfully sure of all this. How much time are you talking about?"

"As long as it takes. I have already waited almost years to have my revenge, I can wait a few months longer."

"A few months?"

"It must be natural, not forced. You will bring me reports of how you are progressing."

Nolan wandered a few paces away to stare out across the plains. The ground hard, unforgiving. The year was moving on and soon the weather would change, bringing with it cold and snow. No matter what the season this was a harsh, barren, and friendless land, not one for the weak of spirit.

Shapiro stepped up alongside him and rested a hand on the young man's shoulder. "You'll be well rewarded, my friend."

"It's not that I'm thinking about."

"Oh? What then?"

Nolan turned his face towards his companion. "Julia. What if ... What if the feelings develop into something real?"

"Then your reward will be greater than any monetary gain, my friend!" Shapiro laughed and slapped Nolan hard on the shoulder.

But Nolan did not return the man's laughter. Instead, he closed his eyes and took a huge, shuddering breath.

Shapiro stared at his new companion, his laughter drifting away. At that moment, he knew Cole would not be the only one to die when this plan came to its inevitable conclusion.

CHAPTER EIGHT

Cole

Several months after Nolan's meeting with Shapiro the first flurries of snow fell, dusting the mountains with soft, white powder. From a distance an observer might think it romantic, wistful almost, the sort of view to turn one's mind to ideas of long winter evenings nestled in front of burning log fires, holding one's beloved close. Cole knew it was none of these things. Nature was turning, transforming the land from baked hard to one riddled with deep ruts hidden under the snow where untold perils could throw a horse, twist its ankle. After that, the chances of finding oneself exposed and alone, to suffer and freeze to death multiplied. Winter was the time Cole feared most. Its uncertainties, its unforgiving nature. Blazing sun he could cope with, prepare himself for, have enough water to get him through, but winter ... No, winter was another animal altogether. And it was not one he trusted.

Beside him, Captain Fleming stared up to the mountain peaks and sighed. "You think they would have come this way?"

"Could be," said Cole. He'd picked up the trail two days ago and hadn't lost it since, but their direction troubled him. The mountains in these parts were high and sheer, impossible for horses to traverse. The only way, other than climbing over the top, was through a narrow gorge. Single file. Slow, laborious.

"Could be?" echoed Fleming, unable to keep the impatience and frustration out of his voice. "You're the one who should know, Cole!"

"The trail peters out roundabouts here, Captain. They is clever. They know we is hot on their trail and they ain't about to make chasing 'em easy."

"So, what's your bet on this? They have gone through the gorge?"

Cole ran his eyes over the tracks, easy to see in the snow, but only an expert could decipher their meaning. "There are six of 'em, travelling on foot and light because they have let their horses loose. You send your men through that gorge, you is sealing their doom I can tell you that."

"Is that all – *Six*? Are you out of your mind? I have twenty good men here, Cole. We can outrun them within a few hours, I reckon."

"Then you'd be reckoning wrong if you think you'll have twenty men at the end of this, Captain. My advice ...?" He looked Fleming full in the face, unblinking. "You circumnavigate the mountain, cut them off at the far end."

"Circum-*what?*"

"Go around. You give me four of your best men and we'll cut a path over the top, whilst you and the rest make your—"

"Hold on, Cole." Fleming, shielding his eyes against the sun with the flat on one hand across his brow, looked to the top of the mountains, "You'll climb that thing?"

"That's all we have. If you can block the far end of the gorge, we will then come down upon them from above. They'll give it up then, I guarantee it."

"That sure seems like a lot of hard work ... You can do it?"

"I've done it before."

"I bet you have..." Fleming dropped his hand and shook his head. "Going around will take us more than two days. By that time, they will be gone."

"They will not be expecting us to do what I've laid out. They will hole themselves up ready to ambush you."

"Six against twenty? I doubt it."

"They is Apache, Captain. They ain't like other Injuns."

"You said Comanch are the meanest."

"They is, but when it comes to ambush, no one gets anywhere close to Apache. Trust me on this, Captain. Please."

Deep in thought, Fleming chewed away at his bottom lip, looking from the top to the bottom of the mountain range. It seemed to Cole that the cavalry commander was involved in a desperate dispute with himself. The scout prayed he would find the right solution.

After a long pause, the captain blew out a long breath and shook his head. "Nah, we simply ain't got the time, Cole. They will be long gone. I doubt they will ambush us," he quickly held up his hand before Cole could interject once again, "I respect your undoubted knowledge on this Cole, but common sense, if nothing else, tells me they would not try and shoot down an entire cavalry troop. So, we'll go through while you, and your selected men, scale up over the top to cover us."

"Captain, they will kill the officers and NCOs first. The rest of your men will then hightail it out of there quicker than a little 'un who's upturned a wasps' nest."

"Well that's easily fixed." Grinning at his own brainwave, Fleming quickly peeled off his uniform jacket and stuffed it behind the bedroll looped across the rear of his saddle. Sweeping off his hat, he threw it across to a waiting trooper, who grabbed it, wide-eyed with bewilderment. "Toss me your kepi, trooper." Recovering, the young cavalryman took off his headgear and, not wishing to offend, gently eased his horse over to his commanding officer. Fleming took the kepi, positioned it at an appropriately jaunty angle and, looking smug, nodded towards Cole. "There! I'm now just an ordinary trooper, or at least I'll look that way to any pesky Apache. Don't you think so, Cole?"

Exasperated, Cole decided it was best to look away. Clearly, Captain Fleming was not going to be persuaded of the foolishness of his plan. "I'll start my men up the rock face immediately," said Cole and signalled to the nearby sergeant, who knew exactly what to do. Within a few minutes, Cole had his men assembled in front of him, carbines and water-bottles at the ready. Cole dismounted. "Give us a head start, Cap'n, before you go through."

"I will that, Cole. See you at the other end."

Grunting, Cole motioned for the gathered troopers to begin their steady and careful ascent.

They were only five minutes into the climb when they heard the first gunshot.

. . .

In accompaniment to mounting gunfire, Cole urged his men ever upwards. The climb proved arduous; the cold biting deep. Even so, by the time they made the crest all of them were soaked in sweat. Worming his way to the edge of the rise, Cole squinted down into the gorge. Fleming and his men were there, scurrying behind cover like so many ants. One lay spread-eagled on the ground, clearly dead. Reaching for the eyeglasses at his hip, Cole adjusted the focus ring to get a more detailed view of what was happening down there amongst the hard, unforgiving rocks. As he scanned the area, he could see his prophesy from earlier had come true – the one fallen dead was the poor trooper who had donned Fleming's cap and tunic.

"Ah, darn it," breathed another young trooper slithering up beside him, taking the proffered field glasses and instantly ducking his head down in reaction to a distant gunshot. He put the glasses to his eyes and hissed. "This is bad, Mr Cole."

"Seems that way." The scout rolled over onto his back and signalled for the others to keep low. "We have to try and get into a position where we have the advantage."

The young trooper handed back the glasses. "They look as though they got round the back of the captain. There's two of 'em pinning our boys down, picking them off every time they show themselves."

Scanning the area again, Cole grunted. "There's one is at the front, blocking off any chance of moving forward. They're hemmed in."

"And the others?" asked another trooper from a position some feet away from the edge and well out of sight.

"I can't see 'em," said Cole. Then, he cursed loudly. "The horses! They've circled back to take the horses." He pounded the ground with his fist. "Darn it! They mean to take the cavalry horses and leave Fleming and his men with no means to travel save on foot."

"I'll stop him," said the young trooper quickly. Already he was beginning his descent when Cole grabbed his arm. They exchanged a look. Cole recognised him of course but, as always, he could not remember the youth's name. He'd done well when they had first hunted down this group of Apaches, learning fast. Cole also remembered his easy manner, his intelligence and quick-thinking. If he could choose any of these men to watch his back, it would be this young trooper. He went to speak, but the youth got in there first. "There's no choice, Mr Cole. You know it."

"Yes, I suppose I do." He gave a wry smile and squeezed the trooper's arm harder still. "You take care down there, son. You'll not hear any of 'em when they comes up behind you."

"You know I've held my own against these savages before, Mr Cole. I know what to do."

Acquiescing, Cole nodded and watched the young man scramble back down the way he had come only moments before. He said, to no one in particular, "What's his name again?"

"Vance. Hyrum Vance," said another, then added in a low, heavy sounding voice, "He's eighteen years old."

Cole winced and looked again through his glasses, saying through gritted teeth, "If he saves those horses, I'll request a citation to U.S. Army headquarters in Denver for his bravery."

"No one in our troop has ever had one of those, Mr Cole."

"Well, it's past time that you did. Anyone who comes out here to face Apache has more sand than can be found in Death Valley."

"We don't have no say in any of that. We just follow orders is all."

Straining his neck, Cole stared at the trooper. "And what's your name, son?"

"Crevis. Boys back in the barracks call me Buster. This here is Larry McDonald and Jason Spooney." The other two nodded without uttering a word.

"We all have choices," said Cole, "and the choices start at the top. If governors and senators and the like hadn't been in the pockets of railroad tycoons, we never would have had so much trouble with the natives."

"But they is savages," snapped McDonald. "Whatever their excuses, we can't allow them to do what they do, murdering and burning and the like. No sir, we cannot allow such things."

"McDonald is it?" The trooper nodded. "Son, I reckon we is all savages at heart. What we have done to these people is nothing more than rape and pillage. They is only giving back what we first gave them. I believe that is something your ancestors were well accustomed to when the English ripped out your homeland during the Highland Clearances."

McDonald gaped at the scout. "I'm impressed with your knowledge, sir."

"I'm a scholar of such things and I see the pattern being repeated everywhere I look."

"I bow to your learning, nevertheless, these Apache are unlike anyone else."

"Perhaps in their efficiency, but not their methods." Cole returned to the view below. "As far as I can tell, they have no awareness of us, so we have to get down there and help Vance to take them out. You'll need to move slow and careful, keep your wits about and do not discharge your firearms until I give the signal."

"And if you fall, Mr Cole?"

Cole chuckled, "Then it's every man for himself, but I won't be caring too much about any of that."

"I'm scared," said Spooney, his voice trembling.

"We all is, son," said Cole. He smiled reassuringly. "Just keep your head down and do as I do. All will be fine."

No one spoke. Cole returned the field glasses to their leather case and motioned the men forward. As one, they wormed their way over the crest and began their descent into the gorge.

CHAPTER NINE

Hyrum Vance

Scrambling over the many rocks and boulders, often losing his footing, which caused him to jar his knees painfully, Vance stopped beside a particularly large boulder and slumped down behind it. Tearing off his kepi, he wiped the sweat from his brow with the back of his hand. This was not what he'd joined the army for. They said it was good pay with three square a day, adventurous, riding out across the plain, but with no danger. He never paused to fathom why they were recruiting so fervently, and he put his name at the foot of the paper, lying about his age without a thought. Back home, his sickly mother broke down at the news, clawing at his shirt front, shaking him, begging him not to go. His younger brother, Nathanial, looked on with a gleam in his eye, chest swelled up with pride. "He's gonna ride with the U.S. Cavalry, Ma! Don't take on so." She rounded on her second son and gave him such a slap across the face that the thirteen-year-old fell to his knees and burst into tears, more from shock and indignation than anything else.

Seizing her by the arm, Vance turned her to him, his eyes also full of tears. "Oh Ma, why must you take on so – why must you make me feel so guilty!"

"Guilty? *I'm afraid!*"

Gaping at her, his grip loosened, and she tore herself free. "There's no need to be. There'll be no fighting and I can send money home every month. It's for the best, Ma, it truly is."

She pulled out a square of linen from her sleeve and used it to dab away at her wet face. "No fighting? Old Santiago over at the livery said there are stories coming down from South Dakota that they've discovered gold up there and some of the Indians are making threats. There's talk of war, Hyrum!"

"War? It's not going to come to war, Ma, whatever it is that is happening up there." Towering over her, he rested his hands on her shoulders. From this close, he could see how weary and old she looked. "South Dakota? That is hundreds of miles away. Besides, all those Indians, they will be in reservations soon. The recruiting sergeant told me that there are only the occasional stragglers who break out and cause mischief. It's all perfectly safe."

A bullet slapped against a nearby rock, ricocheting away at a wild angle and Vance, coming out of his reverie with a jolt, flung himself face down into the dirt. Sucking in air, his head pounding with fear, he clung onto his carbine and wondered what to do. His movement towards the boulder had been slow and cautious. He felt sure nobody could have spotted him.

But, of course, these were Apache.

He waited, forcing himself to count slowly to thirty. Somewhere beyond the cover of the large rock, more shots rang out, returning fire from his comrades no doubt. Tensing himself, he rolled over and got to his knees, chancing a quick look over the rim of the boulder.

He spotted the Apache warrior almost immediately. He wore a bright red shirt and black bandana, the flesh of his naked legs burned the colour of leather. Dipping back out of sight, Vance counted again. If he was quick enough, he could shoot the Indian, break cover and find the others. His orders were to gather the horses, but the thought of felling a savage was too great.

He felt rather than heard something behind him. He span around and for a moment caught the flash of bright eyes, a grimace fixed on a chewed-up face burnished by the sun. He groaned as the knife went in deep. The Apache's face was so close, and he was smiling. For a moment, terror seized Vance's body, but he somehow managed to summon the strength to grip his attacker's arm. He held on, gazing into the other's eyes, hypnotised by their intensity, and all he could think about was a warm, swirling sensation, dragging him forever downwards. "Oh, dear Lord," he moaned, the carbine slipping from fingers growing numb. The Apache titled his head, the smile broadening and he slipped a free hand around Vance's neck, cupping his head to gain more leverage as he pushed the knife deeper still.

"Go to your ancestors," said the Apache in a low, soothing voice and he pushed again.

Vance held onto the man's arm, awestruck by his strength, seduced by the curious feelings washing over him, feelings of calmness, surrender. He knew the blood was pumping out of him, in a thick, warm torrent. He thought he should cry out, try and warn the others, but the Apache's reassuring smile made him realise that nothing could save any of them now and the fight left him. The Apache gently lowered him to the ground, the knife still deep, then slowly withdrew it. Vance gazed into the face of his conqueror, thought he saw something else, regret perhaps, and then there was nothing.

CHAPTER TEN

Cole

Gunfire increased the deeper into the gorge Cole and his men went. More of it seemed to be coming from the far end, drawing fire from the troopers. Fleming was waving his hand like someone possessed, his teeth flashing white in a face red with rage. "Cole, the horses!"

Keeping low and close to the side of the gorge down which they had ascended, Cole and his men scurried along, finding whatever cover they could, edging their way ever closer to where they had tethered the horses.

Crevis spotted him first, drawing up to a sudden stop, Cole and the others almost crashing into him. Then Cole saw it too and he lowered his head and silently cursed.

Hyrum Vance lay pressed against a rock, eyes wide open, staring into nothing, his torso soaked through with blood. Beyond him, where the Apaches had once been, there was now nothing but open plain. Another soldier lay face down in the dirt, dead. The horses gone.

"What do we do now?" wailed Spooney, falling to his knees. "Those horses had our canteens and everything. We're gonna die out here!"

"Shut up," snapped McDonald, rounding on his fellow-soldier, taking him by the arms and shaking him as if he were a naughty child. "You quit that, Jason. None of us is gonna die out here, ain't that right, Cole?"

Cole met the young Scot's desperate stare and did his best to sound positive. "I reckon. But we'll need water if we're gonna make it back to the fort. We're two days out, and that's by horseback."

"Oh, dear Lord," said Crevis, crumbling to the ground. "You can multiply that by ten if we're travelling on foot."

"*Ten days?*" yelled Spooney. "Are you out of your mind? How can we walk ten days without water?"

"There's the snow," said McDonald quickly, becoming animated with his idea. "What do you think, Mr Cole? We can survive by drinking the snow."

"Yes," said Cole slowly, "we can, although snow don't give you that much. Enough maybe, to keep us alive. But the nights will be cold, boys. Maybe too cold. It was different when we had the tents. Outside," he looked at the sky, at its uniform blue, "in this, with no cloud cover, we might freeze."

"Jeez, you're just full of laughs, ain't you Cole." Crevis stood up to his full height, confident he was out of range of the remaining Apache at the far end of the gorge. "I say we rush that lone savage, kill him and take whatever he has, then we can—"

"I got a better idea," said Cole, staring down the gorge. "But it's something I need to do on my own."

CHAPTER ELEVEN

Julia

Sometime before his confrontation with the Apaches, Cole had ridden into the town of Feathernest on a very different kind of mission. She had not been so hard to find. Perhaps she meant it that way. Slowing down to a walk, he spotted her straight away sat in a rocking chair looking like a million dollars and he noted how her eyes followed him. He wondered what he should do now. She'd gunned down an escaped criminal after aiding him in his escape, clubbed Sterling to the ground but then balanced the scales when she later saved Cole's life. Seeing her again, bold as could be, stirred him up inside. Already he was formulating reasons for not bringing her in to face justice. He knew he'd have to find a way because watching her dangle from the end of a rope was not something he ever wished to contemplate. So, mind swirling with confusion over finding a solution, he guided his horse to the livery stable.

From where she sat, Julia could not help but smile. He looked as good as he ever did in that saddle, his back straight, his face tanned and hard looking, just the way she remembered. Old Mrs Roman, who had taken her in the day she first rolled up, poured out a glass of lemonade, cleared her throat and fixed Julia a look akin to that of a schoolteacher. "Is that him?"

Julia did her best to suppress a young-girl-like giggle but failed. Feeling the heat move across her jawline and rise to her cheeks, she turned and brushed away a lock of golden hair from her face. "Yes. That's Reuben."

"He looks a fine man," Mrs Roman said, sipping at her drink. Julia regarded her with a keen interest. The older woman smiled. "I remember the day I first laid eyes on my Clancy. Felt my heart swell right up into my throat, I did." Unconsciously, a hand fell to her breast as her eyes grew misty with the memory. "I couldn't speak. Is that how it is with you?"

"Well," she gave another short laugh, "perhaps not quite the same, but yes, I must admit the sight of him so lean and strong ..." She shook her head. "There's a strength within him I have not known in any other man I've met. I feel safe with him."

"And yet you chose to ride away."

"I wasn't sure how he'd react after what happened. I'd spent a lot of my time making plans on how to deal with Burroughs, plotting my revenge. I wasn't sure if Reuben would accept what I did. He's a man of honour."

"Accept what? The Killing of that horrible man, you mean?"

Julia's eyes bulged wide. "How—?"

Mrs Roman gave a tiny shrug and returned her empty glass to the small table beside her. "You were crying out in your sleep first night you stayed here. Rolling around and lashing out like you was in a fight or something. Then, when you shouted, 'Rot in hell' and a few other, much more choice words, I surmised something quite awful had happened."

"Oh my, Mrs Roman, why didn't you *say* something?"

"To be honest, I didn't know what to think." She looked again at the tall stranger, whom Julia had referred to as Reuben, dressed in buckskin and black, calf-length boots, leading his horse to the livery. "The only thing I do not like is that gun of his, the way it is holstered at a slant across his middle. Clancy often told me of gunmen he'd seen who wore their guns like that."

"He's not a gunman," said Julia quickly, "he's a U.S. Army scout."

"So that's how he found you? He tracked you down?"

Julia's grin widened again, showing her even, white teeth. "No. I think it was more likely the telegram I sent him." She leaned over and squeezed Mrs Roman's hand. "I did a lot of thinking, most of it about how he helped me. I decided I wanted security, a period of calm. I believe he could give me that, so I messaged him."

"So, you no longer wish to run away from the killing?"

Another squeeze before Julia returned to her embroidery. "I'll not try and wrap that up into something it is not. I ended that despicable man's life for what he did. I'm not proud of it, but I don't regret it."

"Despite it being a mortal sin?"

Julia sighed, laid down her needle, and was about to say something when she noticed Reuben Cole emerging from the livery stable. She saw him taking off his battered hat and slapping it against his thigh, a tiny cloud of dust springing up. As he replaced it, he caught her eye and smiled.

Without averting her eyes, she continued talking to Mrs Roman. "I understand your point of view, I do. And yes, I could have watched Burroughs swing for what he did, but ..." She shook her head. "I was consumed ... *consumed* by my hatred for him. I planned it, down to the very last moment. I hooked him and drew him in so that his trust of me was total. I wanted him to realise, as he breathed his last, the depth of my betrayal and the enormity of his error."

"In other words, you wanted him to suffer."

"Indeed, I did. But it's not in my nature. I had to steel myself to see it through right to the very end. I am not a murderess, I wanted revenge. Against him, and nobody else. I'm hoping Reuben will see it my way."

"And if he doesn't?"

"Then I'll face the consequences." Her eyes stared hard at the other woman. "I'm ready, Mrs Roman, don't get me wrong. I did a bad thing and if I have to face trial, then so be it." She straightened her back as Cole approached.

She noticed his smile never faltered.

"Mistress Julia," said Cole, doffing his hat. He looked at Mrs Roman and did the same, "Ma'am."

"Good day, Mr Cole," said Mrs Roman. "Julia has been telling me something about you. An Army scout so I understand."

"Indeed, I am, Ma'am."

"And have scouted your way here, to take Julia back."

"That," said Cole with meaning, "is up to her."

Laying down her embroidery, Julia brushed away some imaginary specs of dust from her dress. "I'm willing," she said.

Sighing, Cole put his hands on his hips and smiled. "Then perhaps I could trouble you for a glass of that delicious looking lemonade. It sure is hot out here today."

Returning his smile, Julia went to lift the jug, but Mrs Roman was already there, chuckling to herself. "Seems like justice has been served after all, Julia."

"Indeed so," said Julia, watching Mrs Roman filling up the glass, licking her lips as the sharp tang of fresh lemons hit the back of her throat. She passed the glass across to Cole.

"What's done is done," said Cole, taking the glass and draining it in one. He smacked his lips and stared at the empty glass with satisfaction. "We can't turn back the clock and no point in trying."

"And your report will declare such a thing?"

Cole frowned at Mrs Roman. "Report? What report?" He winked a little impishly. "This isn't an official visit, Ma'am." He smiled and looked at Julia for a long time. "Purely social."

Both women laughed, and Cole held out his hand for another glass of lemonade.

CHAPTER TWELVE
Hold-Up

The spread's small size meant it proved manageable and with Cole away so often this fact was a godsend. Yes, Julia would have preferred more space for their horses and the two barns required urgent fixing, but all in all nothing would be too daunting over the coming months. Even as the winter took hold, the snow from the mountain tops encroaching downwards to nibble at the outer edges of the fields, she felt comfortable and safe.

Sometimes, if he was not on duty, Sterling Roose would ride over from town and keep her company. She liked Sterling and, now that he had completely forgiven her for laying him out cold when she helped Burroughs to escape, they were good friends, sharing stories and laughter over freshly made coffee. She'd feel a tug at her heart when Cole's friend would announce his departure and she'd stand on the porch watching him disappearing into the distance.

She had previously known long periods of solitude when, married to her late husband, business would keep him away, sometimes for weeks at a time. Of course, back then, she did not know what that 'business' was, and she spent her time in quiet pursuits such as reading, embroidery and taking long walks around their vast ranch. So unlike now when, sleeves rolled up, she'd wash and scrub, fix and mend, no two days ever being the same. Sometimes she missed her former life, the peace, the opportunities to contemplate, study the wisdom of ages past through the many books in the library, but most of the time she relished her new life. Except for one thing. The anxiety.

Often, Cole would ride into the ranch late in the mornings to announce orders had been delivered, orders which meant he would have to leave again. In any given month, he would be out scouting at least every other week. Usually it was mundane tracking duties. Sometimes horses broken free from army stables, fences rotten and easily knocked through, sometimes hunting down deserters, of which there were many. But sometimes it was raiders, be they disaffected ex-army or, more worryingly, Indians. She always knew when it was the latter as Cole could never keep anything from his face. The deep lines of concern written in the creases around his eyes spoke volumes and she'd feel the tendrils of fear creeping across her back once again.

It was during one of his many absences that Julia took the flat wagon into town to pick up supplies. She tended to make the journey every three months or so. Although it was not an arduous journey, it was long and, especially with the cold biting so deep, she wished there was some other way to stock up with oats, barley, coffee, beans, and rice. But there wasn't. Unlike her previous life with her husband, there were no servants to help. Cole had made this abundantly clear when he first invited her to his home. "My father has a place," he told her. "It's large, the house well-built and decorated to a high standard, but I'm not my father. We went our separate ways and I chose the army life. It means I'm a man of meagre means. My home is simple, but comfortable, I guess. I rear horses and manage to sell one or two, but there are no other means and I haven't much to offer a woman such as you. I'm not telling you this to dissuade you, Julia, merely to lay everything before you, openly and honestly."

She had smiled at him, knowing the circumstances were not perfect by any means, but they were all she had. For now. Stroking his rough cheek, she said to him, "Reuben, I'm not looking for a knight in shining armour, just someone who will treat me right and who will never lie."

Blushing, he looked away. "Well, I guess that could be me."

He did take her to his father's place. Not to visit, merely to stand on the hill overlooking the spread, gazing at the house with the smoke trailing from the double chimneys, knowing it was occupied.

"Do you never visit him?"

Cole shrugged. "Sometimes. He has his own life and he's made it plain, on more than one occasion, he does not approve of my choices. He made a fortune importing exotic spices and tea from the east. A sailor, he'd risen as mate on one of the great clippers that set out from San Francisco. He made contacts, developed a network and ..." He gave a short laugh and waved his hand over the vistas before them, "This is the result."

"It's very impressive, Reuben. It's a wonder you didn't follow him in his trade."

"I have no interest in it. My life has always been the prairie. Perhaps, when he's gone, I'll move in ... Who knows."

Now, moving down the main track of the small town, she pushed the memories aside as she steered the wagon towards the large merchandise store. Bringing the pony to a halt, she drew back the hand brake. Turning, she gathered her cloth bag containing her money. The street was quiet, the snow well settled on the ground and those people who did shuffle by were huddled deep inside thick coats, scarves, and hats. Heads down, nobody acknowledged her, not that such a thing concerned her too much. Everyone had their own business to attend to, never mind hers.

Stepping down from the wagon, she was about to mount the steps to the store door when the unmistakeable sound of a pistol being cocked brought her to a sudden halt.

A figure, swathed in voluminous black coat, gloves, scarf and hat, emerged out of nowhere. He gestured with the gun in his hand and spoke, voice muffled behind the scarf concealing the bottom part of his face, a face ruby red with cold. "I'll take the bag, miss."

Unable to register much of what was happening, Julia collapsed on the buckboard steps, rigid with fear, all her attention focused on the huge, black pistol aimed directly towards her.

"*Give me the bag NOW!*"

She jumped, somehow finding the strength to move. She glanced around, hoping someone, anyone would come to her aid, but mere phantoms glided by swathed against the cold. It was as if she were alone in a world suddenly turned brutal and uncaring.

"Don't even think about crying out, or I'll shoot you dead."

She looked at him, the menace clear in his grey eyes and she knew he spoke truth. Swallowing down hard, she managed to say, "I have only about twenty bucks."

"That's more than enough for me." He thrust out his hand. "Pass it over."

With little choice, Julia reached for the bag, turning away from her assailant for a brief moment. But in that small flicker of time, it happened.

Yelping, she turned to see another, much younger man in tweed jacket and cord trousers, grappling with the would-be robber, punching him, gripping his gun hand, slamming him to the ground. She watched, hands clamped to her mouth, as the two men wrestled in the snow, rolling over, kicking, punching, and clawing. The young one had his hand wrapped around the other's wrist, twisting the gun away, out of danger, whilst he repeatedly jabbed his other fist into the robber's ribs.

A knee came up, the robber squealed, releasing the hold on his gun and the young man stood up, triumphant, breathing hard, the Colt in his hand now.

"Get up," snarled the younger man. The robber, groaning, got to his feet with some difficulty. He looked up, the scarf having fallen down to reveal a bewildered expression on what was otherwise a handsome, almost angelic face. Without a pause, the younger man landed a full, swinging punch to the other's jaw and dumped him to the ground where he lay, motionless.

The young man turned to her. "Are you all right, ma'am?"

She gazed in disbelief. This close, Julia recognised him at once, so there could be no escaping who he was.

"Oh my ..." was all she could manage to say.

CHAPTER THIRTEEN

Nolan's Journal

I'd struck up something of a friendship with a thin looking fella by the name of Sam Caine. He was pleasant enough, with a mop of blond hair set upon his smooth face which lent him something of a boyish air. I could understand why the ladies seemed drawn to him so much. He'd laugh about that sometimes, winking, "Oh, there's something else too, but you'll have to guess what." He worked hard out on the range and it became something of a ritual for us to ride out to the far-off edges of the spread to spend the morning repairing the fences. Alone, with just the sky and the distant mountains for company, we'd talk about all sorts of things. It was during one such time, as we sat with our backs against a rocky outcrop munching down the corn bread dear old Miss Tomkins from the kitchen made us – I think she had something of a thing for Sam – that he told me why he was there.

"I'd got into bad company," he said, staring into space as if the memories were difficult to recall, "and took to drinking way too much. I went into town one evening. I was working for Chisum on one of his ranches back then. Anyways, we got to gambling and drinking and a fight broke out, as they usually did." Sam picked at a tuft of grass and put it between his teeth. He shook his head, growing angry. "One of our bunch, a man called Entwistle, he gunned down another who was playing and that was that. We skedaddled but the town got up a posse and ..." He pulled out the grass and threw it away in disgust. "I been running ever since."

"But you didn't kill him."

"No, but I was there, and I was drunk. To be honest, I couldn't swear what I did or didn't do. All I remember is when I woke up next morning we was out on the range and the first thing I did was to check my gun. It had six bullets in the cylinder, so ..."

We continued working after our little talk and from that point we were close. Often on a Saturday night we'd go into town and have ourselves a good time, but none of it to excess. Shapiro did not want me to draw attention to myself. But talk of Sam being involved in a shooting, whether deliberately or not, got me to thinking I could use his undoubted experience in a rough and tumble to help me out with Julia.

So, I came up with the idea of holding her up and me, the hero of the hour, coming to her rescue. If Sam wondered what it was all leading to, he never asked. I gave him a hundred dollars to help and that seemed to satisfy him more than anything.

I'd been going over to Cole's ranch too, whenever I found the right moment. Naturally, I had to be careful unless someone saw me and got to asking questions. But, as far as I knew at the time, nobody did see me. I'd lie down on the rise which overlooked the little spread and I'd watch her for most of the day. I would see her coming out to look after the horses or work in the vegetable patch. Occasionally a wiry individual who I knew as Sterling Roose would visit and they'd stay indoors for a long time. I wondered about that. Something told me that the life Julia was leading was not the one she wanted. Cole, so she confided in me, was almost always out on the range, fulfilling his duties with the Army. Her loneliness ate away at her.

It was while returning to the ranch after one of these visits that I was called over by a big cowpuncher by the name of Lawrenson. He was grinning, showing a full set of chipped, blackened teeth as he stood outside the bunkhouse. As I dismounted, he could hardly contain his eagerness to grab me by the arm and march me inside. No one else was around. It was when he closed the door and locked it that I knew something bad was going to happen.

"All righty," he said securing the door, his back to me. "I need you to tell me where it is you go every afternoon." Before I could offer a response, he swung around in a sudden blur and landed a swinging right across my jaw that put me flat on my backside.

With my head swimming I had no time to react as those big, beefy hands were hauling me to my feet.

"Where d'you go?"

His knee came up and slammed straight into my groin. The pain exploded right across my lower body and I thought for one horrible moment I was going to vomit. This was my only thought, my mind in a mess, and I sagged in his strong hands and blubbered. He struck me flat-handed across the face and followed through with another solid punch. My legs went from under me and I hit the floor so hard I heard my teeth rattle.

I don't know for how long I lay there. The pain was blinding, and my face felt like it had been put through as meat grinder. Weird shapes and colours danced in front my eyes but other than that, I couldn't make out anything as I blinked and struggled to focus. As if that wasn't bad enough, as I tried to push myself upright, a huge deluge of fiercely cold water hit my face, stinging me into full consciousness. Spluttering, confused, but alert, I rolled over and sat up.

Big old Lawrenson leant against the far wall, arms folded across his barrel chest, grinning like he'd won the biggest prize of all. "So, I been watching you, boy, and I want to know where you're going. I also want to know why you've got so friendly with that Caine boy. Seems to me *unusual* and I'm thinking you and him have found a nice little place of your own that you can hunker up together real close."

"What?" I blinked, wiped my mouth, and even managed a tiny, scoffing laugh. "Are you out of your mind?"

"No shame in it, boy." He leered. "Happens all the time out here."

"Shame in *what?*" He gave me an exaggerated wink and I felt my stomach heave as I realised the meaning. "No, no, not to me it don't happen. You got it wrong, Lawrenson. *Very* wrong."

"Is that right?"

"Yes, it is." I went to stand up but before I could even get myself half-raised, he was on me again, taking me by the throat and running me across the room like I was a little child in his enormous grip. He smashed me against the far wall, knocking what air was left in my lungs straight out into his face. I wailed, "Please Lawrenson, don't hit me no more."

Laughing now, he put his big, greasy face straight up against me. "Tell me the truth, little boy. Tell me the truth or I'll not stopping hitting you so bad even your own mommy won't recognise me."

"Oh God."

His grip tightened. I grabbed at his massive forearm, but it was useless, his strength was too much. He was going to kill me, that I knew for sure.

His mouth pressed against my ear, "We is a God-fearing community in this ranch. Mr Rancine, he is a forgiving man, but he lives his life by the Good Book and degenerates are not welcome here. I went to him with my concerns and he told me to find out the truth." He pressed himself even closer. "The truth."

"Please, it's not true what you think."

The pressure from his fingers eased a little, allowing me to speak more easily. "You want me to think you and him have not had any ... relations?"

"I ..." I swallowed. I knew there was only one way to get out this alive, one way to give myself an edge. So, I lied. I took a deep breath and said, as feebly as possible, "All right. It's true—"

"I knew it."

But if I was expecting an eruption of anger, I was wrong. Instead, he released his hold around my throat, stepped back half a pace, a curious softness appearing around his eyes. "You and him, you is lovers?"

I nodded, averting my eyes from his. "I'm sorry. I know it's wrong, but out here, like you say, it's difficult, difficult to keep to a natural path."

"Hot dang." He licked his lips, the sight almost causing me to vomit, this time for real. "I just knew it was true. I just knew it."

"Will you tell Mr Rancine? I need this job, Lawrenson, I truly do."

"I won't tell him, no."

"Thank you."

"But only if you do something for me." He leaned closer again, his lips slack, that great tongue lolling out. "I want you to get close to me, the way you do with Caine."

It all happened so quickly then. Even with the burning continuing to spread across my loins, with my head all full of cotton wool, this horrible, disgusting man with his loathsome mind, it all just snapped. My knife was in my hands before I knew what was happening and I thrust it in him with all my strength. Gasping, he looked down at the blade in horror. Taking my chance, I stabbed him again, not once, but several times until he collapsed onto the floor, writhing in agony and disbelief. Blood frothed and gurgled out of his disgusting mouth. I stood and watched him, my hand and arm covered in him and I looked into his fat face and wanted to laugh.

And then he died.

Some moments later, I am not sure how many, I stumbled out into the fresh air. Steadying myself against the bunkhouse exterior wall, I did what I could to settle myself. Yes, I have killed before, but to be that close, to smell him, to witness the life dying in his eyes, nothing could prepare me for the horror of that.

I made sure nobody saw me as I stepped up to Sam Caine. He was in the little workshop next to the livery, fixing up saddles, stirrups, and stuff. He gave me a quick smile as I slouched in beside him.

"You look like you been working hard," he said. "That's a lot of blood. What you been doing, calving?"

"Yes, I have," I lied. "Can I ask you; do you know Lawrenson?"

"Ugh," he gave a little shiver which I hoped meant he was filled with as much disgust at the thought of that lump of lard as I was. I was proved right. "I hate him, always leering at me. I think he's not a ladies' man, if you get my meaning."

"I do. And can I add, just as a little hors d'oeuvre ..." He gave me a puzzled look. "It's French."

"You can speak French?" he shook his head in wonder and returned to unpicking the stitching around the pommel of the saddle he was working on.

"I can speak lots of things. My momma was Creole."

"You're kidding me."

"Oui."

He sniggered. "You're crazy, you know that. So, Lawrenson. What's he done?"

"Nothing. It's what I've done to him."

So, I told him and as I spoke, Caine grew paler and paler until I thought he was going to pass out. I helped him put away his tools, which gave him something to do and hopefully calm him down a little. Together, we then returned to the bunkhouse. I'd already rolled the big cow-punch in a taupe and now we took to working hard and fast. We carried him out to where we left the horses and tied him up across the back of mine. Lawrenson was big and heavy, and it took us a lot of effort but at last we had him secured. We scanned every angle, but nobody was around. The sun, high in the sky, beat down strong, despite winter being here. Most of the cowboys would be out with the herd, so we pretty much had the time to ourselves. At last, when the grizzly work was done, we rode out across the ranch to beyond the far fences. We put Lawrenson in a dried-up riverbed about four or so miles from the main ranch, covering him with big rocks and brush. Nobody would find him unless they were looking.

We stood there, hands on hips, breathing hard. An exchange of looks, but no words. I guessed that was more than Lawrenson deserved.

Later, we sat down at the trestles outside the bunkhouse and did our best to swallow our supper. Nobody spoke to us. Around about fifteen of us were there, heads down, the cook, a Mexican named Felipe, spooning out dollops of gristle and gravy. It looked vile and tasted worse.

"What you gonna do now?" whispered Caine. I checked no one else was close, leaned towards him and I laid out my plan, nice, slow, and quiet. He had to pretend to hold up Julia and I would punch him, not hard. I promised him that. His expression said he didn't believe me. "Maybe you're gonna take the opportunity to dole out all your hatred and anger onto me. Kick me from here to Kingdom Come."

"Don't be silly." I gave him a wink. "You're my only friend."

"Let's hope."

I didn't comment, deciding to return to my meal. It was to be me my last at the ranch because next day we would get ready to meet Julia. I'd been watching her and knew her routine. Tomorrow was her weekly stopover at the merchandise store over in town. It was all worked out and nothing could go wrong. Nothing.

It was when we were preparing for bed that the unlooked-for trouble occurred. The door to the bunkhouse crashed open and in strode Mr Rancine breathing hard, flanked by two of his top trail bosses. All looked mean, clad in long dusters, guns tied down, hats making 'em seem larger than they actually were, which was all part of the act, I guess.

"You boys seen Lawrenson?"

They were six of us in that bunkhouse, including me and Caine, every one of us in varying stages of undress and, as Rancine's eyes roamed over us, his expression turned to one of disgust.

"Speak up," he spat, making the most it by letting his right hand rest on the butt of his ivory handled Colt.

"Ain't seen him since this morning," said a hasty little squirt by the name of Harrowby.

"Nor me," said the others in quick succession.

"Why, Mr Rancine," said Caine and I almost gagged as I tried my utmost not the glare at him, "what's happened?"

"He's gone missing," said Perryman, one of the trail bosses. "You sure you ain't seen him?" He levelled his eyes on me. "Word is you and him were kinda friendly."

"I would not say that, Mr Perryman."

"Then what would you say, boy?" Rancine's eyes narrowed dangerously, and I felt myself drowning under his harsh gaze.

"I'm not his friend," I managed to say.

"Others have seen you and him talking, sometimes real intimate like."

"No sir. Not in any friendly way. Mr Lawrenson never did like me, sir. Always making me do extra duties and things, never allowing me near the steers. He often laughed at me, the way I rode, said I needed lessons."

"So, where is he?"

"Mr Rancine, sir, I honestly do not know. Last I saw him, like Harrowby said, was this morning."

"You sure?"

"I swear it, sir."

"Because others have said they saw him heading this way around noon time. Where were you at noon time?"

"I was over on the far end, sir, like I always am, mending fences, replacing posts."

"Anyone vouch for you?"

"I can, Mr Rancine," said Caine. "We came back around supper time, having worked out there most of the day."

They all stood looking, chewing at their lips, or twitching their fingers around their guns. They seemed to be measuring up everything we'd said, and it took them a long time.

"All right," said Rancine at last and, shooting us a final disgusted look, flounced out with the trail bosses close behind.

We sat there in the semi-darkness, the only light from a small oil-lamp in the corner casting a feeble, sickly light making everything seem creepy and a little unreal.

"We all know he had desires," said Harrowby from his bed. "Unnatural they were."

"I wouldn't know," I said.

"Could be a reason."

"Reason for what?"

"Why he's gone missing."

"I don't get you."

"Oh, you know ... Perhaps he figured you knew how he was, and he decided to cut loose before Mr Rancine confronted him. Mr Rancine, he's all into that old Biblical way of punishments. I reckon if there was real proof about Lawrenson, Mr Rancine would string him up. What do you say to that?"

"I'd say you could be right – but I'd also say I had nothing to do with it. He never spoke to me about such things. Maybe to you, Harrowby as you seem to know an awful lot about it."

He was half off the bed. Even in the semi-darkness I could see him coming at me, fists bunched, "Why you ..."

But I was there first, and punched him hard in the jaw, knocking back onto his bed. He hit the edge with the small of his back and jack-knifed sideways to the floor, squealing. One of the others went to stand up and Caine stopped them dead as he drew his gun. "Just give it up boys," he said in that calm, unsettling way of his. They all did as he bid and when Harrowby struggled to his knees I put a left across his face and that was that.

From that point on we both knew we could no longer stay there, no matter what.

CHAPTER FOURTEEN

Julia

H e helped her into a chair in the little teashop on the corner. She was shaking and he ordered tea.

"Is she all right?" asked the wizened waitress, a white-haired lady of indeterminate age, who fluttered anxiously around them.

"She will be," he said and leaned across to look at her.

Julia brought her eyes up and a fleeting smile crossed her face. Outside, the would-be assailant had already made himself scarce. "We should inform the sheriff," she said in a tired, frightened voice.

"I think I recognised him."

She raised her eyebrows. "Oh? Who is he?"

"One of the cowboys from the Rancine spread. Name of Harrowby."

"Then at least we can get the sheriff to ride on out there, confront him."

"Yeah, we could, but I've left there now. I was working for 'em, and I needed the job, but their methods, well, they ain't that comfortable for a young, ignorant boy like me." He grinned.

"You're not so ignorant, Trooper."

He leaned back, the grin still evident. "So, you remember me, Miss Julia?"

"I sure do." She paused as the tea arrived. The cup rattled against the saucer as the old lady's trembling hand settled it down on the table. Julia smiled. "Thank you." She took a sip before settling her gaze upon the man opposite. "You were there when they arrested Sergeant Burroughs and again later when he escaped."

"My recollection is that it was you who helped him escape."

"Well, I suppose we both have our reasons for why we ran away." She took another drink, replaced the cup, and studied it for some time. "And now you've come back."

"Just in the nick of time!"

"Yes. So it would seem. Does Reuben Cole know you've come back?"

His eyes flickered, betraying something. Fear, nervousness? She couldn't say, but there was something making him feel uncomfortable.

"You needn't worry," she continued, "Cole has much bigger fish to catch. Right now, he's out searching for some escaped Apache."

"Dangerous work."

"Indeed, it is, Mr Nolan."

He sucked in his breath and sat back, arms crossing over his chest. "I don't go by that name no more. It's another part of me I'd rather leave behind."

"Like I say, I wouldn't worry about Cole."

"I'm not. To be honest, it's that other scout I laid out cold who causes me most concern. Roose?"

"Sterling? Sterling is a good man, honest, straight. He is looking to be sheriff of this town, so perhaps he might be someone you need to steer clear of." Finishing her tea with a loud smacking of lips, she studied him, searching for further reaction. "All of what happened back then is pretty much done and dusted, Mr Nolan. We both made mistakes, things we regret. We no longer have to mention it."

"The past you mean?"

She nodded. "I am in your debt for what you did today, so if there is anything I can do in return ..."

She left it there, the invitation, waiting for him to spring. He took his time then slowly, his arms unfolded, shoulders relaxing, and his own smile developed. "To be honest, there is something ..."

"I thought as much."

Slowly, he told her, and she listened and what he offered seemed perfectly fine. The spread required a work hand, someone to put it into good order, look after the horses, fix the old barn's roof, the list was long.

And he could be the one, as long as Cole didn't find out. Or Roose. God help them all if Roose found out!

"All right," Julia said, coming to her decision quickly. "Whatever happened in the past has little bearing on how you helped me today, Mr Nolan. When can you start?"

He came forward, beaming, "What about this afternoon?"

CHAPTER FIFTEEN

The Ranch

With his horse hitched to the rear of the little buggy, Nolan settled himself next to Julia and tried his best to appear relaxed. Inside he was a jumble of nerves, averting his eyes from every questioning glance. It wasn't until they were well clear of the town that he allowed himself a long sigh and took to studying the surrounding countryside.

"I didn't see him," Julia said without turning, her eyes set straight ahead.

"Beg your pardon?"

"The man who attacked me. I half expected to see him still lying in the street. Where d'you think he ran off to?"

"Anywheres, I guess. As far from here as possible."

"How can you be so sure?"

Shrugging his shoulders, Nolan puckered up his mouth before patting the Colt at his hip. "He wouldn't be so stupid as to try anything like that again."

"He didn't strike me as the frightened kind."

"He'll be more than frightened if he dares show his face again, I can guarantee you that."

"I think it would have been best to report it to the sheriff."

He turned and for the smallest of moments, his hand settled on her knee. Before she could react, he withdrew and sighed. "What could the sheriff do? Send out a posse?" He shook his head. "He wouldn't have the time or the inclination, believe you me."

Nothing else passed between them until Julia steered the buggy around the last bend, the vista spreading out before them, Cole's small ranch set in the midst of rolling fields, some enclosed by white fencing. In the distance, mountains formed a natural barrier to whatever it was that lay beyond. The still unchartered Territories, vast, unsettled for the most part, but an area about to be criss-crossed with the railroad, opening up America to the world.

"Roose told of problems in the North," she said, easing the buggy along the gentle incline that was the last leg of the journey to the ranch. "Tribes resisting calls to send them to reservations."

"That's all hokum," said Nolan. "It has nothing to do with reservations."

"Oh? You saying Roose has got it wrong?"

"Mistaken, maybe. Sold the lie."

"Lie? Whose lie?"

"The government's. Gold has been found in the Black Hills, and that is Indian land. The Sioux own it, but more and more prospectors and the like are encroaching in on what those Indians see as sacred. But whites don't care about that, all they care about is the gold."

"You think there's going to be trouble?"

"If the Army decide to go in and protect those same prospectors, then they will clash with the Sioux."

"Perhaps the Army won't decide to do such a thing."

"When it comes to gold, the United States government will want their share."

"You think this may have an impact on us down here?"

"It's so far away I think we can all rest easy, unless, of course, the Comanch and Kiowa copycat. Then there could be trouble."

"And Apache? Cole is tracking Apache right now."

"Apache are different, tending to travel in small groups. And they fight in different ways. Raiding, burning, looting, and ambushing. Lots of that."

A shadow fell over Julia's face, her face drawn, haggard even. Nolan studied her but did not speak. He had to fight hard to keep himself from smiling.

CHAPTER SIXTEEN

Cole

Moving across the jumbled rocks, Cole kept low, creeping forward without a sound. He had circumnavigated the place where the Apache at the far end sat, virtually buried amongst the boulders. From where he now positioned himself, Cole had a perfect line of sight. Bringing up the Henry, he squinted down the length of the barrel. An easy shot. Within a blink, the Apache would be dead, and then they could all return to the fort, licking their wounds and perhaps learning a good deal from their mistakes.

But Cole did not squeeze the trigger. He remained in his position for long, agonising minutes, whilst inside he debated with himself the best thing to do. The Apache was young, wily, no more to blame for the outbreak of violence than anybody else – white settlers included. Perhaps a show of mercy would persuade the Apache to give it up, maybe even disappear into the endless plains, move farther south into Mexico. It was a risk. Not all Apaches were the forgiving kind, but perhaps this one, being so young, might consider Cole's gesture as an opportunity to begin again. Forge a new life. One without violence.

Standing up, Cole edged closer, the Henry held hip high, his body taut like a spring, ready to go into action if the need arose.

Most could not out-fox an Apache, let alone move up behind one without being heard. Cole, unlike other scouts, had honed his skills to a high degree and, in many ways, was more adept at guerrilla tactics than the ones he tracked. A lifetime out on the plains had equipped him with a set of skills which out-classed almost everyone else. Now, standing some ten feet behind the young warrior, he stopped, again brought the Henry up to his eye, and said calmly, "Don't move, boy."

The only reaction from the Apache was a slight lowering of his shoulders, a resignation of defeat. Slowly, he turned his head and his dark eyes met those of Cole. The two stared into one another's souls.

"All I ask is you lay down your rifle and move away. I'll only kill you if you make any sudden moves."

Then something extraordinary happened. The Apache's face broke into a wide grin. "You are He Who Comes. It is an honour to be killed by you."

"But who would know?"

This seemed to cause the young Indian a flash of doubt. His face creased into a frown. He nodded. "My friends are dead?"

"All of 'em."

"And now I too shall join them."

"Only if that is what you is seeking. You have a choice."

"I have? You will spare me?"

"If you go, leave this place, make your way down south. Never come back."

"That is all?"

"That is all."

Considering his options and realising he didn't have any, the young Apache lowered his gaze, settled his rifle on the ground and stood up. "What of your other friends? They would seek my death."

Cole gestured with his own gun. "I'll say that by the time I found you, you had already gone. No one will follow you."

"Why do you do this?"

"Because I'm sick of it. The killing. I've lost count how many men I've put in the ground. It's time for me to turn away ... but if you cross me, I'll add you to my tally."

A slight smile. "I will not cross you, He Who Comes. I will celebrate you to everyone I meet."

"Yeah, well, you just make sure you do that down Mexico way."

. . .

Cole returned to the rest of the troopers, his heart heavy, unsure if his decision had been the right one. The Apache had been indirectly responsible for the deaths of too many, including young Vance. Had justice been served by what Cole had done? He knew it was a gamble. That Apache could continue with his spree of violence and bring havoc and despair to many more. Families. Prospectors. Settlers. Even soldiers. Or, as he truly believed, the Indian would take the opportunity, turn away from the violence, and disappear in a world that was big enough for everyone.

The dead were laid out in two neat rows. Troopers forming one, the Apaches the other. Standing between them was Captain Fleming, hands on hips, forlorn, deep in thought. He barely moved as Cole came up alongside.

"Anything?"

"He'd gone."

A slight turn of the head. "You didn't track him?"

"He's one Apache, on foot. In that vastness of country, he could be anywhere. I could have gone after him, but with no guarantees I would come back."

"He is that good?"

"He's Apache."

Grunting, Fleming returned to studying the bodies. "We've lost too many good men here today, Cole. I should have listened to you."

Cole's eyes settled on Vance's corpse and he could do nothing to keep the trembling from his voice as he spoke, "We've all made mistakes we will live to regret, Cap'n. Let's just pack up and return to the fort."

"There'll be an inquiry."

"And they'll find nothing to bring your command into question, trust me."

"You yourself said I should—"

Cole placed his hand on Fleming's arm. "I think we've already been punished enough, eh?" Their eyes met again and in that moment, something passed between them. A silent admission of mistakes, of the need for forgiveness.

"I'm resigning my command," said the captain, his voice strangely distant, his thoughts elsewhere.

Allowing his hand to slip away from the officer's arm, Cole did not add anything. The captain's words echoed his own feelings. The horror of the recent moments had brought home to them both how violence achieves nothing, except more violence. A vicious circle that had to be broken if this land was to become a place of prosperity and hope.

After the bodies of the soldiers were draped over horses, and those of the Apaches burnt, the survivors made their uneasy way back to the fort, all of them deep in thought, all of them defeated by the loss of comrades and the realisation that nothing had been gained.

CHAPTER SEVENTEEN

Roose

"I'll do what I can," said Sheriff Perdew, standing on the porch, looking out to the street as the townsfolk ambled by. Next to him, Roose quietly smoked a cigarette. "Your record will set you in good stead, Sterling, and I must say I am relieved. Finding law-officers out here is next to impossible and there are plenty of towns that have no one to enforce the law. I think you'll do well, and I shall endorse your application unreservedly."

"I'm obliged, Nathan. I truly am. I haven't come to this decision easily, but I feel it is the right one. I've had a belly-full of riding across the range, hunting down people for endless weeks. My job for the Army is as a scout, but all too often I've needed to shoot my gun. If I'm to do that I'd rather do it for the right reasons. Cole and me, we've both seen too much killing and for no earthly reason. I need to know I'm doing something of service, of good."

"Well, that's mighty high-talking, Sterling. Not sure if this job will supply you with such things, but it is a job that needs doing and doing well. We're lucky in that we do not have robbers and scoundrels infiltrating the lives of the good people here. On the outskirts there have been some, as you know, but this town is a good one. The occasional drunken fight on a Saturday night, maybe a wife on the receiving end of some brute's cowardly fist, minor misdemeanours, pilfering of church funds, confidence tricksters selling worthless deeds to old, confused folk. All the usual, but nothing serious. Dear Lordy, you might even find yourself bored, Sterling."

"Bored is exactly what I'd like, Nathan."

The sheriff pulled in a huge breath, puffing out his chest, holding it, then releasing it long and slow. "Must say my wife will be mighty pleased. She is forever yammering on about me getting to work around the house, fixing the place up and all. I'm thinking my retirement from law-enforcement will not be the gentle ride I hoped it might be."

"Time with loved ones is just about the most important thing of all, Nathan."

"But you don't have any family of your own, do you Sterling? You've never settled down."

"I've never found the right woman." He felt the heat rising from under his collar, because of course he *had* found the right woman. It was simply that she didn't know it yet.

"Maybe being just about the most important man in this town will bring you some wanted attention."

Sterling laughed. It could well be, or not. Either way, if things panned out the way he hoped, he could find himself sharing a life with someone sooner than anyone, including Nathan, would expect.

And Cole too.

An hour or so and two whiskies each later, a somewhat dishevelled and flustered little lady with white hair and tiny, withered hands, barged into the sheriff's office. Spluttering out a barrage of incomprehensible words, Nathan did his best to calm her as Roose looked on, slightly bemused.

"Just you calm yourself, dear lady," said Nathan, throwing a quick wink towards Roose. "Would you like me to get you something? Tea, coffee?"

"Sheriff," she said breathlessly, "I own my own tea shop so I'm not in the habit of drinking other peoples'."

"No, no of course you aren't." He pulled up another chair and leaned into her, "So tell me what all of this a—"

"I witnessed the whole thing. I thought she might come straight over and tell you, so you could apprehend that villain, but I'm not at all sure ... not at all sure ..."

"I'm sorry, if you could just—"

"Don't you ever wash your ears out, Sheriff! I told you! A villain, threatening her with his gun and that other young fella, knocking him down, saving the day. Why don't you know about it?"

"Because you're only just telling me now."

"You mean to say ..." She looked at Roose, bewildered and confused. "I must say I would have thought ... She didn't come to tell you?"

"Who didn't come to tell us what?" asked Roose, as calmly as he could. There was no point in ruffling her up more than she already was."

"Why Miss *Julia* of course."

Roose was off his chair in a blink, stepping over to the old woman, his body tense, knowing this was bound to be bad news. "Miss Julia? What do you mean? What happened?"

"She was in her buggy, having just got down to buy some goods from the merchant store, as she always does on this day. This villain, he must have tried to rob her, but I'm not sure because I only looked out once the commotion began."

"Commotion?"

"Why yes. This young fella, like I say, he helped her. Probably saved her life I shouldn't wonder. He dumped this robber, this *thief* on his back-side, then brought her into my shop to calm her down. Nice looking fella he was, and Miss Julia, well I could see how grateful she was. Took a shine to him I shouldn't wonder."

"Who was he?"

"I have no idea. Young, good, open and honest face, but my, he was like hell on wheels when he put that other one flat out." She looked from one to the other. "Why hasn't she come to report it? And him? The thief, where's he at?"

The sheriff leaned back, shaking his head. "That I'd like to know."

"But Miss Julia, she's safe? Unharmed?"

"She appeared so. Last I saw her she was getting into her buggy with that nice young man beside her."

"Going back to her place?" asked the sheriff.

"That's Cole's place," snapped Roose, straightening up. "And you have no idea where this other fella, the attacker went?"

"No sir. That's what made me come over. He'd gone and I assumed he was in here, in the jail. But I can see he is not."

"So, where is he?" asked Nathan.

"I don't know."

"Seems like you might have some tracking to do, Sterling, despite what you said."

"Yeah, but first I'm gonna check on Julia."

"You think something is wrong?"

"I'm not sure. But I intend to find out."

CHAPTER EIGHTEEN

Julia and Nolan

They were skirting around the spread, Julia pointing out what needed doing and when they returned to the horses in their paddock, they leaned across the top of the fencing and gazed at those fine animals, both lost in thought.

"They are beautiful looking animals," said Nolan, not taking his eyes from the horses as they nickered and played with one another.

"I think Cole sunk most of his savings into buying them. He's thinking of setting up a stud, sell to the Army."

"Profitable that can be," said Nolan. "I know that was what Rancine was hoping to do, amongst other things."

"You don't think you'll go back to him?"

An image of Lawrenson's dead, bloated body sprang to mind, how the boulders slapped off his swollen belly as he lay in that ditch, and he shuddered. "No thank you! My days of working for that miserable old shyster have ended. I'm working for you if you'll have me."

He turned to her and she quickly looked away, cheeks reddening. He returned to the horses and smiled.

"I never know when Cole will be here," she said distantly. "He's forever scouting for the Army, and living here, so alone and isolated, so far from town, I have to admit I get frightened."

"I'm sure you're safe."

"Maybe, but even so, on a cold, crystal clear night I hear the coyotes howling and I wish there was someone with me."

"Well, you have Cole."

"Cole is not the settling down kind. He's been kind to me, I cannot argue about that, but he is not the most *loving* of men, if you get my meaning."

"I think I do." He turned and leaned back against the fence. He stared at the log cabin, a yellow glow seeping from the open door. A place to settle down in that was for sure. "He sounds to me like he's a man who doesn't appreciate what he has."

"You could be right. He often spends time at his father's spread. My, that is one impressive house, but there is something between them, a distance that prevents Cole from moving in. He's a restless spirit. Perhaps that is why he scouts."

"I have heard he is a dangerous man."

"Oh yes, he is that."

"And his partner, what of him?"

"Partner? You mean Sterling?" Nolan nodded, careful not to be too eager. "He comes by every now and then. Sterling is nothing like Cole. He's warm, kind-hearted, always asks how I am, if there is anything he can do to help."

"Perhaps he is a little in love with you?"

That reddening grew deeper. "Mr Nolan, you should not be so personal. Sterling Roose is a gentleman, and he would never—"

"I apologise, Miss Julia," said Nolan quickly, pushing himself off the fence to look at her with deep, sincere eyes, "I have insulted you and that was not my intention. Please forgive me."

"There is nothing untoward between Sterling and myself. Nothing at all."

"No, no, of course not. I did not mean ... Look, let me accompany you home, make sure you are safe and then I shall pay my leave."

"You don't have to. It's just that I'm ... Living out here ..." She stroked away an unruly lock of hair. "It can be so lonesome. Sterling is kind, but he would never ... He and Cole, they go back years."

"Yes, I understand."

"Perhaps when it is time for me to move on ... But that is wishful thinking."

"Is it? You have plans to move on?"

"Cole has made it clear he does not want a relationship. He was only giving me safe haven. His words, not mine."

"I see."

"Do you?"

"You're hoping that when you do finally move on, Sterling will accompany you. Is that it?"

"Perhaps."

They fell into silence until, quite unexpectedly, Julia gave a heavy sigh, linked her arm through Nolan's, and walked him back to the cabin.

"I'll make you supper," she said.

"I'd like that."

He smiled, but the outward one was nowhere near as big as the huge one developing inside.

Sometime later, with the sun just beginning to dip down below the horizon, Nolan set out for the town of Paradise. Things were developing well, now all he had to do was settle his account with Caine. A good friend, Caine had no place with his plans, however. Shapiro would not take kindly to an outsider being au fait with the robbery, so it would all have to be taken care of. This was real heartbreaker for Nolan. He was fond of the young cowhand. They shared the same attractions and their private moments had been some of the fondest Nolan had ever known. Perhaps not quite as fond as the moment he had just shared with Julia, but close enough. However, business was business and the ends needed to be tied off. He rode with a grim resolve, but with a wide grin on his face. Memories of Julia stirred through him and he looked forward to the next time they were together. Telling her some details of the plan proved not so difficult after all. True, he had left out the part where Cole and Roose would die, but she seemed more than amenable to joining him after the robbery. What passed between them after supper, the urgency of it, the unleashing of so much pent-up lust ... Such thoughts lightened his mood and he rode in a sort of daze.

So lost was he in his thoughts that he failed to see the single rider hidden behind an outcrop of large, jagged rocks. It was arguable he would have noticed the rider anyway, for he was a man of great skill and stealth. Nolan rode, and the man watched and when Nolan was well out of sight, the rider turned his horse and headed towards Julia's isolated cabin, his face set hard.

She was just trimming the candles when she heard the footfall on the veranda outside and froze, wondering what to do. It could be anyone, of course, but at this time, so late? As she stood rooted to the spot, pondering, the tension mounted. The bar was across, so whoever it was couldn't burst in. She had time. The Henry was above the door, and the Wells Fargo Cole insisted she keep in the bedside cabinet drawer. Both weapons seemed like an impossible distance away, but she knew she would have to choose one.

Struggling to calm her pounding heart, she told herself it could be Nolan, back to reassure her that what he had told her in the height of passion was not really true. The story that he had sought her out for her own sake, not as some part of his hair-brain plan to murder both Cole and Roose and so ensure that the town was easy pickings for the bank robbery, which was to come. Could that be it? Could it be that Nolan was, as he told her as they lay on their backs in the bed she shared with Cole, a changed man, that she had captivated him, made him want to strike out on a different path?

She jumped in fear at the sound of the impossibly loud knock. Waiting, she held her breath, gazing wide-eyed at the door.

"Julia, are you in there?"

She gaped, hardly daring to believe who had spoken. "Sterling?"

"Oh, thank God, I thought perhaps ... Open the door, would you? I need to know you are unharmed."

With shaking fingers, she swung away the bar and eased open the door, gasping when she saw the wild, frightened face of Sterling Roose.

Without a word, he wrapped himself around her, holding her tight for several long minutes.

"Sterling," she said into the thick material of his coat, "let me go, you're suffocating me."

"Oh God," he said and released her, instantly putting his hands on her shoulders. "I'm sorry, but I was so worried when I found out what had happened."

"What had happened?"

"Back in town. The attack."

Stepping aside, Julia bade Roose to enter, then shut the door behind him, swinging into place the bar. Sweeping back that same unruly lock of hair, she frowned at his concerned look. "Sterling, it's all fine." She strode passed him. "Can I get you some coffee?"

"No, I haven't ... Julia, who was that man, the man I saw leaving just moments before I arrived?"

She felt her spine grow rigid. With her back to him, swilling out the coffee pot, she nevertheless imagined what his face would be like. Accusing. He knew. He'd seen Nolan and now she had a simple choice – to lie or come clean. She turned around. "Oh. He was, *is,* the man who helped me."

"Helped you with what?" He moved closer, "Julia, I thought I recognised him."

"Did you? I don't see how, he's ... Sterling, why don't you sit, and I'll make us some coffee, then we can talk." She gave him her most disarming smile, but it didn't appear to work this time. The Army scout stood ramrod still, studying her. She became acutely aware of her attire: the dishevelled nightdress, her lack of under garments, her wild, unkempt hair, which Nolan raked through with his fingers, urging her to yield. And she had. And Roose could see it, his smarting eyes, flickering with tears, speaking all of his inner thoughts.

"Who was he?"

A shrug before returning to the coffee. "As I told you, the man who helped me. I was attacked. An attempted robbery. He came to my aid, that is all."

He was with her, turning her, his fingers digging into the soft flesh of her biceps. "Sterling, you're *hurting me!*"

"I said I recognised him. I know now who he is."

"So, what if you do?"

"It was Nolan, wasn't it? The scoundrel who laid me out flat in the jail, almost broke my skull. And now you and he ... Oh dear Lord, Julia. What have you done?"

"Don't be so childish," she said, swatting away his hands. The anger welled up, uncontrolled. "All right, yes, it was Nolan! So what? It's not a crime to invite inside the man who has saved your life."

"Saved your life? From what?"

"I told you – I was accosted, threatened. A gunman, demanding I give him all my money and Nolan, he was there, to help me."

"Just like that?"

"What?" She stopped, not able to understand his point, the anger too great, blinding her reason. "What do you mean by that?"

"Convenient he just happened to be there – the man who clubbed me unconscious and allowed you to break Sergeant Burroughs free."

"He did no such thing!"

"And Captain Phelps, what about him? He died and you were the one blamed for it all. But it wasn't you, was it, as Cole and I both suspected. Was it Nolan? That's why he ran isn't it?" His eyes burned. "Tell me – *was it him?*"

"You're insane, Sterling. None of this is true."

"So why did he hightail it out of here? Looked pretty darn guilty to me."

"There was never any evidence – and even if there was, no one can prove anything. Sergeant Burroughs was the guilty one, the one stealing Army horses and selling them to the Mexicans."

"All right, then you explain to me why Nolan suddenly just showed up, straight out of the blue. Explain it."

"How dare you! I don't have to explain anything to you."

"No, and you won't even explain the real reason why he was here tonight." His eyes dropped and roamed over her body. "I can see very clearly what that reason was, Julia. Very clearly."

She struck him across the face with such force he reeled backwards, stunned. "Get out," she screeched. "Get out of my house, you filthy, despicable—"

Clutching his face, Roose forced a laugh, "*Your* house? I wonder what Cole will make of that after he learns about your little tryst!"

"Get out. Get out now!"

Without another word, Roose did so. Even more than the stinging across his face, it was the stinging in his heart that brought the tears to his eyes.

CHAPTER NINETEEN

Nolan

He dismounts some way off and takes a moment to settle himself. It is late, the evening well advanced now, and he is certain no one has seen him trot up to the entrance to the town cemetery. Readjusting his gun belt – although he has no plans to use the Colt holstered at his hip – he ties up the horse at the gate and moves along the narrow path that winds its way to the top. The neat rows of simple crosses with their simple inscriptions reflect the starlit night from their white surfaces and the glare sends a curious shiver through his body. He has never liked cemeteries, and as he walks, he remembers how he stood next to his father's grave, tears rolling down his cheeks as he watched them lower the rough-hewn coffin into that terrible, black hole. He could have sworn he heard the old man shouting, 'Let me out, let me out!' Now, here he is again, not as a mourner this time, more a purveyor. Of death.

Caine steps out from the deepening night and he is rubbing his ribs and looking more than a little angry.

"How you doin'?" Nolan says.

Caine gapes at his friend. "How am I doin'? A little tap, you said, nothing that will hurt, you said. Well, it hurts, and it hurts like sin!"

"I had to make it look realistic. Anything less she would have suspected."

"I reckon you did it because you wanted to."

"Ah, hell, Caine, don't be so—"

"Because you enjoyed it."

"That's just nuts!"

Nolan takes the chance to look around him. The night has, by now, engulfed everything and there is not a soul – living or dead – that is anywhere close. Nevertheless, he cannot shift the feeling that unseen eyes are watching. Eyes from the graves, eyes which are accusing, cursing him. He shivers and Caine notices. "You see, you know it's true."

"It's not that, I just don't like this place is all."

"Then why'd you choose it? Seems to me you don't know what you're doin' lately. Your brain is all scrambled and seeing that beauty in that buggy I can understand why."

Caine steps closer.

"No, no, that, *she* has nothing to do with any of it."

"Don't lie to me! We had a good deal going, you said. She has money, money we could steal then set up for ourselves up in Wyoming. That was what you said."

"And that's what I still mean to happen, Caine. You and me. Just as always."

"Are you sure?"

"Yes, I'm sure." And to underline his sincerity, he places a hand on his friend's shoulder and squeezes it. "You and me."

"All right." He gives a tiny giggle and rubs the side of his face. "You sure can punch when you want to, I'll give you that. I don't ever want to get into a fight with you."

"Then it's good we're still friends."

"Yeah, you're right. I'm sorry."

Nolan lets his hand slip from his friend's shoulder. "I'm the one who should be saying sorry."

"Well, let's just put it down as part of the deception, okay."

"No, I really mean it. I'm sorry. You were always so good to me."

A slight tensing of Caine's shoulders, a sign of his confusion. "Eh? What do you mean?"

Nolan half turns, swinging his body in a sharp arc, the knife in his hand slicing into Caine's body, thrusting upwards, under the rib cage, through vital organs, piercing the lungs. The power of the blow is enormous, and he grunts with the force of it, but it is Caine who makes most of the noise. A sharp, high-pitched squeal, whether through pain or surprise Nolan cannot tell. He plunges the knife farther still and they both topple over the nearest cross and land with a solid thump to the ground.

Caine's eyes flash bright in the darkness and Nolan sees the anguish there, the sadness. Betrayed. Murdered by the only man he has ever loved. Nolan sees it and he holds the blade deep, deeper and deeper still, the point rupturing the heart and he sees the brightness blink into nothingness.

He stands and he looks.

And then he weeps.

CHAPTER TWENTY

In the Night

Unlike the sound of Sterling's insistent pounding, this knocking is quiet, tentative and she has the time to take the Henry from its place and engage the lever. "Who is it?"

"It's me."

His voice is strained, almost as if he is in pain and she almost throws the rifle aside in her desperation to open the door to him and take her in his arms. She sees him, the light from the nearby oil lamp casting him in an unearthly shade of sickly yellow. But it is not this which grips her attention, unwilling to let go. It is the blood. He is awash with it and his face is as pale as a corpse.

"Oh, my dear Lord," she cries and would hold him if it wasn't for the fear of being covered in all that gore herself. She takes his hand and draws him in. He shuffles forward, like one in a trance, and she guides him to the table where he sits and stares.

Stooping down beside him, she grips his hand and peers into his lost, vacant eyes. "What has happened? Was it Sterling? Oh, dear God, don't tell me he followed you and—"

Shaking his head, he turns to her and although his eyes remain lifeless, he manages a thin smile. "Roose? No, although he will be after me now. No, it was the man who attacked you."

"But you said he would be arrested, that he would—"

He presses a finger over her mouth, a finger filthy with dried, black blood. "Ssshh, my darling. No. He must have escaped because as I rode to Rancine's, he waylaid me. We fought and I ..." He looks away and his body convulses. "It was *horrible,* Julia. Like something out of a nightmare. The way he screamed and ran at me."

"What did you do?"

Another convulsion and he held himself, wrapping his arms around his own body as it shook. "He was strong, full of rage. We fell to the ground and we twisted and rolled. His knife, big, heavy, like a sword, but I managed ... I don't know how, but somehow, I ... It went into him, so frightening the way the blade slid inside him, with no resistance."

Regardless of the blood, Julia slowly lowers her head onto his lap and one of his hands massages her scalp. "Oh, my love ... They will come for me now. No matter why it happened, no matter it was my life or his, they will come for me and Roose will lead the hunt because he wants me dead. For what happened this day, and for what I did to him. His revenge."

Lifting her eyes to his, she knows it is the truth. Sterling would never forgive. It was not in him to make such a gesture, to let the past go. He would track Nolan down and string him from the nearest tree. She has no doubts.

"What can we do?"

His face grows taut, eyes staring to something very far away, and he shivers more violently than ever. "I haven't been honest with you, my love. And I need to be. This night, and what has happened, if there is any good to come out of it, then it is my confession to you."

"Confession? I don't under ... What is it you need to tell me? You have already told me so much."

"I need a drink first. Whisky. Have you any?"

Without a moment's hesitation, she goes to where Cole keeps his bottle. She pours a generous measure into a misted glass and brings it back to the table. Nolan is sitting bolt-upright in his chair, his hands flat on the tabletop, and his eyes stare into the distance. As soon as he sees the Bourbon, he seizes it and throws it down his throat, gasping as he winces. Immediately, he holds out his hand with the glass, gesturing for another and she goes back and fetches the bottle. With her eyes never leaving his face, she takes a chair and sits next to him. The second drink he takes much more slowly and, between sips, he tells her.

"I did tell you some things, but I am not sure how clear it all was. I returned here to trap you, Julia. To trap you into taking me in, but I needed a reason. The reason was Caine. We set it all up, the attempted robbery, my being there to help you. I was then to come back here and take all of your money." He pauses and looks at the way her eyes fill up and something stabs at his heart. "But as soon as I saw you, I knew I could never, ever do anything to harm you. I knew it when I first saw you all that time ago, but of course I buried it, not wanting to believe it. The very moment I saw your face again, all thoughts of swindling you, they disappeared, because in that moment I knew I loved you."

Shaking her head, a tear slips down her cheeks, and her lip trembles. "Oh ... Oh my..."

"And I know you feel the same. Tell me you feel the same."

More than her lips trembles now and he reaches out to hold her hand. She does not pull away because she knows it is true. She has wanted this for so long. A man to love her, not use her. Yet, all of this has happened so fast. Can she be sure, can she allow herself to believe that someone could come into her life the way he did and give her all that she craved? His deceit, his plan to take from her? How about that. If he could do such a thing, then what else could he do? These thoughts, and so many more, skirmish across her mind, but the need for him blows away all her doubts, together with her common sense. "Yes," she says quietly, and he leans into her and his lips brush against her. "Yes, I do."

She watches him ride away knowing he has things to do, knowing that as soon as the daylight returns, they will find Caine's body and Sterling will add everything up. Time is against them, but she trusts Nolan enough to let him go and make his peace with Rancine. This is what he has told her, and she agrees. There is no point in having more than those two scouts hunting them down, for she knows Cole will join with his friend. So, if they can work it right, Nolan will return with money and fresh horses and they will ride south, into Mexico, and their new life will begin.

She leans her head against the door jamb and smiles. He is all she has ever wanted. Yes, he has killed, but what choice did he have? His honesty and his loyalty make her breathless. Life has been so very cruel, but now she has the chance to put it all behind her. Cole never offered her anything except a roof above her head. Yes, she is grateful, but her needs are so much more than four walls could ever provide. Nolan has given her a glimpse of what life can truly hold and she is determined not to let it slip from her grasp. As she turns away to start packing up her few belongings, her heart is pounding, no with regret, but with excitement and contentment. She might even allow herself to think she is on the verge of happiness.

Sleep does not come. She is overly excited with the prospect of starting a new life. So, she makes coffee and sits on the porch, despite the cold, and tries to work things through in her mind.

Any solutions or answers, or any clearing of doubt, do not come easily. She rocks gently in the rocking chair, both hands wrapped around the coffee cup. The wind is getting up and with it comes the cold. A glance skywards and the whiteness of the sky brings the knowledge that snow will soon be falling. At this time of year that could be the precursor to a blizzard and travelling in such is not something she relishes.

But they will have to go.

She cannot stay here any longer. Roose, his manner was so ... *unusual.* Where had the mild-mannered, softly spoken man she had always known disappeared to?

What was it he said which has caused her mind to twist and turn ... Ah yes, something about Nolan turning up 'out of the blue'? She has to admit, here in the quiet with no distractions to befuddle her still further, it was strange the way Nolan seemed to appear just at the right moment. And the story about him running away after what had happened at the jail. He helped her to set Sergeant Burroughs free, but in so doing laid Sterling flat. The sudden, unexpected violence of it shocked her then, and now, with the way Nolan had pummelled her attacker ... although she is grateful, it all seemed too neat, too contrived. As she rode away with Burroughs, her memory of that dreadful moment grows clearer. Captain Phelps, hands above his head, Nolan's gun pointed directly at him. She did not hear a shot as she made good her escape, but she did learn later that Phelps was dead, that everyone believed it was either her or Burroughs who had killed the captain. Could it have been Nolan? Was he capable? Of course he was! His original plan was, as he said, to rob her.

Might he still carry that through? Surely, his confession meant he was honest, that he had had a change of mind. He loved her. Didn't he?

Confused, but also resolute, she decides to go into town, settle her bill at the merchandise store, perhaps speak to the little old lady at the teahouse, thank her, reassure her. Then, returning here, she will leave Cole a note and that will be that. Setting aside her worries, her concerns, her mind is made up at last. She drains her coffee, gives the sky one last glance, and goes back inside to make herself ready.

CHAPTER TWENTY-ONE

Cole

They cross the expanse of the plains in silence, travelling through the night, their thoughts blacker than the darkness. Cole, at the head of the ragged line of broken, defeated horse-soldiers, concentrates on the way his horse's hooves blow up tiny dust devils with each step. In the night, the land appeared white, the recent snowfalls making no noticeable change to the uniform greyness of the earth. Sustained downpours of either snow or rain would need to fall for months for any green to reappear. Perhaps it might happen, but not this night. The wind, a mere ghost of what could be, barely ruffled the mane of his horse. Above him, the sky is cloudless, the stars twinkling as if they too mocked him. He should never have come on this journey. He should have refused the order and gone back to his ranch, to Julia, and made some effort. If effort he could gather. No matter how hard he tries, nothing stirred within him when it comes to her. A vibrant, attractive woman and yet there is something, something he cannot fathom. He knows Sterling feels an attraction. No fool, this knowledge brings little concern, nor the tiniest spark of jealousy. This fact alone makes him realise that Julia is not going to find a place in his heart. Is it her former deeds, her readiness to kill? Could he even trust her? Would there come a dark night, such as this, when she will plunge the knife deep into his heart?

Stirring as a horse sidles up next to his own, even in the night light, Cole catches the captain's haunted look. "I guess we should camp soon, even if only for a few hours."

"If that's what your orders is," says Cole.

"Yes. I suppose so."

"It can only be for a few hours, though. Our cargo is going to be a little ripe if we delay our return."

"Dear God, you're all heart, ain't you."

Cole stiffens and for a moment he is about to remind the captain that if it weren't for his inept handling in the way he went about bringing the Apaches in, none of this would have happened. A good many more wives and mothers would not be crying into their breakfasts for the next hundred days or so. But he doesn't say such things, her lets it go, allows his shoulders to relax, grunts and wheels his horse away to help set up camp.

He sleeps, but it is unsettled and as the first streaks of dawn cross the endless sky, he sits up and stretches out his back. He feels like a million ants have walked across his eyes and he rubs them vigorously with his fists. If only they had found a place close to water and camped by a stream. He needs a wash. Badly. Instead, he decides on using his canteen, calculating they will all be back at the fort before the thirst really kicks in. But even as he starts to soak his neckerchief with water, he senses something isn't right and when the trooper out on picket duty comes rushing into camp, everything is confirmed.

"You better come and see this, Cole. Quick."

Strapping on his gun belt, he follows the quivering soldier across the broken scrub, wondering what awaits but knowing, from sheer instinct, it is going to be bad.

It's worse than bad. It's just about the worst it can get, and Cole sinks down onto a nearby rock and gazes in disbelief at the sight before him.

"What are we going to do?" wails the young trooper.

"You hold his legs and I'll cut him down."

Captain Fleming swings from the sturdy branch of one of the few large trees growing in that otherwise barren place. Perhaps that was why he chose this area to camp? Who could tell? Certainly, the captain would not be telling anybody about it. He is dead and Cole wonders what he will write in his report about this disastrous of all expeditions. The truth simply will not cut it.

CHAPTER TWENTY-TWO

At Shapiro's Hideout

R iding without stopping, Nolan makes good time, taking a direct route because he assumes, rightly as it turns out, that no one knows the position of Shapiro's hideout.

At the entrance to the deserted gold mine, a swarthy, big-bellied man stands chewing on a cheroot. The Winchester he carries is looped over one forearm and his eyes flicker left and right, forever watchful.

Nolan sees the man from a distance and slows down to a gentle walk, raising his hand as he calls out, "Don't shoot, it's me – Nolan!"

The big man is already going into a crouch as he calls back into the depths of the mine for his boss to come out and see who has arrived. The Winchester, now snapped up to his face, is unerringly focused on Nolan.

"Ah, my good friend," says Shapiro as he emerges out of the darkness of the mine. He is accompanied by several others, all hitching up pants or stuffing in shirts. The dawn is barely an hour old and they look dishevelled, grumpy, riven with curiosity.

Edging forward, Nolan puts up both his hands and does not drop them until Shapiro claps his hand on the big-belly's back and sniggers. "Relax *amigo*, this must be good news."

As the gang gather around, Shapiro orders coffee and grits to be made ready. Dismounting, Nolan waits until Shapiro steps forward and puts his arm around Nolan's shoulder. The gang leader leads him over to the remnants of a small fire that Big-Belly used to warm himself through the night. "Get some more wood on this," Shapiro shouts and one of the men hastens to do his bidding. At a nearby outcrop of rock, Shapiro sits and beckons for Nolan to do likewise.

"I have news."

"I hoped you might," said Shapiro. "I must be honest, I was thinking that maybe you had forgotten about us."

"No way. Not with the bank being so full."

This welcome news causes Shapiro's eyes to twinkle with delight and he reaches over and embraces Nolan enthusiastically. "I knew you would not let us down. I always had faith in you, unlike the others." He releases himself and, grinning, checks that someone is making the coffee. Satisfied, he returns to Nolan and grins again. "Tell me, what is this news?"

"They're dead."

Shapiro's mouth falls open and for a moment a silence like a heavy steel door falls down over them, shutting everything else out. "What? You mean ...?"

"In the end, it was easy. They were drunk, celebrating some hunt they had been on. Indians. I snuck into Cole's log cabin and did for them both." He pats the heavy-bladed knife at his hip. "They knew nothing about it."

"That is a pity. I would have liked Cole to have suffered. He made a fool out of me. I am disappointed."

"I didn't really have much choice."

"Log cabin you say?" Shapiro is rubbing his chin, eyes distant. "At Cole's spread?"

Nolan nods his head, averting his eyes from Shapiro when his boss frowns at him.

"You know I went there once."

Now it is Nolan's turn to gape. "To Cole's place?"

"Yes. After I broke free of that damn prison, I intended to go there and kill him myself. It was empty. Deserted."

"He doesn't often go there."

"But this time he did? To a tiny ranch he has no time for?"

Nolan squirms. He cannot help it. Shapiro's eyes study him with an intensity unlike anything he has ever known. Perhaps he suspects and if he does, then Nolan will have to end it all here. It would be touch and go, with his gang so numerous, but not all of them are armed. If luck is with him ...

"I told you," Nolan continues, keeping his voice calm, steady, "he was sleeping off a drunk."

"With the other one?"

"Sterling Roose, yes."

"And you killed them?"

"Yes, I did. Why in the name of sanity would I tell you otherwise, Shapiro?" Hoping this show of anger will divert any more suspicions, Nolan jumps to his feet, fists clenched. "I want that money as much as you do, as much as we all do!" He swings his arm around in a wide arc to indicate the rest of the gang, all of whom are dead still, watching. "The bank is open and ready for taking. Just as you told me to make it."

"I did not think you would be able to kill them. Are you sure no one else will be suspicious? The town sheriff, perhaps?"

"He's a fat old man, not worth a dime. It's safe, Shapiro. We can ride in and shoot up the whole town without anyone brave enough to lift a finger."

Another silence. Icy this time. Shapiro appears to be going over everything Nolan has told him, sifting through the words, convincing himself of their veracity.

"What's the matter, Shapiro? Don't you believe me?"

A long sigh slips from Shapiro's thin, cruel mouth. "I must, *amigo,* because nobody would be foolish enough to lie to me."

And then came the grin, lighting up his face, dispelling the charged atmosphere in an instant. Shapiro stands, embraces Nolan again, and calls to his men to gather around. "We have plans to make, and bellies to fill!"

Someone produces a half bottle of tequila and they all break into laughter.

"It's a little early for that, isn't it?" Nolan looks dubiously as the bottle is handed over to him.

"It is never too early for tequila," says Shapiro, "especially when we have so much to celebrate – to our dear departed friend, Reuben Cole!"

Urged on by them all, Nolan takes the first mouthful and creases up his face as the liquid fire hits the back of his throat.

. . .

338

Later that same afternoon, the third bottle finished, Shapiro kicks one of his men in the leg to rouse him from his slumber. Rubbing his eyes, the man squints upwards to his boss and smacks his lips.

"Check he is unconscious, then ride out to Cole's ranch. I want confirmation."

"Eh?"

Shapiro wants to punch the man struggling to his feet, scratching at his crotch. "I want *proof,* you half-wit. Once you have it, you get back here as soon as you can."

"But boss, I thought we were heading into town to take the bank? Before you got us all drunk, that is."

"You do as I say," snarls Shapiro and juts his chin towards the man who is swaying unsteadily before him. "Check out the cabin and bring me the news I want to hear." Then, taking a breath, he leans towards the man's closest ear and gives him the directions. "Now go, and whatever happens do not be seen. By anyone, you understand."

"Yes, boss."

"Good, now get!"

CHAPTER TWENTY-THREE

Discoveries and Confessions

A cold wind blew in from the west, battering hard against the huddle of men who stood in the cemetery looking down at the blood-spattered corpse at their feet.

"I'm getting too old for this sort of thing," mutters Sheriff Perdew with meaning. His face, ashen, appears drained and haggard. Old before his time, possibly sick with something ravaging through his withered body. Roose stands next to him, and doesn't know what to make of him. He doesn't know what to make of the corpse either. He says so and the sheriff throws him a filthy look. "Murder is what it is."

"I know that much," says Roose and gets down on his haunches. Although the morning is moving on, the cemetery remains eerily dark, as if reluctant to give up the night. Having already had a good look outside the entrance, Roose now inspects the ground. "The murderer made off on foot, down through the gate to where his horse was waiting."

"You can catch him?"

"Certainly. But he'll be desperate, so I'll need at least two more men. Or I can wait for Cole."

"Best do it now rather than later. He may well already be out of the Territory."

"Could be." Roose stands up and stares at the body for quite some time. "Anyone know who he was?"

No one is forthcoming until a lanky youth with buck teeth and a thatch of bright orange hair steps forward. "Could be one of them drovers from the Rancine ranch."

"You know him?"

"Not directly," says the youth. "I do recall his face."

"It is a face to remember," says the sheriff. "More like that of a girl. Or angel."

"Well, if he's one of them he's found his way back home, I would suspect. But yeah, his face ..." Roose frowns. "This could be an argument gone bad, not premeditated, so it could be even harder to solve. I'll take myself across to Rancine's before I set off to find the killer. But it ain't gonna be quick."

"Just another reason for me to put in my badge," says the sheriff.

Some of the men chuckle but Roose takes the comment for what it is – an invitation. This is his chance and he means to take it.

As the group of men start to disperse, someone says, "I'll fetch the undertaker," and the sheriff, wheezing loudly, sits down on a nearby stone tomb, fashioned in the shape of a coffin. The irony is not lost on Roose. "You already settling in, sheriff?"

A scoffing bark of a laugh follows. "You can joke about it, Sterling, but I have to tell you, I don't feel too good. And with this cold weather coming..." He lets the comment hang there, unfinished. He looks up as he gathers his coat around his throat. "I'm feeling my age, that's the truth and if it wasn't for the fact that I'm ..." He stops. "Are you all right, Sterling?"

But Sterling is far from all right. Searching every corner of that lonely place, he slowly pushes his hat back from his brow. "There's one thing I almost missed."

"You never miss anything as far as I can tell."

"That's as maybe, but ... I'm wondering, Sheriff ... where is this dead man's horse?"

Bringing the buggy to a slow, easy halt, Julia climbs down and surveys the street. It is mid-morning, but the cold wind bites hard. Well muffled in thick coat, gloves, scarf, and bonnet she still feels it. There will be snow.

Travelling will be hard. Why have the fates conspired to make everything so difficult?

Securing the horse, she steps up onto the boardwalk and clumps down towards the merchandise store. It is warm inside and she breathes a sigh of relief. Mr Stanley, the proprietor, stacks up a big, pot-bellied stove in the corner and he beams when he sees her. "Why, Miss Julia. How are you this somewhat bitter morning?"

"I am well, thank you Mr Stanley. I have come to settle the bill."

"Oh." He looks stunned, but soon his face wrinkles up into one of pure joy. Rubbing his hands, he dips behind the counter and begins to leaf through a large, thick ledger. "It's a piffling amount, Miss Julia. Cole almost always settles it whenever he gets back from one of his trips. Is he home again?"

"No, not yet." She opens her small purse and extracts the required amount. He does not bother to count it and she likes that. In another world, she could take on the management of such a store as this, fill it out with everything anyone from around those parts could ever possibly want and need. "Thank you, Mr Stanley, for all your past service."

"Oh. Well, I ... you know, it's all in the ... Are you going someplace?"

"Yes ... for a little while. Thank you again."

A brief smile followed by a furtive glance around the shop. There is nobody else.

The shopkeeper tilts his head, puzzled. "There is something else you were wanting?"

"Yes. Reuben – Mr Cole, I mean. He gave me a Wells Fargo, for personal protection, but I'm not very well-schooled in its use. I have heard there are better options."

"Indeed, there are, Miss Julia. That little Colt Navy is old-fashioned, uses powder, cap and ball."

"Might you have something a little more ... *effective?*"

"A Peacemaker is probably the best bet, Miss Julia. It's not so very big and uses cartridges, so it can be rapidly reloaded." He ducks down below the counter and returns with a shiny walnut box. Easing it open, he waves his hand across the contents. His cheeks puff out. Obviously proud of these wares, he beams towards her. "I have to confess; I do not get that many ladies inquiring."

"Is that it?" She points at a bright and shiny revolver sitting snug in a bed of plum-coloured velvet.

"That's top of the range, with ivory grips. There is a cheaper version, just as effective."

Sucking in her bottom lip, she gives herself a few moments to consider her options. She could continue with the Wells Fargo, but she wants her own revolver. She knows how to shoot, has done so on many occasions, and what she is planning might mean using up more than one cylinder's worth of bullets. "I'll take it," she says, lifts it and weighs it in her glove hand. "It's heavy."

"And reliable."

Smiling, she pushes the required amount across the counter and then she is gone, stepping outside again in the raw, bitter weather, her pocket sagging with the weight of the Colt.

A few flakes of snow are floating down from a sky almost uniformly white. Shivering, she dashes along the boardwalk to the little teashop on the corner and goes inside.

A bell above the door chimes cheerfully and almost at once, the little proprietor appears through a beaded curtain. "Well I never," she cries, clapping her hands in genuine glee. "I was only just thinking of you, my dear. How are you? Do please come inside, sit yourself down. I'll make you a nice, hot cup of China tea."

"No, no," she says and holds up a gloved hand, "I'm only here to ... to tell you. All is well and I am perfectly recovered."

"Yes, well, thank goodness is all I can say."

"Yes. It was traumatic, to say the least, but—"

"Thanks to that young man, is all I can say – he saved the day."

"Yes, he did! Thank goodness he was here. Could I ask..." She steps closer, checking the shop for any other customers, even though it is clear there are none. "You saw the whole thing, I suppose?"

"Well, I was here, in the shop, heard the commotion and all ..."

"Yes, but the young man, the one who helped me? You saw him?"

"Yes. Of course, when I stepped outside after he had—"

"I mean before."

"Before? Before your attack, you mean?"

"Yes, did you see him standing anywhere close? Loitering I suppose you could call it."

"Not that I can remember, I was in the back, you see, preparing everything for lunch time and I could not see much from where I was—"

"I did," comes a voice from beyond the curtain. "I saw him." Parting the beads, a thin, angular looking woman, as grey as the proprietor, but considerably taller, appears. She dries her hands on a checked tea cloth as she steps forward.

"This is Sylvie," says the old proprietor. "I'm Noreen, by the way."

"Thank you," says Julia with a smile. "Sylvie? Is that French?"

"I am Canadian," says the new arrival as she folds the cloth over her arm. "I moved here with my family some years ago, but yes, we are French."

"Sylvie makes the most delicious cakes," puts in Noreen proudly. "I've never tasted better."

"I'm sure your customers feel the same," says Julia then, the niceties done with, she grows more serious. "Tell me what you saw please, Sylvie."

"The man you speak of, the one who helped you? I saw him talking with the one who tried to hold you up."

For a moment, Julia cannot speak. It is as if a huge, icy cold cloud has enfolded around her, smothering her. Her breathing grows laboured and she reaches out for something to stop herself from falling. Hands help her, grip her by the arm and gently lower her into a chair.

"Brandy," says Sylvie simply. She drops to her knees, hands clasping Julia's own. "I am sorry, madam. This is a shock."

Mumbling, unable to form words, Julia stares into the face of the French-Canadian. Noreen appears with a small glass in her hand and Julia takes it, sips, coughs, but instantly feels better. Blinking, she holds onto Sylvie's hands. "Are you absolutely sure?"

"Yes, I am afraid so. I did not think anything of it, at the time, but after the attack I went to the sheriff to tell him."

"But he did nothing."

"He did not seem all that interested, saying the matter was sorted out thanks to the other man's intervention."

Nodding, Julia drains her glass and hands it back to Noreen. "Thank you. So, they knew each other."

"There is more," said Sylvie. Julia looks at her and notices a tiny tremor running across her eyes. "I also heard what they spoke about."

CHAPTER TWENTY-FOUR

Roose

The body lay stretched out upon the undertaker's table. Having cleaned up most of the blood, the gaunt looking man in black suit with tails who conducted the preparations of the body, thrust out a crumpled piece of paper towards Roose. "It was in his shirt pocket. I took a look, thought you would be interested."

Taking it with great care, Roose unfolded the paper and read the scrawl. Each word grew larger as he took them in, emotions ranging from startled disbelief to, by the time he finished, desperate urgency. "How long has he been dead?"

"Can't say," replied the undertaker. "I ain't no doctor, but the rigor has passed, so I'd say at least twenty-four hours, maybe less."

Grunting, Roose whirled away and went outside. He mounted his horse and kicked it into a gallop, heading into town and the sheriff's office, all the time his mind filled with the enormity of the dead man's written words. The only part he was uncertain about was the timing. Whoever had murdered him must have got into a dispute over the plans, but what that dispute could be he had no means of knowing. Possibly how the loot would be shared out? And if the murder had occurred the previous day, the robbers could be heading into town at any moment.

Reining in his horse outside the office, he jumped to the ground and was mounting the steps up to the door when it opened, and two people stood there.

He gaped, sucking in his breath at a rush. "Julia?"

"Hello Sterling," she said, her lips trembling as she spoke.

"Roose," said the sheriff, who stood next to Julia, face set hard. "We have some news, and it ain't good."

"I know," he said, brandishing the paper. "Is this it?"

The sheriff took it and read through it quickly. "That's about the size of it. The gang is coming in to rob the bank, and they mean to have you and Cole out of the way when they do it. I'm old, Roose. There is no way I can do this on my own, and the town just hasn't got the manpower or the grit to see this thing through."

"Sterling." Julia stepped forward, taking one of his hands in hers. "I've been a terrible, blind, stupid fool."

"No," he said, unable to keep the tears from gathering under his bottom eye lids, "No, you haven't. It's my fault. I knew you were unhappy, and I should have ..." Shaking his head, he tore himself from her grasp, straightening his back, gritting his teeth. "Where is he?"

"He said he was going to the Rancine ranch. It's where he used to work."

"Dear God," said the sheriff. "Surely Rancine would not be involved?"

"In the robbery? No, I doubt it." He gave Julia a withering glance. "Did he say anything about this to you? Who he was in cahoots with?"

"No, not a word. Sterling, I didn't know anything about this, I promise you! He talked about us going away, starting a new life but never anything about any robbery, or what he intended to do to you and Cole. I swear it."

His eyes held hers for a long time and he could see the sincerity there, but it still hurt him to know what she had done. Sharing her bed with a man she barely knew, and he ... He having feelings for her for so long. And for her to contemplate ... contemplate what? His and Cole's death?

"I didn't know about any of that," she said as if she could read his thoughts. She moved closer and took his lapels in her hands and for a moment Roose believed she was about to shake him. "We have to find him, stop him, and then we have to set a trap for the robbers. We *must*, Sterling. It's the only way."

She was right, of course. Anything she had done, mistakes, misjudgements, call them what you will, had to be pushed aside. What mattered now was stopping Nolan and his gang, if indeed it was his gang. "You're right," he said and smiled. He saw her face change, soften, and then her lips were brushing against his chin. He stepped away, his stomach turning over, not sure how to react. His feelings for her were not changed. "I'll ride out to Rancine's. If Nolan is still there, I'll apprehend him, bring him back. Then we can start to make preparations."

"Be careful, Sterling," she said.

He left with those words emblazoned on his mind. Words which he would never forget.

CHAPTER TWENTY-FIVE

The Ranch

Shaking his head, the sheriff looked at Julia as if he were in pain. "I'm not so sure if that is such a good idea."

"I need to be there when Cole returns, to let him know. Hearing it from someone else wouldn't be right."

"But you can tell him here!"

"No, he'll go straight to the ranch. He always does. Nobody at the fort will know what has gone on here, so he'll follow his usual path. I'll go back, wait for him."

"And what if this Nolan character is there? What if he has not gone to Rancine's? What if—"

"Sheriff, the world is full of what-ifs. If Nolan is there, I'll deal with it." Julia hadn't told anyone about the Colt in her possession, but she now unconsciously stroked the pocket where it lay. "I'll be fine."

"I'll come with you, just in case."

"No, I told you, I'll be fine. Trust me. If Nolan is there and he sees you, he'll spook, make a break for it. God knows, he'll probably kill us both before we got within a hundred yards. Cole's Henry is still above the door."

"All the more reason why I should—"

She gripped his hand. "It'll be all right. Besides, you need to organise some sort of defence. Maybe get the bank tellers out of there, lock everything up, apart from the safe. Clear it out and leave the door open." She caught the sheriff's perplexed frown. "We need to shock them, Sheriff. They are going to ride in here thinking it's going to be as easy as getting drunk on the fourth of July. If the town can't stop them with gunfire, then at least we can make it as difficult for them as possible when they come stumbling outside again, wondering what on earth is going on."

"Yes, yes you're right. But please, you must …"

A simple squeeze of his hand and she was gone, marching across the street to her buggy. She gave a tiny wave, then left the town at a steady trot.

She made good time, following the ancient track out of town, the way she had always come, but never with so much trepidation. The enormity of the situation burrowed into her very heart and soul. Nolan. Everything he'd said, the words, promises, all of it so many lies. He'd preyed on her vulnerability, and all in order to convince her to abandon Cole after luring him from town. Was it also Nolan's plan to ambush Cole and perhaps Sterling as well, to kill them and make the robbery of the town bank so much easier? She cursed under her breath as memories of the moments she'd spent with Nolan flashed across her mind. What a fool she'd been, swept off her feet so easily! Such thoughts only served to make her more determined than ever to thwart him. Make him pay. Yes. Not only had her pride been damaged, but her dignity too. She did not know if she had it in him to kill him, the way she had killed Sergeant Burroughs, but she knew she needed to confront Nolan and show him that his lies had not worked. And more. Show him how devastated she was with his deceit.

The ranch appeared as she had left it. A lonely place, not even the few horses cantering around their fenced field lifting the solemn, oppressed atmosphere of the place. She wondered, not for the first time, why she stayed? Perhaps that was why she had jumped so eagerly at Nolan's invitation? Alone in a lonely place. Was nothing more calculated to send her deeper and deeper into a trough of depression? What Nolan offered was a way out. A chance. But he'd lied, using her for his own purposes. The hatred boiled over. She took out the Colt and studied it before placing it in a canvas bag. She urged the little buggy forward.

———

He'd arrived a little before her, gun drawn, checking the rooms. As the silence continued, he realised that Cole and Roose were not there. No signs of struggle, no upturned chairs, tables. No blood. Nolan had lied. He'd tricked Shapiro. For what ends, he could not fathom. Maybe to buy himself time, to double-cross them all, murder them and claim the reward money. Better than a cut from the proceeds of the bank raid. It could be. Shapiro alone was worth what, five thousand dead or alive? That was a lifetime's worth of money. If the bank held a sizeable amount, how much could Nolan hope to take? Two thousand at the most. Yes, that was it. It had to be. He'd turned bounty-hunter on them all.

The sound of approaching hooves spurred him into action. He rushed through into the little back room and out through the door. The cold hit him like a fist and, with one hand around his collar, and the other on his gun, he crouched down against the rear wall and waited.

From the other side, he could hear the buggy stopping, the handbrake going on, the sound of her boots hitting the ground as the driver jumped down. It was all so very quiet. Like the grave. The thought caused him to shudder.

From inside, the door crashing open, a female voice crying out, "Cole? Cole are you here?"

But of course, he wasn't. Was she aware of Nolan's double-cross? Her voice was tremulous, rattled. Then came the sobs and he decided to move, edging around the side to the open door. He stood in the doorway and watched. A beautiful woman, head down, tears dripping from the tip of her nose to the tabletop. He could have stood and watched her for a long time. Instead, he crossed threshold, easing back the hammer of his gun as he did so.

CHAPTER TWENTY-SIX

Cole

S econd-Lieutenant Morris stood, mesmerised, as Cole dismounted. "What has happened?" he asked, trailing his eyes over the horses laden down with their dreadful cargo. Bodies wrapped in white sheets or blankets. Cole merely shrugged.

"They ambushed us. Took out a lot of our boys. The Cap'n, he … Well, let's just say he's amongst those of us who lost."

"But, his wife. She sent a cable telling us she's coming. To join him."

Taking in the young officer's bewildered look, Cole swallowed down the tiny cry trying its level best to burst out of his mouth. What was he supposed to tell her? It would be down to him to do so, the one surviving officer in the troop. "I'll meet her. Let her know." He blew out his breath. "Get a detail to take the bodies away, Lieutenant. Get them ready for burial. But not these boys," he indicated the bedraggled, dishevelled survivors. "They'll need to be left alone for quite some time."

"I'll see to it, sir."

Nodding, Cole tramped across to the drinking hall. Then a bath. There was no way he could ride out and see Julia in the state he was in. She'd never speak to him again.

He went to the bar and drank, his eyes staring into nothing, wishing to God he had the power to turn back time, or at least the guts to have told the captain not to go down into that ravine. Despite the whisky, or perhaps because of it, he knew this was going to be his last duty. Julia would be relieved, he knew that much too. To see her face lighting up as he told her, that would be everything. He would make the effort, show her the care, yes, the love, to make her feel at home with him. That was what mattered now, more than anything else.

In the upstairs rooms, he lowered himself into the hot bath he had ordered before his whiskies. Luxuriating in the sweet-smelling bath oils, he put his head back, draping his legs over the end. Closing his eyes, he allowed himself to drift, the tension immediately draining from his muscles. Unable to fight against his weariness, he slipped into deep sleep. Within seconds he was snoring.

Persistent and rough, someone somewhere shakes him into consciousness.

"*Cole! Cole, wake up!*"

Eyes springing open, Cole sat upright, blinking in his confusion. A man is there, tall, wide across the shoulders, a face lined with worry.

Sterling Roose.

"What's...?" Suddenly becoming aware of how cold the water is, Cole placed both hands on the bath's rim and hauled himself to his feet. Wrapping his arms around his chest, he shivered violently. "How long have I ...?"

"Never mind that," spat Roose. "Get your clothes on and meet me downstairs. We have a situation."

With only time for a swift gulp of coffee, Cole follows his friend out into the daylight. "I just got back from Rancine's," says Roose as he strides across the empty parade ground to where two saddled horses are waiting. "They told me a few things, all of which fit together to make up quite a picture of our friend."

"Sterling," says Cole, grabbing his friend by the arm. "What are you talking about?"

Grimacing, Roose rounds on his friend. "Nolan. He's planning on robbing the bank at Paradise. Originally, he was going to murder both you and me, until Julia put it all together."

"Julia? Sterling, I haven't a clue what you are talking about."

So Roose tells him. Everything, including what he'd learnt from Rancine. How it must have been Nolan who had murdered one of the main cowpunchers there, then murdering a young cowboy up at the cometary, the young cowboy who Nolan had employed to attack Julia. Everything. Julia's suspicions, how she found out what it all meant, and the note which confirmed everything. Cole listens, body gradually turning to liquid. Weak, disorientated, it takes him some time to make sense of it all. Some of it makes him want to be sick. Why would Julia sleep with Nolan? This, the most devastating part, causes him to die a little inside. "Dear God," was all he can manage.

"Listen," says Roose, ignoring his friend's obvious pain, "I'm going into town to help the sheriff organise things. You get over to your place and make sure Julia is all right. Bring her back into town. She's not safe out there on her own. If Nolan was to come back ..."

"Yes," agrees Cole weakly, putting up a hand, "yes, I understand Sterling."

"Are you going to be all right yourself?"

"I'll be fine."

Not at all convinced, Roose swings himself into the saddle. "Be as fast as you can. None of us know who Nolan is in cahoots with, but it must be a gang of at least half-a-dozen. They won't be expecting the reception committee I'll put in place for 'em, I can guarantee you that."

Nodding, Cole strokes his horse's neck for some considerable time while he watches his old friend ride out through the fort gates.

It's as if his entire world has been cut out from underneath him. Why would she do that? All right, he may not be the most garrulous of people, never giving her any intimation of his feelings, his hopes and plans, but even so ... Dragging in a shuddering breath, he pulls himself into his saddle and gently steers his horse through the gates. Roose is already little more than a black smudge on the horizon, galloping hard in the direction of Paradise. Cole's ranch is in the adjacent direction and it isn't going to get any closer unless he moves himself soon.

Wondering what he will find, Cole finally spurs his horse. With every pounding step, his determination grows. Soon, a hardness returns to his limbs, the queasiness all gone. Resolved to do whatever is required, Cole rides with his back straight, his jaw set solid.

CHAPTER TWENTY-SEVEN

At the Ranch

Looking up, a tiny gasp from her lips, Julia stared into the dark eyes of the stranger. He was grinning, the gun in his hand unwavering.

"My, oh my, *señorita,* how pretty you look." He stepped fully into the tiny room.

Julia did not flinch. In a strange, inexplicable way, she had been expecting someone, if not this particular man, to come. Ever since she learned the truth about Nolan, what he was planning, she knew there would have to be some sort of reckoning. So, although this man's sudden appearance frightened her, she was prepared. On her lap was the canvas bag containing the Colt. She bided her time, watching the little man edging up to the table.

"Where is Nolan?"

A small swallow before she answered. "I don't know."

He tilted his head to one side, frowning. "I don't believe you." Scanning the room, he chuckled. "Has he killed them?"

"Them? You mean Roose and—"

"Roose and *Cole*, yes! Has he done it?"

"Of course he has. I suspect even now he is riding back to your hideout. If you go now, you will catch up with him."

The man's smile turned into a grotesque leer. "Nice try, my pretty one, but I do not think Nolan is going anywhere, except to Hell."

He paraded himself around the room, picking up items, opening a drawer in the writing desk under the shuttered window, which he opened and stared out into the surroundings. "He has some fine horses," he said with his back to her. "You tend for them while he is not here?"

"Yes. Among other things."

"Yes. I can imagine." A wry chuckle. "Where is he?"

"I told you, Nolan, he—"

"Don't *lie to me,*" he screamed, whirling around to face her, the gun coming up in his hand.

His eyes dropped as he centred on the Colt Peacemaker in her hand. His grin broadened.

Then she shot him.

The blast sounded incredibly loud in the small confines of that small room. Thrown back against the window, he stood, gaping, disbelief etched into his features. He watched her as she eased back the hammer to fire a second shot. This act seemed to reanimate his senses and as she fired again, so too did he.

This time, the combined blast sounded even louder.

CHAPTER TWENTY-EIGHT

The Camp

Shapiro returns from his prolonged vigil, standing on a high outcrop to observe and signs of his man's horse. Now he goes to the camp-fire, fills a tin cup with bitter coffee and drains it, throwing the dregs into the fire. His eyes roam across the assembled men. Some are cleaning their weapons, other checking their saddles. Nolan sits a little apart, whittling away at a thin piece of wood. Shapiro readjusts his gun belt and moves towards him. "Tell me again how you killed them."

Nolan stops, the blade halfway across the wood, and he stares into Shapiro's face. "What did you say?"

"You said you killed them. Cole and his friend. How did you kill them, *amigo*?"

"I told you. They were drunk. I killed them as they were sleeping."

"Yes, but I ask you again ... *How*?"

Nolan swallows hard. With a violent swipe, he cuts his knife through the wood and throws it to the ground. "What is this again, Shapiro? Don't you believe me?"

"I am just curious, that is all. You used that," he points at the knife in Nolan's fist. "You cut their throats maybe?"

"As they were sleeping, yes."

Shapiro pulls a face. "It is not so easy to do that." He emphasises his point by running the fingertips of one hand sideways across his own throat. "There is a lot of what is called cartilage there. And ligaments. It surprises you that I know so much, eh? You have to saw through it all, like you might a piece of wood." He cackles and allows his left hand to drop down next to his holstered pistol.

"Not if you get it right here," says Nolan, jabbing two of his fingers into the carotid artery of his neck. "You cut that, then it is goodnight time."

"And that is what you did, eh?"

"Yes."

"Just like that?"

"Yes. Just like that." He emphasises each word, his eyes never faltering. Shapiro is measuring him, looking for a flinch, a blink, anything that would put a doubt in his mind. But Nolan remains impassive. Cold. "They were drunk. I did Cole first, as he is the most dangerous, then Roose. I don't think they even knew."

"Blood."

"Eh?"

"There must have been lots of blood. I remember I shot a man in that place," he jabs at Nolan's artery, "and the blood, it came out like a waterfall. Blood red waterfall." Another smile. "So how come when you came here to tell us, you had no blood on your clothes."

"I changed them."

"Ah. Where, at Cole's cabin?"

"Yes."

"Then you came here directly, is that it?"

"Correct. Shapiro, if you have something to say why don't you just—"

"And your knife? You cleaned that too? Your boots? Your hands? All cleaned. Plenty of time to clean all of that, yes?"

"Obviously, as they were dead, and I didn't think they would be—"

"And the woman?" Nolan stops and blinks. Shapiro's eyes widen, together with his smile. "Cole has a woman, yes? Where was she while all of this was happening?"

"I didn't know he had a woman."

"No? Are you sure, *amigo*?"

"Of course I'm sure. Why would I ..." His voice trails away as he stares in horror at the small, silk handkerchief Shapiro dangles in his hand. Embroidered around the edge is a red motif in the shape of a heart.

"You recognise this, *amigo*? It was in your saddle bag. Whilst you were sleeping, I went through your things. I found this, and inside, a note."

"You sonofa—"

Before Nolan can react, Shapiro's gun hand moves in a blur and suddenly, Nolan is facing the barrel of a Remington Army, hammer cocked. "Her little note is very touching. You may think I am an ignorant Mexican, but I know my letters well. She loves you deeply, so I am thinking you have made a little deal with her. A deal that might include Cole, eh? So, please, no more nonsense. I want the truth, *amigo*, or I put a bullet in your brain."

Three of the gang drag him to a nearby tree. They strip him and now he waits naked, shivering in the freezing afternoon air, as they lash his wrists together with leather thongs. Shapiro stands and examines Nolan's knife. Then he snaps an order and, attaching a rope to the thongs, they throw one end over a branch and hoist Nolan into the air, where he dangles, arms high above his head, shoulder ligaments stretching. He is screeching and the sound reminds Shapiro of the pigs his mother kept when he was a little boy. So long ago. Like a dream.

"Now, boss?"

Shapiro smiles and nods.

The crack of the bullwhip brings even happier memories.

After he told Shapiro everything he needed to know, the gang leader orders his men to saddle up. As they rush to obey, Shapiro takes a moment to squat down next to Nolan's quivering, bloody body. "Know this," he says softly, "when we return, we will bring with us your woman. I shall feast on her and you shall watch. Afterwards, when you see how happy and contented she is, I will kill you. Until then," he pats Nolan's cheek, "stay well."

Laughing, he swaggers away.

"Darius," he barks and one of the gang looks up, frowning. "You stay with him. Make sure he does not die."

"But boss, I want to—"

"If he dies, so do you!"

Crestfallen, Darius stomps away from his horse, head down, mumbling something.

Meanwhile, Shapiro singles out two others. "Take the trail to Cole's ranch. I want no mistakes this time. Kill him."

Shapiro wheels his horse in the direction of Paradise, lifts his hat and waves it like one possessed. "Ride, *muchachos!*"

With much hollering and slapping of horses' rumps, the gang pile out of the camp, every one of them grinning with the expectation of the thrills to come.

"You must drink," says Darius, kneeling down beside Nolan. He offers him a canteen of water, which Nolan gulps at thankfully. "Not so fast, my friend. You do not want to choke to death." He cackles.

Revived a little by his drink, Nolan props himself up on one elbow and stares into the man's face. "They have gone?"

"Yes, my friend," sneers Darius, lifting the canteen to Nolan's lips again. He smiles as Nolan drinks. "That's it. When you can sit up, I shall make us something to eat." He sighs and looks into the far distance where a spreading cloud of dust is the only evidence of the gang's departure. "I wish I was with them."

Grunting, Nolan wipes away the sweat from his eyes with the back of one quivering hand. He studies Darius or, more accurately, the way he wears his rig. Cross-bellied, grip facing his right side. The closest side to Nolan.

He almost smiles at the man's stupidity.

In one flowing movement, Nolan whips out the gun and puts two quick slugs into Darius' guts. The man screams and is blown backwards where he writhes on the ground. Meanwhile, Nolan tries to sit up. The pain in his back, where the bullwhip bit so deeply, causes him to seize up solid and he stifles his own scream through gritted teeth. Giving himself a distraction, he turns his attention to Darius flaying around, bent-double, hands clamped to his stomach. "Darn it," breathes Nolan and shoots him through the head.

Silence descends and Nolan thanks God for it.

CHAPTER TWENTY-NINE

The Ranch

I t looked like something out of a faraway land, gripped as it was by winter. The snow had settled, casting everything in a comforting white blanket. At least from a distance. The air, however, almost burned the throat it was so cold. Reining in, huddled in his coat, and watching, Cole knew there was something wrong as soon as he spotted the horse tethered at the side of the barn. It was a horse he did not recognise, the rig jet black, studded with jewels, not something anyone he knew would ride. Slipping from his own mount, he drew the Henry repeating carbine from its scabbard and moved down the slight incline leading to the cabin, keeping himself low. Darting from one measly piece of cover to the next, his boots crunching through the snow. In the eerie silence, the sound echoed all across the valley and he felt certain that at any moment someone would appear, guns blazing.

Nobody did. Cole crouched down behind a freezing boulder, exposed to the very fiercest of chilly blasts of wind, and engaged his carbine. His face tingled with a myriad of tiny needles forever stabbing at his exposed flesh. If he was forced to remain outside in the night, he knew he would not see the morning. The sun was already low in the sky and he calculated less than an hour of daylight remained. Taking a breath, decisions made, he charged from his cover and zig-zagged towards the open doorway.

Not slowing down, he rushed past Julia's buggy, causing the tough little pony to buck and whinny loudly, and continued up the steps to the doorway. He summersaulted through the opening, hoping to catch whoever was inside unawares. He did not know who to find, but he knew it would not be Roose. If someone was holding up Julia, then retribution was close. Maybe it was Nolan. God help him if it was.

The first sight which confronted him was that of a dead gunman, crammed under the open window, eyes staring into nothingness. Punctuating his body were two huge holes, black with dried blood and, next to him, a gun. That can only mean one thing.

He turned his head slowly, praying he would not find anything, that whoever it was who had killed this man was long gone.

Cole was not a man used to praying. Faith, belief, call it whatever you will, these were not concepts he understood nor had ever bothered with. Perhaps he should because now, looking across the room, he saw her, lying in a crumpled heap, the blood in a wide pool around her, and for a long time he did not have the courage, nor the strength, to move.

She was dead. That much was plain, even from where he sat he could see that, and as this realisation hit him, the tears came. If he had shown some hint of his feelings for her, then perhaps none of this might have happened. He knew nothing of what had transpired, but he knew something terrible had. Creeping over to her, the sobs racking through him, he gently lifted her head into his arms and cradled her there. The bullet had struck her in the throat, her life's blood a deep, dark stream cascading down her bodice. She was so cold in his arms. So cold ...

Later he stood on the porch and smoked a cigarette, the plume of blue smoke mixing with his steaming breath. He watched the sun go down and he knew his life was turning a new page. Julia, gone, his unspoken love drifting away on the wind, along with his heart, now as frozen as the winter landscape.

He did not know how long it would be before the thaw came.

CHAPTER THIRTY

The Robbery

The sun was nothing more than a dim smudge when the riders came into town, muffled in their thick blanket coats, hats crammed down hard on their pinched faces. They all wore gloves and scarfs, but the cold penetrated into their very flesh making them slow, weary. At their lead, Shapiro scanned the streets. He did not expect to see anyone this early and his plan was to find the nearest saloon, wait until the bank opened at nine, then hit it with everything they had. After he had checked, of course, that Nolan's words were true.

With two men left standing outside, stamping their feet, Shapiro went through the batwing doors of the Parody Hotel and Saloon, three of his gang behind him, all of them groaning in ecstasy as the heat from the twin wood burners positioned in the far corners hit them with a heavy blast.

From somewhere a frail looking man, bent over with age, appeared carrying a full pail of steaming water in one hand and a mop in the other. He pulled up sharply as he set eyes on Shapiro and his men. "Oh Lordy," he said.

"We need coffee," snapped Shapiro, pulling off his coat. Around his waist were two guns, butts turned forwards, and across his chest a bandolier bulging with cartridges, ending in a shoulder holster. The others, similarly armed, settled themselves at a large, round table, stretching out their legs and blowing out great streams of air.

"We ain't open yet," said the man, his voice shaking, as were the cleaning things in his hand. He settled the bucket down before it slipped from his grasp.

"You is now," snarled Shapiro, drawing one of his guns to underline his point. "Coffee."

Without a word, the little old man scampered behind the counter and disappeared into a room beyond.

"What time is it," asked Shapiro to nobody in particular as he holstered his gun.

"Beats me," said one of his men. "Too darn early that's for sure."

"It's just gone six-twenty," said one of the others, the proud owner of a silver inlaid fob-watch that he kept on a chain across his ample stomach. He snapped the cover closed and dropped the fob to its home in his waistcoat pocket. "That gives us two and a half hours to kill."

The others groaned.

"Best if we relieve Tweedy and Ramon," said Shapiro, leaning across the counter to find a half bottle of whisky on the shelf there. Grinning he pulled out the stopper with his teeth, spat the cork away and took a slug. Gasping, he studied the liquid inside the bottle before shooting a glance towards the others. "Tell 'em to come inside."

As one of the men did his bidding, Shapiro turned and leaned back against the bar, eyes closed. Two and a half hours ...

Another man came through the rear door, still dressed in nightshirt. He took one look at Shapiro and gaped. "Gentlemen," he began, stepping closer, "it is not usual for us to—"

"Just get the coffee," said Shapiro in a bored voice without looking at the man, "or else I'll kill you all and set fire to this stinking old shack of a place."

Instantly the man, sensibly deciding not to argue, disappeared without a word into the back room.

The batwing doors opened, and the others came in, rubbing themselves briskly. "It is so cold out there!"

"Warm yourselves by the fire, boys," said Shapiro, taking another drink, "we have plenty of time."

"It's as quiet as the grave outside," said one of them, moving across to the nearest wood burner, palms outstretched.

"Just as I like it," said Shapiro and closed his eyes once more.

Pushing the little old man out the back door, the big owner whispered, "Tell Roose they is here."

"You do remember what to say, don't you Lawrence?"

"Of course I do. Now scat!"

The old man scurried off with the speed of a worn-out old tortoise. Lawrence sighed deeply before returning inside and set to preparing the coffee.

He threw the body of the gunman out into the open ground, knowing that as soon as they felt safe enough, the buzzards would be making quick work of him. Naturally, he took more time with Julia, washing away the blood, even combing her hair before he lay her down upon the bed. Stooping close, he kissed her gently – something he had never done while she was alive – and covered her with a blanket. Then he went into the room and did his best to tidy up, cleaning the blood, which almost turned his stomach. Perhaps he caught an hour's sleep, but he soon roused himself, despite his joints aching and the tears stinging his eyes. Forced to break the ice that had formed on the surface of the washing bowl, he threw water over his face and felt a little revived. Nothing, however, could expunge the image of Julia's corpse, images that simply would not go away.

Outside again, he took several deep breaths before unhitching the buggy. He took both the pony and the dead gunman's horse into the paddock to join the others. When he returned, after prioritising Julia's burial, he would take the animals into the barn where they could spend the cold nights.

Normality, he knew, would soon return.

Together with the loneliness.

Sometime later, with the morning advancing, he rode away not knowing what to expect, only that at some time soon, Nolan and his men would ride in and attempt to rob the bank. Roose would have done his job, of that Cole was sure, and he could not stop himself from grinning at the prospect of what was to come.

The loud snap of the fob-watch cover closing made them all jump. "It's just after nine."

Shapiro, who had been dozing in the far corner beside the wood burner, sat up, yawned, and stretched luxuriously. Automatically he reached for the whisky bottle standing on the floor next to him. Finishing it, he stood, rolling his shoulders, easing out the cramps in his muscles. He eyed the bartender arranging glasses and bottles behind the counter and sauntered across as his men checked their weapons for the umpteenth time. He looked at his right hand, the forefinger and thumb misshapen and he flexed and unflexed them, wincing a little. "You're certain Cole is not around?"

The bartender turned, his face serious. "Like I told you, rumour has it he got himself killed on his last outing against some Apaches."

"And Roose?"

"That was nasty, and the sheriff is out investigating even now. Over at Cole's ranch. He left late last night and has not returned."

"Nasty in what way?"

"Woman came in here like a startled hen, screaming that there'd been a fight at the cabin and Roose had been shot. I don't know anymore."

"Sounds convenient."

"Convenient or not, I believe it's the truth."

"If it turns out to be drivel," said Shapiro, leaning across the counter and seizing the barkeep by the collar, "I'm coming back for you, *amigo*."

The man's jowls wobbled as he spluttered, "I'm telling you as it was told to me."

With a hefty shove, Shapiro let the man go then swung around to face his gang. "Keep your wits about you, boys. We hit the bank hard and fast."

They all fell in behind him as he stepped outside.

The chill wind hit them all instantly. Pulling his collar tight around him, Shapiro strode out onto Main Street, head snapping left and right. There was no one. Not a soul. Not even a horse. It had to be the cold, there could be no other reason why this place had suddenly become little more than a ghost town.

If Shapiro all but knew it, there was a simple reason. Sterling Roose, if not the architect then the executioner of the plan, stood in the livery stables, deep in the shadows, watching the gang striding by. He could strike now, gunning them down in a blaze but Cole, who had ridden in a little under an hour ago, held his arm and gave a single shake of the head. "Wait," was all he said.

So, they did, grinding their teeth, anger boiling over at the sight of the gang's arrogant swagger.

"How many you count?" asked Roose.

"Six. There'll be a seventh back at the saloon, with the horses. He'll bring 'em up to the bank as soon as the shooting starts." He drew in a deep breath, becoming concerned. "But Nolan isn't among them."

"That worries me. He could be waiting somewhere, as a back-up."

"As leader, he'd be there, right at the front. Anything else and the others wouldn't follow."

"So, what are you saying? That Nolan isn't their leader?"

"I reckon it's the one at the front. I know him from somewhere, but I can't quite fix him in my mind ... He has something about him, a presence. He's their boss, I'm sure of it."

"And Nolan? Where's he?"

A blinding light instantly blazed in Roose's eyes and, snapping his face around to face Cole, he uttered through gritted teeth, "Julia!"

Roose went to move, but Cole caught hold and pulled him back into the shadows. "Don't be a fool! If they see you, they'll figure it's a trap and ride out of here like the hounds of hell were after 'em."

"But we can't just—"

"We get this done first," said Cole, his grip tightening. He had not yet told Roose the horrors of what had transpired back at the ranch, knowing his old friend would already be racing off to see for himself. He needed to convince him that all was well. "Nolan's gone, Sterling."

"You can't be sure of that."

"What would it profit him to harm Julia?" He had to turn away as renewed tears threatened to spring forth. "Come on, let's get into position and get this thing done."

They rushed through the main door, Winchesters ready, covering the whole interior of the bank.

"What the ...?"

Nothing but a cold, empty space glared back at them. No tellers, no customers. At the counter where clerks would sit, chairs waited empty underneath, papers stacked, pencils sharpened and ready. But nobody to do anything.

One of the gang vaulted over the counter, kicked in the manager's office door, and stood, breathing hard. With his back to them all, he gasped, "There ain't no one here."

Another, lifting up the hatch this time, strode towards the massive, green painted safe and groaned. "Boss, this is open." He swung around, pale faced, lips quivering. "It's been cleaned out."

A dreadful drumming had been growing in Shapiro's ears and now he whirled away, clamping hands to the side of his face. "No, no, no," he blared, not wanting to believe any of it, hoping that once he opened his eyes, he'd find himself back at the hideout, all of it a dream. A nightmare.

"Boss, what in the name of Almighty are we gonna do?"

Bringing his face up to meet every one of his terrified gang, Shapiro slowly gathered himself, overcoming the disbelief, the dread. "Nolan. He's double-crossed us, gave the town warning." Both hands came up, curling into tight fists. "I'm gonna rip out his lungs. *His lungs!*"

Striding towards the door, a charging bull out of control, he reeled out into the cold, ignoring it, barely conscious of how quiet the street was. More than quiet. Deserted. Brandishing his arms in a wild cartwheel, he signalled to his man at the saloon, roaring at the top of his voice, "*Bring the horses!*"

Through a shimmering haze of hate, he thought he saw something. Something that shouldn't be there, not now, not in this dead, barren place. Even as his men spilled out all around him, he still could not believe it. Until that is the vision was so close there could be no ignoring it.

"You," he managed, his voice nothing but a drizzle of something he never wanted to be a part of again. Defeat.

Before him, the vision stopped, nonchalant, detached, almost as if it were the most natural thing in the world for him to be there. For it was a 'him'.

"Hello Shapiro," said Cole.

Stepping out from behind the far side of the bank, Roose held a twin-barrelled sawn-off shotgun in his hands, the Remington in its holster and another in his belt. He was glad he had so much fir-power because from where he was standing, the bank robbers were also well tooled-up. All of them were facing Cole, unaware Roose was at their rear. Once the shooting started, if they chose not to lay down their firearms, it was going to come as a huge surprise to them all.

Cole was speaking, his voice calm, as it always was. "You boys all put down your guns and place your hands on your head. There ain't nothing for you here, so quit now while it is still looking good."

For a reply he received a huge, scoffing guffaw from Shapiro who, even though his own voice was trembling, made out he was as unconcerned at seeing Cole there as he would be at finding a bird flying overhead during a walk in the countryside. "And so speaks Mr Reuben Cole. Boys, this here is the great Army scout of the Territories, a man who took away my freedom and who I have sworn to kill."

"The only person who took away your freedom was you."

"Ah, yes, you would say that, wouldn't you Cole, to disguise your own dishonesty. Whatever happened to the money we took from that bank, eh Cole? Where did it go?"

Shifting his weight to his left leg, Cole frowned. "It was returned. As always."

"You know it was not. And now this bank, empty. By who, I wonder?"

"You talk too much."

"Ah, touched a nerve, eh? Well, not to worry. There are six of us my friend. It is for you to throw down your guns. Then, it will be just you and me." His teeth flashed in a nasty looking snarl.

As his men tensed and prepared themselves, a voice broke out from behind them. "I'd take it real easy, boys," said Roose.

A sudden mood change fell over the gang, one of uncertainty charged with fear. Men turned their heads and, realising the odds were now evened out, shuffled and grumbled.

Shapiro quickly responded, his voice taut with tension. "We're moving out boys. Steady does it and keep yourselves ready."

"Give it up," said Cole. "I can't allow you to walk away from this."

"You are not a lawman, Cole. You have no authority."

"He ain't," said Roose, "but I am, and I have all the authority that is needed. I'm acting sheriff and I'm ordering you to throw down your weapons."

Hesitating, the gang members looked from one to another. "What do we do, boss?" asked one of them.

"We'll take you in," continued Cole, "and those of you who ain't wanted we'll let go again. That's a better deal than dyin', boys."

"It is you who will die if you do not let us ride off," said Shapiro, waving his arm again at the horse-holder outside the saloon. "We shall meet again, Cole."

"No. We won't. You're a wanted man, Shapiro. The bounty says one thousand, *dead* or alive. I'm not a bounty hunter but I can't deny that sum would set me up real comfortable for quite a while."

"I would die first."

A tiny smile trickled across Cole's mouth. He nodded towards Shapiro's hand dangling next to his holstered gun. "Looks like you've been doing some practising."

"You destroyed my right hand true enough but I've had years to learn to do just as well with my left. You'll find out soon enough."

"Your call."

Shapiro made it, flinging himself to his right, hitting the dirt in a roll as his gun came up in his left hand, the pistol spouting smoke. Behind him, his men also went for their own guns and as Cole veered away, Roose opened up, hitting two of the men with the shotgun, sending them screaming to the ground. Fanning his gun as bullets filled the air, Cole winged two more. He made it to the boardwalk and crouched down behind a group of stacked barrels adjacent to the merchandise store. He drew his second pistol and laid down evenly spaced shots into the gang as they fumbled around, firing wildly. One went down, hit in the chest, and Roose joined in, the shotgun discarded, both hands filled with his Remingtons.

Meanwhile, amongst all the smoke and noise, Shapiro sprinted across the street, signalling like a lunatic for the horse holder to arrive.

From his cover, Cole watched it all. The horse holder was now riding up, a string of horses behind him. Shapiro swung himself up into the saddle and loosed off two or three shots in Cole's direction, all of which went hopelessly wide. Ignoring them, Cole sprang forward and shot two more gang members, dumping them in bloody heaps. Without a pause, he swept up one of the gang's fallen Winchesters. As he brought it up to his eye, he looked deep into Shapiro's face, that irritating smile on the man's face. Next to him, Roose was on the ground, clutching at his leg. This wasn't good. There were others still standing.

A loud whoop from Shapiro snapped Cole into action and he whirled around, working the Winchester frantically, emptying the rifle into those gang members still standing.

A bullet zinged past and he fell to the ground, bringing out his last loaded gun but knowing the range was too great. He fired nevertheless as Shapiro struggled to bring his horse under control. He wasn't winning, the horse in a mad frenzy, spooked by the close proximity of so many bullets. The man next to him was faring better and as he kicked his horse into a gallop, Shapiro roared out his frustration.

From his position, Cole had a clear view of the situation. He knew he must take up another Winchester and shoot Shapiro down.

As things turned out, he didn't need to.

From the narrow gap between two buildings, old Sheriff Perdew stepped out, the shotgun shaking in hands which were either too old or two weak to hold it up. Or perhaps it was the fear. Whatever, he managed to bring up the gun and emptied both barrels into Shapiro's body, blowing the gang boss sideways across his horse. Some of the spread struck the animal, not fatally but enough to send into an uncontrollable charge. Shapiro, one foot caught in the stirrup, went with it, his body bucketing and bouncing down the street to disappear into the distance.

Cole watched, horror-struck. All around him were groaning and bleeding men, one of whom was Roose, holding onto his leg as the blood frothed through his fingers. Desperately, not even giving himself time to stand up, Cole rolled over to his friend and held him tightly. "Oh, dear God," he said.

"I'm all right," said Roose, his face white with pain. "Help get my tie around it, stop the bleeding as much as you can, then get the doc. But hurry, Cole, hurry."

It was bad, this close Cole could see just how bad. His stomach turned to mush and turned over. He twisted himself around, screaming at Perdew to fetch the doctor, then he ripped away Roose's tie and applied the tourniquet. He pulled it as tight as he dared, and the blood flow lessened. A tiny flicker of hope ran through Cole's body, but the greyness of his friend's face meant the fear remained. All he could do now was wait. And pray.

Something like a boulder the size of anything found in the Rocky Mountains presses down on his chest and he no longer possesses the strength to lift it away. Instead, Shapiro lays on the ground, forcing himself to breathe, each inhalation and accompanying exhalation ratcheting up the pain.

Something blocks out the sun. A shadow, a figure, he knows not which. The pain is his world now. Nothing else exists.

"You're in a bad way, boss," says a voice. It sounds a long way off but is crystal clear. "I don't think you is gonna last out the next hour. That old guy, he done paid you the Lord's dues."

Shapiro wants to speak, but he cannot voice anything out of throat so dry it has completely closed over. Instead he groans, wanting to tell this man, who he thinks is one of his gang, a man called Tweedy, to take him away, bury him, burn him, anything that will prevent Cole from claiming the bounty. The final ignominy.

"Me," says Tweedy, looking back towards the town, "I'm gonna finish you off now, boss. End the pain. Then I'll claim the bounty. No one will recognise me when I bring you in, telling them I found you out on the plain. You're gonna make me rich, boss. That's about all you have ever done for me, you lousy piece of horse dung." He grins and pulls out his gun, wraps his hat around the barrel and presses it against Shapiro's head.

Shapiro wants to move, squirm away, bring out his own gun, but there is nothing he can do because there is nothing left, save for the blackness swallowing him up whole.

371

CHAPTER THIRTY-ONE

Nolan's Journal

It takes me a long time to drag myself down into the entrance to the old mine. Inside, it is cold but nowhere near as cold as outside. I find a threadbare blanket and wrap it around myself and try to find some slight vestige of sleep.

I wake with a start. With no idea of time, I scramble around, find an old pair of work pants, and, pulling them on, I go outside. The sun is blinding. A new day. Over where they tied me to that tree, there's the body of the man I killed and, about ten paces of so beyond, three scrawny looking buzzards, their eyes on stalks. They have only just begun to tear at the corpse, and they look to me with true hatred for disturbing their breakfast.

Ignoring them, I manage to pick up my clothes and pull them on, gasping as the pain lances through my back. I feel like my back is a single open wound, flesh ripped apart by a giant piece of carpenter's sandpaper. It is difficult for me to ease my arms through the sleeves of the shirt, even worse through a thick coat, some of the scabs on the wounds cracking open, new blood trickling through. If ever I meet up with Shapiro again, I'm gonna take a long time making him pay.

The dead man's gun is lying where I dropped it. I busily put the gun belt around my waist, check the cylinder and drop in fresh cartridges to replace the used ones.

My plan is a simple one – to ride out to Cole's ranch, explain to Julia what I had to do, somehow persuade her that nothing now stands in our way, and make it down to Mexico for a new life. I had toiled with the idea of confusing everyone and going north, way up through Oregon and maybe into Canada. I would see what Julia's opinion is of that. But wherever we end up, I know now that this is where my future lies. She told me that Cole provided her with a home, a roof, somewhere to rest her head, but not a lot else. She had lost so much in her life and I was here to bring some sense of reason to it all. A new start. Perhaps a child, even children.

After I found some stale corn biscuits to munch down, I packed up my horse and rode out. Every step sent a tornado of agony through my back. I knew if I didn't get the lacerations washed and treated, they'd become infected. Perhaps Julia would help. She helped with so much else.

I made good going, despite the pain. A few flurries of snow lapped around my face and I enjoyed the way my skin would cool at their touch. A tiny scratch of worry made itself felt. Perhaps my hot flesh was the first sign of fever. So, I put my head down and kicked my horse into a gallop, trying my best to clear my mind of such nightmare visions.

Some hours later I rein in my horse and gaze down towards the ranch. All seems fine, save for a few more buzzards flying overhead. I put that down to the rank smell coming off my wounds. They must be infected, I reason.

Drawing closer to the little cabin, I see what the true reason is, and I pull up hard.

There is a body. It is black and bloated and the birds are making a meal of him. I ease myself from my horse and draw my pistol. There is no other sound save for the birds squabbling with one another over the choicest pickings.

I give Julia's buggy a half look. The pony is not there but that does not cause me concern. She must have taken it into the nearby barn due to the freezing cold night. The thought reminds me just how low the temperature has plummeted, even during the daylight hours, and I gather my coat around me and edge towards the door.

The smell hits the back of my throat and I gag. I recognise that smell. It is unmistakeable but I force myself to move forward. There is nothing in the little front room, no evidence of any disturbance or anything unusual. I head to the door which leads to the bedroom, the room where we had discovered one another and I stop and stare in disbelief, my world summersaulting into an awful place, filled with pain, anguish and despair.

She is lying on the bed, a blanket over her body, arms like bleached white wooden sticks draped over the top, the flesh of her face a hideous pale green.

Julia. Dead.

I drop to my knees and the tears burst down my cheeks. I cannot hold them back. She is gone and I do not know how. For many moments, perhaps hours, I remain like that, not daring to believe that everything I wanted, everything I *ever* wanted has gone.

Finding the courage, I go to her and take hold of one of those hands, lift it to my lips and kiss. She is so cold. Colder than anything I've endured during my ride or the terrible night in the mine. This is a coldness beyond the living, something one never wishes to experience. Her face, sunken yet still retaining that stark, natural beauty which I so loved, appears peaceful. I sit on the edge of the bed, her hand in mine, and I weep again.

In time, I look at her more deeply. There is a hole in her neck, black, ragged. A bullet hole, but one that somebody has cleaned. Why would someone murder her then lay her down in the bed with such reverence? It makes no sense to me and the more I think about it, the more I simply do not care.

As if in a dream, I leave that ghastly place. I say goodbye to her with a simple kiss on the brow. Ignoring the cold from the snow which now falls much more heavily, I go into the barn. There, sure enough, is the pony, together with the other horses. Acting automatically, without conscious thought, I lead them all to the small paddock, closing the gate, and watch them buck and run. I should feed them, I say to myself, but that task can wait for someone else to do. What I need to do now cannot.

In the barn I find some rope. It does not take long for me to fashion a noose. My years of working in various ranches has taught me well. I no longer care about whoever has ended my life, or why. All I know is that Julia has gone and with her passing all reasons for continuing have also gone. Never to return.

I have taken time to scribble down these last few words in the hope that whoever reads this miserable journal will at least understand what I have done. I have made mistakes and I have so many regrets, but my life has run dry now. Without Julia, there is nothing. Only this final goodbye.

CHAPTER THIRTY-TWO

The End of It

C oles stands in the entrance. He had wondered how the horses had been returned to the paddock and now he knows.

The body swings like a pendulum, the rope creaking with the weight and he remembers the way Captain Fleming's body moved in the same way. No feelings meander through him. He is cold now. As cold as the winter.

After the doc patched Roose up, Cole's old friend insisted coming out to the ranch, so Cole borrowed the Doc's buggy and here they are. Both of them, staring. Cole had shown Roose Julia's body and Roose had wept like a baby. Cole never knew the depths of his old friend's feelings. Another reason for a withdrawal from this world.

"You gonna cut him down?"

Cole looked askance at his old friend. "I'd rather he stayed there and rotted."

"Yeah, but you know you can't do that."

"I guess not."

The silence stretched out between them. Neither moved. Roose swayed, his wounded leg bound and someone, maybe the doc, had given him a walking stick upon which he was leaning. Something on the ground, a thin notebook, the stub of a pencil next to it, grabs his attention. "What's that?"

Cole picked it up and flicked through it. "It's writing. A diary maybe." He looks towards Nolan. "He must have written it."

"Maybe it's a confession?"

"Could be."

They both stare at the body hanging there until at last, Roose sspoke. "So, you gonna cut him down?"

Blowing out a long sigh, Cole's shoulders slump. "We need to bury Julia first."

"Here, at the ranch?"

Cole nods.

More than an hour later they stand before the grave, a simple cross marking the spot. Roose has said some words, but both men know there will never be words enough.

"We'll forget this pain in time," says Roose, replacing his hat, but due to only having one free arm to do so because of the walking stick he leans on, he does not succeed. Reaching across, Cole helps his old friend.

"One day," says Cole.

"Yeah. One day." He lifts his head and stares out across the range. "I'm gonna run for sheriff. My days of scouting are done, Cole. I need to settle, do a job worth doing."

"I reckon that's a good idea, Sterling." Another sigh. So heavy this time, and rattling, as if he is barely able to keep himself under control. "Me too, in a way. I'm retiring, Sterling. No more army for me. There's been too much killing and I'm sick to my stomach of it."

Roose nods. He understands all too well how much these recent events have changed them both. "What will you do with the ranch, after ..." He breaks down again, ramming finger and thumb into his eyes as he does his utmost to control the grief consuming him.

Cole places his arm around his friend and stares at the cross bearing Julia's name. 'Our true love,' it says, 'gone but always here.'

"I'm selling up and moving into Pa's place. He's sick, he needs taking care of. Besides, there is more land there for the stock we have."

Sniffing loudly, Roose drags the back of his free hand across his nose. "Cole, don't you be thinking of doing anything stupid as you rattle around in that big, old house. I don't want you to do what Nolan did."

Cole's face cracks into something akin to a smile. He turns and looks into the distance. Birds are hovering over where the two ex-scouts threw Nolan's corpse. Neither felt they could bury him, so the buzzards have feasted again. "I've always done stupid things, Sterling. But not anymore. I'm done."

Together they look in silence at Julia's grave. Before long, the sun sets beneath the horizon and the air grows chillier than ever, but still they stand and look.

The End

NO ONE CAN HIDE

Reuben Cole Westerns Book 4

For Janice,
hoping you enjoy this one as much as the others!

CHAPTER ONE

Catherine "Cathy" Courtauld lived on the far side of the river in a small log cabin her husband Jude built before he died of scarlet fever in the summer of 1870. Some people from the nearby town of Bethlehem believed he had picked up something awful from one of the many bordellos he was known to frequent, but Cathy did her best not to listen to such spurious, hurtful gossip. People were jealous of what she and her husband had achieved in such a short span of time, and when folk are jealous, they allow their tongues to wag. That was how she saw it, and nothing much had happened since to convince her otherwise. Jude was a good man, and she missed him. Well, "good" in the sense that he provided. She wasn't so certain about everything else.

A slim, strikingly handsome woman, she worked tirelessly to keep the family smallholding in good condition, something in which she excelled. Nevertheless, loneliness gnawed into her bones. The land was uncompromising, the soil hard, the weather lacking in rain. She longed for a partner to share her burdens.

The late afternoon she heard the spattering of gunfire, she was on her knees, weeding through the root crop. She stopped, senses alerted. Cautiously, she raised her head and squinted towards the distant tree line. In one direction, the river formed a natural barrier for her land, another a cluster of trees, interspersed with bracken and shrub, another. It was from somewhere within this area that the gunfire came.

For a long moment, she considered running back to her cabin, to find the Henry carbine she always kept in her buggy. It hadn't been fired since Jude was alive, and she had no idea where extra cartridges were kept. So she squatted and waited and prayed that whoever it was wouldn't approach her place.

But they did.

Four men riding shaggy looking mares, their faces cast into deep shadow by the brims of their dusty hats. She flattened herself, putting her cheek against the earth. Perhaps if she remained deathly still, they wouldn't notice her.

They were close now, steering their mounts around the root crop field. She gave up a tiny prayer of thanks for that.

"We should go see who is in there."

"Could be they heard the gunfire."

"Could be they have seen us."

These three statements came from three distinctly different voices, one clearly Mexican, one old and gruff, the third much younger, a tinge of fear on the edge of his words. The fourth, when he spoke, was that of their obvious leader. A man well used to giving orders, of others doing as he bid. "If they had heard, we'd see 'em running, and I'd kill them dead before they opened their blabbering mouths."

"So who lives there, Jonas?"

"I don't know and I don't care. Maybe they is in town picking up supplies. I don't see no buggy."

This much was true. Cathy did possess a buggy, but it was stored away in the barn. When she needed to, she rode into town on her colt, Pharaoh. Pharaoh had thrown a shoe some days previously, and the blacksmith was due any day now. She sheltered in the small stable, together with her *burro* friend. Being out of sight proved another reason to thank God.

The riders moved on, the clomping of hooves gradually fading away until, ears straining to hear, Cathy caught the sound of water splashing. They were crossing the river and heading away from her place.

She let out a long sigh, rolled over onto her back, and settled herself before climbing to her feet. She gave a look around. Satisfied no one remained behind, she broke into a run. Not towards the house, however. Towards where the gunshots came.

In a dip amongst the trees where the harsh warmth of the sun could not penetrate, she found him.

Shot. Two times. Once in the left shoulder, once in the chest. He appeared to be dead, the pallor of his flesh waxen, drained of color. He was young, had been handsome, smooth-faced. They had taken his gun, his hat, his boots, leaving him to bleed out alone in this sad and dreary place. It was the blood that made her stop and take a closer look.

Dead don't bleed.

Quickly, she got down on her haunches and felt his neck for a pulse. A tiny gasp escaped from her throat.

He was alive.

She dressed his wounds as best she could, fetching water from her well, washing away the worst of it before wrapping bandages torn from the bedsheets she'd only recently purchased from the local town's merchandise store around him. He groaned several times, and she knew this was a good sign. When she put water to his lips, he coughed, and her heart leapt.

Returning to the smallholding at a run, she fetched Brandy, the *burro*. Pharaoh didn't like that, but Cathy ignored her horse and led the donkey to the trees. There she fashioned a sort of sledge from fallen trees, threading them together in the way Jude had shown her to make wattle fencing. It took her a long time to struggle and place the wounded man on the sledge. Her grim determination saw her through, despite the weight of him. She paused several times to wipe the sweat from her brow but before long he was positioned on the sled and, satisfied, she led Brandy back to the cabin.

That night she lay him down by the fire as the fever came, the bullet in his chest the worst of the two. Bathing his brow, she watched him as he writhed around on the cabin floor. She thought he would die and dreaded the thought of having to dig a grave deep enough to deter coyotes. The hard earth would barely cover his body. But he did not die, and the morning dawned to find him breathing, an infection rattling in his chest. She washed away the sweat from his brow, changed the bandages covering his wounds, and made sure the fire was well stacked up.

She nursed him for another day before she accepted the inevitable – she would have to cut out the bullets if he were to survive.

He drifted in and out of consciousness, lucid moments few and far between. Managing to roll him onto an old piece of canvas, she sharpened one of her kitchen knives, held her breath, and worked on the lesser of the two wounds.

It proved a godsend he was unconscious for most of it.

The slug, when it came out, looked surprisingly small. She studied it for a long time, marveling how something so insignificant could cause such distress.

Setting to the second wound proved a far more laborious, stressful, and difficult task. It was in deep, forcing her to use a different knife with a thinner blade. At one point, he arched his back and bellowed, eyes snapping open, wild and afraid. He tried to sit up, but she pushed him back down, put a wet cloth over his forehead, waited until his spasm subsided, then set to work once more.

It took something like twenty minutes to ease the bullet out, although it felt a lot longer. She was exhausted when she managed to lever it free.

The blood pulsed freely, but that had to be a good sign, and she packed the wound like the Kiowa had shown her all those years before, cleaning out the wound with some of Jude 's whisky before making a poultice from dampened, stale bread and herbs.

To her astonishment, as the evening wore on, his breathing grew lighter, the perspiration abated, and his almost constant moaning lessened until, finally, it ceased. He slept soundly. The following day, he sat up, face dry, eyes focused. She studied him from the far corner where she stood, the old Spencer in her hands. Who could guess what this man, now recovered, might try to do?

His lips, when he spoke, trembled slightly, his voice sounded raucous, the throat dry. "I could do with some water, ma'am, if you could be so kind."

Without any hesitation, she twisted around to where a goatskin gourd stood on the rickety table next to the water pump. She placed it on the floor within his arm's reach. Not for a single moment did her eyes leave his as she carefully stepped back.

He nodded his thanks, lifted the gourd to his lips, and drank fitfully, coughing hoarsely as the water hit his parched mouth.

"Take it slow," she said quietly.

Something passed across his eyes as he swallowed some more. A look of gratitude, so overwhelming that the tears came to his eyes and spilt down his cheeks. He looked away, ashamed at this show of emotion. 'I'm so very grateful for what you have done, ma'am.' He broke down and sobbed uncontrollably, head on his chest, shoulders heaving with the power of his outpourings.

Cathy watched, speechless, in two minds as to what to do. It could be a ploy, of course, to draw her to him, lower her guard so he could pounce, over-power her, and ... and then what, she could only speculate. But something about the rawness of his tears made her think that this was no ruse. This was genuine, the sheer relief of being alive causing him to react in such an open, sincere way.

"I'm sorry," he said as the tears abated at last. He dabbed at his eyes with the back of his hand. Pulling a piece of white material from her sleeve, she crossed to him and pushed the makeshift handkerchief into his hand. He mopped at his wet face and smiled his thanks.

Stepping away again, Cathy studied him, the way his dark hair flopped over the left eye, the full, feminine mouth, smooth-cheeked, strong jawline not yet sprinkled with the shadow of a beard's growth. How old could he be? Eighteen? Twenty perhaps? And here he was, in her home, recovering from bullets which should have killed him. Who was he, and what had forced those others to attack him so viciously?

He caught her look, and his cheeks reddened slightly. "As soon as I'm able, I'll be on my way, ma'am. I don't wish to impose upon your hospitality any more than I need to."

"You're not imposing," she said, a slight smile playing across her mouth. "It was me that brought you in. And, besides, you can't go, not until you have some new boots."

He laughed, the relief palpable. "Ah, yes. They took those, I suppose." A sudden darkness came over his features. His eyes held hers. 'Did you see the men who did this to me?'

"No. Only heard them as they rode by."

"But they didn't see you?"

She frowned at the panic in his voice. "No. Don't worry yourself about that. I was on the ground, well hidden."

His shoulders visibly relaxed, and he lay back in the bed. "Thank you."

"Who were they? Why did they shoot you and leave you to die like that?"

She knew it was too soon to ask such searching questions. She had yet to gain his trust and, indeed, for him to gain hers. She held her breath, unable to take back her words, wondering if he would reveal it all or slip into coyness.

"We had a falling out," he said simply, his voice growing distant. "I'm sorry, ma'am. I'm tired. And I need ... you know ... I need ..."

"Yes!" she blurted, understanding immediately what he meant. "There is an outhouse round back. Are you sure you can walk?"

"If you were to put that carbine away, you could help me. At least to the door of the privy?" He sat up, laughing, and the sound cut through the tension which had settled between them.

"We'll see," she said, propped the carbine against the wall, and drew back her threadbare cardigan to reveal the Colt Navy stuffed into her skirt waistband. "My husband's. He taught me how to shoot, saying I'd need to if ever he was away on business and I was left alone."

"Is he away on business now?"

"Kind of." She took a step towards him. "Let's get you feeling a little more comfortable." She smiled and put out her hand. He took it after a moment's hesitation and slipped out from beneath the covers.

CHAPTER TWO

"I 'll swear in a posse and run them down before sundown." Roose worked fresh cartridges into the Henry. He was breathing hard, his anger clear for all to see.

People began to gather around, staring at the bodies, muttering among themselves, commenting on how awful it all was, that such a lovely day could have ended in such a murderous way.

"We need to get these bodies off the street and go check the bank first," said Cole. "Put two armed men outside while we go inside."

Singling out two young men, both wearing tied down guns at their hips, Roose pointed to the bank. "Anyone but us comes out, you shoot 'em."

Appalled, the two young men exchanged nervous glances. Cole chuckled, "Don't worry, boys, I very much doubt there are any desperados left inside."

"Even so," muttered Roose.

"Even so, you just do what you can." Flashing them a wink, Cole inched forwards, alert, carbine ready. Roose scooted past, slamming himself against the wall adjacent to the entrance. He carefully propped the Henry beside him and drew his Colt Cavalry. Nodding to Cole, he eased back the hammer.

Cole went inside, sweeping the room with his Winchester. The three tellers behind the counter had their arms stretched upwards with such strain it looked like they were in pain. Cole pressed a single finger to his lips, gesturing with the Winchester for them to lower their hands. He scanned the rest of the room and, satisfied, lay down his carbine and pulled out his revolver. One of the tellers slowly pulled up the hatch to allow him to slip behind the counter. Cole went to the bank manager's office.

The door was part-open, and, using his foot, he pushed it wide, his gun ready.

There was paper money all over the floor, a lot of it splattered with fresh blood. Against the far wall, a man, clearly dead with his open eyes staring into space, a look of abject bewilderment etched across his frozen face.

A trail of more blood led to the rear entrance, usually heavily bolted with two thick iron bars giving further security. Everything was hanging open, the locks released by one of the keys from a bunch thrown onto the floor.

"He used my keys," explained a well-dressed and badly beaten man slumped in the corner, his mouth so swollen his words were barely recognizable.

Lowering himself to one knee, Cole peered through the crack in-between the door and the jam.

"The other one shot him."

Cole arched a single eyebrow and gave him a questioning glance.

"Young fella, very tall. He shot the both of them. They wanted to kill me, but he stopped them." He tried to sit upright but failed and, letting out a long wail of pain, slumped back down. "He saved my life."

"But only wounded the one who got away."

"Yes. Perhaps he was hoping you'd arrest him, throw him in jail."

"Why do that when there would be a chance he'd tell us everything he knows about the gang – their hideout, who they are, where they planned on headin'?"

"Who knows? Mister Cole, could you please send for a doctor? I'm not sure how much more of this pain I can take."

Returning his Colt to its holster, Cole stood and headed outside, picking up his carbine before gesturing the tellers to follow close behind.

"Anything?" asked Roose, visibly relaxing as Cole stepped up beside him.

"One dead, shot by one of his own according to the bank manager, who needs a doctor by the way. The other one he shot managed to get away. He'll be riding hell-for-leather to meet up with the rest of 'em." He nodded to the two young would-be gunslingers. "Thanks, boys, we won't be needing you today."

Looking relieved, they slinked away and headed towards the nearest saloon.

Roose watched them move away, then said, "Do we know which one did the shootin'?"

Cole scanned the many bodies sprawled out in the street. "Could be any one of 'em. The only witness we have, the manager, won't be able to confirm anything until the doc's checked him over."

"If he's one of the ones who got away, there'll be a reckoning." Roose chuckled. "They might even do our job for us."

"Somewhat wishful thinking there, Sterling. You'll need to hunt 'em down and bring 'em in, then we can get to the bottom of this damned fiasco."

"You're not coming?"

"Sterling, I've done my duty for the day," he sighed. "I'm supposed to be retired, remember?"

"You're too young to retire – besides, I need you."

"Nah, you don't need me, Sterling. You can call on Brown Owl, the Arapaho. He's the best tracker there is."

"Except he's not – you is."

"That's gracious of you, you old skunk," he grinned, "but I need to get back to Pa's place. He ain't too well. I'm not sure he's gonna be around much longer."

Deep in thought, Roose swung away for a moment. Already, bodies were being covered in white shrouds. Several burly men lifted them and stacked them in the back of a flat-bed wagon, destined for the undertakers.

"All right, Cole, if that's how it is."

"You're in safe hands with Brown Owl. He's a good friend, dependable and honest. I've known him for as long as I can remember so I have no worries about placing you in his good hands."

"Yeah, but I'll miss you, Cole."

"Now, don't get all maudlin on me, Sterling. How hard can it be to track down such an incompetent bunch as this?"

"Not very."

"Well, there you go. I'll see you back here in less than two days. Trust me."

"I hope you're right," said Roose and moved away, calling to several men lingering close by.

Cole watched his old friend swear in the men as deputies and couldn't prevent a shudder running through him, his sense of foreboding growing by the second. He couldn't understand why, but perhaps none of this was going to be as straightforward as he'd said it would.

CHAPTER THREE

The old place felt chill as he stepped inside, kicking off the dust from his boots. Hanging up his jacket on the hat stand in the hallway, he moved to the foot of the stairs and looked to the top. "Pa? Pa, are you awake? Got some news for you. From town." He started to climb then stopped as Marta, his father's loyal Mexican housekeeper, appeared from the rear kitchen, face screwed up in anguish.

"Oh, *Señor* Reuben," she said, words laced with tears, "it is *Señor* Martin, he is not eating and seems so weak. I wanted to call for the doctor, but I was too frightened to leave him." She broke down, and Cole went to her, holding her tight. Pressing her face against his chest, she sobbed uncontrollably.

Waiting for the right moment before he released her, Cole drew in a deep breath. "All right, Marta, I'll go to him now. You ride over to the Doc's and tell him to get here as soon as he can."

She scurried away, wringing her hands, muttering incoherent Spanish under her breath. Taking his time, dreading what he would find, Cole climbed the stairs.

His father's room was blanketed in darkness, the heavy drapes shutting out all available light. A small oil lamp flickered pathetically in the far corner, and the air was heavy with the smell of sickness. The only sound was the awful, dry wheeze of his father's labored breathing.

Up until a year ago, his father's health had been robust. Often, he would be found out in the far reaches of his ranch, checking the fences, guiding any errant cattle back to the main herd, a herd which was due to be sold in only a few weeks' time. He'd return to the house, full of vim, grinning like an ape, happy to be alive.

After he'd moved in, Cole marveled at how sprightly his father was. "News was you ain't so good, Pa," he'd said on that first meeting. His father merely laughed for a reply.

Not anymore. Since then, his father's health had deteriorated until just, two weeks ago, he'd taken to his bed and had not yet moved, save for the occasional visit to the bathroom.

"I'm old, Reuben," he said only the other day. "I'm old and I *feel* old."

Here, standing at the foot of the large bed, squinting through the darkness, Cole studied his father and struggled to remember moments from the past. Good times, memories, shared events, but nothing would formulate in his mind. All he could picture was the mound of blankets and the irregular rise and fall of his father's chest.

This was not the man he knew. The man he knew was already gone. As if to confirm this idea, a low, pain-racked moan escaped from his father's lips. It subsided, and Cole stepped closer.

Spasmodically, his father would kick out under the covers, as if struggling against some invisible enemy, or a frantic attempt to free himself of the blankets. Cole knew not what it could be, only that his father was in pain, and there was nothing he could do.

When the call came from Sterling two days previously, Cole had left without a word, not giving a second's thought for what he might find on his return. Yes, his father was old and tired, all tuckered out as the man himself might have said, but never did Cole think he would come home to this. Such a serious and sudden deterioration left him speechless and unable to know what to do. He'd always assumed, perhaps stupidly, that things would just go along the way they always had. That soon, his old Pa would recover, and life would return to its usual, dull routine. Normality.

The realization that those days had now come to an end made him numb.

Sitting down at the foot of the bed, he remained there until Marta returned with Doctor Henson. She might have been away for an hour or half a day, he couldn't tell. Like vague shadows, they fluttered around him, and he wandered outside as if in a dream and sat on the porch, rolled himself a cigarette, and waited.

It was Marta's strangled cries that brought him back to reality. He got up and went to go back inside. Doc Henson stood there, grim and serious. "I'm sorry, Reuben, I did all I could, but ..."

He pressed a hand on Reuben's shoulder. Cole gave a tiny shrug and said, "Thanks anyway. I knew he was sick, but never how bad it truly was."

"Nobody did, except perhaps him. My guess, it was some sort of sickness in his brain. A cancer maybe, or something to do with his arteries."

"His what?"

"Blood vessels. That would account for his forgetfulness of late, his wandering around the house. Marta kept me informed when you were away. It's been a gradual but relentless decline, Reuben, but, like I say, no one knew. He was often lucid, and during those times, he was the same as he always was. At least, now he is at peace."

Cole stared, the guilt overwhelming him. He should have been here more often, spent more time with his father, savoring each precious moment. Now he never would. Life, as always, had turned another page.

"I'll see to all the arrangements, Reuben, so you have no need to worry. He'll be in the family plot, I'm guessing, up there with your mom?"

Cole grunted, shook the doctor's hand, and watched him ride off.

It was only when the sun went down that he returned indoors.

CHAPTER FOUR

S tanding on the boardwalk just outside the entrance to his dry goods
store, Larry Grimes, face lifted skywards, took in the morning
sunshine. With the furor of the failed bank robbery now in the past, the
town had returned to normal. Several passers-by called out to him as they
strolled along the street, and he would nod and smile, raising his hand
occasionally. A popular man, almost everyone frequented his store at
some point or other. Recently, the inclusion of a mail-order catalogue to
his business attracted a growing number of fashion-conscious women, all
keen to discover the latest 'best-thing' from out east. It was to this
purpose that Florence Caitlin mounted the steps and bobbed her head in
his direction.

"'Morning, Miss Caitlin."

"Good morning, Mr Grimes. Another beautiful day."

"Sure is, although I suspect that early morning chill I'm feeling is the
precursor to winter coming on."

"That dreadful robbery was so very terrible, was it not? I hope you
were not a witness to any of it?"

"No, miss, I give thanks I had not yet opened up when it all erupted.
So many killed, thankfully most of them those vile robbers. I have not
yet heard much news, but I do know the Sheriff has gone to track them
down."

"Let us hope it all ends well."

"Indeed," he said.

Smiling, she stepped inside, her patent leather boots clumping across the wood flooring. Larry watched her and sighed. If only he had the courage, he would invite Florence for a Sunday afternoon walk through the surrounding hills, or a buggy ride down to the river. Her cool, blue eyes, blonde ringlets and full, pouting mouth brought uncontrolled heat to his loins. However, he accepted he could never ask her to join him. Everyone in town, including Florence, knew his heart was set elsewhere, yet his roaming eye meant he might never be entirely satisfied with just one woman, no matter how attractive that one woman might be. Believing him to be steady, God-fearing man, nobody could tell what went on behind those soft, gentle brown eyes of his. Perhaps this knowledge was the reason why Florence appeared so comfortable in his presence. She believed him to be faithful, a good man, strong and virtuous. Handsome too, despite his limp. Perhaps if she knew the truth, she would no longer frequent his store. Nor, perhaps, would the majority of his customers. And Cathy, who held the flame close to his heart, may be forced to make up her mind and turn her back on him for good.

Pushing aside these disturbing thoughts, Larry shuffled inside. His leg felt good today, the warmth helping to ease the pain in his knee. The bullet he'd caught at Gettysburg had made him a virtual cripple for the last ten years and more, but his determination to walk unaided meant that few knew the history of his limp. Rumor had it he'd fallen from a horse some years back. Such a belief was fine by him, anything to divert them from the truth.

As he expected, Florence was at the catalogue stand, slowly leafing through the illustrations on the pages. She barely looked up as Larry moved up beside her. "I see they've added some new lines."

"Straight from Chicago, so they say."

"Chicago?" She looked at him. "Didn't you come from there, Mr Grimes?"

"I was born there, yes."

She arched a single eyebrow and stared at him intriguingly. "I've heard it say you joined the Army, Mr Grimes, fought for the Blues, that the horse you rode was shot under you and you suffered a broken knee."

"Something like that." He didn't add that the only factual part of her story was that he had fought for the Union, volunteering as soon as Lincoln made the call.

"You don't mind me asking you, do you?"

"No, not at all." He forced a small bark of a laugh. Had she noticed something in his changed mood, he wondered. He hastily did his best to sidetrack her. "It was all a long time ago, Miss Caitlin."

"Not all that long ago. Ten years. We're still healing."

"Yes, I guess that's so."

"The efforts made to try to reform the south into some form of social Utopia are failing miserably. Soon we'll be right back to where we started before the War even began."

"I can't see that happening, Miss Caitlin. I believe the President has it all under control."

"You think so? Then why didn't he send troops in to quell the outbreak of violence down in Mississippi that time? That Nathan Forrest had been stirring things for too long, in my opinion."

"I don't believe it was Forrest who instigated the violence in Mississippi."

"Possibly not, but it was all thanks to his creation of those lunatics called the Ku Klux Klan that this all started."

Larry Grimes blinked. "Your grasp of politics surprises me, Miss Caitlin."

"Why? Because I'm a woman?"

He side-stepped her caustic retort, continuing to smile despite the growing anxiety spreading through him. It was true; he himself saw similarities to how the country was back in the early 1860s. To think of it all exploding into armed confrontation once again would be enough to have him packing his bags and heading for Canada.

"No, not because you're a woman," he said, as disarmingly as he could. "Because of your passion."

"Passion? I'm not a secessionist, Mr Grimes. My father too fought in the War – for the Union."

"I didn't know that."

"He was killed at Second Manassas."

The unemotional matter-of-fact way she revealed this awful news shocked him. "I'm sorry," he said gently.

"Where did that bullet take down your horse, Mr Grimes?"

He wondered, not for the first time, whether or not he should tell her the truth. He drew in a breath. "Gettysburg."

Her eyes clouded over and then, quite unexpectedly, she reached over and squeezed his hand. "You're hiding something, Mr Grimes. I can tell."

Feeling the heat rise to his jawline, he cleared his throat and gave her a tiny nod. The conversation was growing too close for comfort. He gently tugged his hand free and moved over to the counter. "I'm glad you find that catalogue of interest, Miss Caitlin. Once you put your order in, they say six weeks is the waiting time. That's quite something."

"Indeed it is." She stared at him, waiting for him to continue, perhaps. When he didn't, she returned to the catalogue, wetting a slim index finger before recommencing her search through the many items on offer.

Some hours later, having replenished shelves and served at least a dozen or so customers, he stepped outside again. The street buzzed with people, many walking, some riding by on horses, the occasional buggy or wagon trundling along, wheels in need of grease grating around their axles. Larry blew out his breath and checked his fob-watch. Almost mid-afternoon. Cathy was usually here by now, and he wondered what might have prevented her from coming in. Her visits were the highlight of his day, although she probably didn't know how much he looked forward to her arrival. He never said anything. A woman like Cathy, strong, independent, wouldn't be interested in somebody like him – a virtual cripple. Perhaps he should try his luck with Florence. After all, she'd held his hand, which was something Cathy had never done in the whole two years he'd known her.

Checking both ends of the street, he returned to the store interior, his heart heavy, his mood low.

CHAPTER FIVE

"I'm gonna need to call a doctor," she said, placing the big cast-iron pot carefully upon the stovetop.

"You've done admirably so far," he said from inside the bedroom, propped up by every pillow she had.

"What's the matter," sensing something in his tone, "you don't want to get fixed?" She swung around and stared at him across the tiny cabin room.

"Of course I wanna get fixed."

"Well then."

"I just thought if I could lay up for a couple more days, I´d be fine."

"Fine you may be, but a doctor would know that for sure. That hole in your chest was deep, and the other one is all puckering up."

"You packed it with some stuff, didn't you? Weird stuff."

"I did, yes, but it smells, and I need to get it all cleaned out proper."

Collapsing his head back into the pillows, he blew out a long sigh. "Truth is, I'm scared. Scared they'll come back. If you were out fetching whoever and they burst in here ..."

"All right," she said gently, drying her hands on a rag and throwing it into the corner. Unrolling her sleeves, she moved across the room and entered the bedroom. She sat down on the bed beside him. "I think it's time you told me what went on and why they shot you."

"Do I have to?"

"Yes, you do. And I ain't gonna stop badgering you until you do."

"My, you are nothing but a terrier, ain't yeh."

"I am that. Funny, my husband used to call me that – *Cathy*, he'd say, *you has as much sand, spit, and venom as any rat-catchin' terrier there ever has been!*" She laughed hard and long, shaking her head, looking back through the years.

"I thought you said he was away," he said when, at last, she paused.

Her eyes, bright with the tears of laughter, hardened. "No. I said he was 'sort of'. He's away, but not in the strict meaning of the word. He's dead. Scarlet fever. Cut him down like he was a weak-kneed infant. I did all I could, Doc Henson, too. Up for three nights we was ..." Shaking her head again, but this time in a deep, heavy sadness, she pulled in a huge breath. "I lost him, and there ain't a day goes by that I wish he would come back."

"I'm sorry."

"Don't be – you never even knew him."

"Even so."

"Even so, it's your turn. Tell me your story, then I'll fetch the Doc again and we'll get you right."

He looked deep into her eyes for a moment before slowly turning away. A few deep breaths, as if he were preparing himself for some mighty physical effort, and then he launched himself into the story.

CHAPTER SIX

'We'd set to casing the bank for more than two weeks. A big deposit was coming in from the railroad, mostly gold transported to government storehouses. None of us knew how much, but Bernie Seagrams, our boss, if you wanna call him such, he'd caught a whiff of it from some drunkard over in Amarillo over a card game. He said it was somewhere in the region of fifty to a hundred thousand dollars. Life-changing. The thought of it made us determined to see it through.

'Bethlehem is a smallish town, past its best, but it is on the main railroad line from Chicago. We rode in two at a time, and Pete Mullins and me got ourselves a room in a two-bit hotel near the end of the main street. The plan was for us to wander around, keeping ourselves as inconspicuous as possible, whilst noting down the comings and goings at the bank.

'They'd brought in a group of new guards, well-armed, to protect the shipment. It was to be stored overnight before continuing on its long journey to somewhere deep in Texas. We had no idea where it was headed, and neither did we care.

'We was on the boardwalk of the saloon, chomping on cheroots, when we first saw him. At the time, I had no idea who he was. Tall and lean, grey pin-striped trousers and black tailcoat. He wore his gun across his belly. The star on his lapel was huge, as if he were proclaiming himself as to just who exactly he was – the law.

'Pete grumbled under his breath, saying he would be the first to die as he looked as mean as a coyote. I agreed. I do not think I have ever seen such a look on a man's face as the one he bore. Until his partner arrived. That was when I got scared.

'Something started niggling away at me that this was going to be a darn sight more difficult than Seagrams had ever thought.

'I learned later that the lean one in black was Sterling Roose, sheriff of the town. His companion, dressed in buckskins, was an Army Scout name of Reuben Cole. They had something of a reputation these two, both of 'em as hard as the land upon which they rode. Men who knew about killin' and made light of it with a detached indifference that was chilling.

'The day of the delivery came, and Seagrams met with me outside a millinery shop. I told him of my concerns, and he laughed them off. He was a man on a mission, and nothing was about to force him away from what he saw as his destiny.

'"I'm gonna be rich, as rich as I have ever dreamed of!" He said this with his thumbs stuck in his belt, looking as happy as a little boy on his birthday.

'That was that. Disregarding all I said, the time came for us to go in. Six of us, bandanas over our noses, we went steaming inside, six-guns ready. Three others were outside, two with the horses, old Joey Steiner driving the wagon. The tellers behind the counter were already thrusting their hands upwards as Seagrams shouted, "Get your money from those drawers and don't even think about trying anything foolish!"

'Vaulting the counter, Jonas and I burst into the tiny office at the back where we found a suited man sporting a resplendent handlebar moustache and a quivering look. "We want the combination to the safe," spat Jonas and rammed his six-gun hard into the man's forehead.

'The bank at Bethlehem was one of the new-fangled types imported from Germany. Not only was it large, but it boasted a twin set of combination locks, both of which had to be properly engaged for the great, heavy door to open.

'From the look on his face, I could see the bank manager was not the bravest of men. He gladly gave up the combination, and I set to it while Jonas kept the gun to his head.

'I hollered as the tumblers engaged, and Seagrams came in, beaming. Together with myself and two others, we set to filling the many canvas sacks we'd brought with us. Gradually, an impressive mound of money bags grew beside the safe, and soon we'd be taking them to the wagon outside.

'It was then, perhaps when he saw us begin to take the money away, that the little bank manager said something. "You won't get away with this. That is railroad money, destined for the government. They will hunt you down and hang you all."

'Jonas hit him, the sound of his pistol against the side of his skull making the most fearful crack. The force of the blow tipped him out of his revolving chair and sent him into the far corner, blood already streaming, his moans growing louder by the second. "I'll put a bullet in you if you don't stop," shouted Jonas as Seagrams, distracted from the money for a moment, drew his own gun, and aimed it. "Shut up!"

'The poor man, stricken by pain and fear, did the exact opposite, his moaning becoming a loud wail. A horrible sound, it travelled way beyond the walls of the bank and was better than any alarm to warn the town of what was happening.

'It was then I did a most foolhardy thing. I stepped between the manager and those two fools with their guns. Waving my hands, I shouted, "There is no need for any killin'!"

'If not already incensed, those two became like wild dogs, frothing at the mouth, teeth chomping, eyes flashing. "Get out the damned way," screamed Jonas, but I wouldn't. Behind me, the little manager's yells were continuing, and they were awesome loud. I could see what was stirring behind Jonas' eyes and what I saw scared me, I don't mind telling you. I knew him to be a low life, a simpleton who was quick to violence, so I took no chances. In that tiny lull, with uncertainty dancing across his features, I pulled my gun and shot him high up on his gun arm.

'Everything went crazy from that point.

'As Jonas cartwheeled across the room, Seagrams' jaw hung wide open. All of his plans, all of his dreams, were disintegrating right before his eyes, and I knew he was about to do something awful.

'So I shot him too, not in the arm this time, in the chest. I blew him flat against the far wall and watched him slide down to the ground, his eyes already lifeless, the hole in his body trailing smoke and blood.

'The bank manager's jaw hung open with disbelief at what he had witnessed. Although in obvious pain, his face swelling like a ripe melon, he no longer moaned. Ignoring him, and without another thought, I grabbed up three or four of them money sacks and rushed out into the main room.

'"What is going on in there," one of the gang demanded.

'"Bank manager shot Seagrams," I said quickly. "We have to go."

'No one took to questioning me as the four of us remaining rushed out to join the rest of the gang outside. Grabbing handfuls of money, we stuffed dollar bills into the sacks while we ran. We threw some of the sacks into the back of the wagon. One or two of us went to tie bundles behind our saddles before we jumped onto the backs of our horses and made to high tail it out of there.

'Until Roose appeared.

'He stood in the centre of the street, Henry in his hand, aiming it like it was a turkey shoot, he was so damned calm. His first bullet took out old Joey Steiner, blowing him clean out of his seat. The horses went wild, rearing up, whinnying and squealing in terror, and stampeded down the street. There was nothing we could do but watch. Second bullet took the skull off one of the others, showering those closest to him with his blood and brains. That set off everyone, the hollering of both men and horses sounding like something from the very bowels of hell where tormented souls ranted and raved in the depths of their tortured souls.

'For that was what it was like. Pure hell.

'I was battling to keep my horse under control. Others were moving past me, swearing and cursing, beating at their horses with hands, hats, even drawn weapons. Anything to get those terrified beasts moving.

'More bullets raced through the air, missing some of us by mere inches. The air filled with horse sweat and fear. One or two of us sent some returning shots, but they was as ineffective as they was desperate. Struggling to move forward, I managed to pull my weapon and did my best to aim, but it was useless, my horse too far gone in fear by now.

'The other one came out of a side street. Reuben Cole. I don't know how he did that, sneaking up on us without being seen, but he shot another of our gang dead and wounded Jim-Bob Winters in the leg before we managed to gallop away from that killing zone.

'We were in a sorry state. Four of us dead, Jonas wounded back in the bank, poor little Jim-Bob squealing like a stuck pig beside me. I knew he wouldn't last the night, but there was nothing I or anyone else could do. Our only thought now was to ride, hard and fast, back to our hideout, count whatever money we had, and make our way down to the Mexican border and safety.

'When finally we made it to our camp, the horses blown, all of us in a wretched state of mangled nerves, I did what I could to make Jim-Bob comfortable. With the afternoon drawing on and the heat gripping us like a vice, I took a hot knife to little Jim-Bob's thigh and dug that slug out. We packed it with tequila-soaked rags, and I sat with him as he writhed around in his blanket, consumed by sweat. The others drank what little liquor remained, smoked and mumbled. All of us were numb with shock. We had little to show for all of our efforts, and I was the only one still alive who'd managed to put some money in my saddlebags.

'It was in the early evening when Jonas appeared. As the others whooped and hollered with relief and excitement, I stood like a rock. Our eyes bore into one another. His right arm dangled useless by his side but in his left hand was his Colt.

'I took my chance and bolted, leaping onto the back of my horse as the first bullet pinged over my head. Keeping low, I set off, knowing full well they would be behind me.

'They caught up with me by a trickling brook, and there they shot me, stripped me and left me for dead. It was justice, said Jonas, his eyes alight with murderous glee. "I'll see you in Hell, you traitorous wretch," he said and spat at me before riding off.

'I passed out, and when I woke up, I was in a cabin with the most beautiful woman I've ever seen tending to me. And that's it. The whole thing. I do not know what will become of me now, but it cannot be as bad as what I have already been through during that miserable attempt to rob the bank.'

He lowered his head and blew out a long sigh, seemingly exhausted with the re-telling.

Having listened in silence, Cathy leaned back in her chair and considered the man sitting across from her at the rough-hewn table. He chose to focus on the floor.

"Is that the truth?" she said after some time.

"I swear it is."

"Not sure if a self-confessed bank robber's word is all that believable."

"I understand that, but why would I lie? You saved my life. I owe you."

That was good enough for Cathy. She got up, made coffee and eggs, serving them up on tin plates, and he ate like he hadn't tasted food in days. This brought a smile to her lips, and she felt he was a good man, one to be trusted. Unlike her late husband, whose wanderlust brought her nothing but heartache, despite her loving the very bones of him.

CHAPTER SEVEN

They reined in on the rise overlooking the tired, worn-out collection of warped wooden buildings that someone had once christened the town of 'Haven'. One of the men spat and swore. "This looks deader than a graveyard, Jonas."

"Graveyards ain't dead, only those in 'em."

"You know what I mean."

"All I need is a doctor to patch me up, then we'll be gone." To give some emphasis to his words, he attempted to revolve his shoulder, an action which brought a string of obscenities to his lips. "It's been two days, and I feel it going numb."

"That's good, ain't it? No more pain."

"Are you stupid or you just ain't got a brain."

"Ah shucks, Jonas, no need to say such things to me!"

"*Gringo,*" said the Mexican who sat astride his horse on the other side of Jonas, "if you don't like it, stay here and cook us some food."

"Food? Hell, I ain't your servant, Cruces! Besides, we ain't got no food."

"That's another reason to go take a look," said the fourth member of the gang, a gangly, pock-marked youth with no teeth.

Jonas kicked his horse and eased it down the incline, the others slowly moving in behind.

The sun burned, but not as ferociously as of late. The year was turning, the nights much colder now than they had been. Soon, snow would come and travelling across country would become increasingly difficult. They needed supplies and a place to stay, lick their wounds, and reassess their situation. These thoughts, among others, buzzed around inside Jonas' head. None of this was his fault. The plan had been down to Seagrams, but however clever their former leader was, he made no back-up plan, never considering for a moment anything would go wrong. Now the gang had to somehow extricate itself and move on, and this time, whatever plan evolved, it would succeed. It would be Jonas' plan, if he ever got this arm fixed. He tried clenching and unclenching his fist but could barely manage it, the numbness spreading with frightening rapidity. He pushed aside dark, unsettling thoughts and spurred his horse into a canter.

The single saloon was a sad affair, a single narrow room with four tables and a battered staircase leading to rooms above. Around one table, two men studied torn, dog-eared playing cards. Behind the counter, a tiny, bald man polished glasses. He looked up as the four dust-spattered riders came inside. All at once, his hands started to tremble.

"Easy," said Jonas through clenched teeth, "we is tired, thirsty, and hungry. All we want is to rest up for a spell."

"You got beer?" asked the gangly youth.

The man nodded. "It's cold too."

The youth slapped the countertop with his palm. "Then serve 'em up!"

The bald barkeep disappeared into a backroom. Jonas gave the room a scan and stepped up to the two card players. He doffed his hat. "Gentlemen, would there be a doctor hereabouts?"

The men studied Jonas' blood-soaked arm and shifted uneasily in their chairs. "Doc Farlow is retired now," said one of them, "but he still lives above Maisie's."

"Maisie's?"

"That's our local whorehouse," said the bald man, reappearing with a tray of four beer glasses filled to the top, froth cascading down the sides.

"It ain't in operation any longer," put in the card-player quickly.

While the others attacked their beer, Jonas' eyes never left the two men. "How far?"

"Straight down the street. You can't miss it, the sign's still hanging there. You get to Doc Farlow's by the steps outside. That's where he lodges."

"Obliged," said Jonas, crossed to his beer and downed it in one gulp. Smacking his lips and belching loudly, he went to the door. "I won't be long, boys."

"You want someone to come with you?"

Jonas smiled at the gangly youth. "I'll be all right, Len, but thanks for offering."

Stopping at the foot of the wooden staircase, attached as it was to the abandoned whorehouse, Jonas hesitated. The steps were grey, and the warped planks did not look as if they could take the weight of a child, let alone a man. A rotten door at the top hung on rusted hinges. No sign of life.

Jonas tentatively placed his foot on the first step and winced as it groaned. Applying more of his weight, he began a slow, laborious ascent, pausing, testing the planks one at a time before moving up to the next.

With one more step to go, he levered up his foot. The old door wrenched open, and a small, rotund man wearing stained long johns appeared holding a Navy Colt in his hand.

Surprised by this sudden apparition appearing before him, Jonas jumped back, screamed, lost his footing and tipped over backwards down the steps, splintering several, until he hit the bottom and rolled across the ground, throwing up billowing clouds of grey dust, which slowly settled over him. He lay motionless, aware of the pain spreading through his body, not only from the gunshot wound, but new, even more excruciating rivals from bruises, cuts, and, more than likely, breaks.

"What, in the name of Hades, is you doing creeping up my stairs, boy?"

Aware of the voice, but not its direction, Jonas dared not move. He felt if he did, he would snap his spine in two. Breathing into the dirt, trying not to take too much into his mouth, he groaned, "Help me."

"How can I help you, you darned fool? You've gone and busted my staircase. Now I can't get down nor up."

"Ah no, Lemmy," came the voice of a young woman, "now we're gonna just have to stay in bed all day." She giggled.

"And what about food and water, eh? This darned fool has condemned us to a jail sentence."

"It ain't that bad, is it, Lemmy? Being locked up with me?"

"Ah, Maisie, you know I would wanna spend the rest of my days locked up with you."

Another giggle, the sound of something striking the girl's body, and then the crash of the old door closing behind them, muffled cries coming from within.

Jonas groaned. The old coot had left him out here to die. If he ever got back on his feet, he'd get him to patch up the wounds then put a forty-five caliber bullet through his brainpan.

————

Sometime later, concerned over Jonas' whereabouts, the others moved outside, ambling down the street to find their leader sprawled in the dust, barely breathing. Len broke into a run and got down beside him. "Jonas," he said, shaking his fallen boss by the shoulders. "Jonas, is you dead?"

"Somebody shot him?" asked the Mexican Cruces, drawing his gun and scanning all sides of the street. Len quickly checked Jonas' body and shook his head. "Channi," said Cruces, looking back the way they had come, "cover the far end, and I'll try and see who is in that doctor's place."

"Who did this?" demanded Channi. He peered down the deserted street. "I'll kill 'em when I see 'em."

Reaching the broken steps, Cruces gave a low cackle and eased his flat-crowned sombrero from his forehead with the barrel of his revolver. "No one, *mi amigo*. He fell down these stairs." He pushed a step with his boot and went clean through. He laughed again. "They are rotten. All of them. I wonder who it is who lives there?"

"A doctor, so that chump back in the saloon said." Len cradled Jonas' head, smoothing away strands of hair from his boss's sweating brow. "I don't like the look of him, Cruces," he said, his voice whining. "Call out to that doc and tell him to get down here."

"I do not think anyone will be coming down here anytime soon, *amigo*."

They all heard it then, an outburst of gleeful laughter, the slap of naked flesh, followed by prolonged moans.

"What the..." Cruces brought up his gun and took a bead on the door latch. Holding his breath, he eased off one carefully aimed shot and blew the latch clean off, the retort of the blast echoing throughout the quiet, empty streets.

A terrific hollering and squawking emitted from beyond the door, and soon it was ripped open, a small, disheveled, sweat-drenched man appearing, face twisted into a scowl of pure, uncontained anger.

Before he could speak, however, Cruces' next shot tore into the top of the door frame, inches away from the old man's bald head. Yelling out in alarm, the old man dipped back inside, hands waving above his head. "I'm unarmed, I'm unarmed!"

"Get back out here, you old coot." Cruces loosed off another shot, tearing out a huge chunk of the nearside doorframe. "The next bullet is going right through your wall!"

"Cruces," called Channi from behind him.

"What?" demanded Cruces, without turning, keeping his gun trained on the door.

"Cruces, come here *now!*"

Swinging around red-faced, Cruces spat out several choice words, ending with, "What is it?"

He saw Channi doing a strange little dance as he pointed down the street. Cruces followed his companion's outstretched finger and swallowed down a gasp.

"We got trouble," said Len, standing up.

"Looks that way," said Cruces, replacing the two spent cartridges with fresh ones. Holstering his gun, he took in a breath. "I sure hope this don't take long. Jonas needs tending to."

CHAPTER EIGHT

Cathy came back inside having hitched up her horse to the buggy. Tugging on a thick overcoat, she arched an eyebrow towards her guest and sighed, not liking the way he struggled getting dressed one bit. "Are you fit for travelling? The air is becoming sharp."

"I'll be fine," he said. He'd managed to pull on trousers and shirt from her husband's wardrobe she had so methodically laundered and repaired as he slept. He winced as he pushed his arm through a sleeve. "I can feel it. The infection. Smell it too."

"Well, the doc will sort it, I am sure. I am thinking we cut across to Haven, which is closer. Doc Farlow is a smelly old goat, but he is a good doctor, so everyone says. After my man died, they all told me he is better than the doc over in Bethlehem." She bit down hard on her bottom lip. "Wish I'd known that at the time."

"Perhaps nobody could have done much for him."

"In the end, I think you're right."

He hobbled towards her. She took him by the elbow and led him outside. Immediately, he took to shivering. The sky, no longer blue, was a uniform white, the promise of snow in the air. She'd put one of her husband's overcoats on the buckboard, and, after helping him to step up, she got in beside him and put the coat around his shoulders.

"I'm obliged you doing this for me, Miss Catherine."

"Just Catherine is fine." She shot him a smile. "You never did tell me yours."

"Ah, yeah ... it's Norton," he said, not too convincingly.

"Norton?" He nodded. "Well, if that's your real name or not, pleased to make your acquaintance." She thrust out a gloved hand, and he took it, laughing, an action which soon sent him into a bout of hoarse, raspy coughing. "We need to get moving. You'll be overcome with fever soon." She flicked the reins and they trundled away over the hard, rutted ground, picking up the trail to Haven within barely ten minutes.

Some way out of the town, the horse straining in the harness with its unusual load of two people, they first heard the gunshots. Cathy reined in the horse, which blew out its nostrils loudly with relief. They sat, listening.

"You have a gun?"

She looked at him. "Only the old Henry, here behind me."

"We might need it."

Distant shots rang out, sounding like tacks being dropped into a bucket. "Wonder what it is."

"I don't know, Cathy, but I don't think I am up for any gunplay." He gave a wry smile. "Unless pushed."

Again, she looked, harder this time. Drawn, sweating profusely, his pallor sickly grey, she could see he was deteriorating fast. She also knew she had to get him to the doctor's before he succumbed to the developing fever, the poison running freely through him, bringing him ever closer to death. "Listen, I want you to wrap yourself up in that coat. Put your head down and try and stay conscious."

"Thought you said sleep was a good thing?"

"Mostly it is, but right now, you need to stay awake and focus on fighting that fever. You look like death."

"I *feel* like death."

"All righty," she said, twisting in her seat to pick up the Henry. She worked the lever and engaged a fresh round.

"You sure you know how to use that thing?"

"I do indeed."

"You said that with meaning."

414

Nodding, her eyes misted over as she looked back to that dreadful day not so very long ago when they came. Three of them, stick thin, starving to death by the look of them, their black eyes smoldering from faces ravaged with hunger. Nevertheless, despite this, they moved with mesmerizing grace, sweeping around the log-cabin from different angles. Two had Winchesters, the third a bow, arrow nocked. Jude, who had been out turning potatoes in one of the small vegetable patches when he noticed them, was already running faster than a roadrunner, hollering, "Get the Henry, Cathy!"

Old Beth, their dog, such a faithful, sweet-natured thing, was snarling, showing her teeth. She made a charge for the nearest Indian, launching herself with mindless courage at his throat. He tried to bat her away with the Winchester, holding it by the barrel, but she was determined, that old dog. She got her teeth around his forearm, and they fell to the hard earth in a mess of screams and growls.

The blood spurted from his mangled arm, the Winchester forgotten. Old Beth held on, those teeth sinking ever deeper, shaking him as if he were one of the rats she often killed in the barn.

The one with the bow did for Old Beth, shooting her in the flank with two arrows. Cathy always thought, perhaps truly, that this was the reason why she took out the old Henry from the buggy with such determination, ignored Jude's anguished pleas for her to give it to him, and shot that Indian with the bow right through the head. Without a pause, she put three more bullets into another coming around the well, doing his best to shoot her with his Winchester. He went down and stayed down.

"Cath!"

She shouldered him out the way, working the lever, and strode towards the maimed warrior on the ground. Naked, body alive with sweat and blood, he writhed around in agony, blabbering something to her, a look of abject terror on his face. She silenced him with the remainder of the rifle's load, perforating his torso and enjoying every shot.

"Yes," she said slowly, dragging herself back to the present. "I surely do mean it." And she twitched the reins and urged her poor, bedraggled horse towards town.

CHAPTER NINE

Four riders, black dust coats enveloping their bodies, black hats crammed down upon their heads, masking features, designed to instill fear. They rode with a deliberate, slow advance as if they were well-rehearsed in this sort of intimidation.

Channi edged up close to Cruces. The Mexican stood with his six-gun drawn, eying the approaching riders with increasing anxiety. "They look mean. Twin guns, tied down, they are gunfighters."

"We can handle 'em, Cruces, don't worry."

"But I do," said Cruces. "Wish we had rifles."

"I have my Winchester back with the horses," said Len. "I could pick 'em off with ease if that is what you think we should do."

Looking down at Jonas' inert body, Channi drew in a deep breath. "Jonas would know what to do."

"I say we spread out," said Len. "Cruces, you stay here. Channi, over there to the right, behind those stacked barrels next to the old assayer's office. Me, I'll run back to my horse and put a line on 'em with my Winchester."

"Shoot, Len, you got it all worked out," said Channi, voice buoyant, suitably impressed.

"Do as he says," snarled Cruces from the corner of his mouth. "Meanwhile, I'll talk to 'em, see what it is they want."

"They is Ed Rollins' men," came a voice, and the all looked up to see the doc, on all fours, poking his head out of his door. "I don't know who you boys is, but my advice is to go back to where you came from. Rollins is not a man who takes kindly to strangers, especially those ones who try to shoot up his town."

"*His* town?" Channi chuckled. "If this is his town, he is welcome to it."

"Wasn't always like this. Once it was a thriving, lively place, plenty of money being spent by gold-miners. When the seam was spent, they left. Rollins stayed behind, invested his money wisely, and is now trying to come to some arrangement with the railroad companies. If he succeeds, this town will boom once again."

"I hear that story almost every place I go," said Channi. "There must be more busted up towns than there is flies around a dead body."

"There'll be flies around Jonas if we don't act fast," put in Len. He swung around and dashed back towards his horse.

The riders continued to move inexorably forward, but this sudden burst of activity from Len spurred them into action. Raising their hats, they beat their horses' flanks and broke into a sudden charge.

"Ah hell," growled Cruces and brought up his revolver, fanning the hammer, spurting out a blaze of lead with no effect whatsoever.

Diving behind the stacked barrels, as he was told to do, Channi took his time, gathering his thoughts, controlling his body as the palpitations grew into something closer to hammer blows in his chest. Holding his breath, he rested his gun arm on the top of the closest barrel and eased off shots, one after the other, watching with some satisfaction as one of the riders rose up, clutching at his chest, pitching backwards over his saddle, blood bursting from the wound. He hit the dirt hard and lay still. Channi hollered in his triumph and fed in more cartridges as the riders fanned out in a wide arc.

Meanwhile, Len had reached his horse and scrambled around in pulling out the Winchester from its scabbard. Working the lever, he rested the barrel across the back of his horse and carefully aimed. When he squeezed the trigger, another rider dropped, and Len, not the most vociferous of people, grunted in satisfaction as he prepared to fire again.

Cruces did not fare so well. After leaping over Jonas' inert form, he sprinted towards the ruined steps. He did his best to keep himself low, but the riders were close now. Although their mounts were increasingly out of control due to the gunshots, one of them managed to put a bullet into Cruces' thigh. The Mexican squealed and tumbled sideways, his Colt skidding across the ground, well out of his reach. Clutching at the wound, he tried to shuffle backwards, but before he managed to retreat less than six feet, the two remaining riders were upon him.

Channi, his gun now reloaded despite spilling some of the bullets onto the ground, groaned in anguish at the sight of poor Cruces. Why wasn't Len shooting more rounds? He glanced back down the street and swore when he saw the answer to his question.

Three more riders were approaching from the other side of town. Len was doing his best to react after he'd got wind of their advance, turning, dropping to one knee, lining up the first target. Unfortunately for Len, they were so quiet that now they were virtually upon him. They surrounded him, guns drawn, letting him know with little doubt he was a dead man as soon as he fired his Winchester. He didn't debate the situation for long, and, throwing the Winchester down, he stood up, arms raised.

"You've shot down two of my boys," said the closest rider to the squirming Cruces. "If they is dead, we will hang you. If they is sorely wounded, we'll strip you, whip you, and send you back from whatever hole you crawled out of. Tab, check their bodies."

Tab slowly dismounted. Taking his chance, Channi stepped out from behind the barrels.

"You put that gun away, boy," said the one doing all the talking, "unless you wanna meet your maker within the next ten seconds."

It didn't take those ten seconds for Channi to make up his mind and let his gun drop from trembling fingers.

"My name is Edward Rollins, and this is my town," said the talker and eased himself from the saddle. "Tab, how are them boys of mine?"

Tab, checking the rider that Channi had shot for any vital signs, let out a long sigh. "He's shot up bad, Mr Rollins."

"Yes, but is he dead?"

"Not yet, sir."

"All right, now check Louden there."

Louden was the poor rider who received the Winchester round from

Len. There was a fair-sized hole in his chest, and his eyes were wide open. Tab didn't need to check further. "Nope, Mr Rollins, he's dead."

Upon hearing this, Rollins let out a prolonged sigh, pushed back his hat, and allowed himself a few seconds before he said, "That is a shame. He was a good man. Knew his mother. Knew her well. Thank the Lord she is also dead; otherwise, my wrath would be such that already I would be putting you bunch of vermin in the ground!"

The additional riders had by now steered Len to join the others. A frightened, pathetic figure, he wrung his hands constantly, features strained, already surrendering to the terrible inevitability of his impending doom.

"All right, boys," said Rollins, looking around him as if he were searching for something. "String 'em up."

CHAPTER TEN

From his saddle, Sterling Roose watched as Brown Owl, on hands and knees, studied the land. For all his years of riding with the Army, tracking down renegades and Comanche war-parties, Roose had never developed such a high level of skill as Cole and Brown Owl demonstrated. They were masters of their art, Cole especially. He could tell an escapee's direction from a single broken blade of grass. Now, watching Brown Owl, he was filled with the same sense of wonder as the scout stood, dusting off his buckskin trousers. "They ride fast, but here," he waved his hand over a broken up piece of hard, dry ground, "another is behind them. Not so fast. Perhaps his horse is old, or he is sick, maybe wounded."

"That would tie in with what happened back at the bank. The one who escaped through the back, he was wounded. Bad, so the bank manager said."

Brown Owl grunted and nodded, but did not answer. He swung himself up onto his pony's back. "They are not so far."

"Well then," Roose turned to his motley posse, "make sure your guns are loaded, men. It won't be long now."

Something rippled through them. A nervousness which you could almost taste. Roose looked away and wished, not for the first time, that Cole was riding with him.

. . .

A little farther on, they came to the remains of a camp. It didn't take long before Brown Owl pointed out the areas where the ground was scuffed and broken. "I think one rode away, with others close behind."

"An argument of kinds," said Roose, hands on the pommel, staring out across the endless plain. "That could work to our advantage."

"Don't see how," said one of the posse.

"It might mean we have less of 'em to tangle with."

"Tangle?" The man looked to his companions then back to Roose, panic in his voice. "You never said nothin' about tangling with anyone."

"Don't worry yourself none, Coltrane, I doubt it'll be so bad that we'll be calling on your superior firearm skills."

"Then what will you be calling on, Sheriff?" asked another.

"Who can tell? You're something of a lawyer, ain't you, Philips?"

"I was in law school before my daddy said they needed me back home to help pay the bills."

"But you know a little about the law?"

"A little. I studied in Chicago. A mighty fine city, I can tell you. It was my dream to open up my own little law—"

"I might just call on you to explain to our motley bank robbers the enormity of their crimes. How's about that?"

Philips didn't look impressed. Ignoring him, Roose turned again to Brown Owl. "Which way?"

In silence, Brown Owl mounted his pony and set off.

Slowing down, Brown Owl in the lead, they inched their way across the sad trickle that used to be a river and reined in when the Indian scout slipped down from his mount into the mud and raised his hand.

Roose leaned forward. "What you found?"

For a few anxious moments, Brown Owl continued to read the signs, so deep in concentration it seemed he had not heard Roose's question.

"Maybe he can't see anything," said one of the others, holding back with his two companions.

"Shut up, Knott," spat Roose, "when you got something sensible to say, then you can say it."

"You can't talk to me that way, Sheriff! I volunteered for this and I can walk away any time I choose."

"You do that and I'll hunt you down and throw you into jail!"

The air grew chilly. Knott fumed, face screwed up in a mix of confusion and indignation. His companions averted their eyes and stayed quiet.

"You is what is known as a dictator," said Knott, voice cracking.

"And you is what is known as an idiot, now quiet down before I knock you down."

"There's more," said the scout, continuing to examine the surroundings. "Someone else was here, on foot. Then, more tracks leading in two directions." He stood up and pointed. "Riders went that way. More than two of them. The one on foot took another direction."

"All right," said Roose. "We'll visit the one who was on foot first. They may be able to tell us what went on here. Boys, keep your wits about you."

As things turned out, there was no need for any caution because the small cabin they came upon not very long afterwards, with its small vegetable patch, little barn, and fenced in paddock, was empty. Blowing out his cheeks, Roose turned from pounding on the door to look at his men. "Seems like we follow the riders, boys."

This news did not inspire anyone, but they moved away nevertheless, falling in behind Brown Owl, who constantly checked the ground, until they came to the rise that overlooked a ramshackle town which appeared to be dead.

Until they heard the gunshots.

CHAPTER ELEVEN

"Kicking my heels around this place ain't gonna change my mood," said Cole, going through the papers in his father's desk. "I can't make head nor tail of any of this."

"I will do it, *Señor* Reuben," said Marta, her voice thick with grief.

"Most of it relates to cattle and horse deals from half a lifetime ago." He sat back and looked at the mound of paperwork in despair. "Marta, I reckon most of this could be burned."

"He was a great hoarder, your father," she said, lifted a little by the memory. "I think he felt that he may need these things again another day, so he kept them, just in case."

Running a hand through his hair, Cole gave a long sigh. "I should have gone with Sterling. I'm not ready for this sort of thing."

"You must go if you feel it is your duty," she said and gestured to the papers. "I can deal with this."

"I think I just might do that, Marta, if you're sure it's all right with you?"

A tiny flush spread across her cheeks. "*Señor* Reuben, this is your home now. You make the decisions."

"Well ... Look, I been thinking. You've lived and worked here almost all your life." He noted her eyes widening, and the way she suddenly held her breath. She appeared to be preparing herself for some bad news.

"Marta, if you can, I'd like you to continue working here. I'm not much of a one for—"

Marta gave out a great whoop and threw herself at him, covering his face with kisses. "Oh, *Señor* Reuben, I thought you were going to dismiss me – throw me out!"

"Please, Marta." He managed, with some effort, to extricate himself from her embrace. "Of course I'm not going to do that! No, I need you, Marta. Now more than ever."

As if realizing what she had done, she leaned back, hand covering her mouth, tears tumbling down her cheeks. "*Señor* Reuben, forgive me, I never meant—"

Suppressing his laughter, Cole stood up. "Hey, Marta, don't worry. I'm kinda touched at your reaction." Feeling the heat on his face, he touched his cheeks where she'd kissed him. "I'm never gonna say 'no' to your kisses!"

She gaped at him, and he swung away and strode out of the house before he said anything more.

At the jail, old Clancy Hughes was picking at his few remaining teeth when Cole came in. Dressed in buckskins and high boots, with his Colt Cavalry angled across his middle for a cross-belly draw, he was ready to ride out across the plains once more.

On seeing him, Clancy sat bolt upright, desperate to clear away the remnants of his chicken dinner. "Why, Mr Cole, sir. I was not expecting you."

"Me neither."

Frowning, Clancy took particular care with the almost empty bottle of whisky beside his dinner plate. "Eh? I don't get you."

"Never mind. Where's the prisoner?"

"In the back. Doc Henson patched him up real good. One of the other wounded fellas died. Didn't say a word."

Grunting, Cole went through the heavy door that opened up into a narrow passage. There were four cells, three of which were empty. At the far end, on the left, he found the one surviving bank robber curled up on a sagging wooden bunk, a threadbare blanket covering him. Cole pressed his face up close to the cell bars and coughed. The man did not stir. Cole raised his breath, his voice filling the small jail as he shouted, "Hey, pigswill, wake up!"

Startled, the man rolled over, the blanket forgotten, and sat up, rubbing his eyes. "Who in the name of—"

"Name is Cole, and I'm here to ask you some questions, which you would be advised to answer truthfully. Understand?"

"Questions?" The man, who could not have been more than eighteen years of age, swung his legs over the side of the bunk and put his face in his hands. "Mister, I can barely remember my own name."

"But you do remember shooting up that bank, don't you?"

His face came up, and he peered at Cole, the beginning of real, noticeable fear twitching at his face. "I doubt there'd be much point in denying that."

"Seeing as we've got about a hundred witnesses, I'd say that was sensible."

"But I have little recollection of what happened. Very little, in fact. I remember being shot and hitting the ground, but after that ..." He shook his head. "Sorry."

"What I need you to focus on is the fact that people died. That makes you an accessory."

"A what?"

"An *accessory*. It means you is just as much to blame for what went down as the men who pulled the triggers."

"I didn't shoot nobody, Mister, I swear to God."

"Like I said, in *law*, you is as much to blame as anyone else."

"But no, that can't be!" He jumped up and rushed to the bars, so fast and unexpected, Cole was forced to take a step back, hand instinctively dropping to his gun. "You can't do this. I never killed nobody in my life. Seagrams said to me we would be straight in and straight out, nothing about no killings."

"Seagrams? So this Seagrams was your leader, eh?"

Ashen-faced, the young man retreated a few steps, hands up in surrender. Clearly he'd realized some terrible mistake. "I never said no such thing. I didn't know him so well."

"Son, you have no need to worry. Seagrams, if he was the one led the robbery, is dead."

The young man's relief was clear. "Oh my."

"But there was someone else with him, in the bank manager's office. Who might that be?"

"I don't know, mister. I was outside."

"Outside or in, you must have some idea."

"No, sir, I don't."

"Tell you what, son, you give me your best bet on who it was, and I'll talk to the judge, tell him how well you cooperated in our investigations."

A slight hesitation followed. The young man chewed away at his lip, slumped down on the bunk, and stared. It took him quite a while before his head came around again. "You mean it? You will take away this – what was it? Accessory?"

"I can make it go away, son. Easy as easy is."

"You swear it?"

"As God's my maker."

This had the desired effect. The young man nodded his head several times and said, in a quiet voice, "Jonas. He was Seagrams' chosen one, if you put it that way."

"Jonas who?"

The young man's face came up. "That I don't know, Mister. I only ever knew him as Jonas."

"Well, that don't tell me much. I doubt I will be able to find out anything about him by just that. But never mind," he made an exaggerated yawn, "I'm sure the judge will do what he can...but no promises." He smiled, winked, and turned away.

"Wait!" cried the young man, rushing to the bars again, clinging onto them, face close, panic written into every line. "Falkin. His name is Jonas Falkin." He swallowed hard. "If you mean what you say, I have something else too."

Arching a single eyebrow, Cole moved closer and listened to what the young man had to say. Satisfied, Cole's smile grew wide. He tipped his hat's brim and returned to the outer room.

Clancy stood up as the scout returned. "You got what you needed?"

"I sure did. Don't suppose you happen to know who will be the judge for the trial of that boy?"

"I reckon it'll be Justice Hartley. He's tough. He's also a personal friend of the bank manager."

"Well, well, the world is full of surprises."

"I don't fully understand what you mean, Mr Cole."

"That's all right, Clance. Just means it'll be a quick trial is all."

"He has a reputation as something of a hanging judge. Confessions, they don't mean diddly to Justice Hartley." He shook his head a little sadly. "I don't give much chance for that boy back there."

A wry smile. "No. I think you're probably right."

Deep in thought, Cole stepped outside. He'd need to return to the bank, the scene of the crime, and asked some questions. Most especially, he needed to talk to the manager.

CHAPTER TWELVE

"That's serious gunfire," Norton said. "Perhaps we should turn away and make our way to Bethlehem?"

"We do, and they'll hang you as soon as they see you."

"They won't recognize me."

"If your story is true, they'll remember you for the rest of their lives."

"I was wearing my bandana over my face."

"Is that so?"

He smirked. "It's a sort of disguise."

She studied the film of sweat covering his brow, the chalky whiteness of his face, his eyes so dull. "I'm not sure you'll make it to Bethlehem. We need to get you fixed now!"

"I'll make it." He shivered beneath the thick coat draped around him.

Several shots rang out. Cathy leaned forward, narrowing her eyes. She thought she saw some distant puffs of smoke, but she couldn't be sure. "We'll go in from the other direction. I know Doc Farlow's place, so we can go straight to him. Whatever is happening down there, we can ignore it."

"What if it's them? The rest of the gang, helping Jonas with getting himself fixed?"

"If it is, they could all be dead after all that gunfire."

He cocked his head. Silence settled over the cluster of broken and decrepit buildings. "It seems to have finished. Maybe whatever was happening has ended."

"So you see, no need to be a-worrying."

"But I am," he said, pulling the coat tight around him. "If it is Jonas down there and he catches sight of me, I'm dead. Maybe you too. If some other bunch has shot up the gang, they must be as mean as rattlers. Could be they are even more dangerous than Jonas and the rest of the boys."

"Well, there's only one way to find out," and she flicked the reins and edged the buggy in a westerly direction in order to enter the little town from the opposite side.

She hitched the buggy to a sagging tree and jumped down. She checked the Henry.

"You've got to be careful," he said in a croaking whisper.

"I will. You just sit and try and keep yourself warm." She gave him what she hoped was a reassuring smile and shuffled away.

"Don't take the rifle. Leave it with me."

"You said you weren't up to shootin'."

Norton shrugged. "If they see you with that, they'll shoot first and ask questions after you're dead in the ground."

Considering his words for no more than two seconds, she nodded and gave him the Henry. She forced a smile then turned to go.

Norton worried her. She knew he was close to collapse, and it was vital she got him to Farlow's as quickly as possible. Whatever was playing out in the main street had to be ignored as far as possible. No point in tangling herself up in other people's problems. She had plenty of her own. There was no denying the thoughts and feelings racing around inside. Her place needed a man, a good dependable man. Not like Jude and his womanizing, but an upright one, able to stay and help her with the spread, especially now that winter was coming on. Jude always hated the winter, and when they were snowed in, Jude stomped around the cabin like an angry bear. Norton didn't strike her as being like that. Regardless of the crimes he had involved himself with, she cared little about his past and was prepared to give him the benefit of the doubt.

Whether Norton was his real name or not, it suited him, and when he was fixed, she'd give him her proposal.

Something moved ahead of her and she ducked out of sight. There were voices, some muffled, but one in particular raised high, "String 'em up, boys!"

She shuddered at the thought, took in a large breath, and edged forward, keeping herself close to the wall of the building beside her.

A gasp almost escaped from her mouth when she saw the broken steps leading up to Doc Farlow's place. In disbelief, she stood and gaped and, almost as if in a dream, she stepped away from the wall into full view of anyone watching and stared up to the top of the shattered staircase.

"Well, well, what have we here?"

The voice, mixed between amusement and surprise, brought her to her senses and, snapping her head around, she saw an elderly looking man in a black tailcoat, leering at her. She thought she recognized him but couldn't be sure, until he moved closer, the leer growing wider with every step.

"Ed Rollins," she said.

He pulled up sharp, frowning. "Do I know you, missie?"

"You knew my husband, Jude." His frown deepened. "Jude Courtauld."

Slowly his face cleared, memory stirring. "Ah, yes, Jude. You're his ...? Well, well, Jude Courtauld. He never mentioned you, or if he did, he never said how pretty you are." He looked back at his men trussing up the remnants of the others, some badly wounded by the look of them. "I'm in the middle of something right now, Miss Courtauld." He turned to her again. "It won't take more than a few minutes, then we can talk."

"I came here to see Doc Farlow."

"Did you now? Well ..." Laughing, he shot a glance to the top of the broken stairs. "He's somewhat indisposed at the moment, but I'm sure we can fix it. Are you sick?"

"No, but a friend of mine is."

"Oh, I see. Like I said, let me finish my business, and I'll be right with you."

"What does this *business* consist of, Mr Rollins?"

"It's business that is no concern of yours, Miss. Now, if you'll excuse me."

He doffed his hat and swung away, with something of a jaunt to his step.

Catherine melted into the shadows. The cold was penetrating her overcoat, pinching her skin, and she knew time was pressing. Another glance to Farlow's door brought her only a deepening sense of gloom.

CHAPTER THIRTEEN

"They could be the men we're after – the bank robbers," said Roose, studying the goings-on at the end of the main street.

"Could be," said Coltrane, "but could just as well be not."

"Only one way to find out," said Roose and went to kick his horse forwards.

"Hold on, Sheriff," cut in Knott. "This looks serious, and I can see one or two of 'em down on the ground."

"There's gonna be a-hangin'," said Philips.

"They can't hang those men," said Roose. "They is our men! It's my duty to take 'em back to Bethlehem for trial."

"Shoot, Sheriff," said Coltrane, "dead or alive is what it always says on them reward posters. What difference does it make who it is who does the killing?"

"Our men, you say," put in Knott. "They ain't *my* men. Let 'em hang is what I say."

"I don't believe I've ever rode with such a sorry bunch of whining old women as you!" Roose stared meaningfully towards Brown Owl. "Looks like it's you and me."

The scout grunted, pulled out his Colt and checked its load.

Coltrane looked anxiously from one of his companions to the next. "What are you aimin' on doin', Sheriff?"

"Something you boys would *never* be able to do!"

Roose pulled out the Colt Cavalry from its holster, nodded towards Brown Owl, and set off, kicking his horse hard, breaking into a full charge, with Brown Owl whooping and hollering close behind.

The others stared in disbelief for a few moments before they too, albeit reluctantly and not so fast, spurred their mounts to follow Roose and the scout.

———

They had the three men's wrists lashed behind them when Rollins emerged from the side street, chuckling to himself. His amusement, if that was what it was, soon disappeared when he caught sight of five riders bearing down on them all from the far end of the street. Frozen with indecision, it took him too long to call out to his men. Even as they turned, the riders were amongst them.

Rollins did his best to take some cover. He fanned his handgun as he went to his right, but the first bullet hit him in the back of the leg. He fell to his knees, cursing loudly. As he twisted himself around, clouds of dust obscured what was going on around him. Guns barked, men screamed and horses were out of control. In the swirling nightmare of confusion and blood, Rollins received another bullet in the throat. He fell, gurgling out his last few moments in the dirt.

Sterling Roose managed to control his frenzied horse as it reared up, threatening to unsaddle him. A man, shooting wildly at him, did not help the situation. Roose managed to put a bullet in him, but not before others shot Brown Owl off the back of his pony.

Battling to keep his emotions in check, Roose snapped his head around. The Indian scout lay on his back, rigid. The unmistakable repose of the dead. Gritting his teeth, Roose turned away just as Knott, handgun blazing, received a wound in the guts. He keeled over, anguish and pain screwing up his face. For a moment, Roose believed he would survive, but two more shots burst his head open in a huge red plume of blood and brains.

All around, men were moving and firing. With little idea of how many adversaries he faced, Roose continued through pure instinct, measuring his shots, doing his utmost to keep himself moving whilst he fired. Little success came his way. When Philips crashed to the ground, writhing in blood and gore, Roose dismounted, rolling across the ground, not caring where his horse might go.

On his knees, he expelled cartridges and fed in new. Through the clouds of dust, he spotted them. Two men, rifles in hand, working the levers as if possessed by some mad, uncontrollable desire to kill. He took his time, knowing he must make every bullet count now. He aimed and shot the first of these men through the head. Standing and moving rapidly to his left, he put three more into the second just as he was about to bring his Winchester to bear.

Deathly quiet fell like a great weight around them. Even the horses seemed shocked into silence. Checking around him, Roose reloaded and waited, senses alert, ready to explode into action once more if necessary.

"Oh dear God!"

He turned to see Coltrane falling to his knees, face in hands, sobbing uncontrollably. Ignoring him, Roose tested each of the bodies with the toe of his boot. Seven in all. Everyone dead.

A high-pitched scream shattered the eerie silence and brought everything back into sharp focus. In the narrow side street, a woman struggled in the arms of a man, a man who had a gun to her head.

"You're gonna let me ride outta here," he said, voice trembling with fear, pushing the barrel hard into the side of the woman's head. She whimpered, but the fight was leaving her as the hopelessness of her situation gradually became clear. "I'm taking her with me, as security."

He edged backwards, and Roose watched, going through his options. He didn't have many. He turned around to try and say something to Coltrane and was transfixed in horror. Coltrane had cut through the cords binding the men's wrists and now they were free, shaking and rubbing their hands. How could Coltrane be so stupid? Had he simply decided, without any serious thought, that these men were not the bank robbers?

As if by a signal, Coltrane's face came up, his eyes locked onto Roose, and a wide grin slowly developed as all around him, the robbers retrieved firearms from the bodies of the dead. One of them, a burly looking Mexican, clamped a hand around Coltrane's shoulder. Roose saw it and knew.

Of course, it all made sense. The robbers would have needed an inside man to give them vital knowledge about the bank. And there he was, grinning like a loon, triumph written into every line of his treacherous face.

But Roose had no further time to consider any more options. Another scream from the woman and he turned. The gunshot rang out. A single boom from a weapon of much larger caliber than a handgun. The man holding the woman sort of imploded, his head enveloped by thick blood as it sank deep into his neck. His mouth gaped open in a soundless scream as he slid sideways and crumpled to the ground.

"Come on!" roared a voice from the far end of the street. A man, a large overcoat draped around his shoulders, stood in front of a small buggy, a smoking Henry rifle in his hands.

Paralyzed with fear, the woman stood staring at the dead man at her feet. She was covered in his blood and flecks of bone and brain. Roose, reacting quickly, sprinted to her, scooped up the dead man's gun, took her around the waist and ran with her towards the buggy. The man at the buggy was aiming the Henry. "Get her on top," he said, "and be quick."

Not pausing to debate any of what the man said, Roose bundled the woman onto the seat as the Henry belched fire once again. He chanced a quick look. The released bank robbers were swarming forwards, including Coltrane, guns drawn, murder in their eyes. Roose had a notion to take the Henry and blow Coltrane's head off, but such an action would have to wait. There simply was no more time. Soon, responding gunfire would hail down upon them all.

Roose clambered up onto the seat. This close, the man with the Henry looked ghastly. It was a tight squeeze, all three of them crushed up together, but Roose took the reins and managed to control the horse, turning the buggy in a tight arc. He thanked every angel and saint there is that the buggy was positioned at the far end of the passage, affording enough room to maneuver it away from their attackers.

The man loosed off two more rounds before several bullets came zinging their way. Head down, Roose urged the horse on with violent swishes of the reins. It broke into a goodly gallop, eating up the distance between themselves and the frustrated, screaming robbers, their revolvers firing uselessly, bullets dropping well short.

CHAPTER FOURTEEN

Cole sat in the bank manager's office, leg twitching, anxious to set off and find out what was happening. Next to him sat two other men, dressed in black tailcoats and matching trousers, hats on their laps, side arms prominent, almost as prominent as the large badges pinned to their lapels. United States Marshals, both looking grim and mean.

"Problem is, Mr Cole," the larger and older of the two marshals was saying, "as the money stolen was government responsibility, it falls to the United States Government to retrieve it."

"By whatever means necessary," interjected the younger man.

"You don't know the territory," said Cole evenly. "How you gonna track any of them?"

"We will employ you, Mr Cole," said the older one. "We will pay you far in excess of what the Army paid you during your time with them."

"A daily rate?"

"Indeed."

"Plus a bonus on completion."

"Completion? What does that mean exactly?"

"When we find 'em and bring 'em back here for trial."

The younger one leaned closer to Cole. "Mr Cole, we will take them to Washington for trial. The government is keen to send out a signal that such excesses will not be tolerated."

"So you see, all we need you to do is find them for us." A slick smile. "But we agree to pay you the bonus."

Cole leaned back in his chair, took out a small canvas pouch from his jacket, and prepared himself a smoke. "I was talking to the only surviving member of the gang," he said. "He told me some things, and I said I'd put in a good word for him."

"Things such as what?"

"If I tell you, I need guarantees that he will be spared the rope."

"You know we can't do that."

"That puts me in a somewhat difficult position. You see, with what that young bank robber told me, it sort of complicates things."

"Then you must tell us."

"Not without an assurance." He rolled up his smoke and lit it. He smiled at the bank manager. "You is a personal friend of Justice Hartley, so I understand."

The bank manager turned a shade of puce. "How do you know that?"

A shrug. "Word gets around. I also know there was an insider working for the robbers, feeding them information about the railroad money, when it was due, how much it was, all of that."

"I don't see how any of this is relevant," said the older marshal.

"Well, listen. When I give my word, I stick with it. I gave that boy assurances, so if I'm gonna accompany you gentlemen, I want your word – and yours," he jabbed a finger at the bank manager, "that the boy is given a fair trial. He played no part in the killing. And, because of the information he has supplied, I believe he deserves a break."

"Preposterous!" spurted the manager.

"I ain't got access to any records," said Cole, ignoring the little man behind the desk, "but you have." He looked at the older marshal. "Send a telegram and find out what you can about a man called Jonas Franklin. He's the new boss of the gang, as the original was shot dead in the bank office."

"Oh dear Lord," said the manager, the memory returning. He got unsteadily to his feet and moved over to a drink cabinet in the corner and, with trembling fingers, poured himself a large whisky.

"A telegram? Yes, I can do that," said the older one.

"Good. As for the insider, I want those guarantees."

"Mr Lister," said the older one, nodding towards the manager. "If you know this Justice Harley—"

"Hart*ley*," said Cole.

"Yes. Hartley. Perhaps you can tell the judge that this young man had little to do with the killing."

"He had *nothing* to do with it," said Cole.

The marshal gave the slightest of nods. "So, you will convey that to the judge, Mr Lister. If you could be so kind."

Lister drained his glass. "Very well."

"So, who was the insider?"

"A man called Coltrane."

A squawk and Lister dropped the glass. It shattered across the floor. He looked close to collapse. "He is my assistant! It can't be true."

"Why would he lie?" asked Cole. "Besides, how could the prisoner know that name? Of course it's true, and it makes a good deal of sense. They knew the plan of the bank, how much money there'd be … Who knows what else. It was Coltrane, no question."

Running a hand through his thinning hair, Lister collapsed into his chair. "Oh my, this is all just too terrible." Shaking his head, he produced a handkerchief and used it to dab his sweating forehead. "He is one of the men who joined Mr Roose's posse."

Now it was Cole's turn to react. He stood up, cigarette forgotten. "Then we have to move, gentlemen. And we have to move now, for I fear my good friend, Sheriff Roose, could be in real danger."

"I'll get the horses ready," said the younger marshal, standing up.

"And I will send that telegram." The older one nodded towards the bank manager. "How much went missing, Mr Lister?"

"Hardly anything at all, apart from the money the men took from the tellers and what the other man in my office managed to grab after he'd shot the others."

"And saved your life."

Lister's eyes held Cole's. "Indeed, yes, Mr Cole. Two saddle bags he had. A matter of perhaps twenty-five thousand dollars, I would estimate."

"That's a fair sum, Mr Lister."

"Yes. But they were bank robbers, after all."

The older marshal got to his feet, shook Lister's hand and motioned for Cole to talk with him outside. Lister watched them go, his eyes moving again to the whisky waiting for him in the drink cabinet.

"Will we need more men?"

"No. We'll be just fine. For all we know, Roose may well have tied everything off for us, unless that Coltrane got to him first."

"Which is a possibility," said the older marshal.

"Yes. It is." Cole gave him a measured look. "If we're to ride, I'd prefer to know your name rather than call you marshal."

"Whit. My associate is Deputy Marshal Simpson." He looked at the sky, barely able to contain a shiver. "It's cold, Mr Cole. Will we need extra provisions – blankets, perhaps?"

"And coats. It'll be especially cold at night now that the weather is closing in. Snow is in the air."

"But we won't be on the trail for long, surely?"

"Depends."

"Very well. I shall instruct Simpson to purchase what we need."

"You have rifles?"

"Winchesters."

"Fair enough. I'll meet you in the saloon, but please don't be long."

Cole stepped down into the street, untied his horse from the hitching rail, and walked down to the saloon, aware of Whit's eyes boring into his back but fending off the urge to check. At the saloon, he went straight to the bar and ordered a single whisky then asked for a flask to be filled up. "Gonna be cold," he said by way of explanation.

"I thought you'd retired, Mr Cole," said the bartender.

"So did I," said Cole, finishing off his drink. "So did I."

CHAPTER FIFTEEN

They managed to repair the steps as best they could. Timber seemed to be in short supply, but they ripped off several planks from an old, near-collapsed barn and fashioned them to fit the gaps. Doc Farlow watched them from the top, shaking his head. Beside him stood Maisie, dressed only in her finest Basque, herring-bone ribbed sides accentuating her full figure. She laughed, but could not keep the admiration from her voice when she said, "I do like a man who indulges in manual labor!"

Dragging a forearm across his brow, Coltrane smiled towards her. "And I do like the way you are looking, Miss."

"Name's Maisie."

Her smile grew wider.

"Mine's Jeremiah. Jeremiah Coltrane. It's good to meet you."

"Hey, gringo," spat Cruces, breathing hard. "We need to get this done if the Doc is to fix us." His wound was not healing and oozed a sickening yellow fluid. On the ground, some feet away, lay Jonas. They'd propped him against the wall of the closed-down bordello, and he too looked grim, face swathed in sweat, eyes rolling around. He was conscious but if he was aware of his surroundings, he did not inform anyone, the only sound coming from his slack mouth a long, drawn-out moan every now and then.

By the time they had managed to create a workable set of steps, Doc Farlow could slowly make his way down, although he hesitated at every creak and groan.

"Fix him first," said Cruces, pointing at Jonas as the Doc finally stepped onto the ground.

"You don't look too good yourself," said Farlow. "Boys, help these men to the saloon, gather together some tables and lay 'em both down. Then get lots of boiling water and torn up sheets. Hurry now, time is pressing, and these boys need tending to."

It took them some time. Cruces tried to walk but collapsed after only two steps. Maisie helped, taking the Mexican by the feet whilst Coltrane and Farlow took one of his arms each. Behind them, Len and Channi struggled with Jonas.

Making the saloon, they carried out Farlow's instructions and pressed together several tables and laid the wounded men on top of them. As the Doc retreated into a back room to organize the water, Coltrane went to the bar and ordered whisky all around. Maisie, fanning herself with the palm of one hand, leaned up next to him. "Hot work."

"Sure is," he said and downed his whisky. He slid a glass towards her. She studied it for a few moments.

"How come a man like you has come to this dead-end town and gunned down old Ed Rollins?"

"Ed Rollins got in the way. We're here to rest up, nothing more."

"And those others, the ones who rode off in that buggy. Who were they?"

"You ask a lot of questions, Miss."

"I told you the name's Maisie, Mr Jeremiah Coltrane." Smiling, she lifted the glass to her lips and took a small sip. "I remember yours. If you were a gentleman, you should remember mine."

"I never said nothin' about being no gentleman."

A smile creased her pretty face. "That's what I was hoping you'd say."

The rear door swung open, and Doc Farlow strode in, determination written on his face. Gone was the drunken old man from only hours before. Here he was, the man he used to be. He levelled his gaze towards Coltrane. "I'll need you and your men to hold down the patients. Maisie, if it's not too much trouble, keep the water coming. I have to wash the wounds, extract the bullets and then dress 'em. It's gonna take time and it's gonna be messy."

Coltrane let out a long low whistle. "I'm glad you're on our side, Doc."

"This is not about sides, it's about saving lives. I may be retired, but I still remember my oath. Now let's get to it!"

And 'get to it' they all did. Farlow worked relentlessly, his body leaking sweat despite the cold drifting in through the saloon doors. The barkeep kept everyone well supplied with whisky, Farlow even using some of it to wash over the gaping holes out of which he'd extracted the bullets. Jonas, by now consumed with fever, screamed and writhed while Cruces, a more resolute and stubborn individual, gritted his death and swallowed down the pain.

It took over three hours to get the two men patched up. Jonas was already unconscious. Cruces, drowned in alcohol, mumbled incoherently. At least they were both alive. At least, if they were lucky enough to get through the night, they could ride again.

CHAPTER SIXTEEN

The same could not be said for Norton.

Slowing the buggy down to a steady walk, Roose steered it under the cover of low trees clustered around jagged rocks and smooth boulders. Jumping down, he stretched out his back before taking a look at the wounded Norton. The man's head was lolling on his chest, a trail of saliva mingled with blood drooling from the corner of his mouth. Lifting the man's head by the chin, Roose sucked in a breath. "Wish you'd been able to get him to the Doc's. He's bad, miss. Very bad."

She was sobbing, face in hands. "It's my fault," she said. "I should have tended to him better back at home, but I insisted on him goin' to the Doc's. One of the wounds was festering, and I didn't have the means …" She looked across at the stricken Norton and released a long, shuddering breath. "He's gonna die, isn't he?"

"Maybe," said Roose. "Maybe not. I've seen plenty of men with wounds this bad, some a lot worse, and they pulled through. He's strong and he's young, but we do need to get that bullet out."

"I tried, honest I did. But I think I only managed to get a piece of it, it was so deep."

"That's what's causing the infection, I reckon. Thankfully, he's unconscious now, so we can give it a try. Help me get him down."

The ground was broken, dry and hard. Cathy tried to make the best of it by rolling out an old blanket. Then she helped Roose carry Norton to the most comfortable spot amongst the trees. Breathing hard, Roose stepped back and studied the young man. "He's one of them, isn't he?" He turned to her, her smooth face creased into a frown. "One of the bank robbers we were hunting."

"Yes," she said immediately before turning away, eyes downcast. "I found him close to my home. He was shot. I managed to get him back, tended to him as best I could, but it wasn't enough."

"He told you what he'd done?"

"He told me the story, yes. I'm not sure he did such bad things, mister. He told me he saved the manager of the bank. Is that true?"

"I'm not sure. All I know is that they are a murdering bunch of desperadoes, and now they done more killing. Including my friend. I can't let that lie." He took a deep breath. "But he did help us back there. I won't forget that, either."

They stood staring at one another for a long time, neither speaking, an understanding of sorts passing between them. Roose saw her as a gentle, forgiving woman possessed of real charm. What she was doing living out in the wilderness all alone was beyond him. The fact she'd cared for Norton suggested to him she was needy, desperate to have someone in her life. Perhaps for the first time, he thought. Perhaps, as so many settlers had discovered, starvation and sickness were never far away in this hard, unforgiving land. "Forgive me, ma'am," he said at last, "you have no family?"

Blinking a few times, she opened and closed her mouth several times as if she struggled to find an appropriate response. "I don't see what that has got to do with anything," she said at last.

Roose held up his hand. "Apologies, I did not mean to intrude. It just strikes me as unusual for a woman like yourself to be living a life out here all on your ownsome."

"I don't have much choice."

"And then to get yourself involved in all of this ..."

"I told you, my home is some way off. I found Mr Norton almost dead, and he told me those responsible were the same ones back at the town. My intention was to take Mr Norton to Doc Farlow's, to fix him up." She blew out a forceful sigh. "If you must know, my husband died not so long ago. Fever took him. We were not blessed with children, so I live alone."

"Dangerous."

"I have managed to survive." Her eyes hardened. "Despite being a woman."

"Ma'am," he now held up both hands in surrender, "like I say, I do not wish to cause offence."

"No, well, that's as may be, but now I think we must do our best for Mr Norton before the night draws in."

"Indeed," he said, reached under the back of his coat, and produced a heavy-bladed knife, its keen edge glinting in the thin sun of the late afternoon. "Have you any water?"

"I have two flasks in the buggy."

"And we'll need something to bandage him up with."

"I'll use my petticoat."

With the heat rising to his face, Roose nodded and turned away. "I'll do my best, but get ready to help me. If he wakes, you'll need to hold him."

"I'm prepared to do everything I can."

And Roose could see by the determined look on her face how truthful her words were.

Sometime later, with the sun dipping below the horizon, Cathy finished securing Norton's bandages while Roose sat with his back against a nearby tree, smoking. Having discarded his jacket, his white shirt drenched in sweat, he gazed into nothingness, lost in his thoughts. The Bowie knife lay next to him, still red with Norton's blood. He'd worked as fast and as carefully as he could, finally managing to dig the rest of the bullet out. The wound stank, worse than anything he could remember, and he felt certain, despite his earlier reassurances, that Norton would not last the night. But he'd done all that he could.

Cathy rocked back on her heels and gave a grunt of satisfaction. "He's sleeping, thank the Lord."

"That's the best thing for him. All we can do now is wait."

"He drifted into fever when I first tended to him. He's weak. I'm fearful for his chances."

"Try not to worry. We can only see what the morning will bring."

A faint smile played around her mouth. "Thank you, mister. I appreciate your help."

"The name's Roose. I'm sheriff of Bethlehem."

"Oh my! I did not realize."

"No reason why you should. I can't recall ever seeing you in town myself."

"I live some distance out of town, Sheriff, as I said."

"Yeah, on your own."

"I manage."

"You said that too." He nodded towards Norton. "Could be you've found someone to ease the burden."

"What do you mean by that?"

"Nothing." He studied the glowing end of his cigarette. "We need to get some rest. We'll start out early, but I'm fearful those desperadoes will cut us off before we make it back to town."

"They know where I live. They could figure we might head for there."

"Well, we have to try and make it to one of them. Either town or your place."

"There is somewhere else, Sheriff. I've been thinking on it. About halfway between the two. The smallholding of a friend of mine name of Larry Grimes. They'll never think of looking there. We could rest there, and Larry could ride into town and get help."

Roose considered her words and could see nothing wrong with the plan.

"Then that is where we'll go," he said, stubbed out his smoke, pulled his hat down over his eyes and drifted into sleep.

CHAPTER SEVENTEEN

The two marshals sat astride their horses, both men swathed in thick buffalo coats, those parts of their faces not covered by scarves were blue with cold. They had slept fitfully, forever turning and stretching, trying their best to find some form of comfort to help them rest. The cold bit deep into their bones, the ground was iron hard and sleep avoided them. They finally managed a few hours and woke to the smell of freshly brewed coffee made by Cole, who seemed rested and fresh.

They headed off not long after but soon Cole signaled for them to stop. Jumping down, on all fours, Cole searched the ground, blew out his cheeks, and stood up. "It's confusing," he said at long last.

"What is?"

"The number of tracks. Quite a few horses have passed this way, but these here," he waved his hand vaguely over some broken ground to his right, "are those of a pony, so Brown Owl was among 'em."

"How in the name of creation can you tell that?" asked the younger man.

"What did you say your name was?"

"Simpson."

"Well, Mr Simpson, I've been tracking for the Army since before the War." He stared out across the plain to the distant horizon, lost in his thoughts for a moment. "Fought Comanch, Apache, and Arapaho. I stood and watched that crazy procession of soldiers, women, bands, and house building materials snaking out of Fort Kearny back in sixty-six. They said they didn't need no scouts as the Platte Road leading to the Bozeman Trail was well known. So I stayed behind and when the news came through later in the year of what had happened, I felt lower than at any other time in my life. The Sioux, they called it 'The Battle of the One Hundred Slain,' and that was precisely what it was." He heaved in a breath. "So yeah, after that, I sort of took stock, questioned my usefulness, but then more trouble broke out with Comanch and I found my days filled with tracking 'em and killing 'em. Many broke out from the reservations. A lot of Kiowa too. They was bad times, Mr Deputy Marshal but it was a job I did and I retired from it. Until now. And that's how I know."

He hauled himself up onto the back of his horse and pointed in a north-westerly direction. "They are headed that way. I'm not sure what is out there. As far as I know, it is open, barren land with very few settlements. Almost all the gold has been mined out and those towns which prospered are now dead and forgotten. Either way, we proceed with caution. Sterling has gone after 'em, with Brown Owl, as good a tracker as any. But those men, the bank robbers, they is cold and ruthless. I warned Sterling, but he is an obstinate man. I just hope in the good Lord that he is well." He pulled out his tobacco pouch and proceeded to prepare himself a cigarette. "A well-used trail passes through not so far away. It's going to be simple from here on in. We still need to be alert, though, so keep your wits about you."

Clicking his tongue, he gently urged his horse forward as he lit up his smoke, the two marshals falling in behind, Cole's words bringing a sullen silence to them all.

CHAPTER EIGHTEEN

C ruces was awake, sitting in a high-backed chair, sipping whisky. His sunken cheeks and dull eyes were the only indications of the trauma he'd been through, but he was strong. Coltrane, watching the Mexican from where he sat at another table with Maisie beside him, knew Cruces would be well enough to ride soon.

Through the bat-wing doors came Doc Farlow, stinking of booze, reeling across to the counter, pummeling it with his fists and demanding another drink. The barkeep, a man by the name of Sefton, shook his head, wiping the counter surface for something to do. "You've had enough, Doc."

"To hell with that!" spat the old medic. "My money is as good as anyone's, now give me a drink."

"No."

Farlow swung a wild, loping punch, which Sefton easily dodged. He caught the old man's wrist, twisted it viciously, turned him around, and shoved him across the room. Farlow crashed against Coltrane's table and slumped to the ground.

Jumping to her feet, Maisie put her hands on her hips and glared at him. "Doc, you is a disgrace! Go and get yourself a bath and sober up!"

Muttering a mouthful of abuse, Farlow used the palms of his hands to push himself up. "You know what you can do, don't you, Maisie?" He glared at her through bleary, bloodshot eyes. "What we had was something special, now you've gone and bunked up with this piece of rat filth!"

"Now hold on," said Coltrane, a dangerous tone creeping into his voice. "We're all mighty grateful for what you've done for Cruces and Jonas, but you have no need to talk like that. Who Masie wants to be with is up to her, I reckon."

"She's mine," said Farlow, getting to his feet. He swayed from side to side, legs like rubber, his mouth drooling through slack lips. "You hear me? Mine!"

Without any warning, Maisie rammed a straight left into the old man's nose. Squealing, he staggered backwards, hands clamped to his face, the blood leaking between his fingers. She took two steps towards him and swung her knee into his groin and felled him with a left cross that would have graced any prize-fighter's repertoire.

Coltrane whistled, and Cruces burst into laughter, an outburst that soon turned to a groan of real, biting pain. Clutching his leg, he doubled up, panting, "Oh *Santa Maria*, I do not need this sort of entertainment!" He looked up. "It was good fun, but it hurts."

"Why you so hard on him, Maisie?" It was Sefton, coming from around the counter, stooping down and cradling Farlow's head. "Thought you and him had something going?"

"Sef, apart from you, he was the only man here who could still stand, let alone anything else." A sheepish smile spread across her lovely mouth. She turned to Coltrane. "Until I got myself a better offer."

They all laughed as Coltrane took Maisie by the hand and led her to one of the rooms upstairs.

Afterwards, they both lay beneath the covers, Coltrane smoking, Maisie staring into space. Eventually, she turned into him. He looped one arm around her shoulders, flicking his cigarette across the floor.

"What are your plans?" she asked, voice thick with sleep.

"Difficult to say."

"Try."

He strained his neck to turn to her. "You sure do like asking questions."

"And you sure do not like answering 'em."

He laughed. "True. Comes with my suspicious nature. It's what's kept me alive all these years."

"But you ain't like the rest. The way you dress. You don't carry no gun. I don't see you as a bank robber."

"That's 'cause I ain't. I was the 'inside man' if you wanna put it that way. I'd met Seagrams years ago, and we got to thinking how we could get ahead in this life, make some money. Now he is dead, and I'm left with the remnants of his gang. But you're right, I ain't no bank robber or gunslinger, unlike Cruces and Jonas."

"Jonas. He's the other wounded one, the one that's real bad."

"He's 'real bad' in more ways than you can think! Once he wakes up and his strength is restored, he ain't gonna take too kindly to what has happened."

She propped herself up on one elbow, running the finger of her other hand through the tight, curly hairs of his chest. "What you think he'll do?"

"Blow his top." He chuckled. "We ain't got no money from that bank raid. Norton, he shot Seagrams *and* Jonas. Any money we got was nothing but a few dollars and cents. It's all gone, and Jonas will be itchin' to get more. Once he knows Norton is alive, he'll wanna track him down and kill him. That woman and sheriff who helped him too."

"That ain't gonna make you any more money."

"True, but Jonas is not one to argue with. What he says will happen, will happen."

"What if you show him you've managed to make some money? Maybe that'll calm him down, then ..." She smiled. "I'll not mix my words. I want us to head off to California, start again. You know that."

"Without money, it ain't gonna be possible."

"Which is what I been thinking about. I have an idea."

"Oh really?" He arched a single eyebrow. "What, in this broken-down old town, there's bank filled to the rooftop with gold? Is that it?"

"Not quite. This town was prosperous once and the stage ran right through it. Even though the town is almost dead, the stage still comes through, and it's due in two days."

"A stage? How is that gonna help us?"

"Because this one comes from Denver. It's the main line down to

Santa Fe. It's stuffed with money. You could rob it just outside town, split the money, and you and me head off west. What do you think?"

"Sounds easy."

"It is. "

Coltrane untangled his arm, swung his legs from beneath the covers, and sat on the edge of the bed thinking. "This is genuine?"

"Absolutely." She reached over and massaged his neck. "We could be in California, looking for a place to buy within two weeks."

"How come you haven't done this before?"

"What, who with? Doc and Sefton? Rollins was not interested. In fact, his boys used to ride with the stage as a sort of protection, for which the company paid him handsomely. No, there's never been anyone here I could share my dreams with." She nuzzled into his neck. "Until you came along."

A buzz ran through him and he turned, taking her in his arms, kissing her passionately. "I'll tell the others. Two days you say?"

"It normally gets here around mid-afternoon. They then stay the night to rest the horses. If you ambushed 'em out on the prairie, they wouldn't stand a chance."

"It's guarded, you say?"

"Now that Rollins and his men are dead, there's nobody, except the shotgun rider. Your boys will have no trouble. Then we'll all be rich."

He held her close to him, kissing her cheeks and mouth. "Where have you been all my life?"

"Right here. Waitin'."

Laughing, they both fell back into the bed.

CHAPTER NINETEEN

Somewhere, a rooster made its presence clear as the little buggy trundled into the front yard of Larry Grime's home. A somewhat shambolic building with ill-fitting window casements, warped and roughly shaped wall panels, and a door which appeared to be about to collapse, it seemed to be the product of an unskilled carpenter. Its roof sagged under the weight of a huge bird's nest. When Roose brought the buggy to a halt, he spent a few moments gazing at the building in disbelief. "Is this it?" he asked.

"As far as I know," said Cathy, jumping down from the seat. "I've never been here before, but he's always talking about it."

"You mean he wants people to know he lives in ... *this?*"

"Oh, I think he's mighty proud that he built it all by himself."

Roose pushed his hat back from his forehead. "Built is not the word I'd use, if I'm honest."

"Well, try and not mention that to Larry. He is a man of quiet disposition who takes things very seriously – and to heart."

She crossed over towards the porch steps, pausing for a moment before she placed one tentative foot after the other. Roose watched her and smiled. She was a captivating woman, tussled hair and eyes that danced in a slim, smooth face. How does a woman like that manage to keep herself all alone in this land, he wondered. There had to be a queue a mile long of suitors just itching for a chance to share their lives with her. In another life, he might just join them!

A groan beside him jolted him back to the present. Norton's head slumped onto his chest. His breathing was ragged, the man's shirt front spotted with blood dripping from his mouth. If the poison had infiltrated his blood, Roose knew the man's chances were slim. He'd seen it before, many times. An army doctor told him how medical professors over in England had discovered why people died from wounds in the arms and legs. It was all to do with blood poisoning. He didn't begin to understand it, but he saw the sense in it, how a grown bull of a man, shot in the thigh, could be taken from the field, dressed, cared for, and die three days later in writhing agony. He remembered old Bert Howel, shot in the shoulder by a Shoshone arrow, how he tendered to him, and the following day, there Bert was, covered in sweat, screaming like a demon from the bowels of hell and dying, right before Roose's eyes. It was an image seared into his brain. Old Bert was a good man, a darn good tracker too. Learned his craft from the Kiowa boys who worked for the Army. Life and death. This land never gave you an inch. Not one of us.

"Mr Roose?"

Roose snapped his head around to find himself staring at a tall, gaunt man with a shock of red hair, friendly green eyes creased up in a smile, and an outthrust right hand. "I'm Larry Grimes, pleased to meet you." Roose took his hand and shook it, impressed by the strong grip. "I recognize you as Bethlehem's sheriff, but I do not think we have been properly introduced."

"It's good to meet you, Mr Grimes. Now, if you could, please help me get this fella down before he falls down."

Without a word, Grimes did as asked. Together, they took Norton into the lop-sided edifice Grimes called home. It was something of a struggle for Grimes, as Roose noticed. The man's limp seemed to worsen with every step. It took them both just under ten minutes to settle Norton into a bed in the second bedroom. Roose stripped and bathed him. Cathy then changed his bandages. Grimes studied everything from the doorway, voice sounding serious when he said, "He don't look too good, nor does that wound smell too good either."

"We need to wash it out again," said Roose. "Have you any whisky?"

"About half a bottle. But we'll need more than that. More than clean water and bandages too. We need help – medical help."

"Larry," said Cathy, taking him by the arm and moving him a little away from the bed. "We already been to Doc Farlow."

"Farlow? Dear Lord, Cathy that man hasn't practiced in years. He's a drunk and a fool to boot. Why didn't you go to Doc Henson over in Bethlehem?"

She took a breath, turning to Roose for some support. The sheriff gave a simple nod.

"It's a complicated story, Larry. Have you a mind to listen?"

"I sure have. I want to know what's going on."

"All right, then I'll tell it."

And so Grimes listened to what Cathy had to say. Roose kept himself occupied with Norton, wiping his fevered brow with a cloth, with one ear listening to the details of the story so that he too could have a better understanding.

When she'd finished, Cathy released a long, low sigh. The re-telling seemed to have taken a lot out of her and she moved over to a small wicker chair that sat in the corner. She lowered herself into it. "Things happened so fast," she said to nobody in particular. "One moment I was out in the field, tending my vegetables, the next I'm up to my neck in blood and bullets. You think he'll make it, Mr Roose?"

"Not sure," said Roose, not turning his head, all of his concentration on Norton, concerned with his breathing. "I think whatever is eating through him has got into his lungs. I'm not hopeful unless we can get help."

"I'll go," said Grimes. "It's clear these scoundrels want Cathy and him dead, so they are bound to follow them here. I'm not good with a gun, but I'm assuming you are." He gestured towards the Colt at Roose's waist. "I have a Sharps in the back. It was my papa's from his war days. He served with the cavalry."

"A Sharps would be good," said Roose, looking across to Cathy. "With your Henry, we can hold 'em off for quite some time until Mr Grimes brings help."

"Yes," she said, "I see the sense in it."

"If I go now, I'll make it well before sundown."

"You find a man called Cole. Reuben Cole, you understand? You tell him that I am here and that I need his help."

"Yes, sir. I shall." He smiled and went to a row of hooks on the wall beside Cathy. He pulled down a thick, fur-lined coat and pushed his arms through the sleeves. "You sure you'll be all right here, all on your own?"

"I'm not exactly on my own, Larry." She smiled. "But thanks for asking."

"Cathy, after this is over, maybe we could talk."

"Yes, Larry. That would be good."

"I hope that young fella makes it," and then he was gone. From where she sat, Cathy could watch him limping through the main door into the cold, bright day. "He's a good man," she said. "He never asked me why."

"Why what?"

She turned to Roose. "Why I want Mr Norton to live."

"It's a Christian thing to do, Ma'am."

"Despite him being a robber an' all?"

"Well, from how it's told, he saved the bank manager's life, so I do not believe he is all bad." He sat back, eyes still locked on Norton's feverish brow. "You do know that Mr Grimes is in love with you?"

If he thought this might bring some reaction to her, Roose was wrong. She merely shrugged, a tiny smile developing across her mouth. "I've known that for some time."

Shaking his head, Roose returned to mopping the sweat from Norton's face. "I'll never understand women," he said.

It was later, with Roose sitting out on the porch smoking, the Sharps across his knee that Cathy, with no idea what was occurring many miles away, sat with Norton. He'd rallied a little, the whisky having cleared out a lot of the puss from his wound. What alcohol remained in the bottom of the bottle, he drank, and now his smile was warm and wide. "Thank you," he said, squeezing her hand.

She felt the heat rise up to her jawline, but in the gloom of the tiny room, lit by a single oil lamp in the corner, she knew he could not see. "I didn't do that much. Mr Roose helped more than me, bringing you here."

"I'm not sure where 'here' is."

"A friend's place. He's gone to get help."

"I remember me shooting and I remember seeing Channi's face. Not much else."

"Nothing much else matters. You're here and you're safe and soon you will be better."

His smile changed, from warmth to almost a grimace. "I'm not sure that's true, Cathy. I can feel it, deep inside. The poison. I heard what the sheriff said. It's like a snake, writhing around my insides."

"Don't talk that way. Larry will bring back doc Henson and he will—"

"Listen," his grip tightening, "I want to tell you something, whilst my mind is still clear."

"Whatever it is, it can wait. You need to rebuild your strength."

"No, it can't wait. I took money."

Her heart almost stopped. For a moment, she didn't know how to react. "Money? From the bank?"

He nodded. "I filled up two saddle-bags. I put them inside my bedroll, didn't tell any of the others. They was all shook up by what had happened, so no one noticed. Then, when Jonas turned up, I made a run for it, stopping only to bury the money before I made it to the creek by your place. Where they caught me and left me for dead."

Mouth half open, the images his words conjured up ran through her mind. "But you mean ... you buried it?"

"Something like ten thousand dollars."

"Ten *thousand* ..." Her free hand flew to her mouth. "Oh my. Ten thousand dollars? Are you sure?"

"Well, I could only guess. I didn't have time to count it out carefully. But it's a lot, Cathy. Enough for you to make a good life for yourself."

"A good life for *my*self? What are you saying?"

"I'm saying it's yours. You understand? You get me a piece of paper, and while I am still able, I'll draw a map. It's easy to find, I promise." His face creased up slightly. "Get me a paper, please."

She went out into the main room, rifling through a chest of drawers, finding nothing. In Larry's bedroom, she came across some worn-out old books. She smiled at that, knowing Larry had interests other than running his merchandise store. He was a man of some depth. Even so, the books had the only paper available. She tore out the cover page of one, found a pencil, and returned to Norton. Grunting his thanks, he drew a rough map and handed it across to her. "You follow this route and the money is there in two saddlebags. At least some good will come out of all of this."

"But I don't want to take it ... You're going to get well. Then we can give it back. That would be the right thing to do."

"No. No, it wouldn't. That bank manager, he's a thief. He knew what was going on, I'm sure of it. What he'll do, he'll make a fraudulent claim, telling the bank owners more money was taken than actually was."

"I can't believe that."

"I can. The man's a weasel. Either way, I want you to have that money. You don't tell a living soul, Cathy. You follow my map and you take that money for yourself. You take it and you build yourself a life, a life you can —" He convulsed into a sudden bout of violent coughing. She held him, praying it would stop. When it finally did, he sank back amongst the pillows, exhausted.

Cathy sat, watching him slip into a deep, yet troubled sleep. She sat like that for a long time.

CHAPTER TWENTY

C ruces felt stiff and bad-tempered. Along with the others, he'd been sat hunched up amongst a huge outcrop of rock for what seemed like hours after listening to Coltrane's plan regarding the stage. Reluctantly, they'd ridden out across the range, sullen and silent. Now, however, both Channi and Len were muttering away to themselves, a noise which Cruces found more irritating than squeezing in between the rocks. "Can't you two shut up?" he said at last, the pain in his leg growing worse by the second. Something wasn't right, and he suspected Farlow hadn't done as good a job as the old Doc had said.

"How do we know this is genuine?" asked Channi at last.

"Yeah," put in Len. "Who told Coltrane about this? His new woman? How do we know she is telling the truth?"

"We don't," said Channi. "And how come Coltrane ain't out here with us?"

"He's with that woman, that's why. He ain't left her bed since he first laid eyes on her!"

They both burst out laughing. Cruces watched them but did not join in. He was tired and his leg hurt like sin. Sucking in his breath through clenched teeth, he thought he heard something. He snapped, "Quiet!" and then strained to listen.

The others fell silent.

Senses alert, body tense, Cruces pushed the throbbing in his leg to the back of his mind and peeped out over the top of the rock behind which he sat. The stage, nothing more than a spec on the horizon, was on its way, great clouds of dust thrown up in its wake. "It's coming," he said and pulled out his gun to check the load. "Get ready."

The others did so without argument, repeating Cruces' actions. A new nervousness spread over them, an urgency to get this over and done with. Cruces steadied his breathing and reached across for the Winchester propped against the rock. He worked the lever. "Get ready to run out as soon as I shoot the guard."

"Any outriders?"

"None that I can see. It must be true what Maisie said about Rollins. All his men are either dead or have gone off to find work elsewhere." He carefully rested the Winchester on top of the rock and squinted along the barrel. "I'm not too good with this, boys, so get ready."

"Now he tells us," muttered Len.

"You use it, Len," said Channi, "you're the best of us."

"I can do it," snarled Cruces, one eye closed as he focused his aim. "I just gotta ..."

The stagecoach came inexorably on, those on board unaware of what was about to be unleashed.

They didn't have long to wait.

Cruces eased off the first round.

The bullet sailed harmlessly over the head of the shotgun guard, who immediately shouted out. The driver hauled back on the team of horses, slowing them. "No," yelled the guard, "get 'em moving faster! Faster, I say!"

A second bullet went hopelessly wide. A bead of sweat dripped from Cruces' eyebrow into his eye. Cursing, Cruces worked the lever and pumped out four more rounds in quick succession, none of which hit their intended mark.

In a blur, Len snatched the Winchester from Cruces' hands and stood up, taking careful aim.

The driver, panicking, cracked the whip, and the horses broke into a wild gallop.

Len fired, and the bullet hit the guard in the chest, hurling him from the buckboard to the ground.

"Ah hell, Cruces," spat Channi, jumping to his feet, "this is turning into a mighty mess!"

He ran out into the open without a pause, firing off his gun into the air as the stagecoach bore down on him. Meanwhile, Len busily loaded up the Winchester. Cruces sat, staring into nothing, both hands shaking uncontrollably. Ignoring him, Len stepped out beside Channi, put the Winchester stock into his shoulder and yelled, "Hold up, or I'll shoot!"

The driver needed no further encouragement and reined in the horses.

Slowing down, the horses eventually stopped and stood, flanks heaving, eyes wide and wild. The driver, jabbering, threw up both hands and said, "Don't shoot!"

As Channi held onto the reins, doing his best to calm the horses, Len wandered over to the stage. "Everybody out," he said and waved his Colt in the driver's direction. "You, where's the cashbox?"

"On the roof," the driver replied, hands still aloft.

"Throw it down, then you get yourself down here also."

"It's locked!"

"I don't give a damn. Throw it down. I won't ask you again."

Twisting in his seat, the driver crawled onto the roof and loosened the leather straps keeping the cashbox in place. It was square, made from dark green-colored cast-iron, and he struggled to edge it to the side. Sweating, he managed to tip it over the edge and it crashed to the ground with a dull, hollow thump.

Len stepped back as the passengers spilled out. Three men and a woman, all of them terrified, hands up high. "All right," said Len, "empty your pockets of anything of value. Be quick now." He turned his head, "Cruces, get yourself out here, you sorry piece of trash!"

Emerging from behind the rocks, Len could see Cruces had changed. Perhaps it was his failure with the Winchester, perhaps it was the wound in his leg, but there was something not quite right with him.

"Cruces?"

One of them, a small bespectacled man in a dark blue suit, took his chance and ran. He made it all the way to the stricken guard, who was rolling around trying to reach his shotgun.

Len snarled, "This is all I need."

But it was Cruces who reacted. Pulling out his revolver, he strode forward and put two rounds into the fleeing man's back. Then he turned his gun to the guard and shot him clean through the head. Whirling around, he returned to the stage. "Sorry, Len. I messed up."

"No, no, Cruces, you didn't, you just ain't any good with a Winchester is all."

"No, I messed up and I'll put it right." He turned his gun on the remaining passengers. Before any of them realized what was about to happen, he shot them all down dead.

"Ah, Cruces," said Len in a small voice, "there was no need to—"

"There was every need," said Cruces, a shudder running across his shoulders. He broke open his gun and ejected the spent cartridges. He quickly reloaded. "I messed up, and it ain't gonna happen again."

He swung his gun arm towards the driver and shot him, the blast hurling the man through the open passenger door where he hung, half in, half out of the coach. Stepping up to him, Cruces put three more rounds into him.

"Cruces!" said Len, grabbing the Mexican by the shoulder and spinning him around. He hit him back-handed across the face, stunning him. "Cruces, snap out of it!"

"What's going on," said Channi, approaching them, studying the dead bodies littering the ground. "This ain't good."

"It's all fine," said Len, shaking Cruces by the shirt front. "Cruces, are you listening to me?"

It took a few moments and another slap before the Mexican emerged from the nightmare he had fallen into. Blinking, he tugged himself free from Len's grip and wandered away.

"Is he sick or something?" asked Channi, close now to Len.

"I think so. Something ain't right with him. Maybe it was the gunshot wound. I don't know, but he's acting real strange."

Cruces found another clump of boulders and sat down. Taking his time, he unbuckled his belt and slid his pants down to his knees. The wound in his thigh was well wrapped but soaked through with watery blood and a green fluid which looked and smelled ghastly. Gingerly, he undid the bandaging, releasing the pressure from his leg, which brought some relief and allowed him to examine the puckered, swollen wound more closely. Farlow told him he'd fixed it, but Cruces knew the bullet was still in there. When he touched the oozing white flesh around the hole a jolt of pain lanced through him. He looked back towards his companions and, in that moment, made a decision. Throwing the bandage away, he hitched up his pants and returned to them.

"Get the cash box open," he said, "and go through every body, taking what we can. Put everything into your saddle bags."

"And the horses?" asked Channi.

"Let 'em go."

"We ain't got no key for the box," said Len.

Quickly, Cruces shot through the lock with his gun. "We don't need one. Now get it emptied and hurry up!"

Len and Channi exchanged a look.

"I said *hurry up!*"

Scrambling to do as he was told, Len threw back the box lid and whistled. He rummaged through the collection of bundled up dollar bills, gold coins, letters and rolls of parchment. "There's got to be at least a thousand in here," he said, "and maybe a hundred gold coins!"

"Get it all in your saddle bags. We have to be quick. I don't like being out here in the open. Who knows who might come along?"

"Coltrane is gonna be pretty happy when he sees this," said Len. "It'll make up for that bungled bank job, give us all a—"

"We ain't going back to Coltrane."

Both Len and Channi stopped in their tracks. "Eh?" Len shook his head. "What do you mean, Cruces?"

"I mean we are taking that money for ourselves. Coltrane is the one responsible for what happened back at the bank so he can go and rot. We take everything and ride down to Mexico. I know people there and we can rest up, live easy, and plan our next move."

The others stood in stunned silence, Cruces' words ringing out like a funeral knell.

"But what about Jonas?" asked Channi in a quiet voice.

"He'll kill us," said Len.

"He'll never find us," said Cruces, some of his old fire returning. "So we ride and we don't look back. Our time has come, boys. We have a chance to make things right, so let's go."

Reloading his gun, Cruces limped across to his horse and pulled down the saddle bags.

Shaking his head, Channi looked at his friend. "You think this is right, Len?"

"I think it makes sense." He looked again at the stash inside the cash-box. "An awful lot of sense."

CHAPTER TWENTY-ONE

Throwing up a hand, Cole signaled for the others to stop.

"What is it?" asked Whit, reining in his mount beside Cole.

"A rider." He pointed to a distant plume of dust moving across the plain.

Whit reached behind and pulled out a long leather case from inside his bedroll. He hastily unscrewed the top and tipped it. A brass telescope slid out, which he put to his right eye, twisting the barrel to focus in on the rider. "Yes, it's as you say. A single rider, red-headed and coming this way." He collapsed the telescope and dropped it back into its case. "Simpson, go and intercept him, find out who he is and why he's in such a hurry."

"Yes, sir," said Simpson and spurred his horse into a gallop.

"That's a mighty fine piece of equipment," said Cole, nodding to the telescope case, which Whit was already pushing into the bedroll. "Always wanted one but could never afford it."

"They are wonderful things," said Whit. "Made in Switzerland."

"Where?"

"A country in Europe. Never ever been. I bought it from an associate I met back in Kansas City about two years ago."

"An associate?"

Whit chuckled. "Let's just say he wouldn't be needing it for at least ten years."

They fell into silence and waited until Simpson returned with the newcomer, a gaunt man dressed in store-bought clothes and boasting a thick shock of red hair. Bathed in sweat despite the cold, the man's eyes leaped from one to the other, his speech coming fast. "Thank the Lord Almighty you good gentlemen came across me! I've come from my ranch, a small one but home to me, and it was there that Cathy and a sheriff from Bethlehem brought in a young fella suffering terribly from a gunshot wound, worst I ever seen. I think he is gonna die, and that is why I'm riding for all I'm worth to fetch Doc Henson to try and fix him up. But I am fearful it'll be too late because—"

"Hold on, young fella," said Whit with a smile. "You just ease on down. You been riding long?"

"No more than a few hours. My place is only a short ways away, and I could show you it after we get the Doc."

"That won't be necessary," said Whit. "Mr Simpson here has considerable medical knowledge." The young deputy marshal blushed and looked away.

"A sheriff was with them, you say?" asked Cole.

"Yessir, indeed he was. Out of Bethlehem, on the trail of bank robbers is what he said."

"Catch his name?"

"Yessir, as I own a store in Bethlehem. Merchandise store, selling all kinds of—"He stopped when he saw Cole's face. "Sorry, I'm rambling ... Sheriff Roose, of course. The only sheriff we got."

"Lead us back to where you have come," said Cole quickly before he shot Whit a glance. "We need to get there right now."

"Indeed," said Whit. He flicked his horse into a trot and soon all four of them were cutting across the plain towards Grimes' home, Cole forever wondering what he was going to find there.

What they found was a small, ramshackle old cabin with no square corners and a roof that was in imminent danger of collapse. But there was something else. A heavy, depressed atmosphere and a woman sitting on the creaking porch steps, weeping uncontrollably. Behind her in the doorway, smoking, stood Sterling Roose, in his shirt despite the cold and his face grim and strained. It lightened slightly when he saw Cole and the others ride up and dismount.

"Looks like you've got yourself in a mess, Sterling. As usual," said Cole, crossing to his friend. They embraced, Cole unable to keep the relief from his voice. "It's good to see you." He stepped back and saw the worry lines etched so deep into his friend's face. "Where's Brown Owl?"

Roose swallowed. "Dead."

Cole went deathly white. For a moment he lost the ability to speak. "Dead?"

Roose looked down. "We barely got out alive, Cole. If it hadn't been for Norton laying down covering fire, they'd have shot the rest of us down, I reckon."

Cole's eyes slowly turned away and he stood staring into the distance recalling that day, so very long ago, when he'd rescued his good friend Brown Owl from certain death. And how the debt had been repaid many, many times over.

Whit stepped up. "Did I hear you say Norton? He'll be the one who shot the gang leader?"

Roose nodded. "And now he's gone too. Died just an hour or so ago. You are ...?"

"U.S. Marshal Damien Whit. This is my deputy, Bradley Simpson. As an attempt was made to seize railroad money held in a secure bank, we are agents of the government, instructed to track down the perpetrators and bring them to justice."

Roose watched Grimes moving over to Cathy and noted the man's limp. Sitting down next to her and holding her close, Roose saw how intimate they were. He continued to watch as he spoke. "Well, there ain't many of 'em left, from what I could tell. They shot up some of the locals before they turned their attention to us." He turned again to the marshal. "I calculate there were four or five of 'em."

"And the town they were at?"

"I'll take you."

Whit grunted. "We'll rest up for a little while until the horses have been fed and watered." He looked towards the sky. "It's gonna snow."

"All the more reason why we should leave as soon as we can," said Cole. "So let's get these animals cared for and move out."

. . .

As the law officers moved around in a flurry, Cathy drew in a large breath, wiping the last of her tears with her sleeve. "Oh, Larry," she said, her voice trembling, "what sort of a world is this where all we do is suffer and labor without any just reward?"

"I guess we all came out here because of the promise of a new life, Cathy. An opportunity to grow, to settle down, raise a family."

"You haven't."

"No. Not yet."

"You mean with Florence Caitlin?" She grinned at his shocked expression. "Larry, everybody knows how much you like her."

Shaking his head, unable to conceal his embarrassment, Grimes turned away. "Everybody 'cept Florence herself."

"Well, perhaps you should tell her."

"Tell her? Dear Lord, Cathy, I can't do that!"

They both laughed, but soon Cathy's face crumpled again. "I grew to like Mr Norton. I knew he was with that gang and all, but he did honorable things, Larry. He saved the bank manager's life, and he saved ours too. He was a good man."

"And you was hoping something might come of it?"

"I did my best to make a life of it with Jude, but he was a lying, cheating scoundrel. Yes, I grieved for him, but only because I was alone. When Mr Norton came into my life the way he did, so unexpected, I truly felt the Lord was looking down on me."

"But now you don't think that?"

"Nothing is certain in this world, Larry. And certainly not out here. Yes, there was that promise you mentioned, but when it all goes bad, there is no place to turn, no one to help."

"There's always me, Cathy."

Frowning, she studied him, his face so awkward looking, but expectant also. What did he mean, she wondered. "Well, we're not exactly neighbors, are we?"

"No, but ..." He suddenly stood up, his attention caught by the others unsaddling the horses, rubbing them down, and preparing the feed. "Norton, he ...?"

"He just gave up. The poison got to him in the end. You should have seen it, like green yarn threading through his body. Mr Roose said he'd seen it before. Gangrene he called it. He said once it got into the brain, that was it. Norton would cease to be human." She gasped and broke down again, so unexpectedly that Grimes was left stunned, unable to do anything but watch.

After a few moments, he sat back down beside her, put his arm around her and held her close. Then the storekeeper became the man he'd always hoped he would be, and although his voice rattled with uncertainty, he managed to get out the words he'd longed to say. "Cathy, if you're willing, then we could make a go of this hard life together. My store is doing well and your place, with its possibility to grow vegetables, maybe even crops, then we could—"

"Larry Grimes," she said, sniffing loudly, "is this your idea of a proposal?"

Her bloodshot, black-rimmed eyes peered up towards him and he couldn't help himself in reaching out and wiping away her tears with the back of his hand. "I suppose it is, yes."

She gave a tiny laugh. "Oh, Larry, what a funny man you are."

"Am I?" He couldn't help but sound hurt. "Is that how you see me, Cathy?"

"No, no," she said, taking his hand and holding it, "that's not what I mean." She smiled and sniffed again. "Let's us bury Mr Norton first, then I'll give your words some serious thought."

"You promise?"

Another smile before she leaned forward and kissed his cheek. "Promise."

CHAPTER TWENTY-TWO

They were at crossroads, literally and metaphorically. The old trail slinked down towards the south and, eventually, Mexico. Taking a westerly direction would lead them once more to Jonas and Coltrane. More than once, Cruces had debated within himself how he could broach his decision to the others. He knew they were loyal to Jonas, had ridden with him for years, but what they didn't understand, what they *failed* to understand, was that everything Jonas had ever planned, ever touched, had turned to disaster. The bank robbery almost cost him his life. It had certainly cost the lives of too many of the gang. And Coltrane? His 'insider information' had proved bogus. No, they must now consider themselves, what was best for them. They had money. Enough to start again. He voiced his ideas, and now they sat, the three of them, astride their horses, eyes locked on the trail and the promise of what lay ahead.

"I'm not sure," said Len at last. "Why don't we just ride back to Jonas, tell him your plan, and take it from there."

"I agree," said Channi. Bending one knee over his saddle pommel, he rolled himself a cigarette. "I don't see the point in making an enemy of Jonas. You know how he can be."

"Jonas is close to death."

"Well," continued Channi, running his tongue along the edge of the paper, "you say that, but you don't know for sure."

"I have to say," put in Len, "the way your leg is swelling up, Cruces, I'd say you were closer to meeting your maker than Jonas is."

"Yeah," chuckled Channi, admiring his rolled cigarette with some pride, "who's to say you'll even make it down to Mexico."

Cruces exploded into action. He grabbed for his gun and loosed off the first shot before it barely cleared the holster. Yelping, Channi flung himself to the ground, rolling over in the dirt, scrambling for some nearby cover. Len, reacting as quickly as he could, put a bullet into Cruces' guts before he too received a bullet from the Mexican. It took him high in the shoulder, right next to his carotid artery. He collapsed backwards, the blood pumping horribly from the terrible wound.

Bent double, Cruces slid from the saddle of his terrified, out-of-control horse, clutching at where Len's bullet had struck him. On his hands and knees, he did his best to crawl away, firing blindly to where he thought Channi might be. But all of his shots went wild. By the time he reached a clump of velvet mesquite, which afforded him some cover, his gun was empty, and he realized, in horror, he had no further cartridges.

Channi, however, did not know this. He watched in despair as the horses galloped off, kicking and bucking. He made a quick calculation and decided to cut across country to return to Haven, tell the others what had happened, then come back and do for Cruces once and for all.

Shooting two speculative shots towards the clump of mesquite, he set off at a steady trot, thankful for the cold air. If this were summer, he knew he'd be dead from thirst before the day was out.

Waiting until only the silence engulfed him, Cruces staggered to his feet. Len was lying a few feet away on his back, drenched in blood, fingers of his left hand pressed into the bullet wound, but his eyes were wide open, staring into oblivion.

Dead.

Cruces managed to make his way uncertainly to his former friend. He ripped away the dead man's shirt and neckerchief. Fashioning a crude, padded dressing, he pressed it hard against his stomach and pulled his own shirt tight around it. He knew all about gut wounds, so, with his jaw set hard, he turned about and set off the way he had come, directly opposite to Channi.

CHAPTER TWENTY-THREE

"We may need that telescope of yours again, Marshal," said Cole, pulling up his horse as his eyes settled on the dark bundle some way ahead.

Whit did so, pulling in a breath as he turned the focus ring. "It's a man and he's in trouble."

"Another one?" said Simpson. His voice sounded bored, as if he were resigned to yet another delay in capturing the bank robbers.

Snapping the telescope shut, Whit turned to his younger deputy. "We can't leave a man out here to die. We have a duty."

"He could be one of them," said Cole. "Perhaps an argument, a disagreement over plans? Who knows, but a single man being all the way out here on foot is strange to say the least. Let's take a look at him."

Cantering across the expanse of hard, gradually freezing landscape, they circled the desperate man, who continued his utmost to keep moving despite falling down repeatedly.

"He's wounded," said Simpson. "We should leave him."

Grunting, Whit dismounted and bent down to the injured man. He gently turned him over and hissed when he saw the severity of the man's wound. "It's bad."

"Leave him," repeated Simpson, turning his gaze to the far distance. "We need to get to the town and round 'em up."

"What's eating you, Simpson?" snapped Whit, standing up, brushing off the dirt from his trousers. "You got something else you need to be doing?"

"Not at all, sir, but we were given instructions to apprehend these men and bring them to justice – not nursemaid them back to health."

"All righty," said Whit, "seeing as you are so determined to follow through our instructions—"

"I am indeed, sir."

"Well, you can take this man back to Larry Grimes' home and fix him up yourself."

Simpson's face dropped. "I beg your pardon, sir?"

"He's not gonna make it to the town with us, and he sure as anything can't stay out here, so ... You take him to Grimes, you patch him up and wait for us there. Then, when we return, we will escort the lot of them back to—"

"Bethlehem," interjected Roose quickly. "That's where they'll face justice."

Grumbling under his breath, Whit mounted his horse and pointed to the wounded man. "Get him on your horse, Deputy, and ride back to Grimes. It's barely a couple of hours, so he should make it. What do you reckon, Sheriff?"

Roose shrugged. "A man with a wound like that, I'll give him a day at best."

"Well, there you are," said Whit.

"His leg is bleeding too," said Cole. "He's been shot to pieces."

"And he's Mexican," said Simpson.

"Damn your hide!" snapped Whit. "He's a human being and you'd do best to remember that, Deputy, or I'll revoke your service right here and right now."

Stunned, Simpson roamed his eyes from one man to the next. Everyone stared back, unrelenting, unforgiving. He would find no allies there.

Allowing his shoulders to droop, Simpson reluctantly dropped from his saddle and helped the wounded man to his feet. A pair of black eyes stared deep into him. "*Gracias,*" was all he said.

Cole helped the deputy put the man onto the horse, then held the reins as Simpson mounted up behind him. He nodded towards the scout and grudgingly turned his horse away and kicked it into a lumbering trot.

"Hope it's for the best," said Cole and hauled himself into his saddle.

"If it wasn't for you, Marshal," said Roose, "I'd have put a bullet in his brain after what he's done."

"As a sheriff," said Whit, "you should know better."

"I'm also a man who has been grievous hurt. I lost some good men to that band of vermin. I'll not be lectured by you or anyone else over what is right or wrong."

"Sterling," said Cole evenly, "he'll swing at the end of a rope soon enough, and you can dance a jig in front of him if it'll make you feel better."

"To hell with you, Cole!"

"Brown Owl was my friend too, don't forget."

Leaning over his saddle, Roose hawked and spat into the dirt. "Let's just get this done." He kicked his horse towards the distant town of Haven.

CHAPTER TWENTY-FOUR

With a good deal of care, treading slowly, planting each step without making any noise, Channi approached the jittery, waiting horse before him. Soothing words came from his mouth, low and slow, "There, there, my lovely ... Hush now ... It's all right ... Shush, there's my love ..." Until, at last, he could reach out and take the reins. The relief rushed out of him, and he pressed his face against the horse's neck, closed his eyes, and almost wept.

He checked the saddle bags, felt his knees buckling, and had to hold onto the stirrup to stop himself from falling. The money was there. Drawing in several deep breaths to calm himself, he drank fitfully from the canteen hanging from the saddle, pulled out the blanket roll, wrapped himself in it, and climbed onto the back of the horse. Patting its neck, he nudged the horse forward and settled himself for the ride back to Haven.

Less than an hour later, Channi entered the small, crumbling town, immediately spotting Coltrane standing in the doorway of the saloon.

"Well, well," said Coltrane, coming down the broken steps to hold Channi's horse whilst his friend dismounted. "You took your good, sweet time. Where are the others?"

Channi's eyes, red-rimmed with tears of anguish, so Coltrane suspected, could barely hold his own emotions in check. "It was bad. Real bad." He pushed past him and half-ran up the steps, blasting through the batwing doors. Hitching up the horse and taking the heavy saddle-bags, Coltrane slowly followed.

Channi was at the counter, gulping down a beer that the barkeep provided.

From the far corner, Maisie appeared. She looked troubled, shooting a questioning glance towards Coltrane, who merely shrugged.

"What happened, Channi?"

They all turned towards the voice's owner.

Jonas, sitting at a table dealing himself cards, reached for the whisky in front of him and downed it in one. "Fetch me another, Sef."

"Why not just have the bottle?"

A small chuckle. "I need to stay sober – for now." He slammed the glass down onto the tabletop. "Now, get me a fill-up!"

Sefton quickly did as ordered, pouring another whisky into a small glass and taking it to Jonas, who stared at it for a few moments before downing it in one. Smacking his lips, he leaned back in his chair. "Surprised, Channi, to see me looking so sprightly?"

Swinging around with his back to the counter, Channi held the beer glass in one hand while his other hovered close to his gun. "I always knew you was tough, Jonas."

"So where are the others?" asked Coltrane,

Channi's face dropped. "Dead. You never told us they had guards with 'em, Coltrane. Outriders. Darn good ones too, truth be told."

"Truth?" Jonas stuck his thumbs into his waistband. "You better not be lyin', Channi."

"Why would I do that? I'm here, ain't I?"

"Yes you are," said Coltrane, and he dumped the saddlebags onto the nearest table. "How much?"

"Enough to set us up down Mexico way," said Channi. "That's our best bet now, I reckon."

"Is that so?" said Jonas. "You making all the decisions now, is that it?"

"No, I just think it makes sense."

"Is this your plan, or was it Cruces'?"

"Cruces is dead. Len too. Those outriders shot us all up as soon as we charged in on 'em."

"But you managed to do what was needed?"

Channi jerked his beer glass towards the saddlebags. "Seems that way, don't it!"

Laughing to himself, Jonas rocked his chair forward again and stood up. "Mexico?" He wandered over to the saddlebags and pulled them open. He carefully counted through the paper money and coins.

"We could use it to recoup," said Channi, "before we plan out another job."

"Recoup?" Janus raised an eyebrow. "That's a fancy word, Channi."

"It means rest up, lick our wounds."

"I know what it means." He swung away from the table. "What do you think, Coltrane?"

"You know what I think."

"Tell us again."

"That we go to California. They won't think to look for us there."

"California," said Channi, laughing loudly. "Are you crazy? It'll take us weeks to get there. And what do we do then? Eh? No, Jonas, we gotta head for Mexico. They won't cross the border. We'll be safe."

Rubbing his chin, Jonas went to the bar and eyed the few remaining bottles. "All right, Sef, I'll have that whisky bottle now. In fact, that there Kentucky one will do just fine."

"It *is* the finest, Jonas."

"No arguments then." He grinned and took the proffered bottle. Pulling out the stopper, he savored the aroma and poured himself a glassful. "I shall retire to consider my verdict," he said with a chuckle and made his way back to his table and his cards.

Coltrane looked from Channi to Maisie and sighed.

In one of the bedrooms where once the bar girls had entertained their customers, Doc Farlow lay with his eyes staring at the ceiling. He wasn't seeing anything, however, all of his attention centered on the exchanges down below. So, that was it. Coltrane and Maisie would be setting off to California. How had it come to this? Clenching and unclenching his fists, he did his best to sit upright, but his body ached beyond imagining from where Maisie's blows had thundered into him. Collapsing back down amongst the covers, he gulped in air, closed his eyes, and forced himself to lie still and wait. Every passing minute would make him stronger. And then he knew what he would do.

CHAPTER TWENTY-FIVE

The man stank of sweat and leather, forcing Simpson to screw up his nostrils and turn his face away. Crammed up together on the back of his horse, the deputy found himself wishing he was back in Kansas City with his feet up in a nice, warm office, drinking coffee and not doing much else. Anywhere but here. Cold wind bit deep into the flesh beneath his coat. His ears and nose hurt and his fingers, encased in leather gloves, were numb.

This was as far from the promise made to him when he first volunteered himself for service less than six months before. They said, due to his outstanding character and remarkable pistol skills, he would soon find himself in a Washington post, training others. It was all hogwash, and he felt himself a fool for swallowing it all. Closing his eyes, he tried to rid his mind of images, thoughts, hopes and prayers, and simply allow the animal beneath him to keep plodding on. There really was no other choice.

More than once, the wounded Mexican gave a cry and slid from the laboring horse, hitting the dirt with a painful sounding thud. Each time Simpson would curse, dismount, and struggle to get the big, bulky man back in the saddle. At least the exertions kept the cold at bay. For a few moments, at least.

By the time they reached Grimes' home, Simpson was exhausted. He longed for a hot bath and a good night's sleep, but knew he wouldn't get either.

Miss Courtauld greeted them as they plodded up to the cabin. She held onto the reins as Simpson dismounted then, together with the deputy, helped take the wounded man inside.

Cathy directed them to the same bed where Norton had breathed his last.

Wringing her hands, Cathy stepped back to consider the swarthy, bloodied stranger. "Seems like I should be turning this place into a hospital, Mr Simpson."

"Indeed, Miss Courtauld. I do apologize for all of this, but we found him out on the prairie, and Marshal Whit insisted I bring him here before he is taken back to Bethlehem for trial."

"Well, I don't suppose there is a good deal we can do except make him as comfortable as possible. I have some chicken broth on the stove if you would like some."

"Oh, Miss Courtauld, I would indeed. The cold has developed mightily these past few hours."

"We'll soon be up to our necks in snow, Mr Simpson. I do so wish Mr Roose and Cole are able to return before it becomes impassable."

"They will return, I am certain of it."

"Then let me fetch you that broth. Sit yourself down by the fire, Mr Simpson, and warm-up those bones!"

Simpson watched her go, gave the Mexican a searching look, then went into the main room where he sat in a rocking chair by the fire, warming his palms in front of the flames.

Cathy brought in the broth on a tray, settled it down on Simpson's knees, then slipped into the small bedroom. As Simpson tried not to slurp, he heard her rummaging around inside the room. On her return, he said, without turning his head, "I believe he is a dangerous man, Miss Courtauld, so please take care when you tend to him."

"I was merely checking his wound. It's bad. Much worse than Mr Norton's, and look what happened to him." She came and stood beside the fire. "This is an unforgiving life, wouldn't you say so, Mr Simpson?"

"I'd say it was hard, unpredictable and surprising ... but I do believe those of us who choose to live in this land can make good from it."

"You could be right." She smiled down at him. "I hope you are."

"This is mighty fine broth, Miss Courtauld."

"Oh, do call me Cathy, please."

Nodding, he put another spoonful of broth into his mouth. "Can I ask where Mr Grimes is?"

"In town, tending to his store. He runs a merchandise store, you know. He sells just about everything, and he is successful. I'm hoping he will be more so."

"He has the good fortune to have set-up in a prosperous town, not like many of those 'ghost' towns which are left to rot right across the Territory." He swallowed down the last portion of broth and sat back, contented. "My, that was good. Mr Grimes is a very lucky fellow, I have to say."

Feeling the heat rise to her face, Cathy swung away. "Oh, now hush with all of that!"

He laughed, passed her the empty bowl and stood up. He stretched. "I may have to go back to meet up with the others."

"But you can't – what about the prisoner?"

"Yes, I will do what I can for him and then stay here until Mr Grimes returns. But prisoner is a good description of him. I do not know exactly what he has done, or how involved he has been with all of the troubles, but like I said before, any one of that gang are potential killers. I may have to restrain him before I go. Given that, I shall just go and check on him and make sure all is well."

He went over to the tiny bedroom door and eased it open.

Cruces was grateful for what they had done. He knew that without their help he would be dead by now. But he also knew he would never consent to being taken back to face a judge and jury, people who would want him dead before the hearing had barely begun. So he listened carefully to what the man and woman were talking about, looked around the room and found something he could use. Somewhere along the way, as he crossed the wide-open prairie, he'd lost his own and Len's gun. Fate just didn't seem to be on his side, no matter what.

With the old, knobby walking stick he found in the corner in his hand, he managed to shuffle behind the door, cramping up with pain, the bandages packed hard up against his guts already soaked in blood. He knew he didn't have much longer, but if he could force the woman to drive him over to Bethlehem, there might still be a chance for him.

He heard the clatter of spoon against crockery and sucked in a breath, gripping the end of the walking stick as hard as he could.

The door swung open and in stepped the big, tall deputy marshal, who seemed taken aback by the sight of the empty bed. It was all Cruces needed. He cracked the walking stick hard across the back of the man's head, dropping him to the floor. Quickly, Cruces threw away the stick and reached for the man's gun. His face came up, and for a moment, they locked eyes. But now Cruces had the gun. He stepped back grinning and shot the deputy through the head without a thought.

From the other room came the piercing scream of the woman. Cruces wanted to go after her, but the exertions had cost him. He swayed back to the bed and collapsed onto the edge, wheezing in breaths, struggling to overcome the pain.

She knew what it was, that single, barking eruption from the bedroom. She screamed, the horror of it all so overwhelming. This nightmare was never going to end, she knew that. Racing outside, she ran to the buggy. There was only one thing to do now. Hadn't Jude always told her that in this land, you did not hesitate to do to others what they would do to you?

Throwing back the seat lid, she brought out the Henry, made sure it was loaded, and strode into the cabin.

Alerted to the stomping of shoes upon the floorboards, Cruces managed to get to his feet. He'd compel her to take him to the Doc's in that hellish place they called Bethlehem. There was no choice. He was weak, close to the end, and the only way he was ever going to make good of this, return to Haven, kill Channi, Jonas, and Coltrane and get that money was if he were fixed up good and proper. After that, he would go to Mexico and live out his days in peace and quiet. This life here held nothing but pain and disappointment, and if he could do anything to change things, then he had to—

The door kicked in, and Cruces jerked himself upright. She was there, standing feet slightly apart, a look like something from his worst nightmares etched into her cold, hard features. And the gun. The way she pointed it directly towards him. Surely she wouldn't ...

Not much later, Cathy brought the horse to the buggy and hitched it up. She buttoned her thick overcoat to the neck and clambered aboard. She settled the Henry beside her and steered the horse out of the front yard, heading towards Bethlehem. Larry would be alarmed at what had happened, but at least now it was over. They could move on. Make all of this something to forget.

But even as she bucked along across the hard, uneven ground, she knew she could never forget that look on the Mexican's face moments before she blew him apart and the first of many tears tumbled down her face.

CHAPTER TWENTY-SIX

The bodies lay black and bloated on the freezing hard ground. Whit, despite being used to seeing dead bodies, turned away and vomited. Roose stood in silence, staring, and Cole, flipping open the lid of the cashbox with his boot, let out a long sigh. "These coyotes belong in the ground, Sterling."

Roose's gaze settled on the woman. Dressed in richly embroidered clothes, her bonnet still delicately positioned on top of her curly, auburn hair, in life she had been remarkably handsome. "I reckon you're right, Cole."

Cole checked the ground, studying the tracks. "They made off quickly, which don't surprise me none. No doubt we'll find the place where they argued and from where that Mexican ran from."

"We ain't got time for that," said Whit, taking a long drink from his canteen. "We know what they did, and it makes it even more pressing that we bring them in." He shook his head. "There was no need to do this to these poor people. We'll give them a decent burial later on."

"Buzzards will be finishing off what they've already started by then," said Roose. "We'll do it now."

"We haven't the time," said Whit. "For all we know, they could have already got clean away."

"I doubt it," said Roose. "These vermin will be counting their money from this haul before setting off anywhere. Besides, they don't know we're coming."

"We can't bury them," insisted Whit. "We haven't the tools, damn it!"

"Then we burn them," said Cole. "We put them into the stagecoach and set it alight. It's better than leaving 'em out here to rot."

"That's not the Christian thing to do," said Whit, pressing fingers into his eyes.

"It's the *decent* thing to do, Marshal," said Roose.

Nodding, Cole looked at the sky. "We have less than an hour of sunlight left."

"That might work to our advantage," said Roose. "Let's get this done."

In less than that hour of dwindling daylight, the stagecoach was engulfed in flames, and the three of them stood, hats off, watching it burn. Whit said some words and then they all mounted their horses and rode slowly towards Haven.

Stopping some way outside the town, the three horsemen gathered their coats around them. The chill wind shivered through what little undergrowth there was. As they waited, the first flurries of snow descended from the rapidly darkening sky. Night was almost upon them, and down in the dip, lights appeared in the few remaining buildings.

"It'll be best if we dismount," said Cole, reaching to pull out his Winchester from its scabbard. He checked the load, then did the same for the Colt Cavalry at his waist, positioned as always for a cross-belly draw.

"We'll take either side of the main street," said Roose, getting down from his horse. "Or should I say, the *only* street. You get to the rear of the saloon, Cole. I think it's a safe bet that's where they'll be, and you can pick 'em off as they try to run off."

"You seem to know the layout pretty well," said Whit.

"There's not much to know. There's really only one street with a couple of narrow passages here and there. As you can still see, even in this feeble light, the town's on its last legs. After we've finished here, I reckon it'll disappear into the dust."

"I've a tendency to think that that is the right and proper thing to happen," said Whit. He swung down from the saddle, from which he brought out a scattergun. He cracked it open and fed in two cartridges from a pouch. Putting the remaining cartridges in his coat pockets, he cradled the gun over the crook of one arm.

"We'll hobble the horses," said Roose, "keep 'em here until it's done."

"Gentlemen," said Whit, "may I remind you that these men are to be apprehended and taken to justice."

"Let's just see how it goes," said Cole and worked the lever of the Winchester. He had the image of the murdered passengers in his mind. And Brown Owl. He let out a prolonged sigh. "Move down real slow. This cold night air will amplify any noise, so tread gently."

"I am in the presence of men who have done this type of thing often," said Whit.

"Too often," said Cole.

"Sometimes," put in Roose with feeling, "not often enough."

The street was deathly quiet. No sound came from the saloon, although, from where he stood on the opposite side of the street, Roose could clearly see light from a number of oil lamps through the murky, grime-infested window and underneath the batwing doors. He was under the porch of an old, broken-down dry-goods store, which gave him an idea. He gently eased open the door and went inside. Forced to strike several matches, he found what he hoped would prove useful. Setting it up outside, he positioned himself in an advantageous situation, drew his gun, and waited.

Meanwhile, Whit, following the plan they'd worked out as they approached the main street, stepped up onto the boardwalk leading to the saloon. He waited, listening for anything from inside. There came the occasional cough, a muttering of voices, the clink of glasses. He could not make out how many people were inside, but he could hazard a guess. Although the original gang had been whittled down, he knew them to be ruthless men. He was not about to take any chances. He gently eased back the twin hammers of the scattergun and took a deep breath to settle himself.

At the rear of the saloon, Cole waited in the shadows. When the firefight broke, he would take down anyone who came running out of the door without any warning. Unless it was Jonas. For Jonas, the situation was personal.

Roose, one eye on Whit, rolled himself a cigarette. He stuck it between his lips, where it remained unlit. For now.

Whit closed his eyes. The last time he'd fired his gun in anger had been in a mining town just west of Abilene. Things were bad, and prospectors were close to losing their patience. They'd been sold a lie, that gold was there, and they'd readily purchased mining rights from an unscrupulous fellow called Timothy Bothwell. Bothwell was nowhere to be found, but when a group of miners shot up the stage and murdered the sheriff, who they believed was in cahoots with Bothwell, the US Marshals were called in. The confrontation didn't last much longer than it took Whit to fire two rounds from his scattergun, wounding several miners. One fellow made the mistake of going for his gun and Whit shot him through the throat. They all gave up after that.

Three years ago and counting. He hoped never again to have to face such violence. Hopes now dashed.

Whit ripped off his neckerchief and dabbed the sweat from his forehead. He stuffed it in his pocket, kicked through the doors, and blew out the first one, then a second large oil lamp, sending out showers of glass. Those inside leaped to their feet, a woman screamed, and Whit drew his revolver and shot out another lamp at the end of the bar. One remained, but he didn't have time to do anything about that. The initial shock had worn off and guns were appearing. Before the bullets started flying, he dipped back outside and slammed himself against the wall.

It all got very confused after that.

CHAPTER TWENTY-SEVEN

Acting quickly, Jonas upturned the table at which he'd been drinking and loosed off several shots towards the batwing doors as they flapped shut. He screamed, "Channi, go take a look outside!"

"No way," said Channi, flat on his stomach, edging towards a far corner. The one remaining oil lamp gave enough light for him to find a path to his chosen cover.

"Just take a look under the door, damn it!"

Rolling over onto his back, Channi stared up at the ceiling. He closed his eyes and counted to six. He would have counted further, but he could never remember what came next. He rolled again, three more times, taking himself closer to the saloon entrance. Turning his head, he squinted under the gap beneath the doors.

There was man on the opposite side of the street smoking a cigarette. What an idiot! He must be awful sure of himself, Channi thought with some humor. Well, this ain't gonna be his day. "I see him," he hissed.

"Can you shoot him?"

"Not from here."

"Jonas," said Coltrane from out of the gloom. "I'll take Maisie upstairs."

"You'll protect your own skin, you mean!"

"No, no, I swear. I'll—"

"I have a Winchester up there," said Maisie. "We can shoot down into the street from the bedroom window."

"It's too dark."

"Not if we see the flash of their guns," said Coltrane quickly, grabbed Maisie by the hand, and raced to the stairs. He cracked his shins into the occasional chair as he went, but nothing was going to stop him.

Jonas watched them ascend through the gloom. If there was a Winchester, that would give them an edge, so he waited, keeping his breathing even, knowing this wasn't part of his overall plan. Whoever these people were, they were going to pay for coming up against Jonas like this. "Shoot him, Channi!"

"I'm not in range. But without a light, I might just be able to get closer. He won't see me come out."

He sat up and shot to pieces the last remaining oil lamp. Some of the oil caught fire. Cursing, Sefton the barkeep, ran out from behind the counter and, using a couple of bar towels and a glass of frothy beer, quickly stamped down the flames.

A pall of acrid smoke drifted across the still saloon, now plunged in virtual darkness. What little light left coming from the pale grey sky outside proved too weak to filter into the room.

Channi took his chance. Jumping to his feet, he went through the batwing doors, revolver straight ahead of him, and fired off round after round into the figure standing under the porch. After the third shot, the sound of shattering glass rang out through the silence, but he did not cease firing.

Bemused, some half-dozen paces from where he thought he'd seen the figure arrogantly smoking a cigarette, he stopped, ejecting cartridges. A sound behind him caused him to turn.

There, black against the edifice of the saloon, was a tall man in a frock coat, his marshal's badge glinting dully in the gloom, a halo of fluttering snowflakes giving him an almost ghost-like appearance. In his hands he held a scattergun. He eased back the hammers. "Drop the gun."

Gaping, Channi didn't know what to do. He looked back into the porch. Where was the figure? What had happened to him?

Then, he saw it.

The figure.

Positioned slightly opposite to where Channi thought he was, the man stepped down into the street, still smoking. As he came closer, his boots crushed mirrored glass into the frozen ground. He was laughing.

Channi looked from the figure to his empty gun and groaned.

Lost in the darkness, Jonas decided there was only one option left for him – to flee.

Groping across the room, hoping his memory would serve him well, he managed to find the table and the saddlebags. He threw them over his shoulder and, with one hand outstretched and the other holding his gun, he made his way towards the rear. There had to be a back entrance, then it would be a simple case of sprinting to the livery, finding his horse, and making good his escape.

It was going to take some time, and more than once, he lost his way. Struggling to keep the threat of panic well battened down, he found the far wall and shuffled along it inch by painful inch.

Under the stairs, he found a door and went inside.

Small, airless, this had to be the way.

He clattered into a collection of what felt like metal buckets or pots and fell over, sending the saddlebags skidding across the floor. This was no way out and he cursed loudly, almost losing control. He sat and swallowed down his anger and lack of luck, thinking what to do and where to go.

From the bedroom in which they had spent so many tender moments, Maisie reached under the bed and pulled out the Winchester. Coltrane, meanwhile, put a match to the small, bedside oil lamp and sighed in relief as the sickly yellow light drizzled out to give some respite from the all-consuming darkness.

Moving up close, Coltrane placed a hand gently on her shoulder. Keeping his voice low, he said, "We don't have to do this."

"What do you mean?"

He nodded towards the Winchester in her hands. "We don't have to shoot anyone. We can get the money and go like we said. Make it across to California, start a new life. You and me."

"And Jonas? You think he's going to let us do that?"

"We can take the back stairs, and before anyone realizes, we'll be on our way." Sighing, he sat down beside her. "Jonas is not going to give himself up. He'll try and shoot it out. If we're lucky, he'll get himself killed."

"Or he'll kill them – whoever they are."

"By the time the shooting has died down, we'll be long gone." He nodded again at the Winchester. "Are you any good with that thing?"

A tiny laugh. "Better than most. I've had many years of taking good care of myself."

"And have you ever shot anyone with it?"

"Once. A few years ago, cowboy was beating up one of the girls. Bad. Real bad. I took this rifle, leaned over the balcony, and shot him dead."

"Dear God."

"What's the matter? You think because I'm a weak and defenseless woman I'm not capable?"

"Maisie, I believe you are more than capable." He turned his gaze to the window. "How's about you lean over the balcony again, only this time you shoot Jonas?"

"Are you crazy? What if I miss? In the darkness of the barroom, it's more than likely. Then what? He'll be hell-bent on killing us after that."

Rubbing his face, Coltrane stood up and paced the room. "All right, then we have to take the back stairs. If he comes after us, you try and shoot him then. We have little choice. If he survives, we're more than likely be dead, and if he doesn't, we have a fairly even chance of getting out of this alive."

"Those ain't good odds."

"They're all we have."

They stared into one another's eyes and made their decision.

CHAPTER TWENTY-EIGHT

Hearts pounded in constricted chests.

The horror of gunfights. The promise of almost certain death.

It twists minds, seizes muscle, makes life appear momentary, fleeting. No time to wonder what might have been, all those lost dreams, missed opportunities. No time for anything else except thinking about survival.

In any way possible.

Channi tried.

He turned, hoping to wrong-foot the man in front of him. If he could gain some distance, he might be able to reload his gun, shoot, escape.

But his mind was clouded. The instinct to live.

He spun on his heels, and the other one, the one with the scattergun, dealt him a horrific blow across the side of the head with the stock, pitching him to the ground, all senses gone.

He wasn't quite unconscious. Voices came to him, jumbled up, like tongues. He remembered his old preacher explaining tongues. He never explained how to count, though. Useless old preacher.

Hands were grabbing him, dragging him across the ground, exposed stones biting into his flesh. So hard, so cold. Then they lifted him.

So cold.

The wind rattled through the warped and twisted boards of the crumbling buildings.

He wished he was anywhere else but here. If only he'd made his own way south.

If only.

Channi twisted his neck, tried to focus and recognize the faces of those who were attacking him, wrenching away his future. His life.

A second, heavier blow smashed into his guts, and he thought he would be sick before everything disappeared into an endless black, spiraling hole.

Jonas tried.

Swearing, he managed to find the saddlebags before he clawed the door to the tiny room open and made his way back into the saloon.

"Sefton? Sefton, are you there?"

"Jonas? Is that you? I can't see anything."

"Where are you?"

"Behind the bar, and I ain't coming out – I don't wanna get shot by accident. Who are those men outside?"

"Beats me – bounty hunters or lawmen, it makes no difference – they're out to kill us. Where's the back way to the street?"

"Here, behind the counter. But if you go out there, they'll shoot you dead."

"No. They're too busy with Channi. You have a shotgun behind there, don't you?"

"Yeah, but I'm not that good."

"No need to be."

Jonas groped his way behind the bar. His eyes were much more accustomed to the gloom now and he saw the draped curtain and the promise of a back room. "Is it through this here curtain?"

"Straight ahead. There's back stairs too."

"All right. Put two rounds through the main doors as soon as I shout out to you."

"Hell, Jonas, I don't know if I can—"

"Just do it, Sefton!" and without another word, he went through the curtain.

. . .

Maisie tried.

She knew Coltrane's words made sense, but she also knew none of this would end until those pursuing them were dead.

She had plans.

She had dreams.

All her life, she'd done what others wanted. Men mostly. She believed the Doc offered security. She believed him to be rich. He promised her he'd take her away to the better life she'd always wanted.

But he lied.

They all lied.

Stroking the Winchester, she smiled at Coltrane. "I'm gonna make things right. I'm gonna make sure we never have to live in fear again."

She stood up. Coltrane reached out to grab a handful of her skirt, but she tugged herself free, engaged the Winchester, and went to the window.

Doc Farlow tried.

Tried to get himself out of his bed.

He sat gasping, holding his side, waiting for the waves of pain to die away. They hardly did. From under the pillow, he brought out the old Colt Navy, the only gun he'd ever possessed. The one holstered to his hip during his years as an Army medic during the War. He'd never fired it, but always kept it meticulously clean knowing that one day he would need it.

That day was now.

Steadying himself, he took a breath and stood up, sucking in air as the pain stabbed into his body. Too old for something like this, he chastised himself. Let it go.

But he knew he couldn't and, in a swaying gait, crossed over to the door.

Channi hung in the man's grip. There was nowhere else to go, nothing more to do.

Jonas curled his hand around the door handle. He lifted his head to shout out to Sefton.

Masie raised the window and, kneeling, rested the Winchester barrel on the bottom ledge. The night was black. She saw shapes. She took her aim.

Doc Farlow stepped onto the landing, pausing to gather his strength. Bent over, one hand pressed against the wall, drawing in ragged breaths. He took his time.

Soon. One more effort. Monumental or otherwise, he couldn't live with the shame of it, the ignominy. There was no choice.

Everything came to this.

CHAPTER TWENTY-NINE

From where he was, Roose heard a voice from inside the saloon shouting, "Now, Sefton!" just as a red-hot bullet shot harmlessly above his head. Reacting quickly, he swung Channi in front of him just in time as a second bullet thudded into the bank robber's chest. Holding the stricken man upright and using him as a shield, Roose fired three rounds into the upstairs window from where the shots were fired and, pushing Channi aside, ran to the saloon doors.

Half-a-dozen paces from making it, the doors exploded into a shower of splintered wood causing Roose to hurl himself sideways. Rolling out of harm's way, he glanced up to see Whit going through what remained of the doors. He swore, stood up, and ran after the marshal.

There was a man behind the counter, doing his level best to reload the shotgun. Whit didn't have time for debate and emptied both barrels of his scattergun into him. The spread hit the countertop, sending out a shower of sharp wood splinters straight into the man's body. He was screaming when he went down. Whit broke open his gun and feverishly reloaded.

· · ·

Coltrane was dragging her from the window. "For pity's sake, Maisie, do you want to get us both killed?"

"I'm all right," she said, knocking away his hand and working the lever. "I got one of 'em. I think the other one has come inside.

A shotgun boomed from below. Then, seconds later, another twin blast. Coltrane glared at her, unable to register what was happening. "We're gonna die, Maisie!"

"Man up," she spat and got to her feet.

The bedroom door burst open.

Farlow stood in the open doorway, breathing hard, face covered in sweat. A maniacal grin split his face. "See you in hell," he said.

Dumbstruck, neither Coltrane nor Maisie had any time to react before Doc Farlow put a fusillade of bullets into both of them.

Jonas staggered outside, the cold night air almost taking his breath away. He wore no coat, but such luxuries were beyond him now. The night pressed in all around him, and for a moment, he struggled to get his bearings. A sudden arc of light brought some relief from the darkness, but only briefly. An oil lamp, pitching through the air, hit the ground and burst open, the oil igniting. Behind the orange glow, Jonas saw the outline of a man.

"This is for Brown Owl," said a voice.

Jonas, not knowing who Brown Owl could be, reacted in the only way he knew how. One of them must have managed to hide out back, waiting to ambush him. Well, that was his mistake. Diving full stretch to his right, Jonas brought up his already drawn six-gun and fanned the hammer.

Unfortunately for Jonas, he had no real idea where his attacker was and the shots went wide and wild. Snorting, he climbed to his feet, snapping his head from side to side. "Where the hell are you?"

Cole, who knew exactly where Jonas was, breathed, "Turn around."

Jonas did so. His hands were shaking, his mouth gaping open, voice trembling with dread, "Who ..."

"You killed my friend. Now, you're gonna pay."

"Friend? Mister, I don't know who you mean but I swear I—"

"The Indian scout. Name of Brown Owl."

The beginning of something, a recall, a realization, stirred from within. One hand came up, "Hey, now wait a moment, I—"

Cole put two bullets into him, the heavy slugs throwing the man backwards. He hit the ground, writhing. Cole stepped closer stepped closer, stared into the terrified dying man's eyes, and put a third round into his head.

Breathing a long sigh, Cole ejected the spent bullets, reloaded and holstered his Colt. He turned away. For a moment he allowed himself a brief memory of his fellow scout, Brown Owl, to invade his thoughts. He muttered, "So long old friend," and went through the back entrance to the saloon.

Behind the curtain, he took the gas lamp that was balanced precariously on a lob-sided preparation table and went into the saloon.

Despite the murkiness, he assessed the situation fairly quickly. He saw Whit snapping his scattergun closed. They exchanged a look. "Is that you, Cole?"

"I hope for your sake it is."

The Marshal laughed and went to take a step forwards. A bullet hit him in the left bicep, spinning him around and finally dropping him to his knees, the scattergun falling from numbed fingers.

Several more bullets slapped into the wooden floor around him. Cole turned and saw a small, huddled figure coming down the stairs one at a time and shot him, throwing him backwards against the steps. His firearm clattered down to the floor. Holding the oil lamp aloft, Cole went and checked on him. The old coot, for he was indeed old, lay with his eyes wide open, stone dead.

Roose came crashing through the broken batwing doors, gun drawn, swiveling his head left and right, trying his best to gain some focus on what was occurring.

"Hold on, Sterling," said Cole, and he laid the oil lamp on the countertop. "We have yet another walking wounded to tend to."

Whit groaned, turned over and sat there, right hand flat against his left arm, blood leaking between his fingers. He looked as if he'd aged ten years.

"Does this mean there ain't gonna be a hanging?" asked Roose.

"Seems like," said Cole and holstered his gun.

"There's the fella we found out on the prairie," said Whit, head down, suffering.

"Ah, good," said Cole, "I wouldn't like the party to have been completely spoiled." Then, shaking his head, he went back around the counter, stepped over the ruined corpse of a man lying there, and brought down a bottle of whisky from the shelf.

"You celebrating?" asked Roose.

"Kind of," said Cole, pulled off his neckerchief and soaked it in whisky. Coming around the counter again, he got down next to Whit and grinned. "This is gonna hurt, Marshal," and he pressed it against the man's shot arm with some considerable relish.

CHAPTER THIRTY

"We can't do that," said Larry Grimes, sitting in the back room of his store with Cathy next to him. "It's immoral!"

"I don't really care what it is anymore, Larry. Neither of us have been dealt a good hand in this life, not until now, that is. So we're gonna use that money, pull down that old house of yours and employ some *real* builders to make us a new home – and a bigger one!"

"But, Cathy, don't you think we should—"

"What? Give it back?" Larry nodded. "Well, no, I do not think we shall. I have thought long and hard on this, Larry, since Mr Norton told me about the money. I was like you, at first, but I think we have just as much right to some happiness as the next person. Besides, it was what Mr Norton wanted."

It was late. Cathy had told him the whole story of what had occurred with Simpson and Cruces, of the killing and how she never wanted to set foot in that cabin again. Larry listened and knew she was not to be deterred. The more he thought, the more he begrudgingly came to agree with her. It was a wonderful plan, and he wholeheartedly agreed.

They spent the night in the local hotel, in separate rooms, and the next morning, over the breakfast table, Larry announced that he had sent off to Kansas City for a diamond ring, to make their engagement official. Cathy burst into tears, but for the first time for as long as she could remember, they were tears of happiness.

Towards mid-afternoon, with Larry once again behind the counter of his store, Cathy received Florence Caitlin's congratulations with much blushing. As they both stood exchanging stories about Larry and his somewhat dubious reputation, Cole and Roose rode into town, with Whit behind them looking ashen-faced. A long line of horses, with bodies draped across their backs, accompanied them. Cathy was already running down the steps as Roose reined in his horse.

"Oh, Mr Roose," she said, "what in the name of heaven happened?"

"Nothing that heaven has got anything to do with. I need to know where your doctor is, Miss Courtauld, so we can get this good man looked after. He's as tough as an old mule, but he's lost a lot of blood."

"I'll show you," said Florence, coming down the steps.

Roose doffed his hat and smiled, "Why thank you, Miss."

"Name is Florence Caitlin, as well you should know, Sheriff."

"He don't have much call to be associating with pretty ladies," said Cole from a few feet away.

"That is the truth," said Roose. "I am somewhat busy, as you might say."

Florence gave him a look and crossed to Cole. "I'll show you where Doc Henson's place is."

"Thank you kindly," said Cole, gave Roose a wink, and guided himself and Whit in the direction Florence took them.

Roose looked down at Cathy and pulled a face, gesturing behind him to the string of horses and their grizzly cargo. He wrinkled his nose. "They is somewhat ripe, Miss Courtauld."

"Ain't they just," she said, pressing a handkerchief against her nose.

"I shall deliver them to the undertaker's, then I shall need to come and talk to you. We have some loose ends to tie up."

She watched him go as Larry came down the steps to join her. "What did he mean by that?"

"I'm not sure."

"The money? He knows about it, don't he! Dear Lord, Cathy, we is gonna end up in deep trouble after this."

"No, we ain't, Larry Grimes, unless you open your big mouth."

"I won't, I swear to you."

"Well, all right then," and she pushed past him and went inside the store.

"So that is it," said Roose sometime later, peering at her from across the table.

"Every detail."

"You shot him?"

"I did. And I'd do it again if I had to."

"*Cathy!*" burst out Larry.

Roose held up his hand. "Don't go getting irate, Larry. What's done is done."

Larry gaped at him. "You mean there won't be any charges?"

Sweeping up his hat, Roose stood up. "Well, from where I'm standing, I can't say much wrong has been done. A case of self-defense is how I'd put it." He adjusted his hat on his head and smiled. "How much do you think that young fella you helped took from the bank?"

Cathy's face fell, and, beside her, Larry yelped.

"Well?"

Cathy and Larry exchanged a glance. Dropping her head and voice, Cathy said, "Ten thousand dollars."

There was a long pause before Roose said, "You've lost a good deal. Things have a way of evening out in life is how I see it." Her face came up, wide-eyed in disbelief. "And, I do believe congratulations are in order?"

Cathy gasped. "How did you know?"

"It's my duty to know, Miss Courtauld."

"Cathy."

He smiled again and left.

It didn't take Roose long to wander down to the bank. Cole was waiting for him outside and handed him the telegram as he came up the steps.

"How's Whit?"

"He'll make it. Jim Riley from the telegraph office delivered that to him."

"You read it."

"Whit asked me to."

Grunting, Roose read through the words and sighed. "As we suspected."

"Lister tried to embezzle the railroad out of twenty-five thousand dollars," said Cole. "Can't blame him for trying."

"The man's a weasel."

"How long will he get?"

Roose shrugged. "Depends on the railroad, but no more than six months. He'll lose his job, though, which is probably more of a punishment."

"Crime never does pay."

Smiling, Roose turned towards Larry Grimes' store and sighed. "Almost never," he said, and with that, he went through the bank door, with Cole close behind, to arrest Mr Lister, the bank manager.

The End

MURDERED BY CROWS

Reuben Cole Westerns Book 5

This for everyone.
Janice, of course, but for all those friends and loved ones who have shared my journey. You know who you are.

CHAPTER ONE

THERE was never much to do on a Sunday morning, except maybe to sit on a rocking chair, under the shade, and watch. Not that there was much to see either. The main street of 'Bethlehem' was empty, save for an old mule tied up outside Cecil Bowers' haberdashery store. The owner was nowhere to be seen. The 'Ruby Glow' saloon was closed, as were the adjacent shops. A horse whinnied from the yard of Hedgefield's livery and coral. Not much else though.

Reuben Cole leaned forward, chomping on his tobacco, and let loose a long brown stream of spittle into the street. Sitting back, he groaned, repositioned his hat and did his best to drift off to sleep. Ryan Stone, the young sheriff, newly appointed and as keen as anything, was out visiting the Gower sisters who had reported seeing a 'large black man' poking around in their apple orchard. Amelie, the younger of the two, brought in the news, nervous about leaving Claudette, her sister, out there on her own. Cole recalled the exchange. "Well, there is Joshua, of course, but Joshua is old now. Not sure what use he'd be in a fight."

"A fight?" Stone was busily writing the report down in a large ledger. That's the way things were done now, he had told Cole, everything had to be recorded.

"You said 'fight'. What sort of fight?" put in Cole.

"Oh, I don't know," said Amelie, all flustered. She wore a pretty sky-blue dress with white shawl and matching bonnet. A handsome woman, Cole estimated her age at around fifty and he didn't know of many much younger women who looked as fine as she. Except Maddie, of course. Amelie played with her folded parasol, rolling it in her palms, growing a little more nervous as she continued. "Gunfights and such."

Cole and Stone exchanged a look. "You think this intruder had a gun?" asked the young sheriff.

"Not sure," she said. "But he was black, so he must have."

Cole pulled a face. "Not sure I get your meaning there, ma'am."

"They *all* carry guns, don't they? Violent. Thieves and rapists the lot of them. Isn't that so?"

Suddenly Miss Amelie seemed a whole lot less attractive than before. Blowing out a long breath, Cole shot a glance towards Stone. "I'll be outside."

Later, with Amelie prancing off to the teahouse, Stone stepped out into the daylight, adjusting his gun belt. He checked his Colt Frontier. "She's worried," he said without lifting his head.

"Take the scatter-gun," Cole had suggested, already well ensconced in the rocking chair.

"No need for that Mr Cole, it's probably just some—"

"Humour an over-cautious old man," said Cole without shifting from his position. "Since that business of the break-in at the house, I'm kinda nervous about strangers rooting around." At this point, he tipped his hat back and settled a hard stare upon young Stone. "Take the scatter-gun."

Blowing out a sigh, but chuckling nonetheless, Stone did as asked. He went into the jailhouse and returned moments later with the gun, breaking it open to feed in the load. "You will look after the store whilst I'm gone?"

"Already am," said Cole, easing down the hat over his face, "already am."

That was almost three hours ago. A tiny tingling of something unsettling was becoming more noticeable at the nape of his neck. He didn't like the feeling and thought such things were way behind him. Farther than his neck anyway. Sniggering at his little private joke, he decided to give the young sheriff one more hour before he'd go take a look. Better safe than sorry.

From somewhere far off, the tiny clink of the church bell reminded himself that it was already noon and the padre had ended his service. Soon the faithful and the good would be traipsing back to their homes, and Myron would be opening the bar at the saloon. It was something to look forward to. Snuggling down, arms crossed, he tried again to sleep.

A loud, sharp retort caused him to spring upright, hat falling back. Instinctively, he reached for his gun, which was, as usual, adjusted for a cross-belly draw, the way it always had been since Cole's army days. Almost thirty years had slipped by since he stopped scouting for the United States Cavalry, but old habits do indeed die hard. If they didn't, it might be Cole who would be dying.

Blinking repeatedly, he climbed to his feet and stared in disbelief at the bizarre looking contraption trundling along the middle of the street. A curious, box-like construction, it appeared too flimsy to support the two adults squashed up inside. Open to the elements, they sat on a raised bench seat, covered in dark blue padding. A large, brightly chequered blanket covered their knees, and both wore hats and scarves. The man was the one steering the thing forward, if such a word could be used to describe the ongoing struggle he was making with the small wheel in front of him. Beside him, a slim, elegant looking woman, turned her smiling face towards Cole an action, which caused a tiny thrill to ripple through his abdomen. She possessed a sultry, breath-taking beauty, the kind men found irresistible.

The driver brought the beast to a halt, jerked on the handbrake, and reached to disengage the engine. Unfortunately, he was not fast enough to prevent another loud explosion and a rush of black smoke erupting from the machine's rear.

Clamping a gloved hand over her mouth, the woman stepped down, coughing hoarsely. A piece of black chiffon tied under her chin secured the bonnet. She wore a large grey overcoat, which fell to her ankles, encased as they were in laced patent black leather boots. Behind her, the man stepped up, rubbing his gloved hands together. He prised a set of goggles from his face and pushed them above the rim of his deerstalker cap. A two-piece gabardine coat completed his outfit, all designed to keep him warm and dry when he was perched on the machine's seat.

"Beautiful day," the man shouted. "We've been on the road for quite a while and would dearly love to stretch out legs, find a spot of something to eat. Drink. That sort of thing. Have you anything here?"

Cole couldn't quite catch the accent. He'd heard many in his time, but this one ... It sounded sing-song, like sailors from whaling ships he'd met years before, but a much stranger delivery of the vowels forcing him to strain to catch the meaning.

"If it's eating you're after ..." Cole paused for confirmation.

"Yes, indeed," said the woman, whose voice was clearly discernible. Almost melodic, Cole thought.

"Then you could try either the saloon, or Mrs Desmond, who opens her restaurant roundabout now to accommodate those returning from church."

"That sounds perfect," she said. Stepping forward, she reached out her hand. "I am Mrs Cartwright, but you can call me Sarah." She gestured towards the man hovering at her side. "This is my husband Lewis."

The former scout took her hand and shook it. "I'm Cole."

"Pleased to meet you," she said, releasing her grip. "We've purchased the hotel and have made quite a trip from Nebraska, travelling in Lewis' beautiful horseless carriage here." She stepped aside to allow Cole an uninterrupted view. Lewis beamed, chest swollen with pride.

"Hotel? I didn't know it was for sale."

"Oh yes," said Lewis enthusiastically. He strode forward, proffering his hand this time. "Yes. The Elegance as it's called."

"Ah," said Cole, shaking his hand. "I know the one you mean, a little out of town, not so very far from the rail station?"

"That's the one. Perfect spot."

"It's a wonder nobody has snapped it up before now," put in Sarah Cartwright.

"Well, that could be because of the killing, but who knows."

"Killing?" The couple spoke as one and both looked shocked.

"Some time ago now," said Cole, "but I'm not too clear about the details, not being from here. I live quite a ways out of town myself, but in the opposite direction." To give some emphasis, he pointed towards the distant mountains.

"A killing?" Lewis turned away, shaking his head. "Nobody said anything about a killing ..." Swinging around again, he did his best to force a smile. "Still, it can't be haunted ... can it?"

"Who knows? Besides, wouldn't that be something of a selling point?"

"A selling poi—"

"Good Lord," interjected Sarah, "I think you could have something there," and they all laughed. The mood broken, they bade their farewells and the couple walked off towards Mrs Desmond's restaurant. Cole returned to his rocking chair and, despite the welcome distraction of the newcomers, grew uneasy. Stone was now very much overdue, and he knew, if he didn't know before, that he would have to ride out there and check the situation. He'd promised himself not to get involved in such matters, but here he was once more, doing just that. He offered up a silent prayer that none of it would come to very much.

In that, he was to be proved wrong.

CHAPTER TWO

E VEN though the living nightmare of the proceeding weeks and
months was to prove otherwise, initially it was just what they
wanted. As soon as they stopped their carriage and took in the first, full
view they both knew. It was instinctive. No words were needed. They
simply turned to each other and smiled. In that smile was utter relief.
Months of deliberation, arguing, doubting, had finally led them here. As
far from the leafy avenues of Nebraska City as they could imagine. Nineteen Hundred and Five, but this area still felt very much like the Wild
West. The untamed frontier. The town of Bethlehem, right on the
border with Utah. An old mining town, but as close, both agreed, to
perfect as they could wish as they craned their necks and took in the
'Elegance Hotel'.

With the money dear old, long forgotten Aunt Gwen left Lewis in her
will, it was too good an opportunity to miss, especially with the promise
it held for a good future. Fortunately, or so it appeared, Lewis agreed
with his wife. Childless and reasonably happy, they had no one to
consider but themselves. For the first time in their married life they
could afford to take a gamble. They bought the 'Elegance' without a
second thought and with very little change left from the inheritance.

For over four years, or so they were told, the hotel had stood empty.
No one explained why, and certainly not the agent who introduced them

to the property. "It's ideal," he said, rubbing his hands gleefully as the couple studied the artist's drawing of the place. "The railroad has only recently arrived and soon businesses will take advantage. It's on a direct route to California, and we all know about California, don't we."

The reality hit home as soon as the key fitted into the front door and the door opened, the hinges screaming their objection. A pungent smell of damp and animal droppings immediately hit the back of their throats. Sarah, gagging, held onto the closest wall, hand across her mouth, eyes squeezed shut. "Oh my Lord, Lewis. What *is* that smell?"

"Dead rats probably," he said. He marched forward, taking in the surroundings, despite them being shrouded in dust, cobwebs. Weak, sickly light trickled in from the badly boarded up windows, but adequate enough to pick out the details. "We've got some work to do to get this place up and running."

Sarah moaned. "Haven't we just. It'll be worth it, in the end. If we manage it."

He nodded. "If we don't, we could still make it worthwhile." He kicked his boot through the thick layer of white dust clinging to the floor. "It'll take a lot of hard-work, darling. Elbow-grease and the like."

She did her best to smile, but barely managed little more than a sneer.

During the subsequent weeks they would need to spend ages scrubbing, repainting, fixing and replacing, buying in new beds, furniture, fittings. None of it was going to be quick, but they resigned themselves to making a new life for themselves and both of them were determined to do their very best to achieve their dream.

"You think that nice Mr Cole would help us?" Sarah asked as she trailed a forefinger through the grime of the reception counter.

"Possibly. He would certainly know of some labourers who could help."

"I'll ask him."

"Yes. But let's get our bearings first, yes? I'll check the upstairs rooms then we can begin to come up with some sort of plan."

Smiling, she watched him mounting the broad staircase to the first floor and wished she had invited Mr Cole to help them as soon as she'd met him.

CHAPTER THREE

THE heat pounded down upon him like a hammer of the gods, heavy and relentless. Soaked through with sweat, Cole did his best to maintain his speed but the longer the ride continued the more difficult this became. He decided not to veer off to his home. Maddie would be there, but she wouldn't expect him to turn up until the end of the day, knowing full well that Cole's helping hand to the young sheriff always took longer than anticipated. He found stomping around his father's big old house tedious and, since the break-in and all the horrors that ensued, he much preferred to be in town and while away his days, trying not to think of Maddie too much and the comforts of the wonderful home she had created for them both. But he was a troubled man, as Maddie herself often commented on. A man with a past he could not shake, of a life out on the open range. Army days, scouting days. So much to look back on. So, she encouraged him to go into town and sit, talk to those willing enough to engage him in conversation. Reminisce.

Nights, they were a different matter. The ghosts came then, as they always did, invading his mind. Images of his father and Sterling. Brown Owl. All those he'd lost. Maddie. She got sick soon after he returned following Sterling Roose's death, the news taking a lot out of her. He almost lost her too. Now, she was getting stronger every day. She made everything bearable, but only just.

Clearing his mind, he followed the trail to the Gower house, which was easy and didn't take much of Cole's considerable tracking skills. He prided himself he could still read the signs. Nowadays there was nobody else who had quite the degree of expertise as he. He often wondered if the Army ever came to ask him, would he offer his services. He was old now, early-sixties, and sitting all day in a saddle held little attraction for him. Even the gentle ride into town every morning took its toll on his limbs. Now, reining in his horse to consider the house, he rolled his shoulders and moved around on the hard saddle, trying to ease his discomfort. It didn't work.

The Gower place lay in a small depression. Attractive and well tendered, there were small fields set aside for potatoes, onions, cabbages and the like, a fruit orchard as well as surrounding borders of blooming flowers and shrubs. He marvelled at how the sisters had managed to create it all way out here in the scrub. He'd always thought of it as a life-less place with no goodness in the ground, but there it was, like something out of one of those new-fangled special-interest magazines he sometimes saw in the mercantile store. Soon, within a generation he suspected, what with compulsory education, everyone would be able to read such things. An edition detailing gardens and gardening caught his eye. And here such a garden was, in all its beauty. A miracle to grow such wonders out here.

Despite the blaze of colour something disturbed him.

Nobody moved.

No signs of life.

He spotted the horses in the little coral, the assorted gardening equipment, the wheelbarrow. Reaching behind him he pulled out the telescope he'd been spurred on to purchase after that time with Marshal Whit back in the Seventies who'd used one to such good effect. A wonderful thing it was, even by modern standards. He pressed it against his eye and turned the focus ring to get a better idea.

The body lay face down, amongst the orchard trees, clearly dead. Cole never would have noticed it without the telescope.

Holding his breath, he scanned the rest of the area but saw nothing else. Except for the front door of the house slightly ajar.

That caused him deep concern and, groaning, he put the telescope away, exchanging it for his Winchester.

Easing his horse gently forward, about fifty or so paces from the silent cabin, Cole dismounted. Watchful, he stood behind his horse for a moment, checking for any movement or sound. There was neither. Scanning the surrounding expanse of open plain, he felt sufficiently secure to move forward, leading the horse to a clump of tangled trees. He threw the reins around the stoutest branch and continued on.

Ten paces or so from the building, he dropped to his knees, Winchester at his shoulder. He steadied his breathing.

There was nothing.

Keeping low, he edged across to the body in the field. It was an elderly black man, undoubtedly the servant Joshua. He'd been shot through the head, the exit wound having blown out most of his skull. The blood had dried hard and black, so this had happened some time ago. Buzzards had already started on the corpse. He saw the signs of human feet scampering away and there, not so far, the spent cartridge. Remaining where he was, Cole twisted himself to face the cabin. He spotted more tracks. Horses as well as human beings.

He pulled in a breath and crossed to the cabin. The porch was shaded by a large awning, supported by thick timber poles. A single step led up to the veranda. There was a wide, narrow, shuttered window to the left of the door and a stone chimney stack on the side. The roof was slate. This was a well-built, small yet elegant looking residence, not the usual sort of makeshift building settlers usually erected. With the threat of hostiles long gone, people felt a lot more confident now and were settling down to stay permanently. This would be a nice home to live in. Cole wondered if anybody lived in it now.

Tentatively, he put his weight on the step and hauled himself up to the veranda. A mournful sounding creak beneath him made him freeze, waiting. He had the Winchester at his side now, engaged, ready to fire. He moved towards the door.

He nudged open the door with the point of the Winchester's barrel. Again, the woodwork groaned, the hinges desperate for oil. The sound set his teeth on edge.

Inside, blackness. Not a breath of air stirred.

Waiting until his eyes adjusted to the gloom, he went inside.

Almost immediately he saw the man, slumped in the corner. Quickly checking the rest of the room, Cole crossed to him, put his fingers to the man's throat and felt the pulse. Acting fast now, he went to the window and opened up the shutters. Light flooded in and he turned to see the devastation.

Whatever had happened here had been swift and violent. Not a single piece of furniture or ornament remained upright. Whoever had done this had no regard for another person's property.

Again to the man. Cole saw it was Stone, the sheriff. He was barely alive, a gunshot wound in his chest which must have missed his heart by inches. Outside, he'd noted the water trough, and he rushed to it, fetching water in a pail, returning to mop Stone's brow. Cole soaked up some water with his own neckerchief and squeezed drops from it onto Stone's lips. The man coughed and spluttered. Cole repeated the squeezing action until the man's eyes flickered open.

Seized by sudden fear, Stone panicked, gripping Cole's arm, crying out, "No, please!"

"It's all right, Ryan, it's me – Cole."

"Cole?" Stone's voice was nothing more than a strangulated croak, but his eyes were clearing, senses slowly returning. He shook his head repeatedly, groaning and wincing with pain. "They're here, Cole. They're here."

"No, it's all right. Whoever did this has gone."

Breathing in short, sharp gasps, Stone put his head back against the wall. "Oh God," he said. "I'm shot."

"Yes, you are, but it's gonna be all right. I'm gonna make you comfortable then go back to town and get the Doc."

"No," Stone said, his panic returning. He held onto Cole's arm, squeezing it tight. "No, you can't leave me. They'll come back, they'll—"

"Take it easy," said Cole, mopping Stone's glistening brow. "No one is coming back." He studied the upturned room. "Where's the woman? Claudette?"

"They took her."

Cole snapped his head around to face Stone. "They *took* her?"

He nodded. Eyes closed again, face screwed up, his voice low and trembling as he spoke. "I rode up, not expecting to find anything. There were no horses, no signs anyone was here, but then I went up to the door, knocked on it and came in. She was in a chair, tied up. A man was slapping her, and she was crying. Another one turned to me as I went for my gun but a third one clubbed me on the back of the head." Unconsciously, he raised a hand to feel his skull. "I heard a gunshot from outside and although I was almost unconscious, I tried to pull my gun and that's when they shot me."

"Why did they take her?"

"Miss Claudette?" He shook his head. "They wanted the deed box, they said. I pretended to be out cold so I could hear 'em, every word. She wouldn't tell 'em so they tore the place apart. I heard 'em beating on her some more then she said it was in her lawyer's place and that's when I heard 'em taking her outside. She was kicking up one helluva fight, Cole, but nothing was gonna stop 'em." His eyes sprang open, feverishly locking in on Cole's own. "I couldn't do anything. I swear."

"Ryan, no one could have. You try and rest easy. Her lawyer's place, you say? Do you know where that is?" Stone shook his head. "Well, I could track 'em but it'll take some time. Further to that, they is killers so I'll need more men. Amelie is in town, she'll know where the lawyer is. I'll ride back, fetch the doc, then swear in some deputies for a posse. Meanwhile, I want you to sit here, try not to move. There's water," he tapped the pail, "and I'll find you a cup. I won't be long, you understand?"

Stone nodded, but then his face crumpled and tears sprang from his eyes. "Oh, Cole, I'm so sorry. I should have done more, been more cautious, but I never ..."

"You learn from this, Ryan. You hear me? You learn by your mistakes and you learn 'em fast. *Never* take things at face value, always be prepared and expectant. You're lucky, no one hardly gets a second chance out here." He stepped back, put a hand in the base of his spine and stretched out his muscles. "Darned if I don't feel like I been kicked by a mule. My old joints don't get any easier to move." He chuckled, despite the desperate situation. "I'll go. You hold on."

Stone gave a grudging nod as Cole searched around, found a tin cup, and pressed it into the young sheriff's hand. Without a further word, he went outside again.

Mounting up, Cole gave the surroundings one more scan. It would be simple enough to follow their tracks, but with the woman as hostage he could not take the risk of them spotting him before he got too close. If he was forced to go up against them, he'd need men, good men.

He pulled a face and kicked his horse into a gallop.

It was Nineteen-Hundred and Five. He doubted there were any 'good men' left.

CHAPTER FOUR

NOT everyone in the town was enthusiastic over the re-opening of the Elegance Hotel. Following the church service, words were exchanged between parishioners as they strolled out into the sunshine. The Preacher, Mr Peters, who called himself 'Reverend' – a man not unused to a good drink himself – listened to the comments with feigned interest.

"I'm not sure if it's a good thing," Mrs Collins was saying on her way out. "No doubt they're very nice people, but the town doesn't need that sort of..." She struggled for a moment to find the appropriate word that would convey the depth of her feeling. Not finding one she settled for, "that sort of *thing*."

Her point, if not her use of language, was shared by Mrs Daniels, a stout woman, all full-length overcoat and heavy eyebrows, whose own husband had died two years earlier due to, she maintained, the 'demon drink.' "We don't want drunkards here. Keep them up-country, that's my view."

"They're hardly that, Mrs Daniels," began the Reverend, marvelling at the woman's ability not to perspire, or even look remotely heated in such a coat on such a day. He almost instantly regretted his interjection, however, as the formidable Mrs Daniels fired him a vicious glare. She disliked this preacher, disliked his youthfulness, his 'new' way, his desire to attract more people into the church by offering guitars, choruses, clapping. She bristled with indignation. "I know what I'm talking about, Mr Peters," she said and, wishing him a good morning, she departed. Mrs Collins watched her go. "Nothing good will come of this, Reverend."

"It is only a hotel, Mrs Collins. You never know, it might do the town some good."

"I don't see how. Drink and debauchery never did anybody any good."

"Mrs Collins that is a misplaced and rash judgement if I may say so. I am sure the owners will have nothing to do with such excesses." She didn't look convinced, but he plunged on regardless. "With the ever-expanding railroad system, the town needs a place for businessmen and the like to stay on their way farther west, or even south. It will bring well-needed business to the town."

Pursing her lips, she said, "Where are they from anyway?"

"Not from here, I know that much. East I should imagine, or somewhere up north."

"M'mm, that doesn't tell me a lot. Do they know the history of the place?"

"Now *that* I couldn't say."

"Then it might be a good idea if somebody told them, don't you think?"

The Reverend blinked. "You mean *I* should?"

"Mr Peters, it really is your duty, would you not agree?"

The Reverend wouldn't, but he remained silent.

Mrs Collins nodded to him. Her views concerning him were not as strong as Mrs Daniels', but nevertheless she had her suspicions. She reluctantly supported the Reverend's plans for the re-structuring of services to attract the young to the congregation. No, it was the *man*. She knew about his drinking, of course, but she also knew that it was never to excess. What she didn't like was his idea of creating a boxing club. Wayward young men frequented the old barn just outside the town where they would *train*. She had no idea what that term meant but she felt there was something not quite right about a man of God who kept his body in such good shape, whose swollen chest and shoulders strained against the seams of his vestments and whose hands so obviously bore the marks of manual labour. Here was a man who had a past, a past that was so annoyingly shrouded in mystery. "I shall see you on Tuesday evening for Bible class, Mr Peters. You could tell me their reaction to the news then. Good day."

The Reverend Peters rarely swore, not because of any pious feelings he had on the subject but simply because he was usually unruffled by most of life's little setbacks so had little need to vent his anger with expletives. This, however, was no such moment. He hissed a curse through his teeth before dipping back inside his church. He stood for a moment in the still, stark silence and closed his eyes, drinking in the quiet, allowing the atmosphere to gently waft over him, calm and cool him. The greatest drawback of living in such a small, introvert place was the gossip. It was rampant. And here he was, stuck in the middle, hating it all and yet knowing that now it was up to him to let the Cartwrights know what it was they were living amongst. Forgotten dreams – or, more aptly, nightmares. Perhaps not even forgotten, at least not by the Mrs Collins of this world. He opened his eyes. Why don't people just let go? Why do they cling on to the past, especially the bad parts? Why couldn't the Cartwrights be left in blissful ignorance and why couldn't he find the courage to tell Mrs Collins to go and tell them the story herself? It was all so unnecessary. But what was he to do? He said he would tell them. There was no going back.

He moved down the aisle, sweeping his eyes across the tiny altar. People said it was pre-Revolution. He couldn't imagine anyone living out here back then. He let out a sigh, turned around and leaned back against the cold stone. The dark, yet comforting expanse stretched out before him, rows of pews reeking of history, thousands of ghostly backsides having left their impressions on those polished wooden seats. It was a sobering thought the knowledge that so many had come to this place to find solace, release, hope...all of them looking to preachers not unlike himself for help, guidance, faith. It was a heady responsibility he bore and people, past and present, expected so much from those like him. For the sake of his predecessors he would have to do it. He smiled, finding reassurance in their silent support. He thrived on responsibility. It was what made his calling – for that was how he viewed his work in the Church. So worthwhile, so challenging. God would be his rock and life, as always, and giving the Cartwrights an insight into their new purchase would not prove to be as bad as he thought.

He hoped, because he too had nightmares. Sometimes, the past came to visit, to seize him in its horrible embrace. Faith often came to his aide but recently the memories reared up too strong and so relentless.

He took a deep breath and decided he would go and see the Cartwrights that very afternoon. If he could manage to get this evening's sermon down on paper before then, perhaps he could take a drink or two with the newcomers.

Peters allowed himself a smile. No, life wasn't really all that bad at all.

CHAPTER FIVE

"That's the lot," called Sarah Cartwright as she came round from behind the bar, drying her hands on a towel. She'd decided to work on the reception area before anything else as it would be the first thing potential customers would see and she was anxious to get things moving. A selling point, you could say. An advert. Upstairs, Lewis busied himself in the second of the rooms. Top of the list, he'd cleaned a single, which had proved reasonably easy, but the double was a struggle to prepare. A gaping hole in the roof allowed dust and debris to pile up in the corners, putting a thick film of dirt over everything. As he clumped down the stairs of the two storey hotel, he forced a smile when he saw Sarah with her hair tied back, wearing green overalls, which disguised her fine figure, sleeves rolled up past her elbows. Her determination to make the hotel a success was an inspiration.

Ten years her husband's junior, she was a tall, slim, elegant woman. When not pulled back like now, a cascade of full, brown locks tumbled down around her shoulders, framing her elfin face, producing quite devastating effects on any man that laid eyes on her. Lewis had noted how that old man, Cole, had stopped, mesmerised by her. Lewis had to admit he didn't like it and wondered, not for the first time, if this was the type of business they should be embarking upon. A business which demanded polite and efficient responses from both the owners. He wasn't too sure about that. Sarah always found being friendly so very easy, lapping up those puppy-dog eyes and the drooling mouths, but Lewis, not the most out-going of people, despised it. Not at all gregarious, he preferred to be out of the public eye, locked away in his office, concentrating on the accounts. He found comfort in the knowledge that if they discovered what it was that had brought them here, he could employ an army to keep the place up and running.

Sarah mentioned that once they opened and business developed, they would need to employ additional staff. Already a cook had appeared, the one who had answered their initial newspaper advertisement. Nearly sixty, Blanche Chambers was on trial, preparing them dinner in the compact kitchen. She too had worked tirelessly to ensure the place was ready, at one point emerging, bathed in sweat, a dishevelled mess but beaming nevertheless. "I don't believe that stove has been used for years."

Smiling, Sarah put down her cleaning cloth, held out her hand to Lewis and pulled him to her. "Why don't we all have a little break?"

He kissed her, winked at Blanche, and agreed.

They sat around a small table. Lewis supplied glasses of cold beer and, for a moment at least, a sense of calm settled over them.

"It's a beautiful place," said Blanche, allowing her eyes to roam through the foyer, past the reception desk, the bar, and up the narrow staircase. "How many rooms is it?"

"Twelve," said Lewis.

"Six singles and six doubles," added Sarah. "It's enough."

"If things go well," continued Lewis, "we could build an extension. But we'll see."

"It all depends on what happens after the railroad opens up here. We got in touch with them and they say it'll be no longer than six-moths."

"Well," said Blanche, finishing her beer. "The station is completed. Very fine it looks."

Lewis studied her lined face. He pondered with the thought that a much younger, more attractive barmaid might take some of the attention away from his wife. But he doubted that. Sarah was still the most sensual woman he had ever seen and the fact that most other men agreed with him caused him no end of stress. How much longer would it be, he again mused, before some younger, fitter, and more able man moved in and gave her what she so obviously needed and what he found so increasingly difficult to deliver?

His thoughts were dispelled when Blanche declared that she must "Get on!" and Lewis finished his beer, watched her leave with the empty plates and sat back, sighing. "How long is it all going to take?"

"A couple of weeks," said Sarah. "This reception area needs repainting, furniture replacing, carpets cleaned. It's going to be a full-time job, Lewis."

A thought struck him, and he stood up. "I'm taking a look down below," he said. "For all we know it'll be in a worse state than anywhere."

"Be careful. Take a lamp with you."

Doing as she suggested, Lewis descended into the dark cellar. He had been down there before, during their first inspection of the property in fact, but he still wasn't absolutely certain of his way round. Holding the oil-lamp aloft, he could make out shapes of stacked-up chairs, boxes, rolled up carpets, lots and lots of rotting ledgers and barrels of indeterminate age, which no doubt held beer once. And the smell, thick, heavy. It settled in the back of his throat, causing him to cough intermittently. But there was something else which gripped him. A feeling of unease he couldn't shift. The place had an atmosphere that made it seem strangely out of tune with the rest of the house. He looked about him and through the half-gloom he could just make out a set of dust-encrusted racks on which lay half a dozen or more bottles of some long-forgotten wine. The wood looked rotten, as did everything else. Nothing had been looked at since the place was shut up. He inched forward. Those barrels, precariously stacked, leaned at an impossible angle against the far wall. He rapped one with his knuckles. They were not empty, but what they held only the Lord knew. Lewis sighed heavily. They would all have to be cleared out. During the week, once the rooms were done, he would have to spend some time down here, cleaning, putting in gas lights, trying to make it presentable. His thoughts drifted away, picturing what it must have been like years ago. Who visited then, he wondered, before the War, before it happened. Did it happen down here, amongst the detritus and the dust? Perhaps in the dark, all sound lost in the depths of this mournful place. The sound of the screams. There must have been screams, he assumed...

"Lewis, where have you got to?"

Sarah's voice broke through his thoughtful meandering. He was doing that more and more frequently, he said to himself in a form of admonishment. Forever daydreaming, he must have been down here in the dark for longer than he thought. He really must concentrate on what he's doing.

"Lewis, what are you doing down there? We have the rooms to finish."

"Yes. Just coming."

As he returned to the muggy air of the reception, he noticed that her face had that barely controlled look about it, the look that spelled trouble no matter what the explanation for his prolonged absence might be. "Sorry," he offered limply, and she retorted with her usual, "You will be." He steeled himself to concentrate on the business in hand and stomped upstairs to face the rooms once again. The images of the cellar, however, kept coming back into his head. What was wrong with it? He'd never felt this way about any other place in his entire life. He stood for a while, absently polishing a wall mirror, wondering if there was any way he could find out more, perhaps discover something that would give him the answer to his dread feelings. Whatever it was couldn't linger there. What had happened, the sketchy details he knew about, was over. Gone forever. Ghosts didn't exist. It was only a cellar, he convinced himself – what could possibly be wrong with a cellar? He turned and pulled off the bed sheets, gave an involuntary shiver, considered asking Sarah's opinion, quickly thought better of that and threw himself into his work.

CHAPTER SIX

B EFORE the horse came to a halt, Cole was swinging himself from the saddle. The impact jolted his old bones and he winced, cursing himself for being so dismissive of his aches and pains. There was nothing he could do about the fact that he was getting older. He couldn't remember the last time he'd spent a prolonged time in the saddle, but he needed to remember because the physical effort brought agony to his muscles and limbs. Right now, he needed to focus so, gritting his teeth, he stretched out his back, put the pain out of his mind and went through the door of Doc Wycliffe's surgery.

"What can I do for you, Reuben?" came the shrill voice of Mrs Nelson, the receptionist, who had taken up her usual defensive position behind her desk. A small shrew of a woman, she was nevertheless formidable and only allowed those with an appointment or the most urgent of cases to pass through to the inner sanctum. It was all the thing in New York City, she'd announced, and what was good out east was just as good here.

"We'll be making appointments by telephone soon," said Mrs Tomes one sun-baked morning.

Twisting her lips into what she considered a smile, Mrs Nelson waggled her finger, "Why Geraldine that is *exactly* what Doctor Wycliffe is looking into."

But this was now, and at this moment Cole appeared more agitated than usual.

"You look somewhat flustered, Reuben. Can I be of assistance?"

Cole told her as best he could and, without any discussion, she went directly into Wycliffe's consulting room and within seconds he was out front, glaring at the former Army scout. "The sheriff, you say?"

"He's been shot. It looks bad and I didn't want to bring him as it's in the chest and—"

"Yes, yes, quite so, Reuben. I'm well aware of your knowledge of such things. Where is he?"

"I left him at the Gower's place."

"Amelie?" said Mrs Nelson, looking astounded. "Why, I have only just seen her—"

"I know the place," said Wycliffe, dismissing his receptionist's comment with a wave of the hand. "I'll get my bag and ride on out there. Mrs Nelson, prepare everything for further surgery on my return."

Knowing he could do no more, Cole made his excuses and left. He crossed to the Sheriff's office and eased open the door. He scrambled around, trying to find the appropriate forms. Everything was forms these days. At the back of a desk drawer, he found what he was looking for. Grabbing a pencil stub, he made his way to the saloon.

It being late afternoon the place was fairly full. Something of a private individual who found making a public address difficult, Cole preferred to approach individuals personally, briefly explaining the situation, inviting each to sign up as temporary deputies.

He gained one volunteer.

Keeping his temper, Cole led the man outside. "Best if we talk out here," he said.

"That's fine by me."

"What's your name?"

"Sebastian Monroe. My friends call me Seb, most others just plain Monroe."

"Well, until we're better acquainted ... have you ever used firearms, Monroe?"

"I was in the Army," Monroe said, pulling out a cheroot. He rammed it into the corner of his mouth and lit it. "Fought at Sugar Point. Not something I remember with much fondness. After that, I got myself a job working for the railroad. Shot two men trying to hold up the train just east of here. That'd be ... Nineteen Oh-two."

"Why you give it up?"

Monroe shrugged. "I told 'em I was no assassin and if they wanted to employ me as such they should pay me at least ten times more."

"So, they asked you to leave."

"No severance, nothing." He blew out a stream of smoke. "Since then I been doing odd-jobs here and there. I sometimes serve whisky and beer behind the bar. Been looking at that new hotel. Maybe they might need someone."

"Could be. This job for me – well, for the Sheriff. It's voluntary. No pay."

"But you'd give me a reference for those hotel people?"

"The least I can do."

"So, when do we leave?"

CHAPTER SEVEN

THE day dawned as bright and as clear as any she could remember. She stood on the porch, breathing in the clean air, her eyes wandering over the rambling plains beyond the town limits. This was a staggeringly beautiful place and, if she did have doubts, they were now dispelled. This had been a good move. A decision well made.

She heard the footfall behind her and turned to see Lewis, stretching and yawning as he joined her.

"Isn't it just the most perfect place?" she asked him, slipping her arms around his waist, drawing him close.

"It is," he said, pressing his face into her hair. He kissed her.

"We're going to be happy here."

"Yes," he said. "But it's going to mean a lot of hard work. I've written a letter to the railroad company, asking them about advertising rates. In England they have posters advertising places to visit and where to stay plastered over every station. I'm wondering if our railroad might do the same."

"We'll put more ads in the newspapers back in Kansas. Chicago too. When the line finally opens, we could be inundated."

"We could find an artist to paint pictures, to really sell the place in the adverts I'm proposing." Lewis smiled, allowing his mind to conjure up mountains of dollar bills.

"You really have it all planned out, don't you, my love."

"Well," he chuckled, "let's wait and see."

She drew in a deep breath. "I'm going out this afternoon, if you want anything to eat, I've left you some stew on the hot-plate."

"Thanks. Where're you going?"

She swung away and went back inside, her voice was receding as she climbed the stairs to the bathroom, freshly prepared by her own hand the night before. "Miss Gower said she would give me a guided tour of the town, show me the sights so to speak."

"Very good of her, whoever she is," he was shouting now. "When will you be back?"

"No idea." There was a pause. "Don't worry, I'll get back to work as soon as I return."

"I didn't doubt it..."

He sat down on the porch rocking chair. He heard her moving about upstairs, then the steady thump of her descent.

She appeared all of a sudden, flowing skirt, cream blouse, hair pulled back off her face and tied up with a bow. She looked stunning. "Well?"

He shook his head, his throat sounding constricted when he said, "You look lovely."

She snapped her handbag shut, lay her finger to her lips and then touched his nose as she drifted past him. "Have a nice day, dear." She smiled at him as she went down the steps to the street, almost immediately colliding with the Reverend Peters as he appeared seemingly from nowhere.

"Oh my word!" she hissed, pulling back her feet from under his.

"I'm terribly sorry," he said in a whirl wind of arms, awkward grins, and embarrassed little laughs. "Is your husband...?"

"I'm here," said Lewis quickly coming off the rocking chair, anxiously checking that Sarah was still in one piece after colliding with the powerfully built preacher. Ignoring them both, Sarah strutted towards the main street, tossing her head, unhappy. "I'm afraid," Lewis continued, eyeing her with concern, "we're not yet open..." He glanced at the Reverend's dog-collar and added, "Padre."

"Oh, I realise that. No, no, I'm here in a, how shall I call it, an advisory capacity?"

Lewis noted the tone of uncertainty, and the preacher's air of awkwardness which, he felt sure, wasn't due to his collision with Sarah. "Advisory capacity? I'm not altogether sure if I understand you, Padre."

"Well, that could be the wrong word... Perhaps it's not advisory at all. I really only popped in for a sort of little get-to-know each other chat, sort of thing."

Lewis looked at the Reverend as if for the first time. "Your accent? English?"

"Borders. Scottish borders, I mean. Berwick. You know it?"

Lewis shook his head. "I'm afraid we're not particularly religious, either of us."

"No, no," the Reverend nodded his large head, but the smile never left his face. "I'm not really here for that. Just a chat. About...about the history of the hotel really."

"Oh." Lewis's interest began to stir. "Perhaps you'd better come in."

The Reverend Peters dipped his head and stepped into the murky interior. The ceiling was low, especially for such a big man. The Reverend smiled uneasily as Lewis brushed past him. "I haven't been here for such a long time," Peters said with a faint note of sadness, "I'd almost forgotten what it looks like."

Lewis motioned him into the lounge, almost complete now with an abundance of comfortable looking seating, card tables by the windows, empty fireplace due to the heat. An inviting ambience, or so Lewis liked to think. "You used to come quite often then, Padre?"

"I'm afraid so, yes." He gave a little nervous laugh. "The saloon is not really a place I would ever consider frequenting. I'm not a great drinker, but I do like the occasional snifter...I'm sure you know what I mean."

Lewis thought he did. He pulled up a chair and they both sat. He had an innate distrust of clergy, of whatever denomination. He always felt he was being scanned, as if by some device that could read his very soul. They all had that air of grace, of invulnerability that Lewis found haughty, almost arrogant.

He took in a deep breath and looked at the man who settled himself somewhat awkwardly into the big armchair opposite him. Smiling, prepared to give the Reverend the benefit of the many doubts he had, Lewis said, "So, you have some history to tell me, about the hotel?" He smiled and waited. The Reverend's unease became palpable and Lewis suddenly began to suspect that what he was about to hear would be distasteful.

"Yes, yes I have." The Reverend took in a large breath as if preparing himself for the delivery of something astonishing. "It's about the murder actually."

CHAPTER EIGHT

ITCHING their horses outside the Gower's place, Cole and Monroe waited patiently for Amelie to arrive in the buggy, a buggy driven by another woman, one whom Cole recognised as Sarah Cartwright, the new owner of the Elegance Hotel. She took all of his attention as she stepped down, extended her hand to Amelie and helped the older lady to join her.

Cole doffed his hat. "Good morning to you both, ladies."

Amelie appeared deeply troubled, wringing her hands, all pretence of social etiquette absent. "Mr Cole, I do not understand any of this. When you announced to me earlier that there was trouble, I had no idea you meant here, in my home!"

"I apologize to you, Miss Amelie, but time was pressing. Now that we are here, I will—"

"Perhaps if you just tell us what has happened?" It was Sarah, her voice liquid velvet. Cole noted how her gaze was fixed upon Monroe, who, he also noted, wore a wide smile, as if transfixed. "I don't think I've had the pleasure," she said, extending her hand.

Monroe took it and, to the surprise of Cole and everyone else, pressed the hand to his lips and kissed it. "The pleasure is all mine."

Clearing his throat, Cole stepped aside and beckoned for Amelie to enter. "Sheriff Stone is inside. He'll let you know the details, but please try and be—" He did not make the end of his sentence as, with a toss of her head, Amelie strode into the cabin with Sarah Cartwright close behind, leaving the two men to watch them.

Monroe pursed his lips and emitted a silent whistle. "Dear Lord, she is the most beautiful woman I think I've ever seen!"

Cole gave him a sideways glance. "You'd do best to keep your admiration to yourself. She's a married woman."

"Ah Reuben," said the much bigger man, clamping his hand on the ex-scout's shoulder, "I'm young and headstrong. I can't help myself." He chuckled. "And neither can she, I shouldn't wonder."

Cole considered what a dreadful error of judgement he'd made in enlisting this grossly conceited man's help. He wanted to say something but knew this was not the time nor the place, so he let it go and went into the cabin.

Inside, the air was thick and stuffy. Despite one of the tiny windows being wedged open, the gloom shrouded everything, lending it a depressed, unfriendly and uninviting atmosphere. In the back room the women had gathered. Amelie was crying quietly into a handkerchief, Sarah Cartwright doing her best to comfort her. In the bed, ghastly pale, Sheriff Ryan Stone and standing before them, Doc Wycliffe.

"He's comfortable now," Wycliffe was saying, as he came out of the room, rolling his sleeves down over his thick forearms. "I have to say it was touch-and-go for a moment, but he's young and he's strong. He'll make it."

"Thanks, Doc."

"It's my job, Cole. Yours is to hunt down the varmints that did this."

"I will."

Grunting, Wycliffe studied Monroe from head to toe. "This your deputy?"

"The only one I could muster."

"Good luck with that then," he said and slinked off.

"What in the hell did he mean by that?" demanded Monroe, looking as if he was about to follow the good doctor and accost him.

"Perhaps you could tell me."

A deep frown appeared on Monroe's face. "Listen, I'm the only one who stepped up when you came asking. You'd do well to remember that, old man."

"Ah. Really?"

"You're damned right!"

The big man's hand hovered close to the Police Special at his waist, the type of firearm Sterling Roose had taken to wearing in the later stages of his life, before all of that came to an abrupt and dreadful end. Pegged out to dry in the baking sun like some buffalo skin. Cole drew in a breath, swallowing down the memory of his old friend. "Tell you what, Monroe, we ride, you follow. And in the meantime, keep your mouth shut."

"You think a lot of yourself, don't you, old man? People say you used to hunt Indians."

"Do they?"

"Yeah, they do. They say you killed a lot of men, but that was ages ago, they say. Now, all you do is rock in your chair and pass the time of day chewing backy. You is passed it now."

Cole's eyes narrowed and all of a sudden, he no longer felt old at all. "Let's just see, shall we."

"Yeah. We shall. And when we find these killers, it'll be me who brings it to an end, you can trust me on that."

"Yeah, because you were at that battle, weren't you."

"Sugar Point. That's right."

Cole went to turn away, but pulled up when Monroe said, "How many battles you been in, eh?"

Cole turned, and let out a long sigh. "Enough."

The big man didn't look as if he believed the ex-scout's words, but Cole was no longer in the mood to exchange niceties. He went into the back room to check on Stone.

"Why hello there, stranger," said Stone. Propped up with a mass of pillows, Sarah sat beside him while Amelie fussed around, pulling out drawers and opening wardrobe doors.

Cole grinned and raised his hand. "Ryan, can you tell me any more about the men who came here?"

"Not much more than I told you before. There were three of them. Two white guys and one enormous Negro. They were looking for something and didn't care who they hurt to find it."

"Including Claudette," said Amelie. She came away from the wardrobe she'd been looking through. "Why did they take her?"

"Kidnapped her," emphasised Stone. "No doubt to hold her to ransom, for whatever it is they are seeking."

"But what can it be," said Amelie, her voice high-pitched, close to breaking. She slumped down on the bed. "We're not wealthy. Everything we had we put into this place. And why gun down Joshua the way they did? It is all so senseless."

"Whatever it is they're looking for," said Cole, "it is worth killing for. These are desperate men, capable of anything."

"But this isn't the Wild West," said Sarah. She looked concerned, perspiration across her top lip. This was not what she wanted to find when she decided to open up the hotel. From her expression that much was clear.

"It still ain't tamed," said Cole, "and I doubt it'll be for a long, long time."

Amelie said, "What if they murder Claudette?"

Cole did his best to sound reassuring, but he was no actor and his words failed to have any impression upon the younger sister. "I doubt it, Miss Gower. What would be the point in that?"

"What is the point in *any* of this?"

To that Cole had no answer. These were two spinsters, living alone in this well-appointed home, comfortable but not wealthy. Desperate men, looking to make some quick money, don't break in, kill and kidnap unless there is something worthwhile to be had.

"Miss Gower," said Stone from the bed, voice strained but under control. "Are you certain there were no valuables in the house – jewellery, cash, anything at all."

"Nothing, Sheriff. We are simple folk trying to live out our lives in peace and quiet."

"Besides," put in Sarah, "they surely would know if there was something here, wouldn't they?"

"You're right, Mrs Cartwright. I can't believe this was a random raid," said Stone. "Mr Cole, I will be well enough to ride soon. If you would prefer to wait a little while, I will join you in bringing these men to justice."

"The longer we wait the farther away they get."

"Yes," Stone said, resigned to the reality of the situation. "But you have only one man. I'm not doubting your desire, nor your experience, but—"

"You're no longer young," put in Amelie. She held up her hand as Cole went to speak. "I have heard all about you, Mr Cole. How you tracked down villains and savages and the like, how you mercilessly served justice, but the last time you went up against such men was—"

"Less than a year ago," said Cole quickly, anxious not to listen to any more of this diatribe. "I went to the aid of my old friend, Sterling Roose."

"Yes ..." Amelie Gower's voice trailed away. "Mr Roose was a good sheriff I have no doubt, but the fact that both of you were very much out of your depth just goes to show how age weakens us all, Mr Cole, in so many ways."

"Out of my depth." Cole blew out a long sigh. "Miss Gower, I shot the whole damn lot of 'em. Dead. Now, if you'll excuse me, I have a job to do."

He shot Stone a look, knowing the young sheriff knew the truth of what had happened, and left, leaving Amelie Gower shocked, speechless in fact, and Sarah moved to put her arm around her and give some sense of comfort.

CHAPTER NINE

SARAH Cartwright made Amelie and Stone tea before stepping outside to gaze across the empty land over which Cole and his companion had travelled across. Her mind drifted to other things. Not for the first time, she dwelled on the moment when she had accidentally collided with the preacher. For only the fleeting of instances they pressed together, but in that brief blink of time she had felt the force of his form, sensed the strength of his arms, explored the hard flatness of his stomach. The sensation had thrilled her. It had been two years since she had buried thoughts of the episode that had almost cost her her marriage. She made promises both to herself and Lewis that it would never happen again. However, sweet memories often invaded her sleeping moments, and she knew it was folly to deny simple facts. Lewis was a good, hardworking man, but attentive he was not. He could not tame her wayward spirit.

But could a preacher?

She put such thoughts out of her mind. This was a new place, a chance to start again. She was determined to do all she could to make the hotel a success. Her marriage too. Lewis was under stress. That was all it was. Things would change, of course they would. All it would take was time.

A voice cut into her thoughts causing her to jump. "Sarah, have they gone?"

Amelie's usually good-humoured face appeared lined with worry and strain. "Yes," said Sarah. "I hope they return with good news."

"I pray for that. Claudette is not as strong as she was. I'm worried."

She pulled up a chair and sat beside Sarah on the porch.

"This was a good place," she said quietly. "We had so many hopes and dreams. Joshua was a godsend, working such long hours, without complaint. It's terrible what those monsters did, to butcher him like ... like some poor, wretched animal."

"He must have tried to stop them."

"Yes, and they cut him down and left him to bleach in the Sun." Convulsed with a fresh bout of despair, she pressed a sodden silk handkerchief into her eyes. "Why did this have to happen?"

"I don't know. It seems this town isn't tamed at all. It's still part of the Wild West, isn't it?"

"The Wild West? The stuff of legends, so they'd have you believe. Newspapers and dime novels making it out to be so terribly romantic. Bank robbers, gunfighters, lawmen. It's all too easy to let yourself believe none of it actually happened. But it did happen – and it's still happening."

"You're right. We succumbed to the lure of a good life, of wide-open spaces, of fresh air and endless opportunity. We were so full of hope – my husband and I. We planned to make a real go of the hotel. We were assured Colorado was tamed, but from what Mr Cole intimated at, it is far from the rural idyll the real estate people sold us back in Kansas City."

"They're all vultures those types, only out to get as much money from you as they can."

"We thought we got it at a good price. The hotel I mean. It's very fine. Perhaps once it is ready we can put aside fears and concerns and make it into something special."

"Yes, once the railroad is opened. That's the reason you bought it, so I've heard? The promise of a steady stream of customers?"

"Word gets around fast, doesn't it?"

"A new face in this little place sticks out a mile, especially when it's one as beautiful as yours, Sarah. People are naturally curious, and what with your horseless carriage trundling down the main street, news was bound to travel very quickly."

It was an uneasy feeling, this knowledge that everybody knew you but you knew nobody. Sarah did her best to conceal her unease. What else were they saying, she wondered.

"You'll make a success of it all, I know you will," Amelie remarked

"It'll require plenty of hard work before it'll be ready for opening. But we'll do it. Lewis is very determined."

"Is he?"

"Oh, yes. He wants the elegance to be a success. So do I," Sarah said.

"And what happened, none of that concerns you at all."

"We don't know any of the details. I'm not at all sure if anything actually did happen."

"Oh, it most certainly did, Sarah."

"I'm intrigued."

"Both Claudette and I have talked about how we believed the Territory to be a peaceful place now. But after the dreadful incident with my sister and Joshua, I'm not so sure. What happened here, in the hotel, was not, as most of us hoped, the last stain on our community." Wringing her hands, she turned away, voice tremulous. "Killings, robberies, all of that. Things buried deep. But now ... now, those blights, they have returned." She looked again at Sarah. "This is not the tranquil place it appears to be. I don't suppose it ever was."

"A stain, you said. What sort of stain?"

"It's not an easy tale to tell. I hope I'm doing the right thing if I tell you." Amelie looked up quickly. "Not that I don't trust you, it's not that, it's...it's...Well, it might affect the way you look at things, how you conduct your new life." She pulled in a deep, troubled breath, suddenly making up her mind. She began tentatively, introducing the main characters, the time, the situation – as far as she was aware that is – and then recounted the full horror of what had happened.

CHAPTER TEN

C OLE returned to his horse and stood there for a moment, contemplating the saddle. He felt tired and worried.

"What's wrong?"

Cole turned to Monroe, sitting big and proud on the back of his horse. He looked bored but not tired. Alert, as if he expected something. Cole didn't know what, but his unease grew with each passing minute he shared in this man's company. "Tracks," he said quietly and heaved himself into his saddle.

"What, you mean signs?"

"That's right."

"So, we're on the right path?"

"They ain't making any secret of where they're heading. But one of them is on foot."

"Could be the woman."

"That's my thinking too. She's old, and I'm not sure how much she can take out in this heat." To give his words more weight, he took off his hat and wiped his forehead with his neckerchief. "How are you holding up?"

"Oh, you've no need to worry about me, Mr Cole. I'm well used to living it rough."

"I don't doubt it."

He kicked his horse's flanks and moved on.

The air hummed with the intensity of the sun. Keeping his eyes on the ground, Cole noted how the tracks changed. Those he pursued were slowing to a walk. Soon they would be within sight, then he would need to decide what to do. Three of them, Stone said, but the woman was the problem. Once any shooting started, she would be the first to die. He'd need to wait until nightfall, creep up on them in a surprise attack. He hoped his old bones would respond positively. The thought of crawling over the hard, baked earth was not something he relished.

He took his horse up a sharp incline, away from the fresh, clear tracks. In his bedroll was his telescope, the one which had served him so well over the years. If he could find an advantageous position, he may well be able to figure out how far away they were and how best to overcome them.

As it was, as he reached the top, he had no need for the 'scope.

They were camped in a small dip, sat around an open fire, something roasting on a makeshift spit.

Three men.

To their right, a bundle. A white bundle, big enough to be a person.

Reaching for his telescope, he focused in and sucked in a sharp breath.

It was a woman. Clearly Claudette. She appeared unconscious, lying there in the open, not moving.

Was she dead?

Cursing, Cole snapped shut the telescope and twisted around to face the sound of Monroe's approaching steps. "It seems like—" he began, but got no further.

The stock of the Winchester smashed hard into his face, and he fell back with a loud grunt, senses swirling, flashes of blinding pain overcoming his vision.

Something moved. He knew not what. Strong hands lifted him, Monroe's voice from a hundred miles away saying, "You're too old for this sort of thing now, Cole." And a fist erupting into his guts, jack-knifing him forward. A hand under his chin. Lifting his face. Through bleary, tear-ridden eyes, he managed to make out Monroe. Grinning. Big and burly. Why did he ever recruit him? He should have known, he should have—

The shape of a large fist filled his world. Then the impact. Massive. Total. Smashing bone, clattering his brain around in his skull, pitching him into a whirlwind of blackness, dragging him forever downwards.

He came to hours, perhaps, for all he knew, days later.

On his back, blinking at the sun. A huge, white orb, searing through his face, a face pulsing with pain.

Rolling over onto his side, he let out a prolonged groan and vomited onto the earth. Coughing, he lay that way for some time, struggling to find the strength to sit up. Desperate for water. Desperate for understanding of what had happened. Desperate for sleep.

He succumbed.

The next time he woke, it was almost night, the sun low on the horizon. Late evening. An hour of weak daylight left at best. A buzzard, a huge thing, yellow, virulent eyes studying him, stood only inches away. He shouted, made a wild swipe with his hand, and it screeched, flew backwards a couple of paces, then settled again. To wait. It knew something. Something that perhaps Cole hadn't yet guessed.

He forced himself to sit up. A great sledgehammer of pain exploded through his jaw. Monroe must have hit him with his Winchester, the one he'd left with his horse as he reached the top of the hill and crawled to take a look over the edge. To see Claudette. He remembered that much. Gingerly, he felt his jaw. Swollen, throbbing, his heart beat so strong among the bruises. He ran his tongue around the inside of his mouth and thanked God he still had all of his teeth.

The thirst squeezed his throat in a clamp full of needles. It took him some time to swallow.

Looking around in the developing gloom, he took in his surroundings. Apart from the buzzard, he realised he was still on top of the hill. But that was the best news. Monroe had taken his boots and his gun.

And that was not the worst news.

Making his way down to the flat, he saw his horse was gone.

He crumpled in despair.

This was bad. Worse than bad. This was a death sentence.

CHAPTER ELEVEN

T HE story, as told by Amelie, was bad. Very bad. Almost forty years had passed by, and the murder of Benjamin Mumford remained unsolved. The pub hotel changed hands many times since, but no one ever stayed for very long. The last owners left under something of a cloud. Talk of illicit affairs were rife, but the truth remained unclear, and nobody really cared anyway. That had been four years ago. And now the Cartwrights were the new owners.

Sarah felt numb. The horror that her home was the scene of a murder made her deeply uncomfortable. She shuddered involuntarily. Amelie gave a comforting squeeze of the wrist. "Don't worry, there are no stories of ghosts linked with the ghastly deed."

"Don't joke," Sarah said, not in the mood for brevity. "To think I've actually slept in that place without knowing!"

"Perhaps that's for the best? Imagine the nightmares."

"I hope," Sarah said cautiously, "there are no more gruesome stories concerning our lovely new hotel?"

"Not that I know of, but rest assured that if I can dig any up, you'll be the first to hear them."

"Oh, thank you! That will be a great source of comfort to me in the days to come."

The sound of their laughter dwindled into an awkward silence as both lost themselves in thought.

"I wish we had met in happier circumstances," said Amelie at last.

"I am certain it will end well. Mr Cole seems like a very dependable man."

"Oh, I am sure he is, but he is past his prime. Twenty years ago, I would have no worries, but those men who broke in here ..." She shuddered. "Animals. Savages. I'm not sure if Mr Cole has enough sand to bring them to justice."

"He must have been here when the hotel murder occurred?"

"No, he was working with the army back then. The War was in its last throes, so to speak. This town was nothing more than a sorry collection of broken-down old shacks. I remember the hotel being built in that atmosphere of hope and rejuvenation. I think everyone believed peace would bring us all enormous wealth and happiness." Amelie sighed. "How foolish we were."

"Even so, the hotel was built and the town grew."

"Yes. People were making their way out West once again. The south was ravaged, but out here where the War had hardly touched us, people gathered together to establish new communities and improve the old ones."

"I hope what we do to the hotel will do the town justice – we want to help bring renewed investment, support business, help develop the town into a place in which people are proud, a place where people will come to settle down and live."

Smiling, Amelie reached over and squeezed Sarah's hand. "I wish you every success."

"Thank you, and I wish for you to get your life back."

"I shall, when my sister is home safe and well."

A footfall made them both turn.

Ryan Stone stood in the doorway, his chest heavily bandaged, but a healthy sheen on his face.

"Mr Stone," shouted Amelie, jumping to her feet. "You'll catch your death of cold. What are you doing out of bed?"

She went to him, tenderly taking his arm, preparing to steer him back inside.

Stone gently, but firmly, pushed her hand away. "I'm fine, Miss Gower. Truly."

"Well, it's going to become chilly, Sheriff. I don't want you catching anything."

"Miss Gower." His tone was serious, causing both women to tense up. "I need to know."

"Know what?"

"What were those men after? To kill your servant, bust this place up, abduct your sister?"

Stepping back, Amelie slumped back down in her seat. "I don't know."

"You must!" He followed her, towering over her, face stern, hard. "What could you possibly have that they wanted?"

"I told you," she'd set her face forward to look out across the darkening plain, "I don't know."

"I think you do."

"Sheriff!" blurted Sarah, horrified. "How dare you insinuate that poor Amelie might be lying."

"It's all right, Sarah," the younger of the Gower sisters said.

"No, it's not, Amelie! Sheriff, you have no cause to accuse Amelie of—"

"I haven't accused her of anything, but there's something she's not telling us. I'm lucky to be alive, I know that, but if those men were willing to shoot me dead, and anyone else who got in their way, what they were after must be of real importance. Or value. *Think,* Miss Gower. Is there anything, no matter how insignificant it may seem, that they might have wanted?"

She shook her head, sniffed, and wiped away renewed tears with a silk handkerchief she took from her sleeve.

"Please, Miss Gower, I beseech you. If there is anything you can—"

Her head snapped around, a scowl of abject fury seizing her features. "I've told you, Sheriff, but ..." She drew in a huge breath. "I will sleep on it and tell you in the morning if anything comes to mind."

Grunting, Stone inclined his head slightly, gave a brief smile towards Sarah and turned away, saying, "That is all I ask for, Miss Gower. Goodnight."

The two women sat in silence, neither returning the young sheriff's leaving salutation.

CHAPTER TWELVE

DESPITE his exhaustion, the new day seemed to offer Monroe a little hope. Drenched in sweat, his body glistened slug-like. The night's exertions left him weakened. Time was the great healer, or at least that's how the saying went. For Monroe, waiting was something he had learned to accept. It had not always been a smooth process. Naturally impatient, eager to get on with things, waiting was wasting, as far as he was concerned. Locked in his torment, he felt a little assured that soon he would be able to get on with his life.

He blinked. The sun, warm and bright, brought him renewed energy, and he sat up. The others snored and groaned around him, relieved and secure. Monroe brought them feelings of security. That was his gift, his power. Even the woman, who he believed to be dead when he first came upon them, slept the sleep of the contented. Yes, this would be a good day, he mused.

Closing his eyes, images of the past night invaded his brain, scorching the back of his eyes with the vividness of the memory. An involuntary shudder seared through him. How could so much have happened in so short a span of time?

Knocking down Cole was easy enough. Stripping him of his gun and boots barely caused him to break sweat. Leaving him out in the open with no water and no means to get back to the sister's house meant the old scout would not survive out here. Heat exhaustion followed by crippling thirst. He'd crawl under a clump of sage, wither and die.

Perfect.

By the time a search party came, Monroe and the others would be far away. The old woman would tell them all they wanted to know, and then the riches would flow into their pockets.

Simple.

Except for the horse.

The damned horse would not comply. Cole's horse. A game animal, as soon as Monroe took a step in its direction, it reared up, wild, unpredictable. Making a grab for the reins merely caused it to kick out. And then it bolted, galloping off into the night before Monroe could do anything about it.

Cole must have trained it to react that way.

For some small compensation, Monroe kicked Cole's inert body a few times in the ribs.

He'd enjoyed that.

Releasing a long sigh, Monroe stood up. He needed coffee, so he crossed to the nearest sleeping bundle and roused the man with his boot.

Rolling over, angry, disorientated, still half-asleep, the man lashed out with both hands. They were large, calloused hands, the hands of a manual labourer or farmworker. Ramming his fists into his eyes, he rubbed away the last vestiges of sleep and yawned loudly. "What are you doing waking me up like that!"

"Get up, Constantine, and make me some coffee."

The huge man glared. "Make your own."

Monroe's voice, when he spoke again, held something. Menace. Enough to cause the man to consider his next move. Not used to intimidation, he sensed instinctively there was danger simmering just under the surface. He got to his feet. An inch taller than Monroe, he nevertheless cowered, eyes downcast. "Yeah, sure," he said and staggered across to the remnants of the previous night's campfire and seized the coffee pot. "I'll go swill it out down in the stream. It won't take long."

"Never mind about that," said Monroe, "just get the beans and make it."

The mention of the stream brought concern to Monroe. If Cole could find it, and of course he could, then he would regain sufficient strength to make it back. He cursed under his breath.

"What's that?" said Constantine, shovelling in the last of the beans into the pot.

"Nothing. Just hurry up."

Finding a suitable rock, Monroe slumped down onto it and considered the still sleeping woman. "She told you nothing?"

"Eh? Her?" Constantine shook his head. "Not a word. She's a tough old bird, I'll give her that much. Hemmings slapped her around a bit, but she wouldn't give up anything."

"And the deed box?"

"Empty, save for an old plan of the place. Could be useful, I guess."

"But no lawyer's papers, no deeds, no signed testimonials?"

"Is you deaf, Seb? I said it was *empty*." He looked around. "I need water. I'll have to fetch some."

"Light the fire first."

"Hell, black I may be, but I ain't your slave! We was freed, remember!"

Monroe studied the man's features, the broad nose, the skin that appeared so smooth, gleaming in the sun. Monroe had seen him with his shirt off, knew him to be a superb specimen of manhood, but his insolence riled him something awful. "Just do it!"

"And what you gonna do if I don't?"

In a blur, Monroe produced Cole's gun from his waistband, cocking the hammer and aiming it unerringly in one, smooth motion. "I'll kill yeh."

For a fleeting moment, it seemed Constantine might react, but then something dawned on him – the certainty of imminent death perhaps. His shoulders dropped, and he turned away.

Monroe shot him anyway, between the shoulder blades, and watched the big man fall face-first into the dirt.

Sighing, Monroe sat and waited for the rest of the camp to spring to life, which they did in a mess of flapping arms, high-pitched shrieks, and desperate clawing at firearms. Except for the woman, of course, who sat still as a stone, eyes boring into him as she spoke. "You're going straight to hell, you know that, don't you."

Monroe closed his eyes. Her expression troubled him, unlike her words, which made no impression on him whatsoever. "I've known that for a long time, ma'am."

"Well, I'm glad about that."

Monroe got up to retrieve the coffee-pot, ignoring his companions' screams and their pathetic attempts to revive the dead Constantine. Soon their garbled, excitable voices became nothing more than background noise, and at the trickle of a stream, he sat down, washed water over his face, and already knew the day had turned very bad indeed.

CHAPTER THIRTEEN

S TONE wasn't sure what woke him, but he sat up, alert, and reached for his gun. Wincing as a stab of pain raced across his chest, he slowly rolled out of bed and stood up. Taking his time, calming his breathing, he padded to the open bedroom door and listened for a moment. There was nothing, so he went straight out onto the porch.

It was Cole's horse.

With painful but required slowness, Stone stepped down and moved up to the animal, conscious of the need not to make any sudden gestures. However, the horse appeared calm. Watchful, its eyes never left him as he tenderly reached out a hand and stroked its nose.

"Where's your master, eh?" he said softly.

He scanned the surroundings. There was no sign of Cole, and the fear gradually crawled up Stone's spine. The man who rode with him, the one Cole clearly had misgivings over, was missing also. Nothing about this seemed right.

Leading the horse to the rear of the spread, he entered the coolness of the barn. Working quickly but carefully, he removed the saddle and bridle and, despite his discomfort, wiped the horse down before fetching some oats. The water trough was within a few paces. Drooping the saddle over the rail separating the stalls, Stone noted the empty Winchester scabbard. This definitely was not good.

He went outside again.

Amelie was there, still dressed in her nightdress, stretching out her arms. She smiled as Stone approached, a smile that faded as she saw the obvious stress he was under.

"Sheriff? What is going on?"

"It's Cole's horse," he said, stepping up beside her. "It must have made its way back here."

"But where is Mr Cole?"

Stone shrugged. "I don't know." He allowed his eyes to return to the vast expanse of open, daunting country. "Out there somewhere."

"Oh my Lord," she said. "You think something has happened to him?"

Stone nodded. "That's my guess."

"Something bad?"

"Who can say, but his horse wouldn't have returned here if everything was fine and dandy, that's for sure." A sudden resolve came into his features. "I'm going to go out and see if I can pick up his trail. I'll take Cole's horse, and I'll—"

"You can't," Amelie spurted. "Sheriff, for pity's sake, they've already tried to murder you – they won't fail the next time!"

"I'll be fine. I'll take it real careful, Miss Amelie, I promise."

"At least wait until Doctor Wycliffe returns – he said he would call to check up on your progress."

"Well, I'll wait an hour for Cole's horse to recover a little, but then I'll head on out. Where's Mrs Cartwright?"

"She returned to town after you'd fallen asleep. She too is going to return, with the good doctor, I shouldn't wonder."

"It's a pity none of them have a rifle I can use. I don't suppose you have one lying around someplace?"

"Old Joshua used to keep an old Enfield musket out in his bunkhouse."

"He has some cartridges?"

"I believe so. It's an old gun, so he used powder and lead shot to scare off the coyotes." Her eyes glazed over. "Poor Joshua, he was innocent in all of this. Who are these people, Sheriff?"

"You said you were gonna think on what I'd said, Miss Amelie – if there is anything you can think of that might have brought these men here?"

"I have thought, yes. There is something. The *only* thing. Come on inside, Sheriff. I'll fix you some breakfast and tell you what I know. I should have thought of it before, but what with the attack, Claudette's abduction, Joshua ... I hope it will help."

"It's understandable, Miss Amelie. All this upset, it's a wonder you recall anything at all."

"You're very gracious, Sheriff, but I fear my lapse of good sense may have put everyone in mortal danger."

She took him by the arm and led him inside.

CHAPTER FOURTEEN

COLE knew it was there, he could smell it, as well as hear it. Sometime in the night, he dragged himself to the stream and plunged face first into the cool water. The shocking cold exploded across his skin, revitalising him, and he wallowed in it, allowing himself as much time as he needed to restore strength and mobility to his aching bones.

Later, he slept.

The heat from the morning sun woke him. A further wash, more drinking, and he was on his feet, moving with stealth and speed, keeping the stream close. Soaked through to the skin, at first he shivered with the cold. Soon the heat made its mark, and within the hour, he was dry.

He followed the signs, wondering what had happened to his horse. Monroe must have taken him. He'd taken everything else. Tracking kept his mind focused, forced him to continue despite the throbbing in his jawline and the discomfort of his bare feet on the hard ground. With each step, the jolt caused him to wince. He constantly felt all across his face, searching for broken bones. He was lucky there were none.

The pain from his blistered, bleeding feet at last forced him to seek some shelter. From the position of the sun, he tried to calculate how long he'd been moving across the plain. Guessing it must have been no more than three hours, he found clumps of undergrowth by the stream and managed to fashion himself enough cover to shelter from the sun's glare.

He needed to wait until the air grew a little cooler.

Almost an entire day.

The coming night would bring intense cold, but it would be easier to travel. Not for the first time, he wondered if anyone would miss him. Stone perhaps? If the young sheriff was well enough, he could come out and search. Or, just as easily, he may decide to stay in bed.

Taking in shallow breaths, Cole did his best to rest. The heat sucked all energy from him, combining with his many bruises to make it virtually impossible to continue, even if he wanted to.

But he didn't, and instead, he slept.

At about the same time that Cole curled himself up under the meagre undergrowth, the Reverend Peters was leaving the backdoor of the small church annexe where he lived to begin his daily walk away from the town to the surrounding countryside. As he rounded the first bend before entering the twisting trail, he groaned inwardly when he saw one of his parishioners striding anxiously towards him. Usually, there were very few passers-by in this part of town. Those that he saw were not particularly interested in him. His congregation was small, mostly elderly, and few ventured beyond their front doors unless it was absolutely necessary. Seeing Mrs Jenkins was, therefore, something of a surprise. When she began waving at him furiously, it soon dawned on him that perhaps this day wasn't going to be so peaceful or as uninterrupted as he had hoped. A solitary, private man, he had few pleasures in life; one of them was keeping fit, and it was a pastime that was almost as rigorously pursued as his pastoral duties. He did, however, try to keep his interests well out of the public eye. He knew that his occasional visit to the local mercantile store to purchase his weekly bottle of whisky was frowned upon, but he had never been drunk, not in all the time he had taken his vows, so he could live with the unspoken criticism. But he did guard his other pleasures jealously. The idea of Mrs Jenkins accosting him during the week was one thing, but to see him in an open-necked shirt and work trousers would mean the whole town knowing his business before the day was out. It was a tedious, tiresome irritation that would mar his day.

"Mr Peters, I'm so glad it's you," Mrs Jenkins spurted, gripping his arm as he slowed down beside her.

Noting the woman's stark, worried face, Peters realised this was something more than the usual gossip he often found himself on the receiving end of. She was frightened. She needed him. His impatience, and annoyance if there had been any, disappeared, and he smiled, attempting to comfort her. It didn't work.

"There were three of them. I don't know who they were, but they were an uncouth bunch. I thought I recognised one of them, the biggest of the three, but I couldn't swear to it. I don't know where they are now, but you have to help."

Peters held the claw-like grip on his arm, as much to ease the pain as to reassure her. "Mrs Jenkins, just try and calm down."

"I will not calm down, Mr Peters," she rasped, her eyes flashing. "They were trying to get into my house! I was coming down the stairs when I heard them at my kitchen door. One of them was trying to prise it open with some sort of metal implement when I shouted at them. Mr Jenkins came down with his shotgun, and they ran off." She shuddered. "I hate to think what might have happened if he'd have shot them, but he wanted to, believe you me. They had smashed a window, no doubt to try and open the latch. That's what woke me, you see. Mr Jenkins said I should inform the Sheriff. I mean, it's unheard of here. Robbers and thieves are not something we have experienced, but of course, there is always a first time."

"Mrs Jenkins, please, just try and—"

"Well, we went outside. Mr Jenkins accompanied me just in case they were lurking close by. But, of course, when we reached the Sheriff's office, we discovered he was not there. And that dreadful Mr Cole, usually sitting and watching, he was absent as well. So, of course, you were my only choice, Reverend. My only choice."

"I understand Mr Cole went out to the Gower sisters' place. They'd reported seeing someone."

"Ah, well, there it is! The same gang, no doubt, forcing their way into people's homes, looking for valuables to rob. It's a disgrace, I tell you."

"But nothing was taken, was it? From your home, I mean?"

"Have you been listening to me?" Her face reddened. "I told you. Mr Jenkins chased them off."

"Yes, yes, and everything is all right, isn't it? Are you hurt?"

"I am not, thank the Lord. What would have happened if they had come in, over-powered my husband? Where would I be now? Lying in a pool of blood with no one to care two hoots."

"I doubt that, Mrs Jenkins, someone would have come."

"Who? Who would have come? Would you have come? Too interested in your daily strolls looking at the fields and the sky, daydreaming."

"Friends, neighbour," he said quickly, ignoring her jibes. "Somebody would have come."

"Nobody would have come, Reverend, nobody. Nobody cares. Nobody wants to get involved. I could be dead."

"Well, you're not dead, so we have that to be thankful for." He took a quick glance around. "Have you any idea where they went, in which direction?"

"None whatsoever. But I know what the one who had his hand on my door looked like. Big man. Blond hair, nasty looking, wearing a thin, blue jacket-thing."

Peters frowned. "Someone from the town, perhaps?"

"Folk from town keep themselves to themselves, Mr Peters. They're not thieves." She shook her head emphatically. "No, I'm certain they are not from round here. But the big one ... I've seen him before, I know it. But now they've got away. By the time the Sheriff decides to come back, they will be long gone. It's a disgrace he didn't leave a deputy in charge. That Matthias man isn't worth much and spends all his day sleeping. The town needs a proper law officer."

"Well, I think that's what Mr Cole was doing."

"That scoundrel? Dear Lord, he's worse than any of them. The things I've heard about him are enough to make one's toes curl!"

Peters held his breath. He too had heard the stories, but he did his best to ignore malicious talk. Cole struck him as an honourable man, a private person, but resourceful. Undoubtedly he had a past, but it was a past. It was the present that mattered, and Cole appeared a just person, despite never attending church. "Mrs Jenkins, if I may say so, you and your husband were a touch foolhardy to confront them the way you did."

She looked into his eyes, holding them for an icy moment. "We've no one else to protect us, Reverend," her words hissed out from between her teeth. "If we hadn't stood up to them, they'd be back, thinking that we are an easy target. Well, we're not. Frightened, yes, but you've got to show them that they can't win."

"I wish I had your courage."

She shook her head sadly. "So do I."

"Where is your husband now?"

"He's back home, replacing the glass in the window. When will the Sheriff be back?"

"I said I don't know. Soon I hope." A sudden thought struck him. "Mrs Jenkins, I will do what I can. I shall accompany you to your home, take some details and pass them on to Mr Cole on his return. Perhaps he and the Sheriff will then try and track them ..." It came to him then at a rush. "Oh my, Mrs Jenkins! I've just remembered."

"Remembered what?"

"Mr Cole. He went out to the Gower's place because something had happened. Miss Amelie, she spoke of it, and Cole set off there with another man – a *big* man, with blond hair."

"You can't possibly think ..." She allowed her voice to trail away as her hand came to her mouth. "But no, it must be a coincidence."

"Let us pray it is so, Mrs Jenkins."

"Reverend, if that man is the same, then something must have happened to Mr Cole. Something dreadful."

The Jenkins' home stood in a row of three at the end of a narrow lane leading off from the main street. It was pretty little place, white-painted walls with red-framed windows and an expensive slate roof. A wisteria trailed around the pillars supporting the porch canopy.

"The broken window is around back," explained Mrs Jenkins, opening the small gate which led into the tidy front garden. She led him along the path which circled the house.

The rear porch door hung open.

There was no sound from within.

"Henry?" she shouted, "Henry, I have brought the Reverend Peters, and he wants to ..." The sound of her voice diminished as she disappeared inside.

Peters went to step in behind her and then froze as her scream pierced the still, morning air.

Recovering quickly, he rushed inside and found her standing rigid in the kitchen, hands bunched across her mouth, staring at what she found.

He followed her gaze and felt his knees go weak.

The place was a mess, cupboards torn open and contents thrown across the floor. And in the midst of it all lay Mr Jenkins.

Dead.

CHAPTER FIFTEEN

C OLE sat up, senses on high alert. Unconsciously he reached for his Colt Cavalry and cursed when he remembered Monroe had taken it. So he sat, listening, ready to make a bolt for it if needed.

Two horses, approaching a little way off. Cole's highly developed skills did not desert him at that moment. The sound the horses made were distinctive. Only one bore a rider.

He quickly looked about him. There were numerous rocks, twigs, but nothing big enough to use as a weapon. Then he saw something, a branch lying half-submerged in the gently flowing stream. Stripped of bark, it glowed ivory white under the water. Reaching out, he took it, hefting it in his hands. It would suffice.

Moving quietly, he edged away from the stream. Always looking, always ready, Cole slinked forward, a predator, silent as the night.

The rider drew closer.

Cole could smell the horse sweat.

Only one rider. It would be easy enough.

He burst from his cover, crying out, hands held aloft, the makeshift club he'd found ready to smash down onto the rider.

Taken by surprise, the lead horse reared up, terrified. Battling gamely, the rider clung on while behind him the second, riderless horse kicked and bucked in its desperation to get away.

Cole stopped, recognising both animals and the man.

Quickly, he grabbed hold of the lead horse's reins and struggled to bring it under control. It fought fiercely, alive with terror, its flanks heaving, front legs lashing out. Gritting his teeth, muscles straining, Cole held on, soothing the wretched animal with soft, soothing reassurance. Eventually, with a good deal of gentle coercion, Cole managed at last to calm it. Behind, the other horse seemed to know instinctively what was happening. As its eyes settled on Cole, a sudden change overcame it. Instantly fear was replaced with relief, body relaxing, and it nudged forward, pressing its head into Cole's chest. Laughing, Cole held it with both arms and breathed, "My darling, all is well."

"Cole?"

Cole turned in the direction of the voice and saw Stone, calming his own horse, gawping at him in total astonishment.

"Cole, what in the name of Hades are you doing here?" He jumped down and embraced the old scout warmly in his arms. "I thought you were a goner for sure."

"So did I, Ryan. So did I!"

Stone's face grew serious. "Mr Cole, you don't look so good."

"I took a fearful beating, Ryan, and I was a fool not to be ready for it."

"Who was it?"

"The big fella I recruited to help. Monroe, he calls himself, but whether or not that's his real name, I couldn't tell you. He's in cahoots with the men who attacked Claudette Gower, and I suspect he was hanging around the town to cook up some plan or other."

"Plan? What sort of plan?"

Stroking his horse's neck, Cole gingerly put his bare foot into the stirrup and grimaced. "He took my boots as well as my gun, but I'll repay him." Gritting his teeth, he hauled himself into the saddle and leaned forward to soothe the horse again. "Yes," he said, flicking the reins and easing the horse around in a tight circle, "I reckon they are planning something. Not sure what, but it has something to do with what went down at the Gower's place."

"I agree it is strange, to attack Claudette the way they did, shoot down poor Joshua. But Amelie told me some things, Mr Cole, information that just might solve this mystery." He mounted his horse and moved alongside the old former scout. "I reckon we head back to town, fix you up, and put our heads together in order to plan what to do next."

"Amelie is back in the cabin?"

"Yes, she is."

"I'm not sure it's wise to leave her there all alone. We'll head back there first, then we'll all go back into town."

Nodding in agreement, Stone set his jaw, kicked his horse into a gallop, and before long, both men were making short work of the journey back to Amelie Gower.

CHAPTER SIXTEEN

S ARAH lay in bed staring at the ceiling, making patterns with the cracks, her imagination creating a host of pictures. It was late, but she didn't care. She could hear Lewis downstairs, lugging bits of furniture around, grunting, groaning, sometimes singing tunelessly. She envied his positive outlook. For her, the initial thrill of the arrival was soon replaced by anxiety. They'd taken on too much, she knew it.

Rolling over, she gazed out of the window. Another beautiful day. Against the advice of close friends, she had agreed to come here, doing her best to support her husband. Lewis was a good man. Weak, ineffective in so many ways, he nevertheless wanted to make them a good life, and he believed the hotel would give them that. But they had to make it work. Already Sarah had witnessed first-hand what this area was like. The promise of violence forever lurking in the darkened corners. And the story of what happened in the cellar. She shuddered, threw back the bedclothes, and stood up.

Padding downstairs, she came across Lewis as he emerged from the dining room, sleeves rolled up, lathered in sweat.

"You could do with a drink," she said. He answered with a slight smile and moved behind the bar.

"I haven't fitted any casks," he said. "Not sure who the supplier will be."

"We have some bottles." She opened one and poured him a beer. She watched him drink it. "I went with Amelie to her cabin. The Sheriff is well on the way to recovery."

"Glad to hear it."

"That Mr Cole went off with some brutish-looking character to try to track down the killers."

Lewis jerked the bottle from his lips. "Killers?"

"Don't you pay attention to anything? Where have you been, Lewis?"

"Here, working."

"Well, I have learned a spicy story to do with this place."

"Don't tell me," breathed Lewis with a sigh, putting down the finished bottle and wiping his hands on a bar towel, "let me guess. There was a gruesome murder committed here some years ago. The body was found in our cellar, but the culprit – or culprits – have never been found. Am I warm?"

"You horrible man!" Laughing, she seized the bar-towel and threw it at him. "How did you know all that?"

"Reverend Peters told me."

"The Reverend?"

"Yes. He's a strange one. Did you notice his hands?"

Another laugh. "I noticed his body."

"I thought you might," he grinned.

"Who wouldn't? He's nothing like you'd expect a man of the cloth to look like."

"I guess not. You'd expect a reverend to be all pink and wobbly, not built like a brick outhouse." Lewis shook his head thoughtfully. "There's more to him than he wants us to know. I noticed his hands. Hard hands, gnarled. Been in a fight or two, I'd say."

"You noticed a lot."

"Couldn't help it. He came in while you were out, helped me move quite a few things. He reminded me of someone I met back in Kansas. He had that same sort of *something*. I don't know, an aura. People said he was a prize-fighter."

"You think that's what the Reverend is? Sounds a bit far-fetched, Lewis. A man of the church?" She shook her head. "Perhaps he just keeps himself in good shape. Nothing sinister in that."

"Perhaps not."

They both flinched at the first scream.

Already, Sarah was moving from behind the counter, Lewis close behind.

Stepping outside, they both saw a woman staggering down the main street, overtaken by a sprinting man.

A large man, racing towards the Sheriff's office.

"Oh my Lord," breathed Sarah.

The big man was the Reverend Peters.

CHAPTER SEVENTEEN

O LD man Grimes pushed his way through the murmuring crowd when he saw the horses approaching. He waved them down.

"What's going on, Larry?" asked Stone.

Grimes held onto the Sheriff's reins as Stone dismounted.

"There's been a killing. Matthias has the witnesses inside."

Cole, sporting a pair of old Joshua's boots, jumped down and immediately regretted it. He clutched at his side. "Who?"

"Mr Jenkins. His wife and the Reverend discovered him. Seems like a gang broke into the house and killed him stone dead. Mrs Jenkins, she's in a terrible state. Doc Wycliffe gave her a sedative, but Miss Gower is with her right now."

"Thanks for that, Larry," said Stone and shot a glance towards Cole. "You reckon it's the same gang?"

"Almost certainly."

"But why break into the Jenkins' place?"

"That is indeed the question," said Cole.

"Mrs Jenkins said they tried to break in earlier," said Larry, "but Mr Jenkins ran 'em off."

"Did she see them?" asked Stone hopefully.

"Not sure. She and the Reverend came racing across here in a real state, rousing the whole town. Poor old Matthias didn't know what to do. They're all inside."

Cole sighed. "Larry, I need a new gun."

Grimes frowned. "Oh. I don't think I have anything like your Colt, Mr Cole, but I have some revolvers."

"As long as it shoots straight, I don't care what it is."

The chosen gun did indeed shoot straight. Similar to the revolver Sterling Roose carried, it was a Smith and Wesson Model 10 with a six-inch barrel. Cole liked it for two reasons – one, because it reminded him of his old friend and two; perhaps more importantly, it was double-action.

He took it out back and practised for a while. Satisfied, he bought the gun and holster together with enough ammunition for what he had in mind.

Returning to the Sheriff's office, with the crowd still pressing forward trying to get a view of what was happening, he began to force his way through to get inside.

"Oh, Mr Cole," said a voice.

He turned to see Sarah Cartwright and her husband standing there, both ashen-faced.

"Dear Lord," said Lewis Cartwright in shocked tones. "What on earth happened to you?"

Running his fingers lightly over his bruised face, Cole shrugged. "A slight altercation. What is going on here?"

"That's what we're trying to find out," said Sarah. "I'm very worried for Amelie, who is in there with the Reverend and Mrs Jenkins."

"We think it's more killings," said Lewis. Those close by gave out a collective gasp of shock.

Not wanting to speculate, Cole merely nodded, then continued squeezing through to the door. He pounded on it, shouting out who he was. He heard the bolt drawn back, and he stepped inside. The old deputy, Matthias Thurst, beckoned him forward.

Immediately on seeing Cole, the Reverend Peters stood and thrust out his hand. "Mr Cole, it's a pleasure seeing you so well."

Cole smirked. "Not sure if that's particularly true, Reverend," he said, only too aware of the reaction his swollen jawline brought, "but thank you anyway."

Matthias closed and bolted the door.

Amelie Gower, sitting next to Mrs Jenkins, comforting her, turned a hopeful face towards the former scout. "Anything?"

He turned his face away, not knowing what to say. "Not yet, Miss Amelie. Try not to be too alarmed. We will get 'em, and, I assure you, we will rescue your sister."

"Mr Cole," said Stone, stepping forward and handing the former scout one of the Winchesters he kept in a rack behind his desk, "the good Reverend has managed to extract a description of the perpetrators from Mrs Jenkins."

"The one doing all the shouting was a large, blond man," said Amelie Gower, putting her arm around the older lady to comfort her. "She's in a dreadful state, Mr Cole."

"I can see, ma'am." Cole's tone was grave. He blew out a long sigh as he checked the Winchester. "All right, I'll see what tracks and signs I can find at the Jenkins' house. We'll need men, Ryan. Last time I tried to gather together a posse, I didn't have much success. That was probably down to Monroe intimidating everyone."

"I'm willing to help," said the Reverend.

Cole considered him for a long time. He certainly looked the part, a man of considerable physical advantages. "Can you shoot?"

"If needed."

"I think we can all say it'll be needed, Padre."

"Reverend is just fine, Mr Cole."

"As you wish."

"Mr Cole," said Stone, "I have to remind you, this isn't the Wild West any longer. We have laws now, very strict they are too. We can't just go riding out into the Badlands and gun them down."

"Don't see why not."

"This is what I mean," said Stone, growing uncomfortable. "We have to follow due process. We need to find them and arrest them."

"And if they resist? Ryan, these men are killers. They are clearly after something and will stop at nothing to get it. Whatever it is."

"Perhaps it is all to do with the murder?" All eyes turned to the

Reverend. "At the hotel, I mean. We all know it happened, but none of us know the details."

"I do," said Mrs Jenkins in a low voice.

"Now, you just stay quiet, Mrs Jenkins," said Amelie soothingly. "There is no need to get yourself all upset over any of this. No more than you already are."

"No, it needs to be said. I told that new owner, Mrs Cartwright. I told her everything."

Stone cleared his throat, lowering his voice, as respectful as he could be when he said, "And how come you know it all, Mrs Jenkins?"

"My husband." A tiny shudder. Amelie squeezed her hand. Mrs Jenkins smiled. "I'm all right. My husband was a lawyer, retired, of course. He was in charge of the original sale nigh-on forty years ago. His brother-in-law bought the hotel. I was never happy with any of it. He was a detestable man, but my husband assured me everything was legal."

"But why would these men ..." Stone's voice became pained. "I'm sorry, Mrs Jenkins, but why would these men murder your husband because of something that happened forty years ago?"

"Perhaps if I told you the story, together we might be able to make some sense of it?"

So, as the others sat down and Cole pulled up a chair to do the same, Mrs Jenkins told the story of what happened in the Elegance Hotel all that time ago.

CHAPTER EIGHTEEN

Mumford was his name. He took over the running of the hotel around forty years ago. It was he who christened it "The Elegance," although why nobody knew because it was a squalid looking place, with chipped paint and warped boarding.

The evening it happened, he was closing the bar. Having dismissed Mrs Taylor, the receptionist, a half-hour before, he was alone. Business had been slack recently, and he saw no point in paying good wages for her to simply sit around.

Wheezing, he lifted the hatch to the cellar and climbed down the few damp, dark steps that led into the gloom. He picked one of the torches he always kept down there and lit it. Tinder dry, it flared violently, allowing him a good view of the surroundings. The place stank. He rarely came down here nowadays. Since his wife had left him, there was no one to badger him over keeping the place tidy. Even so, he needed some timber to repair a creaking card table in the lounge, so he set to gathering together several small planks from the stack in the far corner.

Mumford was not a well man. The dank air, combined with particles of dust, had got on his chest, and he was having some difficulty in breathing. He moved away, wheezing painfully now, and decided to take some fresh air before he resumed his work. He blew his nose loudly and placed his foot on the first step, ready to go back up into the bar area.

The kick took him full in the face, tearing his nostrils and upper lip with the force of the blow. He careened backwards, the pain and shock not yet hitting him.

574

As he smashed into assorted crates and barrels, he had the vaguest impression that an army of bodies was charging towards him through the gloom. He screamed, not really sure who or what his attackers were, conscious only of the searing pain wincing through his heavily bleeding face.

He floundered across the dusty floor, his left hand raised in a pathetic attempt to ward off anymore blows, whilst his right hand supported his half-prostrate and trembling body. The blood dripped unchecked from his shattered nose and mouth, and he watched in fascination as it splashed onto the ground.

A dark shape loomed over him, and Mumford at last found the ability to speak. No sooner did his mouth form the first syllable than it was filled with something he did not at first recognize. It was like a blow from a slab of cold, hard metal, so powerful was its delivery. His mind whirled in disarray, and, unable to concentrate properly, he felt like a helpless, foolish drunkard. Nothing was making sense.

Suddenly hands were lifting him up again, propping him against what was left of the stack of barrels. He sat, head on chest, blinking through the tears, watching the blood spreading over his shirt as it dripped from his face, waiting in total helplessness for the next onslaught.

There was silence.

Mumford, at last given the opportunity to think logically, wondered who in the name of God was doing this to him, and why. If it was burglars, why such violence – they could have easily locked the cellar door on him and then ransacked the hotel at their leisure? It was nonsensical and so unnecessary – not a brave man, he would have willingly given them whatever they wanted without any struggle at all.

Distorted images flashed across his consciousness. From somewhere, he found the strength, and courage, to raise his head. A weak, shaking hand moved across his eyes, smearing away the blood and tears that marred his vision. He managed to make out the form of his attacker. He sat opposite, staring in silence, casually filling a bone pipe with tobacco. Mumford marvelled at his audacity and great strength. He was a lone attacker. To lift someone of Mumford's weight would demand an enormous effort, and this man had done it with seeming ease. The realization that here was someone who could destroy him utterly and totally sent new shock waves of horror through Mumford's already battered and defeated body. He could do nothing to defend himself against such an individual, and the knowledge disturbed him greatly.

A match blazed briefly in the gloom, and Mumford caught a glimpse of the man's face. The shock of recognition caused him to involuntarily jerk his head back, a rasp of breath hissing through his chipped teeth.

"Morgan!"

The name was like a slap to the man. He came closer, the pipe clamped in the corner of his hard, handsome face, the lips pulled back in a sneer. "Hello, Mumford," he said, propping one foot next to the innkeeper. "Where's Nancy?"

Mumford recoiled as a stream of smoke was blown into his face. Turning away, he coughed hoarsely. His breathing gargled in his chest.

The face came closer, the words like blows. "I asked you a question!"

Mumford had no idea where his wife was. "She left, a few days ago."

"Is that a fact?" Morgan stepped back, his eyes quickly scanning the eerie half-light of the cellar. Stooping down, he picked up one of the pieces of wood Mumford had chosen to repair the card table. He weighed it in his hand, then advanced on his victim. "You see, she told me she was only leaving for a short time, to teach you a lesson. She said she was going back to you."

"I don't understand. To teach me a lesson? I thought you and she were—"

"We had a tiff. Silly girl found me in bed with..." He smiled broadly. "Well, let's just say she wasn't too happy about it." He let out a long stream of pipe smoke. "Funny things women, don't you think?"

Mumford said nothing. He was concentrating on his breathing, which was becoming a little easier. He looked up into Morgan's maniacal face, the face of a man capable of anything. "You must know she wouldn't come back to me," he managed to say through his already swollen lips.

Morgan looked impressed, but for other reasons. "You mean because I'm a much better lover than you? So much better that she couldn't bear to think of sharing your bed after having shared mine?"

Mumford nodded his head meekly. "Yes."

"I'm glad you've accepted the truth, at long last."

"I always knew she wanted you more than me."

"Really? That's very gracious of you." He pressed his face closer still to Mumford's. "Tell me why you think that's so?"

Mumford swallowed hard. He could smell the man's smoky breath, feel the sweat of his face, sense the insanity that was bubbling just under the surface. But he could also sense that the man's ego was perhaps the most dangerous thing to contend with. If he could keep that sweet then perhaps Mumford could find a way out of this ghastly mess. "Because you are a better man than me," he gushed, guessing it was what Morgan wanted to hear.

Morgan's voice rose in triumph. "Yes! Yes, I am." He stepped back, looking for all the world like a strutting peacock.

The situation was still dangerous, Mumford well aware that only total submission could possibly prevent further violence.

"Tell me more. Tell me how I'm stronger and cleverer than you, that Nancy can't resist me, yearns for me, begs for me to be with her. Tell me all of that."

Mumford did, repeating every word.

Morgan cackled in victory. "You're in awe of me, aren't you? You wish you were like me."

"Yes, yes, I do."

"But you never will be. Never."

From the foot of the stairs, taking both men by surprise, a voice cracked through the fetid air. "You're an embarrassment!"

Mumford stared. Nancy Mumford stood at the foot of the cellar steps wearing a delicately patterned summer dress of powder blue.

"Hello, Nancy," said Morgan.

Mumford took his chance whilst Morgan's attention was diverted. It was desperate, and probably futile, but his only hope. He launched himself forwards, slamming the whole of his considerable weight into the Morgan's midriff, and both of them crashed to the ground.

Morgan's strength proved too much, and he easily disentangled himself, lifted Mumford to his feet, and slammed his knee into Mumford's groin. Mumford yelped and sagged in Morgan's strong hands before a heavy left swung through the air and cracked into his jaw, felling him. Whimpering as he writhed on the ground, Mumford blubbered and begged Nancy to call the sheriff.

But Nancy didn't move. She watched, mesmerised, as Morgan picked her husband up, threw him against the far wall, and used one of the wooden planks to break open Mumford's skull as if it were an egg. She saw, but could not believe, the glint of steel as a long-bladed knife appeared in Morgan's hand. He sliced through Mumford's ponderous belly effortlessly, gutting him like a pig, the contents tumbling out in a gush of blood and gore.

Nancy stared, watching speechless with disbelief.

When it was done and the blood-spattered corpse lay butchered amongst the wreckage of the crates, Morgan stood, limp-wristed, gazing at the consequences, gulping in air, but face blank and impassive, registering nothing.

Waking as if from a dream, Nancy moved to his shoulder and tentatively pulled at his jacket, taking care that no blood splatted onto her. She felt a curious thrill buzzing through her. Although the scene had been horrific, she had marvelled at Morgan's skill and strength, and she now felt elated that this man was hers.

Morgan turned to her. "Bit of a mess," he said quietly, almost in a whisper. Nancy looked deep into his eyes and could find no remorse, fear, or anything else there. "We'd better get the deeds and go," she said.

"Go where?" said Morgan, regaining some of his confidence. "We can't go anywhere that's far enough away. I'm finished."

"No, you're not," she snapped, her resolve hardening. "We can get out of this. No-one knows you're here, and I'm the only witness and," a smile crossed her lovely mouth, "I didn't see a thing."

He went to hold her, but she stopped him with an upturned hand. "Sorry," he said, realizing the blood was all over his shirt front.

"We'll get you a change of clothes, get the deeds, make the claim, and then work out how we can rebuild our lives."

"But what about this," he gestured, without looking, at Mumford's corpse. "Somebody's sure to come along and discover him, and then they'll launch a manhunt."

"And who will they look for? You? Me? Why?" She shook her head. "I'll report it, include a few half-truths and tell the sheriff I left but came back out of guilt; that I found him like this, the victim of a terrible robbery gone wrong. We're going to be all right, I promise you."

He was shaking his head. "But the claim. As soon as you cash it, they'll put two and two together."

"No, I'll put the hotel up for sale, lie low. We've waited this long, we can wait a little longer. When everything is calm, we'll meet up and get away." She stroked his face. "You're everything he wasn't. We've done the hard part, now we just need to stay calm." She leaned forward, careful of the blood, and kissed him lightly on the lips. "I like your arrogance. I like that a lot, but most of all I like your confidence. I like you, or didn't you know that?"

"Nothing more than like?"

She smiled, all thoughts of the nightmare vision she had just witnessed gone from her mind. They were a well-matched pair. "Anything more will come later. Come on, let's get you some clothes..."

CHAPTER NINETEEN

"I told much the same story to Lewis Cartwright," said the Reverend Peters as the others sat in silence, digesting what Mrs Jenkins had told them.

"And how did he react?" asked Stone.

"To be honest, he didn't react at all."

"As if he knew it already?"

"Perhaps, but I don't see how he could have."

"The story is well-known," said Mrs Jenkins. "They tracked them both down, eventually. Silas Morgan was killed in a gunfight, and Nancy Mumford arrested. She made a full statement before her trial. Every gruesome detail was included. Although she wasn't directly responsible for the killing of her husband, a lot of people hated her for her involvement with Morgan and they hanged her."

Stone threw out his hands, exasperated. "And the business about the deeds? What happened to the deeds?"

No one offered any explanation, Mrs Jenkins alone added, "My husband had something to do with it. I think they might have been put into some sort of trust, for Nancy Mumford's grandchildren, but I can't be sure, and of course, now, we can't ask him." Shaking her head, she pressed her handkerchief into her eyes and wept, Amelie holding her tightly around the shoulders.

Stone stood up. "Mr Cole, if you could be so kind as to get the horses ready, I shall wander down to talk to Mr Cartwright in the meantime."

Cole arched a single eyebrow, and he asked, "Something troubling you?"

"Not sure. There's a lot not right about any of this. With what we know, it's almost as if the hotel is the key."

"The hotel?" Peters said, shaking his head. "How can a building be the cause of murder?"

"Well, it already is a place where a murder took place," said Stone. "What happened there forty years ago has some bearing on what is going on here right now. I'm sure of it."

Doffing his hat, Stone made his apologies to the ladies and left. Cole studied the two women, noting their strained faces. He stood up. "Reverend, I'm riding over to my home. I need to explain to Maddie what's going on. She's probably worried sick."

"All right," said Peters. He picked up one of the Winchesters from Sheriff Stone's desk and weighed it in his hands. "Been a while since I've handled one of these." He looked up to see Cole's inquiring glance. "I wasn't always a preacher, Mr Cole."

"You served in the Army?"

Peters inclined his head, thoughtful and quiet. Cole sensed there was a small touch of shame when he again spoke, "Yes. I served in the Spanish-American War. Fought in Cuba and was to be shipped across to the Philippines when I got shot in the calf." He patted his right leg. "I was invalided out." He shook his head. "That was a vicious war, Mr Cole, I don't mind telling you. A lot of things done that shouldn't have been. I spent a lot of soul-searching afterwards as I lay in a hospital bed and decided I wanted to do something of good, if you understand me. So, I joined the clergy. Methodist minister is what I am, although many around here don't seem to care what I am as long as it isn't them standing in the pulpit."

"I wouldn't know. I'm not one for church-going myself."

"Well, after what I saw in that war, I'm not so certain if many people are." He worked the Winchester lever. "I'll wander out back and shoot off a few rounds."

After he'd left, the atmosphere lightened appreciably. Mrs Jenkins was the first to speak. "I knew there was something about him. He's ...

Well, he's very *physical.* I saw him change when we ..." Her head fell, and she sniffed loudly. "When we went back to the house and saw—"

"It's all right," said Amelie. "You don't need to say anymore."

"No, no, I'm fine. But the Reverend, he became quite angry. Muttering all sorts of quite awful things and clenching his fists as if he meant to hit somebody."

Cole didn't say anything, gave a half-smile, and went outside. Deep in thought, he mounted his horse and gently edged it out of town, making his way to his home and Maddie.

CHAPTER TWENTY

HIS aim proved good. After emptying seven rounds into a makeshift target crafted out of an old, rotting piece of tree-trunk, Peters wiped his brow with his sleeve and sighed. His anger boiled. To have killed Mr Jenkins the way they did, then leaving the body so that his wife would find him. Obviously, it was meant as a warning. But why? It had been some time since Peters had experienced such wanton disregard for human life. This latest killing brought it all back.

He wandered through the back streets and entered the saloon by the rear entrance. There was a smattering of customers, but most people seemed to be on the street, wondering what was going on at the Sheriff's office. That suited Peters just fine, and he went to the bar and ordered a whisky. The barman gave him a look, which Peters returned, staring him down.

After the third drink, Peters began to come back to Earth. It took him some time to come to terms with the enormity of what he was capable of. Mr Jenkins' murder conjured up the demons he had kept buried for so long. Changing his direction, living a new life as a preacher, he'd managed to wipe away the memory of what it was like to experience pain. Suffering was a trite word to use; it didn't really say enough. Yes, he was suffering; yes, he *had* suffered; this was something more. He could taste it in his mouth. The bittersweet tang of wanting to punish. He knew it was wrong. He was weak, a failure. Failure in himself, his vows, his Lord. His shame was tangible, and it seeped from the very pores of his soul to mingle with the heavy atmosphere of that lonely saloon that warm summer's day.

Heavy shoulders stooped forward, the slow, deliberate movement of the hand to mouth as he drained the alcohol from the glass. If anyone watched, nobody had any idea that what they were witnessing was the torment of a man of God who had betrayed a promise he had made to himself long ago. The memory of those past times consumed him, and even the drink could not dull the vivid pictures that played across his mind.

In the searing midday heat, the patrol passed down the crumbling street, broken adobe buildings pressing in on both sides, dark faces peering out from within. Some way ahead, an upturned cart with two men furiously exchanging words. Suddenly alert, the soldiers brought up their rifles, fanning out in a thin line.

Peters, young and heavily muscled, had earned his corporal stripes under the heat of the Cuban sun. He recognised something amiss. He had grown old in that place, had visited the bowels of hell more than once, and had moulded himself into a vicious, professional killer, silent and resourceful. These streets had numbed his powers somewhat, but not enough for him to miss the tension that now hung in the atmosphere and was heavier than the warm air itself.

"Shepherd!"

A big lance-corporal turned and gave Peters an inquiring glance. "What's up, Corporal?"

"I don't know," Peters said, working the lever of his Winchester. "Take two others and go and check 'em out. And be careful, all right?"

Shepherd shrugged, called two soldiers over to him, and continued walking towards the two arguing men.

Hill and Stowell ambled alongside. It was too hot for all this.

A yelp of Spanish gave them all a start, forcing them all to reach for their weapons. It was only a boy, stepping out from between houses. They all gave a collective sigh of relief. Dressed in white, his shock of blue-black hair made a stark contrast to the brightness of his garb. He had a cheery, open face, his massive brown eyes like saucers, dispelling all mistrust.

From where he stood, Peters watched transfixed. He saw Shepherd's smile. The boy had an orange in his hand. It was a very big orange. Three more boys, all about the same age standing a little way back, were jabbering to each other. Remarkable how they all looked so similar, small, wiry, burned nutmeg brown by the sun.

Motioning for the other two to move forward, Shepherd tilted his head towards the boy. Peters turned to watching the streets. The quietness was intense.

The boy stepped closer with the orange, holding it out. "Cut, please," he was saying in English. Shepherd smiled again, slung his rifle over his shoulder, and reached for the knife at his belt.

The boy was close now. Thirteen years old at most, Peters calculated, intrigued by the little scene playing out some twenty or so paces from him. The boy seemed small for his age, under-nourished, Peters mused, as so many were.

The boy continued to hold out the fruit for Shepherd to take and begin to peel. He was so tiny compared to Shepherd bearing over him. The lance-corporal bent forward and reached out with his free hand.

From where Peters stood, the whole incident fell into slow-motion. His eyes glazed over, and he felt himself spinning out of control as each minuscule event combined to present before him a scene from his worst nightmare. Time stood still; his body froze. His training, for a few brief and crucial moments, deserted him, and he could do little more than watch.

The boy was fast, faster than anything any of them had ever seen. The knife was like a blue streak, flashing brightly in the daylight, thrusting upwards, ripping into Shepherd's midriff, slicing upwards through his abdomen to his breast bone. Shepherd didn't scream, couldn't scream, the surprise was too great. As his mouth gaped open, he folded forward, holding onto the awful, open wound. The knife flashed again, back and across, the sharp blade slashing across the lance-corporal's throat. The blood spilled, and Shepherd fell.

Hill and Stowell moved, rifles turning, but they turned the wrong way, towards the boy. The two arguing Arabs were arguing no longer. From under their voluminous robes, the ancient pistols spat out a cruel blast of concentrated fire, and the two soldiers died in a hail of ill-aimed but highly effective lead shot.

The firing proved too inaccurate. As the soldiers died, so too did Shepherd's killer, the boy's little body racked by the two old Remingtons. There was another effect too: Peters.

Triggered by the violence, his training kicked in. Already he was rolling across the soft dust that seemed to lie everywhere. Kneeling behind what little cover there was, the Winchester Model 1892 proved highly effective in the big Corporal's hands. The two Cuban men met their deaths before they really knew what was happening. But Peters wasn't finished.

Out of control, thinking clouded by the horror he had witnessed, he strode from behind his cover, working the Winchester lever. The remaining boys reacted too slowly, and even before they were turning, Peters emptied his rifle into them, not caring if they were part of the ambush or innocent bystanders.

Silence settled. Peters stood rock still and watched his victims die.

As the mist before his eyes parted, reality slowly returned, and the enormity of what he had done sank home. The Winchester fell from trembling fingers, all thoughts of his safety gone. The heat, the blood, the scent of death, it was too much. Collapsing into the dirt, his head pressing against the sand, the stillness enveloped him. Overwhelmed by the senseless waste of life, and his shameful part in it, nothing could ever wipe away the image of those boys' faces. Nothing.

At the bar, Peters pushed away the memories and considered his glass. The past had caught up with him at last, the violence he had rejected, the violence he had striven so hard to conceal, to control, to conquer, had risen up and taken hold of him once more. He hadn't changed at all. He still had the capacity to destroy. In Cuba, it had been with guns, guns he continued to know how to use. He had hidden behind his vows, struggling for respectability in what he stood for. It all seemed for nothing.

Blowing out a loud sigh, Peters snatched up the Winchester propped up beside him and wandered outside. Several townsfolk wandered by, giving him curious looks. He wondered if his attitude gave away his drinking bout, but he doubted it. He could still hold his liquor. No, they were probably more curious about his emerging from the saloon. A man of the cloth, and a Methodist at that, did not sit well with any sort of drinking establishment. But Peters was past caring. The murder of Mr Jenkins had brought it all back. The anger at man's inhumanity to man. And the shame over what he'd done. After this, he decided, he would leave the clergy, leave this town, seek out some other means of employment. One that did not require him speaking with people. He needed to escape, start over.

He contemplated the street. Sheriff Stone had mentioned something about talking with Lewis Cartwright, so he decided to go and discover for himself if any developments had been unearthed.

CHAPTER TWENTY-ONE

HELPING him take off his shirt, Maddie screwed up her mouth and groaned when she saw the large bruises across Cole's ribs.

"Don't fuss none," he said through gritted teeth. He moved awkwardly; the kicks he'd received had done damage. He didn't know how much.

"You need to see Doc Evans."

"Doc Evans is dead."

Her hand flew to her mouth. "Oh my Lord, since when?"

"Since about nine months ago." He shook his head but couldn't resist smiling. "Have you been living in a cave, or what?"

She went to punch him light-heartedly, as she usually did in reply to his sarcasm, but stopped herself just in time. "Who's his replacement? I mean, is there one?"

"Yes. Wycliffe. He seems a good man." He tried to stretch out his back, only succeeding in buckling himself up with pain.

"I'll run you a hot bath," Maddie said quickly. "You need to take it easy for a while."

"I can't," he said, sitting down and pulling off his boots. "There's been a killing over in town. I have to try and track them that did it down."

"*What?* Are you crazy? After what happened with that awful man, Soloman and poor Sterling? Reuben, you can't keep doing this! You told me you was retired, that Sterling's death had made you see that time had caught up with you, that you couldn't keep—"

"Maddie, please," he said, holding up both hands in surrender. "I know what I said, but it got complicated. Ryan was shot, and whilst he was recuperating, I sort of—"

"I don't care about Ryan, I care about *you!*"

"Hell, Maddie, he saved my life."

"So, what is this, a debt to be honoured? You're going to get yourself killed."

"No, I ain't."

"Yes, you are – look at you! You're all busted up."

Cole took a breath. He knew she was right, there was no point in trying to deny any of it. His body was telling him with every passing day that even the most menial of tasks caused him enormous effort. "He took me by surprise is all."

She gaped at him, incredulous. "Took you by surprise?" She ran a hand through her hair and Cole could help notice that it was shaking. The fight left her voice, resigned to his stubbornness. "Well, if that isn't a sign that you're too old for this, Reuben, I don't know what is."

"This is the last time, I swear it."

"You've said that before."

"I know, but Maddie, damn it all, I have no choice."

"You have every choice, you stubborn old fool."

She flounced off, leaving him sitting in the armchair, staring into nothingness. "*Old?*" he muttered to himself. "I'm sixty-two, so yes, I'm old..." He sat back, listening to her running the bath, and realised just how lucky he was. She was right, he knew it. Twenty years ago, perhaps even ten, Monroe would never have been able to sucker-punch him the way he did. Perhaps it really was time to give it all up, let others take on the burden.

But what then his sense of duty? There weren't many trackers around nowadays. Almost all Indians who could help, apart from those few Navajos and Yaquis fighting Government forces over in Arizona, were in reservations. Cole was virtually the last of a dying breed.

She came back, drying her hands on a towel. He sat up, waiting for another onslaught. Instead, he saw the softening around her eyes as she spoke. "I'm not going to tell you not to go, there would be no point. But

I'm asking you, Cole – you look after yourself and don't do anything stupid or foolhardy. You hear me?"

"I hear you."

"You really are an old fool, Reuben Cole. There'll be no more of these escapades after this is done."

He nodded and held out his hands for her to help him to his feet.

He held her close and kissed her. "What would I do without you?"

"What would you do? You'd be lying in your damn grave, Reuben Cole, that's what you'd be doing!"

He smiled, knowing he couldn't disagree.

CHAPTER TWENTY-TWO

S TEPPING up to the open double doors, Ryan Stone knocked tentatively before shouting out, "Anybody home?" Receiving no answer, he went inside anyway, taking off his hat and pausing to listen.

From somewhere he could make out the grunts and groans of someone moving things around. Heavy things by all accounts. It was the voice of a man, so he called again, "Mr Cartwright? It's Sheriff Stone, I've come to ask you a few things regarding the hotel."

He waited.

If it was Lewis Cartwright moving things, he clearly did not hear the Sheriff.

As far as Stone could tell, the voice seemed to be coming from underneath the floor. He peeped over the reception desk and frowned.

Spread across the top of the desk were a number of formal looking documents, embossed with stamps to prove their legality. Unable to suppress the urge, Stone picked one up and started to read.

The first thing that captured his attention was the name of the lawyer's office that had drawn up the document. Intrigued, he scanned through that and the other papers, some of which were statements made to the courts. Nancy Mumford's was there, which he found particularly interesting, as well as the legal document which transferred certain holdings to her grandchildren.

Certain holdings. He pondered on what that phrase might mean, but certainly there was enough information here for him to question Lewis Cartwright.

Drawing in a deep breath, he moved into the small saloon bar. Behind the counter, he saw the open hatch. From here, the sounds were louder.

"Mr Cartwright?"

Again, there was no reply, so he descended the steep stairs. There weren't many, but even so, after a few steps, the gloom of the cellar became oppressive.

A small, flickering torch in the far corner dribbled out a poor excuse for light. Bent over, on hands and knees, Lewis Cartwright was using a short spade to dig at the earth. He was muttering to himself as he worked. Next to him was a growing pile of soil.

Stone stood and watched, wondering what it was Cartwright was searching for. The story Mrs Jenkins relayed came to him, that niggling suspicion that all of this was to do with that mention of deeds. Deeds for what? Worth killing for all those years ago, and still now?

"Mr Cartwright?"

Squawking, Lewis span around, his eyes flashing white in the half-light. His face glistened with sweat, his breathing coming in short, sharp rasps. "Sheriff? What is it you want?"

"I can see you're busy, Mr Cartwright. I can come back."

"Eh?" He looked about him, quickly dusted off his trousers, and stood up. "No, no, I'm just fixing some pipes."

"Pipes?"

Cartwright grinned, but it was forced. False. Stone could clearly see the man's panic.

"Yes. Water pipes. I'm trying to fix the supply so it'll reach the upstairs rooms." Laughing, he came forward, took Stone by the elbow, and led him towards the stairs. "Now then, Sheriff, what is this all about?"

"Some questions, Mr Cartwright. About the murder."

Cartwright swayed backwards, Stone's words like slaps across his face. "The *murder*? I know nothing about it. The first I knew was after we'd gone to your office and—"

"No, no, Mr Cartwright, I'm talking about the murder that occurred here. The murder of Mr Mumford."

Cartwright's mouth gaped open as if in shock. Dragging his arm across his brow, he looked around him, reached for the torch, and motioned towards the stairs. "Let's discuss this upstairs, Mr Stone."

They both stomped up the stairs, the brightness of the saloon bar causing Stone to squint as he emerged from below.

Behind him, he heard Cartwright clinking glasses together. "Care for a drink, Sheriff?"

Stone turned to see Cartwright already pouring out two shots of whisky. "Don't mind if I do," he said, taking the proffered glass. He breathed in the smoky aroma and nodded appreciatively.

"Only the best," said Cartwright, downing his whisky in one. Smacking his lips, he raised his glass and studied it. "I'm not such a great drinker, but I do partake now and again." So saying, he poured himself a second shot. "So, Sheriff, what brings you here is the murder? The Mumford case, is that the one? I have to tell you, Sheriff, I don't know all that much."

"I thought the Reverend Peters told you about it?" Stone took a small sip of his drink, his eyes never leaving Cartwright.

The other man stopped, poised in the act of finishing his second glass. "Ah, so *that* was the one."

"Have there been others?"

"Others? What do you mean by that?"

"I mean the murder of Henry Jenkins."

Cartwright kept his eyes away from Stone's, preferring to focus them on his drink. "I wouldn't know."

"Really?" Stone carefully set the glass on the countertop. "I couldn't help noticing the papers you have left lying around, Mr Cartwright. The ones with Henry Jenkins' stamp on them? They detail an agreement made by Nancy Mumford, leaving certain trusts to her grandchildren."

"Ah." Cartwright smiled and downed his drink. Smacking his lips, he spoke in a solemn tone. "I'm afraid none of that has anything to do with me, Sheriff."

"Oh? Then who has it to do with?"

"Me, Sheriff."

Giving a slight start, Stone turned towards the sound of the voice. Sarah Cartwright stood in the doorway, her face blank of expression. She slowly moved forward.

"Mrs Cartwright," said Stone, unconsciously moving his hand to his hat to touch the brim. "I don't quite get your meaning."

"It's simple," said Cartwright, slipping beside Stone to join his wife. He was smiling, an expression made more powerful by the revolver he now held in his hand. "I'll ask you to very slowly throw your gun down, Sheriff. Easy does it, for your own sake."

Staring at the barrel of the gun, Stone knew he had little choice. With finger and thumb, he lifted his gun from its holster and dropped it to the floor.

Sarah dipped down and scooped the gun up.

"This is most inconvenient," said Cartwright. "It's a pity you arrived when you did. Another fifteen minutes or so, we would be gone."

"I don't understand," said Stone, looking from one to the other.

"It's quite simple," said Sarah. "I am Nancy Mumford's granddaughter. The deeds to the gold mine belong to me and my brother. We're here to collect."

"Goldmine?" Stone shook his head. "There ain't been any gold mined here for almost fifty years!"

"That's where you're wrong," said Cartwright. "Mumford found it, you see. Worked it for nearly five years. Dug out a mass of gold which he buried away for safe keeping. The mine he signed over to his wife. He was sick. Dying. He wanted her to have it to pass onto their children's children."

"And then she got herself involved with Silas Morgan, and the situation changed a little. But not so much that the claim was revoked. Our lawyer, Mr Jenkins, saw to that."

"But Jenkins is dead." Stone snapped his head around to Cartwright, lips drawn over his teeth, snarling, "You murdered him, didn't you?"

Cartwright's laughter rang out loud and brutal throughout the hotel. "Murdered Jenkins? Are you mad?"

"We didn't murder anyone," said Sarah quickly.

"Then who did?"

"You know full well – the men who forced their way into his home, to threaten him, demand he hand over the claim to the mine. The same men who assaulted Claudette Gower, abducting her to make her, or Jenkins, give up those deeds."

Stone's frown grew deeper. "Claudette Gower? What has she to do with any of this?"

"You really don't know anything, do you, Sheriff." Sarah shook her head sadly.

"Then maybe you should tell me, before I arrest you both and see you stand trial."

"You seem to forget it's us that have the drop on you, Sheriff," said Cartwright, sneering. To add emphasis, he wiggled the gun in his hand.

"You wouldn't dare shoot an officer of the law," said Stone defiantly. "Now, tell me what this is all about before I arrest you!"

Now it was Sarah's turn to burst out with a loud guffaw. "Arrest us, for what?"

"Holding me up for a start! Hindering my investigation, withholding evidence. The list is long, Mrs Cartwright. You have a lot of explaining to do." He puffed out his chest. "Who was responsible for murdering Mr Jenkins?"

"Sebastian Monroe," said Sarah without a pause. Then, a slight smile. "My brother."

CHAPTER TWENTY-THREE

L EANING with his back against the outside wall, Peters closed his eyes, doing all he could to calm himself. He'd heard everything, the revelations hitting him hard. To think that these two newcomers were capable of such ...

Slowly, he let out a long breath and allowed his eyes to settle on the Winchester. It would take all but a moment to burst in on them, shoot one of them – probably Cartwright – and save the Sheriff and wrap everything up into a neat parcel.

A moment.

It had taken him only moments to shoot down those boys. Innocent boys for all he knew. Their deaths changed him, their faces tormenting him through long, sleepless nights, forcing him to seek a new direction for his life. Turning his back on the Army, he joined a seminary college. A difficult time. So many questions about himself, his motivation, his faith. Faith. What was that, in the end? An acceptance that something beyond knowing watched over us, guided us, gave us the answers if we were willing to look? He didn't know. He thought he did, but not now. Seeing Jenkins lying there, the rage it caused, it made him realise he had never truly changed. He remained that same man, that killer. He always would be.

Checking the Winchester one last time, Peters took a breath, stepped away from the wall, and kicked his way through the main entrance to the hotel.

———

Cole cantered into town, moving easily past the saloon to the Sheriff's office. There he dismounted and tied the reins loosely to the hitching rail. Inside he found Matthias Thurst brewing coffee, and Amelie Gower sat behind Stone's desk, writing furiously.

Mrs Jenkins appeared to be napping in the corner. Perhaps for the best, thought Cole.

Amelie looked up, her face creasing into a frown. "Why, Mr Cole," she said. Her voice held no hint of welcome or relief, more one of thinly disguised distaste.

"Ah, Reuben," said Thurst, pouring out steaming coffee into tin cups, "care for some?"

"No thanks, Matthias. Hasn't Ryan returned yet?"

"Nope," said Matthias, handing a cup to Amelie, whose mouth turned down at the corners. She gave a brief, barely perceptible nod and took a sip.

"And where's the Reverend?"

"He went to see where Mr Stone was," replied Amelie, taking the opportunity to push the coffee away from her. She studied it in disgust as if it were an abhorrence.

"Hotel," put in Thurst, drinking his own coffee with relish.

"Well, we need to get going while there is still light." Cole turned to Amelie, who had recommenced writing. "What is that you're doing, if you don't mind me asking, ma'am?"

Pausing, head down, she appeared to be steadying herself, searching for the right words to say. "It's a testimony, Mr Cole, if you must know."

"A testimony? What kind of testimony?"

"One for the Sheriff." Her head came up, her clear blue eyes piercing, glinting with that look of contempt Cole now recognised so easily. "A lawman, Mr Cole. Not a hired killer."

"Is that what you see me as, ma'am? A hired killer?"

"It's what you do isn't it? You hunt people down and execute them."

Behind Cole, Thurst whistled. "Ma'am, I don't think you fully know what you're saying when you accuse—"

"Excuse me," snapped Amelie Gower, "I know *precisely* what I'm saying." She set her unblinking gaze on Cole once more. "I've heard the stories. I know all about you, Mr Cole. When I have finished this," she prodded the paper with a stiff index finger, "Mr Stone can proceed with a lot more certainty. And by the way," she picked up her pen again, "I am a *Miss*."

Cole and Matthias shared a quick look.

"I'd appreciate that coffee now," said Cole, "if it's all right with you."

As Mathias went to reach for the coffee pot, the first gunshot rang out. He jumped, the tin cup in his hand falling to the floor with a loud clatter.

Amelie gave a cry of alarm.

Cole was already turning for the door when the second shot came.

It took only a moment for the Reverend Peters to assess the situation.

He saw Cartwright's open mouth, Stone's hands held out in supplication, and Sarah, turning, the gun in her hand.

Peter dropped to his knees, making himself as small as possible. He put a bullet into Cartwright, throwing him backwards against the saloon bar counter. Cartwright cried out, grimacing, instinctively grasping for his back despite the bullet in his left shoulder. He fell, his revolver clattering to the ground.

Sarah's gun, the one snatched when Stone dropped it, barked once, but the bullet went hopelessly wild, her chosen target no longer there. Reacting with pure instinct, Stone rushed her from behind and wrestled with her, one arm across her throat, his other hand twisting the gun from her grip. She struggled, screaming insanely, a stream of obscenities issuing from her mouth. Stone held on, gritting his teeth. She was strong, far stronger than he expected, and she was wriggling free, turning, swinging her knee upwards.

Stone screeched high-pitched as her knee connected and released his hold.

"No," said Peters, climbing to his feet, the Winchester aiming. But could he be sure his aim was true? The two of them fought frantically, and if he fired, who would he hit?

Sarah's elbow snapped into Stone's face, sending him sprawling backwards. He fell on top of Cartwright who, bleeding profusely, still managed to bring his firearm to bear.

Peter hesitated.

In those few gaping, terrible seconds, everything flashed before him. Those faces, those boys dying because of him. He should have paused that day, considered his actions before emptying the Winchester into them. Innocent or guilty, they were young, their entire lives ahead of them. Peters had snuffed out their existence without a thought. He was determined not to make the same mistake again.

He stared deep into Cartwright's eyes and saw the man smile.

"Shoot him, Lewis! Shoot him!"

Peters heard the terrible, solid click of the hammer and knew his time had come.

"*Padre,*" came a voice, "*get out of the damned way!*"

Cole moved fast, shouldering the Reverend Peters with a powerful shunt just in time. Cartwright's bullet whizzed past and slapped into the double-door woodwork right behind where the Reverend had been standing. The Model 10 already in his hand, Cole fired twice, the first shot hitting Cartwright in the chest, driving him backwards, the second into his heart. He slumped across Stone, dead.

Screaming hysterically, Sarah Cartwright made a lunge for Stone's gun, but Cole was there first, kicking it out of reach. She rounded on him like a harpy, snarling, hands outstretched, fingers like claws preparing to strike. Without hesitation, Cole swung his fist into the side of her jaw, and it was over.

"I messed up," said Ryan Stone, head in hands, sitting on a barstool in the saloon some thirty or so minutes later.

"Don't be too hard on yourself," said Cole, sliding a full shot of whisky towards the hapless sheriff. "You weren't to know they would turn out that way."

"I should have waited for you. Every manual says never go into a situation alone. I ignored it, and look where it got me."

"Ryan, we learn by our mistakes. Darn it, if I were to count up how many times I've—"

"I could have died, Mr Cole. If it hadn't been for the Reverend, I almost certainly would be dead."

"Yeah," breathed Peters from the far end, rolling his glass between the palms of his hands, "and if it hadn't have been for Cole here, I'd be dead too." He chuckled, raised his glass, and downed it in one.

"What's done is done," said Cole. "We now have to concentrate on the others."

"I'm not going with you," said Stone in a flat, depressed voice. "I'll stay here, take Sarah Cartwright's statement, if she's willing. If not, I can use Amelie Gower's and send a telegram to the circuit judge."

"I've yet to read what Miss Gower had to say."

"Put short, it lays out everything. We know Monroe is Sarah's brother, thanks to what she told us. It seems he met Claudette last year, and they became more than intimate. She told him she had the means for them both to run away, set up on their own in another place."

"Ryan, she's got to be at least twenty years his senior!"

Stone shrugged. "An attractive woman, but you're right. Clearly Monroe encouraged her, and she told him everything – her 'secret' so to speak. She and her sister had been contracted to clean up the hotel for the previous owner. It was while they were doing so that they came across copies of the deeds."

"She stole them?"

"No, she took them to Jenkins, who confirmed they were genuine. It's common for such documents to have several copies made. She kept them, told Monroe all about them. Then, to make things simpler, the previous owner went and died, the hotel was put up for sale, and the Cartwright's swooped."

"Thanks to Monroe's information about the deeds?"

Stone spread out his hands. "Poor Claudette didn't know anything about it. Monroe broke it off with her, and she went into a deep depression. He went to her to get the deeds, she refused, so he kidnapped her, hoping to put pressure on Jenkins. Her life for the deeds."

"And when that didn't happen, Jenkins got himself killed."

"Which leaves," put in Peters, "poor Claudette. I wonder if she's still alive."

"Let us hope so. You saw her, Cole, before Monroe slugged you."

"I saw a bundle lying on the ground. I couldn't tell if she was dead or not."

"Then we have to find out."

Nodding, Cole gave a long sigh. "Could be a U.S. Marshal will come across seeing as all of it is to do with past crimes. It'll get complicated."

"Not if you bring those others in."

Cole cleared his throat, shot a glance at Peters before lifting his glass towards the sheriff and saying, "Tell Maddie, won't you, Ryan. Tell her I'm off out on the range again, only this time I'm with the Padre." He finished his whisky. "I mean Reverend. No offence."

"None taken," said Peters, "but to be honest, I'm all done-in, Cole. As soon as we've brought those no-gooders in, I'll be sending out my own telegram, to the diocese in Denver. I'm quitting."

The others stopped and stared.

"It's a long story," he said, without further explanation. "I'll get the horses ready."

"There goes a man with a lot of problems resting on those big shoulders," said Stone as Reverend Peters plodded out of the saloon.

"I reckon he's had what you'd call a 'moral dilemma.'"

"What's that?"

Cole smirked. "I have no idea, just something Sterling used to say."

"You miss him, don't you, Mr Cole?"

"Every day."

Cole swung around and took a step towards the batwing doors.

"Mr Cole," said Stone quickly, "I sure hope you ain't gonna get yourself into another Monroe situation."

"Only situation I'll be getting into with Monroe is gonna be a mighty troublesome one," said Cole over his shoulder, then added: "For him."

CHAPTER TWENTY-FOUR

ONROE leaned closer, took Claudette's forearm in a vice-like grip and pulled her to him.

"What you really do have to understand, my darling, is that you have no choice in any of this. No choice at all."

Her fear was absolute, but even that could not prevent her from voicing her dissent. "I can't help you. What you're asking me to do ... I can't."

His eyes narrowed, "You're not listening to me," he hissed dangerously. "You have *no choice!*" His companions threw Monroe several inquisitive glances, but his fierce gaze prevented any of them from questioning him. He forced a smile, but there was strain in his face now. "It is time for you to follow my command. When you first came to me, you knew you had to do as you were told. I warned you what would happen if you didn't, that you would be asked to do things that you would find hard, even repulsive. You swore you would do as you were told, and there can be no going back from that. The consequences are total, for you. God will not forget the oath you made, under His name."

Tears welled up in her eyes. Clearly his grip caused her great pain, and all she could manage was a weak shake of the head. "I thought you loved me."

He barked out a laugh. "Love? *You*? You're old and all worn out, Claudette."

"I hate you," she said, tearing her head from those blazing eyes. "You used me, Sebastian. You thought you could control me, and you almost did, but then you left me. Why couldn't you just have stayed away?"

"I need those deeds. I need to know where the gold is buried."

"There is no gold, you oaf!"

He struck her without warning, knocking her backwards. She cowered on the ground, one hand against her mouth where the blood trickled from her cut lip.

"I killed Jenkins, who was as stubborn as you. You'll go back into town, find my sister, and together you'll get to the bottom of this. Jenkins' wife is an old witch, but she'll trust you. You'll convince her to hand over the deeds and then—"

"I'll not do anything to help you," she said, trying to sound brave.

Monroe laughed again. "Oh, yes, you will, or I'll go back into town and kill your sister. And I'll let you watch before I do the same for you."

"You're a monster."

"Indeed, I am, my little pretty one." His smile grew almost pleasant. "Old you may be, but you still is one damned attractive woman. Perhaps when this is all over, we could set up somewhere, you and me? What do you say?"

The only reply he received was a look of utter contempt.

The two men reined in their horses, pausing to lift canteens to dry lips and gulp down water. Peters adjusted himself in his saddle. "How do you manage to sit in one of these things for hours on end," he grimaced. "My backside feels as if it's perched on a bed of nails."

"Bed of nails? What's that?"

"Sore is what it is, Cole. I'm going to have to get down for a moment."

He did so, stretched out his back and rubbed his behind vigorously with both hands. "I can't feel it at all, save for the pain."

"I take it you don't ride a whole lot?"

"Not if I can help it," Peters shook his head. "You think we'll find them?"

"Yup," said the scout, pointing to the broken ground. "Signs are easy to follow. Perhaps too easy. I'm thinking they won't be expecting anyone to come after 'em. They left me out to die, as they did Ryan, so they is brim-full of confidence. My guess is they will be returning to the town soon to make another attempt to find the gold."

"Gold we now know doesn't exist."

"Yeah, but they don't know that."

"And Miss Claudette? What'll they do when they discover the truth? That all of this mayhem has been for nothing and that Sarah Cartwright is in jail, all her plans in shreds?"

Shrugging, Cole allowed his eyes to roam across the open expanse of the plain. "You know what they'll do. What *we* have to do is find 'em and bring 'em in."

Muttering to himself, Peters climbed onto the back of his horse again and twitched the reins. "Let's get to it." And they both set off once more, heads down, huddled up against the pulsing heat of the cruel, burning sun.

Cole spotted the tell-tale clouds of dust and knew what they were before he brought his telescope up to confirm it.

"It's them. Three men and a woman."

"Claudette?"

"I guess so," said Cole, snapping the telescope shut. "We need to take it easy on this, Reverend. At the first sign of trouble, they could well kill her."

"Then we shoot 'em stone dead!" He smacked the stock of his Winchester hanging from his saddle.

"You is awful keen on that, Reverend."

"I'm sick of it all, Cole. I want this done."

"When you said you was quitting the Church, have you a mind to become a bounty hunter, is that it?"

"I've had it with piety and forgiveness. It doesn't do any good."

"An eye for an eye, is that it?"

"Yes it is."

"I understand how you feel, Reverend. I understand a helluva lot, but we cannot sacrifice the woman. We have to be careful."

"How you propose we do that."

Cole motioned towards some broken ground, with sharp protruding rocks jutting upwards. "You wait there. You spook the horses with concentrated fire when they is close enough, and I will come in from the rear to rescue Claudette."

"You think you can do that, Cole? I mean, you aren't exactly a spring chicken anymore, are you."

Through gritted teeth, Cole snarled, "You just do what I say, Reverend, and leave everything else to me." He kicked his horse and set off on a sweeping ride way off to the right.

Peters moved his mount towards the rocks, taking his time, jaw set, eyes to the ground. He felt detached, the forces of fate bringing him to this moment. There was not a single thing he could do to prevent it. He was in Cuba once again, events dictating his actions, taking away his power of choice.

Although, this time, he had already made his choice.

Despite what Cole said, Peters was adamant. He refused to be a pawn in a massive game of chance. He'd seize the initiative, take the appropriate action and end this heinous tale of greed and murder.

CHAPTER TWENTY-FIVE

"Are you sure this is for the best?"

They were moving steadily across the plain, Monroe in the lead with Claudette Gower sitting astride a bedraggled old nag next to him.

With no answer forthcoming, Braddock pressed his companion. "Seb? Did you hear me?"

"I heard you."

"Then answer me! What we're doing, riding back to that town, I can't see as it is the right thing to do. They'll be waiting for us."

"Who?" Monroe eased his horse to a halt, allowing Braddock to move alongside. "Who is there to wait for us, eh? The Sheriff will be dead by now, that Cole is finished. There ain't no one else."

Hemmings cleared his throat as he pushed back his hat and wiped his brow with his sleeve. "The deputy?"

"That old tub of guts?" Monroe cackled and shot a look towards Claudette. "There ain't nobody else to worry about, is there, sweet thing?"

Claudette's icy glare gave him all the answers he needed.

Monroe took a few regular breaths and stared into the distance. "We'll hook up with Sarah and get the gold." He smiled. "Claudette has been forthcoming at last. So, by this evening, we will rich, boys. Rich."

Shaking his head, Braddock lowered his voice. "How you know she is telling the truth, Seb? What if we're riding into a trap?"

"She's telling me the truth because she knows I'll kill her and her sister if what she said is not so."

Something passed between Braddock and Hemmings. "All right, but we need to be careful. Even if that deputy is not much, he could gather together a bunch of townsfolk."

"Nah, I put the frighteners on them when Cole was looking for a posse. No one will dare stand against us."

"But that was before you killed that lawyer," put in Hemmings. "They'll be angry, Seb. They'll be looking to lynch us."

Laughing, Monroe flicked the reins and set off again at a gentle canter. "We'll burn the whole town, boys. Fear is the only weapon we'll need."

"You truly are a monster," said Claudette, body jerking forward as her horse, tethered to Monroe's, moved forward.

"Sure am," cackled Monroe, "but I reckon that's why you're so sweet on me."

From his vantage point far behind the group, Cole watched through his telescope, saw them discussing something, but could not make out their features or reactions. No matter, he sensed there was conflict, something that might work to his advantage. He had faith in the Reverend, knew the man could shoot and was convinced the ensuing confusion caused by his well-placed shots would ensure everything came out well in the end.

Blind faith in a man he hardly knew.

What else did he have?

Snapping the telescope shut, he let out a loud, long sigh. This life, with its constant physical and mental struggle, was proving too much. The years were rolling by, and age was taking its toll and changing him. He remembered how Monroe had slinked up behind him so easily, and he shuddered at the memory. By rights, he should be dead. His luck, he knew, could only last out for so long. Perhaps this was it, the last call. The three men he hunted were hard, vicious, acting without conscience. Especially Monroe. For the first time, he could not predict the outcome. When Ryan Stone had saved him not so long ago, it struck him how fragile his hold on life was. Maddie brought him hope, love, a means to begin again despite the years. His answer was to set out again, on the trail to death. Those men, that swarm of murderous crows, picking at the carcasses, taking and doing as they pleased, they caused him to question his abilities, his desire to get the job done. At least this time, he had the Reverend, a man at odds with himself, but a man who tilted the odds in his favour. For one last time.

He mounted up, checked his Smith and Wesson, set his face against the dwindling, shadowy figures ahead, and moved on.

CHAPTER TWENTY-SIX

P ETERS watched their approach and felt the knot tightening in his gut.

Cole's orders had been precise – shoot to spook the horses. Cole knew, as indeed did he, that once the shooting started, Monroe and his gang would fight. To the death if need be. Spooking the horses might work, but only if Cole acted fast.

From where he sat, crouched behind a cluster of rocks and dried up scrub, there was no sign of the old scout.

Peters' pulse raced, filling up a throat already dry with anxiety. Unable to swallow, he reached for his canteen and took a long drink. The water hit the back of this throat as if it were scalding hot, and he coughed and spluttered, panicked in case any of Monroe's men heard him, and ducked down behind the boulder.

He waited, senses straining.

There appeared to be no reaction, and he chanced a look.

The first shot ricocheted from the top of the rocks, immediately accompanied by wild whooping as Monroe's men kicked their horses into action. The Reverend ducked down as Monroe fired off a second round, the red-hot lead smacking against the boulder inches from Peters' head.

"Damn it!" Peters blurted and tried to bring his Winchester up to at least give some semblance of a retort.

The whooping grew louder. They were close. In that desperate glance he managed to take, Peters saw Monroe wheeling away, taking Claudette with him. She was screaming, and he clubbed her across the side of the head with his pistol. Silenced, she tumbled from her saddle and hit the ground with a sickening, hollow thud.

Incensed, Peters pushed away all his uncertainties. Leaping to his feet, he took a bead on the first rider and shot him out of the saddle. He saw the look of disbelief crossing the man's face, mouth open in a silent scream as he pitched over, blood pumping from the wound in his chest.

Peters froze.

Locked in the moment, unable to tear his eyes away, he watched the man squirming on the ground, frantic fingers clawing at the wound, desperate to stop the flow of that thick, red blood.

So much blood.

He recalled Shepherd, body going into spasm, legs kicking in an insane attempt to escape, to flee from the certainty of his death.

And the blood, of course.

So much blood.

Barely conscious of his surroundings, the Reverend could not prevent the Winchester slipping from his grip. It clattered against the rocks, but he paid no heed. Time stopped. He was there, in that Cuban pueblo once again, Shepherd crying out, "Peters, Peters help me!"

But he could not help. He could do nothing, all of his strength gone.

Trapped and alone in an endless, black tunnel, its sides crushing him, squeezing, forever squeezing, he opened his mouth, battled to force out a scream, anything to help him return to the present, but it was useless.

"*Peters!*"

A bullet hit him in the shoulder, spinning him around, the scorching, instant pain bringing with it a fleeting, tentative awareness of his surroundings. Blinking, the figure of the gunman came into view, striding towards him, handgun held straight out, the grin splitting his sun-blackened face.

"*Peters, get down!*"

Those words did not come from the advancing gunman's mouth.

No, they came from somewhere beyond him. Somewhere far away. But he didn't care. He knew it was too late, and Peters closed his eyes and prepared himself to embrace this long hoped for moment of release.

. . .

Cole was dropping from his saddle before his horse came to a complete stop. The ground was hard underfoot, his running uncertain, ragged. A man past his prime, but a man filled with grim determination. Peters was out of his mind, standing out in the open. What was he doing?

He saw the first gunman falling from his horse, struck by Peters' first shot. Perhaps it was all going to work out fine. Perhaps Claudette could recover from that vicious blow from Monroe's gun. He didn't know. All he did know was what he saw.

Peters, now a statue, mouth opening and closing, lost in a nightmare world of indecision, possibly even fear. He saw him shot.

All of this, everything, so wrong, happening somewhere else in a distant place. Detached, disbelieving, Cole shouted for the Reverend to get down. But the man didn't. He stood transfixed, and when the second bullet streaked past, he didn't flinch.

Cursing, Cole rushed on. He checked to his right. There was Monroe dismounting, sliding the Winchester from its scabbard. There was nothing anyone could do. The inevitable moment, the end of everything. Claudette unconscious, Peters about to die and Cole ...

Damn it, if only Sterling was here.

Cole fired his gun, the bullet slapping into the ground next to the gunman's foot. He spun around, fear mixing with the total shock of this new development.

"Sterling, where are you when I need you?"

The gunman's face changed, the eyes narrowing, the teeth clenched. Cole recognised it. The stone killer gaze.

Cole shot him three times, sending him jumping and jerking backwards, body perforated with tiny eruptions of gore.

Without pausing, Cole raced forward, feeling the tightness in his chest, his lungs bursting, all those years of inactivity, of sitting on the porch watching the world pass by. His muscles screamed, legs like lead, sweat rolling down into his eyes.

Eyes that locked in on those of Peters.

The Reverend's hands spread out, as if he were offering himself, surrendering to his fate. The tears sprang forth and tumbled down his cheeks. "I can't," he said. There was no more.

In those last, desperate strides, Cole wanted to charge into him, send him to the ground, to safety, but the distance seemed so great. Even so, he had to try. As he gathered himself for one, final effort, Monroe's Winchester rang out and Peters' head exploded like a ripe pumpkin, sending out a spray of pink mist to splatter against Cole's shirt front.

Keeling sideways, Peters fell like a great tree, and the silence engulfed them all.

Monroe cackled. This was easier than a turkey-shoot at the local fair. He worked the lever and brought it to his shoulder. "You're gonna die now, Cole," he breathed.

"A monster."

He snapped his head around.

It was Claudette, one side of her head swollen like a huge, purple, overripe piece of fruit. It oozed blood and one of her eyes was almost completely closed over. Despite this, and the obvious pain she was in, she grinned.

Monroe saw why and he understood.

From his horse she'd taken the knife. Its heavy blade glinted in the sun, her knuckles showing white in the tightness of her grip.

She lunged without warning. Monroe dodged and managed to divert the full force of the thrust. The razor-sharp edge sliced through his side, opening up his torso as if it were thin rice paper. He staggered backwards, and Claudette pressed forward, the knife arm coming up in preparation for the killing strike.

Like a drunkard, Cole staggered forward. There was no time to dwell on the poor Reverend because Claudette was in trouble. Serious trouble. Through scalding eyes, breathing laboured, Cole forced his body to eat up those last few paces.

Even then he realised he was too late.

Monroe, gasping from the initial knife attack, worked the Winchester and shot Claudette through the body. As she crumpled, he put another round into her. She floundered, arms outstretched, losing the grip on the knife. She wailed.

Cole roared.

Monroe turned, the wound in his side causing him to buckle. He tried to bring the Winchester to bear, but Cole got there first and emptied the Smith and Wesson into him. Two rounds. But it was enough.

Monroe fell, and Cole was on him, ripping the Winchester from his dying fingers, and clubbed him mercilessly with the stock, pounding him into oblivion.

He didn't stop, and there wasn't anyone left to tell him to.

CHAPTER TWENTY-SEVEN

I N the cool of the evening, Maddie slid closer to Cole on the porch swing they shared and held him close.

"I'm done," he said.

"You've said that before and every time you've—"

"*No,*" he said emphatically, "this is it. No more." He stretched out his hands and they were shaking. "You see that? Never, in all the years have I experienced this. "

She pressed her face into his chest. "You mean I get to keep you here all to myself, every day?"

"Every minute," and he kissed the top of her head. "Out there, in the middle of all that killing, the thought of leaving you ... It was too much, Maddie. It's time to give it up, for good."

She breathed heavily and snuggled even closer. He could not see her smile, but he could feel it and he knew it was all good.

They sat like that for some considerable time until the sound of an approaching rider brought them out of their shared reverie. It was Stone and, as he drew closer, he pulled on the reins and came to a gentle halt. He watched them from a distance and smiled as he slipped down from the saddle. He moved closer, cleared his throat, and mounted the steps.

"Good day to you both."

"Howdy, sheriff," said Maddie. Cole simply looked.

"Mr Cole, I'm sorry to bother you, but it's that marshal I spoke to you about. He's in town right now, doing the investigating, and he says—"

"Ryan, I couldn't give two hoots what some marshal says or doesn't say. I'm finished with it."

"Yeah, yeah, I know that, Mr Cole, but ..." He chewed at his bottom lips as he moved from one foot to the next.

"What is it, Ryan?" asked Maddie, her voice soft and silken in that tense, over-wrought atmosphere. "Just tell it."

"Well, Miss Maddie, he says whoever tried to stop the killing of Reverend Peters and Claudette Gower deserves a medal. He's over-looking a lot of it as those dead pieces of rat-filth were wanted right across Texas for all sorts of heinous things. He said he'd write up his report to show they were lawfully killed."

"And Mrs Cartwright?"

"She's gonna face trial. Poor Miss Amelie, she is in an awful way, crying all the while. The whole thing is ... pardon my language, Miss Maddie, but the whole damned thing was all for nothing. There never was no gold. It was all a lie cobbled together to secure a mortgage for the original purchase of the hotel. Everyone concerned, they all died for nothin'!"

"That's sad," said Maddie, squeezing Cole's hand. "But this land is full of sadness. All we can do is try our best to live with it."

Two days later, Cole returned from his usual early-morning ride to check the stock. He took his horse to the rear of the house, unsaddled her, and made his way back to the house. He stopped when he saw the little rig waiting outside and frowned.

Instinctively, his hand dropped to where his gun would wait. But not any longer. Unarmed, he sighed, chided himself and felt a little silly. Killers don't drive up in full daylight, nor did they drive small buggies.

At least, he hoped they didn't.

"Reuben!" shouted Maddie as Cole came through the door, knocking off the dust with his hat. She came towards him, arms wide open.

"This is Mr Casper from New York City." Sweeping her arm wide, she turned to reveal a small, dapper looking man sitting with his Derby hat on his knees, smiling awkwardly. He put down his coffee cup and stood up. "Mr Casper has a proposition for you, Reuben."

Frowning, Cole studied the little man's reddening face.

"I'm so very pleased to meet you," said Casper, standing up and coming forward. He moved tentatively, a little afraid. The hand he held out shook slightly.

Taking the hand, Cole noted how weak the man's grip was, the manicured fingernails, the softness of the flesh. This was a man who had rarely left the confines of his office. "If this is anything to do with banks or money, then I—"

"Oh no, not banking!"

"Reuben," put in Maddie, "Mr Casper writes for the *Harper's Weekly*. They publish tales about the Old West."

"Perhaps you've heard of us?"

Shrugging, Cole settled himself into his armchair and beckoned for Casper to sit. The little man's smile remained frozen on his lips. "I don't get much chance to read, Mr Casper."

"We have a loyal readership, Mr Cole, who are hungry for *factual* stories. Not Dime Novels, but the real thing."

Maddie busied herself with crossing over to the drinks cabinet in the corner. She spoke with her back to Cole. "Reuben, Mr Casper is interested in hearing your stories, about what you did. You and Sterling."

Cole tilted his head. "What we did?"

"Yes," said Casper, leaning forward, eyes brim-full with enthusiasm. "There is a huge market for such stories, Mr Cole. As the West is now so much tamer, people are interested in discovering what it used to be like."

"Mr Casper, I just recently came back from a fire-fight which was anything but tame."

"That's just it, Reuben," said Maddie, moving up close to him with a full glass of whisky in her hand. "Mr Casper wants all of that, for his magazine. Monthly stories about the Old West. And Reuben," she dropped her voice, "he's gonna pay might handsomely."

Not convinced, Cole took the whisky and considered it for some moments. "To be honest, I'm not sure I want to relive all of that, Mr Casper."

"Oh, Reuben," snapped Maddie. "What else you gonna do, knocking your head against the walls in this place?"

"I have the stock, I have fences to fix, and—"

"Oh tosh, Reuben! It'll liven up your days. You can be out on the range again, with Sterling and the others without ever leaving the confines of this home. With the money we make, we can start to live real comfortable like."

"We already do."

"I want a new dress, Reuben, I want to go into town in a new buggy, to meet my old friends, take lunch ... Why, we could even hire a cook, a maid like Marta who looked after the house when your dear old pa was alive."

Cole drank his whisky, savouring the taste. Slowly, his eyes closed. Marta ...

"What would it entail?" he asked in a low, almost bored voice.

"Why, Mr Cole," said Casper, his voice rising a couple of decibels, "we can write up a contract right now. Payments would be wired to from—"

"No, I mean what do *I* need to do, Mr Casper, about these stories?"

Cole's eyes snapped open and Casper, taken aback a little, spread out his hands. "Nothing at all, Mr Cole. You relay the tales to me, and I write them up. They will be published on a regular basis every three months or so."

"Mr Casper explained he would come here every few weeks, and you tell him what happened," explained Maddie, almost as if she were talking to a child. "It won't take no time at all, will it, Mr Casper?"

"None at all."

"Mr Casper will take the notes then return to New York and prepare them for publication. You'll be famous, Reuben."

"He Who Comes," said Casper.

Cole arched a single eyebrow. "You told him that, Maddie?"

"I did. It's what the Indians called you. I reckon some of the older ones still do."

"It's a great moniker, Mr Cole," said Casper.

"A great what?"

"Reuben," Maddie got down next to him, reached out and held his knee. "Reuben, think of it. The romance of the West. You and Sterling riding out across the plains, adventures, excitement."

"Romance?"

"It doesn't just mean kissing and stuff. It'll be like Robin Hood. You know him, don't you, Reuben."

Cole sat back, face turned to the ceiling, pondering a myriad of reasons why he should turn down the offer. There was no denying the money would be welcome. Times were hard: there was grain to buy, farriers to hire. It all cost. He sighed, surrendering. "When?"

"We can set to work within the next few days, Mr Cole," said Casper, unable to keep the elation from his voice. "I promise you this will be a mutually beneficial arrangement. We have over a million readers, Mr Cole."

"Think of it, Reuben."

His head came down, and he looked into Maddie's beautiful face. "We could do with the money."

"Yes, we could."

"And if it ain't gonna be too taxing ..."

"It won't be," urged Casper.

Cole's smile broadened. "Then why not. It'll be good to revisit the old days, I guess. Without the danger of being shot, of course."

"Yes," said Maddie, grasping his hand and squeezing it. "Without the danger of any kind."

"All right then," and he turned to Casper. For the first time in many weeks, he smiled. "Where do I sign?"

The End

ABOUT THE AUTHOR

Born on the Wirral, I live in Spain for the present, but my dream is to retire (Hah, what is that? Retire?) and live on a narrowboat along one of the many waterways around the Welsh border. I work as a teacher, a profession I've been in for almost 25 years, but writing is my first love.

———

To learn more about Stuart G. Yates and discover more Next Chapter authors, visit our website at www.nextchapter.pub.

Reuben Cole Westerns Collection
ISBN: 978-4-82415-765-2
Hardcover Edition

Published by
Next Chapter
2-5-6 SANNO
SANNO BRIDGE
143-0023 Ota-Ku, Tokyo
+818035793528

17th March 2023

Printed in the USA
CPSIA information can be obtained
at www.ICGtesting.com
LVHW091551231223
767295LV00004B/42

9 784824 157652